Len Deighton was born in London in 1929. He worked as a railway clerk before doing his National Service in the RAF as a photographer attached to the Special Investigation Branch.

After his discharge in 1949, he went to art school – first to the St Martin's School of Art, and then to the Royal College of Art on a scholarship. It was while working as a waiter in the evenings that he developed an interest in cookery – a subject he was later to make his own in an animated strip for the *Observer* and in two cookery books. He worked for a while as an illustrator in New York and as art director of an advertising agency in London.

Deciding it was time to settle down, Deighton moved to the Dordogne where he started work on his first book, *The Ipcress File*. Published in 1962, the book was an immediate and spectacular success. Since then he has published twenty-four books of fiction and non-fiction – including spy stories, and highly-researched war novels and histories – all of which have appeared to international acclaim.

By the same author

Fiction

The Ipcress File
Horse Under Water
Funeral in Berlin
Billion-Dollar Brain
An Expensive Place to Die
Only When I Larf
Bomber
Declarations of War
Close-up
Spy Story
Twinkle, Twinkle, Little Spy
SS-GB
XPD
Goodbye Mickey Mouse

The Samson Stories

Berlin Game
Mexico Set
London Match
Winter: A Berlin Family 1899–1945
Spy Hook
Spy Line

Non-fiction

Fighter: The True Story of the Battle of Britain
Blitzkrieg: From the Rise of Hitler to the Fall of Dunkirk
Airshipwreck
ABC of French Food

LEN DEIGHTON

Yesterday's Spy

TRIAD
GRAFTON BOOKS

LONDON GLASGOW
TORONTO SYDNEY AUCKLAND

Triad
Grafton Books
8 Grafton Street, London W1X 3LA

Published by Triad Grafton 1976
Reprinted 1976, 1977, 1979, 1980, 1981, 1982,
1983, 1984 (twice), 1985, 1987, 1988, 1990

Triad Paperbacks Ltd is an imprint of
Chatto, Bodley Head & Jonathan Cape Ltd and
Grafton Books, a Division of the Collins Publishing Group

First published in Great Britain by
Jonathan Cape Ltd 1975

Copyright © Len Deighton 1975

ISBN 0-586-04347-0

Printed and bound in Great Britain by
Collins, Glasgow

Set in Times

1

'The Guernica network!' said Steve Champion, holding up his glass.

I hesitated. White's Club – *sanctus sanctorum* of Establishment London – seemed an inappropriate place to indulge in revolutionary nostalgia.

'Let's just drink to Marius,' I said.

'Marius,' said Champion. He drank, and wiped his blunt military-style moustache with the back of his glove. It was a gesture I'd noticed that time we'd first met – Villefranche, landing from a submarine, one night when the war was young. It was as wrong for him then as it was now. In those days Regular Army captains of the Welsh Guards did not wipe the froth off their faces with the back of their hand. But then Regular captains of the Brigade of Guards, sent to France to set up anti-Nazi Intelligence networks, were not expected to meet newly arriving agents with a girl on each arm and an open bottle of champagne.

'Marius,' I said. I drank too.

'What a comical crew we were,' said Champion. 'Marius the revolutionary priest, you straight from training school, with your terrible accent and your pimple ointment, and me. Sometimes I thought we should have let the Nazis catch us, and watched them die of laughing.'

'It was Marius who reconciled that network,' I said, 'the Communists and the deserters and the hot-heads and us professionals. It was Marius who held the network together. When he went, we all went.'

'He was past his prime by then,' said Champion. 'He'd

had too much of it. He wouldn't have lasted much longer anyway. None of us would have.'

'Marius was young,' I said. 'Almost as young as I was.'

'Marius died in a torture chamber,' said Champion. 'He died within six hours of being arrested . . . it was incredibly brave and he deserved the medal . . . but he could have saved himself by giving them some useless information. He could have deciphered some ancient codes and given them the names of people who'd already gone back to London. He could have bought a few days, and in a few days we could have rescued him.'

I didn't argue. Even after all this time it was difficult to be objective about the death of Marius. His energy and his optimism had kept us going at times when it seemed that all was lost. And his reckless bravery had more than once saved us.

For Champion it was even more difficult. He'd always blamed himself for the young priest's death. Perhaps that was partly why he'd married Marius's younger sister. And perhaps it was partly why the marriage had now fallen apart.

We both watched the far end of the room, where two Socialist Cabinet Ministers exchanged jokes about their golf handicaps and tips about the stock exchange. Champion reached into the waistcoat of his beautifully cut chalk-stripe suit. He flipped back the cover of the gold hunter that had belonged to his father and his grandfather, looked at the time, and then signalled a club servant to bring more drinks.

'The divorce came through,' he said. 'Caty and me – it's all over. Nowadays I live all the time in France.'

'I'm sorry,' I said.

'Why?' said Champion.

I shrugged. There was no point in telling him that I liked them both, and enjoyed what had once been their happy marriage. 'Those weekends at the house in Wales,' I said. 'Where will I go now to get French cooking like Caty's?'

'Well, Caty still lives there,' said Champion. 'And she'd love to see you again, I'm sure.'

I looked at him. I would have expected him to invite me to his new house in France rather than to that of his ex-wife in Wales, but Steve Champion was always unpredictable. Even more so since he'd become a wealthy businessman. He lit a fresh cigarette from the dog-end of his old one. His hand trembled; he had to steady it with the one on which he always wore a glove – to hide the absence of the fingertips he'd left behind in an interview room of St Roch prison in wartime Nice.

'You never thought of going back?' he said.

'To live in France?' I said.

He smiled. 'To the department.'

'Hah! It's a thought, isn't it?' I said. 'I didn't, Steve, and I'll tell you why.' I leaned a little closer to him, and he glanced round the room with no more than a flicker of the eye.

I said, 'Because the department never asked me to, Steve.'

He smiled soberly.

'And I'll tell you something else, Steve,' I added. 'There are people who say that you never left the department. Whenever we get together like this in London I wonder whether *you* are going to try recruiting *me*.'

'Now you're laughing at me, boyo,' said Champion, in his stage Welsh accent. He reached into his pocket and produced a clear plastic envelope. Inside it were five picture postcards. Each depicted an airship or a balloon, and in the foreground were men in straw hats and women in leg-of-mutton-sleeved dresses, inhabitants of an innocent world that had not quite learned to fly. On the

11

other sides of the cards was a tangle of greetings to long-forgotten addressees, and curious old postage stamps.

'A philatelic auction in Bond Street,' said Champion. 'That's why I came to London. I just couldn't resist these.'

I looked at his purchases. By now Champion should have realized that I was a lost cause as far as his obsession with airmail stamps was concerned. 'And Billy?' I asked. I handed his airships back to him.

'Yes, I'm seeing a lot of Billy this week,' said Champion, as if visiting his young son was no more than an afterthought. 'Caty has been very good about letting me see Billy.'

He went through the postcards one by one and then put them away with exaggerated care. 'The night Billy was born,' he said, 'I was up to the neck in bank loans, promissory notes and mortgages. I was sure I'd done the wrong thing . . . did I ever tell you how I started: with the uncut diamonds?'

'I've heard stories,' I admitted.

He inhaled carefully on his cigarette. 'Do you know Accra?'

'No.'

'The arse-hole of West Africa. I was flat broke, and working hard to buy a ticket home. I was translating export permits for cocoa traders and wangling customs forms for importers – all of them Arabs. My Arabic has always been good, but by the time I finished working with those jokers I could have done the sports reports for Radio Cairo. When I think of it!' He clasped his hands tight as if to stretch the joints. 'I took the bumpf down to the customs sheds one day – June, it was, and bloody steamy, even by Accra standards. I made the usual golden obeisance to the officials and loaded ten crates of Renault spares on to the truck I'd hired. But when I uncrated them back in the cocoa warehouse, I find I'm knee-deep in French MAS 38s, complete with cleaning kits, and spares and instruction booklets.'

'Sub-machineguns,' I said.

'Go to the top of the class.'

'But could you get the Long cartridge?'

'Am I glad you weren't involved, old boy! No, you *couldn't* get them. But the kids who bought them were too young to remember the MAS 38, so they think they are MAT 49s, for which there is 9 mm stuff ready to be nicked from a local police or army unit. Right?'

'Right.'

'But I'm getting ahead of the story. Imagine me – the only man in Accra who'd sooner have Renault spares than sub-machineguns, sitting on ten cases of them. All of them customs cleared, rubber stamped and signed for. It *was* tempting.'

'But you didn't succumb?'

'Oh, but I did.' He took a drag on his cigarette and waved the smoke away. 'Two hundred and thirty-five dollars each – American dollars – and I could have doubled it, had I sold them to the loudmouths with the fuzzy-wuzzy haircuts.'

'Ten to a case?' I said. 'About ten thousand pounds profit.'

'I had to stop my client going down to the customs and raising hell about his Renault spares. I owed a bit of money, I had to get an exit permit, and clearance from the tax office: it all costs money.'

'You came home?'

'I went to buy my air ticket from a crooked little Portuguese travel agent. I started bargaining with him, knowing that he could unload my US dollar bills at a big premium. To cut a long story short, I ended up giving him all my American money in exchange for a bag

13

of uncut diamonds from Angola and a boat ticket to Marseille.'

'You went to Marseille?'

'Old man Tix had just died, his whole set-up was for sale. Caty's sister told me about it. But the Algerian fighting was still on, and the Tix fruit and vegetable importing was no more than a ream of headed notepaper and a couple of fleabitten offices in Constantine.'

'And the quarry was defunct.'

'The quarry – yes.' Champion smiled. We'd both hidden in the quarry during a big German round-up, when old man Tix had chased a German officer out of the house shouting 'Sale Boche' at him, crossing himself as he did so. 'The quarry was finished. They'd mined, too, but it was costing so much to dig that the old boy did better on unemployment benefit.'

'But you sold your diamonds and bought the Tix place from his widow?'

'That was only a down payment,' said Steve, 'but Madame Tix wanted me to have it. She waited a long time for the rest of the money. It was a gamble for all concerned. We were betting on a peaceful settlement of the Algerian war.'

'You were always a good guesser, Steve,' I said.

'The peace between France and Algeria meant immigrant labourers – that got the mine back into profit.'

'Lower wages,' I said.

'But still higher than any they could get in their own country.'

'But you closed the mine and the quarry – you sent the men home.'

Champion smiled. He said, 'It was the *idea* of cheap labour in the mine. That's what enabled me to get my capital. Avaricious little hairdressers with their hands in the till . . . contractors fiddling their tax, and hard-eyed

14

old bastards from the merchant banks. They came to see my quarry and the Arabs sweating their guts out. They liked it – that was the kind of investment those little sods could understand. That was the way their grandfathers – and their friends' grandfathers – had made a fortune in Africa a hundred years ago.'

'And you put that money into the fruit and veg.'

'Much more than money . . . soil analysis, a professor of botany, a programme of seeding techniques, long-term contracts for the farmers, minimum price guarantees for seasonal workers, refrigerated warehouses, refrigerated transport and contracted refrigerated shipping. I put a lot of money into the Arab countries.'

'And now they have oil as well.'

'Oil is a one-crop economy,' said Champion.

'A gilt-edged one,' I said.

'That's what they said about coffee and tea and rubber,' said Champion. 'I truly believe that North Africa must trade with Europe, right across the board. The Arab countries must have a stake in Europe's well-being. The economics must link, otherwise Africa will let Europe die of inflation.'

'I never thought of you as a crusader, Steve.'

Champion seemed disconcerted at the idea. He picked up his glass to hide behind it.

Two men came downstairs: one was a famous poet, the other a peer of the realm. They were arguing quietly and eruditely about the lyrics of an obscene Eighth Army song about the extra-marital activities of King Farouk.

A club servant came to tell Champion that a lady was waiting at the entrance. 'Come along,' said Champion. 'This is someone I'd like you to meet.'

A servant helped Champion into the lightweight vicuna coat, designed like a British warm, and handed him the bowler hat that made him look like a retired general.

15

Someone unseen gave a perfunctory brush to the shoulder of my dirty raincoat.

The snow obliterated the view through the doorway, like static on an old TV. Outside in St James's Street, London's traffic was jammed tight. Champion's girl gave no more than the nod and smile that manners demanded. Her eyes were devoted to Champion. She watched him with the kind of awe with which an orphan eyes a Christmas tree. It was always the same girl. This one had the same perfect skin that Caty had, and the same soft eyes with which Pina had looked at him. Except that decades had passed since Caty or Pina had been this kid's age.

'Melodie,' said Champion. 'It's a nice name, isn't it: Melodie Page.'

'It's a lovely name,' I said, in my usual sycophantic way.

Champion looked at his watch. 'It's a long time since we jawed so much,' he told me. 'My God, but you would have been bored, Melodie. We must be getting old.' He smiled. 'Melodie and Billy are taking me to the theatre tonight. They are going to repair one of the gaps in my musical education.'

The girl hit his arm in mock anger.

'Rock music and pirates,' Champion told me.

'A potent mixture,' I said.

'Billy will be glad I've seen you. You always remember his birthday, he told me.'

'Yes,' I said.

'That's damned nice of you.' Champion patted my arm.

At that moment, exactly on schedule, a black Daimler drew level with the entrance. A uniformed driver hurried across the pavement, opening an umbrella to shelter Champion and the girl from the weather. He opened the door, too. As the girl slid into the real leather seating,

Champion looked back to where I was standing. The snow was beating about my ears. Champion raised his gloved hand in a regal salute. But when only three of your fingers are able to wave, such a gesture can look awfully like a very rude Anglo-Saxon sign.

2

I could see my report about Champion on Schlegel's desk. Schlegel picked it up. He shook it gently, as if hoping that some new information might drop out of it. 'No,' said Schlegel. 'No. No. No.'

I said nothing. Colonel Schlegel, US Marine Corps (Air Wing), Retired, cut a dapper figure in a lightweight houndstooth three-piece, fake club-tie and button-down cotton shirt. It was the kind of outfit they sell in those Los Angeles shops that have bow windows and plastic Tudor beams. He tapped my report. 'Maybe you can shaft the rest of them with your inscrutable sarcasm and innocent questions, but me no likee – got it?'

'Look,' I said. 'Champion was just seeing his kid, and buying stamps – there's no other angle. He's a rich man now: he's not playing secret agents. Believe me, Colonel. There's nothing there.'

Schlegel leaned forward to get a small cigar from a box decorated with an eagle trying to eat a scroll marked *Semper Fidelis*. He pushed the box to me, but I'm trying to give them up.

'He's in deep,' said Schlegel. Puckered scar tissue made it difficult to distinguish his smiles from his scowls. He was a short muscular man with an enviable measure of self-confidence; the kind of personality that you hire to MC an Elks Club stag night.

I waited. The 'need-to-know' basis, upon which the department worked, meant that I'd been told only a part of it. Schlegel took his time getting his cigar well alight.

I said, 'The story about the machineguns fits with

18

everything I've been told. The whole story – the stuff about the uncut diamonds providing the money to start the mine, and then the fruit and vegetable imports – that's all on non-classified file.'

'Not all of it,' said Schlegel. 'Long after the file closes, Champion was still reporting back to this department.'

'Was he!'

'Long before my time, of course,' said Schlegel, to emphasize that this was a British cock-up, less likely to happen now that we had him with us on secondment from Washington. 'Yes,' said Schlegel, 'those machine-guns were shipped to Accra on orders from this office. It was all part of the plan to buy Champion into control of the Tix set-up. Champion was our man.'

I remembered all those years when I'd been drinking and dining with the Champions, never suspecting that he was employed by this office.

Perhaps Schlegel mistook my silence for disbelief. 'It was a good thing while it lasted,' he said. 'Champion was in and out of Egypt, Algeria and Tunisia, arguing about his melons, carrots and potatoes, keeping his eyes open and dropping a few words to the right people, doing us all a power of good. And the *way* that Champion had scored – selling cannons to some freaky little terrorist outfit – all helped.'

'So what was the fadeout?'

Schlegel blew a piece of tobacco off his lip, with enough force to make the bookcase rattle. 'The feedback of information began to sag. Champion said the French were starting to lean on him, and it was getting too dangerous. It was a top-level decision to let him go. It was the right decision. You Brits are good at bowing out gracefully and you'd done all right out of Champion by that time.'

'And now?'

'A guy in German security trying to make a name for himself. He's dug out some stuff about Champion's financial affairs. They are asking questions about the guns at Accra.'

'Bonn gets hysterical – and we have to join in the screaming?'

'If the Champion business becomes a big scandal, they'll say we were careless when we let him go.'

'Perhaps it was a little careless,' I suggested.

'Well, maybe it was,' said Schlegel. He picked up my report exonerating Champion. 'But your whitewash job isn't going to help matters.'

'I'll take another shot at it,' I said.

He slid my report across the polished desk. Then from a drawer he got Perrier water and a tiny bottle of Underberg bitters. He shook the bitters into the mineral water and stirred it with a ballpoint pen to make it a delicate brown. 'Want some?'

'That's just for hangovers,' I said. 'And even then it's got to be a pretty damn bad hangover.'

'I like it,' said Schlegel, and drank it slowly, savouring each sip.

I took the report and stood up to leave. Schlegel said, 'This is going to be a lousy rotten miserable bummer. I hate these jobs where we are shaking down our own. So you don't have to give me a bad time, or give yourself a bad time for not covering up for him.'

'I had that lecture at Indoctrine Four, when I went to the CIA Communications symposium in 1967,' I said.

'Champion saved your life,' Schlegel reminded me. 'If you can't hack it, just say you want out.'

'I know what kind of out I'd get,' I said bitterly.

Schlegel nodded. 'And I'd countersign it,' he said. In a way, I preferred Schlegel's New World directness: the others would have tried to persuade me that such a request would have had no effect on my career.

Schlegel stood up to look out of the window. It was still snowing. 'This isn't just some kind of fancy positive vetting job,' he said. 'This is a hot one.' Schlegel scratched his behind, and reflected.

'Someone across the street could lip-read you,' I warned him.

He turned to look at me pityingly. It was Schlegel's often expressed belief that we'd get more done here in London if we worried less about such details. 'The Germans are sending one of their people down to Nice to investigate Champion,' he said thoughtfully.

I didn't respond.

'Have you been taken suddenly drunk or something?' said Schlegel.

'I didn't want to disturb your deductive processes,' I said. I polished my spectacles and blinked at him.

'Damned if I understand it,' he said.

'You're in Europe now, Colonel,' I said. 'This German scandal has come just when the Bonn government are warming up for an election. When their security people discovered that Champion had once been a British agent it was the answer to all their problems. They wrote "Passed to British security" in the margin and fired it across here. Now the German Defence Minister can refuse to answer any questions about the scandal on the grounds that it would prejudice the security of their British ally. It will give them all they need to stall until the election is over. When they are elected again it will be "Minister requested" and that's the last we'll see of it. I've been through all this before, Colonel.'

'Well, you know more about all this European Mickey Mouse than I'll ever understand,' said Schlegel. It was a double-edged compliment and he bared his teeth to let

21

me know it. 'We'll hold it for the three-month cycle,' he offered, as if trying to come to terms with me.

'Don't do me any favours,' I told him. 'I don't give a good goddamn if you publish it as a whole-page ad in *Variety*. I've done what I was asked. But if the department expected me to return with the synopsis for World War Three, I'm sorry to disappoint. If you want to send me back to spend the rest of the year drinking with Champion at the department's expense, I'll be very happy to do so. But Champion is no dope. He'll tumble what's going on.'

'Maybe he already did,' Schlegel said slyly. 'Maybe that's why you got nothing out of him.'

'You know what to do, then,' I told him.

'I already did it,' he said. 'A short dark kid. Looks ten years younger than she really is: Melodie Page. Been with the department nearly eight years!'

3

'William, come to Mother, darling, and let me give you a kiss.' Champion's failed marriage was all there in that imperious command. An elegant French wife who persisted in calling their small son Billy 'William', and who gave him kisses, instead of asking for them.

She gave Billy the promised kiss, pulled a dead leaf off the front of his sweater and then waited until he'd left the room. She turned to me. 'All I ask is that you don't remind me how keen I was to marry him.' She poured fresh hot water into the teapot, and then put the copper kettle back on the hob. It hummed gently with the heat from the blazing logs. There was a stainless-steel kitchen only a few steps along the carpeted corridor, but she had made the tea and toasted the bread on the open fire in the lounge. From here we could look out of the window and watch the wind ruffling the river and whipping the bare trees into a mad dance. The black Welsh hills wore a halo of gold that promised respite from the dark daylight.

'I didn't come down here to talk about Steve, or about the divorce,' I protested.

She poured tea for me and gave me the last slice of toast. She spiked a fresh piece of bread on to the toasting fork. 'Then it's surprising how many times we seem to find ourselves talking about it.' She turned to the hearth and busied herself with finding a hot place in the fire. 'Steve has this wonderful knack,' she continued bitterly, 'this wonderful knack of falling on his feet . . . like a kitten.'

It was an affectionate analogy. The rejection had hurt, I could see that. I buttered my toast and put some of Caterina's homemade jam on it. It was delicious and I ate it without speaking.

'This damned house,' she continued. 'My sister wrote to tell me how much it would be worth if it was in France. But it's not in France, it's in Wales! And it costs a fortune to keep the slates on, and mend the boiler, and cut the lawn . . . and heating oil has nearly doubled in price just since the last delivery.' The bread started to smoke. She cursed softly, broke the scorched piece off and threw it away into the flames before toasting the other side. Caterina could cope with things. That was her misfortune in a way. She wanted to be cosseted and looked after but she was ten times more efficient than any of the men who wanted to do it. 'So Steve gets rid of the house, burdens me with all its problems and expenses, and everyone tells me to be grateful.'

'You're not exactly poor, Caty,' I said.

She looked at me for a moment, deciding if I knew her well enough to make such a personal remark. But I did know her well enough.

'You know what the arrangement was . . . If he's going down to the river, I'll kill the little devil.'

I followed her gaze to where her small son was dragging a toy cart across the lawn. As if sensing that he was being watched, he changed direction and started back up towards the smart new sauna again. Caterina went back to her tea and toast. 'He's changed a lot, you know . . . I swore to my father that Steve had come through the war unmarred, but it took ten years to take effect. And then the last few years have been hell . . . hell for both of us, and little William, too!'

'He had a lousy war, Caty,' I said.

'So did a lot of other people.'

I remembered the day in 1944 when I went into Nice prison just a few hours after the Gestapo had moved out. I was with the forward elements of the American Army. There was another Englishman with me. We asked each other no personal questions. He was wearing Intelligence Corps badges, but he knew Steve Champion all right, and he was probably sent directly from London, as I had been. The Germans had destroyed all the documents. I suppose London were sure they would have done, or they would have sent someone more important than me to chase it.

'Look at that,' said this other officer, when we were kicking the cupboards of the interrogation room apart. It was a shabby room, with a smell of ether and carbolic, a framed engraving of Salzburg and some broken wine bottles in the fireplace. He pointed to a bottle on the shelf. 'Steve Champion's fingertips,' said my companion. He took the bottle and swirled the brine around so that through the mottled glass I saw four shrunken pieces of dark brown organic matter that jostled together as they were pushed to the centre of the whirling fluid. I looked again and found that they were four olives, just as the label said, but for a moment I had shivered. And each time I remembered it I shivered again. 'You're right, Caty,' I said. 'A lot of people had it much worse.'

Overhead the clouds were low and puffy, like a dirty quilt pulled over the face of the countryside.

'There was all that "we Celts" nonsense. I began to believe that Wales was little different from Brittany. Little did I know . . . My God!' said Caterina. She was still watching Billy in the garden. 'The banks of the river are so muddy this last week . . . the rain . . . one of the village boys was drowned there this time last year.' She looked up at the carved wooden crucifix on the wall above the TV set.

'He'll be all right.' I said it to calm her.

'He never dares to go down as far as the paddock when Steve visits. But he just defies me!'

'Do you want me to get him?'

She gave a despairing smile. 'I don't know,' she said. She tugged at her hair. I was a 'friend of Steve's': she didn't want me to get any kind of response from Billy that she had failed to get. 'We'll watch from here,' she said.

'That's probably best,' I agreed.

'You English!' she said. I got the full blast of her anxiety. 'You're probably a fully paid-up subscriber to the Society for the Prevention of Cruelty to Animals.'

'That wouldn't necessarily make me a child-beater,' I said. 'And it's the *Royal* Society.'

'No one can live with a man who is racked with guilt. And Steve is racked with guilt.'

'You're not talking about the war?' I asked.

'I'm talking about the marriage,' she said.

'Because Steve has no need to feel guilty about the war,' I told her.

'My mother told me about Englishmen,' said Caterina. She raised her hand in a gesture more appropriate to an Italian market than to an English drawing-room. And now her voice, too, carried an inflection of her birth ties. 'You don't have to have something to feel guilty about!' Her voice was high and almost shrill. 'Don't you understand that? Guilt is like pain – it hurts just the same whether it's real or imagined!'

'I'll have to think about that,' I said defensively.

'You think about it, then. I'll go and fetch William.' She pushed the silk cosy down over the teapot to keep the tea warm while she was gone. But she did not go. She kept her hands round it and stared into the distance. Or perhaps she was staring at the silver-framed photo of her brother Marius, the young priest who'd died in that carbolic-smelling basement. Suddenly the sun stabbed into the room. It wasn't real sun, there was no warmth in it, and precious little colour. It spilled over the embroidered traycloth like weak lemon tea, and made a rim round Caty's hair.

They were both like their mother, these Baroni girls. Even as children they'd looked more like visiting towns-people than like village kids. Tall and slim, Caty had that sort of ease and confidence that belied the indecision she expressed.

'I won't stay here,' she said, as if her thoughts had raced on far beyond our conversation. 'My sister wants me to help with her boutique in Nice. With the money I get from the house, we could start another shop, perhaps.'

The sun's cross-light scrawled a thousand wrinkles upon her face, and I was forced to see her as she was, instead of through the flattering haze of my memories. Perhaps she read my thoughts. 'I'm getting old,' she said. 'Steve's getting old, too, and so are you.' She smoothed her hair, and touched the gold cross that she wore.

She was still attractive. Whatever kind of post-natal exercises she'd done after Billy's birth had restored her figure to that of the trim young woman Steve had married. She used just sufficient make-up to compensate for the pale English winters she'd endured for so long. Her nails were manicured, and long enough to convince me that she didn't spend much time at the sink, and her hair was styled in the fashion that requires frequent visits to the hairdresser.

She smoothed the striped silk pants across her knee. They were stylish and tailored. She looked like an illus-tration that American *Vogue* might run if they ever did an article about English crumpet. I wondered if she spent

27

many elegant afternoons sitting by the log fire in her fine clothes, pouring herself lemon tea from a silver teapot.

'Do you know what I think?' she said.

I waited a long time and then I said, 'What do you think, Caty?'

'I don't believe you just *bumped into* Steve. I think you were sent after him. I think you are still working for the Secret Service or something – just like in the war. I think you are after Steve.'

'Why would anyone be after him, Caty?'

'He's changed,' she said. 'You must have noticed that yourself. I wouldn't be surprised what he was mixed up in. He has this sort of schizophrenia and an obsession with secrecy. I don't know if you get like that in the Secret Service, or whether the Secret Service choose that sort of man. But it's hell to live with, I'll tell you that.'

'I think you still love him,' I said.

'You've always hero-worshipped him,' she said. 'He was your big brother, wasn't he? You just can't imagine that some boring little housewife like me would have the effrontery to be glad to get rid of your wonderful Steve Champion. Well, I am glad. I just hope like hell that I never see him again, ever.'

I don't know how she expected me to react, but whatever she expected, I failed her. I saw a look of exasperation. She said, 'I tried, believe me, I tried very hard. I even bought new things and wore false eyelashes.'

I nodded.

'I thought Steve had sent you . . . to get William.'

'No,' I said.

'He'll stop at nothing to get him. He told me that. But I'll fight him, Charles. You tell Steve that. He'll never get William from me.'

She picked up Billy's favourite toy rabbit and went to the door. She looked back at me as if I was a Solomon who would decide Billy's future. 'If I thought he would be happy with Steve, I wouldn't mind so much. But William is not like his father – he's a gentle child and easily hurt.'

'I know he is, Caty.'

She stood there for a moment, thinking of things to say, and not saying them. Then she went out of the room.

I saw her as she passed the window. She was wearing a riding mac and a scarf over her head. She had Billy's rabbit under her arm.

4

That Champion's Master File had been brought from Central Registry was, in itself, a sign of the flap that was in progress. It was seldom that we handled anything other than the Action Abstracts and they were a three-hour task. This Master would have stacked up to a five-feet-tall pile of paperwork, had the Biog, Associative, Report, Vettings and year by year Summaries been put one upon the other.

The papers had yellowed with age, the photos were brittle and dog-eared. The yellow vetting sheets were now buff-coloured, and the bright-red Report dossier had faded to a brownish-pink.

There was little hope of discovering anything startling here. The continuing triple-A clearance, right up to the time that Champion stopped reporting to the department, was in itself a sign that men more jaundiced than I could ever be had given Champion a clean bill of health. Since then the department had shown little interest in him.

I looked at his Biographical entries. Champion's father, a Welsh Catholic, had been a senior lecturer at the Abbasiyah Military Academy, Cairo. Young Champion came back to England to attend public school. From there he won a place at the Royal Military Academy, Sandhurst. For a boy who grew up to table-talk of tactics, battles and ballistics, Sandhurst was a doddle. Champion became an under-officer, and a well-remembered one. And his scholarship matched his military expertise: modern history, four languages and a mathematics prize.

It was Champion's French-language skills that earned

for him a secondment to the French Army. He went the usual round of military colleges, the Paris Embassy, Maginot Line fortresses and Grand General HQ, with occasional glimpses of the legendary General Gamelin.

Champion had only been back with his regiment for a matter of weeks when a War Office directive automatically shortlisted him for a Secret Intelligence Service interview. He was selected, trained and back in France by 1939. He was just in time to watch General Gamelin's defence system surrender to the Nazis. Champion fled south and became 'net-officer' for what was no more than a collection of odds and sods in the unoccupied zone. His orders were to stay clear of the enthusiastic amateurs that London called their Special Operations Executive, but inevitably the two networks became entangled.

It was Champion who greeted me in person that night when I landed from the submarine at Villefranche. I was assigned to SOE but Champion kidnapped me and got it made official afterwards. If I'd gone up to Nîmes as ordered, my war service would have ended two or three months later in Buchenwald.

But Champion used me to sort out his own network and I stayed with him right up to the time the network crumbled and Champion was taken prisoner. Eventually he escaped and was flown back to London. He got a DSO and a new job. Even before D-Day, Champion was assigned to peacetime network planning. He demanded choice of personnel, and got it. His first request was to have me as his senior assistant. It wasn't easy for me now to look at Champion's file with an objective eye.

When you read old files, you realize how the paperwork itself decides the progress of an inquiry. Schlegel gave Bonn's report a twelve-week life cycle, so the coordinator decided not to give it a file number. He attached it as an appendix to Champion's abstract. Then I had to do a written report, to glue it all together. With everyone satisfied, the file would have gone over to Current Storage and then gone sliding down the priorities until it ended in a tin archive box in Hendon.

But it didn't.

It was activated by an alert slip that came from the officer who was 'running' Melodie Page. She failed to report for two cycles. This would normally have meant the opening of an orange Caution File with its own file number. But with Champion's abstract signed out to me, it caused the girl's alert slip to be pinned on to my desk diary.

Suddenly the Champion file was wearing red stickers in its hair, and everyone concerned was trying to think of a 'Latest action' to pin to it, in case the Minister wanted to read it himself.

'I don't like it,' said Schlegel.

'Perhaps she's fallen for Champion,' I said.

He looked at me to see whether I meant it. 'That's all I need,' said Schlegel. 'You coming in here inventing new things for me to worry about.'

'And you want me to go to this flat that Champion is supposed to have kept as some kind of bolt-hole?'

'It's a ten-minute job. Special Branch will send Blantyre and one of the Special Branch break-in specialists. Just take a look round, and file a short report tomorrow. No sweat – it's only to show we're on our toes.'

'Are you sure I'm experienced enough to handle something like this?'

'Don't go touchy on me, bubblebrain. I want a piece of paper: something recent, with a senior operative's signature, to put in the file before it leaves here.'

'You're right,' I said.

'Goddamn! Of course I'm right,' he said in exasperation. 'And Mr Dawlish will be looking in there on his way back from his meeting in Chiswick.'

The top brass! They really expected questions in the House, if Dawlish was going to do an I-was-there piece for them.

Steve Champion's hideaway, in Barons Court. Well, I don't have to tell you what kind of house it was: Gothic horror comes to town! Depressing place, with no sign of any tenants, and a dented metal grille that asks you who you are, and buzzes when it opens the lock.

That bugger Blantyre was already there, chatting away merrily with his 'break-in specialist' who'd already splintered the paintwork on the outer door and left a wet footprint in the hall, and who, on closer inspection, turned out to be Blantyre's old buddy Detective-Inspector Seymour.

There they were, striding all over the clues and pouring each other double portions of Champion's booze.

'I didn't know you were coming,' said Blantyre.

'So I see.'

Blantyre held up his glass and looked at it, like one of those white-coated actors in TV commercials about indigestion. He said, 'We were wondering whether to send samples to the lab.'

'Send a whole bottle,' I said. 'Order a case from Harrods, and give them his Diner's Card number.'

Blantyre's face reddened, but whether in shame or anger I could not be sure. I said, 'Good. Well, if I'm not disturbing you two, I'll take a look round while there's still some evidence left.'

Blantyre gave me both barrels of a sawn-off twelve-bore, sighed and left the room wearing a sardonic smile. His drinking companion followed him.

I'd hardly started having a look round when Dawlish arrived. If Schlegel was hoping to keep our break-in inconspicuous, I'd say that Dawlish screwed up any last chance, what with his official car and uniformed driver, and the bowler hat and Melton overcoat. To say nothing of the tightly rolled umbrella that Dawlish was waving. Plastic raincoats are *de rigueur* for the rainy season in Barons Court.

'Not exactly a playboy pad,' said Dawlish, demonstrating his mastery of the vernacular.

Even by Dawlish's standards that was an understatement. It was a large gloomy apartment. The wallpaper and paintwork were in good condition and so was the cheap carpeting, but there were no pictures, no books, no ornaments, no personal touches. 'A machine for living in,' said Dawlish.

'Le Corbusier at his purest,' I said, anxious to show that I could recognize a cultural quote when I heard one.

It was like the barrack-room I'd had as a sergeant, waiting for Intelligence training. Iron bed, a tiny locker, plain black curtains at the window. On the windowsill there were some withered crumbs. I suppose no pigeon fancied them when just a short flight away the tourists would be throwing them croissants, and they could sit down and eat with a view of St James's Park.

There was a school yard visible from the window. The rain had stopped and the sun was shining. Swarms of children made random patterns as they sang, swung, jumped in puddles and punched each other with the same motiveless exuberance that, organized, becomes war. I closed the window and the shouting died. There were dark clouds; it would rain again.

'Worth a search?' said Dawlish.

I nodded. 'There will be a gun. Sealed under wet plaster perhaps. He's not the kind of man to use the cistern or the chimney: either tear it to pieces or forget it.'

'It's difficult, isn't it,' said Dawlish. 'Don't want to tear it to pieces just to find a gun. I'm interested in documents – stuff that he needs constant access to.'

'There will be nothing like that here,' I said.

Dawlish walked into the second bedroom. 'No linen on the bed, you notice. No pillows, even.'

I opened the chest of drawers. There was plenty of linen there; all brand new, and still in its wrappings.

'Good quality stuff,' said Dawlish.

'Yes, sir,' I said.

Dawlish opened the kitchen cupboards and recited their contents. 'Dozen tins of meat, dozen tins of peas, dozen bottles of beer, dozen tins of rice pudding. A package of candles, unused, a dozen boxes of matches.' He closed the cupboard door and opened a kitchen drawer. We stared at the cutlery for a moment. It was all new and unused. He closed it again without comment.

'No caretaker,' I said. 'No landlady, no doorman.'

'Precisely,' said Dawlish. 'And I'll wager that the rent is paid every quarter day, without fail, by some solicitor who has never come face to face with his client. No papers, eh?'

'Cheap writing-pad and envelopes, a book of stamps, postcards with several different views of London – might be a code device – no, no papers in that sense.'

'I look forward to meeting your friend Champion,' said Dawlish. 'A dozen tins of meat but three dozen bars of soap – that's something for Freud, eh?'

I let the 'your friend' go unremarked. 'Indeed it is, sir,' I said.

'None of it surprises you, of course,' Dawlish said, with more than a trace of sarcasm.

'Paranoia,' I said. 'It's the occupational hazard of men who've worked the sort of territories that Champion has worked.' Dawlish stared at me. I said, 'Like anthrax for tannery workers, and silicosis for miners. You need somewhere . . . a place to go and hide for ever . . .' I indicated the store cupboard, '. . . and you never shake it off.'

Dawlish walked through into the big bedroom. Blantyre and his sidekick made themselves scarce. Dawlish opened the drawers of the chest, starting from the bottom like a burglar so that he didn't have to bother closing them. There were shirts in their original Cellophane bags, a couple of knitted ties, sweaters and plain black socks. Dawlish said, 'So should I infer that you have a little bolt-hole like this, just in case the balloon goes up?' Even after all these years together, Dawlish had to make sure his little jokes left a whiff of cordite.

'No, sir,' I said. 'But on the new salary scale I might be able to afford one – not in central London, though.'

Dawlish grunted, and opened the wardrobe. There were two dark suits, a tweed jacket, a blazer and three pairs of trousers. He twisted the blazer to see the inside pocket. There was no label there. He let it go and then took the tweed jacket off its hanger. He threw it on the bed.

'What about that?' said Dawlish.

I said, 'High notch, slightly waisted, centre-vented, three-button jacket in a sixteen-ounce Cheviot. Austin Reed, Hector Powe, or one of those expensive mass-production tailors. Not made to measure – off the peg. Scarcely worn, two or three years old, perhaps.'

'Have a look at it,' said Dawlish testily.

'Really have a look?'

'You're better at that sort of thing than I am.' It was Dawlish's genius never to tackle anything he couldn't handle and always to have near by a slave who could.

Dawlish took out the sharp little ivory-handled penknife that he used to ream his pipe. He opened it and gave it to me, handle first. I spread the jacket on the bed and used the penknife to cut the stitches of the lining. There were no labels anywhere. Even the interior manufacturer's codes had been removed. So I continued working my way along the buckram until I could reach under that too. There was still nothing.

'Shoulder-pads?' I said.

'Might as well,' said Dawlish. He watched me closely.

'Nothing,' I said finally. 'Would you care to try the trousers, sir?'

'Do the other jackets.'

I smiled. It wasn't that Dawlish was obsessional. It was simply his policy to run his life as though he was already answering the Minister's questions. You searched all the clothing? Yes, all the clothing. Not, no, just one jacket, selected at random.

I did the other jackets. Dawlish proved right. He always proves right. It was in the right-hand shoulder-pad of one of the dark suits that we found the paper money. There were fourteen bills: US dollars, Deutsche Marks and sterling – a total of about twelve thousand dollars at the exchange rate then current.

But it was in the other shoulder-pad that we found the sort of document Dawlish was looking for. It was a letter signed by the Minister Plenipotentiary of the United Arab Republic's Embassy in London. It claimed that Stephen Champion had diplomatic status as a naturalized citizen of the United Arab Republic and listed member of the Diplomatic Corps.

Dawlish read it carefully and passed it across to me. 'What do you think about that?' he asked.

To tell you the truth, I thought Dawlish was asking me to confirm that it was a forgery, but you can never take anything for granted when dealing with Dawlish. I dealt him his cards off the top of the deck. 'Champion is not

37

on the London Diplomatic List,' I said, 'but that's about the only thing I'm certain of.'

Dawlish looked at me and sniffed. 'Can't even be certain of that,' he said. 'All those Abduls and Ahmeds and Alis . . . suppose you were told that one of those was the name Champion had adopted when converted to the Muslim faith. What then . . . ?'

'It would keep the lawyers arguing for months,' I said.

'And what about the Special Branch superintendent at London airport, holding up the aeroplane departing to Cairo? Would he hold a man who was using this as a travel document, and risk the sort of hullabaloo that might result if he put a diplomat in the bag?'

'No,' I said.

'Precisely,' said Dawlish.

A gust of wind rattled the window panes and the sky grew dark. He said nothing more. I took my coat off and hung it up. It was no good pretending that I wouldn't be here all day. There's only one way to tackle those jobs: you do it stone by stone, and you do it yourself. Dawlish sent Blantyre and his associate away. Then he went down to the car and called the office. I began to get some idea of the priorities when he told me he'd cancelled everything for the rest of the day. He sat down on the kitchen chair and watched me work.

There was nothing conclusive, of course: no dismembered limbs or bloodstains, but clothes that I'd seen Melodie Page wearing were packed in plastic carrierbags, sandwiched neatly between two sheets of plasterboard, sealed at every edge, and integrated beautifully into the kitchen ceiling.

The wallpaper near the bed had deep scratches, and a broken fragment of fingernail remained embedded there. There was the faintest smell of carbolic acid from the waste-trap under the sink, and from there I managed to get a curved piece of clear glass that was one part of a hypodermic syringe. Other than that, there was only evidence of removal of evidence.

'It's enough,' said Dawlish.

From the school yard across the street came all the exuberant screams that the kids had been bottling up in class. It was pouring with rain now, but children don't mind the rain.

5

Schlegel likes Southern California. Sometimes I think it's the only thing he does like. You take Southern California by the inland corners, he says, jerk it, so that all the shrubbery and real-estate falls into a heap along the coast, and you know what you've got? And I say, yes, you've got the French Riviera, because I've heard him say it before.

Well, on Monday *I'd* got the French Riviera. Or, more precisely, I'd got Nice. I arrived in my usual neurotic way: ten hours before schedule, breaking my journey in Lyon and choosing the third cab in the line-up.

It was so easy to remember what Nice had looked like the first time I saw it. There had been a pier that stretched out to sea, and barbed wire along the promenade. Armed sentries had stood outside the sea-front hotels, and refugees from the north stood in line for work, or begged furtively outside the crowded cafés and restaurants. Inside, smiling Germans in ill-fitting civilian suits bought each other magnums of champagne and paid in mint-fresh military notes. And everywhere there was this smell of burning, as if everyone in the land had something in their possession that the Fascists would think incriminating.

Everyone's fear is different. And because bravery is just the knack of suppressing signs of your own fear, bravery is different too. The trouble with being only nineteen is that you are frightened of all the wrong things; and brave about the wrong things. Champion had gone to Lyon. I was all alone, and of course then too stupid not to be thankful for it. No matter what the movies tell you, there was no resistance movement visible to the naked eye. Only Jews could be trusted not to turn you over to the Fascists. Men like Serge Frankel. He'd been the first person I'd contacted then, and he was the first one I went to now.

It was a sunny day, but the apartment building, which overlooked the vegetable market, was cold and dark. I went up the five flights of stone stairs. Only a glimmer of daylight penetrated the dirty windows on each landing. The brass plate at his door – 'Philatelic Expert' – was by now polished a little smoother, and there was a card tucked behind the bell that in three languages said 'Buying and Selling by Appointment Only'.

The same heavy door that protected his stamps, and had given us perhaps groundless confidence in the old days, was still in place, and the peep-hole through which he'd met the eyes of the Gestapo now was used to survey me.

'My boy! How wonderful to see you.'

'Hello, Serge.'

'And a chance to practise my English,' he said. He reached forward with a white bony hand, and gripped me firmly enough for me to feel the two gold rings that he wore.

It was easy to imagine Serge Frankel as a youth: a frail-looking small-boned teenager with frizzy hair and a large forehead and the same style of gold-rimmed spectacles as he was wearing now.

We went into the study. It was a high-ceilinged room lined with books, their titles in a dozen or more languages. Not only stamp catalogues and reference books, but philosophy from Cicero to Ortega y Gasset.

He sat in the same button-back leather chair now as he had then. Smiling the same inscrutable and humourless smile, and brushing at the ash that spilled down the same sort of waistcoat, leaving there a grey smear like a mark of penitence. It was inevitable that we should talk of old times.

Serge Frankel was a Communist – student of Marx, devotee of Lenin and servant of Stalin. Born in Berlin, he'd been hunted from end to end of Hitler's Third Reich, and had not seen his wife and children since the day he waved goodbye to them at Cologne railway station, wearing a new moustache and carrying papers that described him as an undertaker from Stettin.

During the Civil War in Spain, Frankel had been a political commissar with the International Brigade. During the tank assault on the Prado, Frankel had destroyed an Italian tank single-handed, using a wine bottle hastily filled with petrol.

'Tea?' said Frankel. I remembered him making tea then as he made it now: pouring boiling water from a dented electric kettle into an antique teapot with a chipped lid. Even this room was enigmatic. Was he a pauper, hoarding the cash value of the skeleton clock and the tiny Corot etching, or a Croesus, indifferent to his plastic teaspoons and museum postcards of Rouault?

'And what can I do for you, young man?' He rubbed his hands together, exactly as he had done the day I first visited him. Then, my briefing could hardly have been more simple: find Communists and give them money, they had told me. But most of life's impossible tasks – from alchemy to squaring the circle – are similarly concise. At that time the British had virtually no networks in Western Europe. A kidnapping on the German–Dutch border in November 1939 had put both the European chief of SIS and his deputy into the hands of the Abwehr. A suitcase full of contact addresses captured in The Hague in May 1940, and the fall of France, had given the *coup de grâce* to the remainder. Champion and I were 'blind', as jargon has it, and halt and lame, too, if the truth be told. We had no contacts except Serge Frankel, who'd done the office a couple of favours in 1938 and 1939 and had never been contacted since.

'Communists.' I remembered the way that Frankel had said it, 'Communists', as though he'd not heard the word before. I had been posing as an American reporter, for America was still a neutral country. He looked again at the papers I had laid out on his writing table. There was a forged US passport sent hurriedly from the office in Berne, an accreditation to the New York *Herald Tribune* and a membership card of The American Rally for a Free Press, which the British Embassy in Washington recommended as the reddest of American organizations. Frankel had jabbed his finger on that card and pushed it to the end of the row, like a man playing patience. 'Now that the Germans have an Abwehr office here, Communists are lying low, my friend.' He had poured tea for us.

'But Hitler and Stalin have signed the peace pact. In Lyon the Communists are even publishing a news-sheet.'

Frankel looked up at me, trying to see if I was being provocative. He said, 'Some of them are even wearing the hammer and sickle again. Some are drinking with the German soldiers and calling them fellow workers, like the Party tells them to do. Some have resigned from the Party in disgust. Some have already faced firing squads. Some are reserving their opinion, waiting to see if the war is really finished. But which are which? Which are which?' He sipped his tea and then said, 'Will the English go on fighting?'

'I know nothing about the English, I'm an American,' I insisted. 'My office wants a story about the French Communists and how they are reacting to the Germans.'

43

Frankel moved the US passport to the end of the row. It was as if he was tacitly dismissing my credentials, and my explanations, one by one. 'The people you want to see are the ones still undecided.'

He looked up to see my reaction.

'Yes,' I said.

'The ones who have *not* signed a friendship treaty with the Boche, eh?'

I nodded.

'We'll meet again on Monday. What about the café in the arcade, at the Place Massena. Three in the afternoon.'

'Thank you, Mr Frankel. Perhaps there's something I can do for you in return. My office have let me have some real coffee . . .'

'Let's see what happens,' said Frankel. But he took the tiny packet of coffee. Already it was becoming scarce.

I picked up the documents and put them into my pocket. Frankel watched me very closely. Making a mistake about me could send him to a concentration camp. We both knew that. If he had any doubts he'd do nothing at all. I buttoned up my coat and bowed him goodbye. He didn't speak again until I reached the door. 'If I am wearing a scarf or have my coat buttoned at the collar, do not approach me.'

'Thank you, Mr Frankel,' I said. 'I'll watch out for that.'

He smiled. 'It seems like only yesterday,' he said. He poured the tea. 'You were too young to be a correspondent for an American newspaper, but I knew you were not working for the Germans.'

'How did you know that?'

He passed the cup of tea to me, murmuring apologies about having neither milk nor lemon. He said, 'They would have sent someone more suitable. The Germans had many men who'd lived in America long enough.

44

They could have chosen someone in his thirties or forties with an authentic accent.'

'But you went ahead,' I reminded him.

'I talked to Marius. We guessed you'd be bringing money. The first contact would have to bring money. We could do nothing without cash.'

'You could have asked for it, or stolen it.'

'All that came later – the bank hold-ups, the extortion, the loans. When you arrived we were very poor. We were offering only a franc for a rifle and we could only afford to buy the perfect Lebel pattern ones even then.'

'Rifles the soldiers had thrown away?' It was always the same conversation that we had, but I didn't mind.

'The ditches were full of them. It was that that started young Marius off – the *bataillon Guernica* was his choice of name – I thought it would have been better to have chosen a victory to celebrate, but young Marius liked the unequivocally anti-German connotation that the Guernica bombing gave us.'

'But on the Monday you said no,' I reminded him.

'On the Monday I told you not to have high hopes,' he corrected me. He ran his long bony fingers back into his fine white wispy hair.

'I knew no one else, Serge.'

'I felt sorry for you when you walked off towards the bus station, but young Marius wanted to look at you and make up his own mind. And that way it was safer for me, too. He decided to stop you in the street if you looked genuine.'

'At the Casino tabac he stopped me. I wanted English cigarettes.'

'Was that good security?'

'I had the American passport. There was no point in trying to pretend I was French.'

'And Marius said he might get some?'

45

'He waited outside the tabac. We talked. He said he'd hide me in the church. And when Champion returned, he hid us both. It was a terrible risk to take for total strangers.'

'Marius was like that,' said Frankel.

'Without you and Marius we might never have got started,' I said.

'Hardly,' said Frankel. 'You would have found others.' But he smiled and was flattered to think of himself as the beginning of the whole network. 'Sometimes I believe that Marius would have become important, had he lived.'

I nodded. They'd made a formidable partnership – the Jewish Communist and the anti-Fascist priest – and yet I remembered Frankel hearing the news of Marius's death without showing a flicker of emotion. But Frankel had been younger then, and keen to show us what his time in Moscow had really taught him.

'We made a lot of concessions to each other – me and Marius,' Frankel said. 'If he'd lived we might have achieved a great deal.'

'Sure you would,' I said. 'He would be running the Mafia, and you would have been made Pope.'

Flippancy was not in the Moscow curriculum, and Frankel didn't like it. 'Have you seen Pina Baroni yet?'

'Not yet,' I said.

'I see her in the market here sometimes,' said Frankel. 'Her little boutique in the Rue de la Buffa is a flourishing concern, I'm told. She's over the other business by now, and I'm glad . . .'

The 'other business' was a hand-grenade thrown into a café in Algiers in 1961. It killed her soldier husband and both her children. Pina escaped without a scratch, unless you looked inside her head. 'Poor Pina,' I said.

'And Ercole . . .' Frankel continued, as if he didn't want to talk of Pina, '. . . his restaurant prospers – they

46

say his grandson will inherit; and "the Princess" still dyes her hair red and gets raided by the social division.'

I nodded. The 'social division' was the delicate French term for vice squad.

'And Claude *l'avocat*?'

'It's Champion you want to know about,' said Frankel.

'Then tell me about Champion.'

He smiled. 'We were all taken in by him, weren't we? And yet when you look back, he's the same now as he was then. A charming sponger who could twist any woman round his little finger.'

'Yes?' I said doubtfully.

'Old Tix's widow, she could have sold out for a big lump sum, but Champion persuaded her to accept instalments. So Champion is living out there in the Tix mansion, with servants to wait on him hand and foot, while Madame Tix is in three rooms with an outdoor toilet, and inflation has devoured what little she does get.'

'Is that so?'

'And now that he sees the Arabs getting rich on the payments for oil, Champion is licking the boots of new masters. His domestic staff are all Arabs, they serve Arab food out there at the house, they talk Arabic all the time and when he visits anywhere in North Africa he gets VIP treatment.'

I nodded. 'I saw him in London,' I said. 'He was wearing a fez and standing in line to see "A Night in Casablanca".'

'It's not funny,' said Frankel irritably.

'It's the one where Groucho is mistaken for the Nazi spy,' I said, 'but there's not much singing.'

Frankel clattered the teapot and the cups as he stacked them on the tray. 'Our Mister Champion is very proud of himself,' he said.

47

'And pride comes before a fall,' I said. 'Is that what you mean, Serge?'

'*You* said that!' said Frankel. 'Just don't put words into my mouth, it's something you're too damned fond of doing, my friend.'

I'd touched a nerve.

Serge Frankel lived in an old building at the far end of the vegetable market. When I left his apartment that Monday afternoon, I walked up through the old part of Nice. There was brilliant sunshine and the narrow alleys were crowded with Algerians. I picked my way between strings of shoes, chickens, dates and figs. There was a peppery aroma of *merguez* sausages frying, and tiny bars where light-skinned workers drank pastis and talked football, and dark-skinned men listened to Arab melodies and talked politics.

From the Place Rosetti came the tolling of a church bell. Its sound echoed through the alleys, and stony-faced men in black suits hurried towards the funeral. Now and again, kids on mopeds came roaring through the alleys, making the shoppers leap into doorways. Sometimes there came cars, inch by inch, the drivers eyeing the scarred walls where so many bright-coloured vehicles had left samples of their paint. I reached the boulevard Jean Jaurès, which used to be the moat of the fortified medieval town, and is now fast becoming the world's largest car park. There I turned, to continue along the alleys that form the perimeter of the old town. Behind me a white BMW was threading through the piles of oranges and stalls of charcuterie with only a fraction to spare. Twice the driver hooted, and on the third time I turned to glare.

'Claude!' I said.

'Charles!' said the driver. 'I knew it was you.'

Claude had become quite bald. His face had reddened, perhaps from the weather, the wine or blood pressure. Or perhaps all three. But there was no mistaking the man. He still had the same infectious grin and the same piercing blue eyes. He wound the window down. 'How are you? How long have you been in Nice? It's early for a holiday, isn't it?' He drove on slowly. At the corner it was wide enough for him to open the passenger door. I got into the car alongside him. 'The legal business looks like it's flourishing,' I said. I was fishing, for I had no way of knowing if the cheerful law student whom we called Claude *l'avocat* was still connected with the legal profession.

'The legal business has been very kind to me,' said Claude. He rubbed his cheek and chuckled as he looked me up and down. 'Four grandchildren, a loving wife and my collection of Delftware. Who could ask for more.' He chuckled again, this time in self-mockery. But he smoothed the lapel of his pearl-grey suit and adjusted the Cardin kerchief so that I would notice that it matched his tie. Even in the old days, when knitted pullovers were the height of chic, Claude had been a dandy. 'And now Steve Champion lives here, too,' he said.

'So I hear.'

He smiled. 'It must be the sunshine and the cooking.'

'Yes,' I said.

'And it was Steve who . . .' He stopped.

'Saved my life?' I said irritably. 'Saved my life up at the quarry.'

'Put the *réseau* together, after the arrests in May,' said Claude. 'That's what I was going to say.'

'Well, strictly between the two of us, Claude, I wish I'd spent the war knitting socks,' I said.

'What's that supposed to mean?'

'It means I wish I had never heard of the lousy *réseau*, the Guernica network and all the people in it.'

49

'And Steve Champion?'

'Steve Champion most of all,' I said. 'I wish I could just come down here on holiday and not be reminded of all that useless crappy idiocy!'

'You don't have to shout at me,' Claude said. 'I didn't send for you, you came.'

'I suppose so,' I said. I regretted losing my cool if only for a moment.

'We *all* want to forget,' Claude said gently. 'No one wants to forget it more than I want to.'

The car was halted while two men unloaded cartons of instant couscous from a grey van. In the Place St François the fish market was busy, too. A decapitated tunny was being sliced into steaks alongside the fountain, and a woman in a rubber apron was sharpening a set of knives.

'So Steve is here?' I said.

'Living here. He lives out at the Tix house near the quarry.'

'What a coincidence,' I said. 'All of us here again.'

'Is it?' said Claude.

'Well, it sounds like a coincidence, doesn't it?'

The driver's sun-shield was drooping and Claude smiled as he reached up and pushed it flat against the roof of the car. In that moment I saw a gun in a shoulder holster under his arm. It wasn't an impress-the-girlfriend, or frightened-of-burglars kind of instrument. The leather holster was soft and shiny, and the underside of the magazine was scratched from years of use. A Walther PPK! Things must have got very rough in the legal business in the last few years.

He turned and smiled the big smile that I remembered from the old days. 'I don't believe in anything any more,' he confessed. 'But most of all I don't believe in coincidences. That's why I'm here.' He smoothed his tie again. 'Where can I drop you, Charles?'

6

Tuesday morning was cold and very still, as if the world was waiting for something to happen. The ocean shone like steel, and from it successive tidal waves of mist engulfed the promenade. The elaborate façades of the great hotels and the disc of the sun were no more than patterns embossed upon a monochrome world.

Trapped between the low pock-marked sky and the grey Mediterranean, two Mirage jets buzzed like flies in a bottle, the vibrations continuing long after they had disappeared out to sea. I walked past the seafood restaurants on the *quai*, where they were skimming the oil and slicing the *frites*. It was a long time until the tourist season but already there were a few Germans in the heated terraces, eating cream cakes and pointing with their forks, and a few British on the beach, with Thermos flasks of strong tea, and cucumber sandwiches wrapped up in *The Observer*.

I was on my way to Frankel's apartment. As I came level with the market entrance I stopped at the traffic lights. A dune buggy with a broken silencer roared past, and then a black Mercedes flashed its main beams. I waited as it crawled past me, its driver gesturing. It was Steve Champion. He was looking for a place to park but all the meter spaces were filled. Just as I thought he'd have to give up the idea, he swerved and bumped over the kerb and on to the promenade. The police allowed tourists to park there, and Champion's Mercedes had Swiss plates.

'You crazy bastard!' said Champion, with a smile. 'Why

51

didn't you tell me? Where are you staying?' The flesh under his eye was scratched and swollen and his smile was hesitant and pained.

'With the Princess,' I said.

He shook his head. 'You're a masochist, Charlie. That's a filthy hole.'

'She can do with the money,' I said.

'Don't you believe it, Charlie. She's probably a major shareholder in IBM or something. Look here – have you time for a drink?'

'Why not?'

He turned up the collar of his dark-grey silk trench coat and tied the belt carelessly. He came round the car to me. 'There's a sort of club,' he said.

'For expatriates?'

'For brothel proprietors and pimps.'

'Let's hope it's not too crowded,' I said.

Champion turned to have a better view of an Italian cruise-liner sailing past towards Marseille. It seemed almost close enough to touch, but the weather had discouraged all but the most intrepid passengers from venturing on deck. A man in oilskins waved. Champion waved back.

'Fancy a walk?' Champion asked me. He saw me looking at his bruised cheek and he touched it self-consciously.

'Yes,' I said. He locked the door of the car and pulled his scarf tight around his throat.

We walked north, through the old town, and through the back alleys that smelled of wood-smoke and shashlik, and past the dark bars where Arab workers drink beer and watch the slot-machine movies of blonde strippers.

But it was no cramped bar, with menu in Arabic, to which Champion took me. It was a fine mansion on the fringe of the 'musicians' quarter'. It stood well back from

52

the street, screened by full-grown palm trees, and guarded by stone cherubs on the porch. A uniformed doorman saluted us, and a pretty girl took our coats. Steve put his hand on my shoulder and guided me through the hall and the bar, to a lounge that was furnished with black leather sofas and abstract paintings in stainless-steel frames. 'The usual,' he told the waiter.

On the low table in front of us there was an array of financial magazines. Champion toyed with them. 'Why didn't you tell me?' he said. 'You let me make a fool of myself.'

It was Steve who'd taught me the value of such direct openings. To continue to deny that I worked for the department was almost an admission that I'd been assigned to seek him out. 'True-life confessions? For those chance meetings once or twice a year? That wasn't in the Steve Champion crash-course when I took it.'

He smiled and winced and, with only the tip of his finger, touched his bruised cheek. 'You did it well, old son. Asking me if I was recruiting you. That was a subtle touch, Charlie.' He was telling me that he now knew it had been no chance meeting that day in Piccadilly. And Steve was telling me that from now on there'd be no half-price admissions for boys under sixteen.

'Tell me one thing,' Steve said, as if he was going to ask nothing else, 'did you volunteer to come out here after me?'

'It's better that it's me,' I said. A waiter brought a tray with silver coffee-pot, Limoges china and a sealed bottle of private-label cognac. It was that sort of club.

'One day you might find out what it's like,' said Steve.

'There was the girl, Steve.'

'What about the girl?'

'It's a Kill File, Steve,' I told him. 'Melodie Page is dead.'

'Death of an operative?' He looked at me for a long time. He knew how the department felt about Kill File investigations. He spooned a lot of sugar into his coffee, and took his time in stirring it. 'So they are playing rough,' he said. 'Have they applied for extradition?'

'If the investigating officer decides . . .'

'Jesus Christ!' said Steve angrily. 'Don't give me that Moriarty Police Law crap. Are you telling me that there is a murder investigation being conducted by C.1 at the Yard?'

'Not yet,' I said. 'There were complications.'

Champion screwed up his face and sucked his coffee spoon. 'So Melodie was working for the department?'

I didn't answer. I didn't have to.

Champion nodded. 'Of course. What a clown I am. And she's dead? You saw the body?'

'Yes,' I said.

'Level with me, Charlie,' said Champion.

I said, 'No, I didn't see the body.' Champion poured coffee, then he snapped the seal on the cognac and poured two large tots.

'Neat. Effective. And not at all gaudy,' said Champion eventually, with some measure of admiration. He waggled the coffee spoon at me.

It seemed a bit disloyal to the department to understand his meaning too quickly. 'I don't understand,' I said.

'You understand, old boy,' said Champion. 'You understand. But not as well as I bloody understand.' He paused while a waiter brought the cigarettes he'd ordered. When the waiter departed, Steve said softly, 'There's no dead girl – or if there is, your people have killed her – this is just a stunt, a frame-up, to get me back to London.' Champion moved his cigarettes and his gold Dunhill lighter about on the magazines in front of him, pushing them like a little train from *The Financial Times* and on to *Forbes* and *Figaro*.

'They are pressing me,' I said. 'It's a Minister-wants-to-know inquiry.'

'Ministers never want to know,' said Champion bitterly. 'All Ministers want is answers to give.' He sighed. 'And someone decided that I was the right answer for this one.'

'I wish you'd come back to London with me,' I said.

'Spend a month or more kicking my heels in Whitehall? And what could I get out of it? An apology, if I'm lucky, or fifteen years, if that suits them better. No, you'll not get me going back with you.'

'But suppose they extradite you – it'll be worse then.'

'So you say.' He inhaled deeply on his cigarette. 'But the more I think about it, the less frightened I am. The fact they've sent you down here is a tacit admission that they won't pull an extradition order on me.'

'I wouldn't bet on it.'

'Well, that's because you're too damned naïve. The department don't want me back in London, explaining to them all the details of the frame-up they themselves organized. This is all part of an elaborate game . . . a softening-up for something big.'

'Something that London wants you to do for them?' I asked. 'Is that what you mean?'

'Let's stop beating around the bush, shall we? The department has given me jobs from time to time. They do that with pensioned-off operatives because it keeps them signing the Act, and also because their pensions make them the most needy – and so the cheapest – people around.'

'Come back to London, Steve.'

'Can't you understand plain bloody King's English,

Charlie? Either the girl is *not* dead, and the department have put her on ice in order to finger me . . .'

'Or?'

'Or she's dead and the department arranged it.'

'No.'

'How can you say no. Do they let you read the Daily Yellows?'

'It's no good, Steve,' I said. 'The department would never do it this way and both of us know it.'

'The confidence you show in those bastards . . .' said Champion. 'We know only a fraction of what goes on up there. They've told you that Melodie was a departmental employee – have you ever heard of her or seen any documents?'

'The documents of an operative in the field? Of course I haven't.'

'Exactly. Well, suppose I tell you that she was never an employee and the department have wanted her killed for the last three months. Suppose I told you that they ordered me to kill her, and that I refused. And that that was when the row blew up.'

'Go on,' I said.

'The department made that contact for me. They said she was from the Palestinian terrorists. They told me that she was a nutty American student, the London contact for five hundred stolen Armalites and two tons of gelignite.' Champion was excited now and smiling nervously, as I remembered him from the old days.

He sipped his drink. 'They sent an American chap to see me. Is his name Schindler? Drinks that Underberg stuff, I remember. I wouldn't believe he was from the department at first. Then they sent a Mutual down to confirm him as OK. Is it Schroder?'

'Something like that,' I said.

56

'He mentioned the killing end. I didn't take him seriously at first. I mean, they must still have special people for that game, surely. But he was in earnest. Ten thousand pounds, he said. He had it all set up, too. He'd organized a flat in Barons Court stacked up with beer and whisky and cans of beans and soup. I'm telling you, it was equipped like a fall-out shelter. And he showed me this hypodermic syringe, killing wire and rubber gloves. Talk about horror movies, I needed a couple of big whiskies when I got out of there.' He drank some coffee. 'And then I realized how I'd put my prints on everything he'd shown me.' He sighed. 'No fool like an old fool.'

'Did they pay the bill for the tweed jacket we found there?'

'There was no reason to be suspicious,' said Champion. 'They told me to order the suits, and they paid for them. It was only when they sent a funny little man round to my place to take the labels and manufacturers' marks out of them that I began to worry. I mean . . . can you think of anything more damning than picking up some johnny and then finding he's got no labels in his suits?'

'There was money in the shoulder-pads,' I told him. 'And documents, too.'

'Well, there you are. It's the kind of thing a desk-man would dream up if he'd never been at the sharp end. Wouldn't you say that, Charlie?'

I looked at Champion but I didn't answer. I wanted to believe him innocent, but if I discounted his charm, and the nostalgia, I saw only an ingenious man improvising desperately in the hope of getting away with murder.

'How long ago are we talking about?' I said.

'Just a couple of weeks before I ran into you . . . or rather you sought me out. That's why I wasn't suspicious that you were official. I mean, they could have found out whatever they needed to know through their normal contacts ... but that girl, she wasn't one of them, Charlie, believe me.'

'Did you tell her?'

'Like fun! This girl was trying to buy armaments – and not for the first time. She could take care of herself, believe me. She carried, too – she carried a big ·38 in that crocodile handbag.' He finished his coffee and tried to pour more, but the pot was empty. 'Anyway, I've never killed anyone in cold blood and I wasn't about to start, not for the department and not for money, either. But I reasoned that someone would do it. It might have been someone I liked a lot better than her. It might have been you.'

'That was really considerate of you Steve,' I said.

He turned his head to me. The swelling seemed to have grown worse in the last half hour. Perhaps that was because of Champion's constant touches. The blue and red flesh had almost pushed his eye closed. 'You don't go through our kind of war, and come out the other end saying you'd never kill anyone, no matter what kind of pressure is applied.'

I looked at him for a long time. 'The days of the entrepreneur are over, Steve,' I told him. 'Now it's the organization man who gets the Christmas bonus and the mileage allowance. People like you are called "heroes", and don't mistake it for a compliment. It just means has-beens, who'd rather have a hunch than a computer output. You are yesterday's spy, Steve.'

'And you'd sooner believe those organization men than believe me?'

'No good waving your arms, Steve,' I said. 'You're standing on the rails and the express just blew its whistle.'

He stared at me. 'Oooh, they've changed you, Charlie! Those little men who've promised you help with your mortgage, and full pension rights at sixty. Who would

58

have thought they could have done that to the kid who fought the war with a copy of *Wage Labour and Capital* in his back pocket. To say nothing of that boring lecture you gave everyone about Mozart's revolutionary symbolism in "The Marriage of Figaro".' He smiled, but I didn't.

'You've had your say, Steve. Don't take the jury out into the back alley.'

'I hope you listened carefully then,' he said. He got to his feet and tossed some ten-franc notes on to the coffee tray. 'Because if you are only half as naïve as you pretend to be . . . and if *you* have put your dabs all over some carefully chosen incriminating evidence . . .'

'Go on,' I said.

'Then it could be that London are setting us both up for that big debriefing in the sky.'

'You've picked up my matches,' I said.

7

'You'd sooner live in a dump than live in a nice home,' said Schlegel accusingly.

'No,' I said, but without much conviction. I didn't want to argue with him.

He opened the shutters so that he could see the charcuterie across the alley. The tiny shop-window was crammed with everything from shredded carrot to pig feet. Schlegel shuddered. 'Yes, you would,' he insisted. 'Remember that fleapit you used to have in Soho. Look at that time we booked you into the St Regis, and you went into a cold-water walk-up in the Village. You like dumps!'

'OK,' I said.

'If this place had some kind of charm, I'd understand. But it's just a flophouse.' For a long time he was silent. I walked across to the window and discovered that he was staring into the first-floor window across the alley. A fat woman in a frayed dressing-gown was using a sewing machine. She looked up at Schlegel, and when he did not look away she closed her shutters. Schlegel turned and looked round the room. I'd put asters, souci and cornflowers into a chipped tumbler from the washbasin. Schlegel flicked a finger at them and the petals fell. He went over to the tiny writing table that wobbled unless something was wedged under one leg. My Sony radio-recorder almost toppled as Schlegel tested the table for stability. I had turned the volume down as Schlegel had entered, but now the soft sounds of Helen Ward, and Goodman's big band, tried to get out. Schlegel pushed the 'off' button, and the music ended with a loud click. 'That phone work?' he asked.

'It did this morning.'

'Can I give you a word of advice, fella?'

'I wish you would,' I told him.

For a moment I thought I'd offended him, but you don't avoid Schlegel's advice that easily. 'Don't stay in places like this, pal. I mean . . . sure, you save a few bucks when you hit the cashier's office for the price of a hotel. But jeeze . . . is it worth it?'

'I'm not hitting the cashier's office for the price of anything more than I'm spending.'

His face twisted in a scowl as he tried to believe me. And then understanding dawned. 'You came in here, in the sub, in the war. Right? I remember now: Villefranche – it's a deep-water anchorage. Yeah. Sure. Me too. I came here once . . . a long time ago on a flat-top, with the Sixth Fleet. Nostalgia, eh?'

'This is where I first met Champion.'

'And the old doll downstairs.' He nodded to himself. 'She's got to be a hundred years old . . . she was the radio operator . . . the Princess! Right?'

'We just used this as a safe-house for people passing through.'

'It's a brothel!' Schlegel accused.

'Well, I don't mind that so much,' I told him. 'The baker next door waves every morning when I leave. This morning, he winked.'

'Wouldn't you rather be in a hotel?'

'Well, I'm going to ask the Princess if the girls could be a little quieter with the doors.'

'Banging all night?' said Schlegel archly.

'Exactly,' I said.

'A cat house,' mused Schlegel. 'A natural for an escape chain. But the Nazis had them high on the check-out list.'

'Well, we won the war,' I said sharply. Schlegel would get in there, checking out the syntax of my dreams, if he knew the way.

'I'll call Paris,' he said.

'I'd better tell the Princess.'

'Do we have to?'

'We have to,' I said. 'Unless you want her interrupting you to tell you how much it's costing, while you're talking to the Elysée Palace.'

Schlegel scowled to let me know that sarcasm wasn't going to help me find out who he was phoning. 'Extension downstairs, huh?'

I went to the door and yelled down to the bar, at which the Princess was propped with *Salut les Copains* and a big Johnny Walker. 'I'm calling Paris,' I shouted.

'You called Paris already today, chéri,' she said.

'And now we're calling again, you old bag,' growled Schlegel, but he took good care to keep his voice down. Already she'd made him apologize to one of the bar girls for saying goddamn.

'That's right,' I told her.

'Just as long as you don't forget the money you're spending, my darling.'

'Darleeeng,' growled Schlegel. 'Will you believe that's the first hearing-aid I've seen with sequins on it?'

He picked up his plastic case, put it on the bed and opened it. At first glance it might have been mistaken for a portable typewriter, permanently built into its case. It was the newest model of acoustic coupler. Schlegel began typing on the keys.

I said, 'Anything fresh on the girl? Body been found, or anything?'

Schlegel looked up at me, sucked his teeth and said, 'I'll ask them what Missing Persons knows.' When Schlegel finished typing his message he dialled the Paris number.

He gave his real name. I suppose that was to save all the complications that would arise if he was phoning from a hotel that held his passport. Then he said, 'Let's scramble,' and put the phone handpiece into the cradle switch inside the case. He pressed the 'transmit' button and the coupler put a coded version of what he'd typed through the phone cables at thirty or forty characters a second. There was a short delay, then the reply came back from the same sort of machine. This time Schlegel's coupler decoded it and printed it on to tape in 'plain English'. Schlegel read it, grunted, pushed the 'memory erase' button and rang off.

'You ask those guys the *time*, and they'd tell you what trouble they're having from the Records Office,' he said. He burned the tape without showing it to me. It was exactly the way the textbook ordered but it didn't make me want to open my heart to him about Champion's version of the girl's death.

But I told him everything Champion had said.

'He's right,' said Schlegel. 'He knows we wouldn't be pussyfooting around if we had the evidence. Even if he enters the UK I doubt whether the department would let us hold him.'

'He must have killed the girl,' I said, with some hesitation.

'He didn't collect that shiner by walking into a lamp-post.'

I nodded. Champion's bruised face was just the sort of blow he might have suffered while overpowering the girl. And the two scratches on his cheek were just like the damage to the wallpaper near the bed. No matter how much I tried to push the idea away, Champion's guilt bobbed up again like a plastic duck.

'You tell me Champion was some kind of master spy,' Schlegel said. 'Well, I'm telling you he's a loser. So far he's fouled up every which way, so I'm not joining the fan club. Champion is a creep, an over-confident creep, and if he steps out of line we'll clobber him, but good!'

'That's the way it looks,' I agreed.

'You're telling me it's all a set-up?'

I shrugged. 'That's one of the new couplers, is it?'

Schlegel stroked the metal case that was intended to make it look like a cheap typewriter. 'I can plug that baby into any computer with terminals. Last week I used the CIA TELCOM from a call-box, and tomorrow I'll abstract from the London Data Bank.'

'London will ring you back?'

'But not here. Not secure enough. That old doll downstairs . . . no, I'll have to get going.'

'Meet her,' I said. 'Otherwise I'll get endless questions.'

'One drink,' he said.

'You could be right . . . about Champion, I mean. People change.'

We picked our way down the narrow creaking staircase before the time-switch plopped. I opened the door marked 'No Entry' and went through it into the bar.

Through the bead curtain I could see a patch of sunlight on the scaly brickwork of the alley. But inside, the room was as dark as night. An ornate table-lamp at one end of the bar made a golden spot on each of the bottles lined up behind the counter, and gave just enough light for the Princess to see the cash register.

'Come and sit here, Charlie darling,' she said, but her eyes were fixed on Colonel Schlegel. Obediently, I took the bar stool she indicated. Schlegel sat down, too. I put my arm round the Princess and gave her rouged and powdered cheek a circumspect kiss.

'Rapist!' said the Princess.

A girl appeared from out of nowhere and put her

hands on the counter to show us how willing she was to serve expensive drinks.

'Underberg,' said Schlegel, 'and soda.'

'And Charlie will have Scotch,' said the Princess. 'So will I.'

The girl served the drinks and, without discussing the subject, put it all on my bill. Schlegel had the coupler at his feet and I noticed the way he kept his shoe pressed against it to be sure it was not removed.

'Does your friend know that you were here in the war, Charlie?'

'Yes, he knows,' I said.

'What war was that, Charlie?' said Schlegel.

The Princess pretended not to hear Schlegel. She craned her neck to look in the fly-specked mirror behind the bar, so that she could make adjustments to her rouge and eye make-up.

'We had good times, didn't we, Charlie? We had good times as well as bad ones.' She turned to face us again. 'I can remember nights when we sat along this bar counter, with the German sentries walking along the sea-front there. Guns in my cellar and the wireless set in a wine barrel. My God! When I think of the risks we took.'

'You knew this guy Champion then?' Schlegel asked her.

'And I liked him. I still do like him, although I haven't seen him for years. A gentleman of the old sort.' She looked at Schlegel as he swilled down his Underberg and then crunched the ice-cubes in his teeth. 'If you know what I mean,' she added.

'Yeah, well, there's a lot of definitions,' said Schlegel affably, 'and most of them are obscene. So you liked him, eh?'

'Well, at least he didn't betray us,' said the Princess.

'Did anyone?' I said.

'That filthy little Claude betrayed us,' said the Princess.

'Claude *l'avocat*? I saw him only yesterday.'

'Here? The little swine is here?' shouted the Princess angrily. 'He'll get killed if he comes here to Villefranche.' She clasped her beads and twisted them against her neck, staring at me as if angry that I didn't understand. 'If only I'd kept the newspaper clipping.'

'About Claude?'

'He got a medal – an iron cross or something – he was working for the German police all the time. His real name is Claude Winkler, or some name like that. His mother was French, they say. He betrayed Marius and old Madame Baroni and poor Steve Champion, too.'

I drank my whisky. 'All that time and he was working for the Abwehr.'

'The Abwehr – how could I forget that word,' said the Princess.

'And they let us go on functioning,' I said. 'That was cunning.'

'Yes, if they'd arrested us all, others would have replaced us. It was clever of them to let us continue.'

'So Claude was a German,' I said. 'When I think of all those months . . .'

'And the RAF escape-route,' said the Princess. 'They let that continue, too.'

I nodded. 'As long as the flyers came through here, London would be convinced that all was well.'

'I would kill him,' said the Princess. 'If he came in this bar now, I'd kill him.'

'Claude Winkler,' said Schlegel, as the Princess got up from the bar stool in order to pour more drinks for us. 'Do you know what he does now?'

'Yes,' said the Princess. 'He still works for the Boche Secret Police.' She poured drinks for us. 'The nerve of the man! To come back here again.'

I put my hand over my glass. She poured whisky for herself, and this time Schlegel too had whisky.

'I'll kill him if he comes in here,' she said again. 'People think I'm a silly old woman, but I'll do it, I promise you.'

'Claude *l'avocat*,' I said. There were more tourists now, peering into the bars, reading the menus and looking at the crude daubs that the 'artists' sold on the waterfront. None of them came into this bar: it was a dump, just as Schlegel said. Fly-specked old bottles of watered-down cognac, and re-labelled champagne. Bar girls with fat legs and unseeing eyes. And upstairs, broken beds, dirty counterpanes and a 'badger man' who came in and shouted 'That's my wife!' before even your pants were down.

'So Claude betrayed us,' I said.

'Are you all right?' said the Princess.

'I'm all right,' I said. 'Why?'

'You look like you are going to be sick,' she said. If you work in a bar for thirty years, you develop a sharp eye for people who feel sick.

8

'We didn't just *want* to murder him; we planned the killing.'

Serge Frankel did not look up. He put the big magnifying glass over the envelope and examined the stamps carefully. Then he moved it to look at the franking marks. 'Yes, we planned it,' he said. He rubbed his eyes and passed the envelope to me. 'Take a look at that cancellation. What does it say?'

I leaned across the desk, careful not to disturb the trays and the tweezers and the small fluorescent lamp that he used to detect paper repairs and forgeries. I looked closely at the envelope. The stamping machine had not been applied evenly. One side of the circular mark was very faint. '"Varick St Sta . . ." Could it be Varick Street Station?'

'Can you make out the date?'

' May something nineteen thirty.'

'Yes, well that's what it should be.' He picked it up, using only the tips of his fingers. It was a foolscap-size cream envelope, with three large US stamps on it and a big diamond-shaped rubber stamp that said 'First Europe Pan-America Round Flight. *Graf Zeppelin*'.

'Is it very valuable?' I asked.

He slid it into a clear plastic sleeve and clipped it into a large album with others. 'Only for those who want such things,' he said. 'Yes, we planned to kill Claude *l'avocat*. That was in 1947. He gave evidence at one of the Hamburg trials. Pina saw it in a Paris newspaper.'

'But you did nothing.'

'Oh, it wasn't quite like that. Our bitterness was based upon our natural aversion for the betrayer – as yours is now. But Claude did not betray anyone. He was a German. He passed himself off as a Frenchman in order to help his own country . . .'

'Sophistry!'

'Can you remember Claude's accent when he was working with us?'

'He said he was from the north.'

'And none of us had travelled very much, or we might have detected quite a bit of Boche there, eh?'

'None of us had travelled enough – except for Marius. So he made sure that Marius died.'

'I think so,' said Serge calmly. 'But Claude's life was in danger all the time he was with us, did you ever think of that?'

'They were our people, Serge. And they died in squalid camps and torture chambers. Am I supposed to admire your calm and rational attitude? Well, I don't. And perhaps it would be better if you stopped being so godlike . . .'

'We Jews, you mean?'

'I don't know what I meant.'

'This is not in character, Charles. You are the one who stayed so calm. Without you we would have been out on the streets fighting, instead of silently building almost the only network that lasted till the end.' He cocked his head. 'Are you now saying that was wrong?'

I didn't reply. I picked up some of his valuable envelopes and went through the motions of studying them.

'You're fighting the wrong enemy,' said Serge. 'That's all over, that war! I'm more interested in what our friend Champion is doing with his import and export business with the Arabs.'

'Guns, you mean?'

'Who said anything about guns?' Behind him was the skyline of old Nice. The afternoon was dying a slow death, spilling its gory sunlight all over the shiny rooftops.

'You've resurrected the old network, haven't you?' I said.

He pointed to a large lamp that occupied most of the sofa upon which I was sitting. 'Move that infra-red lamp, if it's in your way. This weather is bad for my arthritis.'

'The Guernica network . . .' I said. He watched me as I pieced together my suspicions and the hints and half-truths that only now began to make sense to me. 'You're playing at spies . . . for money? . . . for old times' sake? . . . Because you all hate Champion? Tell me, why?'

He didn't deny it, but that didn't prove I was right, for he was not the sort of man who would leap in to correct your grammar – especially when there might be a deportation order awarded for the right answer.

'Curiosity – even nosiness – is not yet against the law, even in France,' he said.

'I saw Champion today,' I admitted.

'Yes,' said Serge, 'at the *Herren Klub*.'

It was a shrewd jibe, not because it described the club or its members, but because it provided an image of the *Fressenwelle* – Mercedes limousines, silent chauffeurs, astrakhan collars, the whiff of Havana and a muffled belch – I'd never before realized how well Champion fitted into such a scene.

'You are having him followed?' I asked.

Serge picked up an envelope and removed it from its clear plastic cover. 'I sent this to a customer last month. He complained that its condition was not good enough for his collection. Today I had it back from a second customer who says it looks too new to be genuine.' He looked up and smiled at me to make sure I shared the joke.

'Yes,' I said. It was no good pushing him.

'It's a pre-adhesive cover – 1847 – by ship from Port Mauritius to Bordeaux. It got that ship-letter cachet in southern Ireland. It was postmarked again in Dublin as a backstamp, and then got stamped at London and Boulogne before arriving in Bordeaux.' He held it close to the desk light. It was a yellowed piece of paper, folded and sealed so as to make a packet upon which the address had been written. On the back of the folded sheet there was a mess of rubber-stamped names and dates and a cracked segment of a red seal.

Serge looked at me.

'He thinks it's fake?' I said finally.

'He says the watermarks on the paper are wrong for this date . . . And the shape of the Dublin stamp . . . that too he doesn't like.'

'What do *you* say?' I asked politely.

He took it by the two top corners and pulled, so that the sheet tore slowly right down the middle. There was an almost imperceptible hesitation at the bottom and then the two halves separated, and the ragged edge flashed in the lamplight.

'He was quite correct,' said Serge. 'It was a forgery.'

'Did you have to destroy it?'

'If I kept it here, and a client wanted such a thing . . . How can I be sure I wouldn't yield to temptation?'

I smiled. It was not easy to think of this Spartan yielding to temptation.

'I was not even fifteen when I first joined the Communist Party. I was so proud. I slept with that card under my pillow, and in the daytime it was pinned inside my vest. I've given my whole life to the party. You know I have, Charles. You know I have.'

'Yes,' I said.

'The risks I ran, the times I was beaten with police

71

truncheons, the bullets in my leg, the pneumonia I caught during the Spanish winter fighting . . . all this I don't regret. A youth must have something to offer his life to.' He picked up the torn pieces of paper as if for a moment regretting that he'd destroyed the forged cover. 'When they told me about the Stalin–Hitler pact I went round explaining it to the men of lesser faith. The war you know about. Czechoslovakia – well, I'd never liked the Czechs, and when the Russian tanks invaded Hungary . . . well, they were asking for it, those Hungarians – I ask you, who ever met an honest Hungarian?'

I smiled at his little joke.

'But I am a Jew,' said Frankel. 'They are putting my people into concentration camps, starving them, withdrawing the right to work from anyone who asks to go to Israel. When these pigs who call themselves socialists went to the aid of the Arabs . . . then I knew that no matter what kind of Communist I was, I was first and foremost a Jew. A Jew! Do you understand now?'

'And Champion . . . ?'

'You come and visit me from time to time. You tell me that you are on vacation – I believe you. But I've always wondered about you, Charles. What sort of work does a man like you do in peacetime? You told me once that you were an economist, working for your government. Very well, but now you are asking me discreet questions about Champion, and all the others. So I ask myself if the work you do for your government is perhaps not entirely confined to economics.'

It was like taking a book down from one of these crowded shelves: you couldn't read the fine print until the dust settled. 'What is Champion up to, then?' I said.

'You mean, what am I up to?' said Frankel. 'Everyone knows what Champion is up to: he's an Arab.'

'And you?'

'I'm a Jew,' said Frankel. 'It's as simple as that.'

72

9

Geneva. Calvin's great citadel is perched precariously between the grey mountains of France and the grey waters of Lake Geneva. The city, too, is grey: grey stone buildings, grey-uniformed cops, even its money and its politics are grey. Especially its politics.

I looked out through the hotel's spotlessly clean windows, and watched the plume of water that is Geneva's last despairing attempt at gaiety. The tall jet fell back into the lake and hammered the surface into steel. The traffic moving slowly along the lakeside stopped, started and then stopped again. There was no hooting, no flashing headlights, no arguments, no complaining. The citizens of Geneva are as well adjusted as its clocks. It was 10 A.M., but the city was silent except for the rustle of banknotes and the ticking of a couple of billion wristwatches.

'You were a fool to come here. And so was I.' He pushed the bowl of cornflakes away untouched.

'You came because you knew I'd make plenty of trouble for you if you didn't come. I came because I had to.'

'You came for yourself! This isn't official; it's just for yourself. And it's bloody dangerous!' His upper-class voice was pitched high and slightly querulous, like some customer complaining about the caviare in Harrods.

'Well, it's too late now, Aziz.' I poured some tea for him and he gave me a wintry smile. Aziz was working for the World Meteorological Organization headquarters on the Avenue Giuseppe-Motta. His masters here in Geneva would have been astonished perhaps to discover that he was a senior analyst for Egyptian Intelligence. But certainly his masters in Cairo would have been devastated to hear that he'd been on London's payroll for nearly ten years. 'And anyway,' I said, 'this one is *going* to become official. Believe me, it is.'

'You said that in New York.'

'That was different,' I said. 'You got nineteen thousand dollars out of that one. This time it's free.'

'I'm glad you told me,' said Aziz. He sniffed. He was a bird-like little man, with thinning hair, large eyes and a nose like a ploughshare. His dark skin was inherited from the Sudanese peasant girl who bore him, while the chalk-stripe worsted, the hand-made shoes and public-school tie were worn with the aplomb he'd learned from the Egyptian mine-owner who acknowledged the boy as his son. The small turquoise pinned into his tie was taken from a mine that has been worked since the first dynasty of Egyptian kings. For such a man it is not easy to adapt to the stringencies of a nationalized land and high taxation. 'There will be no money this time?' He smiled. 'Surely you are not serious.'

'Champion,' I said. 'Steve Champion.' I gave him a few seconds to think about that. 'I need help, Aziz, I really need it.'

'You must be mad.'

I pushed him a little. 'London's request for the Libyan trade figures, the Sinai supplementaries, the Kissinger stuff and the analysis you did in December. That all came through me. You must have stashed away a quarter of a million dollars over the last three years, Aziz. And most of that stuff was a doddle, wasn't it? It's the easiest money you ever earned, Aziz. And all of that came through me.'

'What are you fishing for – a percentage?' He poured

himself more tea, and took a long time spearing the slice of lemon, but he never drank the tea. He toyed with the thin slice of lemon, and then dipped it into the sugar, popped it into his mouth and looked up guiltily. I smiled.

'You'd better let me phone the office,' he said. He looked at the gold quartz chronometer on his wrist, and touched his diamond cufflinks to make sure they were still in place. I suppose that must be the problem with diamond cufflinks, apart from the way they slash the red silk lining of your Savile Row suits.

'Go ahead,' I said. 'I don't care how long it takes. We'll have room service send lunch up here. I've spent half the night checking this room for electronic plumbing.'

He looked around the austere Swiss hotel room that cost as much per night as the average British worker received per week. He shuddered. 'It won't take that long,' he said.

'This time I've got more to lose than you have.'

He looked me up and down, from shoes to haircut. 'I don't think so,' he said finally. He sniffed again.

'Just Champion?' he said. All these people who sell us information are like that. They categorize it, and husband it, and let it go only grudgingly, as a philatelist disposes of bits of his collection, and tries to get rid of the dud stamps first. Aziz smoothed his hair across the crown of his head. There wasn't much of it, and he patted it gently. 'You've always played fair with me,' he said. 'I'd be the first to admit that.' I waited while he persuaded himself to tell me what I wanted to know.

'It's the same tedious story that we know only too well,' said Aziz, in his beautifully modulated English public-school accent. 'London put Champion into some of the rougher bits of the small-arms trade . . .'

'Terrorist weapons.'

'Terrorist weapons. And eventually Champion makes contact with our people.'

'Political Intelligence.'

'Political Intelligence,' repeated Aziz, and nodded. Why the hell he still called them his people, when he'd spent a decade selling them out, was strictly between him and his analyst, but I let him continue uninterrupted. 'London must have seen what would happen,' said Aziz. 'Ask yourself . . . Champion's father spent his whole life in Egypt. The Academy gave him a banquet when he retired. Nasser was a student of the old man, you know, as was Sadat. Even the younger Champion has better Arabic than I can put my tongue to.'

'Do you want to light that cigarette?' I said, 'Or do you prefer waving it around?'

He smiled and caught the matches I threw to him. He seemed surprised to find they burned as brightly as a gold lighter. 'We turned him, of course.' He blew smoke and took a piece of tobacco off his lip with a long fingernail. 'At first it was all quite straightforward; London knew he was a double, Cairo knew he was a double. It was a convenient method of communication between Egypt and you . . .'

'When was that?'

'Let's say until the summer before last. It was just before the Fleet exercises that he delivered the NATO wavelengths to us. That was not part of the plan – as far as London was concerned. They found out when Damascus got the wavelengths. London got a rocket from NATO, or so I heard. Yes, Champion burned his boats when he did that.'

'Champion did it for money?'

'My dear fellow . . .' he protested. 'What else?'

'You seem pretty certain about all this, Aziz. Even you have been known to make a mistake.'

'Have I?' He frowned. 'I certainly don't remember one.'

I got up and went back to the window to watch the lake again. I said, 'Are you just giving me the gossip from the Cairo Hilton?'

'This is all top-level stuff, old boy. There's a very limited circulation for Champion's material – top bloody secret, all the way.'

'How did you get it?'

'My brother-in-law, of course.'

'Of course,' I said. His borther-in-law was a one-star general in Cairo's Department of Political Intelligence that fills – and overflows from – a seven-storey building in Heliopolis.

Aziz was watching me closely as I turned away from the window. 'I can get you Xerox copies of anything special,' he offered. 'But it will take at least two weeks.'

'We'll see, Aziz.'

'Oh, yes, Champion's deep into it.' He stubbed out the cigarette and watched me as I figured out what to do next. 'It's upset you, hasn't it,' said Aziz, with more friendliness than I would have thought him capable of. 'I'm sorry about that, but Champion has gone a lot too far for London to be running him still – he's Cairo's man. He's ours.'

Ours, I thought, good old Aziz, consummate schizoid, that's the way to be. I sat down on the leather armchair and closed my eyes. 'There's got to be a better way than this to earn a living, Aziz,' I said. I had to be back in Villefranche that evening. It was a long drive and I was suddenly very, very tired.

'No doubt about that, old boy,' said Aziz. 'Trouble is . . . a chap's got to have a little bread, while he's figuring out what the better way is.'

10

He was wearing a short fur coat, and a black kerchief knotted cowboy-style, right against the throat. It was a measure of their subtlety that they sent along a man so unlike any policeman I'd ever seen. This youngster was completely different from the wrestlers of the Police Judiciaire in Marseille, or the hatchet-faced PJ boys who work in Nice. I'd noticed him the previous evening. He'd been drinking straight cognac at the far end of the bar when I went in to ask the Princess for the key of my room. It was a bad sign – cognac, I mean; I like my cops to stick to rot-gut.

He was in the same seat next morning, drinking coffee and smiling apologetically, as if he'd been there all night. 'Monsieur Charles Bonnard?' he said.

That was my wartime name: I thought I'd seen the last reel of that one, but now the nightmares came back. He didn't wait for my reply. 'My name is Fabre. Inspector Fabre, Renseignements Généraux, Lyon.'

'That's a relief,' I said. 'Just for a moment I thought you were from the Gestapo.'

He smiled again. 'We weren't quite sure what name you'd be using this time.'

'Well, I'm glad to hear someone wasn't,' I said.

'You'll have to come to Lyon, I'm afraid,' he said.

He could have been no older than twenty-five, but his youth, like his bizarre outfit, made him a likely recruit for the political undercover work of the RG. He was tall and broad-shouldered, but the slim hips would have suited a dancer or acrobat. His handsome bony face was white. In the north it would have gone unremarked, but here in the Riviera it seemed almost perverse that anyone should so avoid the sunshine.

He rubbed his fingers nervously. 'You'll have to come with us,' he said apologetically. 'To Lyon,' he told me again. He stopped rubbing his hands together for long enough to reach into an inside pocket for a tin of throat lozenges. He tore the silver wrapping from two of them, and popped them into his mouth in swift succession.

'You'll need overnight things,' he said.

I smiled. The Princess came in and put my coffee on the counter. She looked from one to the other of us and left without speaking. 'Why not pay your bill now?' he said. 'I'll make sure they hold your room for a few days. I mean, if you are not back tonight, why pay these hotel bastards?'

I nodded and drank some more coffee. 'Have you worked very long for the RG?' I asked.

He swallowed his throat lozenges. 'Forget checking me out,' he said. 'I don't know anybody important there. That's why I get lousy jobs like bringing you in.'

There was no sign of the Princess. From behind the cash register I took the handful of cash slips that were marked 'Charles'. I added fifteen per cent and signed. 'No need to hold the room,' I said. 'They are not expecting a tour-bus.'

He looked around the bar. There was enough daylight to expose the sleazy fly-blown wallpaper and the cracked lino. He smiled, and I smiled back, and then we went up to get my baggage.

Once inside my room, he became more confidential. 'You must be someone important,' he told me, 'judging by all the teleprinter messages and what I hear about the cabinet du préfet complaining to London.'

'Why are you telling me?' I asked.

79

'Cops should stick together,' he said. He opened the door of the battered wardrobe, and spent a moment or two looking at his brown-speckled reflection. 'Last year I followed a suspect to Aachen, in Germany. I grabbed him and brought him back across the border in my car. There was no end of fuss. But luckily the Aachen CID lied their heads off for me. Cops have to stick together; bureaucrats arrest only pieces of paper.'

He pulled my suit out of the wardrobe and folded it carefully while I packed my case. 'They'll take you up to Paris, I think. If you want to make a quick phone call, I won't hear you.'

'No, thanks,' I said. I went into the bathroom and threw my shaving gear into the zip bag. His voice was louder when he next spoke and I could tell he'd started a new throat lozenge. 'And if you have a gun, I'd get rid of it. It will just give them something to hold you for.'

'I don't carry a gun,' I called from the bathroom. I could hear him going all through the drawers of the wardrobe.

I closed the bathroom door. Then I released the plastic bath panels with my knife. I reached into the dust and dead spiders to get the plastic bag I'd hidden there. I didn't have to swing out the cylinder, I could see the 125 grain round-nosed bullets that I'd loaded into the ·38 Centennial Airweight. I stuffed the pistol into the waistband of my trousers and quickly replaced the panel. Then I flushed the toilet and emerged from the bathroom. It had taken me no more than ten seconds.

Fabre said, 'Because if they find a pistol anywhere in the room here, they can hold you under the new emergency laws – one month it is.' He slammed the last drawer closed, as if to punctuate the warning.

'I don't carry a pistol. I don't even *own* a pistol. You know English policemen don't have guns.'

'I was forgetting,' he said. 'And you have *habeas corpus* and all that crap, too. Hell, what a life for a cop. Are you sure you don't want to make a phone call? Call London if you want, but make it snappy.'

'Are you in traffic?'

'Renseignements Généraux,' he said. 'I told you I was from RG. Why?'

'Because you come on like a courtesy cop,' I said.

He smiled. 'I'm one of the graduate entries,' he said. He gave a self-conscious smile. 'I don't believe in rough stuff, unless it's absolutely necessary.'

'Have you got a car here?'

'And a driver. We must stop in Nice, at the Palais de Justice. I must sign the forms and go through the formalities. You don't need gloves: it's not that cold.'

'I've got a circulation problem,' I said.

It was a black Citroën. The driver was a mournful Negro of about fifty. He took my case and locked it in the boot. His skin was bluish black and his eyes heavy-lidded. He wore a shabby raincoat and battered hat. He hardly looked at us as we got into the car. The young one continued talking. 'The other day someone said that we were the Jews of Western Europe. Palais de Justice, Ahmed.'

'Who?' I said.

'Cops. The Jews of Western Europe; we're blamed for everything, aren't we? Everything, from traffic jams to strike-breaking – it's convenient to have someone to blame.'

I grunted.

'Park in the usual space, Ahmed,' he told the driver, as we turned into the Place du Palais. To me he said, 'I'll be as quick as I can. You wait with Ahmed.'

I nodded.

'What's wrong with you?' he said. 'A pain in the guts? Indigestion?'

'Could you get me something? It's an acid stomach. There's a chemist at the end of the street.'

Fabre looked at me for what seemed like a long time. Then he reached into a pocket of his fur coat and found a plastic box. 'You need two of these,' he said. 'I carry all that kind of junk; I'm a hypochondriac.'

'Thanks,' I said. He tipped two small multi-coloured capsules into the palm of my gloved hand.

'They melt at different times,' he explained, 'so you get this continuous anti-acid together with minute doses of regular aspirin and buffer – you must have seen the adverts . . .'

I put them into my mouth with my left hand and tried to look like a man who was holding on to his belly-ache with the other hand, rather than one who had been a little too premature in checking the butt of a ·38 Centennial Airweight.

'Shellfish,' I said. 'That always does it. I'm a fool, really.'

Fabre nodded his agreement, slammed the car door, and walked off across the square to the police offices. The driver was still looking at me. I smiled at him. He touched the evil-eye beads that dangled from the driving mirror, and then gave his whole attention to the horse-racing section of his paper.

Whatever Fabre did inside that imposing building took no more than five minutes. The driver had the engine running by the time Fabre got back in. 'We'll take the autoroute, Ahmed,' Fabre told the Negro. 'You'll see the Grasse exit marked.'

We followed the Mediterranean coast as far as Cannes, and then turned north, into the land of truffles, baccarat

82

and fast cars that stretches from Mougins to Vence. No one spoke. I looked out of the window.

'This is Grasse,' said the driver. He turned to look back over his shoulder, and gave me a sad smile.

Palm Springs on a French hill-top. Daubed on a wall there was a slogan: 'Arabs Keep Out of Grasse.' It was raining in Grasse. We didn't stop.

'We'll be there by lunchtime,' said Fabre.

I tried to wet my lips and smile back, but my tongue was dry. These boys were all soft lights and sweet music, but I had the feeling that it was going to go dark and quiet at some chosen place on the highway north. And they weren't planning to leave long-stemmed roses to mark the spot.

'I'm sorry,' he said.

The driver kept to a steady speed and showed impeccable road manners. To them, it might have seemed convincingly like police procedure, but to me it looked as though they were extremely careful not to be booked on a traffic offence at a time when they had another crime in operation.

'Sorry about what?' I croaked.

'Mentioning food – when you have a *crise de foie*,' he said.

'Is that what I have?'

'I think so,' he said.

Instinct said use the gun and get out of here, but training said find out who, what and where.

The driver chose the N85, the *route Napoléon*. As we climbed away from the sheltered Riviera coast, a hell's kitchen of boiling storm-clouds came into view. The mountain peaks were white, like burned soufflés that some chef had hidden under too much powdered sugar. The sky became darker and darker, and the cars coming south had their headlights on. The rain turned to hail that beat a tattoo on the roof of the car, and at the La Faye pass the mountains echoed with the sound of thunder. Great lightning flashes froze an endless line of toy motor-cars that were crawling up the far side of the gorge. The wiper blades stropped the glass, and the engine's note changed to a whine that provided an undertone of hysteria.

'We'll be late,' the driver warned. It was the hard consonantal French of the Arab.

'It will be clear beyond Barrême.'

'Barrême is a long way,' said the driver. 'We'll be late.' He paddled the brake and swung the steering wheel as the tyres slid on a patch of ice. He lost enough speed to have to change down. There was the scream of a power-horn, and a small Renault sped past us on the wrong side of the road. There was a thud as his slush hit the door, and a fanfare of horns as the Renault prised open the traffic to avoid an oncoming bus. 'Bloody idiot,' said the driver. 'He won't get to Castellane, except in a hearse.'

The equinoctial storms that lash the great limestone plateau of Provence provide Nice with a rainfall higher than even London. But as we hurried north the black clouds sped over us, tearing themselves to shreds to reveal their sulphur-yellow interiors and, eventually, the sun. The inland roads were dry, and as the traffic thinned out we increased speed. I watched the fields, and the huge flocks of birds that circled like dust-storms, but my mind calculated every possible way in which the threat of death might come.

At first they pretended that it would be faster to take to the minor roads, but by the time we were as far as the military exercise zone they had grown tired of their game, or had decided that it was no longer necessary.

Fabre, in the back seat with me, was watching the road with unusual attention. 'You missed the turn-off,' he told

84

the driver. He tugged at his finger joints one by one, as if he was field-stripping his hand to clear a blockage.

The driver made no sign that he'd heard, until finally he said, 'I didn't miss *anything*. There's that tumbledown shrine and the wire, *then* comes the turn-off.'

'Perhaps you are right,' said Fabre. His face was even whiter than white, and he chewed down on one of his tablets in a rare display of emotion. He became conscious of my stare and turned to me. 'We must get the right road or we'll be lost – it's one of those short-cuts.'

'Oh, one of *those* short-cuts,' I said. I nodded.

He rubbed his hands together and smiled. Perhaps he'd realized that there had been undertones in that last exchange which denied any last chance that they were policemen.

Fabre spotted a wayside shrine with a few miserable wild flowers in a tin at the foot of a tormented Christ. 'You're right,' he told the driver. We turned on to the narrow side road.

'Take it easy,' Fabre said to the driver, his face tightening as the suspension thumped the rutted track. He was nervous now, as the time came closer. They were both nervous. The driver had stiffened at the wheel, and he seemed to shrink even as I watched him.

'Not the right-hand fork,' Fabre warned the driver. And then I suddenly recognized the landscape. A few stunted trees on rolling hills: I'd not seen this place since the war. We were taking the high road to the west side of the Tix quarry: Champion's quarry, as it now was. The old open-cast workings had been abandoned since the late 'fifties, and the mine had proved so expensive that it had closed a few years later. The quarry: it would be an ideal place.

As we came up the slope to the brink of the quarry I saw the same dilapidated wooden huts that had been there ever since I could remember. Fabre squirmed. He thought he was a hell of a hard kid, pulses racing and eyes narrowed. I saw him as a grotesque caricature of myself when young. Well, perhaps I was the same 'yesterday's spy' that Champion was, but my heart wasn't pounding. Shakespeare got me all wrong: no stiffening of the sinews, no summoning of the blood, not even 'hard favour'd rage'. There was only a cold sad ache in the gut – no longer any need to simulate it. And – such was the monumental ego a job like mine needs – I was already consoling myself for the distress that killing them would inevitably cause me.

I was concentrating on the pros and cons of striking while the driver had his hands full of car, and Fabre had his attention distracted. But because they were watching the road ahead, they took in the scene some five seconds before I did – and five seconds in this job is a long weekend elsewhere – ten seconds is for ever!

'*Merde!*' said Fabre softly. 'She's escaped.' Then I saw all: the woman in the short fur coat, identical to the one that Fabre was wearing, and the man on his knees, almost hidden in the thorns and long grass. The man kicked frantically to free himself. There were two loud bangs. The man in the grass convulsed at each gunshot and fell flat and out of sight. Then there came the thump of the wooden door, as the fur-coated woman disappeared into the hut.

Fabre had the car door open by that time. The car slewed to a stop in thick mud, almost sliding into a ditch. Even before he was out of the car Fabre had his Browning Model Ten automatic in his hand. Well, that was the right pistol! I knew plenty of French cops with those: smooth finish, three safeties and only twenty ounces in your pocket. A pro gun, and this one had long since lost its blueing. It was scratched, worn shiny at the edges, and

I didn't like it. Fabre stood behind the open car door, ballooning his body gently, so as never to be a static target. He was squinting into the dark shadows under the trees. Only men who have been in gunfire do that instinctively as this man was doing it.

The clouds parted to let the sun through. I glimpsed the face at the hut window. I remember thinking that it must be Madame Baroni, the mother of Caty and Pina, but she had died in Ravensbrück in 1944. Two more shots: one of them banged into the car body, and made the metal sing. Not Pina's mother but Pina herself, Caty's sister, her face drawn tight in fear. There was a flash of reflected light as the sun caught the nickel-finish revolver that she levelled through the broken window.

She depressed the gun and fired again at the man in the undergrowth. I remembered the German courier she'd killed, when we were together at the farmhouse. She'd shot him six times.

'You cow!' Fabre's face contorted, and he brought his Browning up in a two-hand clasp, bending his knees slightly, FBI target-shooting style. He'd need only one shot at this range. His knuckles were white before I made my decision.

I pulled the trigger of my revolver. The noise inside the car was deafening. At a range of less than two yards, the first bullet lifted him under the arm like a bouncer's grip. He was four yards away, and tilted at forty-five degrees, as the second shot collapsed him like a deckchair and threw him into the ditch. My ears rang with the noise. There was the smell of scorched cloth, and two holes in my coat.

Ahmed jumped out of the car at the same moment I did. With the car between us, he was able to cover a lot of ground before I was able to shoot. The bullet howled into the sky, miles away from him. I cursed, and moved

87

back to the place where Fabre had fallen. I was cautious, but I needn't have been. He was dead. The Browning was still gripped tight in his hands. He was a real gunny. His mouth was open, teeth clenched, and his eyes askew. I knew it was another nightmare. I steeled myself to see that face again in many dreams, and I was not to be wrong about it.

Cautiously I moved up the track towards the wooden shack, keeping low and behind the scrub. I was on the very brink of the quarry before the door opened. Pina emerged, tight-lipped, dishevelled, her fur coat ripped so that its lining hung below the hem. The man she'd shot was dead: a dark-skinned youth in leather jacket and woollen hat, his tweed trousers still entangled in the thorns.

'Charlie! Charlie! Oh, Charlie!' Pina pushed the revolver into her pocket and then washed her dry hands, in some curious rite of abnegation. 'They were going to kill me, Charlie. They were going to kill me. They said so.'

'Are you all right, Pina?'

'We must get away from here, Charlie.'

There was a flash of lightning and a prolonged rumble of thunder.

Pina mumbled a prayer into my shirt-front. I held her tight, but I didn't relax. From here I could see right down to the puddles in the bottom of the quarry. It was a spooky place for me, its vast space brimful of memories and fears. In the war I'd hidden here, listening to the barking of the search dogs, and the whistles of the Feldgendarmerie as they came, shoulder to shoulder, across these very fields. Pina clutched my hand, and she felt there the anxious sweat that my memories provoked.

'But where?' she said. 'Where can we go?' Again, lightning lit up the underside of the dark clouds, and a perfect disc of its blue light flashed from the bracken a few yards in front of me. Violently I pushed Pina to the ground, and threw myself down into firing position. With one hand I pushed my spectacles against my face and capped one eye. With the other hand I put the pistol's foresight near the place where I'd seen the glint of reflected light. I pulled the trigger three times.

The sound of the gunfire was reflected off the sloping ground: three loud bangs, and the echo of them came rolling back from the far side of the quarry. Pina crawled nearer. 'Keep down,' I said.

'This grass! I'm soaked,' she complained.

'It's a sniperscope, a perfect disc of light. It must have been sighted on us.'

I rolled over enough to get some bullets from my pocket and push them into the chamber. Then I picked up the empty cases and wrapped them in my handkerchief. There was no point in trying to be clever about powder traces – the bullet holes in my pocket would be enough.

'They will try to get to the car,' said Pina. 'If you could get to that bracken you'd shoot anyone who tried to get down to the track where the car is.'

'You're riding the wrong sideshow,' I growled. 'I'm selling tickets for the tunnel of love.'

'You're going to let them take the car?'

'I'll check their oil, and polish the windscreen for them.'

Pina gave that sort of whistle that well-bred French ladies resort to when they want to swear. It was then that the Negro driver broke cover and went racing off down the slope towards the main road. If there was more than one man, this had to be the moment to rush them. I jumped up and ran as fast as I could to where I'd seen the glint of light. Pina followed me.

'I don't understand,' she said.

I said nothing; I didn't understand, either. There was no sniperscope, no high-powered rifle, no lethal weapons at all. The lightning had reflected from the front element of a zoom-lens fitted to a Beaulieu 16 mm movie camera. I fidgeted with the magazine until I got it open and then I pulled the grey film out into the daylight. A considerable footage had passed through the film-gate but the bulk of it was in the top magazine. Whatever it was intended to film had not yet happened.

I unlatched the camera from its pan and tilt head, and lifted it on to my shoulder. Then, in some irrational fit of destructive anger, I pitched the valuable movie camera over the side of the quarry. It hit an outcrop and bounced high into the air, spilling lenses and sprockets and trailing a long tail of film. It bounced a second time and then fell out of sight before landing with a thud.

Pina gave me the big pistol she had used. 'It's his,' she said, indicating the body of the dark-skinned man, 'I got it away from him.' After wiping it carefully, I threw it into the wooden hut. There was a new plastic-topped table there and two kitchen chairs. Cigarette ends, pieces of loaf and the remains of hard-boiled egg littered the table top, and a length of rope was on the floor. 'I tricked him,' said Pina. 'They had me tied up at first.'

'Go and wait in the car, Pina,' I said.

She shuffled off like a sleepwalker. Half-heartedly, I pressed my ·38 into the dead Arab's hand and threw my cotton gloves down alongside the body, to account for its powder-free hands. But I didn't fool myself that I was achieving anything more than a couple of hours at double-time for some junior assistants in the local forensic lab.

I started the Citroën. There was a full minute of wheel-spinning before the old brute crawled out of the mire and waddled off down the track, spewing mud in every direction. We left everything the way it was, the fur-coated gunny head-down in the ditch, the camera-operator – for so I had decided was the man Pina had killed – stiff in the long grass.

'What did it all mean?' Pina asked me, as we reached the main road.

I looked at her and then back down the road. 'You know what it means, Pina,' I said. 'And, by God, I'm going to wring it out of you, so just start getting used to the idea of telling me.'

We were both silent for a long time. I suppose we were both thinking about the Negro driver, and what he might do. Pina finally said, 'He'll not tell the police anything, unless they squeeze it out of him. They were there to kill you, Charlie. They grabbed me this morning on my way to the hairdresser's.'

'Why you, Pina?'

She didn't answer. My thoughts moved on to more urgent matters.

'Is there a plane service to Paris from Grenoble?' I asked her.

'Air Alpes fly Marseille–Grenoble–Metz, and connect with an Air France Düsseldorf flight. I did that last year.'

'No good,' I said, thinking better of it. 'Passports, credit cards and cheques – a trail of paper.'

'I've got a lot of cash,' she said.

'Give me a minute to think.'

'You'd better think fast, petit, or we'll be in Valence. And that's on the autoroute. It will be thick with cops.'

'I wish I knew whether this was a stolen car.'

'Don't be silly, Charlie. You saw those men. They don't work with stolen cars: they are assassins – cent-mille francs a time men – they don't use stolen cars.'

'Who are they, Pina?'

She picked at the dried mud that was plastered on her

fur coat. 'It's no good shouting at me as if I was a juvenile delinquent,' she said.

'You killed that man, Pina,' I said.

She didn't answer. I found it difficult to be patient with her, and yet I knew there was no other way. I said, 'The Tix quarry . . . Pina, and not far away, the mine, and the house where Champion lives. What the hell are you doing there?'

A police car came speeding towards us, with siren and light going. I watched it in the mirror until it disappeared over the hill. 'And the camera,' I said. 'I think you took it up there to spy on Champion. Is that it?'

She turned her head to see me more clearly.

'You and Champion are in it together,' she said, as if the idea had just occurred to her.

'In what?' I demanded.

She shook her head. Then she looked at her gold wristwatch and fidgeted with it, so that it jangled against the bracelets on her arm.

'You tell *me*,' she mumbled.

The rain mottled the windscreen and I switched on the wipers and the heater. She loosened her coat. 'OK,' I said, 'I'll tell you. You've always blamed Champion for the death of Marius. But your brother was arrested hours before Champion, and you know it because you saw it happen. And I saw it, too.' I waited for her to admit it, but she didn't.

She forced herself to smile. 'I was mad about Champion,' she protested. 'I loved him, you know I did.'

'And that's all part of the vendetta,' I said. 'You never forgave him for marrying your sister.'

She gave a little hoot of laughter. 'Jealousy!' she said. 'What a joker you are!' She took out a tiny handkerchief and wiped her nose. Only after she had taken a quick look at herself, run a fingertip over her eyebrows and clicked her handbag closed, did she speak again. 'It's the way he's *treated* Caterina that I resent so much. Have you seen her lately?'

'A week or so ago.'

'He's made her life hell, and it shows on her face.'

'No, Pina,' I said. 'She's just getting old, that's all.'

'You're pitiless, Charlie, do you know that?' It was a pleasant conversational voice she used. 'You don't have flesh and blood, you have clockwork. You don't live, you tick.' She wiped her nose again. 'Tell me, Charlie: do you ever love, or hate, or weep? Tell me!'

'No,' I said, 'I just blow a fuse.'

'And each time you do it, someone comes along and fits you with a bigger fuse, and finally you can tick-tock your life away, Charlie, without any problems of conscience, or morals, or thought of tomorrow.'

'It's a funny thing, Pina,' I said. 'Every time someone puts a bomb in a supermarket or machineguns a few airline passengers, it turns out that they are doing it on account of their conscience, or their morals, or some goddamned twisted idea of a new Jerusalem.'

I'd said it simply out of anger, but the reference to Jerusalem caused her to react.

'Me?'

Her eyes opened wide and her mouth slackened with amazement and indignation. 'You think I'm working with the Palestinian terrorists?'

'Then who are you working for?'

'The autoroute will be best,' she said. 'The car's not stolen, I'm sure of it. We'd best make for Paris.'

'Who?' I said again. 'Who are you working for, then?'

Pina had said too much and she knew it, and now she hunched forward in her seat and began to worry. The moment had passed.

For a few minutes she was very still. Then she turned her head to see the road behind us.

'I'll watch the road, Pina. You try and rest for a few minutes.'

'I'm frightened, Charlie.'

'It will be all right,' I said. 'Try to get some sleep.'

'Sleep,' she said. 'It's ten years since I was able to sleep without my pills.'

'Well, don't take any of those. We might need to be wide awake.'

A helicopter came over the road and then made off towards the autoroute. Pina leaned close to the window to watch it fly over.

'Traffic police,' I said.

She nodded and leaned back in her seat, her head resting against the window. I glanced at her. Her hair was knotted and her lipstick smudged. In her lap, her hands were clasped too tight, the knuckles criss-crossed with the marks of her nails. When she spoke it was in a different sort of voice, and I glanced across her to see that she had not opened her eyes. 'I must have a drink, Charlie. I must.'

'In Lyon.'

'You don't understand!' She rummaged through the rubbish and dog-eared papers in the car, as if hoping to find a bottle or a hip-flask.

'We'll find somewhere,' I said.

'Soon, Charlie.'

Her hands were shaking, in spite of the strength she used to clench them together. And I saw the way that her face was stiff as if with pain.

'The first place we see,' I promised.

'Oh, yes, petit.'

It was an elegant and yet a forbidding place. A pox of tourist-club badges studded the portals, and the flags of the world's richest nations flew from the battlements. The gravel was freshly raked and the grass clipped short.

'Let's go,' I said. I had already given her my lecture on being inconspicuous – don't over-tip, thank anyone or converse too long with the waiter – and we'd stopped a moment or two while she combed her hair and used tissues to clean her face. After that, we'd gone a couple of miles up the road, in order to enter the drive from the north, and so be remembered as a southbound car.

She left her muddied coat in the car. We came, huffing and puffing from the cold, into the warmed and scented air of the lobby. The tiles were polished and the carpets brushed. Behind the desk a middle-aged man looked up and reached for his jacket. He put it on before greeting us. 'Yes?' he said, as if he could think of no possible reason why people should break their journey there.

'Can we get a drink?' I said.

'I'll see,' he said, and disappeared through a door marked 'Private'.

There was a smell of disaster in the air, along with the scent of tile polish and coffee. About thirty tables had been set with cloths and cutlery but only one table had been used. On it there were two used cups, a coffee-pot and a newspaper folded so that the classified columns could be read.

A second man appeared from the service doors. Behind him there was the sudden sound of water going into a pot and a clatter of plates.

'A table for two?' He gave us a dignified smile. He was about sixty, a balding man with pale face and red hands: the legacy of a lifetime of steamy kitchens and hot water.

'Yes,' I said.

He raised a hand, turned on his heel and led us through the empty dining-room to a table near the window, as if we'd have had little chance of finding an empty seat without his assistance.

'*Omelette fines herbes*,' he suggested. His collar was twisted, as if the coat had been put on hurriedly.

'Give me a brandy,' said Pina, 'a *fine*. We just want a drink.' She sighed, and dumped her handbag on the table with a thud that knocked the cutlery askew. Then she opened the bag and began to search for cigarettes.

The waiter was patient. He handed me a menu.

'Two omelettes,' I said. 'And I'd like a glass of red wine.'

'Fleurie,' he suggested.

'And a green salad.'

'Perfect,' said the old man.

Pina found her cigarettes and lit one. She watched the old man stride away with his order. 'You just gave him his big moment of the week,' she said.

'The way you say it, it sounds like I gave him leprosy.'

She touched my hand on the table-top. 'You were being nice. And I'm being . . .' She shook her head, unable to think of a word, and inhaled on the cigarette again. She propped her hand under her chin, and did not turn her eyes away from the kitchen door, shivering so violently that, for a moment, her whole body trembled.

'Relax, Pina, relax,' I said. But she did not relax until the old man emerged with the drinks. When he placed the brandy before her, she reached out to touch the stem of the glass, and as she did so – just with the possession of the drink – I saw the tension die within her. As if exercising masterful restraint she raised the glass slowly and met my eyes before taking a sip of it.

'It's a good brandy,' she said.

'Drink it down, Pina, you need a drink.'

But she didn't gulp it. She pushed her gold cigarette case towards me, to offer me one.

'No thanks,' I said. 'I'm trying to give it up.'

She smiled, as if at some secret joke, and placed the jacket of the black Dior suit over the back of her chair, carefully enough for the label to be on display. 'Have a cigarette.' She touched her hair as if it was herself that she was offering.

'I'm trying to give it up,' I said again, but I opened the case and took one, in just the same way that I'd ordered the omelette: to be obliging.

The afternoon sun came through the window and lit up her hair. And it lit up the strange grey eyes. 'And what else are you trying to give up?' she said, and waved away her cigarette smoke and my answer with it. 'No, don't tell me, darling, let me find out.'

It would have been difficult to guess Pina's age. She needed no girdle, nor skin treatments. Neither the tiny wrinkles around her eyes, nor the freckles on her cheeks, were disguised under make-up. And when she'd combed through her hair, and tidied up in the car mirror, she'd done so without the narcissistic alarm that you see in the eyes of so many women over thirty. In Pina I could still see quite a lot of the foul-mouthed tomboy who had so alarmed me when I was a teenage subaltern.

'Go and wash your face,' she commanded. 'When I look at the mess you're in, I'm surprised they didn't ask us to pay for the meal in advance.'

I looked at my watch.

'They'll be ages yet,' she added caustically. 'They'll have to go and buy some eggs.'

Unlike the French restaurants that persist in modernizing dining-rooms while retaining medieval toilets, this place had reversed that configuration. The antique wood carvings, dark panelling and worn flagstones of the dining-room ill prepared me for the brilliantly lit stainless-steel sinks, the tinted mirrors and scented air of a washroom designed to look like a space-station.

I used the silver-backed hairbrush provided by the management, and stared at my reflection as I went over the events for the thousandth time. I'd put on my gloves before being brought out of the hotel and I had not taken them off until the shooting was done. Therefore no dabs on the car or at the scene of the crime. My Centennial Airweight had been bought new – in 1968 from a man in Rue Paradis, Marseille. He was well known, and well paid, for his skill at removing numbers from metal, and going deep enough to remove the impacted metal under the numbers. The gun had lived in a rented cash-box deep under a bank in suburban Lyon, until I collected it a week before using it. The gun was all right. They'd discover nothing from that. I stopped brushing my hair to finger the blackened holes in my coat pocket. All that would go for nothing, if the police lab got a sniff at my clothes. Oh, well.

Behind me, the toilet door creaked softly. In the mirror I saw it open just enough for someone to see inside. I turned. Perhaps I would have been fast enough, and even heavy enough, to handle one such man, but there were three of them. They were motor-cycle cops: giants in boots, breeches, black leather coats and shiny crash helmets. I thrashed about, until a butt in the face with a helmet, and a nicely timed kick behind the knee, tumbled me to the floor. As they pulled me to my feet they had me pinioned so tight I could hardly breathe.

There were two other men behind the cops. They were small, white-faced men, with tight-fitting overcoats and expensive gloves. One of them bent down to pick up my spectacles. He examined them to be sure they were not cracked and then placed them on my face.

The other civilian advanced upon me, clutching a handful of paperwork, as a priest might brandish a crucifix at a malevolent Lucifer.

I protested as much as a man can protest when he has a blue uniformed arm choking the life out of him, and the hard corner of a sink prising his vertebrae apart.

And they were still crowding into the place: autoroute police, motor-cyclists, civilians and helicopter pilots. 'Is this the one?' a voice asked, and they shuffled about until the person questioned could get a look at me.

He must have nodded, for another voice said, 'You know that under French law you can be held for questioning for up to forty-eight hours without charges being preferred against you.'

I was gasping for air. I got my arm free, and tried to loosen the arm round my throat. My captor mistook this for an attempt to escape. He gave me a kidney punch, nicely calculated to be less than lethal.

Now I was bent almost double. I could no longer see any of the men. 'This is a murder charge,' said another voice. 'Mrs Helen Bishop, alias Melodie Page, murdered in flat seven, twenty-three Victoria Terrace Gardens, London South-West. It's all here . . . French magistrate's signature, préfecture, as well as the extradition . . . You just cool it. We're taking you to Lyon airport, and then to London. You just cool it, or I'll beat you unconscious personally. Got it?'

It was the voice of Colonel Schlegel. The grip on my throat was loosened so that I could answer.

'OK, OK,' I croaked.

'Get the cuffs on the bastard,' said Schlegel. 'And if he looks like he's even *thinking* of escaping, beat him senseless.'

They let me straighten. There was a ghoulish smile on

Schlegel's face. If he was trying to convince these French policemen that this wasn't a way of getting a colleague out of trouble, he was overdoing it.

I took a few deep breaths. Over Schlegel's shoulder I could see through the open door into the dining-room beyond. Pina had gone.

11

'All you do is complain,' Schlegel told me.

Dawlish was pouring tea and cutting into a fruit cake.

'He's simply trying to irritate you, my dear Schlegel. He knows that that was the only way to do it.' Dawlish turned to me and smiled, challenging me to tell him a better way of getting away from the quarry, and the corpses, and the problems arising therefrom.

I couldn't. I took the slice of cake Dawlish offered.

'You moved quickly,' I said. Schlegel bit into his piece of fruit cake and smiled to show his appreciation of my grudging praise.

He said, 'Your friend – the Princess – came through with a description of the two men, the make and year of the car and the registration number. I'm telling you, she had me high-tailing down that highway in the police chopper before I was fully awake.'

My mouth was hardly open before Dawlish answered my question. 'Colonel Schlegel had the foresight to leave a contact number with her,' he said.

I scowled. Colonel Schlegel was too bloody fond of leaving contact numbers, and what he described as cutting through British red tape and deviousness. It was bloody dangerous.

'She *was* worried about you,' said Dawlish. 'I think the Princess is straight.'

'A pity she wasn't with Schlegel and that French heavy-glove squad when they found me.'

'We didn't know about the quarry and the shooting at

that time,' Schlegel explained. 'We thought we were picking up the hoods who were snatching you.'

'Well, when the cops find the bodies, Colonel Schlegel is going to have a lot of explaining to do,' I told them.

'Not so,' said Dawlish. 'We had one of our people go up to the quarry last night – no corpses, no guns; nothing.'

'Champion has cleaned up the garbage,' said Schlegel. 'No more will be heard.'

They had it all worked out. There was no arguing with them. And anyway, I had nothing to add. I walked across to the window. I rubbed the condensation away with my fingertip, and looked out. This was really gracious living. From the window I could see a few hundred acres of Wiltshire and Sir Dudley's new Bentley parked at the east wing entrance. Did the family know what we used the west wing for? Did the gardener, who watched them bury the Telex cables and the scrambler phone lines under his five-hundred-year-old lawn, know? Did he think we needed the eight Yagi aerials for TV, and the double-glazing to keep us warm?

I turned round to look at them. 'But why would Pina Baroni take a movie camera up there?' I said. 'That's what I still fail to understand.'

'Pin your ears back,' said Schlegel, waving a piece of fruit cake at me. 'Pina Baroni took nothing up there. She was snatched, the same way you were.' He bit into the fruit cake and chewed it for a long time before swallowing.

'Are you sure?' I said.

'Sure, we're sure,' said Schlegel, and Dawlish nodded.

Schlegel said, 'This Pina Baroni was wearing the identical fur coat to one that your guy was wearing. Right?'

'Identical,' I agreed.

'Not just a coincidence,' said Schlegel. 'She was going to get killed in that coat. Killed by you.' He pointed at me in case I needed a little help in following the conversation.

'Killed by you when you mistook her for the gunny in the same coat.'

'No,' I said calmly.

'Don't give me no,' said Schlegel. 'The movie camera was there to film it happen.'

'Why?'

Schlegel said, 'We know Champion killed Melodie Page . . . Oh, sure, he gave you all that crap about us conspiring to frame him – but he did it. So he dreams up the counterploy – and it has just that kind of poetic touch that a psycho like Champion likes – he was going to have you kill Pina Baroni, and with enough evidence to make it stick.'

'Why?' I said again.

Dawlish interrupted Schlegel's act. 'He'd threaten us. He'd offer a deal: we forget about the Page murder, and he lets you off the hook.'

Well, it did have the kind of crazy effrontery that had once been Champion's hallmark. 'It's the film camera gimmick that I find so difficult,' I said. 'The kind of blurred image you'd get on 16 mm film on a winter's day doesn't compare with eyewitnesses, or telephoto stills, that a court of law would want.'

'Court of law!' said Schlegel. 'Don't be so dumb. Champion knows it would never get that far. He wanted something that would capture the imagination. He'd be threatening to give it to one of the US networks or a TV agency. He was more interested in grabbing attention than getting a conviction.'

'It would have given us a headache,' said Dawlish, as if regretful that the department had lost such an employee.

'But why Pina Baroni?' I said. I was still not convinced. 'Why murder his sister-in-law? Why not a movie of me killing just anybody?'

'We thought about that,' said Schlegel, tapping the

103

papers on the desk. 'Sure why Pina Baroni, his sister-in-law? Finally we figured it this way. The girl hates Champion – really hates him. She's convinced that after Champion was arrested he talked. She thinks he betrayed her brother Marius to the Gestapo – you know all about that, I guess.'

'I know all about it,' I said. 'She's crazy. I saw Champion arrested at Nice station. And that was hours *after* Marius was picked up.' I thought about it. 'Yes, *hours* after.'

'It's water under the bridge now,' said Schlegel. 'She hates Champion's guts, and Champion divorcing her sister didn't help.'

'*Marrying* her sister didn't help,' I corrected him. 'There was a time when Pina Baroni was crazy about Champion.'

'Hell hath no fury like a woman scorned,' said Schlegel.

'You should write that down, Colonel,' I said. 'It has a fine ring to it.'

Schlegel was never slowed by sarcasm. He said, 'And the Baroni girl killed men in the war, she got a medal for it. So she's not the kind of doll who is going to sit at home, sticking pins into clay figures. I mean, this babe is going to do it!'

'OK,' I said, 'you've told me why she might kill Champion, but I'm still waiting to hear why Champion would want to kill her. This is someone we were both with in the war. Why her? Why not a stranger?'

Dawlish said, 'Any news agency would drag out all that stuff about you and Pina Baroni in the war. First they find out she was in the resistance, and then they find out you were with her. Then they start asking what work you are doing nowadays . . . It would cause us maximum embarrassment. It was just another perfect Champion touch.'

'But not quite enough,' I protested. 'Not quite enough.'

'Don't baby him along,' Schlegel told Dawlish. Turning to me he added, 'If you'd killed some broad you'd never met, you'd clam up and put your mind in neutral. You're a pro, and your training would make you proof against any kind of working-over the press, the TV or the law could give you. But if you'd killed this Baroni woman – especially in error – you're going to be full of guilt and remorse. With you in that kind of mood, a prosecutor presses the right buttons, and any guy will sing.'

He was right, and I didn't need to tell him so. In that moment any last doubt I'd had about Champion killing the Page girl disappeared completely. Champion was a dangerous bastard. As devious as ever and not too fussy about who got hurt, as long as it wasn't him.

'It all fits,' I admitted.

'Good,' said Schlegel. There was an indefinable change of atmosphere in the room. I felt as though I'd passed some sort of examination. I looked at Dawlish soon enough to see the tiny nod of his head. Schlegel looked down at the piece of fruit cake he was eating. 'Hell!' he said angrily. 'I don't eat fruit cake.' He stubbed it into the ashtray like an old cigar butt. 'You *know* I don't eat fruit cake,' he complained to Dawlish.

'I'm afraid we're all a little on edge today,' said Dawlish. He bent to pick up cake crumbs and put them into the ashtray.

Schlegel grunted a sort of apology and picked up a couple of crumbs.

I sat down in the red leather chair that is usually reserved for visitors. I closed my eyes for a moment. Schlegel mistook my weariness for anguish.

He said, 'You don't need to lose any sleep about the guy you knocked off. A real expensive hit-man out of Zürich. "The Corsican", a rub-out artist, who probably cooled more guys than you've had hot dinners. For my money, you'd get a medal for that job you did. A medal; not a murder rap.'

'Well, I didn't know I was getting either,' I said.

'Keep your voices down,' said Dawlish primly. 'These wretched guns. If you'd obeyed your orders about guns we'd not have to be sending chaps up to the quarry at dead of night, and faking up a lot of extradition paperwork for Paris.'

'If I'd obeyed orders about guns, I'd be D.E.D.,' I said.

'If they trace that handgun back to you, I'll make you wish you were,' said Dawlish.

'Just tell me your problem,' I said wearily. 'You want this in my file? Give me a sheet of paper, I'll be pleased to oblige you. Anything else you want – crimes you need a confession for? Typewriters missing from the inventory? Petty-cash slips without counterfoils? I'll make it all right in one bumper-size confession.'

I sank back in the chair and shook my shoes off. 'I'm very tired,' I said. 'Perhaps it would be easier on all of us if you told me what you had in mind, instead of straining to pretend that you're being hit by a succession of brilliant ideas.'

The brevity of the glance they exchanged in no way lessened its conspiratorial quality. 'There's a chance to stick a transistor radio up Champion's arse,' explained Schlegel.

I knew enough about Schlegel's allegorical syntax to guess that I was cast as the radio. 'If it's all the same to you,' I said, 'I'll stay with the murder charge.'

'We haven't got time for comic backchat,' said Dawlish.

'Don't look at me,' I told him. 'I'm the straight man.'

Dawlish said, 'Of course, Major Champion will guess

that charging you with the girl's murder was just a device . . .'

'. . . but he might believe that gunning down Fabre was too rich for the department's blood,' said Schlegel. 'Got me?'

'No,' I said.

There was a long silence. Finally, it was Schlegel who spoke. They were going to save Dawlish for the replay.

'Right now, you're charged with the murder of Melodie Page. OK, it's very phoney, but we think we could exploit it. We could leak that to Champion, and make it sound convincing. Right?'

'Carry on,' I said. I opened the VIP cigar box and lit one of Dawlish's Monte Cristos. Employees were not permitted access to the hospitality, but this wasn't the right time to remind me.

'Suppose we let the charge ride,' said Schlegel.

I pretended to search my pockets for matches. Dawlish sighed and lit it for me. I smiled up at him.

'Suppose?' said Schlegel, to be sure I was paying attention.

'Yes, suppose,' I said. He need not have worried; I hadn't paid such close attention to the spoken word since the day I got married.

Dawlish said, 'You're here, accused of the murder of the Page girl . . .'

Schlegel said, 'You break bail. You go to France, and ask Champion for a job with his organization. What do you think?'

'You know there's no bail on a murder charge,' I said. 'What are you two setting me up for?'

'No, well, break out of custody, then,' amended Schlegel.

'He's been seeing too many Bogart movies,' I told Dawlish.

'Well?' said Schlegel.

'It would have to make better sense to Champion,' I said. 'If a murder charge was brought against me, and then dismissed on some technicality – he'd see the hand of the department in that. *Then* if the department puts me out to grass . . . That might sound right to him.'

'Well, that fits in with what we know,' said Dawlish, and I realized too late that the two of them had deliberately led me into the planning of their crackpot idea. Dawlish hurried on. 'Champion has a contact with a contact with a contact – you know what I mean. He'd know what was happening to you if you were in Wormwood Scrubs sometime in the next two months.'

Obviously that meant a remand prisoner. 'Just don't ask me to plead guilty,' I said.

'No, no, no,' said Dawlish. The history of the department was littered with the corpses of men who had been persuaded to plead guilty, with the promise of a quiet trial and a release on 'unsound mind' clauses. 'No, no. You'll plead not guilty.'

'And none of those dumb little creeps from the legal department,' I said. 'You manufacture the flaw in the charge but I'll find some crooked lawyer who will discover it and think it was him.'

'Agreed,' said Schlegel.

'I'll go through the motions,' I said. 'But don't rely on it. Champion is a shrewdie: he'll compromise. He'll find me some bloody job with his potato farm in Morocco, and sit back and laugh his head off.'

'We don't think so,' said Dawlish. 'We've been through the reports he sent to London, in the war. He had a high opinion of your judgement then, and he probably still has it. He could use someone like you right now. He's under pressure to increase the Intelligence flow back to Cairo, or so we think.'

Schlegel said, 'But you see why we're worried about the Baroni woman. If this was all a set-up . . . if she was working *with* Champion. If you read the entrails wrong – then . . .' He ran a forefinger across his throat. 'There will be some corner of a foreign field . . .'

'I didn't know you were interested in poetry, Colonel,' I said.

12

It was not the first time that I'd been in Wormwood Scrubs prison. In 1939, at the outbreak of war, the prisoners had been evacuated and the prison building housed Military Intelligence personnel. A few coats of paint and improvements to the plumbing had not changed the place very much. There was still the faint odour of urine that reached every cell and office. And there was still the resonance that made every sound vibrate and echo, so that at night I was kept awake by the coughing of some prisoner on the upstairs floor. And there was still the same strangled silence: a thousand throats waiting to scream in unison.

'And no reason why you shouldn't have toiletries – decent soap, after-shave and bath lotion – and your own pyjamas and a dressing-gown . . .' He looked round my cell as if he'd never seen inside one before.

'You're not defending some East-End ponce,' I said quietly. 'You work on my defence. Let me worry about the deodorants.'

'Just so, just so,' he said. Michael Moncrieff, he called himself, a name just as artificial as 'Michael the Mouth', by which he was known to his gangland clients. Men like him fight their way out of the gutters of every slum in Europe. He was a tall man with broad muscular shoulders, and a face pock-marked and scarred. And yet time had softened those marks, and now his thick white hair and wrinkled face could easily persuade you that he was the genial country lawyer that perhaps he'd liked to have been.

He reached into the waistcoat pocket of his expensive bird's-eye suit and found a gold pocket-watch. He looked at it for long enough to let me know that he was annoyed with me, but not so long that he might be deprived of the rest of the fee I'd promised him.

With some effort, he managed a smile. 'I've been going over the notes I've made. On both my last visits you said something that interested me very much.'

I yawned and nodded.

He said, 'It could just be that our friends have botched up their case even before it comes to trial.'

'Yes?'

'No promises, mind. Lots of legal work yet. I'll have to see a couple of people in Lincoln's Inn – and that will cost you a monkey . . .'

He waited until I nodded my assent to another five hundred pounds.

'I hope you don't think . . .' he said.

'Never mind the *amour propre*,' I said. 'You get your friends working on the legal double-talk. Right?'

'Not friends – *colleagues*. No fee-splitting, if that's what you're hinting at.'

'You get them working on it, and come back in the morning to tell me what they say.' I got up from the table and walked across to the bedside cabinet for my cigarettes.

'Probably take me two or three days to get a meeting – these chaps are the top people . . .'

'What am I?' I said. 'Bottom people?' I leaned over him to take his gold lighter. I used it, and tossed it back on to the table in front of him.

He didn't look round at me. He got out a red foulard handkerchief and made a lot of noise blowing his nose. He was still dabbing at it when he spoke again. 'You sit in here and get broody,' he accused me. 'You think I'm

111

sitting on my arse all day. You think I take your money and then don't give a damn.'

'Is it your legal training that makes you so perceptive?' I said. 'Or have you got second sight?'

'I work bloody hard,' he said. 'Worrying about people who if they had anything between the ears wouldn't be in here in the first place.' He sat down and fingered some papers on the table. 'Not you, I don't mean you, but some of them . . . Look, it will take me a few days to set up this meeting. Now, be patient, just trust me.'

I lit my cigarette. From behind him I leaned down and whispered softly, very close to his ear. 'Do you know what it's like in this lousy nick, waiting while some overfed mouthpiece spares time to earn the bread he's taken in advance?'

'I know, I know,' he said.

'I'm in here for topping this bird, Michael, old pal. I mean, I've got nothing to lose. You know what I mean: nothing to lose, except wonderful friendships.'

'Now, cut that out,' he said, but I'd shaken him. I saw his hands tremble as he put his typed notes back into the pigskin document case. 'I'll see them this afternoon, if I can. But it might not be possible.'

'I've got every confidence in you, Michael. You won't disappoint me.'

'I hope not,' he said, and again managed a smile.

Stupid bastard, I thought. Three QCs from the Public Prosecutor's department worked a holiday weekend to build mistakes into that paperwork. By now, any prison-visitor with *Everyman's Guide to the Law* could have sprung me in ten minutes, but this schnorrer needed ten days, and two consultants, and he was still only nibbling at the edges.

'I don't like the way they are treating you in here,' he said.

'Oh?'

'No association, no sport, no TV, no educationals, and your visits all closed. It's not right. I've complained about it.'

'I'm violent,' I told him.

'That's what they always say, but you're getting your forty-five minutes' exercise, aren't you? You're entitled to that.'

'I threatened a warder,' I told him. 'So they stopped it.'

He looked at me, and shook his head. 'You behave like you prefer it inside,' he said.

I smiled at him.

After he'd gone, I settled down with *Inside the Third Reich*, but it was not easy to concentrate. As a remand prisoner I'd been given a quiet landing, but there was always the clickety-clack of the peep-hole. As the screw passed, I'd hear his footsteps slow and then there was a moment or so as he watched me, to be sure I wasn't doing any of the forbidden things. It was the same when there was a visit. The peep-hole slammed shut and there was a jangle of keys and the clatter of the door-lock.

'Visitor! Stand up!'

It was Schlegel, complete with document case and a supply of cigarettes. I sat down again. Schlegel remained standing until we both heard the warder move away from the door.

'Stir-crazy yet?' Schlegel asked. 'They say the first ten years is the worst.'

I didn't answer. He went across to the wall cupboard, opened it, pushed my shaving brush and soap aside, and threw the cigarette packets well to the back of the second shelf. 'We'd better keep them out of sight,' he explained. He closed the cupboard door, and reached into his pocket

113

to find his ivory cigarette holder. He blew through it noisily.

'And don't smoke,' I said. He nodded.

'Anything happened in here? Champion is in London, *that* we know! Anything happened here inside?' He smiled.

'Not a thing,' I told him.

'You got the butter, and the tea and stuff? Dawlish said it wouldn't be exactly what you had in mind, but we figured that a parcel from Harrods might be a bit too conspicuous.'

'Can't leave it alone, can you, Schlegel,' I said. 'Just couldn't resist coming in to take a look, eh?'

He said nothing. He put his cigarette holder back into his top pocket. A passing warder rattled his keys against the metal railings, making a sudden loud noise, like a football rattle. Schlegel was startled.

I whispered, 'Schlegel, come here.' He sat down opposite me and bent his head forward to hear better. I said, 'If you, or any of your minions, come here again, spy on me, pass me notes, send me parcels, ask for special privileges for me, ask me or even furrow your brow when my name is mentioned, I'll consider it a very, very unfriendly act. I not only will screw up your goddamned Champion project but I will wreak physical vengeance upon all concerned . . .'

'Now, wait just one minute . . .'

'You button up your Aquascutum raincoat, Colonel, and rap on that door. You get out of here in a hurry, before I cut you into pieces small enough to squeeze through the peep-hole. And you *stay* away – a long, long way from me, until I make a contact – and you make sure there are no misunderstandings, because I'm a very nervous man. Remember that, very nervous.'

Schlegel got to his feet and went to the door. He was

about to rap on the door to call the warder, but he stopped, his fist in mid-air. 'Did you hear the ruckus this morning?'

'No.'

'Twelve prisoners coming back from their meal. Staged a sit-down in the offices. Threw a scare into the clerks, threw a typewriter into the yard and tore the locks off the filing cabinets: all good clean fun.'

'And?'

'It was all over in an hour or two. No sweat. They threatened to stop their TV, or cut back on the smokes, or something.' He thumped the door. 'High spirits, I guess. Don't worry, we had all the exits covered, pal.'

If he was expecting some significant reaction from me, he was disappointed. I shrugged. Schlegel rapped on the door. Within a minute the door was unlocked. He tipped his hat to me, and left.

It was only after he'd gone that the penny dropped. Why a sit-in, and why would they break the locks off the filing cabinets, except that they wanted to read the files. There was a dossier for each of the prisoners in that office. It might simply be high spirits; or it might be an indication of how far someone was prepared to go to get a look at my prison documents.

I stayed in London after my release.

For the first few nights, I slept at Waterloo Station. The first night, I used the waiting-room, but the railway police come round asking to see rail tickets. Out on the concourse, it's cold. The regulars steal the unsold newspapers and line the slatted benches to stop the draughts, but you have to be tough, or very tired, to get much rest there.

By the third night I'd learned a thing or two. An old man they called 'the Bishop', who had arrived on foot from Winchester, told me how to choose the trains. The heat comes from the front, so the residual warmth lasts longer at that end. The Bishop preferred dirty trains, because in those he'd be discovered by cleaners instead of by some railway cop who might turn him in. It was the Bishop who told me always to pretend to any inquisitive policeman that my wife had locked me out. His filthy raincoat tied with string, his broken boots and bundle of belongings, gave him no chance to try that story himself. But I used it three or four times and it worked like a charm. But now my shirt was dirty, and the sort of hasty shave I was able to have in the gents' toilet was stretching the errant-husband story thin.

It was the Bishop who found me a billet on Friday night. There were three of us. We got on to platform four, where the Guildford train was about to leave, and then slipped round behind the buffers to a darkened train that would not go until morning. It was the Bishop who had the square-sectioned key that opens the guard's-van doors. The Bishop settled into the narrow pew from which the periscope gives a view along the train top, while I kipped with Fuller, wedged behind some freight. Fuller was a hatchet-faced thirty-year-old. He wore a battered leather coat and a red-and-white woolly hat. He was a sociology graduate from Sussex University who 'weaseled' luggage for the boat-train passengers and was not above stealing the occasional camera or transistor radio. Such items went on sale in The Cut street-market, not thirty yards away, while the owner was still searching the taxi line to locate the 'well-spoken porter' and trying to remember when he last renewed the insurance.

'It's my back,' explained the Bishop. 'Sleeping on the floor plays merry hell with my back.'

'Spare us the details,' said Fuller. 'We know all about the state of your health.'

'You'll be old yourself someday,' said the Bishop.

'You need a bit of exercise,' said Fuller, 'that's what you need. You come and help me with that boat-train tomorrow. It'll be a good one, they say.'

'I wish I could, but I'd do myself an injury,' said the Bishop. He wriggled into the upholstered seat and searched inside his hat. He kept everything in there: paper money, cigarette stubs, string and matches. Finally he found the matches he wanted. Then he searched through his pockets until he found a tin. It was dented and all vestiges of advertising lettering had long since been polished away. Now it shone like silver, and from inside it he took a cigarette-rolling machine. 'Exercise is no good to anybody,' said the Bishop. 'Who lives to be a hundred? These fellers you see jogging down the road in a track suit at night, or those old cows with their poodles and their chauffeurs and their afternoon naps? You answer me that.'

'Trust you to rationalize it out,' said Fuller, but he found no easy answer to the old man's contention.

The Bishop smiled. He was like some down-at-heel Father Christmas, his beard stained with nicotine and his teeth long and yellow. And yet he did not smell: for a tramp, that was quite an achievement.

'Either of you two want a smoke?' he said. He rolled them carefully, thin tubes of white paper, marked with the Bishop's grey dabs, and spilling dried tobacco.

'Thanks, Bish,' I said. But Fuller did not smoke. Even before the Bishop had given me a light, Fuller was beginning to snore.

'First today,' said the Bishop proudly, holding the roll-up in the air.

'My first for six days,' I said.

'You want to give it up, son,' he said. As he inhaled, the burning cigarette lit up his arthritic knuckles and

117

watery eyes. 'Money going up in smoke: my old mother said it, and she was right.'

'And what did your mother do with her bread?' I said. 'Play the stock exchange?'

'You've been in nick, haven't you, son?'

'I was working the North Sea oil rigs. I told you that.'

'Yeah, you told me that,' said the Bishop. 'But I'm saying you've been doing porridge!'

I pinched out the cigarette and pushed it into the top pocket of his tattered overcoat.

'Naw, no offence, son.'

'Get stuffed,' I said.

'No need to get nasty.'

'Think yourself lucky I didn't poke it down your throat,' I said.

'I'm old enough to be your father.'

'But not bright enough.' I turned over and closed my eyes.

I only dozed for a moment or two before I heard the old man's voice again. He was leaning out of the window. 'They're raking everybody out,' he said. 'Like they did last week. It must be another bloody bomb warning.'

We scattered before the police reached the front carriage. I evaded the half-asleep porters and ticket men, and shuffled off down the freight road that bisects the station layout.

'In here.' I was too tired to recognize the voice. For a moment I thought it was the Bishop, or Fuller.

'In here.' It was not any of the layabouts from the station. It was a short thickset man named Pierce, who was from the department, and behind him I saw Schlegel. They were crowded into a phone booth. I moved fast. I hit Schlegel first, and he reeled. There was a crunch as his elbow hit a metal panel. I saw the look of open-mouthed bewilderment on Pierce's face, and then I slammed two body punches into him and hooked him as he doubled up. The two of them were jammed tight into the corner of the phone booth; neither stood much chance against me, for I had room to swing my elbows. I hit Schlegel again, and tapped blood from his nose. I gave him a moment to collect himself. 'Easy, easy,' he grunted. He was tucking his chin in and holding up his hands in a gesture that was neither defence nor surrender, but had a measure of both.

Pierce was huddled almost on the floor, and Schlegel was twisted into a corner, with the phone jammed into his backside. 'What did I tell you, that day in the Scrubs,' I said.

Schlegel stared at me. I not only looked different: I was different. The world had worn me shiny. Prodded awake by cops, cursed by screws, threatened by yobs who wanted your coat, or thought you might have cash. How did a man survive it, except by violence. The world was at your knees, or at your throat. Or so it seemed at the time. But the look in Schlegel's eyes made me realize how far I'd come down the long road.

'You got the passport and everything?' said Schlegel. 'You should be in France.'

'You stupid sod. You people never learn, do you? Champion is one of ours – or was once – he knows all that departmental crap. Our Swiss passports would never fool him for thirty seconds. It went into the furnace along with the letters of credit. Me and Champion set up that payment line back in 1941. It was his idea.' I straightened up, and pushed my fist into the small of my back, to ease the aches and pains of sleeping on the hard floor of the guard's van.

But I kept them both pinned tight into the booth, with Pierce on the floor. Schlegel tried to move, but I forced him back into the corner with my forearm, and he only retained his balance by treading on Pierce's leg. 'Champion is going to come and find *me*,' I told them. 'He won't buy it any other way. And I'm not sure he'll swallow it, even without you stupid bastards trying to hurry things along.' I stopped. I was so tired I could have lain down on the street and sobbed myself to sleep. But I rubbed my face, and blinked, and shook my brains from side to side until I heard a reassuring rattle. 'And if he *doesn't* buy it,' I said, 'I get dead. So forgive me, girls, if I'm a little bit sensitive. Because I've got a whole lot of dances on my programme, I don't need a hand up my skirt.'

'OK,' said Schlegel. 'You're right.' He found a handkerchief and dabbed his bloody nose.

'You'd just better believe it, Schlegel, because next time I won't be just tweaking your nose. You want to give me credentials for Champion? Great! I'll kill you, Schlegel. And I'll cool any of the boys you bring along, and not even Champion will think that was a set-up.'

'You don't talk to me like that,' growled Schlegel, and he coughed as he sniffed his own blood. I had him, and he knew it, and I leaned across and with the knuckle of my left fist I tapped his jaw, as one might when playing with a baby. And he didn't take his eyes off my right fist, that was all set to drive him into the wall.

'Give me some money,' I said.

He reached into his inside pocket and found three crumpled five-pound notes. I took them from him, and then I stepped backwards and I felt Pierce's feet sprawl out. I almost ran down the slope towards York Road.

It was a full moon. 'Hello, son,' said the Bishop, as I overtook him. He was hurrying down the traffic ramp, with his bundle of belongings slung over his back. 'A regular purge tonight, eh?' He chuckled.

'Looks like,' I said. 'But I can buy us a night's kip, and a plate of eggs and sausage.' I brandished the money.

'You shouldn't have done it,' said the Bishop. He was not looking at the notes in my hand, but at Schlegel's blood on my cuff and knuckles.

'We've been together all evening,' I said.

'Portsmouth train, platform eighteen,' said the Bishop.

'Near the front,' I agreed happily, 'in a non-smoker.'

The next day, I tried for job number eighteen on my list. It was a small private bank off Fetter Lane. It specialized in everything from sanction-breaking to fraud. I'd chosen my list of jobs with great care. A man with my qualifications, booted into the street, isn't going to apply for a trainee's job with ICI. These were all dodgy concerns, who knew how to double the five or six grand salary I was asking. But they put a hatchet-man with a big carnation alongside the drinks cabinet, and gave me two glasses of dry sherry and economic-recession talk. I was expecting it, because I had spent nearly five hours on the memo that ensured that each of these companies had a visit from a Special Branch officer at least a week before I arrived.

'Thank the Lord for Saturday,' said the Bishop late Friday night as we sat in our local, nursing one glass of warm beer, and taking simulated swigs at it whenever the landlord glared at us.

'What's the difference?' I said. As far as I was concerned, it simply meant that I couldn't approach the next on the list of prospective employers until the weekend was passed. I leaned back and watched the colour TV on the bar. It was tuned to a comedy show but the sound was turned off.

Fuller said, 'We go to the coast tomorrow.'

'Do you?' I said.

'The Bishop has this fiddle with the National Assistance . . .'

'I told you not to tell him,' said the Bishop. He found a half-smoked cigarette in his hat.

'Everybody knows, you old fool.' Fuller turned to me. 'There's a friendly clerk on the paying-out counter. He calls your name, pays you unemployment money, and then later you give him half of it back. He can't do it more than once a month, or they'd tumble to him.' Fuller produced his matches and gave just one of them to the old man to light his cigarette end. 'Bloody disgusting, isn't he?' said Fuller.

'The Phantom Army, they call it,' said the Bishop. He took a deep drag of the cigarette smoke, and then a swig of the bitter, to celebrate the next day's payment.

'We can row you in on that one,' Fuller offered. 'Can't we, Dad?'

'I suppose so,' said the old man grudgingly.

'You're on,' I said. 'How do you get to the coast? You don't pay the train fare, do you?'

'Couldn't make it pay then, could you?' said Fuller defensively. 'We fiddle the tickets from one of the booking clerks.'

'It's a complicated life,' I remarked.

'You don't *have* to come,' said the Bishop.

'I wasn't complaining,' I said.

'You went after a job today,' said the Bishop.

'That's it,' I admitted.

Fuller looked me up and down with interest. He paid special attention to my newly washed shirt and carefully brushed coat. 'You wouldn't catch me poncing off the capitalist system,' said Fuller finally.

'Same again?' I said. 'Pints of bitter?'

'I wouldn't say no,' said Fuller.

'Thanks, son,' said the Bishop.

Saturday morning. The Southampton train was not full. We caught it with only a few seconds to spare. Fuller led the way, through the buffet car and a luggage van. Even while the train was still stumbling over the points outside the station, I knew that this was the sort of way Champion would make contact.

'Go ahead,' said the Bishop. He indicated the door leading to the next coach and the first-class compartments.

I went forward.

In the corridor, outside his compartment, two men in lumpy raincoats took exceptional interest in the dilapidated back yards of Lambeth and did not give me a glance. Champion looked up from *The Financial Times* and smiled.

'Surprised?' said Champion.

'Not very.'

'No, of course not. Come and sit down. We've got a lot to talk about.' Beyond him the cramped slums became high-rise slums, and then semi-detached houses and sports fields.

In my hand I was holding one of the Bishop's roll-ups. I put it in my mouth as I searched my pockets for matches.

'Been having a rough time?' said Champion.

I nodded.

He leaned forward and snatched the cigarette out of my mouth. He clenched his fist to screw it up, and threw the mangled remains of it to the floor. 'Balls,' he said.

I looked at him without anger or surprise. He brought a handkerchief from his pocket and wiped his hands on it. 'Sleeping on railway stations: it's balls. I know you of old. You can't pass through a big town without dropping a few pounds here, and a gun there, and some beaver bonds in the next place. You of all people – sleeping on railway stations – crap, I say.' He looked out at the factories of Weybridge, and the streets crowded with weekend shoppers.

'You're losing your cool, Steve,' I said. He didn't answer or turn his head. I said, 'Certainly I've got a few quid stashed away, but I'm not leading the band of the Grenadier Guards there for a ceremonial opening.'

Champion looked at me for a moment, then he threw his packet of cigarettes. I caught them. I lit one and smoked for a minute or two. 'And I'm not even taking *you* there,' I added.

Champion said, 'I'm offering you a job.'

I let him wait for an answer. 'That might turn out to be a bad move,' I told him. 'A bad move for both of us.'

'You mean the department will be breathing down my neck because I've given you a job,' he nodded. 'Well, you let me worry about that, Charlie, old son.' He watched me with the care and calculation that a night-club comic gives a drunk.

'If you say so, Steve,' I said.

'You found out what those bastards are really like now, eh?' He nodded to himself. I believe he really thought they *had* framed him for the murder of Melodie Page. That was the sort of man Champion was, he could always convince himself that his cause was right and remember only the evidence he selected.

'Remember when you arrived – that night? Me, and young Pina, and little Caty and the bottle of champagne?'

'I remember,' I said.

'I told you that it would be up to you to keep me convinced you were loyal, not my job to prove you weren't. It's the same now, Charlie.'

I smiled.

'Don't think I'm joking, Charlie. It wouldn't need more

than a wave to a stranger, or an unexplained phone call, for you to lose your job . . . you know what I mean.'

'I can fill in the blank spaces, Steve.'

'Can you?'

'We're not going to be distributing food parcels to old-age pensioners.'

'*No one* distributes food parcels to old-age pensioners, and soon I'm going to be one, Charlie. I'm past retiring age: ex-Major, DSO, MC, and I'm cold and hungry, at least I was until a few years ago. I've done my bit of villainy for God, King and country. And now I'm doing a bit for my own benefit.'

'And where would I fit in?' I asked.

'I need an assistant,' he said. 'And you'd be perfect. Nothing to trouble your conscience; nothing to ruin your health.'

'It sounds a bit boring, Steve.'

'I have a lot of Arabs working for me. They do the tricky jobs. They are good workers, and I pay enough to take the pick of the workforce, from botanists to butlers. But there are jobs that they can't do for me.'

'For instance?'

'I've got to get a school for Billy. I can't send an Arab to take tea with a prospective headmaster. I need someone who can take a suitcase full of money somewhere, talk his way out of trouble, and forget all about it afterwards. I talk Arabic as fluently as any Arab, but I don't *think* like one, Charlie. I need someone I can relax with.'

'Sounds like you need a wife,' I said, 'not an assistant.'

He sighed, and held up his gloved hand in a defensive gesture. 'Anything but that, Charlie.' He let the hand fall. 'You need a job, Charlie; come and work for me. I need someone from our world.'

'Thanks,' I said. 'I appreciate it.'

'There's a Latin tag – "Render a service to a friend . . . to bind him closer", is that how it goes?'

'Yes,' I said, '"and render a service to an enemy, to make a friend of him". You wrote that on the report to London, and told the pilot to make sure the old man got it personally. And we got that reprimand with the next night's radio messages. You remember!'

He shook his head to show that he didn't remember, and was annoyed to be reminded. It was difficult for Champion to appreciate how impressionable I had been in those early days. For him I'd just been another expendable subaltern. But, like many such eager kids, I'd studied my battle-scarred commander with uncritical intensity, as an infant studies its mother.

'Well, you didn't sign up for a course in elementary philosophy, did you?'

'No,' I said, 'for one million dollars. When can I start?'

'Right now.' He pointed to a canvas two-suiter on the floor. 'That's for you. Use the battery shaver in the outside pocket, and change into the suit and shirt and stuff.'

'All without leaving your sight?'

'You catch on quick,' said Champion. The train gave a throaty roar as we rushed into the darkness of a tunnel and out again into blinding rain.

'And at Southampton: a false passport, a false beard and a boat?'

'Could be,' he admitted. 'There's no going back, Charlie. No farewell kisses. No notes cancelling the milk. No forwarding address.'

'Not even a chance to get a newspaper,' I said, reminding him of a device we'd used at Nice railway station one night in 1941, when Pina passed back through a police cordon to warn us.

'Especially not a chance to get a newspaper,' he said. I

sorted through the clothes he'd provided. They'd fit me. If Schlegel had a tail on me, in spite of my protests, they'd need a sharp-eyed man at Southampton to recognize me as I left the train. I was about to vanish through the floor, like the demon king in a pantomime. Well, it was about what I expected. I was changed within five minutes.

I settled back into the corner of my soft first-class seat, and used the electric shaver. Between gusts of rain I glimpsed rolling green oceans of grassland. Winchester flashed past, like a trawler fleet making too much smoke. After Southampton there would certainly be no going back.

'Have you started again?'

Champion was offering his cigars. 'Yes, I have,' I said.

Champion lit both cigars. 'The bearded one – the Bishop – was one of my people,' he said.

'I thought he might be.'

'Why?' said Champion, as if he did not believe me.

'Too fragrant for a tramp.'

'He told me,' said Champion. 'Bathed every day – every day!'

'No one's perfect,' I said.

Champion gave a stony smile and punched my arm.

13

'When a senior officer, like Champion, confesses to being outwitted – that's the time to run for your life.' The quote originated from a German: a Sicherheitsdienst officer giving evidence to one of our departmental inquiries in 1945. Champion – like all other British SIS agents captured by the Nazi security service – faced a board after the war, and heard his ex-captors describe his interrogations. Not many came out of such investigations unscathed, and very few such men were ever employed in the field again. Champion was an exception.

'I think it's yours,' said Champion. He picked up the red king and waved it at me. 'Unless you can think of something I can do.'

'No, it's checkmate,' I said. I am a poor player, and yet I had won two games out of three. Champion swept the pieces off the small magnetic board, and folded it. 'Anyway, we must be nearly there.'

'Nice airport have just given us permission to land,' said the second pilot. I looked out of the window. The land below was dark except for a glittering scimitar that was the coast. We continued southwards, for even a small executive jet must obey the traffic pattern designed to leave jet-noise over the sea. Champion looked at his wristwatch. There would be a chauffeur-driven limousine at Nice airport, just as there had been at the quayside in Le Havre. There was no fuel crisis for Champion.

'You must have questions,' said Champion. 'You never were the trusting type.'

'Yes,' I said. 'Why did you bring your queen forward?

Twice you did that. You must have seen what would happen.'

The limousine was there. It was parked in the no-waiting area. The cop had moved a sign to make room for it. The dark-skinned chauffeur was holding a boy in his arms when we saw him. The chauffeur's gigantic size made the child seem no larger than a baby. But he was a big boy, dressed in a denim bib and brace, with a red wool workshirt: all tailored with the sort of care that only the French expend on children's clothes.

'Has he been a good boy?' said Champion.

The chauffeur stroked the child's hair gently. 'Have you, Billy?'

The boy just nuzzled closer into the shoulder of the dark wool uniform.

It was a starry night. The air was warm, and the white-shirted airport workers moved with a spurious grace. What had these men of the south in common with the stamping feet and placid anxiety of the bundled-up dock workers we'd seen sheltering from the driving rainstorms of northern Europe?

I sniffed the air. I could smell the flower market across the road, the ocean, the olives, the sun-oil and the money.

'Bloody odd world,' said Champion, 'when a man has to kidnap his own child.'

'And his friends,' I said.

Champion took his son from the chauffeur. He put him on the back seat of the car. Billy woke for a moment, smiled at both of us, and then closed his eyes to nuzzle into the leatherwork. Gently Champion pushed his son along the seat to make room for us. He gave no instructions to the driver, but the car started and moved off into the traffic of the busy coast road. A roar of engines became deafening, and modulated into a scream as a jet came low across the road and turned seaward.

'You said you'd bring Mummy,' said the boy. His voice was drowsy and muffled by the seat. Champion didn't answer. The boy said it again: 'You said you'd bring her.'

'Now, that's not true, Billy,' said Champion. 'It will be a long time. I told you that.'

The boy was silent for a long time. When finally he mumbled, 'You promised,' it seemed as though he preferred the dispute to continue, rather than be silent and alone. 'You promised,' he said again.

I thought for one moment that Champion was going to strike the child, but the arm he stretched out went round him, and pulled him close. 'Dammit, Billy,' said Champion softly. 'I need you to help your Dad, not fight with him.'

By the time we got to Cannes, the child's slow breathing indicated that he'd gone back to sleep.

You won't find the Tix mansion in any of those coffee-table books about the houses and gardens of the rich families of France. But the Tix fortune was once a notable one, and the house had been built without regard to cost. The quarry, two miles from it, had been the basis of the Tix empire, and even now in the summer, when there had been no rain for a couple of weeks, the yellow quarry-dust could be seen on the marble steps, the carved oak door and on the half-timbered gables.

A century earlier, the wealth from the quarry had built this great house, and created the village that had housed the men who worked there. But the riches of the quarry had diminished to seams that had to be mined. Eventually even the honeycomb of the mine's diggings yielded so little that it was closed. The village languished, and finally became a training ground where French infantry learned house-to-house fighting. But the mansion survived, its paintings and furnishings as intact as three great wars permitted.

The builder had made it face the entrance to the drive, a track nearly a mile long. It was a gloomy house, for the dramatic siting of this solitary building on the desolate limestone plateau condemned it to dim northern light.

The electricity was provided by a generator which made a steady hum, audible throughout the house. The hall lights dimmed as we entered, for the power it provided was fitful and uncertain. The entrance hall was panelled in oak, and a wide staircase went to a gallery that completely surrounded the hall. I looked to the balcony but could see no one there, and yet I never entered the house without feeling that I was being observed.

'Make yourself at home,' said Champion, not without some undertones of self-mockery.

The tiled floor reflected the hall table, where the day's papers were arrayed, undisturbed by human hand. The roses were perfect, too, no discoloured leaf disfigured them, nor shed petal marred their arrangement. It was as homely as a wax museum, its life measured by the pendulum of the longcase clock that ticked softly, and tried not to chime.

A servant appeared from a room that I later learned was Champion's study. This was Mebarki, Champion's Algerian secretary. He was about fifty years old, his eyes narrow, skin pigmented, and his white hair cropped close to the skull. He pulled the door closed behind him and stood in the recessed doorway like a sentry.

Champion carried his son, sound asleep, in his arms. A man in a green baize apron helped the chauffeur with Champion's cases. But my attention was held by a girl. She was in her early twenties. The dark woollen dress and flat heels were perhaps calculated to be restrained, as befits the station of a domestic servant who does not

131

wear uniform. But in fact the button-through knitted dress clung to her hips and breasts, and revealed enough of her tanned body to interest any man who knew how to undo a button.

'Anything?' said Champion to the white-haired man.

'Two Telex messages; the bank and the confirmation.'

'In gold?'

'Yes.'

'Good. It's a pity they have to learn the hard way. In that case tell the warehouse, and let them collect them as soon as they like.'

'And I confirmed lunch tomorrow.' Mebarki turned his cold eyes to me. There was no welcome there.

'Good, good, good,' said Champion, as his mind turned to other matters. Still holding his son, he started up the stairs. 'I'll put Billy to bed, Nanny,' he said. 'Come along, Charles. I'll show you your room.'

The servants dispersed, and Champion took me along the dark upstairs corridors of the house to my room.

'There's a phone in your room: dial two for my room, one for my study, and ten for the kitchen. They'll get you coffee and a sandwich, if you ask.'

'It's a plush life, Steve.'

'Goodnight, Charlie. Sleep well.'

My 'room' was a suite: a double-bedroom, ante-room and sitting-room, with a fully stocked cocktail cabinet and a balcony that overlooked a thousand acres of scrub. There were books too: carefully chosen ones. I was flattered by the care shown in choosing them, and affronted by the assurance that I'd arrive.

I picked up the phone and asked for tea and ham sandwiches. 'Tea with milk,' I said again. It was the nanny who answered. She replied in English. It was English English. 'Have cold chicken,' she suggested. 'They don't eat ham here – they're Arabs.'

132

'I'll come down to the kitchen,' I said.

'No, I'll bring it up,' she said hurriedly. 'Cheese or chicken?'

'Chicken.'

'Stay there. I'll bring it up.'

I walked out on to my balcony. There was still a light burning somewhere in the lower part of the house, and there were the mixed smells of capsicums being scorched in the style of Arab cooking, and the sweet smell of incense.

I was still on the balcony when the girl arrived with the tray. I watched her as she put it down on the bedside table. She'd unpinned her hair. It was corn-coloured and fell on her shoulders in an attractive disarray. She was tall and slim, with high cheekbones, a generous mouth and blue eyes. She seemed to sense that she was being watched, and she looked up suddenly and smiled, as if reading my carnal thoughts.

'You're English, aren't you?' The voice was home counties, but it had been a long time away from home.

I nodded.

'First Englishman I've seen in an age,' she said.

'No shortage in Nice.'

'These people won't let me borrow a car,' she said. 'Just because I dented their lousy old Fiat. And you change twice on the bus – I tried it once, and once was enough, I'll tell you!' She turned down the cover on the bed and tucked it in, with the quick nervous movements of a trained nurse. 'The maid should have done that before dinner,' she explained. 'No, I'm trapped here.' She smoothed her skirt over her hips as she straightened her body, and looked at me. 'I used to go for walks but I twisted my ankle, and there are mine-shafts out there with no fencing or warning notices or anything – just like the French – you could fall right down them and no one would even know about it.'

'And no cabs?'

'On my salary – you must be joking.' She gave me a knowing smile. It was the sort of smile that only beautiful young girls know about: a provocative smile from moist open lips, as sweet as fresh cream. And as ready to turn sour at the first sign of thunder.

I smiled. She walked across to the balcony where I stood. 'It's fantastic weather for this time of year,' she said. The sky was purple, and from somewhere over the hill there was a glow of red neon, like an electronic sunset switched on all night.

Even before she put her arm round me, I felt the warmth of her body and smelled the cologne. 'I think I'm going to like you,' she whispered. She reached around to clasp her hands in front of me. Then she pressed her body against my back. 'I'm going to like you very much.'

'Why?' I said.

She laughed. 'You're a cool bastard.' She blew on the back of my neck and then gently bit the lobe of my ear. 'I'm lonely,' she said finally, when she grew tired of the game.

'Not tonight,' I said. 'I've got a headache.'

She chuckled, and gripped me more tightly.

'Why don't you drink your tea?' she asked. 'It might start your blood circulating.'

'Good thinking,' I said. I took her wrists and gently broke free from her tight grasp.

I went across to the bedside table where she'd put the tray. It was an impressive spread. There were hand-embroidered napkins, solid silver cutlery and some spring flowers in a vase. The tray was set for two. I sat down on the edge of the bed and poured two cups of tea, and added milk. I heard a rustle of silk; by the time I turned round, with the cup and saucer in my hand, she was stark naked, except for a string of pearls and a heavy gold bangle that denoted her blood group.

'Damn!' she said mildly. 'I wanted to surprise you.' She flipped back the counterpane and climbed into my bed, stretching her legs down into the crisp starched sheets with a sound like tearing tissue paper. 'Oooh! The sheets are cold!'

'You want a chicken sandwich?'

She shook her head. She seemed little more than a child, and, like a child, was suddenly sad. 'You are angry?' she asked. 'Have I shocked you?'

'No,' I said.

'Be nice to me,' she pleaded. 'If you want me to go, I'll go. But be nice to me.' She was tanned, except for the places that would be covered by a small two-piece.

I gave her the cup and saucer. 'You want sugar?'

'You're very English,' she said. 'You don't want it yourself, but you can't bear to turn it away. No, no sugar.'

'Was this Mr Champion's idea?' I said. I turned to watch her as she answered.

She sat up in bed to drink her tea. 'You're his best friend, he said.' A drip of tea had dribbled down her breast. When she rescued it with her spoon she looked at me and giggled. She raised the spoon to my lips, and when I accepted it, giggled again.

'Was it his *idea*?' I persisted.

'Yes, but I told him I'd have to see you first.' She stretched her long tanned arm out, to run a fingertip down my back. 'My name is Topaz,' she said. 'It means yellow sapphire.' She was in her early twenties, with educated speech and calm confident eyes. Forty years ago, girls like this had converged upon Hollywood; now

135

they can be found wherever there are yachts or skis or racing cars, and men to pay for them.

'So he's going to pay you?'

'No, darling, I do it for love.' She chuckled as if that was the greatest joke in the world. Then she drank her tea greedily and put her tea-cup down on the table at her side of the bed. 'Put your arms round me for a minute.'

I did so.

'I get frightened here,' she said in a whisper. 'I'm serious now, I really am.'

'Why should you be frightened?'

'These bloody Arabs arrive by the dozen and then literally disappear!'

'Now, come on, Topaz.'

'I'm not kidding. They arrive in cars in the night, and then next morning there's no sign of them.'

'Oh, yes.'

'I'm serious!' she said angrily. 'Footmarks on the hall carpet, and funny noises in the night. Sometimes I wonder if it's worth the money.'

'Why are you telling me all this?' I said.

'I don't know,' she admitted. 'Because you're English, I suppose.'

'But Mr Champion is English too, isn't he?'

She screwed up her face in deep thought. She was either the greatest actress I'd ever seen in action, or she was speaking right from the heart. I looked at her heart with more than casual interest. 'Not really English,' she said finally. 'They laugh and joke together in Arabic. I don't call that being English, do you?'

'You're quite right,' I said.

Her arms reached out again. 'Do you wear an under-vest?' she said. It was a rhetorical question. 'It's a long time since I met a man who wears undervests.'

'I can always take it off,' I said.

'Yes, take it off.' She had probably been telling me the truth, but I knew enough about Champion not to dismiss the idea that she might be the greatest actress in the world.

I looked at her. What was she: a housekeeper, a cast-off girlfriend of Champion, a nurse brought here just to look after Billy, or a spy planted to check out what I might say in my sleep. Or did she play some other unsuspected role in this strange household where no pork was eaten, and where the night air smelled of burning incense.

I said, 'It's just that I've stopped believing in Santa Claus, reincarnation and love at first sight.'

'And which of those am I supposed to be?' she asked. 'You want me to go? If you want me to go, say so.'

'A man can suss out Santa,' I said, 'without stuffing his presents back up the chimney.'

14

The N562 road from Grasse deteriorates after Draguignan. From its sharp hairpins you can see the Mediterranean on a fine day, or at least the shiny new autoroute that swings inland at Cannes and goes past Aix and Avignon. That – if you have the right sort of car, and keep your foot on the floor – will take you to Paris within five hours.

But to the north of that '*route sinueuse*' is a barren region of scrub and rock that the French Army have possessed since the early years of this century. There are no autoroutes there. In fact, the local people will tell you that there are no roads there at all, although they themselves drive north. The raincoated policemen and armed soldiers who huddle around the *zone militaire* barriers wave the grey corrugated vans of the grocer, the butcher and the baker through the cordon, except when the gunnery ranges are in use.

Champion's black Mercedes was well known to the sentries. Champion had a local resident's pass, for the Tix mansion and the quarry were close to the military zone, and the most direct route was through the barriers.

The chauffeur showed the pass to the sergeant of gendarmerie. The sergeant leaned into the car and stared at all three of us before handing the papers back. There was a buzz as the window was raised, and the car rolled forward into the military exercise zone. With a rattle of gravel we passed over the junction of the communications roads. Soon we reached the reinforced surface that the army built to withstand the weight of the AMX 50s, brought up here to 'the Atelier' for testing under battle conditions.

Even in fine weather it is a grim place. Like all such military establishments, it is an example of decades of neglect interspersed with panic spending. The buildings at the north-western tip were built by the Germans during the war. It is a walled compound, with guard towers and ditches. The emplacement area, which the US Army built in 1946, included a cinema and swimming-pool that are still in use, but a more important legacy from the Americans is the line-up of artillery stands, where the big guns are anchored during the firing trials.

The heart of the Atelier is to the south of the plateau. It is called the Valmy complex. It was built in 1890, and the name of the great victory for French artillery is carved in stone above the main entrance. It's a curious-looking place: probably designed by some architect who had waited all his life for a chance to use poured concrete, for almost every wall is curved. It stands amid the stone barracks and the metal tank-hangars like a set for some old Hollywood musical, and it's not difficult to imagine lines of dancers kicking their way along the curved balconies, tap-dancing on the prow, or poking their smiling faces out of the circular windows.

'Stop a moment,' Champion told the driver.

'They'll move us on,' he replied.

'Go and look at the plugs or something,' said Champion. He turned to me. 'Quite a place, isn't it,' he said. 'That's the research block.'

I pushed the button to lower the window. The clouds were scudding low over the superstructure of the block, tangling in the aerials to make it look more than ever like a ship at full steam.

'Real research?'

139

'Missiles, atomic artillery . . . some interesting heat-seeking ideas, and one of the best electronic counter-measures research teams in the West.'

'And what are you interested in?'

'What are *we* interested in, you mean.'

'That's it.'

Champion had his gloved hands locked together. I noticed him pinching his fingers to find the place from which the tips were missing. I wondered if it gave him pain. 'I wouldn't pass anything to the bloody Russians, Charlie.'

I didn't answer.

He looked at me to see how I'd reacted to his promise about not working for the Russians, but I didn't react in any way. Champion wiped the back of his glove across his mouth as a child might after an indiscretion. 'The Arabs will pay for the best anti-aircraft defence that can be bought . . . defensive weapons, Charlie . . . you've been good not to ask before, but you deserve an explanation of what you are doing.'

'I've never had one in the past.'

Champion smiled grimly. 'No, I suppose not.'

'Fuses? Working drawings? One of the research team, is it?'

'They've taught you to think wholesale,' said Champion. 'Is that the way the department would do it?' He didn't expect an answer. He looked through the rain-specked windscreen to watch the driver prodding the engine. The bonnet closed, and Champion spoke hurriedly to provide an answer before the driver came back inside the car. 'You know what I'm trying to say, Charlie. If you've got any doubts about what I'm doing, for God's sake tell me.'

'OK.'

'Not just OK, Charles. Promise me!'

I smiled. It was not like the Champion I used to know. 'Scout's honour, you mean? Will it make you feel more secure if I say I won't betray you?' I asked him.

'Funnily enough,' said Champion irritably, 'it will.'

'I'll give you a contract,' I offered. 'And then if I shop you, you can sue me.'

Then even Champion saw how ridiculous it was to seek assurances from men who were professional betrayers. 'You killed the men at the quarry,' he said. 'Admit it!'

The driver opened the door and got in. I nodded.

The car turned away from the Valmy complex, and took the main road west. There is a large hotel only ten miles down the road. Crowded into the smoke-filled bar there were civilians from the administration and from the laboratories. In the restaurant sat a few off-duty artillery officers in uniform eating lunch. Three of them had wives and children with them.

Champion pushed his way through the noisy men at the bar and ordered drinks. He had dressed to be inconspicuous here – a short brown leather jacket and a stained hat. He made some joke to the bartender and the man smiled. We took our drinks to a battered wooden table under the window, and an old woman put a checked tablecloth on it and set the cutlery for four. She gave a nod of recognition to Champion. We had come a long way round by road, but as the crow flies Champion was almost a neighbour.

'One of the lab workers will be here,' said Champion. 'An old-time Communist, he thinks I make regular trips to Moscow. Don't disillusion him.'

'I'll try not to.'

'The test firings begin next week. He'll let you have whatever he can get hold of, but we might have to lean on him.'

The waitress brought three beers, and the menu. Champion tapped the plastic menu on the edge of the table and said to me, 'Remember what I told you, Charlie. I'm trusting you.'

I reached for my beer and drank some. It seemed unlikely that Champion trusted me, for he'd told me countless times that a spy should trust no one.

Champion stared at the menu. '*Choucroute!* It's a long time since I last had *choucroute garni*,' he said. He pursed his lips as if he was already tasting it. But he didn't order sauerkraut, he had fillet steak and imported asparagus.

15

It was my idea that Gus – Champion's contact in the Valmy depot – should get a local contractor's pass for me. He had doubts about it, but the application went through within seven days and they gave me the pass the following Monday. With it I was able to crisscross the whole military zone. Providing Gus came down to the door of the administration block, I was also permitted to enter the buildings there.

From the top floor I saw the flash of the guns far away on the other side of the range, and I could look down to the bottom of the old fault on the edge of which Valmy was built. On the firing days, yellow helicopters scoured the range for warheads and the striped dummy atomic shells. They clattered across the rift to deliver the target-graphs to the administration block's front lawn – that is to say, the wind-scoured piece of scrubland where stood two ancient field guns, an old missile ramp, and a sign saying 'No Admittance'.

'The French are being very co-operative,' said Schlegel.

'Too bloody co-operative,' I said. 'When that pass came through within seven days, this fellow Gus couldn't talk about anything else.'

Schlegel stopped pacing up and down and looked at me. He recognized other unspoken criticisms in my voice.

'We've got to keep in contact,' said Schlegel defensively. 'And this was the only place.'

I didn't pursue the argument. Schlegel was right. He looked at his watch. 'Mustn't keep you too long, or our friend Champion might wonder where you are.' He put the papers that Gus had given me into my document case and clicked the locks closed. 'Worthless,' he pronounced. 'If Champion can sell that to the Arabs, he deserves every penny he gets!'

'A dummy-run perhaps. Just to see if I'm going to blow the works.'

'What for?' said Schlegel. 'Who needs you, one way or the other? Why try to convince you that he trusts you – where's the percentage?'

'That's right,' I agreed.

'Now don't go all hurt on me. Champion doesn't need you, or any other cut-out. He's met Gus – Gus knows his face – Jesus! It doesn't make sense, does it?'

I blew my nose. Then I walked over to the window and looked down at the other buildings. I was suffering the first symptoms of influenza, and the weather promised nothing but thunder and lightning and endless torrents of rain. I put my hands on the radiator and shivered.

'Come away from that window, bird-brain,' said Schlegel. 'You want your pal Gus to see you?'

'It *could* make sense,' I said, moving away from the window. 'It would make sense, if there was something very big coming up. Something that the French don't want to talk about.'

Schlegel pulled a horrified face and waved his flattened hands at me to warn me to stop.

'I know, I know, I know!' I said. I looked round at the soft furnishings, the hand-tinted portraits of nineteenth-century generals and the faded plastic flowers. Such a reception room – in such a place – was sure to have electronic plumbing, but I continued anyway. 'If they are putting something really important through the Atelier in the near future, Champion will get his hands on it.'

Schlegel shrugged at what most people in the department would have considered a major breach of security.

'Not if our pal Gus goes into the cooler. That's the way they'd reason.'

'And perhaps that's the way Champion hopes they will reason.'

Schlegel sucked his teeth in a gesture that was as near as he ever came to admiration. 'You have your lucid moments, fella. For a Brit, I mean.' He nodded. 'You mean he might have *two* contacts here.'

'Champion was brought up on second network techniques.'

'Well, you should know. You were with him, weren't you.' He walked over to the plastic flowers, took one and snapped its petals off one by one, tossing them into an ashtray. 'There are still some questions, though.' He looked down at the broken pieces of plastic that remained in his hand and dropped them as if they were red hot. 'I'm trying to give up smoking,' he said. 'It's tough!'

'Yes,' I said.

Schlegel pulled a face, trying not to sneeze; sneezed, and then wiped his nose carefully. He went over to the radiator to see if the heat was on. It wasn't. 'You want to give me one of those aspirins? I think maybe I'm getting your virus.'

I gave him two tablets. He swallowed them.

He said, 'Champion has been made a colonel in the Egyptian Army.'

I stared at him in disbelief.

'It's true,' he said. 'It's not promulgated, or even distributed, but it's official all right. You know how these army chiefs like to get their claws into promising sources.'

I nodded. The army would want to get the allegiance of a man like Champion, rather than let his reports go back to the politicians. Giving him a colonelcy was a simple way of doing it.

'A colonel of the propaganda division, with effect from

January the tenth.' Schlegel folded his handkerchief into a ball and pummelled his nose with it, as if trying to suppress another sneeze. 'Propaganda division! You think that could be on the level? You think this could all be a propaganda exercise?'

'Propaganda? A sell so soft that it's secret, you mean?' I asked sarcastically.

'He's not through yet,' said Schlegel, with some foreboding.

'That's true,' I said.

'You'd better move,' said Schlegel. 'I know Champion likes you back there in time to dress for dinner.'

'You're a sarcastic bastard, Colonel.'

'Well, I'm too old to change my ways now,' he said.

There was a tiny mark on Schlegel's face, where I had punched him in the fracas at Waterloo Station. 'That other business . . .' I said.

'My Waterloo,' said Schlegel. He smiled his lopsided smile, and explained, 'That was Dawlish's joke.'

'It wasn't like me,' I said apologetically.

'Funny you should say that,' said Schlegel. 'Dawlish said it was *exactly* like you.'

16

'So this is the south of France?' I said, as the servant took my coat. Champion leaned forward in his big wing armchair, and reached for a log. He placed it upon the fire before looking up at me. The logs were perfect cylinders cut from young trees, a degree of calculation that extended to everything in the house. The three matching antique corner cupboards, with their japanned decoration, fitted exactly to the space outside the carpet, and the colours harmonized with the painting over the fireplace and with the envelope card table. It was the sort of home you got from giving an interior decorator a blank cheque. After a lifetime of bedsitters and chaotic flats I found the calculated effect disconcerting. Champion had the whisky decanter within arm's reach. That morning it had been full. Now it was almost empty.

Billy was full-length on the floor, drawing monsters in his animal book. He got to his feet and advanced upon me with an accusing finger.

'The fishes can't *hear* when you call them.'

'Can't they?' I said.

'No, because they have no ears. I spent hours and hours today, calling to the fishes, but Nanny says they can't hear.'

'So why do they follow me?'

'My nurse says you must have thrown bread into the pond.'

'I hope you didn't tell her I did, because she gets angry if I don't eat all my bread.'

'Yes, I know,' said Billy wistfully. 'I won't tell her, you needn't worry.'

Champion was watching the exchange. He said, 'You'll give him a complex.'

'What's a complex?' Billy said.

'Never mind what it is,' said Champion. 'You go with Nurse now, and I'll come up and say goodnight.'

Billy looked at me, and then at his father, and back to me again. 'I'd like a complex,' he said.

'Don't worry, Billy,' I said. 'I know a man who can get them wholesale.'

There was a discreet tap at the door. Topaz entered. She wore a white apron. Her face had no make-up, and her blonde hair was drawn tight into a chignon high on the back of her head. I knew it was what she always wore when giving Billy his bath but it made her look like some impossibly beautiful nurse from one of those hospital films.

She nodded deferentially to Champion, and smiled at me. It was the same warm friendly smile that she gave me whenever we saw each other about the house, but she had not visited my room since that first night together.

Love has been defined as 'a desire to be desired'. Well, I'd been in love enough times to think it unlikely that I was falling in love with Topaz. And yet I knew that curious mixture of passion and pity that is the essence of love. And, in spite of myself, I was jealous of some unknown man who might deprive her of this exasperating composure.

I looked at Champion and then I looked back to her, always watchful for a hint of their relationship. But the secret smile she gave me was more like the *rapport* two sober people share in the presence of a drunken friend.

'Come along, Billy,' she said. But Billy did not go to

her; he came to me and put his arms round me and buried his head.

I crouched down to bring our faces level. Billy whispered, 'Don't worry, Uncle Charlie, I won't tell her about the bread.'

When Billy had finally said goodnight and departed, Champion walked round to the table beside the sofa. He opened the document case I'd brought from Valmy, and flicked his way through it with superficial interest. 'Crap,' he said. 'The same old crap. I'll look at it later. No need to lock it away upstairs.'

'Does Gus know that it's crap?' I said.

'It makes him feel he's part of the class struggle,' said Champion.

'He won't feel like that if he gets ten years for stealing secrets.'

'Then you don't *know* him,' said Champion. 'I fancy that's his most cherished dream.'

'What's for dinner?'

'She's doing that bloody *tripes à la mode* again.'

'I like that.'

'Well, I don't,' said Champion. 'Don't you ever think about anything but food? How about a drink?'

'You do that journey up the road to Valmy three times a week, in that little Fiat, and maybe you'll start thinking about it, too.' I waved away the decanter he offered.

'All right. You think it's a waste of time seeing Gus. But we'll need Gus soon – really need him – and I don't want him getting a sudden crisis of conscience then.'

'This is just to implicate him?'

'No, no, no. But I don't want him picking and choosing. I want a regular channel out of that place. I'll sort it out when it gets here.'

'Dangerous way of buying crap,' I said.

'For you, you mean?'

149

'Who else?'

'Don't worry your pretty little head. If they are going to clamp down, I'll hear about it. I'll hear about it before the commandant.' He gave me a big self-congratulatory smile. I'd never seen him really drunk before, or perhaps until now I'd not known what to look out for.

'Well, that's wonderful,' I said, but the sarcasm didn't register upon him.

He said, 'You should have seen Billy this afternoon. Ever seen those toy trains the Germans do? They sent a man from the factory to set it up: goods wagons, diesels, restaurant cars and locomotives – it goes right around the room. Locomotives no bigger than your hand, but the detail is fantastic. We kept it a secret – you should have seen Billy's face.'

'He wants his mother, Steve. And he needs her! Servants and tailored clothes and model trains – he doesn't give a damn about any of that.'

Steve furrowed his brow. 'I'm only doing it for the boy,' he said. 'You know that.'

'Doing what?'

He drained his Scotch. 'He wants his mother,' he repeated disgustedly. 'Whose damn side are you on?'

'Billy's,' I said.

He got to his feet with only the slightest hint of unsteadiness, but when he pointed at me his hand shook. 'You keep your lousy opinions to yourself.' To moderate the rebuke, Champion smiled. But it wasn't much of a smile. 'For God's sake, Charlie. She gets me down. Another letter from her lawyers today . . . they accuse me of kidnapping Billy.'

'But isn't that what you did?'

'Damn right! And she's got two ways of getting Billy back – lawyers or physical force. Well, she'll find out that I can afford more lawyers than she can, and as for

150

physical force, she'd have to fight her way through my army to get here.' He smiled a bigger smile.

'He wants his mother, Steve. How can you be so blind?'

'Just do as you're told and keep your nose clean.'

'*Tripes à la mode*, eh,' I said. 'I like the way she does that. She puts calves' stomach and ox-foot in it, that's what makes the gravy so thick.'

'Do you want to make me sick!' said Champion. 'I think I shall have a mushroom omelette.' He walked round the sofa and opened the document case. He shuffled through the Xerox copies that Gus had made at considerable risk. This second look at them confirmed his opinion. He tossed them back into the case with a contemptuous Gallic 'Pooof!' and poured the last of the Scotch into his glass.

I was surprised to find how much his contempt annoyed me. Whatever Champion felt about my fears, and Gus's motives, we deserved more for our pains than that.

'Yes,' I said. 'She puts those garlic croutons into the omelettes. Perhaps I'll have one of those as a starter.'

17

Thursday was a free day for me. I spent it in Nice. That morning I walked slowly through the market, smelling the vegetables, fruit and flowers. I ate an early peach, and put a blue cornflower in my buttonhole. From the market it was only a stone's throw to Serge Frankel's apartment. He was not surprised to see me.

'We'll have coffee,' he said. He ushered me into the study. It was in the usual state of chaos. Valuable stamps were scattered across his desk, and there were piles of the old envelopes that I had learned to call 'covers'. Catalogues, their pages tagged with coloured slips of paper, were piled high on a chair, and some were placed open, one upon the other, alongside the notebooks on his desk.

'I'm disturbing you.'

'Not at all, my boy. I'm glad of a break from work.'

I looked round the room, carefully and systematically. I tried to be discreet about it but there could be no doubt that Serge Frankel knew what I was doing. He waited for me to speak. I said, 'Aren't you frightened of burglars, Serge? This stuff must be worth a fortune.'

He picked up some creased stamps that he'd lined up under the big magnifier. Using tweezers, he put them into a clear paper packet and placed a small weight upon them. 'This is only a small percentage of what I have. A dealer has to keep his stock circulating to prospective customers.' He plugged the coffee-pot into a wall socket. 'I can give you cream today. It will make up for last time.'

'Is Steve Champion still buying?' I said.

The telephone rang before Frankel could answer my question. He answered the call, 'Serge Frankel,' and then before the caller could get launched into a long conversation, he said, 'I have someone with me at present, and we are talking business.' He watched the coffee-pot and interjected a few laconic and noncommittal words and a farewell. The coffee-pot was bubbling by the time he rang off. 'A stamp dealer faces a thousand problems,' he said. 'One or two of them are philatelic but at least nine hundred and ninety are simply human nature.'

'Is that so?'

'This woman, for instance,' he made fastidious movements with his fingers to indicate the telephone. 'Her husband died last month . . . a decent sort: a printer . . . well, you can hardly respond to his death by asking her if she wants to sell her husband's stamp collection.'

I nodded.

'And now,' said Frankel, 'she's phoning to explain that a Paris dealer called in to see them, was shocked to hear that her husband had died, offered to advise her on the sale, and wound up buying the whole eighteen albums for five thousand francs.' He ran his hand through his hair. 'About one quarter of what I would have given her for it. She thinks she's got a wonderful deal because her husband would never admit how much he was spending on stamps each month . . . guilty feelings, you see.'

'You get a lot of that?'

'Usually the other way about: the husband with a mistress and an apartment in the Victor Hugo to pay for. Such men tell their wives that they are spending the money on stamps. When that sort die, they leave me with the unenviable task of explaining to the widow that the stamp collection that she thought was going to pay off the mortgage, give her a world cruise and put their sons

153

through college, is just a lot of "labels" that I don't even want to buy.'

'Those collections you *are* offered.'

'Yes, dealers from Paris don't just happen by when there's a death in that sort of family. Worse, the widows so often suspect that I've been through the albums and stolen all the really valuable items.'

'A stamp dealer's life is tough,' I said.

'It's like being Cassius Clay,' he said. 'I thump this desk and proclaim that I'll take on all comers. You could walk through that door, and for all I know you might be the greatest authority on Ballons-Montes or the stamps of the Second Empire or – worse still – telegraph stamps or tax stamps. Everyone wants an instant valuation and payment in cash. I've got to be able to buy and sell from experts like that, and make a profit. It's not easy, I'll tell you.'

'Do you ever sell to Champion?' I asked.

'Last year I did. I had three very rare French covers. It was mail sent by a catapulted aeroplane from the liner *Ile de France* in 1928. It was the first such experiment. They ran out of stamps so that they overprinted the surcharge on other stamps. On these the surcharge was inverted . . . It's all nonsense, isn't it?' He smiled.

'Evidently not to Champion. What did he pay?'

'I forget now. Twenty thousand francs or more.'

'A lot of money, Serge.'

'Champion has one of the top ten airmail collections in Europe: Zeppelins, French airships, balloon mail and pioneer flights. He likes the drama of it. He doesn't have the right sort of scholarship for the classic stamps. And anyway, he's a crook. He likes to have the sort of collection he can run with, and unload quickly. A man like Champion always has a bag packed and a blank airline ticket in his pocket. He was always a crook, you know that!'

I didn't follow Serge Frankel's reasoning. It would seem to my non-philatelic mind that a mobile crook would prefer classic stamps of enormous price. And then he'd never need to pack his bag. He could carry his fortune in his wallet everywhere he went. 'You didn't tell him he was a crook in the old days,' I pointed out.

'Didn't say that when he ambushed the prison van and set me free, you mean. Well, I didn't know him in those days.' He drank the rest of his cup of coffee. 'I just thought I did.'

He brought the pot and poured more for both of us. He spooned some whipped cream on to the top of his strong coffee and then rapped the spoon against the edge of the cream jug to shake the remains off. The force of the gesture revealed his feelings. 'Yes, well, perhaps you're right,' he admitted. 'I must give the devil his due. He saved my life. I would never have lasted the war in a concentration camp, and that's where the rest of them ended up.'

'What's he up to, Serge?'

'You're out there in the big house with him, aren't you?'

'But I don't know what he's up to, just the same.'

'This oil business,' said Serge. 'It will change the lives of all of us.' He picked up the jug, and in a different voice said, 'Have some cream in your coffee?'

I shook my head. I would not provide him with another chance to move away from the matter in hand.

'I'm not a Communist any more,' he said. 'You realize that, I suppose.'

'I'd detected some disenchantment,' I said.

'Did the czars ever dream of such imperialism? Did the Jew-baiters dream of such support? The Russians have us all on the run, Charles, my boy. They urge the Arabs to deny us oil, they pass guns and bombs and rocket launchers to any group of madmen who will burn and maim and blow up the airports and hijack the planes. They brief the trade unionists to lock up the docks, halt the trains and silence the factories.'

I reached for my coffee and drank some.

'Makes your throat dry, does it?' he said. 'And well it might. Do you realize what's happening? In effect we'll see a movement of wealth to the Arab countries comparable to the movement of wealth from India to Britain in the eighteenth century. And *that* generated the Industrial Revolution! The USSR has now become the biggest exporter of armaments in the world. Algeria, Sudan, Morocco, Egypt, Libya – I won't bother you with the list of non-Arab customers – are buying Soviet arms as fast as they can spend. You're asking me if I help the Israelis! Helping the Israelis might be the West's only chance to survive.'

'And where does Champion fit into this picture?'

'A good question. Where indeed! Why should the Arabs bother with a cheap tout like Champion, when all the world's salesmen are falling over each other to sell them anything their hearts desire?'

'Don't keep me in suspense.'

'Your sarcasm is out of place, my boy.'

'Then tell me.'

'Champion has promised to sell them the only thing their money cannot buy.'

'Eternal happiness?'

'A nuclear device. A French nuclear device.'

There was a silence broken only by my heavy breathing. 'How can you know that, Serge?'

Serge stared at me, but did not answer.

'And if he delivers?'

156

'Two hundred million pounds was mentioned.'

I smiled. 'You are taking a chance on me . . . suppose I went back to the house and told Champion . . .'

'Then either he would give up the plan – which would delight me – or he'd continue with it.' He shrugged.

'He might *change* the plan,' I said.

'I wouldn't imagine that alternative plans spring readily to mind for such a venture.'

'No,' I said. 'I suppose you are right.' I reached into my pocket, found my cigarettes and matches and took my time about lighting a cigarette. I offered them to Serge.

He waved them away. 'You haven't told me your reaction,' he said.

'I'm trying to decide whether to laugh or cry,' I told him.

'What do you mean?'

'You've been overworking, Serge. Your worries about the Arab–Israeli war, the oil crisis, your business, perhaps . . . you think that they form a pattern. You have invented a nightmare, and cast Champion as the arch-fiend.'

'And I'm right,' said Serge, but as soon as he said it, he realized that it would confirm my diagnosis. He was a lonely old man, without wife, child or very close friends. I felt sorry for him. I wanted to calm his fears. 'If Champion can steal an atomic bomb he deserves whatever it was you said he'd get.'

'Two hundred million pounds was mentioned,' said Serge, repeating the exact words he'd used before as if it was a few frames of a film loop that never stopped running through his mind.

'Why a *French* atomic bomb?' I said. 'Why not an American or a British or a Russian atomic bomb?'

I wished I'd not asked him, for he'd obviously worked out the answer to that one long ago. 'A French nuclear *device*,' he corrected me. 'The technology is simpler. The French made their bomb unaided, it's a far simpler device, and probably less well guarded.' Serge Frankel got to his feet with all the care and concentration of the arthritic. He steadied himself by touching the windowsill where there was a brass inkstand and a carriage clock that always stood at four minutes past one o'clock. I wondered if the hands had become entangled. But Serge was looking not at the cluttered sill but through the window, and down into the street below.

The word 'probably' left me an opening. 'Now, you don't really believe that the French leave their goodies less well guarded than anyone else in the world. Now, do you, Serge?'

'I take back the less well guarded,' he said over his shoulder. From his window there was a view of the market in Cours Saleya. I went over to where he was standing, to see what he was staring at. He said, 'Any one of them could be working for Champion.'

I realized he was talking about the dark-skinned North Africans, so evident among both the sellers and the customers.

'That's right.'

'Don't humour me,' he said. 'Champion's bringing Arab cut-throats into the country by the dozen. Algerians don't even need immigration papers. It was all part of de Gaulle's sell-out to them.'

'I'd better get going,' I said.

He didn't answer. When I left he was still staring down through the window, seeing God knows what terrible scene of carnage.

As I started to descend the stone steps, I heard someone hurrying behind me from the floor above. The metal-tipped shoes echoed against the bare walls and I moved aside cautiously as he came closer.

158

'Vos papiers!' It was the age-old demand of every French policeman. I turned to see his face, and that was my undoing. He struck my shoulder, from behind. There was enough force in it to topple me and I lost my balance on the last few steps of the flight.

I didn't fall on to the landing. Two men caught me and had me pinioned against the landing window, with no breath left in my body.

'Let's have a look at him.' He gave me a sudden push to flatten me against the wall.

'Wait a minute,' said the second voice, and they searched me with the sort of precision cops achieve in towns where the favourite weapon is a small folding-knife.

'Let him go! I know who it is,' said a third voice. I recognized it as that of Claude *l'avocat*. They turned me round very slowly, as a vet might handle a fierce animal. There were four of them: three coloured men and Claude, all in plain clothes.

'It was you who phoned Frankel, was it?' I said.

'Was it so obvious?'

'Serge went into a long explanation about stamp collectors' widows.'

Claude raised his arms and let them slap against his legs. 'Serge!' he said. 'Someone must look after him, eh?'

'Is that what you're doing?'

'He has acquired a lot of enemies, Charles.'

'Or thinks he has.'

Claude looked at the French plainclothes men. 'Thank you. We'll be all right now.' He looked at me. 'We will, won't we?'

'You assaulted *me*! Remember? What are you waiting for, an apology?'

'You're right,' said Charles. He held up his hand in a gesture of appeasement. Then he indicated the way

159

through the lobby to the street. The Nice cops had given him one of their stickers and now his white BMW was askew on the pavement under a 'No Parking' sign. 'I'll give you a lift somewhere.'

'No thanks.'

'We should talk, I think.'

'Another time.'

'Why put me to all the trouble of making it official?'

I said nothing, but I got into the passenger seat of his car. The anger, despair and humiliation of Claude's wartime betrayals boiled up inside me again.

We sat in the car for a moment in silence. Claude fussed around to find his cheroots and put on his spectacles, and dabbed at his natty gent's suiting. I wondered whether he'd spoken with any of the others and whether they'd told him that I wasn't likely to congratulate him about earning his medal and his pension.

He smiled. Claude smiled too often, I'd always thought so.

'We said you'd never last,' said Claude. 'When you first appeared on the scene, we had bets that you wouldn't last out.'

'In the war?'

'Of course, in the war. You had us fooled, Charles.'

'That makes two of us.'

'*Touché*.' He smiled again. 'We thought you were too headstrong then, too direct, *trop simple*.'

'And now?'

'We soon learned that you are anything but direct, my friend. It's unusual to find a man so ready to let the world think him a clumsy unschooled peasant, while all the time his mind is processing every possible permutation for every possible situation. Headstrong! How could we have ever thought that.'

'It's your story,' I said.

'But in one respect our first impressions were correct,' said Claude. 'You are a worrier. *After* the event, you worry. If it wasn't for that you would have been the greatest of the great.'

'The Muhammed Ali of espionage,' I said. 'It's an attractive idea. Serge just told me he feels like the Muhammed Ali of stamps, except that he called him Cassius Clay.'

'I know you're here for your government. I'm here for the German government. We're both after Champion. We might as well co-operate.'

He looked at me, but I said nothing. He looked away from me, to where the figs, apricots and new potatoes from Morocco were on sale alongside the oranges from Jaffa. A man stole a bean and walked on chewing it. Claude looked round at me to see if I'd noticed the larceny. His reaction was too studied. It was all too studied. I doubted whether Claude had been told anything about me – he just wanted to see me at close quarters. Perhaps he reasoned that if I was still in government service, I'd have to deny it hotly, while if I now worked for Champion, I'd want Claude to think I was still official.

What he decided about me I don't know. I opened the car door, and began to get out. I said, 'I've no inclination for all this play-acting, late-night TV spy stuff. If you, and that old man up there want to re-live the great days of your youth, very well, but leave me out of it.'

'Your youth, too,' said Claude.

'My childhood,' I said. 'And that's why I don't want to repeat it.'

'Close the door,' said Claude. 'Get back in, and close the door!'

I did so. I wanted to know what Claude was going to say next, because if he really had been tipped off by his office in Bonn, this would be the time to throw the details in my face and watch it dribble down my chin.

I had to know, because if Claude knew . . . it was only a matter of time before Champion found out.

But Claude was silent.

It was lunchtime. We both watched the stall-holders folding up their stands and stacking away the unsold fruit. As each space was cleared, the motor-cars – which had been circling the Cours for the last half-hour – dashed in to park. More than once there was a bitter argument between drivers. It was a famous local amusement. Claude's strong-arm men were still standing on the far side of the market. They had bought slices of hot pizza, and were eating them while watching both Claude's car and Frankel's window.

'Are they really cops?' I asked him.

'Yes, they are cops all right. Harkis – auxiliaries who worked for the French in Algeria. They can't go home and the French don't like them.'

'You realize that Frankel is terrified of the Arabs. If you have these jokers hanging around to protect him, you are probably giving him his nightmares.'

'They keep out of sight. And are you sure Frankel is terrified of the Arabs?'

'You don't know much if you don't know that,' I said. 'Frankel, the onetime exponent of Marxism and the brotherhood of man, now comes on like . . . Goebbels.'

'A Fascist, you mean, comes on like a Fascist. Don't worry about hurting my feelings. Yes, we're all fighting a new war: the battle-lines have been drawn afresh. Frankel is a racist, I've become a champion of parliamentary government, you are working to defeat the Communists you once fought alongside, and Champion has become an active anti-Semite.'

'Has he?'

'You don't do your homework very thoroughly, Charles. He's working for the Egyptians. Are you getting too old for this business?' He smiled, and touched the hair that was carefully arranged over his almost-bald head. 'You are a strange race, you English,' he said. He searched my face, as if he might find some answer there. 'I work in security in Bonn. We turned out our files, to keep London fully informed of what we are doing. We sent the usual notification to French security before I came down here to take a closer look at Champion. The French have been very good. I have an office with the police here in town. They keep me informed, and they've let me have those Harkis to help me. But you English are so arrogant! You'll never be a part of Europe. You don't reply to our correspondence. Your people come here without proper clearance with the French. And now, when I put my cards on the table and suggest some co-operation, you adopt the superiority of manner that we've learned to expect from the English.'

'You've got it all wrong, Claude,' I told him. 'I don't work for British security. I don't work for any kind of security. I'm not concerned in your problems with London. And I'm not interested in your simplistic generalizations about the British character.'

'Champion has bribed German government officials and senior officers of the Bundeswehr, and he threatened a police officer. He has conspired to import arms into the Federal Republic, and forged official documents. Within a week or ten days he'll be arrested, and there will be no point in his running away because, with the charges we're bringing, we'll extradite him from any country of Western Europe or the USA.' A car took the corner a little too widely. The driver hooted angrily before he saw Claude's police sticker and steered away. 'Have I made myself clear?' Claude asked me.

'You've made yourself clear, all right,' I said. 'You mean you want Champion to run, or else you'll have to start putting some real evidence together. If that happens, some of those bribed officials might get angry while they're still in a position to fight back. And, in that case, you and some of your colleagues will be out of a job.'

'You're protecting Champion!' he said.

'He doesn't need any protection, Claude. You found that out in the war, when you took him down to the Rock and removed the tips of his fingers without getting a squeak out of him.'

For a moment Claude looked as if he was going to argue, but he swallowed his anger. He said, 'Champion still has that same charm, doesn't he? He had us all eating out of his hand in the war, and now he's still got you in his pocket.'

'There's something you should know, Claude,' I said sarcastically. 'I work for Champion. He pays me every month; and I work for him. Have you got that? Now write it down in your notebook and send a carbon to your office in Bonn, so they can file it in their secret archives. And make sure you put your address on it, in case they want to send you another Iron Cross.'

I fiddled with the door catch, which was designed to baffle foolhardy children. This time I opened the door and got out.

'Frankel will make an attempt on Champion's life,' said Claude. 'You tell your boss that.'

I rested one hand on the roof of the car, and leaned down to talk to Claude. He wound the window down hurriedly. 'Do you believe everything that Frankel tells you?' I asked. 'Or do you just pick out the bits you like?'

'I'm looking after the old man,' said Claude.

'Just where does your concern end, and where does house-arrest start?' I said. 'You have men outside his

164

door – dark-skinned men who terrify him – you tap his phone, and you rough-up his visitors.' I waited for Claude to deny it; but he didn't deny it.

Claude didn't want to discuss Frankel; he was interested only in Champion. He said, 'Champion is an Arab terrorist, and no matter how many times you tell me which side he fought on during the war, he'll be treated like an Arab terrorist. And he can't even claim to be some perverted form of idealist – he's in it just for the money.'

'We're all in whatever we're in for the money, Claude. I forget the last time I met an unpaid volunteer.'

I'd got as far as this without realizing that Claude had the same bitter contempt for me that I had for him. But now, as he bit his lip, I could see that Claude had not escaped the war unscathed. His wounds had come after the surrender, as he co-operated with his conquerors and learned the apartheid of crime that all German policemen had to learn during the Allied occupation, but his wounds were none the less crippling for that. 'At first I'm a Fascist, and now I'm a mercenary. And I've got to smile, and take it all the time, have I?' He brought a clenched fist down upon the car's steering wheel with enough force to break it, except that German cars were so well made and safe to drive in. 'Well, I was never a Nazi – *never*! I hated those people. But I am a German, and I did my duty then as I do it now.'

'And if you'd been living just a few miles farther east, you'd be doing your duty on behalf of the Communists, I suppose.'

Claude smiled. 'I can remember a few nights during the war when you were telling us all how much you favoured theoretical Communism.'

'Yes,' I said. 'Well, almost everyone's in favour of *theoretical* Communism. Maybe even those bastards in the Kremlin.'

18

An atlas might show Marseille and Nice as two identical dots on the map. But Marseille is a sprawling Sodom-on-Sea, complete with bidonville and race riots, a city of medieval confusion, where the only thing properly organized is crime.

Nice, on the other hand, is prim and neat, its size regulated by the niche in the hills into which it nestles. Its cops nod politely to the local madams, and Queen Victoria shakes a stone fist at the sea.

Friday's sky was blue, and the first foolhardy yachtsmen were beating their way up the coast against a chilly wind.

I went through the usual contact procedure. I phoned the sleazy little office near Nice railway station, but I would have been surprised to find Schlegel there. In his present role, I knew he'd stay well away from a small place like Nice. And well before the secretary told me that Schlegel wanted to see me urgently, I guessed he was staying with Ercole out at the restaurant – '*vue panoramique, tranquillité, et cuisine mémorable*' – because it was the one place I did not want to go.

Old Ercole would greet me with a bear-hug, and a kiss on both cheeks, and he'd talk about the old days, and look up to the wall behind the bar where his citation hung. And where a silver-framed Ercole was frozen in an endless handshake with a stern-faced General de Gaulle.

There was nothing perspicacious about that guess. It was a natural place for Schlegel to hole-up. There'd be no resident guests there at this time of year, apart from the occasional use of a private room, booked with a wink and paid for with a leer. Ercole still had top security clearance with the department, and it was not only secluded but it was as luxurious a place as Schlegel would find anywhere along this coast. Had I been a computer, I would have put Schlegel there. But I'm not a computer, and try as I may, I could never get to like old Ercole, and never get to trust him either.

It all went as I knew it would. Even the fast drive along the high Corniche – that dramatic mountain road you see behind the titles of TV documentaries about the French Miracle, just before they cut to an economist standing in front of the frozen food cabinet – even that was the same.

All of these hill villages depress me. Either they have been taken over by souvenir shops and tarted-up restaurants with the menu in German, or, like this village, they are dying a slow lingering death.

The wind had dropped. Out at sea, the sailing boats, like neatly folded pocket handkerchiefs, hardly moved. I parked alongside the defunct fountain, and walked up the village's only street. The houses were shuttered, and the paintwork was peeling and faded except for the bright red façade of the Communist Party's converted shop.

It was damned hot and the air was heavy. The cobblestones burned my feet, and the rough stone walls were hot to the touch. An Air Tunis jet passed over, obeying the control pattern of Nice. From up here, I seemed almost close enough to touch the faces of passengers peering from its windows. It turned away over the sea, and its sound was gone. In the quiet, my footsteps echoed between the walls.

A newly painted sign pointed the way to Ercole's restaurant. It was tacked to the wall of a roofless slum. From its open door a lean dog came running, followed by a missile and an old man's curse that ended in a bronchial cough. I hurried on.

Built with the stone of the mountainside, the village was as colourless as the barren hill upon which it perched. But at the summit, there was Ercole's restaurant. Its whitewashed walls could be seen through a jungle of shrubs and flowers.

From somewhere out of sight came the grunts, puffs and smacks of a tennis game. I recognized the voices of Schlegel and Ercole's grandson. There were kitchen noises, too. Through an open window came steam, and I heard Ercole telling someone that a meal was a conversation between diner and chef. I went in. He stopped suddenly as he caught sight of me. His greeting, his embrace and his welcome were as overwhelming as I feared they would be.

'I had this *feeling* . . . all *day* I had it . . . that *you* would come here.' He laughed and put his arm round my shoulder and clasped me tight. 'I *hate* this man!' he proclaimed to the world in a loud voice. 'I hate him! That he comes here, and does not come to Ercole straight away . . . what have I *done*? This is your home, Charles. You know this is your home.'

'Jesus, Ercole. What's this goddamned mouthfest?' It was Schlegel. 'Oh, there you are, kid. They said you'd phoned. All OK?'

I didn't tell him whether or not everything was OK.

'Staying to supper?'

'I'm not sure I should,' I said. 'I said I'd be back in the late afternoon.' But Ercole was going into an encore, and I decided not to get too neurotic about Champion, lest I stir up the very suspicions I was trying to avoid.

'Give us a drink, Ercole. Splice the mainbrace! Right?'

'Right,' I said, with the sort of enthusiasm I was

expected to show for Schlegel's studied forays into English idiom.

'Sure, sure, sure,' said Ercole.

I looked round the empty dining-room. Soon it would be crowded. Ercole was making money, there was little doubt about that. He'd torn down most of the old buildings and built anew, spending additional money to make it all look old again.

On the far side of the room, two young waiters were setting a table for a party of fifteen diners. The glasses were getting an extra polish, and special flowers and handwritten *table d'hôte* cards were positioned on the starched cloth.

Ercole watched them until they'd finished. 'A drink, a drink, a drink,' he said suddenly. 'Apéritif? Whisky? What is the smart thing in London now?'

'I don't know what's the smart thing in London now,' I said. And if I did know, I'd make a special point of not drinking it. 'But a *kir* would suit me very well.'

'Two *kirs*, and an Underberg and soda for the colonel,' Ercole ordered.

'Bring ours down to the pool,' said Schlegel. He stabbed me with a finger. 'And you come and swim.'

'No trunks,' I said.

'The fellow mending the filter will show you,' said Ercole. 'There are all sizes, and plenty of towels.'

I still hesitated.

'It's a heated pool,' said Schlegel. I realized that he'd chosen the pool as a suitable place for us to talk.

The drinks arrived. Schlegel changed into nylon swimming trunks patterned like leopard's fur. He timed his activities so that his running-somersault dive off the board coincided with my emergence from the changing-room in a curious pink swimming costume about two sizes too big.

169

Schlegel devoted his entire attention to his swimming, just as he gave undivided attention to most of the other things I'd seen him do. For me, the pool merely provided a diversion for my arms and legs, while my mind grappled with Champion. Eventually even Schlegel grew tired, and climbed out of the water. I swam across to where he was sitting. I floated in the water as he sipped his drink.

'It's a long time since I did any swimming,' I said.

'Is that what it was?' said Schlegel. 'I thought you were perfecting a horizontal form of drowning.'

'Spare me the swimming lesson,' I said. I wasn't in the mood for Schlegel's Catskill comedy. 'What is it?'

Schlegel picked up the packet of cheroots that he'd placed ready at the side of the pool. He selected one and took his time lighting it. Then he tossed the dead match into the undergrowth.

Ercole had planted quick-growing bamboo, but it was not yet tall enough to hide the little village cemetery, with its decorated family tombs, faded photos and fallen flowers. There was a small child there, she was putting flowers into a tin can and singing to herself.

It was only the middle of the afternoon, but already the mist was piling up in the valleys so that the landscape became just flat washes of colour, with no dimensions at all, like a stage backdrop.

'Cu-nim. We'll have a whole week of this,' Schlegel predicted. He sniffed the air with an aviator's nose and looked respectfully at the clouds.

I waited.

Schlegel said, 'There's a Panamanian freighter coming in to Marseille from Alexandria tomorrow night. Dangerous cargo wharf. Five articulated trucks will be there to load. Those trucks belong to the Tix outfit – Champion's trucks, in other words . . .' He puffed on the cheroot. 'Know anything about that?'

'No,' I said. 'But if it worries you, get the dock police to turn it all over.'

He shook his head. 'Uh-uh-uh! Diplomatic cargo. Going to the embassy in Bonn. It will be sealed. Breaking into that baby and finding anything less than Hitler seated at the Wurlitzer is a sure-fire way to get yourself busted. That cargo has exactly the same protection as a diplomatic bag.'

I related my conversations with Serge Frankel and with Claude.

'And now you're going to start telling me that Champion is going to stash a nuclear bomb into those trucks,' said Schlegel.

'I'm just telling you what Frankel said,' I told him. 'Do we know the route the trucks will take?'

'Don't mastermind me, bubblebrain,' said Schlegel. 'We're checking out all likely targets along the routes. Including airfields where nukes are stored,' he added. 'But Champion is not after a nuke.'

'How can you be so sure?'

'Nah! If you'd ever seen a nuke, you'd know why. They bring those cookies in on freight cars, shielded with lead, and crawling with guys in protective clothing . . . and even if Champion got his hands on one, what does he do – take off down the road in an articulated truck?'

'Threatening to detonate it,' I offered.

'You've got a nasty overdose of Serge Frankel,' he said. 'For all we know, he's in this with Champion.'

'Frankel's a Jew,' I protested.

'Spare me the schmaltz, buddy: my violin is in my other pants. If your pal Champion was planning to hijack canned pork, I wouldn't eliminate the chief rabbi.'

'If Champion was planning to hijack tinned pork,' I said patiently, 'we wouldn't have to worry about the Arabs dropping it on Tel Aviv.'

'But how would they move a bomb?'

'Steal a loaded bomber?'

He stared at me. 'You are determined to lay this theory on me, aren't you?' He kicked the water, very hard, with his heel. It splashed all over me.

'It's the only theory I've got,' I said. I wiped the splashes from my face.

'Bombers loaded with atomic weapons are guarded like . . .' Unable to find a comparison, Schlegel shook his head. 'I'll do the necessary,' he promised. 'The people who guard nukes scare easily.'

'I know the feeling,' I said.

Schlegel nodded. 'Come into town Sunday morning, when Champion goes to Mass. I'll see you at the port – Ercole's cabin-cruiser: the *Guilietta*. Right?'

'I'll do my best.'

'Let's hope the smoke's clearing by then,' he said. He wrapped his sunglasses and cigars in his towel and gave them to me. 'You want to take my stuff round the pool while I swim back?' Schlegel gave orders in the American style, as if politely inquiring about certain aspects of obsessional behaviour. I didn't answer him and I didn't take his towel.

'There's something else you want?' said Schlegel.

'I want Melodie Page's reports, contacts and sheets – anything, in fact – for the month before she died. I want to look at it for myself.'

'Why? Of course you can have it, but why?'

'Murdering the girl was the only hurried and uncharacteristic move Champion has made so far. Something must have panicked him, and it might be something that the girl discovered.'

Schlegel nodded. 'Anything else?'

'See what you can find out about this Topaz kid.'

'OK,' said Schlegel. He pushed the towel into my hand

172

and dived into the water, leaving barely a ripple. He swam underwater, turning his head only enough to bite air. I envied him. Not only the ability to swim like a basking shark, but also for his jet-jockey readiness to press buttons, pull triggers and dive into the deep end of life, while people like me drown in indecision, imagined loyalties and fear. If Champion was yesterday's spy, Schlegel was tomorrow's. I can't say I looked forward to it.

By the time I started walking round the pool, Schlegel had taken a fresh towel from the rack and disappeared into a changing-room. I took my time. The sun was moving behind the hill-tops, so that the landscape was turning mauve. But high in the stratosphere, a jetliner caught the sun's rays and left a contrail of pure gold. In the cemetery the little girl was still singing.

'Did you enjoy the duck?' said Ercole proudly.

'One of these days,' said Schlegel, 'I'm going to fix you one of my special cheeseburgers. With all the trimmings!'

For a moment Ercole was taken aback. Then he roared, 'I hate you, I hate you,' and kissed Schlegel on the cheek.

'That'll learn you, Colonel,' I said softly.

Schlegel smiled bravely while Ercole placed a large piece of goat's cheese on a crust of bread, but stopped smiling when Ercole put an arm-lock on him and forced it into his mouth. 'It's not possible that a man won't eat a fine cheese like this,' shouted Ercole. 'I make it myself – with my own hands.'

It was in Schlegel's mouth by now, and he pulled a face as he tasted its sharp flavour.

Louis – Ercole's grandson – watched the cameo, disapproval showing clearly on his face. He was in his late teens, dressed in the dark well-cut suit that befitted the heir to a gastronomic mecca, but it was difficult to imagine

173

him presiding over it with the sort of passion that his Falstaffian grandpa never failed to show.

Ercole leaned back in his chair and sipped a little of the vintage Burgundy. He turned to Schlegel. 'Good?' he asked Schlegel finally.

'Wonderful,' said Schlegel, without conviction.

Ercole nodded. It was enough.

We dined that night in Ercole's office. It was large enough to hold a table and half a dozen chairs, as well as the tiny desk at which he did his paperwork. The office was a glass-sided box situated between the dining-room and kitchen, and providing a clear view of both. Such a 'cash-control booth' was not unusual in large restaurants, but perhaps only Ercole's was walled with the mirrored-glass exterior that provided such privacy.

We could see the whole dining-room and kitchen, but the clients and staff saw only their own reflections. We watched a bearded boy walk from table to table, holding aloft carefully drawn landscape sketches. He said nothing, nor did his expression change. Few people for whom he displayed his work granted him more than a casual glance before continuing their meal and their conversation. He moved on. It was a sad society, in which all these property salesmen, plastics executives and car rental tycoons could not only humiliate this boy, but inure him to it.

I asked Louis to purchase a drawing for me. It cost no more than a bottle of Ercole's very cheapest wine.

'Have you gone off your trolley?' asked Schlegel, with no more than passing interest.

'It's a good drawing,' I said.

'At least you can tell which way up it's supposed to be,' said Schlegel. He took it from me and examined it, and then looked through the mirror-glass to see the artist. 'Well, now he'll be able to buy himself some soap,' he said.

'What's so special about soap?' I said. 'Why can't he buy himself some food and wine?'

Schlegel didn't answer, but Louis smiled approvingly and was emboldened to ask me a question. 'Is that Ferrari yours?' His voice was almost a whisper, but it was not so quiet that Ercole didn't hear. He'd moved his chair so that he could watch the restaurant. He answered without turning his head.

'Table twenty-one,' he said. 'The flashy fellow with the open-neck shirt. He arrived in the Ferrari. I wish now I'd made him put the tie on. They both had the hundred-franc menu. He owns a handbag factory near Turin – she's his secretary, I should think.' He took a long look at her, sniffed, and jerked a thumb at Louis. 'Cars and football: that's all this one thinks about.'

'But you said Louis prepared the duck,' I protested.

Ercole reached forward and ruffled his grandson's hair. 'He's not a bad boy, just a bit wild, that's all.'

We were all too polite to remark that the boy's conservatively tailored suit, and deferential whispers, made it difficult to believe. But already Ercole's attention was elsewhere. 'Table nineteen have been waiting hours for their coffee. Tell that fool Bernard to pull himself together.' As Louis slipped quietly away, Ercole said, 'Or you do it.' He didn't take his eyes from the restless people at table nineteen for more than a few seconds at a time but he was able to continue talking as if using some different part of his brain. 'You know what the theory of relativity is?'

'You tell me,' Schlegel invited.

'Bernard's let those two tables in the corner get to the fish course at the same time. They all want it off the bone. Now, for Bernard, the minutes fly like seconds. While for those people who asked for coffee three, perhaps four, minutes ago each minute seems like an hour.'

'So that's the theory of relativity?' said Schlegel.

'That's it,' said Ercole. 'It's a miracle that Einstein discovered it, when you remember that he wasn't even a restaurateur.'

Schlegel turned to follow Ercole's gaze. 'That guy's impatience is nothing to do with Einstein,' he argued. 'With a plug-ugly broad like that facing you, *every* minute seems like an hour.'

It was Louis who served the coffee to them. He did it well, but he didn't once look at the people he served.

'And the special hand-dipped chocolates,' remarked Ercole approvingly, after Louis had sat down with us again. 'She'll gobble her way through them, just watch. Did you notice her ask for a second portion of the *profiteroles*?'

'Are you going to the football match on Sunday morning?' Louis undid the lace of one shoe and rubbed his foot. He lacked the stamina of the professional waiter.

'He's staying out at Champion's house,' said Ercole.

'Yes, I know,' said the boy. I saw contempt in the glance he gave the old man.

'I think I might have a morning in bed,' I said.

'No Mass for these heathens,' said Ercole.

'It's just a friendly match for charity,' said the boy. 'Really not worth the journey. But next month it will be a good one.'

'Perhaps I'll come next month, then,' I said.

'I'll send you tickets,' said the boy, and seemed strangely pleased at my decision.

19

Compliant with Schlegel's prediction, the next few days brought perfect spring weather. When Sunday morning came, there was a clear blue sky and hot sun. I went into Nice with Champion, and Billy decided that he would come too. The chauffeur stopped outside St François de Paule. Billy asked why I wasn't going with them to Mass, and I hesitated, searching for a reply.

'Uncle has an important meeting,' said Champion.

'Can I go too?' said Billy.

'It's a private meeting,' Champion explained. He smiled at me.

'I'll leave my coat,' I said, anxious to change the subject. 'The sun is warm.'

'See you later,' said Champion.

'See you later,' said Billy, but his voice was almost lost in the pealing of church bells.

There was a rehearsal in progress at the opera house across the road. A few bars from Verdi's 'Requiem' were repeated over and over. The red carpet was laid for the 'Caisse', but in the shabby doorway marked 'Paradis', a policeman barred the way.

I cut through the market. It was crowded with shoppers, and with country people in their well-brushed black suits, black dresses and shawls, arguing over cages of rabbits and chickens and snails and brandishing brown eggs.

Out at sea, a yachtsman hopefully hauled upon an orange-striped spinnaker as he was passed by a ketch. The sea still had the milkiness of winter, but the surface was calm. The waves lapped the shingle with no more than a gentle slap, and disappeared with a deep sigh of despair.

There is always a blustery wind around the great hillock of rock under which the port of Nice shelters. There was everything there, from a sailing dinghy to tramp steamers moored close to the cranes. The quayside was piled high with pale-yellow timber, and on the far side of the water I saw the *Giulietta* tied up along with half a dozen yachts and cruisers. There was no sign of Schlegel on its deck.

The main port of Nice is not the sort of place where you see the fancy yachts double-parked, with film stars dining *al fresco* on the poop deck, and borrowing a cup of caviare from the tycoon next door. This is a strictly business-only mooring, the Club Nautique is another call. But for a Sunday morning, it was unusually crowded: a dozen men stood around a Peugeot van, and watched two frogmen having their equipment checked. The metal barriers that divide the car-parking area had now been rearranged to cordon off the quay, and a uniformed policeman guarded the only gap in it.

'Where are you going?'

'A little walk,' I said.

'Little walk somewhere else,' said the cop.

'What's happening?' I said.

'Did you hear me? Get going!'

I walked, but kept to the other side of the fence until I came to some other spectators. 'What's happening?' I asked.

'A body, I should think,' said a woman with a shopping bag. She didn't look round to see who'd asked, in case she missed something.

'A suicide?'

'Off one of the yachts,' said another man. He was dressed in an orange-and-yellow yachtsman's wind-cheater, with a heavy-duty zip in bright red.

178

'Some millionaire, or his fancy piece,' said the woman. 'On drugs, probably – an orgy, perhaps.'

'I'll bet they are Germans,' said the man in the wind-cheater, anxious lest the woman's fancies should be so elaborate as to eliminate his own prejudices. 'Germans can't hold their drink.'

The officious policeman came back to where we were standing. 'Move on,' he said.

'Move on yourself, you dirty pig,' said the woman.

'I'll put you into the van,' said the policeman.

'You ponce,' said the woman. 'What could you do with me in the back of the van?' She let out a cackle of dirty laughter and looked round at the rest of us. We all joined in, and the policeman went back to the barrier.

The unity of our gathering thus demonstrated, a hitherto silent member of the crowd was encouraged to speak. 'They think it's a tourist,' he said. 'Tangled in the anchor ropes of one of the boats – the *Giulietta* or the *Manxman* there – they think he went in during the night. The frogmen will soon get him.'

'It will take them an hour,' said the man in the yachting-jacket.

Yes, I thought, it will take them an hour. I moved away from the spectators, and walked slowly up the steep connecting street to the Boulevard de Stalingrad.

Everywhere seemed closed, except for the bakers across the street and a large café, its name, 'Longchamps', in white plastic letters on a hand-painted acid-green background. The floor was cleared, as if for dancing, or a bout of bare-fist fighting. There were a dozen or more customers, all men, and none of them dressed well enough for Mass. In a far corner, a man in a booth accepted bets, and all the while the customers were prodding the racing papers, writing out slips and drinking pastis.

I ordered a cognac, and drank it before the girl behind the bar replaced the cap on the bottle.

'That's an expensive way to satisfy a thirst,' she said. I nodded, and she poured a second one. This one I took more slowly. The radio music came to an end and a weather forecaster started a lot of double talk about areas of high pressure. The woman switched it off. I sipped my brandy.

A man came up, put a one-franc coin into the machine on the counter and got a handful of olives. 'Have one,' he offered. It was Schlegel.

I took one without comment but my eyes must have popped.

'Thought they were untangling me from an anchor chain, did you?'

'Something like that,' I said.

Schlegel was wearing native costume: stone-coloured golf-jacket, dark pants and canvas shoes. 'Well, you started celebrating too soon, blue-eyes.'

'Did you ever think of wearing a black beret with that outfit?' I asked.

We took our time before moving to the quietest corner of the café, alongside a broken juke-box.

'Here's what you asked for,' said Schlegel. 'The contacts that Melodie Page made with her "running officer" and the report dated six weeks before her death.'

I opened the brown envelope and looked inside.

'She stuck with Champion – very close,' said Schlegel. 'She went with him to stamp exhibitions in Zürich and Rome. The last three cards have special exhibition cancellations, you'll notice.'

I looked at the postcards that Melodie Page had sent to her cut-out. They were the sort of thing that several aerophilately firms sell: picture postcards of the *Graf*

Zeppelin airship anchored at some place in South America, the *Hindenburg* airship flying over New York and a grim one that showed the same airship exploding in flames in Lakehurst in 1937. The last card was a picture of an American airship, *Macon*, sent after her return to London.

'Nothing complicated about the code,' explained Schlegel. 'She met her contact five days after the postmark date. Seven days after if the postcard was coloured.'

I went through the cards again.

Schlegel said, 'Why did she suddenly become interested in aerophilately?'

I said, 'The cards were easy to obtain. Champion likes using them to send to his collector friends. And if she's at these stamp shows, what could be more natural?'

'This couldn't be a big stamp racket, could it?' said Schlegel.

'Champion might transfer money that way. A stamp is a bit like a bearer-bond but it's not much of an investment. After all, the value has got to go up at least thirty per cent before you've covered the dealer's mark-up.'

'What about forgeries or stolen stuff?'

'No,' I said.

'How can you be sure?'

'On the scale we're talking about, it would be impossible. The word gets around. A stamp crook has to nibble a mouthful at a time. Making a halfway decent forgery of a stamp is a long expensive business. And you can't recoup by suddenly putting a hundred forged rare stamps on the market, or prices would slump to nothing. Even with genuine stamps they would. And what kind of dough are we talking about? Even in the swish Bond Street auctions you won't find many single stamps fetching more than fifty pounds sterling. That kind of swindle isn't going to meet Champion's wine bill!'

He opened his case and brought out the five-page report that the London office had sent. It was an analysis of Champion's movements, and the spending and activities of his companies, during the previous six months. Or as much as London knew of them. 'Not to be taken away,' said Schlegel, as I opened it hurriedly. He went to the counter and brought two espresso coffees. By the time he'd returned, I'd scanned it.

'Nothing there, is there?' He tapped the coffee with his spoon. 'You'd better drink that. Two brandies under is no way to face that boy, even if he's half of what you say he is.'

I drank the hot coffee, folded up his sheets of typing, and handed them back to him.

'And the trucks in Marseille?'

'They are being loaded. The manifest says engine parts, chemicals and heavy-duty plastics and fabrics. It's a diplomatic load, just as we were warned it would be.'

'Did you find out anything about the Topaz girl?'

Schlegel studied me carefully before replying. 'She's twenty-five. British subject, born in London. Only child. Doting parents to whom she writes each week. Her father is a retired research chemist, living on a small pension in Portsmouth, England. She hasn't lived at home since she first went to college in London. She graduated with honours in thermo-chemistry but she's never had a proper job. She's worked as a waitress and gas-pump attendant . . . you know the kind of thing. Seems like she's hooked on kids. Her last three jobs have been as a children's nurse. She's not a qualified nurse, of course.'

'No,' I said. 'She's a qualified thermo-chemist.'

'Oh, Jesus!' said Schlegel. 'I knew this was going to start you shovelling that Serge Frankel shit all over me. Thermo-chemists don't manufacture nukes.'

182

'No,' I said patiently. 'Thermo-chemists don't manufacture nukes. But thermo-chemistry does relate to the explosion of nukes.' I opened the manila envelope he'd given me, and I found the photo postcard of the *Hindenburg* disaster. 'And the conversion of hydrogen into helium also relates to the explosion of nukes.' I stabbed my finger at the great boiling mass of flame erupting out of the airship.

Schlegel took it from me and bent close to look at the photo, as if he might discover more there. He was still looking at it when I left.

20

The cars of Nice are mostly white, so Champion's black Mercedes was easily spotted on the Place Massena. The driver was in the car, but Champion and his son were sitting outside a café-bar under the stone arcades. Champion was drinking an apéritif, and Billy was arranging sweet-wrappers on the circular metal table-top. Billy waved when he saw me. He'd saved me two cubes of chocolate, which by now were soft, misshapen and coated with pocket-fluff.

Champion got to his feet too. They'd clearly had long enough sitting there, and he didn't offer me a drink. The chauffeur had the door open as we reached the car, and there was a discussion about whether Billy was permitted to sit in front. Billy lost and was seated between us in the back.

Champion opened the window. The sun had heated the interior enough to explain why most cars were white.

'Now don't get chocolate all over the upholstery,' said Champion. He got a handkerchief from his top pocket.

'I'll be careful,' I said.

'Not you, stupid,' said Champion. He grinned, and wiped Billy's hands and mouth.

'You can't always be sure, these days,' I said.

'Don't say that, Charlie.' He seemed genuinely hurt. 'Have I changed so much?'

'You're a tough cookie, Steve,' I told him.

'Welcome to the club,' he said. He looked to Billy to see if he was listening to us.

Billy looked up at me. 'I'm a tough cookie, too,' he told me.

'That's what I said: Billy is a tough cookie, Steve!'

Billy looked to his father to check me out. Steve smiled. 'We don't want too many tough cookies in the family,' he said, and straightened Billy's tie.

By this time we'd reached the airport turn-off. The chauffeur was overtaking the Sunday drivers creeping along the promenade. An Air France Caravelle came down alongside us, to land on the runway that runs parallel to the road. There was a roar, and a scream of rubber as its jets reversed.

Billy watched the Caravelle until it disappeared from sight behind the airport buildings. 'When will we go in an aeroplane again, Daddy?'

'One of these days,' said Champion.

'Soon?'

'Perhaps.'

'For my birthday?'

'We'll see, Billy.'

'Will Uncle Charles come too?'

'I hope so, Billy. I'm counting on it.'

Billy smiled.

The car sped on over the Pont du Var and to the toll-gate of the autoroute. Like any good chauffeur, our driver had the coins ready, and so we joined the fast-moving lane for the *automatique*. A few cars ahead of us, the driver of a VW camper tossed his three francs into the plastic funnel. The barrier tilted upwards to let the VW through. Before it dropped back into position again, a lightweight motor-cycle slipped through behind it. The long lines of cars at the other gates kept the gate-men too busy to notice the infringement.

'Young bastards!' said Champion. 'Bikes are not even *allowed* on the autoroute.'

By that time we were through the barrier, too. The two youths on the motor-cycle had pulled into the slow lane and were weaving through the traffic. The pillion passenger had a golf-bag on the shoulder, and kept turning round to be sure there was no pursuit. They were a sinister pair, both in black one-piece suits, with shiny black bone-domes and dark visors.

'That's what I mean, Steve. There was a time when you would have laughed,' I said.

He'd been watching the motor-cycle riders through the rear window, but now he turned away. 'Perhaps you're right,' he said tonelessly.

The traffic thinned. The driver pulled out to the fast lane and put his foot hard down. The car leaped forward, passing everything on the road. Champion liked speed. He smiled, and glanced triumphantly at the cars that were left behind. The motor-cyclists were the only ones who chased us. We went faster and faster still, and they kept on our tail.

I put my hand out to steady Billy as we accelerated. As I did so, Champion's face tightened with rage. The light inside the car changed dramatically. The windows frosted, one by one, as if whitewash was being poured over us. Champion's hand hit my shoulder and knocked me aside. I toppled, falling upon Billy, who let out a loud yell of protest.

Champion seemed to be hammering upon my back with all his strength, and under both of us, Billy was squashed breathless. The Mercedes rocked with a succession of spine-jarring jolts, as if we were driving over railway sleepers. I knew that the tyres had torn, we were riding on the wheel-rims. As the car struck the verge, it tilted. The driver was screaming as he fought the steering-wheel, and behind his shrill voice I heard the steady hammering noise that can never be mistaken.

'Down, down, down,' Champion was shouting. The car began to roll over. There was a sickening thump, and a squeal of tortured metal. The horizon twisted, and we fell upwards in a crazy inverted world. The car continued to roll, tossing us around like wet clothes in a tumble-dryer. With wheels in the air, the engine screamed, and the driver disappeared through the windscreen in a shower of splintered glass that caught the sunlight as it burst over him like confetti. For a moment the car was the right way up, but it started to roll for a second time, and now fir-tree branches, clods of earth and chopped vegetation were coming in through the smashed windows. When upside down, the car slowed, tried to get on to its side, but with a groan settled on to its roof, wheels in the air, like a dead black beetle.

If I expected hordes of rescuing Samaritans, I was to be sadly disappointed. No one came. The trees made it dark inside the narrow confines of the bent car. With great effort I extricated myself from under Champion's bloody limbs. Billy began to cry. Still no one appeared. I heard the buzz of traffic speeding past on the autoroute, and realized that we were out of sight.

I struggled with the door catch, but the car had warped enough to jam the door. I rolled over on to my back and braced my hands behind my head. Then, both feet together, I kicked. There was a sound of breaking glass and the door loosened. I clambered out. Then I got Billy under the armpits and pulled him clear.

Any last doubt I'd had about the two motor-cyclists machinegunning us was dispelled by the bullet-riddled body of Champion's driver. He was dead, shiny with bright-red blood, upon which thousands of particles of safety glass stuck, like sequins on a party dress.

'Daddy's dead,' said Billy.

I fumbled around for my spectacles and then took

Champion's limp arm and dragged him from the car. It was now an almost unrecognizable shape. There was the stink of petrol, and the loud gurgle of it pouring from the inverted petrol tank.

'Go over there and lie down, Billy.'

Champion wasn't breathing. 'Steve,' I whispered. 'Don't kid around, Steve.'

The irrational thought that Champion might be shamming was all I had to comfort me. I pushed a finger into his mouth and found his dentures. They were halfway down his throat. I tipped him face-down, and thumped him in the small of the back. Billy was staring at me wide-eyed. Champion gurgled. I hit him again, and shook him. He vomited. I dropped him flat on his face and began to pump the small of his back, using a system of artificial respiration long since discarded from the first-aid manuals. Soon I felt him shudder, and I changed the pressure to coincide with his painful inhalations.

'Where's Billy?' His voice was cruelly distorted by the absence of his dentures.

'Billy is absolutely all right, Steve.'

'Get him away from the car.'

'He's fine, I tell you.'

Champion closed his eyes. I had to lean close to hear him. 'Don't send him to wave down a car,' he mumbled. 'These French drivers will run anyone down to avoid being late for lunch.'

'He's right here, Steve.'

His mouth moved again, and I bent close. 'I said it would be like old times, didn't I, Charlie?'

21

'Don't ask me for a medical reason,' said the doctor. He finished dressing a cut on my arm. 'Let's just say that it wasn't Monsieur Champion's time to go.'

'But how sick is he now?'

'Most people would need a couple of months' convalescence. But then most people would probably have died in the smash. Most people would need an intensive-care unit, instead of sitting up in bed asking for whisky. But the police can't talk to him until next week. I told them that.'

'I'm sure he stopped breathing,' I said. 'I thought he was dead.'

'Will-power,' said the doctor. 'You see a lot of it in my job. Had he been in a depressed state, he might have died. As it is, he's probably got all manner of plans that he simply won't give up.'

'You're probably right,' I said.

'You saved his life,' said the doctor. 'I told him that. It was lucky that you were only slightly hurt. You saved him. Those damned dentures would have choked him: he wouldn't have been the first, either. Airlines tell people to remove them if there's the danger of a forced landing.'

'We've known each other a long time,' I said.

'Don't talk to him tonight,' said the doctor. 'Well, let's hope he's around to do the same thing for you some time.'

'He already has,' I said.

The doctor nodded. 'There are tablets for the pain. He'll go to sleep now, I've given him a powerful dose of sedative – big frame and very restless – I'll keep him well sedated for the next few days. I don't think we'll have to move him into the clinic.'

'And the boy?'

'He needs a good night's sleep, that's all. Children have an extraordinary recuperative facility. I don't want to give him my knock-out drops. I suggest that you give him some warmed wine with plenty of sugar in it. Nature's remedy, the grape. Better than all the chemicals.'

'Thank you, doctor.'

'Don't thank me. I am pleased to be of service. I like them, you see. The child has inherited his father's charm, hasn't he?'

'Yes, he has.'

'He made me promise you'd say goodnight to him. I told him his father's asleep. I don't think he's anxious, but . . .'

'I'll go and see him now.'

I need not have tiptoed in.

'Did you see Henry? He was covered in blood.'

'You must go to sleep, Billy.'

'Where's Daddy?'

'He's got to have a good night's sleep, the doctor said so.'

'Is Henry dead?'

It was a trap to test my story about his father. 'Yes, Billy. Poor Henry is dead, but your father is just shaken up, and you and me are just fine. So we must count our blessings.'

Billy corrected me. 'We must thank God,' he said.

'That's what I meant,' I said.

'Can I see Daddy?'

'If you want to, you can. But I thought you'd take my word for it.'

'Yes, I do,' said Billy. 'I *do* take your word for it.' He

190

wriggled down into his bed and put his face into his pillow. I waited for him to peep out at me. When he did, I pulled a face at him. Usually he laughed, but this time he was very serious. 'Is Aunty Nini in prison?'

Pina had always been called Nini, ever since Billy had found her real name too difficult to pronounce. 'Why, Billy?'

'For shooting Henry.'

'Who says she shot Henry?'

'I *saw* her,' said Billy. 'She was driving the motor-cycle. I saw her and she saw me.'

'It looked like her, Billy. But Aunty Nini would not shoot us; we're friends, aren't we?'

Billy nodded, and swallowed. 'It looked like her, though,' he said.

'I'll bring you a glass of wine,' I said. 'Then we'll put out the light, so that you can sleep. In the morning we'll try talking to the fishes again.'

22

'Don't switch on the light, lover man.'

Topaz was waiting in my bedroom. She'd pulled the curtains open and stood near the balcony, so that the moonlight made her hair shine like polished silver.

I moved towards her. She threw herself into my arms. 'It gives me the creeps, this house.'

'Is everything all right?'

'All right? How could it be, in this dump? Those Arabs eating couscous and watching me all the time. And Mr Champion in some sort of coma.'

'He's only under sedation,' I said. 'And I like couscous.'

'Gives me the creeps,' she said. 'This whole house gives me the creeps. If it wasn't for poor little Billy, I would have packed my bags weeks ago.' As she put her arms round me, I could feel the thinness of the white cotton dress, and I could feel that she wore nothing under it. She kissed me.

'Don't undo my shirt,' I said.

'What are you, a poof or something?'

'Some other time, Topaz,' I said. 'Right now, I've got things to do.'

She hugged me tighter, confident that she could make me see reason.

'You know enough of those English words for "go away" without forcing me to use them,' I whispered.

'I am English,' she said.

'And that's another reason,' I said.

'What have I done?' she said. 'Am I using the wrong sort of toothpaste, or something?'

'You're a doll,' I told her, 'but for the next hour I'm going to be busy.'

'Oh, an hour.' She gave me her sexiest smile, and a sigh to match. 'I might be able to last out an hour.'

'Well, don't blow a gasket,' I said, 'the steam fogs up my glasses.'

There was enough light coming from the night sky for me to see her as she smiled, and kicked off her shoes. She plumped up the pillows and sat on the bed. She kept her handbag close to her and began to rummage through its contents.

Footsteps came hurrying along the corridor outside my room. An Arab voice called softly for Billy, but there was no answer. The footsteps moved away downstairs, and I heard the call repeated somewhere down in the hall.

'They are all leaving,' said Topaz.

'Sounds like it,' I said. Now they were calling for Billy from outside in the grounds.

'I'm not involved in any of this,' she said.

'I'll see you in an hour,' I said.

'No,' said Topaz.

There was enough light to see that she was holding a small pistol. 'I thought it might be like that,' I said.

'Sit down on that little chair.'

I sat down very quickly. She gave a mocking laugh. 'What are you?' she said. 'A man or a mouse?'

'Do I have a choice?'

She looked at me for what seemed like a long time. 'I'll bet you keep your small change in a little purse.' She waved the gun to show that she didn't like the way I was leaning towards the door. Her position on the bed gave her a clear field of fire should I go to either the balcony window or the door. There was enough moonlight coming through the window to make such a dash very dangerous.

'You shouldn't have got into this one, cream bun.'

'Stay here until morning, and you'll be safe, and I'll collect one hundred thousand francs,' she explained. 'Go downstairs, and you'll be knocked unconscious, and I'll lose my money.'

'Sweet talk!' I said. 'These people pay debts with bullets.'

'You let me worry about that,' she said.

I moved. The little gold-painted chair creaked. Such chairs are not designed for sitting on.

'It will be a long night,' she said. 'It's too bad you wouldn't do it the easy way.'

'I'll get my cigarettes,' I said. I reached into my jacket for them. Topaz smiled her agreement. She had already run her hands over every place I might have hidden a gun.

I smoked my cigarette, and gave her no cause for alarm. She held the pistol as if she knew how to use it, and she'd left the room in darkness, so that if I tried to get away I would be silhouetted against the light from the balcony window or the light from the hall when I opened the door. I wasn't sure how much of this was luck, and how much of it judgement, but neither was I in a hurry to learn.

Elsewhere in the house there were sounds of movement. Footsteps came up the stairs, past the door, and returned slowly and with enough deep breathing to make me sure that Champion was being carried downstairs.

'Light another cigarette,' said Topaz.

I did as I was told. At that range its glowing ember provided her with a target that she could not miss.

What was the plan, I wondered. If the girl was going to kill me, she could have done so already. If they were going to take me with them, there was no need for her to get me into bed for the night. If she was going to delay me until morning, how would she prevent me then from giving the alarm. Holding me at gun-point was one thing, locking me up, or knocking me unconscious was another.

I wondered how much of this was Champion's idea.

'If they kill Champion, you'll be an accessory,' I said. 'And they still have the death penalty in France.'

My eyes had become accustomed to the gloom. I could see her stretched out on the bed, her hands clasped loosely in front of her. In her hands, the gun. 'I'll have a hundred thousand francs,' she said. 'You don't think I'm going to hang around here, do you?'

'The Riviera,' I said. 'Why not?'

'I've had one winter in this lousy climate and I'm not planning another. To think that I believed all that travel-poster bilge about hot sun and swimming all the year. No, mister, my future is all planned.'

'Husband?' I asked. 'Or someone else's husband?'

'You should have been on the stage,' she said. 'I don't need anyone to help me spend. Especially I don't need *men* to help me.'

'Where in the sun?' I persisted.

'Close your eyes and go to sleep,' she said, as if angry with herself for revealing too much. 'Or I'll sing out and someone will put you to sleep.'

There was the sound of heavy diesels coming slowly up the road. Topaz slid off the bed and went to the window. 'Four huge trucks,' she said. 'No, five, I mean. Really huge. They've stopped down near the lodge.'

'Use your brains, Topaz,' I said. 'We've got to get out of here.'

'You're frightened,' she said.

'You're damned right,' I said.

'I'll look after you,' she said sarcastically. 'If they were going to hurt us, they wouldn't have let me have the gun, would they?'

'Have you tried it?'

'Funny man – just don't give me an excuse, that's all.' She went back to the bed.

'Champion's badly hurt,' I told her. 'The Arabs have taken control. They are not just going to leave us here.'

'Oh, shut up.'

I chain-smoked that night, my muscles so tense that I hardly inhaled the smoke, and I don't know how many cigarettes I used before there came a soft tapping on the door.

'Topaz!' The voice was no more than a whisper but I could see Mebarki, the Algerian secretary, as he came into the room. 'Are you both there?' Already some reflex action had turned my cigarette to conceal its light behind my palm.

'Yes,' said Topaz. The man stepped forward to the bed. There was a blaze of light. I might have mistaken it for a photo-flash, except that it was a rich yellow colour, rather than a thin blue. The flash of light printed Mebarki in full colour upon the black negative of the room. He stood leaning forward, like a man digging his garden. His eyes were half closed and his lips pursed in mental, moral and physical effort. The resounding bang of the gun he held seemed to come a long time afterwards. It was followed by the sound of gun-shot buzzing round the room like angry flies. Then he pulled the second trigger.

There was a clatter as the shotgun was dropped upon the floor, and a softer noise that I later discovered to be the leather gloves he'd thrown after them. From outside came the sound of the diesel engines. They revved and then moved away, until the sound of the last truck faded.

Topaz was past help. I could see that without even switching the light on. The point-blank shotgun blasts had torn her in two, and the bed was soaked with warm blood.

I owed my life to a semantic distinction: had Mebarki said 'Are you both in bed?' instead of 'Are you both there?', he would, no doubt, have devoted the second barrel to me.

I reached forward gingerly to retrieve her gun, and rinsed it under the tap in a process that was as much exorcism as it was forensic science.

Poor Topaz. Even traffic casualties who have played tag in the road deserve our tears, but I could find none. In Portsmouth two would grieve, each Sunday morning of their final years marred by long bus rides to a chilly cemetery.

Armed only with the little pop-gun that the Arabs had given Topaz, and equipped with a torch from beside my bed, I went through the house.

Billy's room was empty, but I threw some of his clothes into a canvas bag and hurried down to the back door and went outside. I moved quickly and spoke softly: 'Billy! Billy!' There was no response. I went round past the kitchen door until I got to the fish pond. 'Billy! It's Uncle Charlie.'

There was a long silence, and when an answer came it was no more than a whisper. 'Uncle Charlie.' Billy was behind the summerhouse from which we played our games of calling to the fish. 'Is that you, Uncle Charlie?'

'Were you banging the doors, Billy?'

'It was those men – did you see the big lorries? They made the doors bang twice.'

'That's all right, then,' I said. 'As long as it wasn't you.' I picked him up. He was dressed only in his thin pyjamas. I felt him shivering. 'We must hurry, Billy.'

'Are we going somewhere?'

'Perhaps Aunty Nini will take you to England. Take you to Mummy.'

'For always?'

'If you want.' Keeping off the gravel path, I carried Billy down to the copse where I'd left the Fiat under the trees.

'Promise?'

'You know I'll try.'

'Daddy says that when he means no.' Billy put both arms round my neck. 'Aunty Nini shot Henry,' he said.

'But only in the game,' I said.

'Was it?' he said, coming fully awake and staring at me.

'You and I always play jokes on Sunday,' I reminded him. 'There was the man trapped inside the fire extinguisher, and the toy rabbit who hid . . .'

'And the fishes you talked to.'

'There you are,' I said.

'Daddy will be awfully cross about the car,' said Billy.

'That's why he went to bed,' I explained. 'I've had to promise to mend it.'

'Oh dear,' said Billy with a deep sigh. 'But I'll help you, Uncle Charlie.'

I found the Fiat parked where I had left it. I unlocked the front door and put Billy inside. As I looked back towards the house I saw a light shine from one of the upstairs windows. I got into the car and closed the door without slamming it. Another light shone from the upstairs windows of the house. I was beginning to understand how they worked now: someone had come back to sweep up the remains.

I started the Fiat. 'Hold tight, Billy!' I said. 'This might be a rough ride!' The car careered over the rutted tracks.

'Yippee! Are you going to drive right across the back fields?' said Billy excitedly.

'Yes,' I said. 'It's so dull always going out through the front gate.'

23

There was a bright moon, but cloud was building up with every sign that the promised storms would arrive by morning. I kept up a good speed on the dry moonlit roads. I took my own route into Nice rather than follow the obvious one. I crossed the River Var high up, leaving behind the chic region where wealthy psychiatrists throw poolside parties for pop-groups.

East of the Var is another landscape. Routiers and quarrymen work extra time to buy a few hundred breeze blocks for raw little villas, that squat upon steep hillsides and at the weekends excrete small cars. In record time we were at St Pancrace. I raced through the empty streets of the northern suburbs and along the Boulevard de Cessole to the station. From there it was only two minutes to the Rue de la Buffa where Pina Baroni lived.

I found a parking place near the Anglican church. It was still only about one A.M., but as the sound of the Fiat's motor faded there was not a sound or a movement in any direction.

Pina lived on the fourth floor of a new apartment block, at the fashionable end of the Rue de la Buffa. Across the street was Pina's boutique. Its neighbours included two foreign banks, a poodle-clipper and the sort of athletic club that turns out to be a sun-lamp salon for fat executives.

In the moonlight the white marble entrance was as bright as day. The foyer was all tinted mirror, concealed lighting and locked glass doors, with a light behind the intercom and a thief-proof welcome-mat. 'It's Charlie,' I said. The door opened with a loud click, and a sign lighted to tell me to push the door closed behind me.

Pina was dressed as if ready to go out. 'Charlie – ' she began, but I shook my head, and at the sight of Billy she bent down to him. 'Darling Billy,' she said, and embraced him tightly enough to squeeze the breath from his body.

'Aunty Nini,' he said dutifully, and stared at her thoughtfully.

'He got his feet wet,' I told her. 'He went down to talk to the fishes in his pyjamas.'

'We'll give you a hot bath, Billy.'

'These are clean pyjamas and underclothes and things,' I said. I indicated the bag I'd brought.

'Your Uncle Charlie thinks of everything,' said Pina.

'But always a bit too late,' I said.

As if anxious to avoid talking to me, Pina took Billy into the bathroom. I heard the water running, and Pina came out and fussed about with clean sheets and pillow-cases for the spare bed.

'I want you to take him to England, Pina. Take him back to Caty.'

Pina looked at me without answering. 'Hot milk or cocoa?' she called loudly. 'Which would you like, Billy?'

'Cocoa, please, Aunty Nini.'

'I can't,' said Pina.

'It's all over, Pina,' I said. 'Even now I can't guarantee to keep you out of it.'

She pushed past me and went into the tiny kitchen. She poured milk into a saucepan, mixed cocoa into a jug and added sugar. She gave it all her attention. When she spoke it was without looking up. 'You know about the others?'

'Serge Frankel masterminding the whole thing, with you and old Ercole's grandson doing the commando stuff? Eventually I guessed.'

'Is Champion dead?'

'No,' I said. 'They took him away when the big trucks came. Where are they going, Pina?'

She bit her lip and then shook her head. 'It's a mess, Charlie.' The milk boiled and she poured it into the cups. She pushed one cup towards me and took another one to Billy.

I sank down into an armchair and resisted a great desire to go to sleep myself. I heard the water running, and the voices of Pina and the child. I looked round the room. Amongst the colour TV, indoor plants and the sort of steel-and-leather furniture that looks like office equipment, there were one or two items still remaining from the farmhouse where she'd lived with her parents during the war. There was a sword that some long-dead Baroni had carried in the Battle of Solferino, at a time when Nice and Savoy were speaking Italian. Alongside it hung a faded watercolour of a house near Turin, and a photo of Pina's parents on their wedding day. In the glass-fronted cabinet a place of honour had been found for a Staffordshire teapot with a broken spout. In the old days that had been the hiding place for the radio crystals.

'He's asleep,' she said. She looked at me as if still not believing I was real.

'I'm glad you kept the teapot, Pina.'

'I've come close to throwing it over the balcony,' she said tonelessly. She went over to the cabinet and looked at it. Then she picked up the photo of her late husband and sons and put it down again.

'I should have come here and talked to you,' I said. 'Every day I planned to, but each time I put it off. I don't know why.' But really I did know why: it was because I knew such a conversation would probably end with Pina going into custody.

'A husband and two fine boys,' she snapped her fingers.

'Gone like that!' She pouted her lips. 'And what of the kid who threw the bomb. Someone said he was no more than fifteen years old. Where is he now, living there, in Algiers, with a wife and two kids?'

'Don't torture yourself, Pina.'

She took Billy's coat and mine from a chair, and with the curious automatic movements that motherhood bestows she straightened them, buttoned them and hung them in a closet. Then she busied herself arranging the cups and saucers and the small plates and silver forks. I said nothing. When she had finally arranged the last coffee spoon, she looked up and smiled ruefully. 'The war,' she said. 'It makes me feel so old, Charlie.'

'Is that why?' I said.

'Is that why what?'

'Is that why you tried to kill Champion today, and damned near killed me and the kid as well?'

'We didn't even know Billy was in France.'

'So it was Champion's fault,' I said bitterly.

'Did you recognize me?' she asked.

'Billy did.'

'We came back,' she said. 'You were on your feet, and Billy was all right. So we didn't stop.'

'You and old Ercole's grandson,' I said. 'Bonnie and Clyde, eh?'

'Don't be bloody stupid, Charlie.'

'What, then?'

'Someone's got to stop Champion, Charlie.'

'But why you? And why Ercole's grandson?' But I didn't have to ask. I'd heard Ercole's stories about the war and the glorious part he'd played in the liberation of France. Who could miss the citation, and the photographs, so beautifully framed and well displayed near the lights ostensibly directed at the Renoir reproduction?

I put more sugar into the cocoa.

'I said you'd guess,' said Pina. 'He sounded you out about the football match, to make sure you wouldn't be in the car at the time. But I said you'd guess.'

'It will be a fifteen-year stretch,' I said. 'The driver's dead, do you know that?'

'We talked about it,' said Pina. She took her coffee and drank some. 'But finally we decided that we'd go ahead, even with you in the car, we'd go ahead.'

'So I noticed,' I said. I drank some cocoa and then I sniffed at it.

'It's only cocoa, Charlie,' she said.

I drank it. 'And did you decide to go ahead even if Billy was in the car?'

'Oh, my God, Charlie. What have we come to?' Her eyes filled with tears. 'Will you forgive me, Charlie? We didn't see Billy. You must believe me. You must!'

'I believe you, Pina.'

She reached out and clung tightly to me, but there was no passion, just that terrible wail of despair with which survivors lament being left alone.

'Take Billy to his mother, Pina.'

She nodded, but her face was contorted with grief and she soon began to cry again. I put my arms round her, and tried to steady her as the sobs racked her frail body. I felt the hot tears on my cheek and I caressed her back as a mother might calm a fractious child.

'I'll phone my people right now. I might be able to arrange a plane immediately. In any case, you mustn't stay here.'

She stopped crying, and looked at me. 'Serge Frankel said you were an important man.'

'Go to Caty, in Wales. Stay, until I tell you it's safe to return.'

She gripped my arm to tell me that she understood. I pulled myself away from her and stood up. She huddled in the corner of the sofa and sobbed into her hands. I remembered the tomboy who had never shed a tear, not even when the Germans took her mother away. Pina had a lot of crying to catch up with. Or perhaps she was crying for all of us.

24

I was too late. We were all too late. If you are trying to do a totalitarian job within the permitted limits of a free society, you are always too late. The vegetable market, that after dark is as deserted as anywhere in the city, had become a copper's carnival.

Where the vegetable stalls usually stood, there were the shiny black police cars of the Divisional Superintendent, the police doctor and the examining magistrate. Parked tight to the pavement there was an ambulance and the Criminal Records van.

The entrance to Serge Frankel's apartment block was rigged with lights, and guarded by two policemen, their pinched faces blue with cold.

'Everybody wants to get into the act!' It was Claude.

He nodded to the guards and I was permitted inside. 'It looks that way,' I said.

There was a cop on each landing, and the residents stood about in pyjamas and dressing gowns as plainclothes men searched through every room. But when we got to Serge Frankel's study there was hardly room to move.

Frankel was spreadeagled across the threadbare carpet, one thin arm extended to the wing armchair in which I'd sat that day in 1940. There were enough valuable stamps and covers scattered around the room to make some casual observers believe that it had been robbery with violence. Claude did not look directly at Frankel. He found excuses to look at other things in the room, and to examine the stamps and covers on the desk, as the policeman entered them into the evidence book. 'It was clean and quick,' said Claude.

I picked up the sheet. 'Through and through wound,' I read aloud. 'Grease collar on the entry side . . .'

'He was a big man in the 'thirties,' said Claude. 'He brought a lot of people out of Germany in 'thirty-three and 'thirty-four. He helped the Princess escape, did you know that?'

I looked at him. Claude was taking the old man's death very badly. Very badly for a professional, that is. I realized that my suspicions about Claude's intentions were unfounded: he simply liked the old man.

'He was never bitter,' said Claude. 'Never suspicious.'

'This time, he wasn't suspicious enough,' I said. 'No break-in. He must have opened the door for whoever did it.'

Claude nodded.

Dawn was breaking, chiselling the horizon open like a blue steel oyster knife. The first of the market-men were throwing boxes of vegetables about, with all the noisy glee of men who are early risers.

'Schlegel said that you would know what to do,' said Claude.

'Here?'

Claude looked towards the Divisional Super, who was near enough to be listening to what we said. The policeman nodded, and looked at me. 'Schlegel said you know more than any of us.'

'God help us, then,' I said.

A plainclothes officer was outlining the position of Frankel's body in white chalk upon the carpet. As he finished and stepped aside, a photographer did the necessary three-shot set. Then two men in white coats put Frankel on to a stretcher, tied a label to his wrist, and carried his body away.

'The end of an era,' said Claude.

'Only for us, Claude,' I said. 'For these boys it's just another night of overtime.'

'It's shaken you, too, hasn't it?' said Claude.

'No,' I said.

'They should never have sent us,' said Claude.

Well, perhaps Claude was right, but as soon as the ambulance men had removed Serge Frankel's body I took hold of the situation. 'Three of your men,' I told the Divisional Super. 'Get all the rest of them out of here. Three of your best detectives must go through all this stuff, piece by piece.'

'Looking for what?' said Claude. 'A piece of paper?'

'This man Frankel had some sort of inside line to the Champion household. By some kind of alchemy this arthritic old man sat up here in this apartment, plotting and planning everything from murder to geopolitics. Until yesterday I thought his contact was Champion's English nanny, but now I'm sure it wasn't her.' I turned to look at the amazing chaos of the study: thousands of books, thousands of covers, countless stamps and a muddle of bric-à-brac. 'Somewhere here something will tell us who, what, why and where Frankel's contact was.' I sighed. 'No, I don't know if it will be a piece of paper.'

A plainclothes officer stood behind Frankel's desk, putting keys and money and personal papers into separate plastic bags and labelling each one with the same number that was registered in the evidence book. 'Stop him doing that,' I said. 'We'll need those keys: I want to open these drawers and boxes and filing cabinets.'

The Divisional Superintendent gave the necessary orders, until the room was almost empty. His chosen detectives took a handful of keys and began to work methodically.

'What's the latest on the big trucks?' I asked Claude.

Claude straightened the shoulder strap of his impeccable white trenchcoat, coughed and said apologetically, 'We can hardly put out an all-stations alert, can we?'

'It might look that way now,' I said. 'But if it all fouls up, you'll have lots of little men in pin-stripe trousers explaining exactly why you could have.'

'Five trucks,' said Claude. 'Still all together, and following the expected route to Bonn. At first light, the traffic helicopters will take a look at them.'

I didn't answer.

Claude said, 'You're blown, Charlie. You're not going to get back into Champion's set-up again. The whole thing is blown wide open. Schlegel sent you across to investigate Frankel's death. It's absurd to go on pretending you are just a bystander.'

'You're right, Claude,' I said.

'Your request about the plane for Pina Baroni and the Champion child came to me,' explained Claude. 'I got permission to use the plane belonging to our ambassador in Paris. So I know all the details.'

'Schlegel talks too much,' I said.

'You're wrong,' said Claude. 'Colonel Schlegel is brighter than you. He knows that he can get more co-operation from people who know what is happening.'

One of the detectives had found the key to the big safe behind the door. It looked like a rusty old refrigerator and was about as invulnerable.

'You think this Algerian secretary has taken control?' said Claude.

'How do we know he is Algerian? He might be an Egyptian – a nuclear physicist, a general or an executioner. If I hadn't been in that shoot-up on the autoroute, I'd even be suspecting that that was another of Champion's tricks.'

'He's got us all like that,' said Claude. 'But perhaps Champion's ultimate trick is simply to pull no tricks.'

We both turned to see the two detectives hammering the handle of the gigantic safe. With one final heave they wrenched the door open.

Just for one moment, I thought he was still alive. He was sitting inside, cross-legged, on some dented cash-boxes, with box-files resting on his shoulders. Then, very slowly, Gus tilted forward, and crashed on to the carpet, in an avalanche of stamps and covers. He had not yet stiffened, and, under the weight of his body, his arms and legs reached out, so that he seemed to be trying to crawl out from under the debris.

'Gus!' I exclaimed loudly. 'The Spanish Civil War – the International Brigade. Why the devil didn't I think of those two getting together.'

'Someone murdered both,' said Claude. It was a guess, but it was obviously the right one.

One of the detectives leaned close to look at the body. 'Same wound as the old man,' he said.

'Damn, damn, damn,' I said. 'Every time they are a jump ahead of us.'

Claude's Teutonic reaction was a more practical one. 'Get the doctor and the photographers and the records people back,' he told one of the detectives. 'Now we start all over again.'

A uniformed policeman brought me a small green official envelope from the police station. His raincoat was shiny with rain and I had already heard the rumble of thunder. I tore open the envelope. Schlegel had sent a Telex from the CRS office at Nice airport. He wanted me there as quickly as possible.

'I've got to go,' I said.

'Schlegel is probably taking you up to talk to our Border Police in Aachen.'

'Where the hell is that?' I said. I knew where it was, but I was angry that Claude knew more than he told me. Perhaps that was what was wrong with all of us.

'Nordrhein-Westfalen,' said Claude. 'The German frontier with Belgium and Holland. It's a health resort.'

I waited, but Claude said nothing more. 'Well?' I said. 'He's not going up there to take a cure, is he?'

'There was a tip-off . . . a shipment of guns being smuggled. Schlegel felt it might have a bearing on the Champion business.' Claude's face was quite impassive. It was impossible to know whether he agreed with Schlegel.

'We have a car here,' said the uniformed policeman, in a polite attempt to hurry me.

'One more thing,' said Claude.

I bowed my head and pinched my nose waiting for it.

'It was Champion who betrayed the network. The rest of us all worked through cut-outs. Only Champion knew that Marius was collecting the radio messages from the Princess, and circulating them through the confessional.'

I looked at him for a long time before replying, wondering why he wanted to hurt me. 'I was there at Nice railway station when Champion was arrested,' I told him. 'You know that Marius and the others had already been arrested about five o'clock that morning – seven hours earlier!'

Claude shook his head. There was the sound of distant thunder, and dawn was making the windows red enough to see the dabs of rain hitting the glass. When Claude spoke, it was in the dull monotone of a speak-your-weight-machine. 'That was part of the deal. We arrested Champion the previous morning. It was part of the deal that we would let him come down on the train, so that you would see him being arrested.'

'The departmental inquiry after the war. Your people cleared him.'

'We all lied. We thought it would be clever to have a hold over a man like Champion. But it was never of any use.' He sighed as though his life had been filled with brilliant ideas for blackmail that he'd found no chance of using.

'Why tell me now?' I asked. 'After all this time. Why tell me now?' It was all happening as I knew it would if I came back here to find the remembered magic: I was stumbling over broken wires, bent pulleys and jammed trapdoors, left over from a bungled stage conjuring act.

'You've been assuming that Champion is some kind of entrepreneur. He might be the victim of blackmail.'

'I'll write it into the report,' I promised. 'Meanwhile, dig out something on that old bastard Santa Claus. Why do the poor kids get the paper-hats, and the rich kids get the ponies?'

'Have a good time in Germany,' said Claude. I heard the thunder again. Or was it some old man in the wings, shaking a sheet of tin?

25

Monday morning: Germany: the helicopter touched down on the rain-soaked earth, and lurched slightly as it settled into the mud. I opened the Plexiglas door, and jumped down, landing with a loud squelch. Schlegel jumped out too, and the mud spattered over my trouser-legs. 'So Champion was taken away by force?' asked Schlegel. He squinted through the driving rain to the far side of the clearing, where a group of foresters conferred beside a fallen fir tree.

I didn't answer. Schlegel asked me again. It was one of those examination questions; any square you tick loses you marks.

'Billy went into the garden and hid,' I said. 'I can't imagine Champion moving off, and leaving his boy there.'

'I'm glad to hear that some of it's not going according to plan,' said Schlegel, with uncharacteristic low spirits.

'I just can't decide whether the death of Gus, and Serge Frankel, was part of the plan – or a reckless way of dealing with an emergency,' I said. 'If we knew that, it might all fall into place.'

Schlegel sighed, wiped his face and nodded, all at the same time. Behind us I heard the helicopter blades chug to a halt. 'Come along,' he said. For a moment or two there was no sound except the squelch of our shoes, and the splash of rain running off the firs that made this path as green and gloomy as the ocean deeps. But then the first axe fell, and the chopping continued like the beating of a heart.

'We should have put a transponder into Champion's cars,' grumbled Schlegel.

'Yes, we should have,' I said. It was like wishing that Champion was sporting enough to leave a trail of paper.

We came off the pathway on to the road, stepping along a wooden duckboard to cross a drainage ditch. On the road three cars and a small van were parked askew to improvise a roadblock. The cars had the insignia of the state police, but the van belonged to the Border Police, a force with federal authority. There was no way of recognizing which men were which, for they were all wearing the same wet raincoats and sou'westers. They had adopted the relaxed and patient attitudes with which outdoor workers endure steady rain. One of the men detached himself from the group and hurried towards us.

He was an elderly man, and under the collar of his oilskin I saw the badges of a captain. He saluted gravely. 'We're holding them in the truck.' He spoke good English, with just a trace of an accent. 'They'll admit nothing.'

'While you get wet!' said Schlegel. 'Bring the little creeps out, and let them get rained on.'

'We'd have to handcuff them,' said the policeman. He handed Schlegel two detonators, and a map drawn upon a page torn from a school exercise book.

'So?' said Schlegel aggressively. 'So?' He looked down the road in the direction of Roetgen. It was several kilometres to the Belgian frontier. There are many such minor roads crossing the border. Some of them are little more than fire-breaks through the mighty wilderness of the Eifel. Even when the Ruhr disgorged its hunters, campers and holidaymakers, you could still get lost among these hilly forests that have to be cut by handsaw.

Here the US First Army faced Germans fighting on home-soil, for the first time. The Americans had been fed into the dense mine-strewn forest like coffee beans

213

into a grinder. There was no room for a tank to pass between the trees, so the infantry had dug deep and listened to the artillery barrage. It chopped the limbs off the trees, and left a legacy of steel that even today tears the teeth out of power-saws.

'Grim bloody place,' said Schlegel. He brought out his cigars, but thought better of it and put them away again.

'Here they come,' I said.

There were two of them: wretched-looking hitch-hikers, bearded, tired and crumpled. It was surprising that they had strength enough to manage the gigantic rucksacks and bedding rolls that were on their backs. The policeman had not handcuffed them, having probably decided that the equipment and accessories were more than enough to hamper their escape. Now the policeman stepped back from them.

The police had found twelve detonators, two Sten guns and some maps – including one of the USAF–Luftwaffe air-base at Ramstein – buried in their camping gear. The taller of the pair looked back at the uniformed officer, and then at Schlegel. 'I want a lawyer! This is the twentieth time I've asked for a lawyer. I know my rights!' Even Professor Higgins would be hard-pressed to place such an accent: Birmingham, England, at first-hand, perhaps, Brooklyn, New York, at second-hand and a sprinkling of Hollywood, California.

'So you can count?' said Schlegel. He didn't look up. Schlegel seemed oblivious of the pouring rain that was fast reducing the maps in his hands to pulp.

Schlegel passed the maps to me. There were half a dozen of them: small practical Xerox copies of the suburbs of Bonn, the centre of Bonn – some of the more important buildings indicated in additional felt-pen notes – and a Michelin map of this area with the cross-border roads scribbled upon.

Without a word to me, Schlegel reached back for the maps and I gave them to him.

'Yeah, I can count, Yank!' said the boy. Schlegel still didn't look at him. The boy glanced up at the sky, as if looking for some reassuring patch of blue. But the only break in the dark clouds revealed a kingdom sulphurous and fiery.

The boy used both thumbs to ease the weight of his pack and equipment. 'And you'd just better know it, Yank. 'Cos you'll find out I can count real good.' They both wore red-star badges, pinned into the sort of beret that Che Guevara wears in posters.

Schlegel looked up at him and then at his silent companion, who was a few inches shorter, and carried notably less equipment. 'I haven't got a great deal of time,' Schlegel explained, as if the boy had invited him to take tea and cucumber sandwiches. 'So just tell me where you got the maps, the Sten gun and the detonators, and then I can get some lunch and go back to my office.'

'Drop dead, Yank.'

'This is no time to be cute, sonny. Tell him, Barrington. This is no time to be cute, is it?'

Schlegel often made up names on the spur of the moment. I recognized his use of Barrington as a sign of his impatience with my Island Race. 'It's not the time,' I said obediently.

The boy's lips moved as if he was salivating to spit but it was simply a show of anger. 'Get stuffed!' he said. His voice was pure Birmingham now.

Schlegel moved so fast that both boys were caught off balance, but it was only the silent boy that he hit. He walloped him twice, swinging his elbow back in a great show of force, so that the blows looked far harder than they were. But, for a boy with forty or fifty pounds strapped on his back, and metal studs in his shoes, it was

215

more than enough to send him reeling and sliding. A third jab tumbled him into the rain-filled ditch that gurgled under a jungle of thorns and weeds. The boy landed with a splash, and was trapped by the weight of his burden. He let out a scream that was strangled as the cold water took away his breath.

'You bastard,' said the Birmingham boy. It was a different sort of voice now: just as bitter, and even more angry, but there was an undertone of defeat there, too. 'Jerry's not strong,' he shouted. 'Leave him alone, you old bastard. It's not fair!'

Schlegel had not used his left hand, in which the map and detonators were still clasped. He spared no more than a glance at the boy who was struggling to climb out of the ditch. He stared at the talkative one. 'It's fairness we're talking about now, is it? I thought we were talking about dynamite. About blowing the bourgeoisie into hamburger.' He waved the detonators about. 'Not strong, your friend Jerry, eh? Strong enough to carry a machine-gun and two hundred shells, right? And strong enough to pull the trigger, providing both you punks think you'll get away unhurt.' By now Jerry had hauled himself up the side of the steep ditch. He was on his hands and knees, shaking the water from his head and whimpering to himself.

Schlegel was close to him. He looked down at him for what seemed like ages. Shivering and wet, the boy did not look up. Schlegel gently put his foot on the boy's shoulder and pushed. He grabbed Schlegel's ankle but could not hold on to it. There was a cry of despair as he tumbled back into the ditch.

'He'll get pneumonia!' shouted the boy from Birmingham.

'Are you a medical student?' said Schlegel, with polite interest.

'The boy swallowed. 'I'll talk,' he growled. 'I'll talk. You win, I'll talk.'

The rain lessened but the wind was cold. Schlegel buttoned his collar tight against his throat, and flicked the brim of his corduroy hat to get the rain off it.

From the clearing where our chopper had landed, there came the sudden clatter of a two-stroke motor, and then the terrible scream of a chain-saw biting into wood. I shivered.

'You heard me, Yank. I'll talk!'

Schlegel said, 'Go ahead, son. I'm listening.'

'Outside the American Express in Amsterdam – that place on the pavement, you know . . .' He looked at his friend sprawled in the ditch.

'I know,' said Schlegel.

'A guy named Frits – he bought hot dogs for us. The next day we went back to his pad and smoked. He had a friend . . . least, he said he had a friend. There was a thousand guilders for starters. Another fifteen hundred for delivery of the stuff to an address in the village of Schmidt. We thought it was pot, honest we did.'

'Sure. And the Sten guns you thought were pipes, to smoke it,' said Schlegel. 'Come out of there, you stinking little fairy.' He reached down and grabbed the rucksack straps of the boy in the ditch. With apparent ease, he hoisted him back on the road. 'OK,' said Schlegel. 'I'll believe you.'

'Can we go?'

'You sort that one out with the German cops,' said Schlegel. 'Come on, Barrington. Just standing downwind of these little creeps makes me throw up.'

'We could identify Frits, the man in Amsterdam. Do a deal . . . huh?' said the boy.

'A man for all seasons,' said Schlegel. 'I don't do deals with kids like you – I squeeze them; and they drip.' He flicked the boy away, as he would some insect buzzing around his head.

'In Schmidt. We had to meet our contact in the Haus Rursee,' added the boy anxiously. The police officer took the boy's arm.

'Come on,' said Schlegel to me. He turned and I followed. The scream of the chain-saw grew louder. When we reached the clearing the tree was dismembered, the amputations marked by bright circular wounds, and pools of sawdust.

The police pilot sat at the controls of the helicopter waiting for the order to go. Schlegel did not give it immediately. We sat back on the seats, with rain forming puddles underfoot, and the world multiplied ten thousand times in the raindrops on the Plexiglas.

'It's Champion, no question of that,' said Schlegel. 'He wanted us here, but what the hell are we supposed to do?'

'They are just stupid kids,' I said.

'I know they are,' said Schlegel. 'But I had to know if they were more than that.'

'Could those trucks be across the border by now?' I asked.

'They were going like hell all last night,' said Schlegel. 'No reason why not.'

I looked at Schlegel.

He said, 'Why should he stage a diversion like this, while the trucks cross the border? They have diplomatic protection: borders make no difference in this case.'

'There has to be a reason,' I said. 'Something happened when those trucks went across the border. And that something would have told us what the plan was.'

'The drivers were all checked at the dock gates. All of them are French-born professional drivers, with at least eight years' experience. Already we have checked their fingerprints with London, Washington, Paris and Bonn. Not a whisper of a clue.'

'No, it must be the vehicles.'

'You think Champion is inside one of those trucks?'

I said, 'I only wish I had a theory.'

'What happens to trucks when they cross a frontier?' Schlegel asked the pilot of the police helicopter.

'They check the manifests and the personal papers. They make sure the load is firmly secured. Perhaps they check the brakes and the roadworthiness. It's according to how busy they are.'

'No,' I told Schlegel. 'It's not going to be something that the customs men would notice. It's something that would only seem strange to you or me, or to someone who knows the situation. Otherwise there would be no point in staging a diversion that would take our attention.'

Schlegel sat hunched forward in his seat, while the rain beat down upon our plastic bubble. 'They must be on the Autobahn to Cologne by now,' he said finally. He reached for the pilot's map and opened it on his knees. 'If they are going to Bonn, they will turn off the Autobahn at that big clover-leaf there – *Autobahnkreuz Köln West* – and follow the circular road as far as the next clover-leaf.' He stabbed the place on the map. 'From there, it's only a lousy twenty kilometres to Bonn.' He looked at me and then at the pilot. 'When those trucks get halfway between Cologne and Bonn – we stop them, and screw the diplomatic ruckus.'

'You want me to radio for permission?' the pilot asked.

Schlegel looked at him unenthusiastically. 'I'm giving the orders, Baron von Richthofen! You just pull the levers! Let's go!'

The pilot clipped his helmet chinstrap tight, and twisted the microphone wire so that it was close to his mouth. Schlegel, having made his decision, twisted his nose in his hand, and then pinched his own cheeks as a physician might help a patient recover from a coma.

I looked at the pilot's map. On both sides of the River Rhine, from Cologne to Bonn, the land is flat and, by the standards of the great industrial complex of the Ruhr, comparatively lightly inhabited. But there were towns there – Wesseling and Niederkassel – I wondered how they would like being expendable in favour of the great cities each side of them.

The starter banged and I watched the pilot's lips moving as he began his litany of radio signals. I guessed he would call the traffic police who had been tailing the convoy of trucks at a discreet distance.

The helicopter tilted forward and lifted away over its cushion of downdraught. It, too, belonged to the traffic police and the pilot was used to flying through this sort of weather. Even at tree-top height, black puffs of cloud scudded past us like Indian signals. I stared at the scenery. The forest stretched as far as I could see. To the south, yellow sky was reflected in the ruffled water of the Rursee, so that it looked like a fiery volcano just about to boil over.

26

By the time the River Rhine gets to Bonn, it is wide and grey and cold, smeared with fuel oil and flecked with detergent. And north of the capital it meanders through flat featureless land that continues all the way to Holland and the North Sea, and the wind makes the river choppy.

The police helicopter came low over the waterway, lifting enough to clear the masts of a liquid-gas tanker, and then of a big Dutchman, low in the water, with a deck-cargo of yellow bulldozers. Once over his cranes we crossed waterlogged fields and high-tension cables that sparkled in the rain, like a spider's web wet with dew. And then we saw them.

The helicopter reared, and turned abruptly as we came to the concrete of the rain-washed Autobahn. The five trucks were keeping to a steady fifty miles per hour and the pilot had timed our approach to coincide with a burst of speed by the two white Porsche cars that had been following them.

The flashing police-lights made long reflections on the road, and the trucks slowed and followed the police cars into the heavy vehicle park of a service area. Our helicopter put us down gently just before the huge diesel trucks cut their engines, one by one.

'Perfect,' said Schlegel. I'd never heard him use that word before.

The policemen got out of their Porsches, put on their white-topped caps and stretched their limbs. They had been providing us with a commentary for the last half hour. Now they saluted Schlegel and awaited instructions.

'Ask them for their driving licences,' said Schlegel derisively. 'Jesus Christ! Don't tell me a traffic cop can't find something wrong with everybody.'

They didn't smile, and neither did the men who climbed down from the cabs of the trucks.

'Check the manifests, check the customs seals, check the brakes,' said Schlegel. He tapped my arm. 'You and me are going to give them the once-over lightly, before we open them up.'

They were gigantic fifty-ton diesels: twelve forward speeds and two reverse. Cabs like glasshouses, ergonometrically designed seats, and behind them a rest bunk. There were racks for vacuum flasks of coffee, and cheap transistor radios were taped to the sunshields. A set of Michelin maps was duplicated for each of the five cabs, and there was a German phrase-book and a repair manual. They had been on the road for almost twenty-four hours. The cabs had become a smelly clutter of empty cigarette packets and butts, squashed paper cups and discarded newspapers.

'We would see it,' Schlegel reminded me. 'Champion was frightened that we would see it, smell it, or hear it. Otherwise there was no point in arranging that charade with those kooks.'

One of the traffic policemen brought the manifest to Schlegel. It was the same as the ones we'd got from the dock office in Marseille. It described the load as a general consignment of engine parts, construction materials, fabrics and chemicals. Schlegel handed it back. 'Frisk all of them,' he told the policeman. 'If you find as much as a pocket knife, it might be enough to hold them for inquiries. And I want the exterior of the trucks examined by someone who knows how many differentials a truck like this needs and where to find them.'

'Yes, sir,' said the policeman.

There was a steel towing-cable padlocked to the underside of the chassis and, in special cradles behind the cabs, there were steel wheel-chocks. Schlegel rapped one of them. The metal was too heavy to get an echo out of it.

Schlegel looked at me and raised an eyebrow.

'Why?' I said. 'When you can put it inside so easily?'

'I suppose you are right,' said Schlegel. 'We're going to have to bust them open.' The vehicles were so large, and the wheels so big, that we were able to get right under the chassis without crouching very low. 'Look at the suspension,' said Schlegel. 'With one of these brutes you could schlepp Cologne cathedral away in the middle of the night, and still throw the opera house in the trunk.'

'And it could take plenty more, too,' I remarked. We looked at the massive leaf springs. The upper one was still curved, and the lower, supplementary spring not yet tensioned.

'That's got to be it!' said Schlegel, in great excitement. 'You've hit it.'

'The weight!'

'Exactly. These trucks must be almost empty. Look at that! We should have noticed that from the way they were sitting on the road.'

'And a customs man would have noticed. In fact they might have put them on a weighbridge while the manifest was stamped.'

'Why? Why? Why?' said Schlegel. He punched the great rubber tyre.

'So that we would be talking about fifty-ton diesel-truck suspension, somewhere on the banks of the lower Rhine, while Champion is earning a promotion from colonel of propaganda to general of god-knows-what.'

Schlegel grunted, and came out from under the truck. He waved to the policeman. 'Forget it,' he called. 'Let them go.'

'They say they are going right the way down the Autobahn to Munich,' said the policeman.

'Are the papers in order?'

'They say they are going to get new papers in Bonn.'

'Let them go,' said Schlegel. 'They can keep going all the way to Vladivostok for all I care.' He smiled. 'That's all, boys: go get yourselves some coffee.'

The policemen looked at Schlegel with that same inscrutable superiority with which they look up from your driving licence.

Schlegel turned back to me. 'Munich,' he said with disgust. 'And after that, Brindisi or Lisbon – it's a merry dance he's been leading us.'

'There's something else,' I said.

'Like what?'

'I don't know – but he didn't send five empty trucks from Marseille docks to Bonn just to grab our attention.'

'Why not?' said Schlegel. 'He did it! And while we chased them, he got to where he wanted to go.'

'You don't know Champion,' I said. 'That's not fancy enough for him.'

Littered with old food wrappings, smelling of spilled fuel and warm fat, these coffee shops on the Autobahns are the most desolate places in Europe. An endless succession of strangers gobble mass-produced food and hurry on. The staff are glassy eyed and melancholy, trapped in a river of traffic, which swirls past so that the fumes, noise and vibration never cease.

'And lousy coffee,' added Schlegel.

'Do you know how much it costs to hold a chopper on the ground while you dunk that doughnut?'

'You're a lot of fun to have around,' said Schlegel. 'Did I ever tell you that?' He opened his shirt and scratched himself.

'Not lately,' I admitted.

'Hit me with one of your dust-packets, will you.'

I gave him one of my French cigarettes.

'Why?' he said for the hundredth time. He lit the cigarette.

'There's only one explanation,' I said.

He inhaled and then waved the match violently to put the flame out. 'Give.'

'He brought something off that boat.'

'And unloaded it during the night,' finished Schlegel. 'On the other hand, they've been making such a good average speed.'

'It's all double-think,' I said.

'Let's get back to Nice,' said Schlegel. He scratched himself again, but this time there seemed to be an element of self-punishment in it.

27

When Champion broke from the department, we set up this small office in Nice. The modest entrance bore the trademark of a well-known British travel company, and three of our staff gave their full-time attention to legitimate travel business.

Schlegel had taken an office on the top floor. He was standing in the window when I entered, looking across the square to Nice railway station. When Cimiez, in the northern part of Nice, had been chic, this section had also been fashionable. But now it was dirty and run-down. The tourists arrived at the airport, and they wanted hotels near the sea. I walked over to the window.

The railway station had hardly changed since the day I waited for Champion to arrive, and watched him being arrested. The tiled floor was a little more chipped, the mural of the Alps a little dirtier, but what else had stayed so much the same? Certainly not me.

Schlegel could always find himself a clean shirt, but his suit was creased and baggy, and the oil-stain on his knee was the one he'd got from the wheel of the big truck. His eyes were red, and he rubbed them. 'They should tear this whole lousy district down. Put the bus depot and the railroad station in one complex, and stack twenty floors of office accommodation overhead.'

'Is that why you sent down for me?' I said.

'What are you doing downstairs?'

'Trying to catch up on my sleep. First time since I got up on Sunday.'

'You want to learn to cat-nap. No. I mean what are you working on down there?'

'I sent out for some maps. I'm waiting for them,' I told him.

'I know all about that,' said Schlegel. 'When people in this office send out for things, I get a copy of the requisition. Your goddamn maps have arrived. I've got them here.'

'I can see you have,' I said.

'That's the way I work.'

'Well, good luck, Colonel. I'll go back downstairs and try to get a little more sleep.' I got up and went to the door.

Schlegel suppressed a yawn. 'OK, OK, OK. We're both tired. Now come over here and show me what you want the maps for.'

I went around to the other side of his desk and sorted through the survey maps of the country round Champion's house, and copies of the land registration, and some data about drainage and changes of ownership. I tipped everything – except the map that showed the whole region – into Schlegel's wastepaper basket. 'That stuff was just to make it look like an ordinary lawyer's inquiry,' I said.

'You want to tell me what's on your mind?' demanded Schlegel.

'Those five empty trucks. Suppose they unloaded the contents at the Champion house.' I spread the map.

'No, no, no,' said Schlegel. 'I thought of that, but the gendarmerie patrol that area up there. They fixed a new lock on the back door. They go in there to look round.'

'Let's suppose,' I said patiently.

'That Champion is sitting in the dark up there, testing the spark plugs in some reconditioned dragster?'

'Engine parts,' I said. 'That might mean pumps, to get the old workings going again.'

227

'The mine.' He snatched the map and unrolled it across his desk. He used the phone, a paperweight and his desk-set to hold the corners. He sucked his teeth as he looked at the full extent of the mine workings: the shafts, seams and the long haulage roads. 'That was quite a layout.'

I rapped my knuckle against the telephone with enough effort to make the bell tinkle. 'And just about here, remember – the artillery depot, Valmy.'

'Jesus!' whispered Schlegel. 'They've got atomic shells in that store.' For the first time Schlegel took the idea seriously.

'Nuclear artillery shells – at Valmy! And you knew that all along?' I said.

'It was need-to-know,' said Schlegel defensively.

'And I didn't need to know?'

'Keep your voice down, mister. You were going to sit in Champion's pocket. Telling you that there were nukes in Champion's back yard would have been stupid.'

I didn't reply.

'It wasn't a matter of *trust*,' said Schlegel.

'You're a stupid bastard,' I said.

'And maybe you're right,' he admitted. He ran his thumb and index finger down his face, as if to wipe the wrinkles from his cheeks. It didn't work. 'So what do we do about this?' He smacked the map with his fingers so that he made a tiny tear in the brittle paper.

'We'd better tell Paris,' I said.

'If we're wrong, they'll hate us. If we're right, they'll hate us even more.'

'You'd better tell them,' I said.

'You don't know those people like I do,' said Schlegel. 'Champion was once one of ours – that's all they will need to blame us for everything.'

'We've had these maps from the municipal authority – and that's on record – you've been told about the atomic

228

shells – and that's on record, too. They will crucify us if we don't tell them immediately.'

Schlegel looked at his watch. 'They will have packed up by now. I don't want to spend an hour explaining things to the night-duty officer.' He looked up at me. 'And I know that you don't, either. Let's go out to the house and take another look at it. It might be just another false trail. If it's worth a damn, we'll tell Paris in the morning. What do you say?'

'I don't like it,' I said.

'Why not?'

'I don't like it,' I said, 'because when we get out there, you'll want to go inside. And then, you're going to want to find the entrance to the mine. And then you're going to want to go down there . . . and all the time, you're going to be holding me in front of you.'

'How can you say that! Did I ever do that to you before?'

Before I could answer, Schlegel picked up the phone to get a car.

28

It was dark. I fidgeted enough to send the blood back through my dead arm, and looked round to where Schlegel was hiding, in the scrubland just a few feet away. The western horizon was still pale. But there was not enough light to see the Tix house, except through the night-scope that we'd set up on the rise behind it.

There was precious little moon, just a well-honed sickle, cutting its way out of the clouds every few minutes. But it was during such a flicker of light that the 'scope showed a movement at the back door. I held my breath: it was a man, tall enough to be Champion. He had a gun slung over his shoulder, and was wearing a helmet and some sort of boots or gaiters. I released the trigger on the night-scope so that the intensifying tube could build up a fresh charge. I used it again as the man started to walk across the yard, picking his way past the mud, and then climbing the wooden stairs to a vantage point on the platform outside the hayloft. It made a good sentry post; too good – if he turned this way he'd need no night-scope to see us moving.

Schlegel moved closer. 'Champion's people,' he said. On the cold air his voice was dangerously loud. He rubbed his mouth, as if to punish it, and when he spoke again it was in a whisper. 'Not real policemen; I checked the patrol times before we left.'

The dew had soaked my clothes and there was enough of a breeze to make me shiver. I nodded, lest the tone of my voice revealed the state of my morale.

We'd already seen another such man, standing at the

place where the tracks divided for the house and the quarry. Equipped with a radio-phone it would be easy to warn of the approach of the gendarmes on their regular patrols.

Schlegel elbowed me aside, and took the eyepiece of the 'scope for a moment. There was a movement beyond the clump of half-dead olive trees that we were depending upon to screen us from the house. Lying full-length in the grass, I felt the vibrations of a man stamping his feet to keep warm. He was not more than forty metres away from us. Perhaps only the woollen scarf wrapped round his head, plus the numbness that comes from long spells of sentry duty, had prevented him from hearing Schlegel's voice.

When the second man stamped his feet, a third sentry moved. This one was up the slope to the rear of the house. I swung the night-scope to see him. He'd unbuttoned his overcoat and, after a considerable search of his clothing, he brought out cigarettes and matches and lit up.

'That lame-brain is asking for it,' whispered Schlegel.

It was true that he'd offered himself as an easy target to anyone within range. For a moment I was puzzled by his action.

Even an imbecilic sentry should know enough to step behind cover while he strikes a match, if only to keep it secret from his sergeant. And then I understood. 'They're not sentries,' I told Schlegel. Each one of them was facing the wrong way, which was probably why we'd got so close without being detected. 'They're *guards*.'

I crawled forward to get under the shelter of the low stone wall that separated the yard from the long meadow. Would they patrol, I wondered, and which side of the wall did our fellow keep to?

I waited while Schlegel moved up to me. 'Champion is in there,' I said. 'They are holding him.'

He didn't answer for a moment or two. Then he said, 'The imbecile would be our best chance.'

The kitchen door opened, making a bright-yellow smoke-filled prism. Out of the kitchen came a man. A smell of burning fat confirmed that he was the cook. To be that indifferent to the police patrols they must obviously be about to pull out.

'Champion is a prisoner in there,' I told Schlegel.

'I heard you the first time,' he said.

'I want a closer look.'

He thought about it for a moment or two. 'Give me that night-scope.'

'I'd better look inside the house,' I said. He didn't reply. I wondered if he'd heard my whisper.

He stretched forward to hand me a Walther P·38 and four magazines of bullets. I pushed it into the waistband of my trousers.

I waited until the nearest guard moved down to exchange a word with the man who was still coughing his heart out in the back yard. I vaulted over the low stone wall, lost my balance on the dew-wet stones, and slid down the incline, to land in a heap against a neatly stacked log-pile. I remained dead-still, hardly daring to breathe, but the lung-racking coughs were loud enough to prevent the clatter of my fall from reaching the men in the yard.

I looked back to where Schlegel lay hidden. The lens of his night-scope caught the light from the kitchen window, and flashed like a searchlight. Seen from this end, it was a dangerous toy, but I could do nothing to warn Schlegel now.

Beyond the stacked logs there was the door to the dairy. I crawled forward, and pressed gently against it. It was ajar and swung open with hardly a sound. There was a smell of cheese. A glimmer of light, from the kitchen at the other end of the hall, glinted on the big stone crocks that held the separated milk. I could hear the cook still coughing, and I could feel the draught of air that was clearing the kitchen of smoke.

If I was to get to Champion's study, I would have to get through the kitchen while it was still empty.

I peered into the smoke. The spilled fat was still burning with fierce flames on the coal-fired cooking stove. I held my breath but the acrid fumes made my eyes water, and took a layer off the back of my throat. I ran into the smoke.

I remembered the two steps down to the scullery, and the slippery mat that was at the bottom of the back stairs. When I reached the entrance hall, I planted myself in the recess under the stairs and listened. Someone was coming. I heard unhurried footsteps on the upstairs landing. The balcony creaked as someone put his weight on the rails, and looked down into the hall. There was a whirr of clockwork and then the longcase clock struck the half hour. The footsteps moved away.

Before I could move, the front door opened and one of the guards came into the hall. He was a huge man, an Algerian, in raincoat, helmet and gumboots. He wiped his feet on the doormat, plucked the chinstrap loose, took off the helmet carefully, and placed it on the hall table. Then he discarded the raincoat, too, leaving it in a heap in the hall, like the skin shed from some shiny black insect. Under the policeman's coat and helmet, he was dressed in blue overalls. He came past me close enough for me to smell the garlic on his breath, but he looked neither to right nor left. He stopped in front of Champion's study. He sorted through a bunch of keys, then opened the door and went inside. I waited. Soon there was a noise that I'd always associated with the generator that supplied electricity for the household. Now I had another theory.

I looked at my watch. Fifteen minutes had already passed. I stepped across the hall and to the door of the study. I put my ear to it. No sound came from inside and I leaned forward to look through a crack in the door. As far as I could see it was empty. I pushed the door and went in.

I walked through Champion's large study. I looked behind the curtains and behind the inlaid Sheraton bookcase. There was no sign of the Algerian sentry and there was only one other door. It was open, and I stepped into a small ante-room, in which Champion kept filing cabinets, typewriter and office materials of a sort which might make his elegant study unsightly. I stepped inside. The second of the filing cabinets was unlocked. I slid the drawer open and found inside, not documents, but a phone and a panel with buttons marked 'open doors', 'close doors', 'top floor' and 'lower level'. I pressed the last button. The sliding door closed. A motor mechanism whirred, and the lights dimmed. This was the sound that I'd mistaken for that of the generator. Very slowly at first, the whole room began moving. It was not a room at all: it was a lift.

It stopped at what I guessed was about fifty feet below ground level. I pushed against a heavy metal door, keeping flat against the cabinets, but when the door was fully open I saw only a short corridor, brightly lit by fluorescent lights. There was no one in sight. I pulled the gun out of my waistband and moved warily along the corridor until I reached a large office-like room. It too was empty. I breathed a sigh of relief, and tucked the gun away again.

It was a square room, with cheap wall-to-wall carpet, and a plastic sofa arranged to face an office desk, swivel chair and telephone switchboard. It could have been the reception office of any penny-pinching little company, except for the notice that said 'No Smoking' in both French and Arabic.

But now I knew what to look for, I had no difficulty noticing the tiny gap that ran down the mirror from floor to ceiling. And then – on the telephone switchboard – I found a switch around which the paint was exceptionally worn and dirtied. I pressed it. The mirrored doors slid apart.

This was another shaft, but quite different to the one behind me. This was a part of the original nineteenth-century workings. From up the shaft there came the draught that is the sign of an active mine. And the draught smelled sour, as the dust it carried hit my face.

The Tix mansion was built on a rise that brought its ground floor level with the old winding gear. The lift from Champion's study had brought me down to the level of the old fan drift. This was the upcast shaft, which had been built only for the filled tubs to come out.

This was not a lift – it was not a padded box with concealed lighting, Muzak and seats for the elderly – it was a cage. It was an open-fronted cage, with rusty chain-link sides, a wire-netting top, to catch falls of rock from the roughly hewn shaft, and an expanded-steel floor, through which I could see a glimmer of light a thousand feet below me. I stepped inside and the cage jiggled and clanged against the stay-wires. The sound echoed in the dark shaft, so loud that I expected some reaction from below, but I saw none. I locked the safety bar in place in front of me, and swung the crude lever mechanism to close the outer doors. For a moment I stood in the pitch darkness, listening to the whirr of engines and cables. Then, with a sickening lurch, the cage dropped, gathering speed as it went. The winding mechanism screeched loudly, the pitch of its cry growing more shrill as the speed increased.

The cage stopped suddenly, so that it bounced on the springing. I was at the bottom of the mine. It was dark. There was a steady beat of the pumps and the hum of fans. I reached forward, to touch the rocky face of the shaft, but a crack of light showed that I faced doors with a crush-bar opening device.

I could hear the pumps somewhere close at hand, and under my feet, in the bottom of the shaft, there was the sump and its running water. I opened the doors, and found the shaft-landing brightly lit with fluorescent light. This must have been one of the earliest shafts sunk. The landing was a large one, with concreted walls and lockers and safety notices, and a time-keeper's box that contained all the comforts of a ramshackle home. These 'No Smoking' notices were only in Arabic. From here stretched three galleries, forming a junction at the corner of the landing. One gallery was sealed. The other two had rails for the tub-trains. One gallery's tracks were rusted and dirty, but the other's were shiny bright and slightly oiled, like a guardsman's rifle.

Keeping close to the wall, I moved out of the light into the gallery that seemed still in use. Its walls were wet, and there was the steady drip of water, its sound magnified by the narrow confines of the tunnel. For illumination there was only the dim yellow glow of a few safety lights, recessed into wired and armour-glassed fittings. The line of bulbs showed me the inclines and curves of the workings, but there was not enough light to prevent me stumbling into pot-holes and falling over outcrops of rock. More than once, I went ankle-deep into the syrupy liquid that the dust and water made. Times without number I barked my shins and ankles upon the uneven sides of the gallery. There were rats everywhere: pairs of

236

tiny green lights that stared at me, before disappearing with a scamper of feet that sometimes disturbed the litter of paper and tin cans.

I was a hundred and fifty yards along the gallery when I heard the train start. I looked around for somewhere to hide. The dim wall lights glinted on the sides of the gallery. I could see no recesses or cross-cuts ahead, and I'd certainly not passed anywhere that could conceal a man.

The sound of the train grew louder. I guessed that it was pulling a train of empty tubs, for there was a metallic rattling as the trolley wheels bounced on the poorly made track. It moved slowly, and as it turned the curve the diesel loco and its driver obscured the safety lights. I pressed myself flat against the wet rock-face.

The train was only fifty yards away by now, and its noise was almost deafening. I sank down on to my knees, and then went flat. It was a gamble, for if they did spot me, I'd have no chance to defend myself. I turned up my collar to hide the whiteness of my neck, and tucked my hands out of sight. The locomotive roared close to my ears, and its diesel exhaust scorched my arm. One of the tubs had been left in the inverted dump position. The edge of it struck my arm. I bit back an involuntary yell, and then the noise of the train overwhelmed my gasp of pain.

I remained still for several minutes after the train passed. When I got to my feet again, it was out of sight, although I could hear its rumble as it crossed the junction at the shaft landing. I heard voices, too, as the driver exchanged greetings with someone. The winding gear started again.

I moved forward, and this time I kept the gun in my hand. Now I heard other voices from the distant shaft landing. There were lots of men, and even my lousy

237

Arabic was enough to tell me that a new shift of workers was coming on duty.

I hurried forward. Behind me I could hear the voices of the men as they climbed aboard the train. There were curses, and cheers, and the unfunny jokes that men exchange at moments of tension. The men's voices were amplified by the narrow mine workings, and for a moment I panicked. I ran forward, hammering my fist against the rock, and desperately praying for any small niche in which to hide. My prayer was answered and I groped my way into a low tunnel that gave off the main gallery. It was wide, but there was so little head-room that I was almost bent double. I realized that it was not a gallery: it was a working face. I stumbled, banged my head and fell heavily. I felt the blood trickle down the side of my cheek and reached out to help myself to my feet. It was then that I touched the chilly surface of a steel rail. The tracks ran along this working, too. I went cold with fear. I realized that the train – filled with the workers – would not return along that same gallery down which I'd seen it go. The mine would be sure to work a one-way system, so that the unloaded trains could complete a circuit, to return the empty tubs to the work-face.

The train was coming up this road to meet me.

I turned and ran along the tunnel, now crouched even lower to avoid hitting my head. To my left there was the ancient conveyor and to my right what had once been the working face. The face was not flat, like a wall, it was an endless series of 'rooms' eaten out of the rock. Some of them were no more than a few feet wide, while others were just a black void. But that side of the workings was closed off with wire fencing. Several times I almost lost my balance as I tripped upon the loose uneven surface. I grazed my hand on the sharp edges of the conveyor-belt, with all its pulleys and rollers. Growing panicky, and

238

ever more careless, I blundered into a wooden pit-prop and momentarily was knocked senseless. I doubled up over the conveyor, and heaved deep breaths that took the sharp dust deep into my lungs.

I looked back. The tunnel shone yellow. The driver was using the headlight on the locomotive. When it turned the corner this time, they surely must see me.

Desperately, I decided to crush myself into the space between the conveyor-belt and the bench over which it ran. I got my legs inside but only the great beam of yellow light, and the noise of the locomotive, persuaded me to cram myself into a space far too small.

I held my breath as the train approached with agonizing slowness. On it there were a dozen or more men. Most of them were dressed in the same dungarees that the others had been wearing, but four of the men were differently dressed. I blinked in amazement to see that they were wearing the leather helmets and goggles of old-time aviators. And, in case I was still in doubt, each of them was nursing on his lap the heavy canvas harness and unmistakable brown canvas pack of a parachute.

29

I watched the tub-train as it trundled away from my hiding place. There was enough light now to see that this track was entirely new. The air-doors at the end of them were also new. The train, with its strange subterranean aviators, thudded through the air-doors with a flash of lights and a shrill call of its whistle.

I waited a long time before extricating myself from my hiding place. When I was sure there was no one following them, I made my way along the track to the air-doors. I opened them and stepped through quickly.

The air-door shut behind me with a muffled bump, and cold night air hit me in the face like a custard pie. I was standing on a ledge, some twenty feet up one side of a vast underground cavern. It was about fifty yards across, and just as deep, but it must have been well over one hundred yards in length. Suddenly I realized that the roof was the sky, and I recognized it as the Tix quarry where I'd hidden for two nights and days of the war. But far more astonishing than the man-made hollow was the huge black metallic egg that completely filled it.

It was smooth and symmetrical, elegant and futuristic like those storage tanks that the oil companies depict on the covers of their annual reports, when shares have tumbled. On an airfield, perhaps I would have recognized it more quickly, but only when I saw its whole shape against the starry sky did I realize that the quarry was being used to house an airship.

An airship. Melodie Page had died after sending us the postcard photos of the *Graf Zeppelin* and the *Hindenburg*, and it had been too obvious to see. Not that this was a giant rigid, like those airships of the 'thirties. This was no more than a blimp, of the sort I'd seen drifting over the cities of Europe and America advertising drink and cigarettes. This, then, was the consignment of engine parts, heavy-duty fabrics and plastics, and hydrogen or the plant to manufacture it – hence all those 'No Smoking' notices in Arabic.

Lacking a proper mooring mast, its nose was tethered to the shovel of a rusty excavator, and dozens of ropes held the restless shape down, close upon the floor of the quarry. The Dacron envelope had been roughly covered with matt black paint, and the gondola had been modified for freight-carrying. The engine nacelles were fixed to each side of the gondola. One engine had a servicing platform still in position. Three mechanics were bending over it, clanking spanners. They stood upright and exchanged looks of satisfaction.

As I was looking down upon them, one of the mechanics signalled to someone at the pilot's controls, in the gondola. The engine started with a bang. It roared and came up to full revolutions, before being throttled back to a steady tick. They let it run for a couple of minutes, and then cut it. The quarry was silent, except for the generator that powered the lights and tools, and, from behind me, the faint hum of the fans in the mine.

I still had the P·38 in my hand, and my first impulse was to fire into the gas envelope, but there was little chance that such pin-pricks would do it any great damage. Also it would be dangerous. I was still thinking about it when a voice said, 'Put it down, Charlie!'

I looked round, but I could see no one, apart from the mechanics who were displaying the same sort of interest in the voice as I was. It was Champion's voice and it had come from a loudspeaker – or several loudspeakers. His voice echoed as the sound of it travelled back from the farthest loudspeaker and bounced off the gas-filled envelope and the quarry walls.

'Put it down, please!' A bird fluttered fearfully and flew across the airship. I still did not move.

'I have a marksman here. The gallery behind you is sealed, and there is no way out of the quarry, except up the cliff side.'

I looked at the sheer sides of the quarry from which his voice still reverberated, and I put my pistol back into my belt.

Champion took his time, crossing the bottom of the quarry and climbing the crude steps to the ledge where I'd emerged from the mine gallery. I suppose I would have been equally cautious, or perhaps I would have shot first and parleyed afterwards. But Champion climbed up the steps, smiling his tired old smile and smacking the quarry dust off the knees of the grey, multi-zippered flying-suit he was wearing.

'You cost me fifty francs,' he said. 'I bet you'd get Schlegel to come in.'

'You knew we were out there?'

'No, no, no. First thing we knew was that the cage was left at the bottom. We guessed then. Someone had got in. You and Schlegel, was it?'

'And a couple of battalions of CRS.'

'You wish!' said Champion. 'Well, we probably have Schlegel too, by now. You got through the road block but I brought them close in afterwards. They'll phone down to me.'

'I'm way ahead of you, Champ,' I said.

'Don't tell me you thought of the airship.'

'No, that was a surprise. But I knew that whatever it was it would be here.'

He walked to a door built into the cliff at one end of

242

the ledge. It was his control room. Inside, there were a couple of chairs, and the control console for launching the airship. There was a battery of telephones, an intercom, and six small TV screens that provided a view of the airship from each direction. Champion indicated a chair and sat down at the console. The little control room was glass-faced, and before sitting, he lifted an arm to the mechanics below us, to tell them that all was well.

'Why here?' he said.

I said, 'Remember that day we were caught by that German spot-check at St Tropez, and the German guard shot at the kid who stole the chickens?'

'I remember.'

'You told them we'd found the Renault on the road. And then, after we'd watched them taking the car away, you phoned the police station, and said there was a Renault with RAF escapers inside, going to a safe house in Nîmes.'

Champion smiled.

'I was pretty impressed, Steve,' I said. 'The cops followed those German soldiers in the Renault. They followed them all the way to Nîmes . . . stake-outs, checks . . . mobiles . . . all kinds of stuff . . .'

'And meanwhile we put Serge Frankel, and his junk, into the submarine at Villefranche,' said Champion. He frowned.

I said, 'Afterwards you said, "Make the deceit do the work". I remembered that last week.'

He nodded.

I said, 'You deliberately let us suspect the manifest. You let us think you'd go to all kinds of trouble to get some mystery cargo into position in Germany. While all the time the trucks *were* loading at Marseille docks – loading this airship, envelope folded and engines crated – and then you drove here and unloaded.'

'It worked,' said Champion.

'Like a conjurer – you told me that: make enough sly play with your left hand, and they won't even look at your right one. You made them look at your empty trucks and see loaded trucks, because that's what they wanted to see.'

'It worked,' repeated Champion.

'Almost,' I said.

'You didn't discover it,' said Champion, 'you *sensed* it. No plan is proof against a hunch.' He grinned. 'You told me there was no place for hunches any more. So perhaps we are both yesterday's spies.'

'It had crossed my mind,' I admitted.

'And . . . ?'

'You're going to have to kill me, Steve. And that's another hunch.'

He looked at me and wiped his moustache. 'We'll see, Charlie.'

'You don't teach an old dog new tricks, Steve. You know it, I know it. Let's not kid around, at least you owe me that. There are thoughts I might need to have, and things I might have to do.'

'Like . . . ?'

I shrugged. 'Like getting out of here!'

He looked at me and smiled wearily, like the governor of Devil's Island indenting for more shark food. 'It doesn't have to be like that,' he said. 'We'll work out something. How's the boy?'

'Billy's fine. We're going to build a plastic model of the *Cutty Sark* before he goes back to school.'

'You sent him back to Caty.'

'That's it,' I said.

'It will make no difference in the long run,' said Champion. 'The important fact is that he'll grow up with a bit of money in his pocket.'

244

'The money you'll get for this caper?'

Champion nodded. 'If my old dad had left me a bit of money, it might have worked out differently.' He reached inside his flying-suit and found the big gold pocket-watch I remembered from the old days. He held it up to show me that it was all his father had left him. Or perhaps it was just Champion's way of checking what the time was.

'Inconsiderate of your old man,' I said. 'Not to sell out.'

'Thirty-five years teaching in Egypt,' said Champion. 'Scrimping and saving to send me to school, and the only time he ever hit me was when I didn't stand up for "God Save the King".'

'What an incurable romantic he must have been, Steve. Old fools like that can never match the wits of realists like you.'

Champion stared at me. 'That's not cricket, old pal.'

'I thought we were all-in wrestling,' I said.

'You have to learn cricket *and* all-in wrestling, if you are the only boy at Sandhurst who plays cricket in second-hand togs.'

'And that kind of resentment spurred you on to get all the prizes.'

'Perhaps,' admitted Champion. 'But don't ask me to say thank you.' He wiped the back of his hand across his mouth, as if wiping away a bad taste. 'By God, Charlie, you're a working-class boy. You know what I mean.'

'I know what you mean,' I said, 'but I am not planning to deliver an atomic bomb to back up the demands of the Trades Union Congress, or the Monday Club.'

If he detected a note of irony in my remark, he gave no sign of it. 'Shells, atomic shells!' He obviously hoped that this distinction would bring about a change of my attitude. 'I wouldn't get involved in nuclear *bombs* – not accurate enough. But atomic shells are tactical, Charlie.

They can be put into a vehicle park, or a dump – no fall-out, and very tight destruction pattern.'

'You've been reading too many of those Staff College appreciations, Champ,' I said. 'Save the rationalization for your memoirs: what are they paying you?'

'They'll cross my hand with silver,' he admitted.

'Thirty pieces?'

'Thirty *billion* pieces, if I ask for it. And every currency in the world, Charlie. When we needed money to fight starvation, disease and poverty, Europe couldn't be bothered. But when they had to start walking to the railway station . . . then they put their hands in their pockets!' All the time the airship moved restlessly, rearing up suddenly to the limit of its mooring ropes, and then being hauled down again by the ground crew at each end of the quarry.

'You know how it works, Champ,' I reminded him. 'I didn't come out here without leaving a forwarding address. They will soon find your hole in the ground.'

Champion turned away to look at the TV monitoring screens. There were half a dozen of them, relaying pictures from cameras set high on the cliff side, and facing down to the airship. Using these, the pilot would be able to see how much clearance he had, on every side, as the moorings were cast off and it floated upwards.

'Helicopters, you mean?' Champion said, without looking up from the console.

'I don't know what they will send.'

'With half a dozen cookies on board with me, I don't care what they send. They are not going to shoot me down over mainland France. Not with a cargo of nuclear explosive aboard, they're not.'

'And over the sea?'

'A civil aircraft, registered in Cairo? We do sixty, perhaps eighty, miles an hour in this bladder. By the time they get permission to shoot, I'll be over Tunis!' His mind went back to Billy, or perhaps he had never stopped thinking about his son. 'How could Billy adapt to Cairo? Answer me truly, Charlie. How could he?'

'You mean you're frightened that he might adapt too well. You're scared in case he becomes the chief assassin for the Palestine Liberation Organization.'

'Perhaps I am.'

'But you'd give them the means by which to bomb themselves to power.'

'Not the PLO . . .' he waved his hand wearily, as if deciding whether to enlighten me about the distinction between the government in Cairo, and the terrorists who throw bombs into airport waiting-rooms and set fire to jumbo-jets. He decided against it. 'Billy stays in Europe where he was born – he's vulnerable to smallpox, malaria, cholera and a million other things.'

'You'd be separated from him?' I couldn't believe it. 'The judgement of Solomon, Champ.'

'You didn't say "You can't get away with it,"' he complained. Then we both looked up at the great black shape of the airship.

'But you *can*!' I said. 'That's what I don't like about it.'

'You can't see it, and even with the engines running the only sound is a faint hum, like a distant car. People just don't look up.'

'Radar?'

'We're keeping well clear of the air traffic lanes. The military radar is mostly facing seawards: the stations at Arles and Digne can read inland, but we keep behind high ground.'

'Flying low.'

'Yes. One hundred metres or less. There's no risk: even if some radar operator did see us . . . a huge blob, moving at no more than sixty miles an hour? . . . he's just going to log it as what radar men call "an anomalous propagation" and everyone else calls a machine failure.'

'You're flying it?'

He shook his head. 'We don't take risks,' he said. 'An airline captain, qualified on 707s. He went to America and did the course, said he was going to fly it for advertising.'

'How soon?'

He looked at his watch. 'We'll start cutting into the explosives store at Valmy sometime within the next hour.'

'From the mine?'

'We've dug thirty kilometres of gallery,' said Champion. 'We are now underneath the nuclear explosives store. Some of the most experienced mine engineers, from all the Arab states.'

'Brought in as waiters?'

'. . . and labourers, foundry workers and garbage men. All they need is an Algerian ONAMO card, and the French immigration can't stop them.'

'Suppose you hit an alarm system?'

'From under the earth?' said Champion. He laughed. He knew it was a perfect plan, and he was enjoying this chance to tell me about it.

From some tiny ledge, high up on the side of the quarry, birds began to sing: not one but a whole chorus of them.

The stars were bright, and cold air coming over the lip of the quarry was striking against the warmer airship and causing it to rear against the mooring ropes: superheat, they call it. This was the time of maximum lift.

Champion smiled.

Only the inevitable is tragic. Perhaps Steve Champion's tragedy was born out of his obsession about providing money for his son. Perhaps it was a need to provide for his son a future at least as affluent as the boy's mother could have supplied. Or perhaps it was simply that Steve Champion was the same romantic, desperate man that he said his father had been.

'The money's safe,' said Champion. 'Billy will never want.'

'Wouldn't you have chosen your father, rather than any fortune, Steve?'

'No!'

'Too emphatic!' I chided him. 'Top marks for self-deception.'

'Well, it's a pretty poor liar who can't even deceive himself,' said Champion, and, like an elderly soprano defying the critics, he gave me one of his famous coloratura smiles, and held it long enough to deserve a round of applause.

It was the smile that was his undoing. Until then, I had been listening to Steve Champion, and making excuses for him. I was trying to understand his concern about Billy, and struggling to believe that he'd spend the rest of his life separated from his son. But now somewhere far behind his eyes I saw, not bonhomie, but bravura.

I looked down to where the ground crew was standing by on the moorings. As each completed his task, he looked towards the platform where we were standing – they were looking to Champion.

Champion's story about cutting into the bomb store within the next hour was nonsense. They must have done it already. The shells must be aboard, and the airship ready to go. Champion's last laugh was in keeping me talking until a moment before take-off.

No one intended to stay for another hour, or even another few minutes, if the bustle around the gondola was any indication. The mooring ropes were hitched into quick-release hooks, and the covers were now being clamped over the engine casings.

The canvas screens that extended around the rim of the quarry, to protect the airship against rock-falls, were now fully retracted. Champion leaned forward and tapped the wind gauge, but the needle didn't move.

Champion got up and walked outside, to the open balcony. I followed him. He leaned forward to see the tall vegetation that grew along the edge of the quarry. There was no movement in it. 'The wind is always a worry,' said Champion.

'There's no wind,' I said. I was watching him carefully now.

'No.' He sniffed the air. 'You can "free-balloon" up on a night like this . . . start the engines when you're in the air.'

'Is that so?' I said. He was thinking aloud. They would need to 'free-balloon' up if they were to go, without someone controlling the ascent, from this console.

'You'll look after the boy?'

I didn't answer him.

'Good,' he said, and patted my arm.

Perhaps if I'd been listening to him more closely, or remembering old times, I would never have hit him in the sudden and impulsive way that I did. He reeled against the rail. I followed the straight right with an uppercut from my left. It wasn't anything to write to *Physical Fitness Magazine* about, but Champion was already off balance. It sent him down the staircase: backwards. Even while my left was connecting, I was bringing the P·38 out of my belt. Champion landed at the bottom of the steps in a heap. He groaned, and dragged his arm from under him, but it carried no gun. Champion was too damned Sandhurst to brandish pocket guns, and his sort of tailor can't set a sleeve to hide a shoulder holster. And anyway, Steve Champion had no trigger finger. He fixed me with a look of hatred and despair, but pain closed his eyes.

I offered a silent thanks to Schlegel for the P·38. The well-oiled safety slid to fire. There was no time to thumb the hammer back; I pulled hard on the trigger and felt the double-action. I fired, and put the whole magazine of bullets into the gas bag. The Walther twisted in my hand, as all big pistols do, but I wasn't trying to win a prize at Bisley; I wanted only to puncture the envelope and let the hydrogen gas escape near the engine. I pushed the magazine catch, and shook the gun hard enough to bring the empty magazine out. It clattered to the floor. I banged the full magazine into place and brought it up two-handed style. These were the ones that had to hit. There was only the faintest glimpse of light on the foresight, but as it came up the engine nacelle, I squeezed the trigger. I'd known old P·38s, with worn trigger bars, to rip off a magazine like a burp-gun, but this one was a gentleman's pistol. It was too dark to see what my grouping was like, but inside the engine cowling, ricocheting bullets were playing close-harmony tin, like a drunken steel-band at Mardi Gras.

As the hammer nose clicked on the firing-pin, I threw the gun aside, and ran for the mine entrance. I already fancied I heard the gurgle of petrol running from the punctured fuel tank. I pictured the hot engine that it would fall upon; the thought propelled me head-first through the doors. They thudded shut behind me and the sound of the fans was in my ears, until the beat of my pulsing veins drowned it out. I stumbled in the darkness but fear beats any after-burner as a means of propulsion, and I was at the far end of the main gallery when the airship's hydrogen ignited. I knew that, in theory, an atomic shell could not be exploded by fire, but did that extend to the temperatures at which hydrogen burned?

The bang ripped the doors from their hinges, and the end of the mine gallery became a red glowing rectangle. A giant breaker of hot air picked me up and slammed me to the floor, and then did it again. I twisted my head to see what was chasing me. The patch of light was boiling whiteness. It was like staring into the sun through a square telescope. I screwed up my eyes as the main blast of heat hit me. This time the smell hit me too; not only the carbonized rubber, and the stink of hydrogen and scorched dust, but the awesome smell of burned hair and flesh. I clamped my hands over my face and found that some of the burned hair and flesh was my own. I rolled over, shouting some incoherent mixture of prayers, oaths and promises.

With the roar of the great furnace I'd created still in my ears, I crawled towards the shaft landing. Each movement was painful and the dust had been sucked up into a blinding black storm. After the first few tottering steps I knew I could go no farther.

But it wasn't going to end like this, I told myself. A man doesn't spend a lifetime working for that damned department, and die in a mine, without pension or gratuity. But a few minutes' rest . . . that was different: a man must be allowed a moment's rest.

30

'And do you know what I say?' said Schlegel for the tenth or eleventh time.

'You say "crap",' I replied. I was tired. As I wiped a hand across my forehead I smelled my scorched clothes and my scorched hair. And I looked at the burns on my hand.

'Don't go to sleep on me,' said Schlegel. 'There's a whole slew of paperwork for you to finish before you sack out. Yes, that's right: I say crap. And if it wasn't for Dawlish being so soft, I'd have your arse in a sling.' He nodded to me, and scowled at the same time. 'I wouldn't let my own mother come out of the other side of this one unscathed.'

'I believe you, Colonel,' I said.

'Well, now we can see why the girl sent that picture postcard of the Zeppelin. She got on to it too early for Champion's liking. But how could you be sure it was filled with *hydrogen*? No one fills blimps with hydrogen any more.'

'Helium is too difficult to get.'

'Helium would have left you looking pretty damned stupid, fella,' said Schlegel. 'Non-flam helium would not have burned. That would have left you with egg on your face. It would have given Champion a big laugh, and you a tail filled with lead.'

'You would have preferred that, perhaps,' I said.

'I would have preferred that. No perhaps about it.'

He picked up a newspaper that had just arrived by messenger. The headline said, 'Gas Leak Kills Twelve', with a subhead that said it had happened at a 'remote chemical plant' owned by Tix Industries. Schlegel held the paper up and flicked it with the back of his hand, so that it made a loud noise. 'A lot of trouble went into getting us that newsbreak the way we wanted it,' he said.

Schlegel opened a new box of cigars and selected one. He didn't offer them to me. 'Atomic shells!' said Schlegel. 'Would it interest you to know that Champion had not even *tried* to dig a passage to the artillery school?'

I didn't answer.

'You pleading the Fifth Amendment?' said Schlegel. 'Or did you just go to sleep? The whole thing was a bluff. And you fell for it . . .' He shook his head sadly. 'Do you realize what you did?'

'OK,' I told him. 'It was a bluff. But let me tell you what kind of bluff it was. Champion was going to fly that blimp to North Africa – there's no doubt about that.'

'So what?'

'He would have claimed to have stolen atomic shells.'

'And the French would have denied it.'

'And which of them would we have believed?' I asked him.

'I would have believed the French,' insisted Schlegel primly.

'Well, the Israelis might *not* have believed the French. And if you were the Israeli negotiators at the treaty talks, perhaps you'd have had your doubts, too.'

'And lost out in the negotiations, you mean?' Grudgingly, Schlegel conceded an inch to me. 'Champion wouldn't put his head on the block just to provide psychological advantages for those goddamned Cairo politicians.'

'He wasn't putting anything on the block,' I said. 'It was an aircraft, registered in Cairo, flying over France without permission. Who was going to press the button?'

'Nukes in French air space . . . and the Quai d'Orsay in a panic . . . ? Champion would be taking a big risk, I'd say.'

I said, 'Champion knew they'd phone the artillery commandant and find that there were no atomic artillery shells missing. They sign those things in and out, every shift: a thirty-second response.'

Schlegel didn't answer.

I said, 'All along, I was puzzled by the way that he let us know it was going to be a nuclear device. I wondered why he didn't try to disguise the *object* of the operation as well as the *method*.'

Schlegel nodded. It was beginning to get through to him. 'He did it so that you would strong-arm me into alerting every damn official in NATO. When the Egyptians claimed to have got a nuke, there were going to be a lot of our top brass saying where there's smoke there's fire.'

'It was a neat idea, Colonel,' I said. 'And since we were going to keep on denying that any kind of bomb had been stolen, Champion could come back and live in France, get Billy again, and even go to London for his stamp auctions.'

'Knowing that any attempt to hit or hassle him would look like a confirmation that he'd got the damned thing.' Schlegel nodded a grudging concession to Champion's cleverness. 'The only thing he didn't figure was that the Melodie Page kid would put the boot in.'

'And that I would put the boot in, too.'

'Umm,' said Schlegel. He rubbed his chin. He'd not shaved for forty-eight hours and his suit was filthy from poking around in the embers of the fire.

Out of the window, I could see Nice railway station. It was dusk, and the lights were on. Facing it was the Terminus Hotel. Once this had been a fashionable place to stroll and to sit, but now the great hotel was dark and empty, its windows dirty and its fine entrance boarded up. I remembered the café, with outdoor tables and fine cane chairs. I'd been sitting there, that day in that war so long ago. I'd waited for Champion, and seen him arrested by the Germans as he emerged from the station. He knew exactly where I would be, but he didn't look in my direction. Steve was a pro.

Now Steve was dead. The hotel was dead, and the café was gone. The chairs and tables were replaced by a corrugated iron hoarding. Upon it there was layer upon layer of posters, advertising everything from Communist Party candidates to go-go clubs and careers in the Foreign Legion. Across them, someone had daubed 'Merde aux Arabes' in red paint.

'Are you listening?' said Schlegel.

'Yes,' I said, but I wasn't.

THE SEA STAR

"Rana, get th[...] [...]o the water and row! Have you fo[...] [...]at you're carrying? Getting the J[...] [...]lian is more important than my life, [...] [...] Rana, please! You must go now or a[...] [...] done will be in vain!"

The pain [...] his voice came from something more than fear, but Rana could not stop to analyze it. He was right. Though her throat ached with grief, she knew it, and already she was bundling the cask and foodbag into the skiff and shoving off. In a moment the complaining of sand under the keel gave way to the slap of waves; resistance eased suddenly, and the skiff was bobbing in uneasy response to the swells that washed the outer cove.

For a last moment she hesitated, torn between conflicting fears. Then she caught the ugly note in the shouting, and remembered why she had decided that a clean death in the sea would be better than remaining here. On the rock above her, Fredric stood waiting with drawn sword, like an image of the Defender. The sea-wind ruffled his fair hair, but his face had somehow regained its serenity.

"Rana, they are coming—" he said quietly. "Don't be afraid for me. You know they'll save me for ransom if they can. When you see Julian, tell him he still has my loyalty.... Go now, girl, in the name of the Maker, and may the Guardians protect you!" he cried. His boots rang on rock as he strode to face their foes.

**Also by the same author,
and available from NEL:**

Westria Series:
Lady of Light, Lady of Darkness (Westria 1)
Silverhair the Wanderer (Westria 2)
The Earthstone (Westria 3)
The Wind Crystal (Westria 5)
The Jewel of Fire (Westria 6)

White Raven

About the author

Diana Paxson is a science fiction and fantasy
writer living in Berkeley, California. She studied
medieval English and French for her Master's
Degree at the University of California, and this
knowledge has been used as the basis of many
of her short stories and novels. Diana Paxson is
married with two sons. She spends her spare
time playing the harp and writing poetry.

The Sea Star

Diana Paxson

NEW ENGLISH LIBRARY
Hodder and Stoughton

First published in the USA in 1988 by
Tom Doherty Associates, Inc.
First published in Great Britain in
1991 by New English Library
paperbacks

An NEL paperback original

Second impression 1992

British Library C.I.P.

Paxson, Diana L.
  The sea star.
  I. Title II. Series
813.54[F]

  ISBN 0-450-53718-8

Printed and bound in Great Britain for
Hodder and Stoughton Paperbacks, a
division of Hodder and Stoughton
Ltd., Mill Road, Dunton Green,
Sevenoaks, Kent TN13 2YA (Editorial
Office: 47 Bedford Square, London
WC1B 3DP) by Clays Ltd, St Ives plc.

To Fiona—

*may you always bear the blessing
of the Lady of Moon and Sea*

PART ONE:

The Sea

Julian is standing on the shore of the ocean, just where the foam expires upon the sand. It is night, and his comrades are laughing around a bonfire. Some of them are men he served with in the Border Guard, and he wonders what they are doing on the coast. What is he doing here?

But more recent companions from Seagate are there too: Frederic of Bongarde, his friend; his uncle the harper; and Rana, the red-headed girl. They call to him to join them, but the ocean is sighing restlessly. The glittering billows heave as if some great animal were breathing in the dark. Anything could be out there. He tries to tell his friends to watch out for danger, but they do not seem to hear.

Suddenly Julian's shadow pools at his feet and spills down into the sea. He turns, and sees that the moon has appeared behind him, huge, misshapen, its face scarred *by forgotten wars. Cold light chills him as it rises, and the moon grows larger—nearer, not higher, looming above him until his body trembles at its dreadful proximity.*

He shouts out a warning and struggles through the sand toward higher ground. At last his boots clatter on bare stone. The others are still singing around their puny fire. They do not seem to hear him, nor do they see the menace of the moon. But though his friends have not noticed the moon, huge swells lift as the sea responds to its pull with an eager roar. Foam-flecked water glistens in the pale light, curving like a hungry maw above the land.

And the monster moon swings down to meet it. The sea engulfs the shore with a thunder of waters and sucks everything back into its gullet. The fire is gone. His friends are gone.

Julian wakes, screaming, as the mad moon falls. . . .

Chapter One

Water clucked and gurgled against *Sea Brother*'s smooth sides as the ship moved southward under reefed sails, given just enough momentum by the seaward current to keep the heavy holding nets taut below the waves. A morning's fishing had filled the nets with striped bass and surfperch, sole and turbot, and young salmon just beginning their journey to the sea.

Nearby, the other ships of the Seagate fishing fleet drifted like butterflies across the Great Bay, and like the return of the butterflies, this blossoming of bright sails signified that summer had arrived. Surface ripples netted the sunlight, keeping the eye from seeing what lay below.

Entranced by that ceaseless flicker, Rana stretched herself more comfortably along the arched back of the dolphin figurehead and drew in a deep breath of the tangy air. If only this momentary mating of sun and sound and sea could go on and on and on!

3

The soft speech of men murmured counterpoint to the whispering of the waters.

"We've nearly filled our nets already, and it's only mid-afternoon—we'll have a fair offering for the ritual!" That was Arn's voice, full of pride in the ship his father had given him when he and Rana's sister were married. *Sea Brother* was one of the larger members of the Seahold fleet, a gaff-rigged schooner fifty feet from bow to stern.

"We need it," came the reply. "The catch has been poor this year. But what should we expect? Nothing is right in the land. A sorcerer on the Red Mountain is bad enough, and now we're expected to follow this Prince Julian, who comes from the Guardians know where!"

Rana's copper braids thumped against the smooth wood as she stirred. *She* knew where Julian had come from. He was son to the last king, brought up unknowing until he had come to the Master of the Junipers last Midsummer to learn his name. But that was not what had put the odd note in old Bertram's voice. Julian had been struck down in a duel of sorcery and buried in the Sacred Wood. She herself had been the first to find the Prince, with eyes like a wild thing and the earth of the grave still on him, walking in the Sacred Wood on Midwinter Day. No wonder the men of Westria looked at him strangely. Her own skin prickled at the memory.

Rana squinted back along the deck. In a moment she identified the broad shoulders and dark head she was looking for, as motionless at the stern as Rana was at *Sea Brother*'s prow. But even she could not imagine what a man who had been to the land of death and back might be thinking as he gazed at the green-gold hills and scattering of whitewashed houses that bordered the bright bay.

*   *   *

4

Julian gripped the rail as a shift in the wind altered the ship's motion, then forced himself to let go. Reason told him that if Rana could go to sleep on the figurehead, the sea must be calm. But reason could not still the panic that threatened him every time *Sea Brother* moved. He was not seasick; even that would have been understandable. What had troubled him ever since they left the pier was the unsteadiness. He felt as if he had been uprooted and was floating aimlessly away.

Frederic was picking his way past the people on the port side, his fair hair blazing a deeper gold in the long rays of the westering sun.

"What are you doing all alone back here?"

Julian shrugged his heavy shoulders uncomfortably and tried to smile. Seeing Frederic eased him immensely, for he had been alone with the Master of the Junipers on the Lady Mountain for the past four months, learning to use the Earthstone, but somehow he could not find the words to say so. Frederic laughed.

"When I came home after my first year at the College of the Wise it was a week before my brothers dared to tease me! It will get easier."

Will it? Julian knew how to talk to the trees, but he seemed to have forgotten how to communicate with men. He heard Rana's laughter and saw that she had joined Arn and some of his crewmen amidships. He felt a spurt of envy for that easy companionship. Frederic leaned back comfortably against the rail and Julian shuddered, aware once more of the unstable depths below.

"Do you think your father will attack the sorcerer again?" he asked quickly.

"One of these days—he can't leave Blood Gard to fester like a canker in the heart of Westria!" Frederic frowned. On the other side of the ship someone was

5

shouting for a net as he fought a big striped bass to the side.

"But he has failed once already—" Even from here Julian could see the tip of the Red Mountain, poking above the eastern hills.

"He attacked too soon. . . ." Frederic answered him. "Well, we all thought you were dead, Julian! My father felt he had failed you, and he had to wipe out the shame. He sent every fighter who had come to Laurelynn for the Midwinter Festival into an attack against the Mountain. But the trees would not fight for us there, and our men were willing to give their lives, but not their souls. . . ."

"Strength of arms will not defeat Caolin," Julian said heavily. "What about the College of the Wise?"

"I don't know—" Frederic's voice tightened with the pain of that admission. "There is much knowledge there, but little application. There are some of us who want to learn to use the old skills again. But for now . . ." He shook his head.

"It's my job," said Julian. Frederic looked at him anxiously, and Julian shook his head. "Not yet, but I know that I will have to face him one day. . . ."

Images of the last time he had faced Caolin flooded his vision. He extended his awareness earthward as the Master of the Junipers had taught him, seeking the power to resist them, but the deep currents swirled his will away. Then pain prickled through the tracery of silver scars at his temple where the sorcerer's blow had marked him, bringing him back to the present again. Julian's gaze focused on Frederic's face and he recognized fear in his friend's blue eyes.

It's no use, he thought then. *They should have let me go to the Sacred Wood . . .*

"Well, if the sorcerer cannot be conquered, at least he is doing us no harm!" Arn's words came to them in an

6

odd echo of their own. "The sea wolves are another matter. They strike ever more boldly along the coast, and our men are afraid to sail outside the Bay. They're brave enough at sea, but they're fishermen, not warriors, and even if they could learn to fight, our boats don't maneuver very well. We have never needed a navy until now."

Julian remembered the burned steading they had seen on the way to Ravensgate and shuddered, imagining Seahold in flames. Frederic raised one eyebrow and moved along *Sea Brother*'s side toward the others, and after a moment's hesitation Julian followed him.

Rana saw them coming and raised a hand in welcome. She could feel the constraint around her as the others recognized Julian, but she gave him her widest grin. His shoulders twitched as they always did when he was nervous, but he nodded a greeting.

"I couldn't help hearing," Frederic said cheerfully, easing down among the others. Julian remained standing behind him, holding onto the mast. "But my father's not likely to beg the Prince of Elaya for the loan of his warships! We'll have to find some other way!"

"The sooner, the better!" exclaimed Arn, pushing the sun-bleached hair out of his eyes. "I've a wife to worry about now, and a child coming soon!" He blushed as he said it, as if he could still not quite believe in his approaching fatherhood.

Rana could hardly believe it either. It did not seem so long ago that the children of Registhorpe and Seahold had risked their lives in leaky rowboats and chased each other up and down the steep paths to the village. And now her sister's belly was rounding. In a few months she would look like a beached whale.

"Yes, I heard that Bella was blooming. When is the baby due?" Frederic asked.

7

"Near Harvest-tide—" Arn blushed once more. "Last year she made the Beltane offering, but now the very thought of getting into a boat makes her stomach churn."

"So I'm standing in for her," said Rana briskly, fighting down the discomfort she felt when she allowed herself to think for too long about what was happening to Bella. Pregnancy was a natural thing; everyone else was rejoicing. But it seemed to Rana that she would rather face a reiver, sword in hand.

"And it's almost sunset!" exclaimed Arn. Swiftly he began to gather in his line. Carefully he unhooked an undersized turbot and tossed it back over the side. "Frederic, Lord Julian, excuse me, and Rana—you had better get dressed right now!"

He picked up his pole and started forward, preparing the crew for a course change. Julian was still standing by the mast.

"Are you all right?" She stopped short, afraid she had offended him, but his eyes lost their distant look and he smiled.

"It's nothing that matters. . . . You go along now—I'm looking forward to seeing you in the ritual!"

Rana made a last check on the sun, which was now dropping swiftly toward the Lady Mountain, and squinted into its dying flame. Then she opened the stern cabin door. As soon as her eyes had adjusted she began to strip off her tunic and the short breeches she usually wore onboard.

Be still, she told herself. *Pay attention to what you are doing! You are going to act as priestess here!* Biting her lip, she wondered if she would remember what she was supposed to do? What would happen if she failed?

With trembling hands she poured fresh water from the bottle and began to sponge herself, and the cool touch of moisture on her skin calmed her so that she was able to unroll the linen without fumbling and lay out her gown.

8

Water . . . It is all water—water on my skin, in my body, in the sea . . . there is no reason to be afraid.

The aqua silk of the Festival dress shimmered even in that uncertain light. It had been made for Arn's mother when she was young and *Sea Brother* was new; Lady Leonie wore a new gown now that she was offering for *Wind Dancer*, but this one belong to *Sea Brother*, and in the other ships it was the same. If Bella had a son, his woman might wear the dress one day.

Shells tinkled musically as Rana lifted the gown, and the embroidered sea-creatures seemed to move. She let the soft fabric slither over her head and fall in loose folds, and fastened her own silver and abalone-shell necklace around her neck before she began to brush out her braids.

There was a clatter of feet outside and then a rhythmic squeak as the crew raised the main sail. The deck tilted as the ship came about. Rana realized that they must be turning toward the rendezvous point, gave her copper mane a last swipe with the brush, and flung open the door.

The sun had dipped below the ragged black wall of the hills, but the sky still glowed. *Sea Brother* seemed to be gliding across a sheet of fire that shattered into embers as she passed. In the shadow of the Lady Mountain, little lights already winked from the windows of Seahold, but they were pale beside the splendor of sea and sky. A few thin clouds caught the last rays of sunlight and streamed across the heavens like banners of gold. The other boats were dark specks against the brilliant water, moving towards the same invisible point near the center of the Bay. The tide was on the ebb, but here in the lee of Stag Island the water was almost still.

Rana moved toward the prow and found Frederic already standing there.

9

"Beltane Eve—" he said softly without turning. "I have never before celebrated it upon the sea. It will seem strange not to have the flower-decked pole and the fires. But I know the principle is the same—to invoke fertility for predator and prey, so that we all may live."

"There will be fires—" Rana responded, "and the ocean has its own flowers!" She gestured toward the tangles of wet kelp that, like the fish, had been kept fresh in nets beneath the surface until now.

"I hope Julian enjoys it. . . ."

Rana did not answer him. Julian had gone back to the stern again, and was gazing at the Lady Mountain. Despite old friendship, Seahold's Beltane Festival did not usually merit the participation of the Lord Commander's household, much less that of a royal heir. But the barriers between the worlds thinned on Beltane Eve, and there was reason to fear that if Julian saw the tree-spirits dancing he would never return to the world of men.

A soft order from Arn brought *Sea Brother* around on a new tack. Rana swayed to the motion instinctively, but Frederic staggered and clutched at the rail.

"I hope I can remember my part. . . ." she said nervously.

"It will be all right." Frederic looked at her now. "The words are important, but less so than the will. Do you know *why* you are making the offering and wearing that gown?"

Rana smoothed back her hair, burnished by the westering light to an even brighter flame. "The tides of a woman's body obey the moon like the tides of the sea, so a woman must be the celebrant," she answered as Lady Leonie had taught her. "If the fishing boat is captained by a man the role goes to his closest female kin. I must ask Sea Mother to make Her creatures flourish,

10

and give what we have caught this day back to Her in token of our willingness to take no more than our share. The fish that we release will be our messengers . . ." She paused as a drumbeat sounded from the stern. "Listen! It's beginning now!"

Pulse pounding, she gripped the rail as a dull *boom* drifted across the water like an echo. Others, fainter, followed it, coming from the other boats as they neared. *Wind Dancer* had pulled away as they tacked, but they were all drawing together now. Louder and louder the drums boomed, crescendoing like a breaking wave, then soft again. The beat throbbed across the water; the ships were borne by waves of sound. Above them, the brilliant sky had faded to rose and the quarter-round of the waning moon was already high.

No, not beginning—it has begun. . . . Suddenly, she was caught by the momentum of the ritual, and she knew that like a swimmer swept away by the current, her only safety lay in allowing it to carry her along.

Now the boats formed a great circle on the water, which tightened as they converged. The drumbeats had become more distinct; soft, soft, loud, loud, LOUD, and then soft again. *Sea Brother*'s big mainsail had been furled once more, and the fishermen stood at attention along the sides, allowing the ship's momentum to carry her along.

From across the water came a long horn call. Arn gave a quiet order, the foresail went down, and the ship's headway carried her the last few feet to her position. Arn spoke again. The *splash* and *thunk* as their anchor hit water was repeated all around the circle. The boat lurched slightly as the anchor bit, then *Sea Brother* was still.

The drums, finally, were silent. For a moment Rana

stood still as well; then she met Arn's anxious glance and realized that he was nervous too. She took a deep breath of salt air.

"Oh my brothers and my sisters, who are you?"

"We are the People of the Sea!" came the full-throated reply.

Rana nodded. "Indeed, we are sea-hunters. Like the creatures who feed us, we are people of the sea. Let us proclaim that kinship by wearing Ocean's garlands!" She bent to the pile of glistening garnet-brown kelp, pulled free a long strand and draped it about her shoulders, then grasped at more, wreathing it about Frederic's neck, and Arn's, and up and down the lines of fisherfolk until everyone was garlanded.

The west still glowed crimson, but overhead the sky had turned a rich indigo against which the brightening moon rested like a rind of pearl. The waves lapped quietly against *Sea Brother*'s sides, and her dolphin figurehead nodded greeting to her companions— *Wind Dancer, Cazadora, Sea Otter, Ballena, Gull*, and *Orca*, as if the Guardians of the Sea were meeting there.

The stillness deepened. The silence was within her now, and Rana could not move. But she drew breath sharply as against the violet sky the summit of the Lady Mountain suddenly quivered with flame. A horn sounded and torches sprang to life around it, light springing from prow to prow. Almost directly above, the cold moon glowed; to the west the Mountain was crowned with flame, and below them, a circle of fire floated upon the sea.

Deep as the voice of the ocean, the hymn began. The tune was simple, repeated over and over again, but Rana felt the gooseflesh rising on her arms.

"See! the year has turned again—summer's in:
we who bore the bitter storms, and alarms

now need fairer winds to fill every sail. . . .
So favor us who love the sea—Lady, pray!"

The music rose around her, and instinctively Rana lifted her face to the moon and heard her own voice soar.

"We seek Thy bounty anywhere wind may bear
our little ships, and as the tide may decide,
return to harbor once again, landborn men,
so favor us who love the sea—Lady, pray!

"The Sea-People near and far our brothers are.
Together taking what we need, our young to feed,
to Thy will obedient, we submit—
so favor us who love the sea—Lady, pray!"

The singing ended. Rana, remembering who she was and where, made her way to *Sea Brother*'s prow. A horn blew once more, and a rope came flying through the darkness on their right just as Arn cast *Sea Brother*'s line toward the ship on the left. Men wound it round a pulley, and flung it back, while the same thing happened on the other side. The pulleys squeaked as the fishers hauled on the ropes.

"Scaled swimmers, now hear us! Will you be our messengers?" Rana's fingers tightened on the rail as she leaned forward, staring at the glitter of silver in the dark waters below. "Kindred of the Sea, we offer you all honor! Go to Sea Mother and tell her how we have treated you. Beg Her to bless us and give us what we need to live!"

As she finished, the lines between the ships grew taut. They were attached to the nets which had been filled during the day. As they were drawn together, the nets fell open, so that ships and nets together formed a circular pen. The discouraged fish quickened to confused life as the nets freed them, and the sea boiled as the seething mass sought open water.

"From the Sea we have taken them—to the Sea we

13

return them again!" came a many-throated cry.

The vibration pulsed through the water, adding its impetus to the deeper currents that already bore the scent of the fish and the boats themselves and all things touched by the waters through the Gateway to Mother Ocean.

"It's more than fish we should be giving Her. . . ." muttered old Bertram. "Dead men should stay buried, and if earth won't hold them perhaps the water will!"

There was an uneasy murmur as folk stared toward the stern, where Julian's dark figure was silhouetted against the torchlight. Rana felt a cold fist clutch in her belly. Was this the kind of talk that was going around? She hoped desperately that he had not heard those words.

"In the old days the land's best blood bought favor from the ancient powers. . . ." said Bertram more loudly. One of the fishermen gave him a sharp look and bent to his companion, whispering.

Julian had turned and Rana could see his face clearly now, heavy brows a little bent as if he were striving to understand. Why didn't somebody say something? Rana glared at Arn.

"The old days are dead and gone—" he said lamely. "We know better now."

"We know that it is not blood but beauty that makes a worthy sacrifice!" Rana exclaimed. "We win favor by giving what we value away." She had their attention, but they still looked dubious. She would have given her life for Julian, but that wasn't the point now. She frowned, thinking, then reached up and fumbled to loose the clasp of her necklace.

"Here is the fairest thing I own! Let the Sea take this necklace if there must be a sacrifice!" For a moment silver glittered in the firelight. "Behold my offering—

14

now all debts are paid!" she cried, and flung the necklace in a glittering arc over the side.

Bertram grinned sourly. "Eh, lass, that was foolish, to give something of your own. The necklace stands for you—it is you that the Sea will claim now!"

"So be it!" Rana's defiant reply was lost in Bertram's laugh.

They were all still gazing at the spreading ripples where the necklace had disappeared when they heard a crash from the stern. The deck tilted suddenly and Rana staggered as one of the men fell against her. Painted teeth gleamed from the darkness behind them, and as *Sea Brother* righted herself Rana glimpsed a long dark shape slipping alongside. Grappling irons snapped accurately over the rail.

"Reivers! Reivers!" She found her voice as the night exploded in sound.

From across the smashed circle the ceremonial horn blew frantically. Tangled in their own lines, the fishing boats wallowed helplessly as more raiders reached them. Arn shouted to his people to take up poles and push back the boarders; he grabbed a net and tried to entangle a raider's sword.

Rana started toward him, tripped over the skirts of her gown and crashed into a bench. For a moment she lay where she had fallen, gasping. Across the circle a ship was burning. Elsewhere, most torches had been doused. Dark figures struggled in the uncertain light—impossible to tell friend from foe. She put out a hand to push herself up and felt the horn haft of a scaling knife. Crushing the wadded folds of her gown against her with one arm, she crouched, prudence overwhelmed by rage.

A helmed figure darted toward her. She slashed and dodged as it clapped hand to arm and dropped its sword. Beyond she could see another reiver jerking away Arn's fishnet. She shouted and kicked the sword across the deck to him, turned and glimpsed a man in leather armor sweeping his cutlass toward Frederic's side. Shrieking, she dove at the raider, bringing her knife up beneath the armor. Astonishingly, it sank in. Then the man fell, dragging the knife from her hand and pinning her beneath him.

Rana's head struck hard against the deck, and there was a blessed moment of darkness. Then feet thundered past. Panicking at the thought of being trampled, she struggled free. A man hurtled towards her, was thrust aside by another. Frederic shouted to her to get to the rail. She heaved convulsively, got her legs from under the body of the man she had downed, and scrambled toward her friend.

Frederic was parrying the blows and the bodies that came his way with a three-legged stool and striking with his ceremonial sword. Rana grabbed a broken pole and crouched beside him, thrusting it out to trip raiders who came past.

"Have you seen Arn?" she panted when for a moment they were free. It would be hard for Bella to be widowed so soon.

"Not lately. He was over there with Julian—" Without expression, Frederic nodded toward the heaving mass of bodies in the stern. A rush of raiders cut them off from the others.

"Sea Mother save us!" Rana breathed. For a moment a great quiet weighted her ears. As if from very far away she saw a slim figure in a shirt of gilded mail, face hidden by a golden helm. She felt the stare of shadowed eyes. The raiders surged around them.

"There's two still on their feet—a wench, by the Lord—a redheaded wench, and a man!" a deep voice exclaimed. "Hurry now, but handle him carefully— we've netted their Regent's own cub this time!"

Frederic's hand clenched on the hilt of his sword, but there were too many of them. The harsh sound of their laughter broke through Rana's shock and she was suddenly painfully conscious of the slap of waves against the hull, of moans from the deck, of cries from the other end of the ship. Where was Julian?

"Put down your weapons. . . ." Graybeard's sword threatened.

Frederic's glance flickered to the water and then back again. For a moment he stood very still. Then he flung the sword to the deck and let the stool bounce into the hold. Why had he given in so easily? Rana felt her stomach churn with shame. Then she realized that something was moving beyond them, silent as the shark-ships had been, but larger. She clamped lips tight against sudden hope, then flung down her pole.

The big man pulled thongs from his belt-pouch to bind their wrists behind their backs. Rana gasped as he lifted her, then she fell.

Julian wrenched his blade from the body of a reiver and looked up just as Rana disappeared over the side. The other reivers were retreating now, but he was almost the only one of *Sea Brother*'s defenders still fighting. Arn lay curled beside him, blood welling between his fingers as he clutched his side. Others lay still.

He pushed away from the sternrail to follow, and staggered as *Wind Dancer* loomed up suddenly beside them. Timbers groaned as the bigger ship scraped along *Sea Brother*'s side.

"This way!" shrieked Julian. "They've got Frederic and Rana!"

The two ships lay grappled now. Westrians poured over the rail and after him, waving whatever weapons they had been able to find. Julian's blade bit deep and the nearest reiver went down. Another turned to fight, snarling. Julian struck again, felt the momentary resistance of leather armor, and let his own weight draw the stroke the rest of the way through.

"For Westria!" he cried. "For Westria!"

Now there were only a few men between him and the sharkship. The rush of the counterattack carried him forward. Steel clanged as an enemy sword came up to parry. Julian's strong wrist flexed; disengaging, he thrust and the man fell. A flicker of movement brought him around, sword lifting. He felt the sting as the reiver's blade sliced across the top of his arm. Then his own stroke sent his assailant screaming over the side.

There were no others.

Julian grasped the rail, staring stupidly at the strip of black water that was opening between the sharkship and *Sea Brother*'s side. He could just see the copper gleam of Rana's hair. A mallet hit wood with a hollow knock, and two dozen oars dug into the waves. The galley surged away. Against the silver water he saw the dark shapes of the rest. They must have crept in on the afternoon floodtide and hidden in the lee of Pelican Island, he thought dimly. Now they would have the full ebb to help them out again.

Frederic, Rana, can you hear me? His thought sped after them. *In the Guardians' names I swear it—I will do whatever I must to get you back again!*

Julian's breathing steadied as his battle-fury drained away. The ship rocked gently, and he was aware of the treacherous water beneath him for the first time since the attack began. But he watched the sharkships until they disappeared, while blood from his wounded arm dripped unheeded into the sea.

Almost as swiftly as the sharkships, the fish the folk of Seahold had released moved through the Bay's chill waters toward the sea. But the waters carried other tales as well, borne seaward by the ebbing tide. There was blood in the water now, and the bodies of men. Scavengers gathered to feast on the unexpected bounty. But both kinds of information came to Sea Mother at last. For a time she pondered. Then she sent out her own messages, summoning the Guardians of the Sea.

The ship rocked in the long ocean swells, lifting and dropping in an irregular rhythm that was different from the purposeful surges that had brought them here. The change in motion roused Rana, and she twisted awkwardly to see. Frederic drew a painful sigh.

"Why have we stopped?" he asked miserably.

"I do not know. . . ." His face was a dim blur against the darkness, and beyond him the shapes of the rowers bulked deeper black against the sky. But she shouldn't be able to see anything.

"Dawn . . ." she breathed. "They must be waiting for more light before they go on." She shivered violently and Frederic curved his body against hers in a vain effort to shield her from the wind. She could feel the tension in his body, and the effort it took to control his breathing. He had been very silent since they left the Bay, concentrating, she supposed, on controlling the responses of his body with the resources of his trained mind.

A whistle twittered and the rowers grasped their oars. Rana grunted and wriggled upright once more. A shape loomed before them, ghostly in the fog. At its base a faint line of white flickered and disappeared. Surf! But not enough for the coast. Could it be an island?

Outlines grew more distinct as the boat swept forward. Now the oarsmen broke their nightlong silence with broad jokes about food, beer, and bed, and the fight they had just won. Rana found their accents strange, and some spoke a language she did not recognize. Considering the nature of the comments she did understand, she was glad to know no more.

A horn blared sharply from the sharkship's prow and was echoed, eerily, from across the waves. The rowers bent to their work, and the shape before them was revealed as a fantastically weathered dome of rock whose base was still veiled in swirling fog. A crisp order brought the ship around to starboard, and a jagged slope and more pinnacles, smaller but equally alien, appeared.

"These must be the Far Alone Islands—" Frederic said softly. "We've not been out long enough to go anywhere else. The only one of the islands where boats can land is the Isle of Birds, but humans cannot live here!"

The oarsmen pulled strongly, holding the ship steady against the treacherous currents. Light glittered on restless waves as mist-haloed torches flared from the shore, and Rana glimpsed bright eyes and then a swift swirl in the water as a sea lion dove out of their path. Ahead of them the land shelved outward to meet the sea in slabs of rock festooned with seaweed. But the sound of waves clashing against rock was only a background to the incessant shrilling of innumerable birds.

Another order brought them into the shelter of a small cove. Frederic struggled to right himself as the rowers upped oars and let the gentle waves ease them nearer to the shore, then sculled to hold their position there. Now Rana could see a narrow opening between rock walls that ended in a crescent of dun sand. There was some kind of rude shelter above it, and a hoist made of ropes and crossed timbers. Then one of the sharkships darted suddenly toward shore, letting the last wave slide it up onto the sand. In moments the crew were out of it, carrying the heavier booty, and then the ship itself was swung up to the ledge and hauled out of the way.

A sharp command brought the ship that carried Rana suddenly to life again. Oars lifted like the wings of a hovering hawk, then dipped, and they swooped toward the rocks with a precision that left no room for fear. She felt sand grate beneath the keel, and the boat canted over. A knife sliced through her bonds, and hard hands lifted her over the side.

"Up there—" One of the men pointed to the rock wall, then turned to the boat again. Rana forced numb limbs to carry her forward and saw steps roughly cut into the stone. A threat to hoist her up with one of the boat ropes gave her the strength to clamber up them, and she found herself standing on the ledge, coughing as she breathed in moist air weighted with the overpowering odor of birds. In a few moments Frederic appeared, white and shivering, but pathetically glad to be back on solid ground.

Now that they were out of the way, no one seemed to care what they did, and why should they? Rana shivered with new despair as she realized that more surely than bonds or bars, the ocean prisoned them here. Even on the borders of Elaya she had never felt so far from home. The Far Alone islands lay no more than twenty-five miles from the Gateway, but they existed in another dimension to which even the reivers were only temporary visitors—the world of the sea.

Men were already carrying their spoils up a path that wound past the hut and over the shoulder of the ridge. There would be fire where they were going, and perhaps food as well. Too exhausted even to wonder at the sea-birds that flew squawking out of their path, Rana and Frederic followed the path around the shoulder of the hill.

On the long slope below it rough wood shanties and bright tents were set in a straggling circle around a blazing fire, dominated by a pavilion of crimson and gold. Supporting each other, Rana and Frederic stumbled down the path. They pressed through a confusion of colors and costume. Ignoring the malice in the men's laughter, Frederic pulled Rana toward an iron kettle that steamed above red coals.

"Hey, Macko—better feed those two plucked chickens—we'll get no gold for their bones!" someone cried.

Rana flinched as the man by the cauldron looked up and grinned broadly, revealing stained teeth and a ragged gap where his tongue should have been. He filled an earthenware bowl with corn gruel in which gobbets of fat meat bobbed. The rich aroma surrounded them. Frederic looked down at his bowl as if he did not know what it was, but Rana brought hers clumsily to her lips and drank eagerly, not caring if the stuff ran down her cheeks and chin.

By the time Rana finished the last drop and set the bowl down, life was welling through her bruised body once more. A dark man with a scar that turned up one side of his mouth in a perpetual scowl winked at her and smacked his lips. She looked quickly away and saw amusement in the eyes of a big man whose grey beard spilled over his chest like a waterfall . . . the man who had taken her and Frederic prisoner.

Rana's eyes narrowed. Beside him stood someone smaller, shrouded in dark wool. As the figure turned, gilded mail caught the light of the fire.

"I see you appreciate our hospitality . . ." The voice was as clear as a boy's, with an edge of mockery.

Rana felt Frederic's hand tighten on her arm. The person in the cloak moved towards them, a gold wristguard flashing as the hood was thrown back. It was a young woman. Earth-brown eyes stared into Rana's blue ones from a dark, fine-boned face; ash-gold hair stood out like a cloud around the arrogant head; full lips smiled.

Then the proud gaze moved from her to Frederic. Rana felt him straighten beside her as the woman looked him up and down, and saw her grow still. For a moment there was silence, as if two warriors were measuring each other.

"I am Frederic of Bongarde. I demand speech with your Captain—" Frederic said finally, with the unconscious arrogance of one born to wealth and power.

"I am the Lady Ardra," came the answer, given in exactly the same tone. "I command here."

Chapter Two

Pale sunlight glinted on Ardra's golden wristguard as she turned it back and forth on her brown arm. On the top of the dome of rock that crowned the island, the sea-breeze had cleared the air, but mist still blanketed the waves. There was an illusion of warmth and privacy, here at the top of the only world they could see, with only the murres, flapping awkwardly from their nests on the rocky slopes to the sea and back again, for company. After two days of the Isle of Birds, Frederic had been glad to parley, sure that what he remembered of Ardra from their first brief meeting had been a fancy born of his exhaustion.

But five minutes alone with her had undone him. Frederic's gaze followed the hypnotic flicker of gold gratefully, not wanting to look into her face again. Ardra was honey and amber and crimson fire in the midst of a colorless universe, as if the sun had burned through the clouds just to look at her.

She was his enemy.

The Master of the Junipers would have told him that an adept has no enemies. But had the Master ever looked at skin with a matte sheen like tan velvet and wanted to touch it so badly that he could feel the tingling in his palms? Frederic could have mastered a simple stirring in the flesh, but neither was this the tempered and enduring love that had illuminated his parents' lives. What Frederic was feeling now had no place in his cosmology.

Her lieutenant, Don Esteban Lorca, was watching them from just out of earshot down the hill, though she had a sword while he was unarmed and weakened by three days on poor food in captivity. But if once he touched Ardra, Frederic knew that they would both be in a very different kind of danger. He licked dry lips and thought that perhaps it was his own body that was the enemy.

"I trust that you have been treated well?" Ardra's voice was velvety too, and Frederic shivered. She spoke with the accent of Elaya, but her speech was cultivated, precise.

"I have lived harder and fared worse," he answered with an attempt at pride. "But never in captivity. What of the girl who was captured with me? She is of good family. Has she been treated equally well?" Worry about Rana had been a painful distraction from Frederic's own misery. Elayans made obscene jokes about the freedom Westrian women enjoyed.

Ardra shrugged. "She has been working for her keep, but she is only a child. I have ordered the men not to touch her. . . . The girl may be well-born, but you, my lord, are nearly royal." She eyed him speculatively. "I am sorry for the lack of ceremony attending your arrival.

25

You understand that in war one cannot always observe the amenities."

"I was not aware that we were at war. . . ." he said with conscious steadiness.

"Those who have little are always at war with those who have more," she answered softly, "and my men have no fortune but their swords!"

Frederic's gaze went back to her armlets, good gold, close-fitting as if they had been made for her. The workmanship was exquisite; the royal lions emblazoned on the filigree seemed ready to roar. He had never seen anything like them before, but Silverhair had, on the wrists of the Prince of Elaya. Was Westria's southern neighbor behind these attacks after all? It was hard to believe any Elayan would allow his womenfolk to wage war.

"And what of you?" For the first time his eyes challenged hers. "You do not belong with men like these! What are you fighting for?"

"For freedom!" Her dark eyes flickered away. There was a short silence, then she turned back to him like a riposting swordsman. "But it is not for you to question me! The only question now is how much your father will pay for you!"

He could hear the crash of the waves that rolled endlessly down from the north to batter this lonely piece of rock and, defeated, to claw at the sky with fingers of spray. Frederic's face stiffened. During the past three days that question had occurred to him with painful regularity.

"The wealth of the Lord Commander of Seagate is in well-tilled land and healthy stock, not ready gold," he said carefully.

"And yet you have bankers in your Free Cities—and your father is not only Lord of a Province but Regent of Westria . . . Surely the Kingdom still has a treasury. . . ." There was mockery in Ardra's smile, and Frederic felt his gut clench. For a moment, her beauty had no power over him. He lifted his head defiantly.

"As Eric of Bongarde he will raise what wealth he can to ransom me and the girl who was taken with me—but the Regent of Westria has no right to spend the Kingdom's resources! I would be dishonored if he was false to his trust for me!"

"Ah—honor!" Ardra sat back with a sigh, staring out over the mist-shrouded sea. "For me, that is the greatest of all considerations, but my men may think differently."

"But you are their commander—" he pressed her. "When I arrived here you told me so!" Her profile had a painful beauty against that featureless gray.

"Yes, I am!" she answered with unexpected vehemence. "I *will*—" She broke off abruptly, pressing her hand against her forehead.

"Tell them they will get more by moderation," Frederic went on. "If the demands are too great my father may attack you. He is not a patient man—"

"First he will have to find us . . ." she said abstractedly. "Here we are invulnerable, but we do not tempt fortune." She shut her eyes.

She thought she had intensified her threat, but she could not see Frederic's involuntary relaxation. He knew that in his own inarticulate way his father loved him, but he knew also the strength of the Regent's integrity. Lord Eric would sacrifice his son rather than betray Westria, with Frederic's full agreement. And if his father knew where he was held, that knowledge would inevitably come to Julian. The possibility that Julian would throw away his life in an attempt to rescue him and Rana was something that Frederic *did* fear.

He realized that for some moments Ardra had been silent. He looked back at her and saw that her face was closed, all her awareness intent on some thought, or

27

perhaps some pain, deep within. The wind was suddenly very cold.

"Ardra! What is it? Lady—" he corrected himself, "should I get help? Are you ill?"

"Leave me—" she whispered. "Go away!"

"Back to custody?" Bitterness warred with his anxiety.

"No . . . Give me your parole and you may have the freedom of the island. Tell Lorca. But now, please, you must leave me alone!"

She was shivering, her skin like clay beneath the brown. Frederic trembled with the need to put his arms around her, and soothe the trouble away. But her man was watching him, and she had told him to go.

Frederic rose to his feet and bowed to her. "Lady, you have my pledge—" Then, dizzied by conflicting desires, he picked his way back down the mountainside.

He scarcely thought about the word that he had given her. He was on an island, unarmed, surrounded by enemies. Where, after all, could he go?

Wincing, Rana set the empty garbage basket down in front of the cookshed, straightened up, and wiped sweating palms on the coarse stuff of her gown. It still disturbed her to dump garbage into the sea, but the bruises her protest had earned her were just beginning to heal. After a week as cook's drudge, she thought she would never again complain about the chores her mother gave her. That was, of course, if she ever got home. But it was better not to think of that, better to wall herself off from the reality of this captivity and not think at all.

A step behind her made her turn, but not quite fast enough to escape the stinging blow. Macko grimaced, gobbling deep in his throat, and pointed at the buckets.

"All right! I'll get the water, but can't I rest?" Rana moved quickly as Macko drew back his arm again. For a man without speech, the old Elayan made himself understood very well. Limping, she lifted a bucket in each hand and moved slowly down the path to the shed where a man guarded the casks of water that were perhaps the most precious booty the reivers brought in.

When she returned, two men were sitting on a rock beside the path throwing dice for a skin of wine, ignoring the cormorants who squabbled over each other's nests a few feet away. Their faces were unfamiliar, but she supposed they belonged to the crew of the new ship that had come in the night before. She had stayed huddled in the cookshed when the others went out to welcome them, glad enough to lie out of sight and out of mind for awhile.

"Hey girlie, stop and give a drink to some thirsty men—" One of them, a wiry man with sun-bleached brown hair and a gold ring through one ear, put out a hand and grabbed her gown.

"You already have something to drink!" Rana nodded toward the wineskin. "This is to cook your evening meal." She started to move on, but he was still holding her.

"I'm hungry now. . . ." the man said hoarsely. He winked at his companion, grizzled and scarred and even dirtier, and jerked her towards him. Water splashed and Rana set her buckets down, glancing quickly around her. No one else was in sight. She twitched like a startled horse as a hard hand squeezed her buttocks.

"Let me go! It's the lady's order—I'm not to be harmed!"

"Order? I heard no order!" He grinned. "Besides, we're Zoltan's men!"

His hand slipped suddenly under her skirt and groped up the soft skin of her inner thigh. Rana gasped and twisted, reached for the heavy bucket and heaved, drenching both men with precious water.

Sopping, sputtering, the reiver grabbed her ankle and jerked hard, bringing her down. The fall drove the breath from her body, and before she could move his weight pinned her. A rough hand covered her mouth while the other tore at the neck of her gown. Her fists clenched in his shirt and she tried with all her own wiry strength to thrust him away. He swore, and suddenly another pair of hands closed on her arms and jerked them over her head.

"That's right, you Westrian whore!" her attacker said softly. "Now you'll learn to be nice when a man asks you." He pushed aside the ripped gown and squeezed her breast, then pinched the nipple painfully.

Rana bucked furiously, glaring, but he had gotten his legs between hers and pushed her skirt up; she could feel his sex growing harder as she moved.

"That's right, vixen, fight me—I like my women with a little fire!" His voice had gone hoarse and his eyes glowed. His companion was laughing. Rana stilled. She did not yet believe what was happening to her. It was the constriction that panicked her.

The Elayan's hand left her breast and fumbled at his breeches. As he shifted position his other hand moved on her mouth and she twisted her head and bit hard into the fleshy part of his palm. With an oath he jerked it away, and just as his fist struck Rana's temple, she screamed.

Half stunned, she felt a clumsy battering at the softness between her thighs. She jerked one arm free and clawed. Then running footsteps shook the ground, and the Elayan was heaved off of her. Rana felt her other arm released and lay dazed and gasping. There was shouting, but she could not make out the words.

Someone bent over her. She flinched as her skirts were pulled down and a hand touched her shoulder. Blinking, she recognized Frederic, with Lorca behind him, standing over her attacker with drawn sword.

"Rana—it's over—it's over! You're safe now!"

The rage in Rana's belly exploded. With a convulsive

movement she sat up and her hand closed on one of the stones that had bruised her side. Breath caught on a sob as she scrambled toward the man on the ground and lifted the stone to smash the limp pink thing with which he had assaulted her.

Lorca caught her arm and hauled her to her feet. The stone fell from her hand and rolled down the path.

"Don Esteban, I'm at your mercy, I didn't know!" The Elayan shut up as the tip of Lorca's sword moved toward his throat.

"That's enough, *niña*. Let it end now—"

"Is that an excuse? Geld him!" Rana hiccupped as she tried to get her breath again. "And he did know—I told him about the lady's order. He said he was Zoltan's man!"

Lorca's hand tightened on her arm, then he sighed. "Nevertheless, the lady must judge him."

"Then her judgment had better fall hard!" Rana said venomously. The fury that had filled her was ebbing, and she began to feel her bruises now. She could not tell for certain what damage the man had done her; she was cold and dizzy and she hurt all over. As she swayed, Frederic supported her.

"Don't touch me!" She jerked free. "Don't anyone touch me. I have to wash his filthiness off of me. Leave me alone!" Rana felt them watching her as she picked up the other bucket and stumbled down the path. Lorca had the frown of a badly worried man, but it seemed to her that she saw shame in Frederic's eyes.

Ardra hanged the man who had assaulted Rana and flogged the one who had helped him. She also gave Rana a long dagger. After that, even Macko treated her more respectfully. It made for bad blood in the encampment, though, and the crews of the different ships snarled as

31

venemously as the battling birds. Rana wondered how the Elayan woman had retained her authority over them so far, and how long it could last.

Ardra sent off most of her men. Whether her purpose was to ease the strain on the island's limited resources or for further raiding was unclear. Only her crew and Zoltan's remained. Rana found it difficult to care. Since the assault she had been numb to all emotion. There had been no sense of triumph even when she saw her attacker dangling above the sea, and her thoughts were as gray as the perpetual fog.

Then came a morning when the mist grew luminous, and fitful gleams of sunlight sparkled from the waves, and Rana felt her depression lifting. Breakfast was over and all the cooking things put away when Ardra came down the path with Frederic and Don Esteban a little behind her.

"Look, the fog is thinning—we may even see the sun today!" Ardra spoke with an unaccustomed gaiety. "Come fishing with us and see what my men can do!" She was looking at Frederic. His face brightened and then grew troubled again.

"I would be glad to get off of this rock, but what if the answer from my father comes while we are gone?"

For a moment Ardra's eyes grew vague. "They will not come. The fog still blankets the coastline."

Lorca nodded. "It will be hours before the Gate is free, and longer before anything comes through it, if indeed the answer comes today!"

"If that is so, then I thank you." Frederic relaxed and smiled. Rana frowned, wishing she knew if that were true. How easily Frederic accepted the Lady's word!

"You come too, and you also, Macko—" Ardra seemed to focus on Rana for the first time. "It will be a holiday for us all!"

The island glimmered behind them as the two lean

ships pulled away, the weathered white-streaked beige of the rocks turning to palest gold as the sun broke through the clouds. The elephant seals and sea lions that lived at the sea's edge barked as if rejoicing that the humans had gone. Sulking in the cookshed, Rana had not realized there was more life on the island than the ubiquitous screaming birds.

From the second boat they could hear Zoltan's sardonic laughter. With the other sharkships gone, the island looked abandoned. The driftwood huts could have been there forever, and a high wind some nights earlier had blown Ardra's bright pavilion down. But when the weirdly humped shapes of the islands had faded to shadows in the mists behind them Rana was glad to forget them for awhile. Where the sun shone the turbid gray of the waves glowed like liquid tourmaline, deepening to a vibrant blue as they moved farther out to sea.

Ardra stood in the bow, balancing easily as the boat breasted the waves. She had put on a sleeveless white tunic in the Elayan style, overlapping and embroidered down the front in red, above loose, knee-length trousers of maroon. A crimson scarf was tied over her hair. The mast had been stepped and the square scarlet sail unfurled. Now it swelled proudly behind her.

"Ah, now our lady is herself again . . ." said one of the men, working an anchovy onto his hook and tossing it over the side. "Like she was at Serpent's Bay, when a good ship was all she wanted mastery of." His hair was dressed in little braids all over his head, bound with copper wire.

"This is well enough for sport," said his mate, "but I've no mind for the life of a fisherman!" He laughed deeply.

The first man nodded. "Aye, but I still say we'd be better off without that crew of sea-vultures—" He jerked his head toward Zoltan's ship.

33

"Maybe, but admit they have a nose for the women and the gold!" His eyes slid towards Rana—who felt suddenly ill—then met Frederic's cold gray gaze. He laughed again, but after that the two men kept their voices low.

"Well, this is better than the last boat ride we went on—" Frederic said with self-conscious cheerfulness. He was a little pale, but so far he had not been sick again.

"Be still, Frederic." Rana turned away. If she ignored them, perhaps awareness of what had happened on the island could be washed away by the clean beauty of the sea. The sharkship slipped through the water as easily as any sea-creature, its flexible hull responding to the rhythm of the waves. Gulls and skuas circled screaming above them, and once Rana saw the fountain of breath and a luminous flare of aquamarine just below the surface as a blue whale spouted and dove.

Frederic had given up trying to talk to her. When she looked for him again he was helping Ardra to brace a pole. The line slackened suddenly and they fell in a tangle of limbs. For a moment both were very still; then Frederic pulled abruptly away. Ardra's laughter echoed across the water, and Zoltan glared.

Frederic grabbed the pole, which was making its own way over the side, and hung on as the line sang like a bowstring. Better braced this time, he and Ardra played the big fish until it tired and was pulled glittering into the ship. With a merciful blow Frederic quieted its flopping and held it up.

"A beauty, my lord Frederic—full four feet long. Silver salmon are rarely found in the waters of my home." Ardra smiled.

"Your home?"

"The bay below the Serpent's Head south of Santibar, in the Campos del Mar where I was born."

There was a cheer as one of the seamen hauled a ling cod over the side. Several of the men had bites now, and soon the bottom of the boat glistened with wriggling proofs of their skill. By the time they had caught as many fish as their baskets would hold, the sun was high.

"Well, my lord, what would you now?" Ardra's smile was enchantment, and Frederic's eyes lit in response.

"We are at your command, lady. Do what you will." The trouble had left Frederic's face finally, and Rana felt shame at resenting his brief happiness.

For a moment Ardra looked at him speculatively. Then she turned to her men. "Well, lads, are you tired out by all that fishing? Or do you have enough strength to show these northerners what the men of Serpent's Bay can do?"

They grinned and cheered her, and those in Zoltan's boat turned to see what was going on.

"For all their boasting, I think yonder sharks less strong than they say. Shall we challenge them to a rowing match? I've a bag of gold for the boat that wins!" she added as they cheered.

"Aye, my lady—we will row for you until our arms drop off—no mercenary can outdo true men!" Lorca laughed.

Ardra's grin was reflected in two dozen bearded faces as she cupped her hands to challenge the other boat. Zoltan's reply was short, and his men made no sound. In a moment both crews were lowering their masts and unshipping their oars. The mallets began their ominous beat.

"The wind is free, and so are we—
We go where we will on the open sea!
To safely stay is a landsman's way—"
Lorca sang, beating out time from the stern.

"We follow the life of a rover!" chorused the men,

35

muscles rippling beneath skins tanned every shade of bronze and brown. Urged on by Ardra's cries, they beat Zoltan's boat to the floating log that was their goal, startling a basking otter who dove for safety like an old man disturbed from his nap. Everyone laughed, and the steersman brought the galley around.

Rana sat back and unclenched her hands from the rail, realizing only then how much she had wanted Ardra to win. She could see Zoltan quite clearly now, and the look in his eyes reminded her of the man who had tried to rape her. *"Like master like man,"* she thought then. But he accepted Ardra's authority. Rana wondered why.

"I've a challenge for you now, my commander," called Zoltan as his boat slid alongside. "Something a little more useful than simple speed."

Ardra leaned over the side to hear him. Her kerchief had come off during the race, and her hair was like a golden cloud. "What do you suggest?"

"War games, Alteza. In a seafight, the victory goes oftener to those who can maneuver than to those who run. Let the next prize go to the boat that can best contrive to sheer oars and board. We shall, of course, turn away at the last moment lest we cripple you!" His teeth flashed in his black beard.

"Never mind about that," snapped Ardra. "The victor can pick up anyone who gets ducked. I hope you do not mind being crowded on our way home . . ." she added to her own men. They laughed, then sobered as her face grew intent. Zoltan was already turning to align his vessel with the waves. "Steady now, *compadres*—we shall have to work this time. . . ."

Slowly the two boats slid over the water, careful orders moving them sometimes only a few feet at a time. Ardra seemed to be trying to force Zoltan to face the sun. They could not guess Zoltan's plans. Ardra had forgotten

Frederic, forgotten all of them now. Her unhesitating orders were instantly obeyed and the boat moved beneath them like a live thing.

"I hope we are not the ones who sink—" Frederic touched Rana's shoulder. "Look there!"

Rana's skin prickled. Dark triangles, sickle-edged, sliced through the waves a few yards away, and she sensed, rather than saw, powerful bodies arrowing beneath them. They stared as the movement of the dark fins reflected the motions of the two galleys. They were picking up speed.

There was a *whfft*! close by, and a small jet of spray. A short-beaked dark gray head broke the water and disappeared. In a moment another did the same. Rana's tension dissolved in laughter.

"Dolphins!" she breathed, and their sparkling eyes seemed to laugh back at her.

As the ships closed, the dolphins leaped across their bows and sped beneath them again, white bellies and the pale side-patches flashing in the sun. Rana's attention was torn between the human contest and the dolphins' dance.

"Can she do it?" Frederic's whisper was anguished. "Zoltan is so fast!"

Ardra directed her men in a level voice, matching Zoltan's moves. The ship rocked as they swiveled, picking up speed. The dolphins grew bolder. Smooth backs slid neatly beneath the oars. One of the dolphins belly-flopped full in their path, drenching everyone with spray.

Ardra swore and dashed water from her eyes. "Hard to port!" she cried as the dark shape of the other galley swept down on them. Rana grabbed for the rail.

The whole craft shuddered and there was a rending screech as Zoltan's prow gouged the side. The air crackled with the sound of breaking oars. The other ship slid close by them. Browned hands reached for their rail, and metal flashed as a gray body rose into the air close by.

Rana's cry was lost in Zoltan's laughter as his harpoon drove through the dolphin behind the right flipper where the dark skin of its back turned pale.

"Well thrust!" cried Ardra. She lifted her own harpoon.

"No!" Frederic struggled forward, and she turned. The wounded dolphin was writhing on the surface in a crimson cloud, its blow hole filled with pink froth, while its companions held it up to breathe. But before the echoes of Frederic's protest had faded, the dolphin arched in a last convulsion and was still. Without a ripple, the others disappeared.

For a few moments the only sound was the slap of waves against the hull. The dolphin floated aimlessly beside them, its blood already dissipating into the sea. One of the men stretched out an oar to pull it in.

"No. . . . " Frederic spoke again, and Ardra's eyes met his. Then she glanced up at the westering sun. Slowly the animation left her face.

"Leave the carrion be—we will have enough to do to get ourselves home. You have won fairly, Captain Zoltan." Her voice was oddly flat.

The wind was against them for using sail. There was little talk as the oars were redistributed and they started back, Zoltan's galley keeping pace alongside. To Rana, who was trying to keep from being sick, it did not seem long before their island prison was in sight once more. By now the sea mist had lifted entirely, and the whole Seagate coast from Kings' Point to Whale Head shone in sunlit majesty. She could even see the dark tip of the Red Mountain beyond the coastal hills. Then she felt Frederic stiffen beside her.

"No—holy Guardians, no!" His whisper sent a premonitory thrill through Rana even as she turned to follow his stare. Eastward, sails glowed golden in the setting sun, bright against the dark cliffs that warded the Gateway. Even at this distance, Rana recognized the silhouette of *Waverider*.

She tensed to rise, then slowly subsided onto her bench again. Low in the water, with no sail set, they themselves could not be seen, and no shout would carry so far. They watched in silence as *Waverider* tacked and tacked again, straight for the Gateway. And Rana was abruptly certain that she had already been out to the Far Alone islands, perhaps had sent a boat ashore to discover the camp abandoned. And beyond all those other certainties, Rana was sure that one of those on the Regent's great-ship was Julian.

She looked over at Frederic, and saw that he was staring not at the vanishing Westrian ship, but at Ardra, and his face held despair.

Rana forced herself to take another bite of stew. Frederic's untouched bowl sat before him. Unwillingly she looked across the fire to Ardra.

There was no emotion in the Lady's face, but her bowl was as full as Frederic's, and the tension between them was almost visible. The atmosphere would have been unpleasant in any case. A ship had come in just after they did, and one man had knifed another over the division of the spoils. Now his body dangled over one of the cliffs that edged the cove, at rest neither in earth nor air nor sea, and Rana was reminded sickeningly of the way her attacker had died. Their captain sat alone away from the fire, nursing his disgrace with his wine.

One of Zoltan's men strode into the circle and knelt by his captain, whispering. Zoltan rose, bowed to Ardra, and started off, and after a moment Lorca excused

39

himself and followed. Frederic moved, but before Rana could speak to him he had started toward the empty place. Rana's bowl clicked loudly against a stone as she set it down.

She had seen a parody of this arrogance on Frederic's face when he played the great lord to fool the town guard in Santibar. But this was the reality. Frederic stopped before Ardra, drawing himself up to his full height. He tipped back his head and said something in a low voice. His hair gleamed gold in the light of the fire.

"Why should I answer you?" Ardra sounded a trifle bored, but her reply came clearly.

"Do you deny that you expected my people to come out this afternoon?" Either Frederic had forgotten they had an audience, or he did not care.

"Why should I deny anything? You have already decided what to believe."

"Because . . ." He spoke more softly. "Because you led me to believe myself not a prisoner, but a guest here." He moved a little and Rana saw Ardra's face, all shine and shadow like a gilded mask. She shrugged.

"Whatever I knew or did not know, they are gone now. Would you rather they had found us and battled here?"

"They came to negotiate, Ardra!" he exclaimed.

She shrugged again. "So you say—"

"You will have to deal with them sometime, unless you mean to keep me here lifelong! Send a message to my father, telling him to return."

"I would not hazard my men on such an errand."

"Then set me and the girl ashore." Question and answer came quickly now.

"I might forego the ransom, my lord, but I have promised my men this spoil."

"I will have the ransom sent to you, of course."

"I do not doubt *your* honor, but will your father be bound by your word?"

40

Rana drew in her breath as Frederic stiffened. What had possessed the woman to say that, to him?

"My father's honor is as my own, and mine is his!" Frederic snapped. "Would *your* father do differently?"

There was an angry murmur from the men, but Ardra's face had gone chalky and she was on her feet now. "Take care, *prisoner*, take care! I swore that you should come to no harm and that is all I swore. Mark me, as you prate of honor—I have kept to the letter of my bond. But beware of making me forget that honor which you doubt I have! And speak no more of my father, you, whose sire warms a throne he has not the courage to claim . . ." Her voice deepened and the words thundered out. "Until you know my father, speak no more of him!" She drew breath, then spat, "Now get you from my sight!"

Zoltan, returning to the circle around the fire, halted, and began to grin.

"Willingly," said Frederic coldly. "It should not be difficult to find more worthy company . . ." His words were cut short by Ardra's shriek.

"Zoltan! Take this proud gentleman where he need suffer no one's company—the stone hut, and bar and guard the door." She shot a last look at Frederic. "We shall see how bold you speak after some time alone in the dark!"

Before she had finished speaking, Zoltan motioned to one of his men and they seized Frederic. He began to struggle when he understood her meaning, but they had him fast. Still fighting, he was marched away from the fire. Rana heard the door of the hut slam shut and the heavy bar fall.

No one dared speak while the fury faded from Ardra's eyes. Her face grew grayer and she swayed, looked anxiously around her, then stumbled toward her pavilion.

"Another of the lady's spells—" said one of her men. "We'll have to watch out when she comes to herself again!"

"Quiet!" said his companion. "You know what the orders are—"

Rana reached for her bowl, trying to pretend she had not heard. But her other hand went to the hilt of her knife as she realized that, even as her fellow prisoner, Frederic had protected her. And her heartbeat pounded out the question again and again—*How are we going to get out of here?*

Frederic sat cross-legged on the bare dirt floor, his hands open upon his knees. This prison was dark and cold, but for the moment, he was almost happy to be here. While he was here, he couldn't see her—couldn't listen to that velvet voice, need not resist the urge to touch that smooth skin. What called to him was only another human body, a form of flesh like his own. Without the spirit, its beauty meant nothing, and he knew now that Ardra's ardent spirit was a snare.

How could she have deceived him? Had she even asked for ransom? And if not, what did she want with him? He steadied his breathing, seeking the awareness that lies beyond words, but his thoughts chased each other round and round again.

Only a form of flesh—and yet the poise of Ardra's elegant head and the lift of her arm held a truth beyond physical reality. She had misled him, played with him; she lived a lie. But the beauty that shone through her like sunlight was real. When they had fallen together in the boat their flesh had touched with a sweet certainty. And Frederic knew with a sick despair that for him no other woman would ever be so bright a vessel of divinity.

Breathe in . . . and out . . . and in . . . and out

again. . . . He was falling back on his earliest training now.

Ardra was false, but her beauty was true. He must worship that beauty even if she betrayed it, and him. That thought brought a measure of peace to his tormented spirit. He wanted to be a Master; an adept loved all things while depending on none. He could love Ardra—he must love her—as the true Master loved the brilliance of the lightning even as it struck him down.

Again Frederic controlled his breathing, and felt the barriers that held consciousness prisoner ease at last. The darkness around him had brightened to a featureless radiance like a silver sea. But forms swam within that brilliance; he floated among them, for the moment at peace.

Then the silver shattered into opalescent rainbows that arched downward into darkness. But standing at the head of that shimmering bridge was a bright figure of triumphant masculinity, carrying a great horn.

"Strong One, help me!" Frederic cried.

"I am as close to you as your dreams—"

A gesture of the glowing hand brought Frederic toward Him. Then He lifted the horn to His lips. The deep vibration echoed through every particle of Frederic's being, and for a time he knew no more.

Chapter Three

The fickle winds of spring shifted from southeast to northwest and back again. Days of fog were succeeded by crystal mornings ·when the distant coast of Westria glowed with heartrending clarity. On those days, Rana explored the southern and western flanks of the Isle of Birds, keeping the doomed peak between her and that inaccessible beauty. Westward, other islands studded the sea. When the weather was clear, she saw them as hard spires of rock wreathed in birds, but when the mists descended, they glimmered as if some enchantment were dissolving their substance away.

Rana learned to pick her way among the nests of the combative cormorants, and to avoid slopes where an unwary step could crush the burrow which some hapless auklet or petrel had made to protect its nest from the gulls. These past weeks she had come to hate the gulls—agile, aggressive, and as voracious as the human reivers who were her captors. Sometimes she found herself waving her arms at them and screeching with a fury she did not dare show to men.

The clamor of nesting changed in tone, though not in volume, as the chicks pecked free of their shells. After dark, the auklets and other nightbirds took advantage of the gulls' sleep to deafen the island with their cacophony. After a time Rana no longer noticed the noise, just as she had become inured to the smell. Since Beltane Eve she had become hardened to many things.

Ardra's favor gave her some protection from Macko's ill-treatment, and dirt and the fishy sacking in which she wrapped herself decreased her attractiveness to the men. She grew lean, but stronger, and when her work was finished she was free to wander—if freedom had any meaning on a barren piece of rock hardly a half-mile long, even when surrounded by the limitless freedom of sky and sea. Frederic was still confined by Ardra's wrath, but she did not miss him. He had saved her from complete violation, but he was still a man.

Days became weeks. The golden flowers of the tar-weed faded, and the gray-green foliage dried to match the rock to which it clung. Venus brightened and extended her reign over the evening sky. But as the season advanced, the fair weather out to sea stabilized, and the winds settled to a steady flow from the northwest, following the current that swept ever southward and away. Warm, moist air moving across the Sea of Peace was chilled by the cold current and condensed into a fog-bank that blanketed the islands with perpetual mist even as it ebbed and flowed through the gaps in the coastal hills. Now the cliffs of Westria were hidden, and Rana extended her explorations all the way around the island.

But though the land grew barren, the sea teemed with unsuspected vitality. The constant current drew chill, nutrient-rich water from the depths where the continental shelf ended, and the multitudes Rana could see bore witness to the abundance beneath the waves. The bulbous-nosed sea elephants swayed and sparred while their cows lay in obese abandon around them, and sea lions lolloped across the slippery rocks of the shore.

But what Rana liked best was to climb the rocky points where the waves cast coverlets of lace across the shelving stone, and to gaze at the constantly changing gray plains of the sea. The waves knew neither past nor future, only a restless shifting of form. From them she learned to live in a state of emotionless acceptance in which she felt neither hope nor fear. The days passed like the waves that washed the rocky shore. But each dawn was earlier, and each evening the sun set further to the north as the great solar tides drew the planet herself inexorably toward Midsummer Day. And it was on a silver morning a week before the Solstice that everything changed.

Rana had gone down to dig for shellfish in the tiny cove where the reivers landed. The barnacles were poisonous at this time of year, but she thought the sand might be deep enough for clams. Not that it really mattered if she found anything, she thought as the chill water frothed about her legs and washed the dirt of the island away. Her skin stung with the cold, but the touch of the water was clean, and the keen air made the blood tingle through her veins.

For a moment Rana exulted in the sensations and forgot how she had come there. Then a shout from the sea brought her around, heart pounding. One of the shark ships was returning from a foray; heavy with plunder, she wallowed in the waves as the helmsman headed her in. They had not seen Rana yet, but they would in a moment. By the time she could reach the path above the cove they would have landed.

Perhaps because for a moment she had been almost

happy, Rana could not face them. But it might just be possible to reach the sea-cave at the western point of the cove. She scrambled over the rocks, and as she reached it she heard the sharkship's belly scrape sand behind her. Breathing harshly, she settled down against the rocks. She might have a long, cold wait, but she felt as if she had scored a victory.

Wind and water had worked on the rock's natural fissuring to create an angular tall cavern. Waves crashed on the rocks outside, but even the minimal protection of these walls had created a stillness stirred only by the regular flow of the tide. Rana blinked as featureless shadow resolved suddenly into a richly-textured arch of lichened stone. The sun was burning through the mists, and the air darkened and brightened again. She looked down, and saw color flare from the pool.

Pale sunlight struck the water like an adept's wand, touching it with translucent aquamarine above the white sand. Rana knelt carefully, marveling. She had learned to appreciate the island's grim beauty, but this was something other, an enchanted garden that could perhaps exist only in this place that was neither wholly of the land nor of the sea.

The pastel fronds of sea anemones waved in an invisible breeze. Masses of garnet seaweed with grape-clusters of bulbs mingled with a lettuce-like emerald weed. The walls were studded with starfish, not only the simple stars she knew, but a multi-armed creature like a sunflower, and another that radiated lacy white branches. Hermit crabs toiled over the irregularities of the floor, and red-and-white-striped prawns and tiny rockfish darted among the rocks like animate jewels.

Rana held her breath lest she trouble the serenity of that water. This miracle had been here all the time, and she had not known! In her wonder, fear and fury were both forgotten, and love and longing, captivity and home. There was only beauty. The sea roared in her ears. The shimmer of light on water was one with the blaze that dazzled inner sight as for an endless moment she understood the Glory at the heart of things.

Then abused lungs gulped air. Rana's vision cleared, and she blinked at a radiance that glowed through the water, reflecting the sunlight like a miniature moon. Surely that was more than a trick of refraction! Bracing herself on a rock, Rana reached in.

The anemones flinched and drew in their fronds as her hand brushed by, and tiny fish flickered away in panicked flight. Then her fingers closed on something smooth and hard. Carefully Rana eased back and opened her fingers to see what she had found.

The world's sounds faded to a silence in which she could hear the blood rushing through her veins and the sea's pulse throbbing in rhythm with her own. Outside the cavern a wave rose like a wall of sapphire glass.

Slim figures within it beckoned; eyes sparkled; pale hair foamed. They rose until it seemed as if they would burst into the air, then swept down with a fluid undulation. Their eyes met Rana's, and they laughed. She heard that laughter, heard them calling, stood and took one step toward the wild sea.

Then the great wave fell. A cascade of cold water knocked Rana back into the rocks as it replenished the pool. She struggled upright, gasping. Her arm had been grazed when she fell, but the thing that she had found was still clutched in her left hand.

Rana looked at it again.

A clear stone lay in her palm, colorless as water. It was about two inches in diameter and perfectly round, and for an instant she thought it a water-polished piece of glass. Then another shiver shook her hand, and the jewel gathered light and gave it back in a blaze of blue luminescence as if another moon had kindled in her palm. Rana felt the rushing of an inner tide; once more the sweet sea voices called. She gasped and opened her hand.

Metal clinked on rock. Blinking, Rana realized that the jewel was framed by two silver dolphins, joined head to tail. On its back were fittings for a buckle. Where had she heard of such a thing? Momentarily she closed her eyes. Like an echo, the voice of the Master of the Junipers came to her, telling the tale of the four Jewels of Westria.

Rana's eyes flew open and she stared down at the thing she had found. How could she not have known? She felt a moment of vertigo, an undertow of the spirit that carried her from the safe shores of her old assumptions into uncharted seas. Even this momentary contact with the elemental world had jarred her faith in ordinary human perceptions. She could not guess what would happen if she touched it again.

As she must, if she was to bring it to Julian.

And that realization suggested another pattern that was in its way even more disturbing—for if a brutal captivity had not forced her to take refuge here, how could the Sea Star have been found by someone who could recognize it and who would deliver it to its rightful lord? After Julian had found the Earthstone they had all known that he must gain possession of the other three Jewels of Westria, but even the Master of the Junipers had not been able to tell him how. Was some other power at work here—some power that had made Rana its instrument with no consideration for either her sufferings or her will?

That thought was worse than the other. Rana gazed down at the shimmering splendor of the Sea Star, wondering what would happen if she chose to claim it. *I won't be a puppet, even for the Guardians! I do have the choice*, she thought desperately. *I do*!

But whether or not she was free to choose her path, Rana knew that she was not ready to make a decision now. Frederic had given Julian a piece of silk with which to insulate the power of the Earthstone so that he could carry it. Beneath her rough wool tunic she still wore the remnants of her silken Festival gown. Shivering with reaction, she cut off a portion large enough to wrap the Jewel, tied it with the lacing from her tunic, and hung it around her neck. She could still feel a muted throb of power from the stone, as even above the clamor of the birds on the island one was always aware of the regular pounding of the sea. But she could bear it. Now she could think again.

The reivers had finished unloading, and the cove was empty of men. The sharkship had been set next to the others in a rough cradle of stone, but a smaller craft was still drawn up on the sand. That was new, and Rana stopped a moment to look at it. It was little more than a rowboat, but it had a short mast and a sail. One or two people could handle a craft like that. The skin along her forearms prickled with possibility. Then she took a deep breath, picked up her empty bucket, and began to climb the path.

As she came over the ridge and headed down toward the camp, Rana met Lorca. The big man's face cleared as he saw her, and he paused.

"I was hoping I would find you—"

Safe, and alone . . . Rana understood with gratitude the other words he did not say. Ever since Zoltan's men had attacked her, Don Esteban had done his best to watch over her, as if Ardra's protection had also transferred some of his loyalty. She smiled at him now with wordless complicity.

"I was looking for clams, but the tide was in. Is something wrong?"

"Quite the contrary!" Lorca grinned. "My lady's come out of her sulks at last. She's planning a feast for Midsummer, and she has released your friend Frederic!"

Rana's eyes widened. She had not been surprised to find her own apathy banished by finding the Jewel. Even in the short time it had taken to return from the cove she had found her back straightening, her step becoming more purposeful. The power that throbbed at her breast had changed everything, and she would have to take care to conceal the transformation.

Had the unveiling of that power caused other changes? Rana had the abrupt sensation that when she plucked the Sea Star from its sandy bed she had unplugged a dam that held the sea at bay. But now the waters were trickling through the gap. She wondered how long it would take for that power to sweep all barriers away. . . .

"You say she's let Sir Frederic go?" Rana forced her attention back to Lorca. "Where is he now?"

Lorca waved upward. "On the peak. After three weeks in a hut, he wants to drink in the clean wind, and maybe he can get above the bird-stench there!" He heaved a sigh and eased down on a boulder, ignoring the indignant squawking of the murres. "It's not a bad idea, but a sailor's legs were never meant for such scrambling. I think I'll just rest here until my lady needs me again!"

Again an unspoken message passed between them. With Lorca on guard, no one would follow her. He understood that the two captives would need the comfort of each other's company. It was a courtesy made possible only by his assurance that there was no escape from here, and for a moment his confidence in that assumption chilled the fragile hope that had just been born. But Lorca did not know about the Sea Star!

As Rana mounted the path she clutched the knowledge to her as she held the Jewel against her breast.

Frederic was sitting on the rough bench the lookouts used, as still as the rocks behind him. Rana stopped short, for his face held the same disciplined peace she had seen in the Master of the Junipers' eyes, and she had the sudden superstitious fear that she might be interrupting a prayer. She made no sound, but after a moment he turned, and his eyes lost that inward focus that had frightened her.

"Rana—" Frederic's voice creaked. His hair was lank and lightless; his clothing soiled.

"Are you all right? You look like something that's been under a stone!" she said accusingly, joining him.

Frederic shrugged his shoulders. "I have been . . . but everything considered, I am well."

Rana looked at him curiously, seeing the strong sculpturing of the bone beneath the pale skin. Strangely, he looked more like *himself* than he had before.

"I can see that you are—" she said abruptly. "How did you survive? I would have lost my wits in such a hole!"

Frederic gave a faint smile. "The lady did me a favor, though you need not tell her so. I had time to remember the path I follow. She . . . had almost led me away from it for a little while."

"But what did you do?"

"I meditated, as the Master of the Junipers has taught me to do."

"And what help did that bring?" Rana could not quite keep bitterness from her tone.

"For myself I found comfort," he shrugged apologetically. "But I could not reach the Master. It's as if this island were surrounded by a psychic fog. Then I tried to touch the minds of those here. Some of them I could recognize—you, and Lorca, and Zoltan . . . Ardra . . . But there were two strange things. Once, when I sought

Ardra, I found another mind instead, which thrust me back with such force it was hours before I could think again. . . ."

"And what was the other thing?" Rana asked at last.

"Why, this morning, just before they let me go, I felt a blast of power as if the sea had risen to sweep us all away. And yet everything here seems just the same."

Slowly, Rana smiled. "I can read you that riddle. . . ." She looked around her, but the only movement was the fluttering of an auklet as it rowed air frantically to get aloft. With nervous fingers she pulled the clumsy package from beneath her tunic and unwrapped it. There was a flash of light. Instantly, Frederic covered it with his hand and thrust it back at her.

"Wrap it up again! Keep it hid! It's the Sea Star, isn't it? That must be what I felt before!"

Rana nodded. Of course, Frederic had been with Julian when he found the Earthstone. He would recognize the Jewels' particular brand of power.

"But how did you get it?" he added when his breathing had steadied again.

Rana was surprised at the relief she felt in sharing her burden, though she had carried the stone for less than an hour. "And so we have another reason for wanting to escape, now—" she finished, looking at him with a hope she could not deny.

Frederic laughed bitterly. "If only I could! The Sea Star, here!" he exclaimed again. "I will have to think. . . ."

"While you're thinking, can you tell me why this stone is set in a buckle? I would have expected a pendant, somehow."

"It's so the King could wear all the Jewels together," Frederic answered absently, "though he would rarely do so, except on his coronation day."

"Then even if the Council had confirmed Julian in the kingship he could not have been crowned!"

"No, but that's not what matters. The Council's approval would unite the Kingdom behind him—without that it's going to be hard for Julian to deal with the sorcerer. If Caolin were out of the picture, he could take his time about retrieving the rest of the Jewels. . . ."

"But the Blood Lord still lives. Without the Jewels, how can Julian defeat him?" Rana asked softly. Her notions of possessing the Jewel faded like mist before the sun. The Sea Star was not for her! Shuddering, she yanked the thong over her head and held the little bundle out to Frederic.

"You take it! I don't know anything about magic. Can't *you* use the Jewel to get us out of this somehow?"

Frederic jerked away as if she held a serpent in her hand. "No! It does not belong to me! That was how Caolin fell, didn't you know? He wanted what belonged to the King! And it might well be too strong for me!"

"Could it kill you?"

"Maybe—but it's not death I fear." He stopped speaking, but then, as Rana continued to stare at him, continued reluctantly.

"A talisman like the Sea Star is a great temptation to a student of the mysteries, even to one who, like Caolin, has been cast out of the school. I don't know if I could resist the desire to try and use it, if I had it in my hands. Caolin couldn't. He put on all four of them, which tells us that even then he had more power than anyone knew. But the Jewels nearly destroyed him, and when he tore them off, they were whirled away out of the knowledge of men."

"Until now—" said Rana. She remembered how the stone had tempted her in the sea-cave. Was he right? And if he was not, what was she going to do?

"Until now," Frederic agreed. "But now the time for all the Jewels to be found seems to have come, and the only question is, by whom?"

Ardra's pavilion was like something a Lord Commander might go campaigning in. Rana brushed her fingers across its golden fringe as Ardra led her inside and wondered, *What does she want with me?*

In the past week, the Elayan commander's mood had shifted between elation and anxiety, and her preparations for the Midsummer feast had involved everyone in furious activity. The men were as excited as children. If Rana had not remembered too well how they behaved in other moods it would have amused her. As it was, she had been too preoccupied with the Sea Star to care. Until now, when the lady had singled her out for the first time since her would-be rapist had been hanged.

The commander motioned to her toward one of the embroidered cushions. The interior of the tent was a study in contrasts: a hard chair was drawn up to a table ornately carved and inlaid with bits of shell; the plain bedroll was spread below a tapestry of a lion hunt, worked with threads whose gold had tarnished in the sea air; a variety of weapons, including Frederic's sword, were suspended from the crossbars by tasselled silken cords. Books and rolled maps lay on a small brass-bound chest by the bed, and a larger chest stood against the opposite wall.

Ardra offered Rana a silver dish of green jellied globules dusted with sugar. The girl bit into one dubiously, and looked up in surprise as tart sweetness exploded through her tastebuds. Bearing the Sea Star had made her more sensitive to all the messages of the senses. After weeks of Macko's cooking, the shock was almost overwhelming.

"They're good!" she said inadequately. "I've never tasted this kind before."

The Lady smiled, then crossed to the larger chest. She fumbled with the hasps, then with a swift jerk lifted the lid. A mass of color blazed from inside.

"Midsummer Eve is a great Festival in the south—is it so with you?" Ardra asked. "It seemed to me that you would find more joy in our celebration if you had something pretty to wear. And here I have all kinds of clothes—" Ardra hurried on, "and so I have brought you here to choose."

Rana wiped sticky hands on her tunic and stepped toward the chest, eyes widening as she took in the profusion of silk and brocade. She had not expected Ardra to have so many things. She began to lift out garments, recognized a man's surcoat, a child's gown. . . . Suddenly Rana realized from where these things had come. She dropped them, and glared at Ardra accusingly.

"Yes, I know—" said the Lady, almost apologetically. "But the garments are here now. Why not make use of them? Surely you like beautiful things?"

Rana glanced around her. "I think we both do."

A little unexpected color warmed the matte tan of Ardra's skin. She held out a dress of emerald silk embroidered with golden flowers. Rana held it against her and shook her head as the skirt pooled on the floor.

"It's too long for me—could you wear it? Green and gold would suit you—"

There was another silence, and Rana realized that Ardra was as unused to this kind of conversation as she was. She turned back to the chest and pulled out a man's tunic of fine indigo wool.

"This might fit Frederic," she said neutrally.

"Yes—I am afraid his fine garments have suffered

56

here. He looked like a Prince when he arrived, but he says that he is not?" Ardra's voice sounded strained.

This is important to her, thought Rana. *But why?*

She answered aloud. "His father has been Regent, it's true, but Prince Julian will soon become King."

"I have heard about that. . . . But why should they choose this Julian? Surely the lord Frederic is better prepared for such a high position?"

"I don't think he would accept the throne if they offered it," answered Rana. "Not only is Julian the true son of the last King, but Frederic doesn't even want to be Lord of the Province of Seagate, much less of the Kingdom of Westria. He has renounced his heritage in favor of his brother so that he can become a Master of the College of the Wise. The kingdom he seeks is of the spirit alone." In Ardra's face she saw a mixture of confusion and disbelief.

"You speak as if you know the lord Frederic well," said the lady. "And yet I think you are not kin?"

"He might as well be—" Rana laughed. "The children in our families played like puppies when we were growing up, and I travelled with him for several months last year—" Briefly, without giving away its purpose, she described the journey she had made in search of the Earthstone with Julian and Silverhair, old Eva and her grandson, and the tree-woman, Lady Madrone.

"Do the people of Westria let their daughters go about so freely then?"

Rana flushed, for she had not had permission to go, and countered with another question. "Is it different in Elaya, then? Surely *you* are free!"

Ardra's smile held a touch of bitterness. "Only because I stand in my brother's shoes. He died when I was a child, and I was the only other heir, so I have been raised like a boy. And I cannot be sorry for it—the women in my country live through their men, whispering in their ears, manipulating them from behind their veils, and the men never know that they are being led! I have no women friends."

Rana sat still, thinking, *Neither do I! I have never wanted to make a friend of another girl, and I have far less reason to dislike my own sex than she has. . . .* Only since those reivers had attacked her, she, could not love men either. *There's no help for it! I'll have to become a hermit somewhere!* Maybe she could get a one-man fishing craft and spend her life in the clean expanses of the sea, she thought wryly, but first she had to get away from here!

She glanced up, but Ardra was staring at the tent wall, her face like a mask. Rana turned quickly back to the chest, ashamed of having seen. She must find a gown and be done with this. There—a glimpse of purple silk—she burrowed for it and touched the hard leather of a medicine case. A quick glance showed her bottles labeled as infusion of willow-bark and tincture of poppy. Swiftly she rolled them into the purple gown and bundled it up with the blue tunic she had suggested for Frederic. Then she turned again to Ardra.

"I thank you, my Lady," she faltered. "Sir Frederic and I will try to do you credit at the feasting."

Ardra looked surprised to find her still there, and forced a smile. "That is well then—farewell."

Rana bowed awkwardly, and clutching her treasures to her breast, slipped out of the pavilion. And when she would have looked back, she forced her mind to the plan she and Frederic had spent the past week devising. There were only two days now until the feast—and then they would be gone.

The reivers had transformed the rocky plain into a festival ground. Rana nibbled at a piece of strong southern cheese. Her face glowed from the heat of the great fire. An entire shipload of wood had been brought in to build it—at least that was one trip that had done no harm to Westria. Behind her, torches on poles burned pale against a sunset sky. The cloths that had been laid on the ground around the fire looked like carpets in the ruddy light.

"It seems strange just to be sitting here. I'm glad it will be over soon . . ." murmured Rana to Frederic. He frowned in warning, but no one was listening to them. Her eyes slipped sidelong from Frederic to Lorca, who was draining a silver-mounted horn. The Westrian wine was already circulating freely. Three dark-skinned men fluted minor harmonies over the murmur of the crowd.

"They don't need your help—" said Frederic more loudly. "More boats must have come in—I haven't seen half these men before."

"That's true enough, my lord. They've heard of my lady and they come to serve her!" Lorca bowed toward the empty place beside him. Beyond it sat Zoltan, talking with some of his men. "Indeed, I think we have men from every state in Elaya here."

Rana saw calculation in Frederic's glance. Was Ardra's force increasing then? Information on their numbers and origin would be useful to Julian.

"I have never seen folk from so many far places before—" Rana's tone held simple curiosity, and she smiled at Lorca. "Those men playing the flutes—where are they from?"

"From the Tambara, lass, where lions haunt the plains. See, those others are more of their kin." Lorca pointed to a group of tall men, very black, who were laughing together. They wore kilts of bright cotton and short cloaks clasped at the shoulder to leave one well-muscled arm bare.

Then Macko uncovered the fish that had lain baking beneath the fire. The music faltered as the feasters began to cheer. Macko stripped off the seaweed which had covered it, and carefully tipped the young corn that had been buried with it into baskets which the servers passed around.

"I myself come from the Freehold, but the rest of our men are mostly from the Campos del Mar and the coastal villages, or from Los Leones itself," Lorca went on.

"Is the Campos del Mar the largest of your provinces?" asked Rana. The smell of the approaching food was distracting. It had been too long since she had eaten well—who would have thought that old Macko could cook such a meal?

"Not the biggest, but the richest, and my lady's inheritance! Some fine warriors from the Palisada are here."

Rana glanced toward the crimson pavilion, whose sides glowed ruby from the light within. Where was Ardra?

Frederic nodded soberly. "This looks like more than mere raiding to me. Does your Prince know?"

Lorca grinned engagingly, setting down his drinking horn. "Well, he didn't come out to see us off, if that's what you mean . . ."

"It seems an original method of declaring war," Frederic suggested.

Lorca started to reply, felt Zoltan's eyes upon him, and choked on his wine. "No, it is no war at all—just a little commercial venture of our own while your Kingdom's affairs are still adrift."

Frederic frowned at that, but he did not answer. Rana swore as she touched the smoking fish, managed to get some with the tongs, and then took an ear of corn.

"Are your fingers burned?" asked Frederic quietly. Rana looked up at him, and realized she was grimacing.

"It's not that—I'm just wondering whether this corn came from Longbay. It ripens early there."

"I suppose we could draw up an itinerary for the past month's raiding from this night's menu," he answered bitterly. "But we may as well get some strength from it." He spat out a fish bone.

The next course was an assortment of roasted fowls and spiced millet in earthenware pots. The flutes were playing again, supported by a drum. Three of the Elayans began a line dance, arm in arm. It was almost dark by now, and the round moon was glimmering like a disk of pale gold above the distant land. Full moon and sovereign sun—it should be a night of great power. Rana hoped so. They were going to need powerful magic. Someone threw more driftwood on the fire and sparks scattered upward like looted coins. The dancers made a last circuit and collapsed, sweat glistening on their dark skin. For a few moments it was quiet, and above the chirring of the birds Rana heard the restless sigh of the sea. Her hand sought the Jewel hidden at her breast.

Her attention was recalled abruptly as Lorca leaned forward, calling her name. "I told you," he repeated, "everyone must entertain us tonight. Surely you have something for us, *doncellita*?"

Rana stared at him in consternation. He *had* said something about entertainment, but she had not understood him. She had not wanted to draw attention to herself. For once she wished her little brother were here! But that gave her an idea.

"I'm no performer, so I ask your kindness—" she said humbly. "This is just a little song the children sing at home, and you must help me with the chorus—" Her eyes flickered around the circle and then lowered again.

Childish—that was the idea. She rounded her shoulders to minimize her breasts, and widened her eyes.

There was a lad, a little fisher lad,
And for his dinner, fish he would have had—

Her voice gathered strength as she went on, but she kept it thin, like a little girl's.

He baited his hook, and flung it in the sea,
Saying, "Is there a fish that's big enough for me?"

Frederic gave her a quizzical look and joined in on the last line. Rana smiled at him gratefully and went on.

He felt a tug, he pulled it in so fine,
And there was an anchovy dancing on his line,
He left it still hooked, and flung it in the sea,
Saying, "That is not nearly big enough for me!"

The song continued, as the greedy boy caught a rockfish, a striped bass, a mackerel, and finally a sunfish, all with the same results.

He fished all day—when it was nearly dark,
The great big sunfish was gobbled by a shark!

An approving murmur from the audience nearly stopped the song.

He left it still hooked, and flung it in the sea,
Saying, "That is not nearly big enough for me!"

Now she took a deep breath, glanced at Frederic for support, and began the last verse, drawing the words out with a certain grim satisfaction.

Along came Orca, and what did he do?
He snapped up the shark, and ate the boy up too!
And when he was done, he swam off through the sea,
Saying, "Well, that was nearly big enough for me!"

Rana shouted out the conclusion with an extravagant flapping of her arms and an awkward little dance which moved the insulted reivers to laughter as she sank gratefully into her place again.

"What in the name of Sea Mother was that supposed

to be?" Frederic asked her when she had gotten her breath again.

"Well, I've never seen a killer whale. It worked, didn't it?"

While she was singing, someone had put down a bowl of fish stew, drowning in a rich sauce of onions and herbs. It smelled wonderful, but Rana was still too shaken to eat. Frederic had not touched his. In fact, despite his admonitions, she realized that he had hardly eaten at all. The raiders were retaliating with a warsong whose chorus, shouted from nearly a hundred wine-smoothed throats, echoed from the steep slope behind them.

There was a little stir beyond the fire, and the chorus began to fade like a failing wind. Frederic became very still, and Rana turned to see what he was watching. Ardra had come.

Lorca walked a pace behind her, and every man there stood up. This was an Ardra they had not seen before.

Her head was turbaned in ruby silk whose buillon-fringed ends hung down her back. A sleeveless vest of pale damasked gold revealed the bronze swell of her breast and clung to her body above full-length flowing trousers of scarlet and gold brocade. From her slim shoulders drifted an open caftan of sheerest crimson gauze; from neck and ears came a glitter of pearl and garnet and gold.

As she neared, they could see that her lips were painted, and gold dust sparkled on her heavy eyelids. Around her wafted the breath of all the gardens of Al-Kaid.

"Hail, Princess, and welcome to the Festival!" Frederic bowed.

Ardra smiled and pushed back the caftan so that her bracelets glittered in the light of the fire. "Indeed, my lord, you have named me well. My mother's cousin sits on the Lion Throne."

Rana surveyed her critically, thinking that if she had seen all this while dressing, she had spent the time well. Her men were cheering her until Rana thought they must hear it in Bongarde. But at last Ardra lifted one slim hand and the clamor stilled.

"My friends—nay, my *compadres*!" Her clear voice rang across the circle, and her words stirred them to cry out again. "I am glad we are together to celebrate the longest day. We are the children of the sun, and it is good that we should rejoice in his triumph. Song and dance and meat and drink you have had already, and you shall have more. Be glad then, and know that my love and faith are set on you, as yours is given to me! Rejoice, and let all be equal tonight in revelry!" She paused, her eyes holding them.

"And since we are the children of the victorious sun, from this day forward, let us go forth to conquer, trusting to our own courage and to each other's valor to gain the victory!"

They were shouting again, the men of Los Leones and the Campos del Mar and the Tambara, with hoarse throats and shining eyes. Zoltan's men grinned widely, waving wineskins and ale flasks in the air.

Rana felt her heart pounding heavily as the noise rose and fell, for in her own throat an answering cry was aching for release. Ardra stood before them, arms lifted like a goddess of victory jeweled in red and gold. And then a cold voice spoke within her—*Victory for what, and over whom*?

They stopped at last. Shivering slightly, Rana stared into the fire. She could hear the murmur of Frederic's graceful compliments, and Lorca's garrulous chattering. There was a flurry of movement at the other end of the clearing, and her nostrils flared at the scent of roast meat that came with it. Singing, men carried in the sides of beef which had been roasting over coals in the firepits nearby since the day before. They heaved them down on the green hides, one for each side of the fire, and began carving with a flourish of bright knives.

Suddenly Rana felt very tired. Frederic was talking about court life to Ardra, their mingled voices murmering counterpoint to the love songs one of the *Campaneros* was singing to his guitar. They were so obviously of the same world. Would he even want to escape now?

There was a lull, and Ardra's voice came clearly. "My lord Frederic, your young friend has paid for her supper already. Have you a song for us tonight?"

"Ah, lady, I fear to disappoint you. I am no bard!" Frederic shook his fair head, but his eyes smiled.

"You will not disappoint me. . . ." Her words were something between an assurance and a command.

He sobered. "I have no songs for camp or court—my studies have been at the College of the Wise, and I can only give you a sea-song I learned there."

Gilded eyelids hid Ardra's dark eyes from his direct blue gaze as she nodded.

Frederic settled back then, hands open upon his knees, and sang.

Of all things secret in this world, most secret is the sea;
What lies beneath her restless waves remains a mystery.
Though men plumb every valley, and climb earth's every hill,
Survey the heavens in a glance, the sea's unfathomed still.

The lands lie lapped in her embrace; she sends the clouds to bear
Sweet waters to the thirsty earth, yet man may hardly dare

*To venture where her children dwell, and share the
liberty
His kin the dolphin know among the People of the Sea.
    Deprived of this desire, they say, some have dreamed
of an isle—
Secret, safe, where land and sea might mingle for
awhile.
Of woven seaweeds is it made, nowhere does it abide,
Nor is it drawn by any will save that which draws the
tide.
    'Tis there the Mover of the Moon finds harbor for her
feet,
And there the Guardians of the Sea in highest conclave
meet.
And if by favor of those powers, the seeker might draw
near,
All secrets would be known at last, all mysteries made
clear.*

Rana's memory was stricken suddenly with memory
of the vision she had seen when she uncovered the Sea
Star. She listened, clutching the hidden Jewel at her
breast, and when the last notes died away, still she heard
the song of the sea.

The bubble of stillness that had enclosed them burst.

Macko was hovering nearby with a basket of pastries.
The men brought out the rest of the ale casks, and the
hogsheads of fortified wine, and voices, mournful or
riotous, were raised in sporadic song. Some already
snored peacefully.

*"Ay de mi, ay de mi! Will she still love me when I am
far away?"* came the lament from across the fire. Rana
shivered. Soon they would be drunk enough to forget
Ardra's prohibition regarding her. Even if the plan had
not required it, it was time she disappeared.

The plan! Lulled by Frederic's music, she had almost
forgotten it. She turned, and stopped. Frederic and

Ardra had gone. Someone laughed and pointed. Rana followed the movement and glimpsed a departing glimpse of red and blue on the path.

She felt the bile rise in her throat and put her hand to her mouth.

"Is it too much wine, you've had, *niña*?" asked Lorca. "Don't worry about your young friend and my lady— they'll need no more companionship from any of us this Festival! You'd best be off to bed now—you'll feel better on the morn!"

Rana nodded and stumbled away from the firelight, then straightened, swallowing her sickness, staring into the darkness where Frederic and Ardra had disappeared. Her weakness had not been all acting. Even now, her stomach threatened to betray her when she thought about Ardra and Frederic drawn into that mindless degradation that men called love.

How could Frederic betray their plan? And how could he make love to their enemy?

And, in an odd way more painfully, another thought echoed it—

How could Ardra welcome him?

Chapter Four

"You say you enjoyed our celebration—I am glad. . . ." Ardra hesitated. "I know how to order a battle, but I have never needed to manage a feast before."

Ardra moved swiftly, and Frederic lengthened his stride to come up with her. Rana must be watching and worrying, for they had planned to meet at the boat landing as soon as the men had been incapacitated by their festivities, but she must know that there was no way he could disobey the commander now.

The commander . . . As he followed the graceful flutter of her draperies toward the lookout post, Frederic repeated that title with bitter awareness of his self-deception. It was not as his captor that Ardra had commanded him to walk with her, but as a woman, and that was a subtler captivity. Even after she released him from the hut, Ardra had avoided him. What did she want with him now?

I will only stay for a little while, he told himself, *to allay suspicion. I will flatter her, and then she will let me go. . . .* But even as he thought it, he realized that too was a lie. The smooth grace of Ardra's movement set the blood singing in his veins, and he knew that what he said to her tonight would be more than flattery.

She paused to look back at him, and he realized that he should have answered.

"You were magnificent—you appeared at just the right moment—" he stammered, but she interrupted him.

"Do you think I delayed my arrival for effect? You were all gorging yourselves. I did not think that . . . anyone . . . would be wondering about me. No—" She went swiftly up the last few feet to the top. "I was gathering my courage to come out to you. . . ."

Frederic followed her, struggling for a reply. She stood still with her back to him, gazing out over the glistening splendor of the ocean. A faint veiling of mist was forming on the horizon, but the island was still clear, and the sky glittered with stars like the ripples of the sea. To the northwest the Great Bear lumbered across the sky, searching for her cub, while overhead, the torso of the Hunter straddled the heavens.

"Your silence says you don't believe me—" Ardra continued finally. "I don't think that anything that frightens a man would cause me fear—but to come before you all as a woman—of that, I was afraid! The ladies at my uncle's court scorned me because I was not dark and rounded and lovely like them. My men would not have laughed to my face, of course, but I thought that they might, later on. . . ."

Frederic found himself reaching out to her, turning her

toward him so that the moonlight polished the smooth planes of her face. Even in that cold light she seemed to glow.

"Ardra! Don't you know that you are beautiful?" His voice was hoarse with strain. "If sunlight took the form of a woman it would be like you. Laugh? You are such as those men might hardly dare to look on, something a man might dream of when his dreams gave loveliness a form and name!"

Unwilled, his other hand came up, and gently, as if he were touching a butterfly, he traced the pure line of her cheek and brow. Her eyes were pools of darkness in which a man could drown. Abruptly he believed that there had been no artifice in her entrance to the feasting. She was not flirting with him, nor was he flattering her; something else moved both of them, now. At the base of her throat, a pulse was fluttering.

Frederic gave a little sigh, like a man who has fought to the limit of his strength and sees his death upon him, and let his hand fall. Lips parted, she tipped her head a little to look at him, and he surrendered, seeking her mouth with his own.

The first kiss was a butterfly touch, but Ardra's lips were full and soft, sweeter than fresh water to a man on a desert isle. Frederic bent again, desiring that sweetness, dizzied when he tasted it, afraid that his senses would fail him if he took her in his arms. The lips he kissed searched his as desperately as his own, but in some last attempt at control, Ardra kept her own hands clenched in the folds of her robe.

Then the need for breath tore them apart, gasping. Ardra gave a little lightheaded laugh.

"I was never like the others, you see. I wanted a horse, a ship, a sword in my hand! I wanted people to know my name not because I was Prince Palomon's niece, but because of my own deeds."

She was chattering, as if by continuing their conversation she could deny what had just happened, but Frederic understood. His own heart was still pounding. *I have touched her*, he thought, *and the heavens have not fallen.* But when he looked up, the stars swirled dizzily, and he wondered if that were true.

"I know," he answered, fighting for calm. "All my life I was told to thank the Guardians because I was the Lord Commander's heir."

"Yes, you *do* know," she said shyly. "I never met a man whom I thought might understand. . . ."

Ardra took a step closer, and her scent surrounded him. Her caftan had slipped off one shoulder, and he could see the smooth swell of her breast. His hands tingled with the need to taste that smoothness. Frederic stepped backward swiftly and took a deep breath to clear his head.

"But why this way?" He gestured toward the camp where her warriors still caroused beside the fading red glow of the fire.

"At home there was nothing for me but marriage to someone who would use my name to rule my father's lands. Here, I have followers, ships, freedom . . . and a dream! We do not mean to remain plunderers. These lands are without a leader—no trade between the kingdoms, no communication of ideas and knowledge. With a strong power on the sea there could be a flowering on these coasts such as the world has not seen since ancient times!" Ardra's voice rose, vibrant as a trumpet call. He felt the shock as she gripped his arm.

"Together we could do it! A union of north and south! Why not?" she exclaimed. "What is there for *you* if you return? Now that this yokel prince has appeared you have no hope of the throne. Your father will live for many years. What will you do with your talents, your powers?"

After a few moments, Frederic realized that the silence

had gone on too long. He wondered, *Can I betray everything I have loved, and been*? The air seemed to have gone dead between them. Desperately he sought support from the image of the Master of the Junipers, but he could see only Ardra, waiting in the moonlight. He must resist her by sheer will then, though all senses and emotions were her allies.

"Ardra—" his voice cracked. "If I could give my life to any woman it would be you. What you offer is beyond my meriting. But before I ever met you I gave my love to my Master, and my loyalty to my Prince. I have no wish to fill my father's shoes, but that is because I have chosen another way. I am trying to follow the road to Awahna now. . . ."

"Awahna?" she said uncertainly, letting go of his arm. "That is one of your legends, is it not so? How can you consider becoming a worker of illusions, a persuader of other men's deeds, when you have such an arm for a sword, such a mind . . . such a heart? Perhaps that way attracted you when you had no other choice, but surely it cannot any more—it is not worthy of you, Frederic!"

He shook his head. Somehow they had moved apart, and he felt the distance as a physical pain.

"It may be worth more than I can ever give. But even if it were not, it is worth my honor. And if I could renounce my oaths so quickly how could I be worthy of you, Ardra? I told you—I have given my word to Julian. There is no way that I could follow you. Come to Westria with me instead—you will have freedom there!"

Julian's face came clearly to Frederic as he spoke the name—calmly intent as they guarded each other in battle; agonized as Julian called him back from the delirium of fever; transfigured as he walked in the Sacred Wood, reborn with the Midwinter Day. That had been just six months ago.

Ardra looked him up and down, and although her

voice was not quite steady, it held only scorn. "Honor? Do you say that honor prevents you? Honor is a fine cloak for fear! You have deceived me—pretending love, you have tricked me into telling you all my plans!"

Frederic stared at her, stopped by the one truth in her accusations. He *had* deceived her—he meant to leave her even now. But by the Moonlord, he had not pretended love!

"Ardra!" Agonized, he reached out to her.

"Do not presume to touch me! You will escort me back to the camp, and then return to confinement in your hut!" She started down the path.

Frederic followed her. If Ardra imprisoned him now, Rana would wait in vain. She must already think he had betrayed her—whatever he did now, he was going to have to betray somebody. If he ran from Ardra would she follow him? Were any of her men sober enough to search for him?

Thoughts chased each other distractedly, but still his feet moved in Ardra's footsteps, as if some invisible tether linked them. And then they were before her pavilion, its crimson walls cold in the moonlight. The men by the fire were passed out or sleeping. They might have been alone.

She turned to face him as if some other force had compelled her, and in the pale clarity of the moonlight he saw upon her cheeks the crystal glitter of tears.

"Ardra . . ." Frederic had never spoken her name—or anyone's name—in that voice before.

"Ah, damn you, damn you!" she wailed softly, and then she was in his arms, and without thought for past or future he was trying to kiss away her tears.

For almost a quarter hour, the boat guard had not moved. Rana sat back on her heels, biting her lip. If only Frederic would get here! The guard would surely wake

73

when they tried to get the skiff down to the water. For safety, the man must drink the poppy-sleep in her flask, and she was going to have to give it to him soon!

Only what if Frederic never came? She would be risking herself for nothing, and even if the guard did her no harm, he would remember, and talk, and the men would begin to think of her as available again. That is, if the fellow believed her in the first place. She and Frederic had argued about that, for a man dangling at a rope's end was memorable evidence of her feelings, but Rana suspected that male vanity would quickly convince her target that he was an exception, especially if he thought she had had too much wine.

The moon lifted above the island like a silver shield. On this shortest of all nights, the dawn would come early. Rana stood up. If she believed that Frederic would, and could, keep faith with her, then she must move now to keep faith with him. Though her flesh prickled with fear and revulsion, she must wake the guard now!

A snore told her where to find him. For a moment Rana stood looking down, disgusted, then she nudged him with one toe. Snorting and clutching at his cutlass, he came upright, staring. Then he rubbed his eyes and began to grin.

"You're 'sleep!" Rana said reproachfully. "I'm lonely, looking for someone to talk to, and you're *sleeping*!"

"You ain't goin't' tell on me, is you, girl?" The man looked her up and down suspiciously, and then grinned. Short and wiry, no dirtier than any of the others, Rana supposed he was no better or worse. They all seemed alike to her now. "Of *course* not," he went on. "You want comp'ny!"

Rana produced a giggle and pretended to drink deeply from her mug. She uncapped the wineskin and started to pour more into it, splashed a little on the ground, then shook her head and sat down on the nearest boulder.

"Guess I better not!" She giggled again. She started to cap the wine again, but did not resist as he grabbed it from her. "I guess I've had enough!"

"Well, *I* haven't!" the man exclaimed, lifting the wineskin and sending a sparkling stream of liquid down his throat. She could see the muscles working as he swallowed. His grab for her waist surprised her, and it took all her will to control her revulsion.

"There, missy—now we'll be comfy—jus' you 'n me!" His grip tightened, and Rana tried to relax. She had no idea what the proper dosage for the tincture of poppy she had stolen from Ardra might be. What if it only made him drowsy?

"M' name's Andri—third oar on *Gaviota Azul*—if we're t' be friendly, y' should know. . . ." He lowered the wineskin to stare earnestly into her face. "'M not like those others, y'know—guess y' *do* know that, or y' wouldn' be here!" He laughed delightedly, and upended the wineskin.

The torch crackled and hissed. A guillemot fluttered toward them and veered awkwardly away, the white patches on its wings flickering. Rana followed its flight into darkness, trying to ignore the man's heavy breathing and the clumsy touch of his hands. And then one of those hands closed hard on her breast and before she could think, Rana jerked away.

"Didn' mean t' hurt ye—" he said slowly, shaking his head. Rana stared at him, wondering if it was only her imagination that made his speech seem more slurred than it had been. "Come 'ere, missy, lemme make it up t' ye, huh?" He pulled her back, and before she could think of evasion, pressed his lips loosely against hers.

For a moment Rana was shocked into stillness. And in that moment she realized that she could not go through with this—she would kill the man if she couldn't get away. Then he pulled back with a sigh and began to paw at the neck of her tunic.

"Oh, Andri—" some reservoir of deception provided her with words. "If we're going to get *that* friendly, there's some business I better attend to first, you know what I mean?" She forced a last giggle and edged away. "I'll be right back! You just stay there and finish your wine!"

He sighed again. His eyelids were drooping—he opened them wide to grin up at her. "Pretty—" he said. "Hair like th' torch flame . . . Bet it's jus' as hot down . . ." His hand fell in mid-gesture and his eyes closed once more.

Scarcely daring to believe that it was over, Rana crept toward the shadows of the hillside. When she reached them, reaction overtook her. She retched painfully onto the barren ground, and when it was over, scrubbed at her lips with the sleeve of her tunic to wipe the reiver's touch away.

The sun and the moon had lain down together, and the crimson pavilion blazed with their splendor.

In those moments when Frederic was capable of thinking, he realized that it had all been planned. The austere bedroll was already unfolded, its limited comforts reinforced by Elayan cushions and embroidered coverlets and looted furs. On the carven clothes-chest wine and little cakes waited to assuage a lesser hunger. Incense had been burned in the pavilion and its perfume still intoxicated the air.

But it would have been the same if they had come to rest in the cookshed.

Whatever measured seduction Ardra might have planned for him, what was happening was at once a mutual surrender and mastery. As the Regent's son he had been courted by women, and festivals at the College of the Wise offered periodic chances to reinforce the earth's fertility. But whether from an innate fastidiousness, as he hoped, or inability, as he had sometimes feared, Frederic had never taken advantage of his opportunities. Or perhaps it was because in those moments when the world fell away and he entered the Great Silence, he glimpsed a union which it seemed the joinings of the flesh could only travesty.

Until now.

In the light of the little lamp Ardra's slim body was as radiant as the morning, and Frederic embraced it like a prisoner kept too long from the light. When for a moment they parted, he saw his own long body pale and glowing, and remembered the erect splendor of the being he had seen once in vision, guarding the rainbow bridge to the Otherworld.

But he was on the bridge now, with Ardra, moving with her and in her and moved by her, seeking that same goal. Hovering on the brink of final frenzy, he paused, hands still compulsively caressing the velvet of her skin, and saw her eyes huge and unseeing, as if she had been blinded by too much light.

And then she gave a soft cry and wrapped her arms more tightly around him, and he fell endlessly into bright darkness.

When Frederic came to consciousness once more, he was lying on his back. Above him floated a sword. For a time he considered it without interest or understanding, until the flicker of lamplight showed him the cord that suspended it. And then, gradually, he realized that it was the sword that had been taken from him when he was captured, and that he was lying in Ardra's pavilion, with Ardra herself by his side.

Desire for the moment exhausted, he raised himself on one elbow to look at her. Lying half-curled against him, she had the defenceless grace of a kitten, or perhaps a lion-cub, anything that was feral and proud. Looking further, he saw a smear of blood on her thigh, and realized that for all her command of men, she had come to their joining as innocent as he. At the time, neither of them had been aware of any barrier.

He sat up, and his movement stirred the air. The sword above his head began to turn. Frederic's gaze fixed on the slow swing of the blade, and his bare skin pebbled with an inner chill. Nothing was changed, even though he and Ardra had just remade the world. She was still his captor, and his enemy. And although he had given her his soul, he had given his faith to Julian, and to Rana, who must be waiting for him even now. Stifling a groan, he rested his head in his hands.

If what he had just experienced was real, surely it superseded all other loyalties!

But if that was real, then that place he reached in meditation was real too, then what of his loyalty to the disciplines which had taught him to get there, and the world to which they belonged?

The inner truth of his being had spoken through his flesh to forge a bond with Ardra that would last to death and beyond it. How could that be denied?

But if his unconscious could make such a commitment, what of the vows that he had made with all the conscious power of his will?

For an unmeasured time Frederic sat there. But presently, moved by a response that had been trained into him for so long it was almost as instinctive as the divine frenzy with which he had loved Ardra, he got up, searched stealthily for his scattered garments, and put them on. Carefully he untied the sword and belted it around him, feeling as if it had split his heart in two.

Then he left her.

* * *

Rana was attempting to wrestle the skiff down to the landing when a soft whistle brought her upright, heart hammering in her chest. For a moment the man was a dark shape against the moonlight, then he came down the last slope and the torchlight showed his face. Reason told her that it must be the effect of the shadows, but for a moment it was hard for her to recognize those haggard features as Frederic's.

"Help me with the end of this thing—" She did not trust herself to ask what had kept him.

"You've dealt with the guard?" Frederic bent to grasp the skiff's stern and Rana saw the red glitter of the swordhilt at his side. For a moment she was silent, digesting the implications, and repressing the first stirrings of curiosity.

"He's asleep. Over there—" At least she could match Frederic's silence with her own, and then perhaps the memory of the Elayan's groping hands and wet mouth would go away.

Frederic nodded and lifted his end of the boat. Grunting, they got it to the edge of the landing.

"The water cask and the bag of food are already down on the sand," Rana said, between gasps. "How are we going to get this thing into the water? The winch needs three men."

"Slide her over—" Frederic peered at the rocks, then began to loop a rope around the stanchion at the stern. "If we're careful, we can get the skiff down without tearing the bottom out of her. We'll get her balanced on the edge, then you go down to guide her while I lower this end."

Rana clambered down the rough steps to the landing. As she reached the bottom, two sea lions barked their astonishment and slid off the rocks into the sea. The tide was beginning to ebb now, and the narrow crescent of wet sand shone in the moonlight. Rana planted her feet firmly in the shallow water and waited as the bulk of the skiff swung round and began to dip towards her, keel grating on stone.

Rana had just touched the bow when a shout startled them both and for a moment the whole weight of the skiff pressed down against her braced hands. Then Frederic took up the slack on his rope, and gasping, she looked up the hill.

Torches were bobbing down the path, and she saw the red glitter of drawn swords. They had been missed, then. It was hopeless—they had been fools to think they could get away with such a plan. She felt her knees weaken and blinked back tears, then realized Frederic was speaking to her.

"Rana—quickly now—we're almost done! Once the skiff's in the water you can get her out of the cove, can't you? I'll hold them until you're gone!" He spoke hoarsely between gasps, and the boat was moving again. Automatically Rana eased backward, steadying and guiding its weight until the bow ground sand.

It was still hopeless, she realized as she dragged it forward and Frederic lowered the stern. While Frederic defended the winch, none of the sharkships could be launched to follow her, but however well schooled he was not *that* great a warrior. He would not be able to hold them off for long. And how could she abandon him?

Frederic let the stern fall the last foot and dropped the rope, turning to face their enemies. And then, as if he had heard what she was thinking, he began to speak in a low hoarse tone she had never heard him use before.

"Rana, get that boat into the water and row! Have you forgotten what you are carrying? Getting the Jewel to Julian is more important than my life, or yours! Rana, please! You must go now or all we've done will be in vain!"

The pain in his voice came from something more than

fear, but Rana could not stop to analyze it. He was right. Though her throat ached with grief, she knew it, and already she was bundling the cask and foodbag into the skiff and shoving off. In a moment the complaining of sand under the keel gave way to the slap of waves; resistance eased suddenly, and the skiff was bobbing in uneasy response to the swells that washed the outer cove. Even on such a calm evening, the currents around the island were treacherous. Rana had assured Frederic that she could row them out to sea, but these were not the protected waters of the Bay.

For a last moment she hesitated, torn between conflicting fears. Then she caught the ugly note in the shouting, and remembered why she had decided that a clean death in the sea would be better than remaining here. On the rock above her, Frederic stood waiting with drawn sword, like an image of the Defender. The sea-wind ruffled his fair hair, but his face had somehow regained its serenity.

"Rana, they are coming—" he said quietly. "Don't be afraid for me. You know they'll save me for ransom if they can. When you see Julian, tell him he still has my loyalty. . . ."

Rana's throat ached furiously as she strangled the cry of grief that struggled there. A larger wave swirled around the keel and sucked the skiff toward the sea. From the hill behind them a clear, angry voice shouted Frederic's name.

"Go now, girl, in the name of the Maker, and may the Guardians protect you!" he cried. His boots rang on rock as he strode to face their foes.

Chill water gurgled around Rana's legs as she ran the skiff out to deeper water. She scrambled over the side, snatching at an oar to fend it away from the rocks. The boat bucked beneath her like an unbroken pony. There was more noise from the shore, but she was too busy fumbling the oars into their locks and trying to guide the skiff through the complicated eddies of the cove to dare a look.

Not until she had gained the comparative safety of open water did she draw breath. A swell lifted the skiff suddenly, and she saw the landing, torchlit like a stage at a festival. Upon it stood the two main characters in the tragedy, one with silver-gilt hair shining above his dark tunic, the other resplendent in golden mail, and the red light ran like water along the blades of their naked swords.

"A traitor you are, and a traitor you will always be! But what else should I have expected out of Westria?"

Frederic flinched involuntarily. He had never heard a voice so icy. That it should be *that* voice, which he had last heard warm as honey pooling in the sun, was an obscenity. And Ardra's eyes were like black stones.

"My lady, if I had stayed I would have been a traitor to oaths sworn long ago!" He said as steadily as he could manage.

A quick glance showed him more men crowding down the hillside. Birds screamed as booted feet crushed burrows and the precious eggs inside them. Some of the reivers were still befuddled with wine, but too many were wide awake and avid for battle, or perhaps, he thought as he considered the odds, for simple slaughter. But at least he had their attention. Dazzled by torchlight, perhaps they would not see the skiff slipping silently out to sea. . . .

"Words!" She spat scornfully. "Actions reveal a deeper truth than words! Will you deny your deeds?"

Frederic felt himself flush, then schooled his features, unwilling even now to shame her before her men. Lorca, faithful as always, was closest, his forehead creased in a worried frown. Zoltan stood with the other captains, grinning nastily. Or perhaps, Frederic thought then, it was his own sensitivities he was protecting. What he had shared with Ardra had been a sacred thing. Desperately he marshaled the arguments he had used against himself not so long ago.

"I deny *nothing*, Ardra," he said quietly, "neither the heart nor the will. But if I broke faith with my own people, how could you ever trust me to be true to you?"

She took a step forward, and he saw in her expression the faintest hint of softening.

"Perhaps it will not matter," she said thoughtfully. "You are still here, after all. There's no harm done." He could hear the faint musical clink of her mail as she came toward him.

A man's voice broke the silence, still blurred with sleep or wine. "Missy, where you goin' now? 'M cold!"

There was a murmur of surprise from the men. Then someone shouted, "It's Andri!" Torchlight flowed toward the beached ships.

"Wha's ever'body doin' here?" came Andri's plaintive response, and then, "Where's the *girl*?"

The men were laughing, accusing him of having been drunk on guard and dreaming, but Ardra's eyes narrowed as she looked at Frederic. Moonlight from above haloed her fine hair with silver even as the torchlight lent her face a red glow.

"Yes indeed," she said with chilling softness, "where *is* the girl? Now you will tell me the truth, Westrian, and no soft words will deceive me! You were going to escape together, weren't you! This flight was no sudden impulse —you must have been planning it for a long time!"

"Of course I was going to take her!" Frederic burst out suddenly. "Do you think I would leave her here? Rana was my responsibility!" At his temples a pulse pounded painfully. Too much had happened, too quickly, and Ardra was looking at him with hatred in her eyes.

"Do you expect me to believe you? You and that red-headed whore have been plotting together since you came! Plotting together, lying together most likely, and laughing at me because I pitied her! That bitch cost me a good man—I should have thrown her to my wolves!"

"Mistress!" came another shout. "The skiff is gone!"

Unexpectedly, Ardra laughed, but it was not a pleasant sound. "Has she gone off and left *you*, then? How disappointing. But never mind, we'll bring her back and you can watch my men avenge their shipmate on her while I meditate on *your* punishment. Zoltan, get your ship in the water—the bitch can't have gone far!"

Zoltan was snapping out his orders before the echoes of her voice had died. Men scurried towards one of the sleek raiding vessels, and timing their motions to Zoltan's count, lifted it from its cradle. Frederic remembered how he and Rana had struggled to wrestle the skiff this far, and shifted his grip on his sword.

"Stop!" he said loudly as the men began to move the ship forward.

"What?" Ardra turned back to him, her face disbelieving.

"You can't lower the boat without using the winch, and to do that you must get past me. . . ."

Ardra shrugged disdainfully. "All I need do is whistle, and my men will knock you into the sea!"

"Your men!" Frederic tried to match her scorn. "And you will enjoy watching them do it, won't you, as you have been pleased to play at war? But not to the point of dirtying your aristocratic hands. . . . You are a fraud, Ardra—" he pitched his voice lower, "with all your dreams of independence and glory! Your men must laugh at your pretensions. What will you do when they tire of humoring you?"

He felt the words leave his lips like a flight of arrows,

and like arrows they hit home. But within him a voice was crying, *Ardra! Ardra!* How could she not hear?

It was then that her sword hissed from her sheath. As the blade came up to guard, she gathered up her cloak and wound it around her left arm, then settled into a balanced half-crouch, facing him. The coordinated precision of those moves told Frederic that she had been well taught. But then, despite what he had just said, he had never doubted her.

An equally well-trained instinct was already moving him to face her. Then, for a moment, both of them were still.

"Zoltan, Lorca, don't interfere!" she called, without taking her eyes from Frederic. "You heard him challenge me. This is my fight now."

Frederic was aware of a ripple of excitement from the men. He supposed it would be good sport for *them*. To some of them it might not even matter who won. They were probably making bets on it already, in low voices so that Lorca would not hear. To him, he supposed, it would not matter who won either. Even if he defeated Ardra, she would still win. He knew he could not kill her, but he did not think that she could afford to leave living a man who had taken her, in either sense of the word.

At least that way he would be out of his torment. The thought gave Frederic a curious comfort. He did not have to worry about winning, then, or making any more of these choices between love and duty that had been tearing his heart in two. All he had to do was to hold Ardra as long as he was able, to buy Rana time.

"Why are you smiling?" hissed Ardra. "Are you mocking me? I will put a different look upon that fair face of yours."

Her attack came with no other warning. Only a quick step backward saved Frederic's arm, but then his blade was up and responses trained into him by dutiful hours in the practice yard were directing it. Seeing that her first try had failed, Ardra retreated, holding her sword low. As if they had been tied together, Frederic moved after her.

Her blade swept in again on the same low line; his own started down to deflect it, then twisted as he realized her intention. The feint ended and her sword slashed toward his throat, but Frederic's sword was there to meet it. The two blades clashed and hers was instantly disengaged again. She danced to one side, seeking an opening.

Ardra favored a rapier style of swordplay, in which speed and agility could compensate for the mass her slim body would never attain. But Frederic's body remembered vividly the whipcord strength of hers, straining against him. She would not quickly tire.

He must press her a little now, or she would think he was only playing. Abruptly Frederic leaped forward, pulling his blow at the last moment, as if this had been a practice bout, so that the point only grazed the gilded mail. There was a shout from their audience, and Ardra's eyes blazed. She came after him immediately, beating him back with quick feints that darted in and out like a serpent's tongue.

Frederic's muscles had loosened now. Existence narrowed to this dance of the swordblades and the glitter of Ardra's eyes. And like dancers they moved back and forth across the cold stone in a deadly choreography that after a time began to turn the sporting fever of the watchers into simple admiration.

And somehow Frederic was always able to turn Ardra's keenest blows. Presently he realized that she was anticipating his moves as well, so that he no longer had to worry about hurting her. Muscles strained and relaxed again in sweet contention. Never had he felt such exaltation in swordplay, even when he was working out with

Julian. Until now, he had never understood what his swordmaster meant when he spoke of the swordsman, the sword, and the opponent as a unity.

It came to him finally that it was their earlier joining that had forged this harmony, and that this swordplay was only a continuation of the loveplay in her pavilion not so long ago. But a greater oblivion would follow the climax of this ecstacy.

Frederic was aware of the moment when Ardra understood it too. A widening of the eyes, a sudden flush beneath the golden skin betrayed her, and the redoubled fury of the assault that followed called forth all of his skill. He saw also her realization that she could not defeat him, and that whether or not he could have killed *her*, he was not even going to try.

Ardra's eyes grew brighter, with fury, or perhaps with tears. She stopped short suddenly. Light shimmered along the edge of her blade, betraying the faint, uncontrollable trembling of her arm.

"This has gone on too long. . . ." she said in a dead voice. "I would fight you until we both fell exhausted, but by then the dawn would have given place to day. We cannot afford to have that girl to reach Westria, so I must allow duty precedence over pride. I am sure that you will understand," she added bitterly.

Frederic lowered his sword and took a deep breath of the damp air. The moon was past its zenith now, haloed by the faintest of rainbows. If the wind had been favorable, Rana might be many miles away, and hard to locate in that expanse of silver sea. He hoped so. He had done all he could for her.

"Zoltan!" she cried suddenly. "Have you brought your bow?"

Frederic looked up sharply. "Does the blood run true then? At the Battle of the Dragon Waste your uncle's crossbowmen shot my father down. Kill me with your

87

own hand, Ardra, with the sword—or don't you have the courage?"

"No—" she shivered violently, "no more than you. And now we both will pay for our deficiencies." She was weeping, as she had once before, but there was no pity in her face for either of them.

Out of the corner of his eye Frederic saw Zoltan, lifting the short bow. He tried to seek that refuge of the spirit that the Master had shown him. But as Zoltan released the string all that he could remember was the beauty of Ardra's body in the lamplight. He turned as he had turned to her outside her pavilion, and the arrow came.

Chapter Five

Rana dug deep with the starboard oar and leaned into it, holding the stroke to let the swell lift the boat past the last projection of rock. She could still see the glow of torchlight from the island, and there was no telling how long Frederic would be able to hold the reivers. Ardra's pride would never allow the escape of even one of her captives. Sooner or later, the sharkships would take to the sea.

The little boat lifted again, and she saw the long swells ridging the sea with momentary regularity. Rana headed the stern at an angle across them. A light breeze ruffled her hair and she frowned. With the mast down, the little boat could hide in the long troughs of the ocean, but Rana could feel the strain of the unaccustomed labor in her shoulders already. She must get under sail before her strength gave out or she would drift helplessly, at worst an easy prey for her pursuers, and at best no closer to her goal.

She could still see the weathered granite towers of the Isle of Birds, luminous in the moonlight and distorted as something seen in a dream, or perhaps a nightmare. As she got farther away the irregular silhouette became a fortress enchanted into existence by some sorcerer of the sea.

The exercise had set blood singing through her veins. The only sounds were the whisper of the wind, the slap of waves against the hull, and the splash as her oars bit the water. The sense of release was dizzying. Perhaps it was the proximity of the men that had made her feel so threatened, or the constricted space of the island. Her spirit, as well as her body, had been in confinement, and now she was free.

Slowly the island shrank behind her. Surrounded by the featureless waste of the sea, it seemed to Rana that it was not she who was moving, but the island that was slowly being towed away. When the swells lifted her, she could turn and see the pale moonwashed line of the cliffs of Westria, twenty-five miles away. With the moon and stars to steer by, she could find her way.

Rana had set her course eastward, but the current was carrying her south as well. For the moment she did not fight it. The Gateway lay almost directly east of the islands, but there was no need to battle the outcoming tide when by tacking she could avoid it. Time enough to set a course straight for her goal when the pillars of the Gate rose before her. But that was hours away. Now the Far Alone islands were out of sight completely. Rana drew in the oars, then began the struggle to raise the short mast in the bow and bend on the gaff-rigged sail.

She blessed all the stolen hours spent with Arn and the others at Seahold, talking to the fishers, watching the ships go in and out and criticizing their handling, and messing about in any boat they could find. Eventually Lord Austin had given up and let Arn have his own small sloop, which she and Bella crewed for him whenever they had time. Of course once Arn had taken his name he had gone on to command *Sea Brother*. But three years was not long enough for the ways of a boat to be forgotten, and the unfamiliar fittings did not puzzle Rana long.

By the time the moon was halfway down the western sky, she had got the big sail up on its gaff and battened, and shoved the daggerboard down. With a sigh of relief she sank down on the stern bench and unlashed the tiller, lowering the rudder into the water and completing the transformation from rowboat to sailing craft. A dry breeze was coming from the northeast. She turned the tiller to starboard, reaching across the wind toward the coast, and eased the mainsheet until the irregular trapezoid of the sail bellied out and sent the little ship swooping over the waves.

Overhead, the Dolphin swam through the sky. The western horizon was blurred, as if the sky were indeed merging with the sea. There was no sign of sharkships. Swaying to the skiff's lively motion, Rana could have been alone in the world, as she was alone upon the restless sea. Now, for the first time since Frederic had joined her at the landing, she could sit back and draw breath. But while her body rejoiced in its release from physical effort, she had no way to keep the torments of the mind at bay. Thoughts of Frederic haunted her. Ardra would be merciless if she thought he had betrayed her.

As, of course, he had. But Rana's own flight was also a betrayal, even though Frederic had urged her to it. How could she have left him? To what fate *had* she left him? He could very well be dead by now. She tried to imagine bringing that news to Eric and Rosemary. Would they consider the Sea Star an acceptable trade for the life of their son? Would Julian?

There were too many questions, and no answers. She could only go on. One hand still gripping the tiller, she set the other around the silk-wrapped bundle that hung at her breast. *Sea Mother!* Rana prayed. *Let me get this thing safely home!*

There was no answer, but after a time she felt calm enough to nibble on the hard bread, and sip some water from the cask. The boat's motion became jerkier as the shore drew nearer, and she braced her feet against the side. She was too far south, thought Rana, for she could see the froth of breakers at the foot of the cliffs—and she prepared to tack again. The sail shivered as it lost the wind, and she ducked to let the boom swing over her and the sail fill once more.

The wind was backing to the northwest now; the blur on the horizon seemed thicker, and there was a rainbow aureole around the westering moon. The summer fog-bank had been dispersed by the hot northeast wind, but it was forming again, and Rana shivered. If the fog came in before the sun rose she would have to decide whether to hug the shore and risk going on the rocks, or seek sea-room and possibly lose her way.

She trimmed the sail and then tacked to port again to correct her course for the Gateway. The wind was driving the fogbank shoreward. The moon sank behind it, its mirror brightness dissolving into a misty glow. As it disappeared, the shoreline dimmed too, until she had only the stars overhead for guide.

Like the sky, time dissolved then into a dream of motion disturbed only when Rana trimmed the sail to match the veering of the wind. Fatigue became her greatest enemy. Once she knew she had been asleep only when the wind changed and she was nearly knocked senseless by the swinging boom. If Frederic had been there they could have traded watches. Tired as she was, even her grief as she remembered him was dull. Fog veiled and unveiled the fading stars, and sent damp streamers past mast and sail. Rana huddled into her cloak, focusing all her awareness into hearing.

The mournful clang of a bell startled her into full consciousness. Somehow it had become light, if that was the right word for it. There was hardly any wind, and the confused bobbing of the floating strands of kelp suggested slack water, though the currents were so complicated here it was hard to tell. Fog brushed the wave crests, and she could scarcely see a boat's length away, but the bell could only be the one that King Alexander had ordered built on Seal Rock, so she must be nearing the Gateway at last. If she could hold position for just an hour or two longer, the mist might lift enough for her to see her way, and the floodtide would carry her in. She stood up with an excitement that burned away the worst of her exhaustion and, balancing carefully, began to fumble with the sail.

Rana had gotten the first sheet half-untied when she heard a sneeze. She dropped the tangled line and stared into the fog. The sound came again, with a muffled obscenity. It could be a fisher, becalmed in the fog. It could be, but a sudden knot in her belly told Rana that it was not. She knew the accent of Elaya only too well by now. She crouched in the bow, peering across the waves.

There—something darker lifted in the swell, sleekly curved with a line of gilt along the rail. Rana cowered into the bottom of the skiff. Reason told her it was no use hiding unless she could make her boat invisible as well, but for the first few moments, reason was powerless against the terrified creature that whimpered within her skull. After a time she realized that the creature was herself, and clamped shut her lips, trying to think.

Rana had been so relieved when the reivers did not follow her—so smugly triumphant at having eluded pursuit. But the sea wolves did not have to search for her. They had known where she was going, and all they needed to do was wait. If there had been no fog, Rana would have seen the ambush long ago. But without the fog they would have been able to see her as well. It was a miracle that they had not noticed her already.

At any moment the fog could shift and betray her. Grimly, Rana felt for the hilt of her dagger. She had forfeited Ardra's protection, and the men would know how to take their revenge.

But something stubborn within her was not yet ready to surrender. As long as they had not seen her, surely she could do *something*. Carefully she picked up one of the oars, and began awkwardly paddling. The skiff had never been built for such propulsion, especially in seas that became increasingly unpredictable as the last of the ebbtide met the heavy swells that were beginning to come in. The skiff's tendency to go in circles when paddled could only be offset by quick switching from side to side, but the oarlocks squeaked too loudly to be used until she was farther away.

A rogue swell caught the boat broadside and nearly capsized her. The wind was freshening, too, plucking at the limp sail. In a moment it would be luffing—Rana set down her oar and released the sheet just as another gust caught the sail and swung it round with a boom that echoed like a thunderclap in the damp air.

Rana braced herself against the sheet, grabbing for the tiller and pointing the boat's bow across the waves. Mist swirled off the waves like smoke. She heard a shout and cast a quick glance over her shoulder. The sharkship was fully visible, oars waving wildly as she started to turn. A second reiver bobbed just beyond her; the fog was lifting, and now she could see past both ships to the steep cliffs of the Gate.

She could neither outrow nor outsail them. Even if the seabreeze had held, the two reivers were between her and the Bay. But it was a breeze from the land that was lifting the fog, and driving her out to sea. Heart pounding, Rana leaned on the tiller and set the skiff on a port heading toward Wolf Point at the southern end of the Gate. The fishers avoided it, because the shelving seabed between the point and the two black rocks they called the Twins was rocky, but there was a shallow bay just beyond it, and with the centerboard up the skiff drew so little water she might be able to pass.

Even if the boat went onto the rocks Rana herself might still make shore. And it could be the sharkships who struck instead—following her, they would assume the passageway was clear. Even drowning was better than certain capture!

Now it took all Rana's strength to steady the tiller. Above the noise of wind and wave she could hear the regular grunt and splash as the reivers' oars bit into the water. But they had enough breath left to pepper the air with gleeful obscenities and to describe in detail what they were going to do to her soon.

Sea Mother! she prayed desperately. *Deliver me from my enemies! Open those stony jaws I see frothing ahead of me and swallow them! Save me from the sharks, and please Lady, if it be Thy will, let me come safely to shore*!

As she passed beneath the cliff the wind fell off and the sail flapped loudly, but the current had the skiff now. Rana hauled on the sheet, trying to win back some control. The Twins loomed up suddenly to starboard, twenty-foot black towers slick with spray. Between them and the shore the water was churning. One of the reivers shouted a warning and Rana laughed.

A wave lifted her; the skiff's side scraped rock as it fell back again. Behind her she heard the crackle of snapping oars. As the skiff dipped, a wave broke high beside it, drenching Rana and leaving the bottom awash. She could feel the difference in the skiff's motion, but there was no time to bail. A quick glance back showed her the first sharkship on the rocks, oars upended like the legs of an overturned beetle and men spilling into the sea.

Rana could see clear water ahead of her, but the skiff was wallowing like a cow in a bog. *Just a little farther! Just a little more now. . . .*

The rudder hit something and the tiller was wrenched from Rana's hand. Zoltan's voice shouted across the chaos, ordering his men to back oars. Grabbing for the rail, Rana looked back, and at that moment the skiff tilted and crashed down on stone.

The world tipped crazily and the rail was wrenched from her hands. Then a world of black water fell upon her. Flailing weakly, she slammed bruisingly against the rocks; she tried to hold to them, but the treacherous current whirled her away. For a moment it lifted her and she gulped air. Then the crosstide sucked her under and away. When it released her, barely conscious and coughing, she being carried with the rest of the wreckage out to sea.

A shattered oar from one of the sharkships bobbed on the waves. Beyond it, her own water cask floated half out of the water, miraculously whole. With the last of her strength, Rana stroked over to it and clung.

For a time she was content simply to float without struggling, cradled by the sea. In a moment she must force herself to action again and attempt to swim to shore. She had been so close! Like a dancer raising her skirts, the drifting fog revealed the black cliffs below

96

Wolf Point. But for the moment, battered limbs could do no more. In just a little while. . . .

Exhaustion betrayed her then, and Rana passed into a state between sleep and waking, retaining only enough awareness to keep holding onto the cask.

She was awakened by her body's shivering. Overhead the air glimmered with diffused brightness, but the mist was still thick around her—*all* around her. With a chill that owed nothing to the cold of the water, Rana realized that she could no longer see the shore. She was a single point of life poised in a vastness of silver sky and pewter sea. Even on the island she had not been so alone. She was moving, but with neither shore nor stars to steer by, she could not tell if she were being carried toward the land, or whether she had been caught by the great current that ran southeastward along the coast and out to sea.

Salt tears ran down her cheeks to mingle with the salt of the sea. Rana kicked out, furiously, futilely, but only succeeded in driving the cask in a wobbly circle and then pushing it under. Startled by her movement, a murre that had been floating nearby rowed air frantically with stubby wings. The cold water on her face startled her back to self-control, and she began to think again.

The shivering warned her that the chill was beginning to weaken her. The fishers of Seahold used to argue, sometimes, about how long a man could stay alive in the water. The ocean off Seagate was not cold enough to kill quickly, but it leached heat from the body until the muscles stiffened and the mind became confused, until eventually consciousness fled. The end would come quickly then, as the heart failed or the body slipped beneath the waves. The longest anyone had ever been known to survive was five hours.

But Rana had been cold and exhausted when she went into the water. For her, the end would probably come more quickly. At least it was not a painful way to die. But why, she wondered then, should she put herself through even a few hours of suffering? If the end was certain, why not release the cask now and let herself slide into the sea?

She looked down through clear gray-green water and saw the distorted shape of her lower limbs, the rags of her purple gown wavering like sea weed. She tried to loosen her fingers, but they would not let go. Clearly the body was not yet ready to accept the mind's conclusions. And maybe it was right. The capricious mists could lift at any time, and if they showed her the coast close enough, she might still make shore under her own power. A friendly ship might come. . . . Rana smiled then, a little grimly. It was not reason, but the same simple, instinctive drive toward survival that had kept her from accepting rape that would keep her struggling as long as she had the power.

Once more Rana scanned the sea. She had thought the skiff put her close enough to the water to become thoroughly familiar with all it had to offer, but at eye-level yet another universe was revealed. A few feet away from her a gull's breast-feather, far more delicate than she was, rested on the wave. Farther off, a torn branch bobbed gently, leaves fluttering in the light breeze. There was an odd comfort in knowing she was not the only land-creature adrift upon the sea.

The sun was burning through the mists. Rana felt the skin on her face stiffening, and knew it would begin to burn soon. There was a dull throb behind her eyes. Feather, branch and castaway floated onward at the same steady pace. But where were they all going?

She tried to remember what the fishers had said about the currents that were the highways of the sea. Once away from the complexity of tides and eddies that guarded the entrance to the Bay, the northwest current came down, swirling along the coasts of Westria and then outward in a great circle that sometimes brought back strange tokens from stranger shores.

In the hall of Fisher Castle hung a piece of wood carved and inlaid with shell after a fashion no craftsman in Westria knew. And there was an old ballad she had heard from Silverhair, about a stone flask that a fisherman found, so encrusted with barnacles that its surface could scarcely be seen. But its seal was unbroken, and it still held a dark and dream-filled wine. The fisher drank, and without speaking a word he launched his boat and headed out of the Gate. His friends could not stop him, and his family waited 'til a year had passed, and then carved his name with those of other lost seamen on Ghost Rock, just above the mark of the highest tide, but never did he sail back into the Bay.

Would Rana be borne to the land from which that strange drink had come? Would this current join another, and yet another, until she had measured the circumference of the sea? She closed her eyes, overwhelmed by the insignificance of one piece of flotsam in the vastness of the sea.

She tried to shift her grip upon the cask and found her fingers stiff and clumsy. Treading water with her legs stimulated the circulation a little and she started to shiver again, but she knew that the improvement was only temporary. Soon her muscles would grow rigid. She would lose her hold on the cask, and unknown and unnoticed, sink and add her substance to the sea. But even that would be better than staying afloat until she starved, and all that remained was a bleached and withered shell to be the plaything of the waves.

I am going to die. . . . she realized in wonder, and felt a sudden dizziness as she tried to imagine her own nonexistence and a world she would not see. As the fog lifted, the wind picked up, and the swells were growing higher. Instinctively she tried to resist them, and swallowed bitterness. Overhead the sky glowed blue, striking an occasional sapphire shimmer from the waves. Dazzled, Rana closed her eyes again, feeling the strength seep away from her body as if her blood were draining into the sea.

The nameless minutes wore on. Rana dozed and woke again to a stomach cramped with hunger, a mouth parched by thirst. There was water in the cask, perhaps even still good, but her limbs would not function well enough for her to try and drink. She tried to remember her mother's face, the voice of the Master of the Junipers, Julian's stride, and could not. *May they remember me . . . may all be well with them . . .* the vague hope came, and then, *perhaps the Sea Star wishes to return to the sea. . . .*

The waters moved between the brightness above, and the darkness below. Rana knew that she had arms and legs, but she could scarcely feel them. She knew that she had a name, but she could not remember what it was. She knew only the great movements of which she was a part—the eternal heave and swell of the open sea.

Is this what a baby feels, being born? This irresistible movement into the unknown? Her lips were cracked. When she licked them she tasted blood, salt as the sea. The Master had said that, originally, all creatures came from the sea; perhaps they would one day return to it, and she was only going on before.

She felt a confused compulsion to be rid of everything that still encumbered her. The remains of the purple gown came away easily. She tugged impatiently at the clasp of her belt and felt the weight of Ardra's dagger slip past her thigh and disappear. As the waters swirled around her naked body, for a moment she thought she was bathing in the lake near Registhorpe, or in the shallow waters of the Bay, in the ritual bath at Awhai.

100

She had no power to resist the cold waters that curled between her thighs. Only at her breast did any warmth remain. The Sea Star was still swathed in its wrappings. Numbly she thought that must be wrong—if she was naked, the stone, too, must be free. Awkwardly she tugged at the bindings, sensed a flare of radiance as they came away.

In contact with both her bare skin and its own element, the Sea Star blazed with power. Consciousness wavered, scraps of image, sound and sense kaleidoscoping in patterns of increasing splendor and complexity. A final glimmer of reason told her that she was very near the last unconscious slide into the depths below.

"Mother . . . back to your womb . . ." Her words were swallowed by the sea.

As the Sea Star touched the water, its energy radiated outward. In every direction the great currents bore the message, *The Sea Star has returned to the Sea.* . . . Where it passed, the sea creatures felt a tingling, and returned to their ceaseless quest for sustenance with increased zeal.

The message moved westward to lap the shores of the island where for so long the Jewel had lain hidden, and seabirds took wing to circle the barren rock in a yammering cloud. Even Ardra heard it in her pavilion, but she would have had cared little even if she had understood. Frederic lay unconscious on the bedding where they had made love not so long ago, nearly as white as the sheet beneath him. Only his bandages were red with blood, and stayed red, it seemed, no matter what she or Lorca could do.

And yet even there the power of the sea was present, for as Ardra worked over Fredcric she whispered words of love to him, knowing he could not hear. And knowing that only Lorca would see, she did not fight the stinging beneath her eyelids or the healing saltwater tears.

To the Great Bay came the message, borne inward on the tide. To the cove of Seahold it came, where Rana's sister gazed out over the water and counted the months until her child should be born, and if there was an added shimmer to the water, Bella thought only that it was the work of the Midsummer sun.

And after many a slow percolation, it passed finally from the Bay's saltwater to its brackish mingling with the flood of the Dorada, and up the river to Laurelynn, where Julian's hand dangled over the side of the royal barge while he pretended to watch the Midsummer pageant on the shore. The pageant was pretty enough, but to Julian, mired in anxieties, retellings of old legends seemed of little importance. The sun was very warm, and the motion of the barge lulled him into a dream of green depths and cold splendors, and a haunting music that was the call of the sea. He came to himself with a start, shivering, wondering why his heart shook at once with anguish and with joy.

And the power of the Sea Star pulsed out to sea also, past the life-rich green waters of the continental shelf to the sapphire waves of deep ocean, and down and outward again until it came to a region where an undersea volcano rose steeply from the depths of the sea. There also, cold water welled upward, bringing nutrients to flourish in the light of day, and there the greater creatures of the ocean played. Dolphins, blue whales, and orcas, humpbacks, fins, and grays all sought the rich feeding there.

And the message came to a lightless grotto at the roots of the undersea mountain, a place where Sea Mother often stayed. Perceiving it, she understood its meaning, and in undulant majesty, she rose to the surface of the waves. A humpback whale was feeding there, sieving tiny shrimp through his baleen, and with him a pod of whitesided dolphins. Sea Mother summoned them and impressed certain directions into his brain, and he turned and began to propel his massive body swiftly eastward through the sea.

Not this way—not unawares! If I can no longer hold on, at least let me go of my own free will!

Rana forced her arms to unlock, pushed the cask away, and clumsily stroked forward with the swell. It lifted her, and like a child soothed by the motion of its mother's breathing as it lies upon her breast, Rana understood the harmonious motion of the waves. The Sea Star's splendor was growing, and with it came awareness of tide and current, nutrients and minerals in the water, and the myriad members of the chain of life they fed.

Rana's dimming awareness focused to a small drop that was pure joy. A slight motion turned her over, arms stretched wide, back arched. The water softly supported her, washed across her face and soothed the burning of cheek and brow. The light of the Sea Star was too brilliant to be borne, and she shut her eyes.

She could no longer feel her body now. Cradled by the waves, she drew a harsh breath and let it out again.

Cool darkness took her. Without breath in her lungs she had little buoyancy. The waters closed over her head and her long hair swirled like kelp on the tide. The blood roared in her ears; the tightness in her chest was growing. A last effort of will kept her lips closed. If she breathed water, her body would panic and the struggling spirit would be forced from it, instead of the peaceful parting she was striving for.

And then something bumped violently from below. There was another shock, and then a powerful push sent her rushing toward the surface. Propelled half out of the water, Rana's lips opened automatically and she gulped air. She felt herself falling back, but the same force that had lifted her before was beside her—instinctively she tried to grasp it, and felt slick, rubbery skin. A burst of whistles and clicks startled her. She turned her head and saw the bright eye and beaked snout of a dolphin.

As her brain began to work again she realized that there were two of them, holding her pressed between them while another leaped nearby. In her confusion, she wondered if perhaps she had already died, and these were spirits in dolphin form who had come to take her to some Otherworld reserved for those who drown. But every breath rasped painfully, and the water was still cold.

A swell lifted them, and Rana began to slip under again. The dolphin squeaked in apparent consternation, and then, more clearly than if she had heard them, Rana was aware of words—

"Put your flipper over me . . ."

Startled beyond wonder, Rana tried to obey. Her arm lifted, but the muscles were too chilled to exert any pressure, and it slipped off the dolphin's smooth back. The two dolphins moved closer together, and for a moment Rana could relax while she gathered her strength to try again. Her ears tingled, but if the dolphins were vocalizing, it was in a frequency beyond the range of her ears. She pulled in as much air as she could, trying without success to force some life back into her limbs, and as the dolphins pressed against her, she found her eyes wet with salt water that was not from the sea. They had made her want to live again.

"Thank you, my brothers." Rana found words for her feelings, hoping that as the dolphin's message had come to her, they would somehow be able to hear. "I'm sorry you have come too late to help me, but at least my death will not be so lonely now."

Whether or not they had heard, the dolphins continued to support her in the water. Rana wondered how long it would be before they gave up, or she lost consciousness again. Overhead the sky was a pure blue. Light sparkled blindingly where the wind wrinkled the surface of the swells, and the stone upon her breast shone with a matching radiance. Blinded, Rana looked down and saw the depths beneath her glowing jade and tourmaline.

Through that jeweled splendor came a long dark shape that grew ever larger as it rose toward her. Rana's frightened cry brought a chorus of clicks from the dolphins, and then the message, *"Elder brother—a friend!"*

The sea heaved as a powerful stroke of its tail sent the creature swiftly upward, and Rana struggled wildly to hold on. She heard a loud *whfft*! as it surfaced, and warm vapor misted her cheek as it spouted five feet into the air. It was a whale! Joy fountained in Rana's heart as she understood. Water cascaded back into the sea as the dark bulk turned, revealing a vast expanse of corrugated white belly, and, scattering droplets like crystals, the whale's narrow, ragged-edged flipper lifted over her like a giant wing.

The other flipper swept past her as the whale continued to rotate, and the turbulence pulled Rana under again. But before she could begin to struggle, the whale's dark, slightly humped back came up underneath her and suddenly she found herself lying on a broad, smooth surface just above the waves.

The dolphins shrilled and chittered, and one of them breached exultantly. Rana could feel the slight shifting of muscles, and lifting her head a little, saw the bump of a brow ridge some ten feet ahead of her, and below it a glimpse of the whale's wise eye. The entire creature was probably almost as long as Arn's fishing boat, but it was living flesh, not wood, that now bore her, directed by a vast and ancient brain.

"Do not fear, little sister. I will not let you fall . . ."

The thought seemed somehow deeper in tone than the dolphins' sending, and louder, though Rana did not hear it with her physical ears. But before she could wonder, the whale's body flexed and they began to move forward through the sea. Though she had to hold her breath when the waves washed across her body, the whale's back was broad enough to keep her from slipping off, and whenever she was in danger of doing so it arched and once more lifted her free of the water. And even if she had slid off, the dolphins were still on escort duty to either side.

Gradually the sun began to warm the feeling back into Rana's stiff limbs, though she still had no strength in them. Arms spread to embrace the broad curve of the whale's back, she lay with her ear against the smooth hide, and presently, transmitted through the bulk of his body, she heard a sweet moaning song.

There were no words in it that she could understand, but there was a pattern that was repeated with variations, rising and falling, lulling her with the music of the sea. Half-conscious and exhausted, Rana lay in a peace beyond wonder, linked to whale and dolphins by the Jewel she wore, and dimly aware of the ocean as they perceived it, not a place of cold and terror, but a limitless, multi-dimensional playground where the flesh was weightless and movement was free.

The whale continued to sing, bearing her onward at the same steady pace to some unknown destination in the sea. Rana had not the strength to try and form a question. For the moment the gentle movement and the whalesong were sufficient, and she did not really care what lay at its end.

But after a time the humpback's motion slowed, and lifting herself a little, Rana saw something looming ahead of them. Not rock, and not shore—here were neither waves nor tide—but neither was it like any kind of ship she had ever seen.

It looked rather as if a flexible wicker platter were floating on the sea. As they came closer, she realized that what she had taken for vines were giant kelp stems, interlaced to form a mat two or three feet thick. The whale eased alongside it and she reached out to grasp one, but her strength was not sufficient to pull her even that far.

Abruptly the humpback rolled out from under her, but before Rana could sink, the dolphins shot upward and propelled her out of the sea. She sprawled half over the edge, clutched, and with her last strength wriggled her legs over, and then collapsed on a soft mat of fine sea-grass.

For a moment Rana was aware that this surface was also undulating gently. But it was warm and dry, and almost instantly her eyes closed and she slid into an unconsciousness that was even darker and more secret than the sea.

Chapter Six

When Rana opened her eyes again, it was dawn, and the rising sun was touching the sea mist with color like the inside of a shell. Her sunburnt skin was stiff and painful, and her muscles sore, but she was alive, and the sea lions whose furred bodies had kept her warm during the night showed her where water had collected in an upturned turtle shell.

When she had drunk, Rana looked around her. The island looked almost as large as the games field at Bongarde. The interlace of seaweed was surfaced with fine bleached sea grass and soft white sand. The waves that sometimes broke across the island had left pieces of seaweed behind, and fragments of coral, shells, and driftwood—all the treasures of the sea.

But there was one feature which could not be the work of the waves. What Rana had taken for the largest heap of driftwood was a shelter, roofed with a basketry of seaweed over a framework made of driftwood and the great rib bones of whales. Humans must have been here before, though the place had no other land-dwellers now. Abruptly a line of song surfaced in her memory—*"Of floating seaweeds is it made . . ."* and her eyes widened. The myth that Frederic had sung about at the feast was true! Beyond all hope or expectation, she had been received into the secret sanctuary of the sea.

Rana's stomach growled, reminding her that though she might be living a legend, she was still a living creature. A shrill whistle from the ocean drew her attention. She saw a dolphin leap, trailing a glittering arc of spray. A moment later, two mackerels were flipped onto the sand.

Rana began to regret having cast her dagger away, but a sharp piece of shell served as a fishknife, and she found the flesh, perfectly fresh and still cool from the sea, to be sweet and good. She sat down on the edge of the island to eat, dangling her legs in the cool water. The water was like glass, and the sunlight seemed to extend downward forever. Below the dolphins, fish flickered in their hundreds, and below them swam scores more. Where sight failed, a fertile darkness deepened to a greater immensity still.

"Friends, my thanks for this meal—I have never needed feeding more!" Rana spoke aloud, hoping that the tone, if not the words, would communicate some of her astonished gratitude. For whatever reason, the dolphins seemed to have adopted her. The largest of the three dolphins rose half out of the water and deposited a red-striped rockfish almost in her lap. Eagerly, she gutted it and scraped the scales away.

The big dolphin was resting on the surface, watching her. One of his companions broke water, a wriggling ling cod in her jaws. Rana tried to wave her away, for she was not sure she could finish what she had now, and with a quick flick of her head, the dolphin tossed the fish and swallowed it herself as it came down again. Rana began to laugh.

"Oh, how I wish I could really talk to you!"

Had the dolphins and the humpback really communicated with her during her rescue, or was that only part of her delirium? It seemed impossible, but surely it was no more unlikely than that she should be sitting here eating raw fish in the middle of the sea. If Rana really had heard the dolphins, her hold on her body must have by that time been so tenuous that mind-speech came easily. But she was very much alive today!

Frowning thoughtfully, she watched the dolphins play. And suddenly a faint memory surfaced—one of Silverhair's stories, about a man he had met on his wanderings. . . . An old man . . . an old merman, who used to live with the dolphins upon the sea. And this old man had told the harper that he and his bond-kin had used a whistle-language, which could be managed both by human lips and whatever internal apparatus dolphins used to make their squeaks and squeals.

"Listen, sea-brother—will you teach me that speech too?" She willed him to understand her as forcefully as she could, and the Sea Star pulsed at her breast. "Look, here's something to start with—" she held up the half-consumed rockfish. "What's the sound for fish, huh? Surely you must know!"

The big male dipped beneath the water and came up almost touching her. As his bright eye fixed on the fish, she felt suddenly certain he had understood her. At the edge of hearing she heard him squealing, and then, quite clearly, a whistled trill. Pursing chapped lips, Rana tried to imitate that sound.

That night the sea lions came to warm her again. She slept soundly, but despite her exhaustion, or perhaps because of it, she dreamed.

Rana is with Frederic on the Isle of Birds. She identifies it as the island, even though she knows this is not the way it appears to waking eyes. The island she sees is larger and more precipitous. Its rocks soar in fantastic towers of stone, and birds fill the air with cries of haunting beauty. Frederic is telling her that he has found a way off the island that no one else knows.

That is hard to believe, but she follows him up the path around the tallest peak, through silver mists that obscure the world until there is only the fog and the path. The mists begin to glimmer like mother-of-pearl; the moon is shining somewhere above. Frederic assures her that he has come here often. A powerful protector is teaching him.

At last they reach the summit. The veiling vapors thin, and Rana sees an iridescent pathway arching into the purple depths beyond. Standing upon that arch is a luminous figure robed in changeable pale purples and greens and blues. In one hand he holds a drinking horn, in the other, a silver chalice set with moonstones. As they approach him, he pours sparkling water from the horn into the chalice and holds it out to them.

"Behold the water of life! Take, drink, and you shall be reborn!"

Frederic starts forward eagerly and receives the chalice from the Being's hand, but Rana hangs back.

"Go on—" she tells him. "This is not my way. . . ."

"But I cannot leave you here!" Frederic cries.

"Do not be afraid," says the Being, "your way and hers will lead to the same place in the end."

Frederic begins to climb the rainbow bridge. His figure grows transparent and finally disappears. She turns, and

111

realizes that on this side, the peak is a cliff above a moonlight-sequined sea. Its glimmering waters beckon her. For a moment she fears, but then the longing grows too strong for her. She steps to the edge of the cliff and lets herself go, falling forever into indigo darkness that cradles her securely until dawn.

Days and nights passed uncounted. The moon waned and disappeared, and began to swell once more. For the first few days, Rana could do little but rub fish oil on her sore skin, eat what the dolphins brought her, and rest in the lean-to's shade. Every night the turtle shell collected her ration of dew while she slept with the seals, lapped in greater luxury than a queen. But she was not lonely even when her friends were away, for the island was a cross-roads for the people of the sea.

Birds swooped to investigate her—the gulls and terns she had grown to know too well on the Far Alone islands, and once the great pelagic albatross, whose spread wings made a black cross against the turquoise sky. But the sea around the island was also full—groups of white-sided dolphins like the ones who had rescued her, and another species with longer beaks and more delicately shaded markings, who appeared one day in such numbers that their leaping seemed to lash the entire ocean into spray.

The larger cetaceans also were sometimes to be seen. More than once she saw the luminous turquoise flare and stately breeching of the great blue whale, the largest creature on land or sea. Humpbacks came also, rising majestically until the whole huge head and pale under-jaw were visible, then spinning and subsiding back into the sea in an explosive burst of spray. One of them seemed to have taken up station near the island, and Rana could not help but wonder if he was the one who had brought her here. Distant fountains marked the passage of other whales, usually too far away for her to identify, though once, by moonlight, she thought she saw the great blunt brow of a sperm whale rising from the sea.

As the days passed, her sunburn healed and she became sleek and brown, impervious to sun and water, as if the fish-oil had been an enchanted ointment to protect her from all dangers of the sea. The heat of the sun refined her hair to a pale burnished copper like the shimmer of dawn on the waves. Though the diet of fish put no fat on her, she grew strong and healthy once more, and her circulation improved until she stayed warm even when the silver mists hung low over the sea.

Slowly she began to acquire some facility in the whistle speech. The notes for "come" were first, then those for "land" and "sea", "dolphin" and "human", the piercing alarm call when an orca passed and again when two white sharks ventured near. There was also a dolphin equivalent for human laughter—perhaps the one they used most often of all. Rana learned it, but only to laugh with them at herself, for she was never able to catch one of the dolphins off-guard.

She learned names for her rescuers which she interpreted roughly as Flasher, Sharksbane and Pearlgray. And as her sunburn healed, Flasher began to teach her how to swim. A dolphin would not have considered it serious swimming, but it was vastly superior to the thrashing stroke with which she used to exhaust her strength swimming in the Bay. Instead of fighting the water, now she passed through it with a swift undulation produced by a flexible harmony of motion in all her limbs.

That gave her the freedom of the sea. Sometimes she let the dolphins tow her through the water until she tired and let go to lie on her back, sculling gently to maintain position, gazing up at the sky's pure and endless blue. With a little labor, she could make a breathing tube from a giant kelp stem, keeping the upper floats and leaves to maintain contact with the air, and that gave her access to the world underneath the island.

Kelp stems hung from the base of the island like elongated trees, broad leaves glowing like amber where the sunlight passed through gaps in the matted structure above. Rootlike holdfasts anchored them to the rocky sides of the seamount over which the "island" was stationed now, slopes bright with shrubby garnet seagrapes, the vivid purple flare of iridessa, emerald clumps of sea lettuce and the fern-like rockweed, flowered with the feathery pastels of anemones.

Fish darted among the swaying kelp stipes like birds among the trees of some faerie forest. A school of sardines rippled like silver as they passed; a three-foot sheepshead heraldically divided in red and black swam slowly by. Deeper still, wolf eels peered from their holes in the rock of the seamount; the long armored forms of white sturgeon proclaimed their age. Rockfish hid in the depths where Rana could not go, their bright patternings apparent only when one of the dolphins brought one into the light of day.

There were salmon, growing to adult majesty in the freedom of the ocean, and once she glimpsed a greater shape among them, shimmering so that she wondered if perhaps she had seen Grandmother Salmon herself, the Spirit-Keeper of the West whom they invoked at home to send them the bounty of the sea.

Each day there was some new lesson, another place to explore, and more wonders than she had ever imagined. In the evenings Rana would watch the sun go down in a sky of coral and mother-of-pearl, and as the moon ripened she saw figures made of mist and moonshine dancing upon the edges of the waves. By day, she answered to a whistled call, and she might have forgotten that she had ever had a life on land or a human name if it had not been that at night, the dreams continued to come.

Rana is sitting in the Moonlodge with the other girls. On the other side of the fire, the old women clap and chant, chant and beat the water-drum. Rana tries to explain that she had her passage into womanhood three years ago. But she cannot make herself heard.

One by one, the girls go through the dark tunnel for initiation. When Rana's turn comes, the doorkeeper puts her finger to her lips to stop the girl's protest, and pushes her through.

Rana emerges into a cavern. Women are standing there, singing the hymn Rana learned from the priestess who taught the women's mysteries—

"Thou art the Womb of Darkness, the Doorway into Light,
From Thy breast draw we motion, and rest when comes the night.
When all men build lies broken and only pain is sure.
Like children we cry to Thee and know Thou wilt endure."

As Rana enters, the women fall back before her. Behind them is a huge black woman robed in silver and blue. Her draperies curve over her belly, which is distended with pregnancy. The women continue to sing.

"Thou art the Maiden's promise, the Mother's lasting love.
The Crone whose smile holds secrets of earth and sky above.
When learning makes men foolish and earning makes them poor,

Ever constant, ever changing, Thou renewest us once more.”

"Come, my daughter—" The woman's voice fills the cavern. *"Touch my belly that you may be fruitful!”*

Rana shakes her head. *"I don't want children. I don't need anything from You!”*

"Will you spend your whole life sterile and alone? Whether you bear children of the spirit or of the body, they must come from Me. . . .”

"No—" says Rana. *"I am afraid.”*

"Come here! Take My hand—" The woman rises, beckoning, and Rana is drawn towards Her. As the firm clasp of Her cool hand enfolds Rana's, the cavern disappears. They are surrounded by a glimmering vastness through which dim shapes undulate, surrounded by a pearly glow, or dart, trailing sparkling wakes of light.

"What you perceive is the life in all things. You yourself are the same—"

Rana looks down, and sees her own body limned in light. She looks up—now the Lady is as radiant as the moon. She can still hear the women singing—

"Sister, Mistress, Mother—eternal Holy One;
In this world transitory, Thou art surer than the sun;
Thy beauty in the darkness blazes 'till it blinds our eyes.
Wisdom past our understanding, Gateway into Paradise.”

The Lady continues to brighten until Her light fills Rana's vision. As she begins to lose awareness of who and where she is, she hears the Lady's voice again.

"When you see Me again, you will understand. . . .”

Once more, the moon was at the full. Rana sat at the edge of the floating island, watching the dolphins chase moonbeams. Were they playing a game or performing a dance? Perhaps for them, the two were the same. First one, then another exploded from the glittering water in a fountain of crystal spray. For a moment the perfect curve of the dolphin's body was silhouetted against the moon's perfect round, and then the falling form flashed silver again.

And then, suddenly, it ended. Rana saw the three dorsals knifing seaward and whistled in inquiry, for except in emergency, the dolphins had always paused to say goodbye. She stood up, scanning the water for danger. The sea was an abstraction in silver and shadow, endlessly shifting so that whatever pattern one saw altered almost before it could be identified. Rana blinked as her eyes blurred from the strain, then blinked again, as she realized that part of that pattern of black and white remained the same.

It was as if all the shadows had flowed together to form a massive body with a sharply outlined triangular fin the size of a knight's shield, and all the white had fused into the patches that marked the huge head now upraised above her own. Rana scrambled backwards. *Orca!* No wonder the dolphins had got out of the way!

But if her friends were fleeing the orca, why were they still holding station nearby? They could not hope to protect her, and they had not given the danger call. She watched the whale warily, distrusting the twinkle in that humorous eye.

"Come . . ." The orca whistled the summons like a bass shawm playing a tenor recorder's line. Rana edged further away.

Water broke over the edge of the island as the orca subsided back into the sea. Rana stared, for the whale did not seem to be sinking, but dissolving, no, changing, as contours flowed into a different form. The fine hairs prickled along her arms and back as she realized where she had seen something like this before.

Memories of another lifetime came to her—a sunlit glade in the Sacred Wood where the Lord of the Trees had taken the form of a Man. Abruptly she knew that it was not fear that had disturbed the dolphins' game, but awe.

Even in human form the Guardian was huge and hairless, dark-skinned, robed in shining black and white. The island dipped as he rested muscular forearms on its edge. Teeth flashed very white in his dark face as he laughed at her astonishment. As if that laughter had been a signal, the three dolphins leaped in unison.

"Human child, come here!"

Rana felt his deep voice vibrate in her bones. Slowly she obeyed, frightened for a different reason now. Had her distrust offended him?

"Do not fear me, child of men. I am Lord Orca, but I am not hunting now!" Amusement reverberated in his chest. "Indeed, tonight I am only a messenger for One greater than I." He sobered. "Climb upon my back, and I will carry you where you now must go. . . ."

Rana felt gooseflesh pebble her arms, but she dared not disobey. She knew well that the power that saved could also slay, but she could not believe that whatever will had watched over her so lovingly would betray her now. She would have to trust, as she had been doing ever since she gave herself to the sea.

Anticipating her agreement, the Orca had resumed his cetacean form, laying his whole length alongside the island like a boat by a wharf, inviting her to mount in front of his dorsal fin. As soon as she was settled, he surged forward, but the great fin behind her supported her, and her legs gripped the whale's sides and steadied her. She could feel the Orca's great muscles working beneath her, and thought that no Queen had ever ridden such a steed. Thus enthroned, she progressed through the sea, and the whale's wake fanned out behind them in a glittering train. As they drew away from the island, the dolphins took up escort formation: Pearlgray behind them, and Flasher and Sharksbane to either side.

Soon the moonlit oval of the Floating Island dwindled behind them. Now they fared between the mutable sea and the unchanging stars, and Rana, lost in the glory of that riding, forgot that she had ever been afraid.

In that vast expanse of ocean there was no way to judge their speed, but after a time she felt the Orca's motion ease. Presently he halted, rolling a little with the swell. The dolphins floated nearby. Rana looked at them curiously. She had never seen them so still. The quality of their attention froze the question on her lips. What were they waiting for?

Shivering, she gazed around her. They were in the middle of the ocean. There was nothing to see here except the play of moonlight on the waves. With nothing else to focus on, she watched that tantalizing glimmering, until, so gradually that she hardly knew when the change began, the light began to disappear. A quick glance told her that nothing had gone wrong with the moon. It was some darkness arising from the depths that made that shadow. Every story of horrors from the deep she had ever heard began to surface in Rana's memory, and she wondered if the cetaceans' apparent friendship had been only a preparation for some elaborate vengeance by the People of the Sea.

But Rana's life had belonged to the ocean since her boat capsized. And besides, there was nowhere she could go.

And now vision tricked her with alternate glimpses of uncoiling tentacles and a great fringed cloak and sparkling lines of light that formed a pattern that was both and neither. Suddenly the shadow solidified into massive shoulders and a hooded head. Slowly it turned. Rana saw a dark face with a beak of a nose and pointed chin and two wonderful, shining eyes.

"What is your name, my daughter, and where do you dwell?"

It was a woman's voice, deep and liquid, that seemed to come from beneath the waves.

Rana gazed into those eyes, too amazed to fear. "I dwell on the Floating Island, but I lost my name in the Sea."

"You are a child of the land—" The voice held now a hint of sternness. "What are you doing here?"

"The great whale bore me to the island when I would have drowned. The sea lions warmed me. The dolphins taught and fed me. Have I done wrong to take what was so graciously given there?"

"Nay, daughter—no one reaches the Island without the favor of the Sea. It was by my order that Long-Fin bore you there to be tended, taught, and tested. Like the ocean itself, the island is governed by the moon. It is there that the Lord of the Waters, whom men sometimes call the Boatman, meets with the People of the Sea, and sometimes it is a refuge for castaways."

"Like me—" said Rana.

"Not quite like you," said the other. "*You* bear the Sea Star. But you are not, I think, of the royalty of Westria. Why did you take the stone from the place where it lay?"

Rana looked down at the unshielded Jewel that lay upon her breast. She had become so accustomed to its presence that it seemed a part of her. But now, like circulation returning to a frozen limb, she felt it warm as the question awakened memories. She pressed her hands to her eyes and shook her head.

"I am Sea Mother. . . ." her questioner said quietly. "Each part of the ocean has its own guardian, but responsibility for all seas and their creatures is mine. As long as the Jewel you wear stayed quiet, washed by my waters, all was well. But loosed, it will bring harm or healing to my people, depending on how it is employed. And so I ask you, why did you take the Sea Star from the sea? Where were you carrying it, and why?"

"I was carrying it to . . . Julian." Rana clung to the name as to a rock in a tide-race, and slowly, as if she were remembering something that had happened to someone else, she told Sea Mother of the journey she and the Companions had made to Awhai and back again to help Julian search for the Earthstone, and how he had found it, and battled the sorcerer, and died the death of a shaman and waked to life once more.

"And then the reivers captured me, and when I found the Sea Star, I thought some power had meant it to be. For Julian is the true King, and he must have all four Jewels to rule Westria!"

Sea Mother subsided into a darkness upon the water, and there was silence for a little while. Then that wise face took shape again and Rana felt the Guardian's eyes searching her.

"It is not our custom to concern ourselves with the doings of those who live on land. But the Sea Star gives landsmen power to concern themselves with *us*. If it is to be restored to Westria, I must be satisfied that it will be used well. Tell me about this Julian. . . ."

Rana stared at her, wondering what to say. *Julian* . . . What after all did she know of him? At first she had thought him just a friend of Frederic's, but on their journey, so gradually that she hardly knew when the knowledge precipitated in her awareness, she had realized that he was much more.

She frowned, trying to picture him—dark eyes, and dark hair brushed back from a square face . . . a clipped beard that made him look older than his nineteen years . . . arms and shoulders developed to the verge of distortion by cutting granite in the Snowy Mountains . . . But that was not what Sea Mother needed now. Slowly Rana began to speak, remembering things she had not known she knew.

"I would trust him with my life—I think we all would. Julian isn't very comfortable with courts and diplomats, but he understands responsibility and courage very well. No one can push him onto any path he doesn't choose, and he always thinks before he acts. If Julian gets the Sea Star, you needn't worry that he'll use it lightly. The problem will be getting him to use it at all!" She looked at the Guardian in frustration, for even this was not the truth she wanted to tell. How could she convey the steadfastness with which Julian had led them, the dedication with which he had sworn service to the land of Westria, or how the light of the Otherworld had shone in his eyes when she found him in the Sacred Wood upon Midwinter Day?

But the Guardian nodded as if she had understood all the things Rana could not say. "From such a one we have nothing to fear. But this story of the sorcerer troubles me. It was his meddling that scattered the Jewels to the elements before, and from what you say, he has acquired new powers. If the Sea Star came into his hands again, he could break the cycles of the sea, stem the tides, pervert our rhythms to serve his will."

"Caolin has great power over the elements already. Without the Sea Star, how can Julian oppose him?"

"That is true. And it is also true that by right of birth the Jewel is his. Only a power greater than I could deny it to him. Let it be so then. Take the Sea Star to this Julian!" Light shimmered along the edges of Sea Mother's cloak and was gone.

Appalled, Rana perceived where her eager championship of Julian had led her. Perhaps Julian was different,

122

but her experiences on the island had given her a horror of the world of men. Knowing now that there was another existence, how could she return?

"Yes, the Jewel must go to Julian," she exclaimed, "but do I have to take it? Couldn't the dolphins carry it to shore? By this time my people have finished mourning me—why must I go back to them? I have been so happy here!"

The Guardian's deep eyes grew stern. "You have not been a part of the real life of the sea. Each of my people must play his appointed part in the cycle of living. You have only been an observer. Would you have the dolphins deny their natures so that you may live at ease?"

"But they enjoyed it—" she began, and then, "I would do anything for them—what can I do?"

"Nothing. Nor should you. As you say, it has been their pleasure to serve. But you are a child of men. For good or ill, your foremothers long ago abandoned the ocean. Their nature and potential is different now, but your people still have the power to harm their kindred in the sea. You must take the Sea Star to the Prince of Men and teach him what you have learned here. Thus shall we be repaid."

"I will go—" Rana said hopelessly, tasting tears as bitter as the sea. "But I think you would have been kinder to let me die in the sea than to make me live away from it, now that I have been here. I have heard stories about men who died of the sea-longing and thought them only tales. Now I know that they were true. The ocean rebirthed me, the dolphins renamed me. The girl they used to call Rana of Registhorpe is gone." A tidal wave of sorrow rose within her. "You have taught me to be a sea-creature! How can I live away from the sea?"

"You carry the sea within you," Sea Mother answered gently. "In your salt blood and the hollow of your womb;

in the ebb and flow of your life; in the rhythms of love. When you understand that, you will no longer be alone."

Rana stared at her, trying to imprint upon her memory everything her senses could perceive. In the long dry years to come, all she would have was what she could remember now. But the Sea Mother she saw was only a semblance, a form adopted so that the Guardian could talk to her.

"One gift, Lady, before you send me away. Let me see you as you really are!"

"As I really am?" Soft laughter bubbled from below. "My real form is such as human eyes have not the power to look upon! Do you mean that you wish to see me as I appear to the People of the Sea?"

When Rana nodded, Sea Mother laughed again. "Are you sure you will not be afraid? Some of my race have evil hearts, and those, men justly fear. I am a legend of terror at many hearths of men."

"I do not think that the Sea will ever frighten me again," Rana said simply.

For a long moment the Guardian looked at her, and Rana read in those liquid eyes sorrow, and laughter, and a love as deep as the sea. Then the Guardian's outlines blurred. The fringes of her cloak lengthened and solidified, and suddenly eight tentacles were coiling lithely on the surface of the sea. The hood had become a mantle that glistened in the moonlight, nose and chin the wicked beak of an octopus of legendary size.

Of course, thought Rana, *no mammal returned to the sea could hold authority over mailed fish and creatures with and without shells. Even the smaller, short-lived species are among the cleverest dwellers in the deep. Surely the great ones, whose marks we see sometimes upon the backs of the toothed whales, must have wisdom beyond the reckoning of men!*

The limber form before her seemed to flow with the sea, and two luminous eyes looked back at her. But Rana was not afraid.

The night before she left the floating island, Rana dreamed.

She is riding a big piebald horse, black and white, following Julian and the other Companions on an endless trail through a hollow land. Each step the ponies take kicks up a cloud of choking dust, and the wind that whirls it away rustles in the dry stems of the brown grasses on the hills, and rattles the skeletal limbs of leafless trees. The streambeds are all scoured dry, scattered with boulders like bleaching bones. Clearly this is a land that had water once, but there is none any longer. Rana licks parched lips as she rides.

As the dry day wears on, she finds herself moving forward in the line until she is riding behind Julian. As always, he is just a little tense in the saddle, broad shoulders hunched forward as he watches the trail. And so when he stops, she urges her horse up beside him.

The way before them is hidden by a lake of dark water. Silent and still, it reflects the sunlight like a sheet of glass.

"It is a mirage—" says Julian.

"I don't think so," Rana answers him. "But does it matter? We have to go through."

"Of course it matters. If that is really water, it may be too deep for the horses to wade." He begins to rein his horse around.

Rana stares at the dark surface. It seems to her that there is movement just beneath it—an upwelling of sweetness that she can almost smell.

"Are you afraid, Julian? Are you afraid even to try?" She calls to him, kicking her horse past his.

"Rana!" He turns again to come after her, and at the

*very edge of the lake he catches her rein. Now the others
are coming up behind them, and their questions tell Rana
that none of them can see the lake at all. She faces Julian.*

*"My lord, I have followed you through darkness and
danger. But here you must follow me—" Her mount
moves without urging, drawing Julian's after it, and as its
forefeet enter the water, Rana feels a rush of coolness. She
holds Julian's gaze with her own.*

*Sweat beads Julian's forehead. His eyes are as dark as
the lake, but Rana's will compels him. And now she
breathes in the sweet scent of water, and the soft lapping of
waves against the shore soothes her ears.*

*"Oh Julian, don't you feel it now? Come!" She splashes
forward in a cloud of sparkling spray. She sees Julian's
face behind her, blurred by falling water, and realizes that
even though the world is turning green around them, he is
still afraid.*

The dolphins had brought Rana lengths of the giant
kelp to weave into a raft. It was not watertight, but the
bulbs kept it afloat, and more bulbs served to store
enough water for the journey. Flasher and Pearlgray and
Sharksbane and a dozen of their Pearlgray kindred
towed her in relays. Those who were not pulling the raft
leaped exuberantly through the water ahead and around
and beside it, so that at all times Rana was escorted like a
Queen at a festival.

She wept when she lost sight of the Floating Island.
The dolphins had told her that it moved from time to
time, sometimes anchoring at other places even farther
out in the ocean, sometimes drawing landward, so that
the fisherfolk thought they saw a mirage, and sometimes
floating freely with current and tide. They themselves
never knew where they would find it. She might well see
it again. But Rana knew that no one found the Island

except by Sea Mother's favor, and it was the Guardian who was sending her back to the land.

Still, to voyage with the dolphins was itself a wonder, and she thought that perhaps she might become one of the mer-folk, like the old man that Silverhair had known, and spend her summers roving with Flasher's tribe.

In this way for three days they traveled. On the fourth day they sighted land, but it was no coast that Rana had ever seen. Instead of the familiar heights that guarded the entrance to the Bay, she saw fold upon fold of coastal hills dappled with patches of ripe grass. A high, jagged peak dominated a row of outcroppings like the spine of a buried dragon that sloped down toward the sea. At the edge of the land a great dome humped out of the water, perhaps five hundred feet high, and nearer still, a volcanic cone which still trailed a faint wisp of vapor jutted through the waves.

Rana crawled to the edge of her raft and whistled for Sharksbane.

"Where are we? This is not my home!"

"Sea Mother said, bring you here—" came the answer. The dolphin curved under the water and then reappeared beside the raft. "Land people call us—see!"

The sun was westering now. Rana no longer needed to shade her eyes to peer toward the shore. The great rock and the volcano marked the middle of a broad bay. Below them a strip of sand protected a narrow lagoon. Waves lapped gently along most of the bar, but near its southern end the water was being beaten to a froth. And it was not only her own dolphins that were answering the call. All around her she saw dolphins leaping, spouting, sharp dorsals cutting through the waves.

A crowd of people darkened the sandbar. She heard singing, and the pulse-beat of drums. Between people and dolphins the sea boiled with mackerel, a school so great the sea seemed turned to silver as the approaching dolphins drove them toward the shore.

The dolphins drawing the raft slowed, and it rose and fell uneasily on the swells.

"Water gets too shallow to pull," whistled Flasher, who had surfaced nearby. "Sister come—I carry to shore—"

For a moment Rana fought the desire to beg the dolphins to take her back out to sea. But she did not suppose they would do it. They were bound by Sea Mother's law, as was she. She set her hand over the Sea Star, feeling its familiar cool light fill her, remembering why she had come.

"Yes, but remember, when hours of day and night are same, come to Great Bay. You promise farewell before winter wandering!"

"Yes, yes!" the dolphin agreed. "Come now, good fishing!"

Rana laughed, tucked her hair back behind her ears, and slid over the side of the raft. The dolphin's smooth body slid up beneath her, and she grasped the dorsal fin and let him tow her forward, sputtering when she got a faceful of spray. Sharksbane and Pearlgray swam to either side, as they had so often in their days at the island, and for a time Rana could not be sure if the salt that stung her eyes was from seawater or tears.

The sea floor began to shelve rapidly; she could feel the motion of the water change. Flasher slowed, and Rana pulled herself upright on his back so that she could see.

Fish were leaping all around them. The light of the setting sun turned their silver to red gold and lit the laughing faces of the people on the sandspit who were casting their nets to draw the rich harvest in. Someone shouted—they had seen her! First one, then another, pointed. Laughter and movement stilled. Silently they stared as Flasher bore her toward them.

And in the midst of that throng she recognized Julian. He shaded his eyes as if dazzled by the setting sun, but in his face she could see relief beyond hope, and wonder, and fear.

Then Flasher turned broadside to the shore. Rana did not need his whistle to know that he dared swim no closer. She forced herself to focus on Julian's dark gaze, ignoring all the murmuring tongues and staring eyes. As if he had understood, he started toward her. For a moment longer Rana stayed, caressing Flasher's smooth body with one hand. Then she swung her leg over his side and felt sand a few feet beneath her, let her weight down upon it, and for the first time since Midsummer, stood upon solid ground.

PART TWO:

The Moon

The moon is dark.

Julian marches through an endless shadow, in which the blank face of the planet above is matched by the featureless expanse below. Or perhaps it is the earth that has been darkened, and Julian is moving across the hidden face of the moon.

He is searching for something. . . .

Memory of what it is and how he lost it comes and goes, but the urgency and desolation of his search remains constant. He is aware that this march is part of a continuing journey. While Julian walks the waking world he forgets it, but almost every night, now, he dreams, and his quest goes on.

A harsh wind sweeps the sands of this place where he is wandering. The dry grains rattle against his boot and he realizes that they sound so loud because he is a hollow man. He looks back and sees that faceless folk are *following him. How can he lead them when he is missing his soul? Then he realizes that they are hollow too. The whole world will be empty until he finds what he is looking for. Julian aches with a dull sorrow, but his dessicated eyes produce no tears.*

Ahead he can see something gleaming faintly under starshine. As he draws closer, he recognizes the slatted ribs and curving spine of some great sea creature stranded upon an alien shore. Or is it a shore? Julian scuffs his boot across the sand and realizes it consists of a million shattered shells. He is walking upon the dry bed of a long dead sea.

"When the seas die, everything dies. You must find water if you wish the world to live."

Julian looks around him for the speaker and sees a cloaked and hooded figure standing by the skeleton. "Who are you?"

The figure does not answer, and as he approaches, it moves effortlessly away. Julian pursues it, and as it goes faster its draperies are blown aside and he sees a woman's pale flesh gleaming beneath them. The hood falls back, revealing flowing hair. The face is Rana's, and Julian increases his pace in an unavailing effort to come up with her.

"Rana!" he cries. "Are you dead too? Rana, wait for me!"

"You will find life when you find me. . . ."

The swirling sand sweeps around her form, and the whisper of her voice is carried away by the wailing wind. When the wind settles to silence once more, he is alone.

Chapter Seven

Julian woke dry-mouthed and gasping. Gradually he realized that the air he was gulping had the coolness of dawn, and was moist with the damp breath of the sea, and his galloping heartbeat slowed.

You fool, he told himself. *It was only another dream.* The bleak landscape through which he had struggled still seemed appallingly real, but now he could remember other wakings and equally vivid memories of another reality. At least this time he had not awakened the others. A quick glance showed him Silverhair still cocooned in his blankets, and the smaller huddle that was the boy, Piper, nearby. It took Julian a little longer to remember where they were—they had guested at so many holdings on their way down the coast. But presently he recalled their arrival in the tiny village of Los Osos the day before. This was the house of the headwoman, then, and it was dawn.

The rawhide lacings of the bed creaked as Julian sat up, feeling the cool dampness pebble his skin. He focused on the physical sensation, trying to increase his grip on present reality. The dreams had begun the night before the Beltane Festival. He knew now that he should have told the Master of the Junipers, but he had been ashamed to mention a few bad dreams when the Master's whole will was bent on determining whether Frederic and Rana were still alive. But they had been travelling for over a month now, and the dreams had become a second life that had nothing to do with his activities during the day.

He swung his legs over the bedframe. Through the window he glimpsed ghostly cypresses. It would be near noon, he guessed, before the fog burned away. Now, even the waking world seemed part of his dream.

The image of Rana superimposed itself upon the fog. She had been in many of his dreams, gradually changing from the sturdy companion he remembered from the quest for the Earthstone to an unearthly figure who led him ever deeper into the Otherworld. In a curious way, that was reassuring. He did not believe that it was her ghost he was seeing—he had walked in the land of the dead, and he thought he would recognize it again. The country of his nightmares seemed to be some other realm in which their spirits both wandered. Or perhaps his unconscious was only weaving her image into the tapestry of his own fears.

He pulled on his tunic and pushed past the hide that curtained the door. Moisture sparkled in the air, carrying the crisp scent of cypress and the rich odors of the marshland beyond it. His bare feet found the earth damp and yielding; for a moment he stood still in the doorway, letting his skin sense the composition of the soil that booted feet had barriered when they arrived the night before.

When Julian came back from the privies, the village was waking. Two women carrying waterjugs paused to look at him with frank appraisal. Meeting his dark gaze, one giggled behind her hand. Then her eyes widened, and Julian knew that she had seen the tracery of silver scars that marred the left side of his face from temple to cheekbone. His deeper awarenesses were still open from his dreaming. He felt the women's uneasy awe like a physical touch and his inner shielding slammed into place as if he held the Earthstone in his hand, walling him away from human contact.

Their eyes flickered uneasily, and they hurried off toward the distant spring which in this dry season was the only source of water the village had. Julian realized with an all-too-familiar dread that even if no tales had reached Los Osos ahead of him, there would be stories in the village now. He did not know why he was surprised, or why he continued to try. In the other settlements where they had stopped on the way south it had been the same.

Suddenly he could bear it no longer. Wordless, he plunged through the line of cypresses that edged the path. Beyond them lay the still expanse of the lagoon. Julian picked his way down the bank where the reeds were thinnest and stepped out onto the mudflats beyond. At his first step he sank ankle-deep in black muck. For a moment he stood with the other foot poised in the air like a heron, almost in shock from the impressions that the rich precipitate was sending through his skin. Then he let the silky slick mud close over his foot. The stink of composting vegetation filled his nostrils. The muck was so rich in nutrients it was almost animate, but mixed with the familiar identities of plants and soil he sensed the organisms that lived in the brackish water, and more faintly, the swirl and pulse of the nearby sea.

As he stood, Julian felt his spirit beginning to steady.

135

He let his awareness sink through the soles of his feet and drew up strength through them, learning this new land to which he had come. The birds who had been frightened away by his sudden incursion began to return, ruddy ducks and teal floating farther out on the water, and stilts stabbing the mudflats with stiletto bills. A great white heron stalked the shallows, pausing with one foot lifted and sinuous neck recurved to survey the lagoon.

That imperial progress soothed Julian's spirit. He let his gaze go farther, knowing that this place had shaped the people of the village, and if he could understand its spirit, he would be well started towards knowing theirs.

The lagoon parallelled the coastline, connected to the sea at its southern extremity. The sandspit that protected it was dimly visible across the still water, and he saw an occasional glitter of sea-spray from the incoming tide. The people of Los Osos lived on clams and waterfowl, on the fish they could catch from the shore or from the rowboats he saw drawn up to the platform farther down the lagoon. To the northwest, the great bulk of the rock they called the Sentinel loomed through the fog.

With that fog still hiding the horizon, the place seemed secret and secure. Only the half-seen waves hinted that if the mists should lift, the sandbar was all that would separate this sanctuary from the alien realm of the sea.

"Would you like some breakfast, or are you planted there?"

Silverhair's familiar mockery brought Julian back to awareness. For a moment the mud held him, and he wondered if he might have taken root indeed. Then, first one foot and then the other popped free, and he squished back toward solid ground.

The harper's dark eyebrows lifted. Julian followed his gaze downward to a pair of feet as black as the muck from which he had come. He looked up again and grinned.

"You don't think it makes me look like a native?"

Silverhair shook his head, nose wrinkling as the rich reek of sludge began to disperse through the damp air. He waved toward the stream.

"My Prince, if you want any company at breakfast, I suggest you wash!"

Still smiling, Julian made his way around the edge of the water to the stream. When his uncle used the title which still seemed so strange to him, things were either very serious, or Silverhair was teasing him. But his communion with the mud of the lagoon had made him a part of this place in a way that talking could ever do. Perhaps the people would sense now that he belonged here, and his strangeness would not matter.

He finished washing his feet and climbed the bank to rejoin Silverhair. But as they turned toward the enticing scent of cooking sausage, the lookout shouted from across the lagoon.

"A ship! A ship!"

A horncall echoed mournfully through the fog.

"It's a fishing vessel from the north," came the word, "they're looking for the entrance to the lagoon—"

As Julian reached the circle of beaten earth at the center of the village, the headwoman came hurrying up. She was a good leader in her own sphere, but she was turned to the slow cycles of the sea, and this talk of war had unsettled her.

"Is it danger, my lord? What should we do?"

Julian mastered his impatience. "It's only a fishing boat, but she may carry messages. Tell your men to guide her in."

Presently a sail loomed out of the mist, flapping in the still air. The men of Los Osos had taken two of their rowboats to tow her in. Julian recognized the carven dolphin on her prow and began to grin. If this was *Sea*

Brother, then the wounds Arn of Seahold had gotten in the Beltane fight must have healed.

Soon the ship came to rest in the still waters of the lagoon. A line moored her to one of the cypresses, and the crewmen began to clamber over the side. Arn came toward them and started a stiff bow. Julian felt the weight of sorrow he had carried since Beltane ease a little at the sight of him.

Then another man leaped from the rail to the quay with the grace of a young stag, his curly hair the warm brown of a deer's hide.

"Robert! What are you doing here?"

Lord Robert of the Ramparts grinned, his blue eyes suddenly alight as he gripped Julian's hand.

"I persuaded my brother and Lord Eric that their reports needed a personal explanation, but I think they really wanted someone to keep an eye on you!"

Julian began to laugh, remembering some of the escapades Robert had led them into on the borders, and still laughing, they went back to the village.

Julian set down his mug with a sharp rap, steadying it automatically to keep the tea from sloshing across the Regent's dispatches as he stared at Arn.

"The reivers burned the College of Bards?"

He was remembering buildings that looked as if they had grown from the redwoods among which they stood, echoing with music even when there was no sound. They had stopped there just two weeks ago. Why did this destruction sicken him so? It was no worse than the burnt holdings he had seen so often this past year. He cast a quick glance at Silverhair, who had studied there, and saw his knuckles whitening as he gripped the bench.

"The smoke was still rising when we put into the cove a week ago," said Arn. "The reivers must have arrived just at sunset and waited offshore. Just before dawn two sharkships slipped in and set the buildings ablaze. They were waiting when the people came out, and there was some fighting. But by then the villagers had seen the fire and came up in force to help fight it. They thought they had scared off the raiders, but once all the men were out of the way at the College, the sharks looted the village and then escaped out to sea."

"What about the people at the College—" Julian asked quickly. He gripped his uncle's arm and felt the older man trembling.

"Master Andreas did not try and resist the raiders. Two students were killed and several wounded, but he got the rest of them into the forest. One of the masters died—Master Sebastian, they said it was—when he went back into the building where the piano burned." Arn's eyes held a stark awareness that it could have been Seahold.

Julian remembered the charred skeleton of the holding on the coast where they had found Piper and his grandmother the summer before. Mute and wide-eyed, the boy had crept closer to Silverhair now, huddling against the harper as if for protection from the memory.

"The walls must have wailed like dying violins, with smoke like flutesong as all their stored music blazed up into the sky," said Silverhair. "And all because of me. . . . There was no wealth there to tempt them. Caolin set them on to it to strike back at me!" The others stared at him, uncomprehending.

"The Blood Lord has reason to hate me," Silverhair said heavily. "A year ago I helped to drive him from the north. Ten years ago what he saw as my treachery cost him the lordship of Santibar. Nearly twenty years ago I helped to deny him rule over Westria. There is a certain justice in his attacks on me. I knew my presence would endanger them, but Caolin once loved music—has his malice mastered him so far?"

Julian stared, finding it difficult to imagine a Caolin who was not the incarnation of malice whom he had known. His brow tingled where the sorcerer's power had struck him. He forced himself to think again.

"Caolin was behind the trouble in the mountains, but how could he gather forces on the sea?"

"For almost ten years he governed the Campos del Mar on the coast of Elaya. He is master of all the land's outcasts, why not those of the sea as well?"

Julian frowned. They had come southward slowly, stopping at each coastal settlement to evaluate their fighting strength and defenses. But until now, the raiders had confined their attentions to isolated holdings. Everyone assured Julian that the sharks would never dare to attack a village, and it was hard to press the point when he knew the Regent's strength was still tied up protecting Laurelynn.

"Is the Blood Lord still on the Red Mountain?" Julian turned to Arn again.

The young man shrugged. "Rumor says he is. Maybe the dispatches will tell you more. The peak is still shrouded in shadow, so there must be something there. But though Lord Eric's men watch the base of the mountain, supplies are still getting in. Where something can get in, someone could get out again. If the sorcerer used his arts to leave his fortress, we might not know."

"I shouldn't have left—" said Julian. He more than half suspected that the Regent had sent him south to get him away from the Red Mountain. He held out his hand to Arn.

"No!" said Silverhair with sudden fire. "Don't you see what is happening? It was too peaceful during our journey south, but if the reivers have begun to attack the villages, perhaps the folk will listen to us now."

"He's right!" exclaimed Arn. "The Regent can't spare

140

any men to defend the villages, so let's attack the reivers instead! Come back with me by sea! If you come by boat, my lord, the sailors will listen to you. We'll raise men and ships at every village with a harbor and build a naval force that can bite back again!"

"But I don't know anything about the sea!" An odd flash of memory brought back the dead seabed of Julian's dream. He could command the powers of earth, but even the Master of the Junipers had not been able to tell him where to start looking for the Sea Star.

The Earthstone had been buried underground; the water jewel was probably at the bottom of the sea. If it was there it would be equally inaccessible to Caolin, but Julian realized that it was not enough to keep the Sea Star from the sorcerer. With or without the jewel, he was going to have to master the sea.

Arn looked at the prince and grinned. "Come home with me on *Sea Brother* and by the time we get back to Seahold you'll be a sailor!"

"If Julian is going by sea, then so am I—" Robert gave Julian a half-smile. "I have not yet forgiven him for going after the Earthstone without me; I refuse to miss all the fun a second time!"

Julian would not have described last summer's journey as *fun*, but he knew that what Robert resented had been Frederic's admission into a companionship which he had thought all his own. Julian met his cousin's blue gaze steadily. Robert did not yet understand that Julian belonged to others now—to all of Westria, if the land would accept him. Still, it would be good to fight side-by-side again.

"I will come with you whatever he does—" added Silverhair with a kind of feverish eagerness that made Julian uneasy. The College of Bards was the closest thing the harper had to a home. Julian had heard that Silverhair fought like a berserker after Lord Theodor died, and wondered if his uncle was going to go battle-mad again.

"Are you trying to shame me, uncle?" he said gently. He looked back at Arn, seeing a maturity that had not been there six months ago despite, or perhaps because of, the wound he had taken then. Eric had sent the Prince south to keep him safe, but there could be no safety for him as long as there was danger to Westria. He remembered the oath he had sworn at his knighting and felt a flicker of anger at the solicitude that would dishonor him. But the Regent's well-meaning protectiveness was about to backfire. Suddenly he grinned.

"If you will have me on your crew I will be glad for the teaching, and try to do you credit. And it may be that on the way back you'll need not only men who can raise a sail but those who can swing a sword!"

"My lord! It would be an honor—if you are ready, we could be out of here with the afternoon tide!"

Arn was gazing at him with an all-too-familiar light in his eyes. Julian remembered how Frederic had looked when he pledged his loyalty, and silently swore that he would not lose this boy too.

"No—take a night to provision and rest your crew. If we're going to raise a navy, we might as well begin here!" He glanced across the circle. The headwoman was standing with her holders, calming them while she kept one eye on her guests. Arn's sailors must have spread their news then, and the folk of Los Osos were wondering what the strangers would do. Julian forced a smile.

"I can't leave here until tomorrow in any case—I have promised the headwoman I would participate in their festival."

The Regent would like the idea of his precious Prince upon the sea even less than having him near the Red Mountain. Eric had already lost a son to the reivers, and he had treated Julian like a cat with one kitten ever since Spear Island. But Arn and Silverhair were right. Offense was their only defense now, and if they could not recover Frederic and Rana, at least they would avenge them!

The village throbbed with the hollow echo of the water drums and the sky blazed silver as the sun burned the mists away. Even the newcomers had been absorbed into the preparations for the Festival. Inland, they would be getting ready to invite the animal kindreds to the Feast of the First People. On the coasts the rite was different, though here too they celebrated the alliance of sea people and humankind.

Nets stretched like spiderwebs across the central circle as the fishers, stripped already to a twist of bright cloth and adorned with clattering necklaces of shell, made a final inspection. Arn's crew had already been parceled out among them. Fishers themselves, they checked the nets with a professional eye, arguing amicably over the value of various knots and weaves. Naked children ran screeching among them, brown all over from the summer sun and flourishing flat paddles that had been painted with the undulant sigils of the sea.

Householders had decorated their rooftrees with the carven sea-beasts of their clans, and in the field behind the village, women were raking the earth over firepits filled with ears of corn. From everywhere came the smells of baking and the sound of singing. The grace notes of Piper's fluting lilted among the other musics, sweet as the piping of one of the little birds that darted along the shore. Even Silverhair had taken out his harp again, though the morning's news still etched his lean features with pain.

Only Julian found it hard to join in the revelry. Why

should sharing a feast induce anyone to follow him? Better to leave the sea to those who understood it, he thought, seeing the easy acceptance that had grown already between Arn's crew and the fishermen. There was no way he could share that comradeship.

The sweet sonority of a horn call floated through the air, and the activity became at once more intense and more purposeful. Crew by crew, the fishers gathered their nets into careful swags; households formed up chattering excitedly, paddles waving in the air. Soon the flat-bottomed boats were busy ferrying folk across the lagoon.

The headwoman, her weather-bronzed features barely containing her pride in the show, invited Julian and Silverhair to cross in her own boat. They were nearly the last, and as the keel crunched sand, Julian saw that the whole village was strung out along the bar.

"Look, the sun has blessed us! We will have a fine harvest for the Festival!" The headwoman gestured seaward, and Julian blinked at the sudden glitter of sunlight on the waves. The last of the mist was vanishing, and the water shone like silver-gilt. Julian was glad to get under the shade of the shelter of boughs. He took his seat and Robert eased down on the sand beside him. The people were singing, the downbeats punctuated by the liquid boom of the water drum, and rattles made of shells filled with pebbles that hissed like the foam when it kisses the shore.

"Down to the depths of the billowing sea.
Over the waves goes our calling—
Out with the tide, from the hills flowing free.
Down with the raindrops swift-falling—"

The voices soared with a lilt that was like the rhythm of the waves. As the music quickened into the chorus, the people with the paddles moved into the shallows and smacked out the tempo.

"Silver they shimmer, bright the swift swimmer!
Leaping in laughter, joy will come after!
Come brothers, dear brothers.
Herd the fish here, brothers!"

The paddlers stayed where they were, water foaming about their ankles, while the others took up the melody. The paddles splashed out the chorus as the singers moved farther into the sea. Glittering arcs of spray followed them and they laughed, splashing each other eagerly.

"Won't the splashing drive the fish away?" asked Julian.

The headwoman smiled. "If the Guardians are kind the fish will be driven, but not by our splashing. You will see!"

Courtesy forbade Julian to spoil the woman's enjoyment of her mystery by probing. He shaded his eyes against the glare of sun on water. Now the sea was clear all the way to the horizon, blue waves dancing beneath an azure sky, while a playful breeze added an edging of lace to the wavelets in the shallow bay. The sand beneath his bare feet was warm and dry, but lifeless. All the life was in the water here.

Verse by verse the song continued, and chorus by chorus the beaters moved farther into the sea. The sun was westering now, and Julian saw them in silhouette, aureoled with glistening spray.

"Sea brothers, sea sisters, bless us again,
Fountaining white breath above us—
Honor the covenant once made with men.
Show that sea spirits still love us!"

Julian laughed then, having finally figured out just what power the villagers were invoking, though he was as

145

far as ever from understanding how that was going to provide fish for the Festival.

"Silver they shimmer, bright the swift swimmer!
Leaping in laughter, joy will come after!
Come brothers, dear brothers,
Herd the fish here, brothers!"

Suddenly the singing faltered. The horns blew again, and the song was taken up with renewed fervor.

"Splash! Splash!" By now the beaters were waist-deep in the waves. The paddles slapped lustily, sending up showers of spray. The fishermen marched into the water behind them, fanning out so that the weighted nets hung free.

Julian was on his feet with the others, shouting. In the distance he saw a white line of foam as if a reef were shearing through the sea. And now the waves glittered; gleaming bodies thrashed wildly, leaping into the air in frantic flight and tumbled back again.

"Come brothers, dear brothers,
Herd the fish here, brothers!"

Shouting with excitement, the people had given up on verses, and now only the last lines were repeated with increasing intensity. Drum and rattle and paddle beat out the compulsive rhythm until Julian felt it in the beat of his heart, in the pulse at his throat, resonating in his belly, vibrating in his bones. Everyone was in the ocean now, whistling, cheering, stripping off excess garments. The sea seethed with silver, and the fishers braced themselves as the mackerel were flung against their nets and tangled there.

And now, beyond the maelstrom of shining bodies Julian saw the sleek dark grey shapes of the hunters leaping through the water in clouds of crystal spray as they snapped up thrashing fish in strong jaws. As they had for generations, the dolphins had honored their bond with the people of the village, and both partners to

146

the agreement would come full-fed from this Festival. Grunting, the fishers began to draw the long nets closed.

Still standing on the sandspit above the others, Julian was the first to see in the midst of all that flashing silver one gleam of gold. But in a moment the headwoman sensed his stillness, and shaded her eyes to see.

"It must be the sun—" said Julian. The spark of gold was moving steadily shoreward with a motion quite different from the darting of the dolphins or the panicked dashing of their prey.

"Yes, but what is it shining on? I have never seen such a thing in my lifetime."

"Dolphins," said Silverhair. "There are three of them, and one of them carries something gold." Piper pointed, dancing with frustration and excitement. The murmur spread as people gaped, their attention distracted from the frenzy around them. Now they could see the dolphins clearly, and the men fell silent, for on the back of the one in the middle was a girl, limned in shades of red gold. The dolphin shifted direction, and blue light flared.

"Is it a sea-sprite?" said someone. "No, one of the Guardians!" "Is it the Lady of the Sea?" The chanting had faded to silence, but still the whispers ran.

But Julian felt that radiance pierce him, and his head swam with visions to which he could give no name. Yet the light had an aching familiarity, and he felt his heart begin to pound, slow and heavy, in his breast. Without willing it, his feet were carrying him to the water's edge.

As the dolphins neared the fisherfolk gave way to either side. The rider was a girl, golden-skinned, with hair the color of the setting sun. Between her young breasts a silver-set pendant glowed with pale fire.

They halted a boat's length offshore. Julian heard a burst of clicks and whistling; the girl's eyes focused and met his. He blinked, dazzled by the twinned light of the jewel at her breast and her blue gaze. He read confusion, and the pain of approaching loss, and fear. And he read recognition there as well.

Reluctantly she slipped off the dolphin's back and cast her arms around it in a desperate embrace. The other two slid forward and nosed at her hand. Then they began to ease away. The girl staggered, but by that time, Julian was already striding into the water. She bit her lip, trying to balance, looking at him in desperate, mute appeal.

And then he had reached her, and she leaned into the support of his strong arms.

"Julian—" Her voice cracked, as if it had not been used for too long. "I found it for you . . . the Sea Star. . . ." She fumbled at the cord around her neck.

But of course by then he had realized what it must be. The lucent glimmer of the stone half-blinded him, and the pulse of its nearness rocked him like the buffeting of the waves. But the body he was holding was warm, and solid, and alive!

"Rana"—he was finding it as hard to speak as she— "you are a greater gift than the stone!"

"It comes with the favor of the people of the sea!" She had got the Jewel off now, and seemed steadier. Her face shone with a terrible beauty, and he saw for the first time fully revealed the Goddess within. Rana's eyes fixed his and he could not look away, could not even move as she reached to slip the thong over his head and pulled it down so that the Sea Star rested above Julian's heart. The soaked cloth transmitted its power as if it had been touching his bare skin. A great wave was rising above them, purple and blue and sea-green dazzling vision; the roaring deafened him.

"Use it well!"

Only Rana's words came clearly as the great wave fell.

Like a tidal wave spreading outward from some under-sea eruption, the unleashed power of the Sea Star pulsed through the planes. Sensing it, Sea Mother knew that Rana had been true to her trust, and waited to see how this unknown prince would fulfill his. In Awahna, the blue cloak of the Lady of Westria suddenly deepened in hue, and the air around her echoed with the sighing of the sea; the figure of the Lord of the Waters manifested within the greatest of the waterfalls. On the Lady Mountain, the Master of the Junipers felt his heart quicken and guessed what had happened, for in spirit he was often with Julian.

And in his study on the Red Mountain, Caolin dropped the list of losses to Westrian maritime trade and clung to his desk as a dark tide flooded over him, tearing at the moorings of his mind until he feared to be carried away, for he too had been Master of the Jewels for a little while. The places in his psyche where the contact had been broken when he was forced to cast them away throbbed like the nerve endings to a missing limb.

When Julian had first put on the Earthstone, the sorcerer had been struck senseless. But that had happened deep in the bowels of the Red Mountain, at the roots of Caolin's own power. This contact was more distant, and broken off more quickly as something muted the Sea Star's energy, but this time the sorcerer recognized it sooner. Rallying, he focused his awareness to follow that flood of sensation back to its source, but almost immediately it dwindled and disappeared.

Gasping, Caolin came to himself again. How had the boy found it? Julian had not been searching for the Jewel, not this time. The Blood Lord had kept watch on him and would have known. But he felt as if he had stepped into quicksand. He had been so sure that the Sea Star was at the bottom of the sea!

And yet, even this chance might be turned to advantage, for the sorcerer was as eager as Julian for the Four Jewels of Westria to be found. Perhaps even more so, thought Caolin as he remembered how reluctant the boy had been to make use of the Earthstone's power, for the Blood Lord *knew* that he could master them. Let Julian find them and save him the labor, then.

Now that he thought about it, the brevity of the contact suggested that Julian already feared the Jewel's power. The People of the Wood had taught him about the Earthstone, but who would teach him how to rule the Sea Star? Julian had never yet sailed upon the open ocean. His very mastery of the land might make it harder for him to learn the sea.

But the Blood Lord needed more information in order to plan, and he dared not spend his own strength getting it when there was so much yet to do. Swiftly he slid the report back into its case, rose from his hard chair and swept toward the door.

He emerged from his study like a spider from its hole and soon the word was passing through the fortress— "*The Blood Lord is hunting again. . . .*" Men checked their equipment, lest some slight slackness bring down his wrath. They looked also to the cracks and corners of Blood Gard, ready to root out any hidden sprout of green. The Wolfmaster hunted rarely and no one knew how he chose his victims, but since last winter it had become clear that any vegetation on the top of the Red Mountain would surely bring down his wrath. Every stone of the fortress had been scraped and scoured, but there was always the fear that some windborne seed would flower.

Now, the ruddy light of the setting sun dyed the sorcerer's robes with a lurid splendor as he stalked across the parapet. In the courtyard below men had gathered to relax before the evening meal. For such as these, that meant smoking the harsh tobacco they favored, a little dicing, an occasional fight, and the perpetual gossip of any garrison. But as they glimpsed the crimson figure above them, slouched backs straightened and laughter failed. They waited, still as if his will had already bound them, trembling at the touch of the Blood Lord's veiled gaze.

"Captain Esteban . . ." Low pitched, the voice still carried to every corner of the yard. "That man—bring him to me!"

The gloved finger stabbed downward, and men edged away until the armsman at whom Caolin had pointed was standing alone. He was very young, but he had lost his boyhood in a rough school, and his shoulders had grown massive with hard labor. Shaggy brown hair fell to his shoulders; dark eyes sought desperately among his fellows, but no one would meet his gaze. And then the captain's hard fingers were gripping his shoulder. Unresisting, he allowed himself to be led away.

Caolin paid no attention to the nervous rattle of conversation that broke out as the victim disappeared. He knew already the ribald commentaries with which the men, in a desperate search for reassurance, would try to account for their fellow's fall. They were well-fed and well-paid in the Blood Lord's service and had regular opportunities to indulge a taste for cruelty. It would take a great deal more than this to wear out their capacity for rationalizing injustice.

In fact, the boy had done nothing wrong. Nor was the resemblance the sorcerer was looking for a particularly close one. But it would serve for what he had to do. Caolin moved swiftly to the main stair, arriving on the landing at the same time as Captain Esteban brought in his prisoner. He snapped his fingers, and frightened brown eyes lifted to meet his.

"What is his name?" he said without letting the boy escape his gaze.

"Jorge, my lord—" The Captain's voice held no emotion at all.

· "Well, Jorge, there is no need to be afraid. . . . You haven't done anything wrong, have you? No, I thought not . . . that's why I chose you for this job. I need your help, lad, that's all—you're willing to help me, aren't you?" Automatically the sorcerer noted the subtle easing in muscle tension, the little sigh.

"Y—yes, m'lord—"

Immediately the gloved hand came up, the crystal it held kindling the light that shafted through the narrow window to pale flame. As the boy's gaze fixed on that flicker, Caolin's voice continued its seductive murmur. It was easier when the attention was distracted by some bauble, and when they consented, however unwittingly.

"I have him now—you may leave us—" he murmured presently, and the Captain bowed and turned away. "Come now, lad, there's good fortune in store for you," he said more loudly. "Follow me."

There was a guestchamber on the next level of the tower, the only richly appointed room in the fortress. Caolin opened the door to it and pointed to the chair across which lay a tunic of purple brocade.

"Put it on, lad—yes, now you are dressed in a manner more befitting your station! Does that surprise you? The fact is that the boy they are calling the Prince in Laurelynn is a pretender—a nobody the Regent has foisted upon the people to bolster his power. You are the true Prince! Did you never suspect it? But who should know better than I what really happened to the Queen and her child? I have watched over you in secret, but now it is time to prepare you for your destiny."

The sorcerer's sharp eyes saw every changing play of expression on the boy's face as he put on the rich robe. Did the lout believe it? Did every child growing up in a shanty dream he was a royal foundling? But Jorge's blunt features had relaxed now into a complacent smile.

"My Prince, there is one final test I must perform. Will you come down to the Temple with me?"

The boy followed, still fondling the smooth stuff of his robe.

Darkness greeted them. Then Caolin lifted his lamp and glimpsed the familiar glitter of metal and stone. He moved to the western altar and lighted the sea-green candles there. Suddenly the corner glimmered with sea-green and purple and the rainbow iridescence of mother-of-pearl. The sorcerer started the incense, and soon the air was cloudy with sweet, choking swirls.

"Breathe deeply now—yes, that's right, relax and breathe in. . . ." He saw the boy's eyes dilate as the narcotic smoke began to affect him. He would be ready soon.

"Who are you?" asked the sorcerer softly.

"The Prince. . . ." came the slow reply.

"What is your name?"

"Jor—no, m' name is Julian!"

"Yes, Julian! You *are* Julian. . . ." Swiftly Caolin sketched in a history that deftly mingled fact and fancy. "And if you are the Prince of Westria, then you are rightful Master of the Jewels! Think about the Jewels, my prince—think about the Sea Star, a blue moonstone surrounded by silver dolphins . . . do you see it? See how it glimmers, how the light pulses now. . . ."

The smoke of the incense had set the candles to flickering hypnotically—dark, light, dark, bright. . . . Caolin felt his own focus wavering and fought to maintain control. He slipped the little knife from its sheath and reached out to slide the brocade sleeve back from the prisoner's arm.

"One last test . . . you'll hardly feel this . . . yes, that's right, just let it flow. . . ."

The boy scarcely flinched as the blade sliced across his

153

wrist. As the bright blood spurted the sorcerer sheathed the knife and held the silver bowl that had been on the altar under his hand. Jorge's face paled beneath the tan and he began to sway, but the bowl filled quickly. Caolin could feel the life in it, and knew he must work quickly. There was a stirring in the mountain beneath him as he lifted Jorge's arm and a few drops of blood spattered across the floor, but that was not the power he needed just now. He set the bowl back on the altar and his strong fingers closed on the boy's wrist, pressing shut the severed skin.

"That's enough—let it stop now! Seal the skin and stop the bleeding, that's right—now sit down and rest . . ." He lowered the half-conscious boy to the floor and swiftly bound up the wound. There might be other uses for this creature later, and there was no point in letting him bleed to death here.

Then he took up the bowl of blood. The dark liquid reflected the glimmer of the candles with a dim sheen; light moved slowly across the surface, drawing the gaze. Caolin drew a deep breath and felt the smoke reaching for him again, but this time he did not fight it. Instead he eased down before the altar with the silver bowl between his hands.

"Lifeblood, flowing salt as the sea . . . Julian's blood, speak now to me!" whispered the sorcerer. His body settled swiftly into the rigid stillness to which he had trained it. His eyes fixed on the shining liquid in the bowl, then unfocused as his awareness sank towards that surface and through.

Consciousness floated in a red darkness. Slowly and with dream-like distortion, the images began to form—a long curve of bay guarded by a great hump of stone . . . people splashing in the waves of a sunlit sea . . . fish fleeing the jaws of hunting dolphins, and with them, a golden girl on whose breast blazed a blue jewel.

When Caolin came to himself again, he understood who had brought Julian the Sea Star, and where he and the stone were now. He permitted himself a small, satisfied smile, for he knew already which of his many secret servants he would contact to deal with this, and how he would instruct him.

Chapter Eight

As if the power of the Sea Star had banished the fog, the evening remained clear. With no moon to dim their splendor, the heavens pulsed with glittering stars as the fish in their multitudes had filled the sea. When the men of the village cast more logs on the bonfire in the center of the green, sparks darted upwards like stragglers hastening after the great schools in the skies. The night air was murmurous with snatches of harpsong and soft laughter as the people feasted on the bounty of the sea.

Only Julian, sitting in the place of honor with Lord Robert and Arn, was silent. Rana sat beside him, great-eyed and shivering in one of the headwoman's gowns. Her sea-bleached hair had been pulled back in a braid that left her face a mask of browned skin stretched over the good bones of the skull. Julian remembered the sturdy girl who had plagued him through the quest for the Earthstone and sighed.

The air was balmy; most of the people had not troubled to resume the clothes they had taken off that afternoon. Julian understood quite well that it was not the temperature, but the presence of so many people that was troubling Rana. He had eaten as much as he could in an attempt to ground himself after the shock of putting on the Sea Star, but he still felt as if he were missing a layer of skin.

Robert had pulled him and Rana from the waves when they fell, and Silverhair had given him the piece of silk he used to polish his harp in which to wrap the Jewel. Thus shielded, it hung around his neck once more, but he was constantly aware of it, and of Rana as well. He did not know whether it was because they had been linked in the moment when she gave him the Sea Star, or whether something of her personality had been imprinted on the stone, but he seemed to feel her emotions as his own.

He hoped that a night's sleep would help settle him. It was hard enough to deal with his own alienation without the added burden of hers, though he had to admit that for the villagers, the wonder of a Prince who had risen from the dead paled beside that of the girl who had risen from the sea. It was unfortunate that their bond denied him the relief that the shift in attention might have given him. If he had had the Earthstone with him it might have been easier to ground, but the Jewel was in the keeping of the People of the Wood, hidden in the grave that had for a short time been Julian's. Even if all other defenses should fail, the sorcerer dared not seek it there.

"I had no idea that mackerel could taste so good!" Robert leaned back against the trunk of the cypress, eyeing the fragments that remained on his basketry platter regretfully. Firelight gilded the perfect planes of his face and glinted on his curly hair. "The only sea-fish I ever had before was salted. I only wish I could eat more!" Most of that afternoon's catch had been set aside to dry for the winter, but there had been plenty for the night's feasting.

"I am glad you enjoyed it, lord—we feared you might find our hospitality poor after Laurelynn—" The headwoman's brown face lit with pleasure, and Julian felt a spurt of delight that his cousin had come. Robert did not have Frederic's sweetness, but he moved through life with the same unconscious assurance, and his beauty would have won him favor even if his manners had not. The village women had been trying to flirt with him all evening, but as usual, he ignored them.

"Come, Rana—why don't you finish this for me? You've scarcely eaten, and the Lady knows how long it's been since you ate properly!"

Robert held out his platter to Rana with courtly grace and she flinched away. Instantly Julian reached to intercept it, understanding already that she did not like to be touched and, unlike the headwoman, was repelled by Robert's charm.

"Let me try—I was still too unsettled to eat much before." He forced a few mouthfuls down. Rana sighed and turned to the headwoman.

"You must forgive me," she said in a low voice. "It is not your cooking, only that I am not used to it. It is all so rich—it would make me ill."

"Ah, you poor child, I had forgotten! You know you are welcome to recover here—after such an experience, you might well fear to travel home by sea!" the headwoman said comfortably.

"No—no, I just need time, that's all!" For a moment panic showed in Rana's gray eyes, and abruptly Julian understood. He had seen her head lift to listen when a shift in the wind brought the sound of waves on the shore, and what her face showed then was not fear. The Sea Star pulsed at his breast, and for a moment he was shaken by longing for something he had never known. He would have to watch Rana on the way home, he thought then, or some moonlit night she would slip over the side.

For a moment there was silence, and he heard Silverhair's trained voice beginning the tale of the greedy fisherman who tried to cast his nets in the Milky Way.

"Not that the land is likely to be so much safer, these days—" the headwoman said then. "Do you truly think the sharkships will strike so far south?"

"Mistress, they are *from* the south!" said Rana harshly. "The scrapings of Elaya man those galleys—to call them sharks is an insult to the People of the Sea."

Her voice shook, and Julian recoiled from the wave of hatred that came with the words. Rana had told him a little of her escape, but nothing of her captivity. Open as he was to her, he sensed a torment of the spirit that would take more than food and rest to heal. But it was men who had hurt her, not the sea.

"Perhaps they will not come here, but you must be prepared," said Robert.

"We could make a boom to close the entrance to the lagoon—" the headwoman said thoughtfully.

"Their ships have no keels. The reivers can run them ashore on the sandbar and swim the lagoon," answered Rana. "They'll do it, if they think you're worth plundering!"

"Build the boom by all means, but post lookouts as well," added Robert. "Can that great rock we passed coming in be climbed? A watcher there would see anyone coming in from the north, and a beacon fire would warn you."

Julian recognized with relief the echo of lessons he and Robert had learned the hard way when the two of them served in the Ramparts in the border patrol. At least there would be someone with experience to stand in while he was trying to deal with the Sea Star. But the headwoman was shaking her head anxiously.

"Not on the Sentinel! We could put a man on the headland, maybe, but not on the rock. It is an evil place—no one goes there."

"What is wrong with it?" asked Julian.

"In the time of the Ancients, it was a great place of power. Our traditions say that the men of old compelled the service of demons that never die and imprisoned them there." Even in the firelight, the woman seemed to pale.

"When the Cataclysm came, the walls were broken and invisible death filled the air. The people died, and all around here the land sickened as well. Then the Guardians caused a new volcano to burst from the bed of the sea, and molten rock covered the old temple and the worst of its demons and barred the channel to the sea. After that a great wave made the southern passage so that the lagoon would not die, and we rebuilt our village here. But there are still evil spirits near the great rock, and people who fish there fall sick, or their children are monsters. . . ."

"There is a place like that near the Far Alone islands," said Rana. "The Sea People do not go there. . . ."

Julian nodded. Most of the evils as well as the wonders of the old ones had been buried by the Cataclysm, but not all. The Master of the Junipers had mapped for him the places where ancient evils still haunted the land— the earth itself told him sometimes when poison lay buried beneath it or was seeping upwards through the soil. But the sins of the Ancients were not his responsibility—it was the evil of living men that he must deal with now.

"Set a watch on both headlands," he told the headwoman, "and place your boom. Make your people practice getting out of the village quickly, and prepare hiding places for your boats and food. You may not be able to prevent the reivers from burning the buildings, but you can save lives!"

"Build blinds from which you can ambush them—" added Robert.

"Set sharpened stakes in the mud of the lagoon!" said Arn. "Show them that we fisherfolk have teeth too!"

"Then bite back!" Rana exclaimed. "We must never stop fighting them! We will only have peace from the reivers when the fish have cleaned their bones!"

Harp music chimed as if in echo, and a child asked Silverhair for more.

"But there is no more—" came the harper's reply. "When the fisherman got tangled in his nets the star fish nibbled at him until he was all gone, but his ship continued to sail the heavens, and for all I know, it is sailing there still. . . ."

Julian shivered and looked quickly at the others, but no one else seemed to have heard. There had to be an end to the fighting someday, and to the search that drove him on. His hand moved to touch the unfathomed, ambiguous power that throbbed at his breast. If he learned to understand the Sea Star perhaps he could stop it.

If he could learn in time. . . .

Sea Brother prepared to depart the next morning with newly filled water casks, and well-provisioned with saltfish, cornmeal, and dried fruit. The headwoman came down to the platform to watch as her men prepared to tow the ship back out to sea. They had rigged canvas between the cabin and the half-deck in the stern to protect the stores, and Arn moved with only a hint of stiffness from deck to shore and back again, directing the loading.

"He's recovered well—" said Silverhair, watching.

"Yes," answered Julian. A night's sleep had settled him somewhat, but he was still abnormally aware of the scent and sound of the sea. Yet for a moment present awareness gave way to memory of a circle of fire disintegrating into the Bay as the sharkships came. Once more he tasted the bitterness of seeing his friends in danger without being able to go to their aid, and the despair of the moment when he realized that Frederic and Rana had been taken prisoner.

"Why such a black look?" said Robert, coming up beside him with a spring to his step that belied the amount he had had to drink the night before. "Did all that fish disagree with you?"

"It had better not," Julian made an attempt to answer in kind. "Or I'll starve on the way home!"

"What's wrong?" Robert sobered, looking at him. Clearly, Julian's attempt at humor had not been successful. "I was wondering about Frederic. . . ."

Robert's smile was a little twisted as he nodded his understanding. "I shouldn't be envious, considering the position the lad is probably in now. And I flatter myself that you would be just as anxious if it had happened to me!"

Wordless, Julian gripped his cousin's arm and felt Robert's hand close over his own. It was true, for both Frederic and Robert had offered him the gift of their loyalty, at moments when either of them would have been justified in asking for his instead. It often seemed to him that both of his friends were more princely than he was, and Robert, at least, had as good a claim to the throne. That they should vie to serve him always astonished him.

Through the skin of their linked hands Julian felt a wash of anxious affection, and his eyes stung in involuntary response. He gave Robert's arm a quick squeeze and turned away, trying to hide his emotion. What was happening to him? It had been months since he had wept for anything, so how could a passing thought threaten him with tears?

"At least one of your lost lambs is safely returned to the fold—" came Robert's voice behind him.

Julian blinked to clear his sight and saw Rana's rigid figure at the end of the quay. She was staring at the band of blue water beyond the sandbar, and the naked longing her face revealed struck him with sudden wonder. Rana had returned from a realm as strange as any in Silverhair's tales, and now they were going back to it. He felt his pulse quicken with anticipation.

The supplies were all aboard. Arn beckoned to them from the stern. Almost instantly, it seemed, Rana had swung herself over the side to join him, the boy Piper scampering after. The rowers were in their boats, coiling the towlines. Julian saw that the villagers had gathered on the bank. It was time to go, but something must be said, or they would hover here forever like ghosts waiting for the Boatman to ferry them to the farthest shore.

Julian waved back at Arn, then turned again to bow to the headwoman.

"Mistress—I have to thank you for your hospitality. Should I say a few words to your folk as well?" He nodded toward the people who were watching them.

Her face brightened. "We would be grateful. They are still confused and afraid."

So am I! thought Julian. He set his hand around the shrouded Sea Star and was immediately submerged in an intensified awareness of their emotions. What could he say?

He licked dry lips and summoned up the trite phrases with which he had made shift before—gratitude for such a kind reception, the good cooking, the beauty of the setting. . . . But once started, his words flowed more easily, and suddenly his heart went out to them. His

163

awkwardness was obvious; could they hear also how much he cared for them?

"But the beauty of your home can be a burden if you are afraid to lose it. Does the news we brought frighten you? It should! I have seen gutted villages—" Julian's throat closed as he remembered. "But—but Los Osos doesn't have to be one of them!"

"You fear the reivers because they are dangerous and unknown. Make that fear work for you! Let it help you work harder, and remember—they don't know *you*. You can be dangerous too if you're ready for them!" He paused a moment to consider the ripe gold of the hills behind the village, dotted with oak trees, and the dark sweep of the cypresses that grew nearer the shore.

"That tangle of brush behind the village could hide an army. Even the muck that I almost got stuck in yesterday could be a weapon if you know how to use it!" He gestured expressively and was rewarded by their laughter. That warmth dissolved some last barrier, and he felt the tide of feeling lifting him again.

"This land is your blood and bone! As the body fights off infection, it will help defend you. You may feel alone here, but you are the heart of Westria. If you—and the many other places like you—resist evil, then Westria will survive!" Julian stopped suddenly, swallowing. A gull's call split the silence, and then the people of Los Osos responded with a roar like the incoming tide.

The cheering bore him backward to the ship. He clambered on board, and the headwoman cast off the ropes that had tethered *Sea Brother* to the quay. The ship jerked as the towlines grew taut, and then settled to a smooth glide as she followed the rowboats across the still waters of the lagoon. A startled heron flapped away with awkward grace, and the swimming ducks went bottoms-up, bobbing back a few moments later in the boat's wake, quacking indignantly.

Julian stood in the stern, watching the thatched roofs of the village dwindle behind him, peaceful and perfect in the summer sun. Would it still look like that a year from now? *Lord of the Waters*, he prayed, *help me use your power to protect them all!*

And then the deck lifted beneath him. Rana laughed as Julian staggered. They were turning into the channel, and for the first time he felt the motion of the sea. The rowers pulled strongly, and in minutes they were through. Arn began to snap out quick orders; the towlines were cast off and he used the last of *Sea Brother's* momentum to bring her round. The ship rocked uneasily and Julian clung to the rail. Instinctively he sought to ground himself, but instead of earth's solid support, he linked into an unstable fluidity that he could not understand and, panicking, broke contact.

Pulleys squeaked as the sailors hauled on the sheets and the mainsail went rattling up the mast. For a moment the canvas flapped loudly, then the sailors got it trimmed, and the big sail bellied smoothly to port with the breeze. A quiver ran through the ship's timbers and Julian felt her come alive beneath him. Ever more swiftly she began to move, rolling in rhythm with the waves.

Haze hid the jagged wall of the Ramparts where at summer's end the snows had shrunk to icy patches on the highest slopes and the rivers to trickling mountain streams. Even from the highest point on the Red Mountain, only the occasional peak was visible, and then only at dawn, when the dew had partly settled the dust of the day. That same dust, lifted by the dry wind that scoured the Dragon Waste and gleaned the chaff from the newly harvested fields, covered the Great Valley with an impenetrable shroud. Even the fortifications at the foot of the Mountain where the Regent had encamped his futile guard could scarcely be seen.

But Caolin, stalking the parapet of his tower with the dark flame of his robes licking the dry stone behind him, was not watching them. The Blood Lord looked westward, where the cool grey mists of summer veiled the sea. He unfolded the papers he was carrying. As the light strengthened, Zoltan's bold scrawl became ever more visible.

"The Regent's whelp continues to live. Knowing his value as a hostage, I shot to disable without killing, but his hold on life is not strong. The lady nurses him like an old dame with a sick lapdog. But she cannot be there always. If you desire his death, instruct me—it can be easily accomplished. This Frederic recovers like one not sure whether life is worth the trouble. . . ."

Caolin read in those lines the scorn of a man who had never hesitated over either his goals or his means. But the sorcerer no longer made the mistake of underestimating his enemies. Both Julian and his friend had already troubled his peace too much for him to entirely despise them, but the Blood Lord had already given orders that would immobilize Julian, and perhaps this brush with death had taken the heart out of Frederic.

The challenge and countersign of the changing guard came faint from below. The Blood Lord straightened, and let some lingering tension flow from his limbs. Blood Gard was well-supplied and well-garrisoned, scornful of all the Regent's efforts against it. Caolin had bested the enemies of his own generation, and the young ones had not the backbone to carry on the fight for long.

Now the sun was fully risen, and the messenger who had brought Zoltan's letter was still waiting below. Caolin retreated from the brightness outside into his study, took ink and paper, and began to write rapidly. Zoltan was to let Frederic live, for now. The boy could be held in reserve until Westria was conquered, and the Blood Lord could make Eric's death more bitter by killing his favorite son before his eyes. There was no longer any reason to endure the annoyance of this siege. When Zoltan received his letter, the reivers would make a conflagration of the coast that would stretch Westria's strength until it was broken by Caolin's power.

The burning of the College of Bards had only been a warning. Caolin allowed himself to feel satisfaction at the thought of how Farin Silverhair would suffer when he heard. He knew how to kill the man's spirit before the inevitable day when the harper's body came into the Blood Lord's power.

When his response was finished, he summoned Captain Esteban, with orders to escort the messenger through the cordon of Eric's troops and back to the little cove just above Longbay which for months now had been in the hands of Caolin's men. He knew that it would take neither violence nor sorcery to get through the Westrian lines, only a little patience, until one of the men who had taken the Blood Lord's gold was on guard. In a week or two, the message would be in Zoltan's hands, and then things would begin to move.

It was not until Caolin re-read Zoltan's letter that evening that he took note of the bitterness in Zoltan's reference to Ardra. That the girl venerated noble birth he knew, but even respect for Frederic's rank did not quite explain the devotion that Zoltan had implied. Was this Zoltan's jealousy? The reiver had not been able to hide his lust for Ardra, and Caolin found it amusing to tantalize him with the possibility that possession of her might eventually reward his labors.

There was only one way to find out, and as he descended the stairs to his temple, the sorcerer realized how long it had been since he had made contact. If there was something wrong, perhaps he should deal with it personally. For the moment there was nothing at Blood Gard that could not be handled by Ordrey, and the sea war would be managed more effectively from the islands, especially now, when Julian was blundering about the coast with the Sea Star. The sorcerer's step quickened with anticipation.

Swiftly, he set incense and candles to burning on the western altar. He had given the false Julian's blood to the Mountain, but a dark crust still darkened the bottom of the silver bowl. That did not matter. What he had to do tonight was much simpler. From the altar he took a piece of granite from the Far Alone isles. The candles were burning steadily now, but the smoke of the incense blurred the colors of the altar. The sorcerer drew in a deep breath, letting the scent trigger his shift to the level on which he could make the journey he intended now. Already he could feel his awareness deepening.

He picked up the piece of stone, and holding it, let himself sink inward. His body stilled. Now the swirling of the incense was the only movement in the room. His eyes were focused downward, sight and touch fixed on the rock until he lost awareness of all else, and then the surface of the stone itself disappeared.

On the Isle of Birds, the light of a single lamp burned low in the red pavilion. Frederic stirred restlessly and moaned, tormented by nightmares. His face was achingly thin, and nearly as white as the sheet beneath him, for he had lost a great deal of blood before Lorca managed to stanch the arrow wounds. Reaching out to soothe him, Ardra paused, and as her eyes unfocused, her hand fell slowly to lie in her lap again.

"*Ardra*—" the call came again, familiar as memory. "*Ardra, listen to me*—"

"*Master, I hear you . . .*" her spirit replied. She sat unseeing now, rigid as stone. Frederic, half-waking, saw her stillness and thought it part of the horror of his dream.

"*My princess, you seem weary . . . Tell me . . .*"

"I have watched over him with all my will, but still he does not mend. His strength wanes with the moon. I am no healer! How can I make him want to live again?"

"Does his life matter so?" Caolin's thought came measured, even kindly. But, controlled by the link, for the girl there was no dissembling. Ardra's response was powered by an anguish that she might not herself have consciously recognized.

"It matters to me!"

For a time there was no reply. The sorcerer felt Ardra begin to lose focus and drift toward consciousness again.

"You shall have a healer. Send a ship to Bull Cove a week from now. He will be waiting there."

When the link with Ardra faded, Caolin did not at once pull free. Here, in this suspended reality, all minds which had submitted to his will were open to him, and he must not waste the opportunity to gain information. Carefully he cast his mind southward, seeking *Sea Brother*, and the member of her crew who belonged to him.

Sea Brother's passage south had been a swift one, running free before the wind. But now the wind was against them, and even if they had not been obligated to make every possible landing to give their warning, the return would have taken more time. To Julian, inundated by new awareness, the voyage was an extension of his dreams.

For most of that first day they tacked out from the Bay, anxious to avoid the evil that haunted the Sentinel. When they had enough sea room to pass the point they found that the bluffs were becoming higher while the grassy hills drew down to the shore. For a time the two boys who had joined them in Los Osos could name both the visible rocks and the more dangerous ones that they could not see; then they passed beyond local knowledge, and Arn had only his chart for guide. Near sundown the country opened out, and they saw the smoke of a village above the pines on shore, but the shore was rocky and shoaling, and without a pilot there was no way for them to land. They spent that night on the ocean with a good watch to make sure that the sea anchor kept them from drifting too close to that treacherous shore. Julian slept fitfully, adrift on a sea of dreams.

By noon of the second day, he had recovered enough to ask Rana the names of Arn's crew.

"The stocky girl is Marta—none of the other women who usually crew on *Sea Brother* wanted to leave their children this long. The one with the white chin-whiskers is Will. He taught Arn most of what he knows about the sea. He'll tell you, too, if you have a year to listen. It's not that there's so much information, but every point he makes is illustrated by some long and usually unbelievable story!" Rana grinned. Being at sea had restored to her all of the confidence that Julian had lost. "But don't ask me to listen! When I was growing up I spent a lot of my time at Seahold, and I think I've heard them all!"

Julian nodded, then put out his hand to the rail once more as the ship heeled. Rana stood with her arms crossed, balancing easily and leaning a little into the wind.

"What about the boy with the new scar?" he said when *Sea Brother* had righted herself again.

"That's Raymond. He got married last year, just before Arn and Bella. I guess he got the wound at Beltane. Theo is the little one next to him, and the big man coiling line is Fernando. You need to watch out for him, too—he's as bad as a herald for making awful puns."

The ship heeled again, sending a flutter along the foresail, and Arn called out to Gully, the skinny black youngster who was steering, to alter course a little to port to catch the wind. An old man was sitting cross-legged on the deck beside him, whittling a tiny figure of a dolphin with precise strokes of a very long knife. The ship's changed motion had not caused him to miss a stroke, and Julian stared. He had noticed the old fellow making such carvings before, and supposed he meant them for presents, or perhaps to sell when he got home again.

"That's Bertram—" Rana grimaced at the word.

"What's wrong with him?" Julian responded to her tone.

"Nothing. I suppose. He's very clever with his hands, and useful enough if a line needs splicing, or any of the fittings need repair. He's gloomy though. At Beltane—" Rana stopped suddenly, and her eyes shifted away from his.

"What happened at Beltane?" asked Julian, when her silence had gone on just a little too long.

"Nothing really, it's just funny—" She shrugged, her gaze still on the horizon. "I threw my necklace overboard as an offering, and he told me that now I belonged to the sea!"

"And it was true. . . ." said Julian quietly.

"Yes—" the answer came on a sigh, and once more the girl looked at him, with a shining in her gaze he had not seen since she came ashore. His awareness stirred with impressions of green depths and silver shapes moving silently.

"But the sea sent me back again," she added sadly.

Julian, his hand on the Sea Star, shook his head. "No—you are still part of the ocean. You carry it within. . . ."

Both of them looked up as the ship began to turn. Ahead of them, a low, wooded point curved out from the shore, forming a small, protected bay. One boat lay anchored there, and two more were fishing offshore. Above the low bluff, whitewashed buildings were scat-

171

tered among the pines. As they drew closer, a bell clanged from the nearer fishing boat, and both craft began to pull for shore.

"They're not taking any chances, are they?" said Robert, picking his way along the deck to join them. "I'm glad somebody has believed our warnings."

Still holding onto the rail, Julian worked his way around to the bow, where Arn and Will were casting the lead to feel their way in.

"Can you hoist our banner?" he asked the captain. "No sense in frightening them when there's no need!"

Arn nodded, and soon the green Seagate pennon was fluttering from the mast. Moving slowly under reefed foresail, *Sea Brother* eased toward land. Their banner had been seen, and the fishermen came out to escort the larger ship in.

"There's hard sand bottom in the middle there, if y' mean to anchor—" came the shout from below.

"Thank you," cried Arn. "What is this place called?"

"Hurst Bay," came the answer. "Yer welcome here, an' yer friendly."

"We are. This is *Sea Brother*, headed north to the Bay with the Prince on board. I'm Arn Austinson of Seahold, commanding."

"Come on then, and tell us all the news!"

The settlement was small—a few families who lived by fishing and the vegetables they could grow, trading for beef and bread with holdings farther back in the hills. Far from having heard of Julian's coastal defense appeal, they had not even heard of Julian, and it took a fair deal of explaining as well as a generous serving of Seahold wine before they would believe in him.

"But if you didn't hear the proclamation, why were you so quick with the warning when you saw us coming in?" asked Arn.

"Well, captain, those sea wolves have bit us before!" said the oldest of the fishermen. "Not right here, mind you, but a holding aways upcoast. There's a bit of a beach just in from Cross Rock, and we figure they landed there and were up to the house before the folk knew. They burned the holding to the ground, the bastards, and killed the whole family!"

Julian heard an inarticulate wail from the other side of the fire. By the time he got there Silverhair had already pinned a thrashing figure that struggled with eel-like agility.

"No, Piper, it's all over now! Piper lad, be still—it's all past and there's nothing you can do!" The harper kept up a running patter in his captive's ear. Julian squatted down and gripped the child's ankle firmly in a broad hand whose muscles had been hardened by years of cutting stone.

"Piper! Listen to me—" For a moment the boy stilled. "Your family is gone. But your grandmother is waiting for you at Bongarde, and Silverhair and Rana and I are right here, remember? We love you, lad—we're your family now. . . ." He let his voice ease into the soothing murmur he had learned from the Master of the Junipers. He felt Piper jerk once more, and tightened his grip, but it was only weeping, and after a little he let go and the harper gathered the sobbing child into his arms.

"What is it with the lad?" asked the fisherman.

"Don't you recognize him?" countered Julian. "We came down from the north by land last year, and found that holding you spoke of just after the raiders had gone. There were only the old woman and this boy left alive, and the child was running wild in the hills. He liked the harp music, though, and they came with us when we went on. Piper still doesn't speak, but he seems content most of the time. I'm afraid that coming here has brought it all back to him. . . ." He looked back at the

boy and shivered for, even muffled, the Sea Star amplified his emotion, and for the first time he understood the
anguish that had shocked speech from the child.

"So that's what's wrong with him!" said Robert. "I did
wonder, but with the chick running after the harper like a
little shadow, I didn't think it would be tactful to
enquire."

"You thought he was a love child?" asked Julian.
Sometimes he forgot that Robert had learned cynicism
as well as courtliness, growing up at his brother's court in
Rivered. "No, my uncle has no child of his blood."

But Robert might well be forgiven for the suspicion,
Julian thought as he watched Silverhair smooth back
Piper's hair and then give him his handkerchief. The
harper had mellowed from the acid-tongued bard who
had set out with them from Bongarde over a year ago,
but it was still unexpected to see him comforting this
damaged child with such tenderness.

"There, isn't that better?" murmured Silverhair. "And
now I'll play you to sleep. What would you like to hear,
hmm?" Agile fingers drew a delicate music from the
strings. "I know one you like—lie down now, lad, and
listen!"

As if all that unexpressed emotion had exhausted him,
Piper slid down against the harper and curled up with his
head resting on Silverhair's thigh. Rana tucked a cloak
around him, and the harper began to play.

"Boat, bear me back, over the sea—
back to the land where the heart is!
Weary the soul of the wanderer must be,
far from the land where the heart is. . . .

Fair are the meadows, and noble are the hills,
and the folk of this place are well-seeming,
but the speech of my kinfolk to me is fairer still,
and the sun on my own waters gleaming."

For a few phrases the harp carried the music. Julian

saw that Piper's cheeks were wet with tears. The Prince closed his own eyes, seeing in memory the sun bright upon the great Bay, and realized for the first time that he had begun to think of the lands around it as home.

"My heart remains restless, my feet want to roam,
from yesterday's task to tomorrow's.
I serve without master, no hearth is my home,
and I leave each new land without sorrow."

Silverhair's gaze had gone inward, and Julian knew he was remembering the years of his own wandering.

"Yet one day my keel will turn shoreward at last,
as a bird turns at dusk to her homing.
I will sit by the fire and turn tales of times past,
for I will be done with my roaming."

The harper looked up and met Julian's eyes with a wry smile, as if to say that his days of sitting by the fireside must be somewhere in the future. But it seemed to Julian that despite his self-mockery there was a peace in Silverhair's eyes that had not been there a year ago, a peace that was mirrored in the sleeping face of the boy by his side.

That night Julian dreamed that they were picking their way down the coast trail again. In front of him rode a figure with a harpcase slung across his back, and a boy clinging to the saddle behind him. Julian shouted and tried to come up with them, and as he did so, the harper turned, and he saw that it was Piper, grown to manhood. The boy turned too, and shouted out some greeting, and Julian saw that he was a stranger, but a stranger with brilliant blue eyes and Rana's blazing hair.

Chapter Nine

By the time *Sea Brother* set sail the next morning, the men of Hurst Bay had promised to send one of their vessels to Seahold, fully manned and equipped for war. The date for the gathering was a matter of some dispute, for it would take time for Julian to gather and train forces sufficient to give battle, and yet the fighting must be over before the winter gales. The beginning of October was finally agreed upon.

Squinting at the sparkling surface of the ocean, Julian found it hard to imagine a seafight. He had fought on shipboard once, at Beltane, on vessels safely anchored in the protected waters of the Bay. When *Sea Brother* was moving, he could hardly get from bow to stern without holding on to something. If other people had not depended on him, there would have been something comic in the vision of himself leading a battle upon the sea.

Coming around the point, the full force of the breeze

176

hit them, and the ship bucked and shuddered as she tacked close-hauled back and forth across the wind. For the rest of that day they struggled along a low coastline of small bluffs and rolling treeless hills. From the breakers the ocean floor shelved gradually, dotted liberally with kelp-fringed rocks that discouraged any attempt to go ashore. They anchored early that night in the shelter of Cross Rock, for the folk at Hurst Bay had warned them that the coast became even more unfriendly beyond.

The mist still hung heavy above the water when they got underway the next morning. The wind had dropped, but they could hear the sound of surf on rocks from the shore. Arn steered a conservative course until the freshening breeze blew the fog away. Then they were grateful he had done so, for the land was rising rapidly in a series of rocky points that jutted out from cliffs several hundred feet high. Beyond them mountains rose sheer to the sky, broken here and there where a gorge slashed downward to the sea. They could see seals sporting in the waves that dashed themselves upon the toothed shoreline, but the snarling surf warned *Sea Brother* away.

They headed out to sea then, and as the ship plunged and rolled northwestward, Arn decided that it was time for Julian's education to begin.

"This is a sheet—"

Automatically Julian took the rope that Arn held out to him.

"What's the matter?" Rana laughed. "You look as if he had dropped a seasnake into your hand!" Julian glared at her, feeling his fingers become even clumsier because she was watching him.

"But this is a rope. I thought that sheet was another word for sail," he protested. A larger swell lifted the ship and he grabbed for the rail. Rana laughed again.

"Once it's on shipboard, it isn't even a rope any

more—" explained Arn patiently. "It's called line. The sheets are the lines that *control* the sails. The ones that raise sail are called halyards, and the masts are held steady by stays and shrouds. All of them together are the rigging, but each part of the rigging has its own function and name."

"I'll never remember them all!" Julian gazed up at the webwork of lines radiating from the great mast.

"You must, my lord, if you intend to command the men of the sea!" answered Arn, and Rana, serious now, echoed him.

"Think, Julian—how would you judge a soldier who talked about the *handle* of his sword?"

Julian lifted his other hand as if to deflect her words. She was right, of course, but a soldier could concentrate on his weapons and his enemy without worrying about keeping his footing on the battlefield. He faced Arn again, but he was still aware of Rana behind him. He wished she would go away, though reason told him that on the ship there was really nowhere for her to go. Even when she was silent, he could feel her presence— unwilling, as if the Jewel drew her; resentful, as if she chafed against that internal compulsion; malicious, as if she found his discomfiture a modest compensation for her own. Was she sorry she had given him the Sea Star? At that moment Julian would happily have given it back to her.

With an effort, he focused his attention back to Arn, who was still talking.

"So if I told you to haul in the mainsheet, what would you do?" Arn paused expectantly, and Julian thought furiously, reluctant to be shamed in front of Rana again.

"I'd be doing something to this big sail, wouldn't I? Do you mean I should pull on this ro—this line," he corrected himself, "here?" He touched the line that was attached to the boom.

"That's right," said Arn rather more heartily than Julian thought necessary. "Now if you wanted to lower the mainsail—" he was interrupted by a shout from the bow, and they all turned.

"Captain, could you just come over? We seem to be taking in a bit of water here." Gully spoke lightly, but Julian felt his skin chill, and did not know whether it were his own fear speaking, or he had sensed some hidden meaning in the boy's words.

"I suppose I'll have to look at it—" said Arn, equally casual. "Rana, why don't you show him the right way to coil a line?"

"Come on—" Rana's invitation sounded ungracious, and as Julian was about to resent it he realized that she would rather have followed Arn. And that was only natural, he thought with an abrupt shift of feeling.

"I'm sorry—" he said as they sat down in front of the locker and she began to pull out a coil of line. More than he could put into words lay unspoken between them. He was sorry that the reivers had captured her, that the sea had claimed her, and that she had had to give up the Sea Star to one who was obviously so unworthy of it. But there was nothing he could do. "I know it's a bore for you to teach me something you've probably known since you were two years old!"

"Not quite that long." Rana gave him an unwilling smile. "Remember, Registhorpe lies inland too. I didn't start learning about boats until I was big enough to ride over to Seahold alone, but Bella and I had to learn fast then, to stop Arn's teasing!" She gestured toward the locker.

"Even if you're in a hurry, don't ever just bundle loose line in there! For one thing, unless all the cordage is coiled neatly, there won't be room. But more important, undoing a tangled line could take time you don't have to

179

lose." She had spilled a coil of line across the deck, and now she offered it to him.

"Hold it up and hand it round deasil—keep it even, now—until you've got just enough left to go around and through. Yes, that's right—" She watched critically as Julian wound the rope with growing confidence. This, after all, was not so new to him. Anyone who worked with animals could do it, even though he called it rope, not line. Deftly, he wrapped the loose end around the coil, and drew it through the top.

"Very good—" Rana inspected his work, and then smiled. "I suppose we could do knots now . . ." she went on.

Julian shook his head. "I would rather find out what is making Arn look so worried up there, wouldn't you?"

Rana shaded her eyes with her hand and looked where Julian was pointing. A shift in the wind brought Arn's next words clearly.

"We went over every inch of this hull when we had her out of the water after Beltane and she was sound!" He sounded as if someone had insulted him. Gully murmured something they could not hear. "Yes, yes, I know—" Arn went on. "It would be easy enough to fix on shore, but right now we don't have that option. Get out the pitchpot and do what you can." He grimaced, then jumped to the foredeck.

"Fernando, Will, bring her around to port now." He watched as Will hauled on the mainsheet and Blackbeard adjusted the rudder. As *Sea Brother* rolled onto the new tack, he jumped down again to check the leak, patted Gully's shoulder, and then moved down the deck, frowning.

"What's wrong?" asked Julian.

Arn looked up. "A leaking seam—just a small one, but it puzzles me, because it shouldn't be there. We've gone about to reduce pressure on that side while we do some

180

caulking, but we'll be on those rocks if we follow this course for long. Reducing sail may help, but it will delay us, and no seaman wants to spend any more time than he has to off such an inhospitable shore."

As Arn made his way aft to speak to Fernando, Julian shifted focus from the small stage of the boat to the jagged backdrop of the coastline. He blinked, for a moment dizzied by the abrupt change in perspective. When you were inside it, the ship seemed not a stage, but a world, kept from crowding by division into territories. From the foredeck to stern locker was a journey, and the deckspace occupied by a man's outstretched legs a domain. It occurred to him that the land was not always so different. When he had crept along those cliffs the year before the world had been shrunken to the next difficult bit of trail. But now he saw the mountains in their harsh totality, an alien universe that bared its teeth at the fragile floating world of men. They were hard, those mountains, stripped by wind and water to the enduring bone. They had resisted the other elements for centuries; the strength that had survived that endless war could splinter slim timbers and tear the flesh of men with casual cruelty.

Julian's belly clenched. He could feel the instinctive panic responses of his body amplifying his anxiety—or was it *his* anxiety? He made himself let go of the mast and turn. Rana was crouched beside him, her face chalky beneath its tan and sweat beading on her brow. He heard her harsh breathing, found his own echoing it, and forced control, counting until it was steady again.

"Rana—" his voice was low, but without thinking he had put the hard edge into it that he learned to use on the borders when one of his men seemed about to give way to fear. "Rana, sit up! That's right—now look at me! Take a deep breath and let it out again, slowly. . . . Feel the deck beneath you. You're safe now—safe with me!"

On impulse, he took her hand and set it over the hard lump at his breast that was the Sea Star. For a moment the wave of shared emotion nearly overwhelmed them both, then Julian felt a steadying, not the solid cessation of motion with which one came to rest on land, but a flexible suspension, as if some other power held him and Rana in balanced harmony.

"The Sea—" whispered Rana. "Safety is in the sea. . . ." Her eyes were shining.

"For you, and perhaps for me—" answered Julian, in that moment believing it. "But for these others it is the ship. We must do what we can to help them!"

"Yes . . ." Rana drew a long, shuddering sigh and pulled her hand away. "Of course. I don't know what happened to me!"

Julian, feeling his own heart resume its steady beat, thought that perhaps he was beginning to understand. His own panic had set off in her a sea-creature's fear of the land, and the emotion that resonated between them had nearly overwhelmed them. It was the fault of the Sea Star. It would probably link them as long as he and she and the Jewel were all in such proximity. The bond was an uncomfortable byproduct of his possession of the Jewel, but now that he had realized what was happening, he thought he would be able to compensate. He wondered if Rana understood what had happened. With both of them back to normal, he could not tell, and he found himself curiously unwilling to ask her.

The rocks were closer now. Waves crashed against jagged pillars of stone in fountains of white spray. Arn was ordering a reef in the mainsail now, and Rana and Julian got out of the way as the excess canvas was lashed to the boom and another order swung the reduced sail around. For a moment *Sea Brother* pitched uneasily, then the wind filled the sail and they were rolling seaward again, and Gully, with his eye on the patched seam in the bow, got ready to bail.

Drawn by the heat of the land, the fog that had blanketed the sea began to move toward the shore. *Sea Brother* passed through its first wisps as though a thickening veil had been drawn between her and the coastline. Arn got out the lodestone and ordered another reef in the sail, and they crept onward as an early darkness fell.

Farther north, the fog breasted the coastal hills like a breaking wave and rolled swiftly through the gap of the Gateway across the Bay. Here, the hills of the Royal Domain slowed it, but in time the pressure behind pushed it over these crests as well, and tendrils of fog found the passes and rolled through.

From the Red Mountain they could see it coming as if in ghostly repetition of the Cataclysm when tidal waves had devastated the land. A breath of cool air heralded it, and the men whom the Regent had set to guard the Mountain reached for the tunics they had laid aside during the heat of the day. By midnight, mist lay heavy in the hollows and sparkled in the air where the nightguards' torches passed. Now men went cloaked and hooded, identifying each other by the countersign.

No one saw the secret door in the side of the mountain opening, or noted the brown-cloaked shadow that stole down the path. When it came to Eric's perimeter, the guard thought he saw his captain, and even if he had not, the man in the brown cloak knew the password. When the guard went off duty later on he did not even think to mention that anyone had gone by.

But Caolin moved swiftly through the camp to the horselines, laid a compulsion upon the man who watched there to select a sturdy beast and saddle it, and was riding along the river toward the Bay Ferry by the time morning came. It took him another two days to reach Bull Cove.

When, on the third morning, Zoltan's sharkship crept past the rocks and beached itself upon the sandy crescent of the cove, they found a nut-brown man in a healer's yellow robe warming his hands over a tiny fire. Neither then nor later did Zoltan realize who he was.

For a week *Sea Brother* crept northward, nosing shoreward to check her position when the mist lifted, and fleeing seaward again as the breakers warned them away. The seam in the bow continued to leak, requiring constant bailing, and though it got no worse, it was a constant anxiety. Three days after the leak appeared they discovered that one of the water casks had gone bad, and Arn put them on half-rations. Now the mountains with their trickling waterfalls seemed like a paradise guarded by watchful dragons. But all they could do was go on.

There were other difficulties—ropes that should not have broken, stores that should not have spoiled, incidents that were insignificant in themselves, but whose impact was cumulative. The Seahold men began to whisper. It was certainly true that none of these accidents had happened before they came to Los Osos. At times Julian thought that it was only the men's inability to decide whether it was the two lads from the village, Rana, or he himself who was most likely to have jinxed the vessel that kept the fishers from making one of them a sacrifice to the sea. Or perhaps they were discouraged by the knowledge that Julian and Robert and Silverhair were all trained swordsmen and that Arn would fight along with them.

By the end of that week those aboard *Sea Brother* were divided, with Arn unhappily caught between them. At night the newcomers retreated to the stern, and tacit agreement divided the watch between the three fighters.

By day, Arn and Julian tried to go on with their lessons in seamanship, while unhappiness showed in every line of Rana's body as she gazed out over the waves. Only Silverhair could sometimes defuse the tension with a song.

They had been a week and a half at sea, and the harper's sweet voice was covering the sound of a quarrel between Gully and Raymond.

"I sing, brothers, now of a man called Arion,
a harper great, in a great king's hall,
who, though he with gold and with prizes was laden
did nonetheless answer the blue sea's call."

Rana, who knew the chorus, turned from her place by the figurehead to lead it.

"Sing now, and praise the sweet people of the sea,
that they still strong to save may be!"

The harper continued with a smile.

"One day he desired to a far land to travel,
and found him a ship fair and swift to go.
High was her prow and her sails were of purple,
golden her hull, and her decks like snow.

But when they were far out upon the bright ocean,
the sailors conspired to have his gold.
Taking their swords, they came then to Arion,
said by sea or steel, he should not grow old.

Pleaded he then, he, the master of music,
that he at least might his death song sing.
He rose, and clasping his bard's cloak around him,
set hand to the harp that had pleased a King."

Listening, one remembered that the purple cloak of a master bard was waiting whenever Silverhair cared to claim it, and that the harp he played had been given him by the King of Westria. Julian saw the anger leaving the sailors' faces, as if the music had mastered them as well.

"To hear him, the white clouds did stop in the heavens.
Fish leaped to know what the song might be.

He finished, and then with a blow snapped the harp-
strings,
bowed, and committed him to the sea."

Strings twanged as Silverhair struck them, startling everyone, but the harper went on mercilessly, challenging them to think where hatred could lead.

"The sailors sat down to count over their booty,
nor thought of Arion in his wet grave,
who sank, while the ocean washed over his body,
'till there was no music except the wave.

But lo, there waited one of the sea people—
sweet brother—who loved to hear the song,
who on his back brought Arion from under
and bore him to safety, a journey long."

And as if the harper's song had been a summoning, the dolphins came.

Gray shapes out of gray mist appearing, smooth backs rising from the curve of a wave, of a sudden they were gamboling around *Sea Brother* as if her figurehead had come to life and returned to the sea. Triumphantly, Silverhair finished his song.

"And when the sailors came at last to harbor,
and swore they had done as the bard them bade,
Arion came forth like a ghost to confound them,
and so they died with no dolphin to aid!"

Rana cried out a welcome, and leaned over the side, questioning them in a queer mixture of whistles and squeals. The Sea Star throbbed at Julian's breast and he drew closer. The sight of the dolphins met some need in him he had not known was there.

"Where did they come from?" asked Arn. "They act as if they know you!"

"They do!" answered Rana. "They saved my life not so long ago!" She saw Julian close beside her and taking his arm, spoke to the dolphins again.

A burst of chattering came in answer, and once more

the dolphins leaped high. Julian did not flinch from the spray that doused him as they re-entered the water, but his throat was tight as suddenly he sensed something of what Rana had sacrificed to bring him the Jewel.

"They give you their greetings and their homage—" said Rana. Julian nodded.

"I honor them—say that they shall have whatever protection I can give."

Once more the girl spoke to her strange friends. Then she laughed.

"Sharksbane says that here it is we who need his protection, and wonders what we are doing so far out to sea?"

"It's no choice of ours!" exclaimed Arn bitterly, gesturing at the mist around them. "If we had dolphin senses, perhaps we could find our way to shore."

Julian frowned. "Rana—ask your friend if he knows where the nearest harbor is?" Rana's eyes sparkled as she understood him and she turned to the dolphins again.

"He tells me that there's a small one with a man-place—a village—a little behind us, and a very large bay with several villages around the point ahead."

"Have we passed Lady Bay?" asked Arn. "I suppose we must have, Sea Mother knows we could never have found our way in with this fog. The big bay must be Montera—can he tell us how far it is?"

"Not the distance, but at the speed we've been going he thinks we could be there tomorrow," came the reply.

Julian leaned over the rail and met the dolphin's bright eye. "Ask if he and his companions will pilot us in—"

Through the night they followed the dolphins, and as the sun rose on a new day the fog began to lift at last. Julian felt as if the cloud of suspicion that had haunted them was disappearing too.

The dolphins had set a course for their namesake that brought *Sea Brother* around the Point of Pines at dawn, and now, as the changed motion of the sea told them they had entered protected waters, the mists began to thin and a glimmer of sunlight broke through. Silently they watched as gray-green hills appeared in the distance. A band of dark pines was swiftly revealed and then hidden again. But the fog was losing its battle against the strengthening sun, and the glimpses of land grew steadily more substantial, until they could see the twenty-mile sweep of pale sand that curved from point to point of the bay.

The dolphins left then, and though Rana wept as they disappeared back into the mists that still shrouded the ocean, the others were too excited by the sight of land to mourn them for long.

Now the sunlight was striking sparkles of brilliant blue from the sea. They moved gently through glowing waters dotted with clumps of floating kelp, past rocks where sea lions barked challenge and startled pelicans rose in clumsy flight. Screaming gulls wheeled around them, but nobody noticed them. All eyes were on the thin spirals of smoke that twined above a white-walled village midway along the shore. A wharf extended into the bay before it, and as they drew closer they could see bare masts sharp against the pale sky.

"That'll be Elkhorn," said old Will. "I wintered there once, long ago. The Salt River makes those marshes where it empties into the bay. It has no defenses, but the Lord of Las Costas used to maintain a watchtower on the northern headland, above the village there."

"Not anymore," said Silverhair bitterly. "For certain it gave no protection to the College of Bards when the reivers came . . ." There was an uncomfortable silence.

"We stopped at Elkhorn on our way south," said Julian finally. "I didn't recognize it from the sea. I never thought I would be so happy to see it again." Everyone laughed.

There was movement on the shore now. Arn's men crowded to *Sea Brother*'s bow, waving. Julian stood with Silverhair and Robert by the mainmast, while Rana remained in the stern, looking behind her out to sea. The fishers had begun to cheer, and only Julian heard Rana's cry.

He left the others and went to her. Too upset to speak, she pointed toward a clump of seaweed. For a moment Julian could not see what she was trying to show him, then his eye made sense of the shapes and colors and he realized that in the kelp a sea otter lay tangled, stiff as one of old Bertram's carvings, its silky fur matted with blood from a long cut as if it had been sliced open with a sword. In a clump of kelp beyond it were two more. One of them had been a female, and her cub lay dead, perhaps of starvation, nearby.

Julian had seen men killed in battle, but something about this wasteful destruction of an animal sickened him. He opened his mouth to call the others, but at that moment Arn ordered his men to lower the jib and hold the mainsail ready to luff as *Sea Brother* came alongside the quay, and by the time it was quiet enough for him to be heard, the clump of kelp and its burden had been left behind.

"I don't like that—" said Julian. "I thought the fisherfolk considered it ill-luck to wantonly slay the people of the sea."

"More than ill-luck," whispered Rana in answer. "No fisher would do it, but there are others who prey on the sea—" Her fingers clenched on the rail.

"The reivers? They might have done it on their way south after they burned the College of Bards," said Julian. "But surely we'd see damage to the village if they had been here recently!"

Sea Brother was barely moving now. Arn hailed the shore, and after a moment a man with the rolling gait of a seaman emerged from the crowd and answered him. After a few moments' discussion, someone threw a rope from the jetty and hauled them in. While the men were dousing the sails Arn came back to Julian.

"Well, we're safe to shore, but there's something not quite right here," said Arn slowly. "The headman was eager to have us, but when I asked for help in repairing the ship he started talking about difficulties."

"You feel that too?" Quickly Julian told Arn about the dead otter he and Rana had seen. "But I don't see how the reivers could have known we were coming. With a little luck, we'll be gone before they return, and if not—I'd just as soon meet them with solid land underfoot as on the sea!"

The Isle of Birds was solid rock, but its sterile beauty pleased Caolin. This was surely the strength of earth, withstanding all the force the waters could bring against it with no soil to weaken it. Within a day of his arrival he knew all the paths of the island and within a week he understood the souls of its men. These wolves of Ardra's were the seagoing equivalent of the men he had gathered at Blood Gard, easily led by their lusts or driven by their fears.

Only one man on the island had so far proved resistant, and Caolin suspected that was the result of his illness rather than of any unique strength of spirit. When Ardra had brought him to Frederic, the cub had closed his eyes and turned away. Caolin's mental probings had encountered an almost painful resistance, and he had broken off the attempt for fear that before he could reach Frederic's soul, the boy's fragile hold on his body would give way. Any shielding could be broken eventually, but first Frederic must be made strong enough to survive it.

Looking at that white, defenseless face, it seemed to the sorcerer that Frederic could be a very useful tool in time, and it would be the best of vengeances upon the Master of the Junipers to make him so. But for now, he had a war to run. While Frederic slept, Caolin pulled out his crystal. As Ardra leaned forward to look at it he spoke to her, and in a moment her mind was captured, as it had been so often before. Quietly he began to give her his instructions.

Julian wiped greasy hands on his tunic and sat down on a driftwood log. They had managed to buy a dozen tough chickens from the villagers, and the rich odor of roasting still hung in the air. But land food tasted strange after eating fish for so long, and Julian could not be sure if the uneasiness in his belly was from the dinner or from anxiety. Things had been quiet enough, and the cooperation of the villagers, though grudging, had enabled them to careen *Sea Brother* on the beach and set about a plank by plank repair.

The sailors lay about the fire, some already asleep, some talking softly. It seemed very quiet without Silverhair to give them a song, but the harper had gone inland with Lord Robert to try and trade for some nails. Piper had taken out his flute and was working out a new melody—the same three or four notes, repeated, then a variation tried out and rejected, then another, and on to a new set, repeated again and again. Some of the men looked up, grimaced, and then turned to their talk again.

Arn sat to one side, tracing letters in the sand with a stick and then smoothing them out again. As Piper continued, Arn jabbed at the ground and glared.

"Piper, you sound like a tinker mending a pot. For heaven's sake, if you have to practice, go somewhere we can't hear!"

Color flooded the boy's surprised face, then drained away. He stood up, brushing sand off his tunic, and ran into the darkness without a word. The others stared after him, and Rana got to her feet and stalked over to her brother-in-law.

"Well, great captain, did you enjoy that?"

Arn looked up at her. "What? Oh—I suppose I shouldn't have been so sharp, but damn it, how can a man think with that kind of thing going on?"

"Well, if you are going to be a father you had better learn!" she said tartly, sitting down. Julian, overhearing, stifled a grin.

Arn's face softened. "That is what I was thinking about," he said, then looked at her in appeal. "Bella *will* be all right, won't she? But that's a silly question, I know. I suppose every man worries when his wife is having her first child."

"Well, *our* mothers both survived it, and Bella has always been strong as a horse. . . ."

Julian heard the strain in her voice and gave her a quick look, but Arn, who seemed to have noticed nothing, went on.

"I suppose so. I would feel better if she had not begged me not to leave her. I didn't expect to have all this trouble and take so long, and I didn't know it would be this hard to be apart from her. I feel silly, worrying about my wife when a war is starting. The men would probably laugh themselves silly if they knew. That's why I've been driving everyone so hard to finish the repairs."

Julian heard him with a pang of longing for something he had never had. He supposed that the other married men shared Arn's feelings, and he did not think they would have laughed at him. But it was not the sort of thing one told another man.

"Yes—I understand," said Rana. "I think I should go look for Piper now." As she got to her feet Julian received an impression of mingled fear and revulsion that made him wonder if Arn had been right to tell this

192

woman, and why the thought of her sister's pregnancy upset her so.

"He might have gone down by the water. I'll come with you," offered Julian.

"Don't stay out too long or go too far," said Arn. "I still don't trust these villagers."

Julian's hand dropped to the pommel of his sword, and Arn grinned. "I know—it would be a relief to deal with open hostility—but until *Sea Brother* is in the water again I'd rather not have to fight a war."

"Yes, captain!" answered Julian, sketching a salute, then he followed Rana.

Drifts of high fog obscured the full moon, and as they walked they could feel the dim murmurous presence of the ocean heaving gently in the dark. Wavelets lapped their bare feet, and sand crunched faintly. They strolled forward, calling Piper in soft voices when they dared disturb the secrecy of the night. To Julian it seemed that he had walked like this before, but he could not think when. Perhaps it had been in a dream. His dreams had stopped after Rana brought him the Sea Star, but he still remembered vividly how he had followed a veiled woman who had worn her form.

He was trying to find a way to tell her about those dreams when a hard hand gripped his ankle and he fell. There was a moment of silent struggle, and then he realized that the arms he was pinioning were thin, the body small—that it was Piper himself who had pulled him down.

"Piper! What do you think—" Julian stopped as the boy's finger touched his lips. "You want me to be quiet, is that it?" he whispered. Rana crouched beside them.

"Is something wrong, Piper?" she breathed. "Can you show us? Take my hand—"

Wishing with a fervency that owed nothing to pity that

193

the boy could talk, Julian followed them. Clearly Piper wanted to communicate as much as they needed to hear him, but the trauma that had blocked his speech still held him mute, and all they could do was trust him now. The boy went up the beach for a little and then turned inland, following a narrow path through the long grass that held down the dunes. It meandered along the north side of the hill, turning to earth pebbled with little stones over which bare feet had to pick their way.

Julian wondering how long they should go on with this when Rana stopped, pointing up the hill.

"A fire!"

As they watched, the red glow grew. Cautiously they crept forward and crouched behind a clump of coyote-brush a few yards from the bonfire. A dark shape moved before it, mechanically throwing pieces of wood onto the fire until the watchers could feel its heat.

"The hill must hide this from our camp—" said Julian.

"But it can be seen from the sea," Rana replied.

They fell silent again, hoping to see the fire-builder's face. A cloak hid all but sandals such as anyone might wear. When he stopped to stare out to sea, a hood shadowed his features. Standing there, he seemed to be listening, but the only sounds Julian could hear were the crackling of the fire and the sighing of the sea.

Then the man laughed. In that lonely place the sound was shocking, and horridly familiar. While it was going on, Julian was incapable of movement, and when it ended, he sat back, shaking, with the sweat starting on his brow.

Then Rana gripped his arm. She was staring out to sea, and as he turned he saw a flicker on the horizon as if a red star had come to rest upon the waves.

Julian lurched to his feet and leaped forward. His

194

quarry scrambled around the fire, but Rana had moved also, as if they had planned it, blocking the fellow just long enough for Julian to seize him. For a moment he struggled, then seemed to collapse, as if knowing there was no escaping those powerful hands. In the struggle his hood had fallen back. Julian hauled him around to face the fire.

"Bertram!" exclaimed Rana in astonishment.

"What're ye holdin' me for, eh? I'm too old t' be so mishandled. Served Master Arn since first he took a tiller in hand. He'll have somethin' to say t' them that treats an old man this way!"

"He'll have something to say to a man who sneaks off to signal to his enemies!" said Julian dangerously.

"Signal? What signal? Can't an old man light a fire t' warm his bones?"

Without releasing his grip, Julian looked back at the sea. The spark of light was gone.

"An' as for sneakin' . . ." The fear in the old man's voice had become malice. "It's the two of ye who're sneakin', and up to no good, I'll warrant, alone in the dunes! Call yerself Prince—think that gives ye a right to our women?" he spat at Julian, "and as for *you*—" He turned to Rana. "Ye ran after him like a bitch in heat before—were y' his whore then, too?"

Julian glimpsed the flicker of fire-lit steel as the blade came up and in instant reaction reached out to deflect Rana's arm. In the same moment Bertram twisted free and ran.

"Don't touch me!" screamed the girl.

"He was a prisoner, unarmed!"

Julian stood panting, wondering if she would attack *him* now. He heard Bertram blundering through the dune grass, and then only silence. And still he waited, while the madness slowly faded from Rana's eyes.

"He got away. . . ." she said finally, looking down at the knife as if wondering how it had gotten into her hand.

"Yes—" Julian said quietly. "Does it matter? If he runs away, surely he's no loss. It might be better that way. We can't prove he betrayed us, and accusations will only divide the men. I only wish he had told us who he was signalling to before he ran!"

"I'm sorry. It's my fault, isn't it? But he said—he said—" Rana's face flushed, and she jammed the knife back into its sheath as if she were sinking it into Bertram's heart. "I should have killed him. . . ."

Why? What did they do to you on that island to make even the suggestion that we might be lovers so terrible? The question echoed in Julian's heart, but he shut his lips upon the words, aware of a sorrow for something blighted before it had even begun to grow.

Chapter Ten

"Julian, the reivers *did* come here!" Silverhair slid off his horse and limped quickly down the path. Lord Robert drew rein behind him, shouting for someone to help with the bags bound behind their saddles.

"We had to go halfway down the valley before we found a blacksmith who could forge the right kind of nails," said Silverhair. "At the inn there folk were saying that the reivers attacked Elkhorn right after they hit the College of Bards and took hostages!"

"Hostages! But what for?" asked Arn.

"Think, Arn—" said Robert, who had gotten someone to take his horse and joined them. "What could they want from poor folk like these?" Except for those who were unloading the supplies, the crew of *Sea Brother* stood in a circle around them, listening avidly.

"To compel cooperation where they could not look for loyalty . . ." answered Julian, setting his hand on Arn's shoulder. "I'd guess they were told to delay us if we came back this way—"

Silverhair nodded. "They took the four best fishermen in the village, and the headman's young son. They were supposed to burn the ship if necessary to keep us here until the raiders could come."

Arn took a swift step toward his helpless ship as if he already saw her timbers smouldering. Then he stopped with a bitter laugh.

"They didn't need to do much, did they, although this news makes me wonder if there might not be some of those nails hidden under somebody's floorboards after all." He turned to gaze toward the reed-thatched roofs of the village, peaceful in the afternoon sun.

"How long to finish the repairs now that you've got the nails?" Julian asked Arn.

"Two days, maybe. I hate to risk poor work, though. Is it really so desperate? We've seen no sign of strangers, and the villagers have been fishing close inshore. How will the reivers know when to come?"

"Because of the signal—" Rana's clear voice cut through the babble. Her eyes were hard, and Julian realized that she was ready to face whatever gossip the news inspired. They could no longer hide what they had seen.

"Three nights ago someone built a bonfire up on the dunes," he said slowly, "and a light on the ocean answered it. I think the reivers already know we are here." For a few moments a babble of speculation drowned discussion.

"But why haven't they attacked us?" Robert's deep voice surfaced finally.

"I've been wondering about that myself. Perhaps there was only one of them on watch, and they're waiting for reinforcements."

"We'll give them a fight, then!" said Will eagerly.

"But first, let's burn the village and give those traitors their reward!" exclaimed Fernando. "Let's see how the sea wolves interpret *that* signal!"

"And make them tell us what they've done with Bertram!" added Gully.

"Westrians do not burn their own!" The uncertainties that had held Julian's tongue were swept away by a great anger, directed as much at himself as at the men. They stared at him, abruptly remembering who he was and by what right he commanded them. "Even had we proof they had betrayed, as well as delayed us, I would forbid it. Think, you—if it were your own brothers who had been taken, could you have resisted as well as the people of Elkhorn?"

"But Bertram *is* gone, and you yourself saw the fire—" protested Arn.

"Yes . . ." Julian answered heavily, "and I saw Bertram feeding it. . . . There is our traitor—not a man of the village, but one of our own."

There was a moment of silence, then a babble of disbelief from the men.

"I could not believe it either! Why do you think I kept silence?" exclaimed Julian. "But now we have answers to the questions I would have asked Bertram if he had not run away—" he turned to Arn. "How long until *Sea Brother* can put to sea again, now that you have your nails?"

"At least two days. Some of the other planks cracked when we removed the damaged piece. We'll have to set the new ones and allow the varnish to dry." Arn was already moving towards his ship with the expression of a young mother who thinks she has heard her baby cry.

"Very well—meanwhile, those who are not needed to work on the ship can take turns watching from the dunes. We'll have a night guard as well. Robert, can you set that up?"

"Of course, but I don't like this, Julian. If you *know* they're out there waiting, wouldn't it make more sense to take the inland route home?"

"Yes, if my only purpose was to get back to Laurelynn," Julian answered him. "But if I do that, I might as well concede the coasts to this pirate Queen. Who will join our navy if word gets around that at the first hint of danger I fled?"

"I suppose you're right, but I wish we were all safe home!"

"Doesn't every soldier wish that?" Julian gave him a playful punch, and Robert grinned.

"All right, but what are you going to do now?"

"Now that we understand what is going on, I mean to have a talk with Elkhorn's headman and see if we can get their cooperation. The men who were taken are my people too!"

"I'm coming with you—" said Rana grimly. "If they won't believe you, perhaps they will listen to someone who has been in the hands of their enemy!"

That night Julian dreamed.

Since Rana had returned with the Sea Star his nights had been untroubled. But now, the knowledge that his enemies might be waiting stimulated a deeper level of his awareness. He dreamed of the sea.

It seems to Julian that he moves through green depths without the need for breathing. But he is not a fish. A call draws him, though he cannot explain how or why. After a time he rises—into consciousness, he thinks—but when he finds himself on land, he is not rolled in his blankets on the beach of Montera, but walking in darkness on the Isle of Birds.

He is picking his way across the shelf of land where the reivers have made their encampment, aware that his vision of the place comes from Rana's description of it to the headman of Elkhorn. And yet it seems very real to him, as if this is an actual landscape through which his spirit body makes its way.

Ahead of him, lights glimmer through canvas. Julian wills himself toward them. He senses the life force within the tents—a shimmer in a spectrum of shades, or perhaps it is a tone that resonates in an endlessly varied scale of frequencies. But most of the colors seem dull, and the sounds jar on his spirit's hearing like instruments out of tune. Only from one tent does the light come faint but clear. As if it were a beacon Julian homes on it.

Now he is in the pavilion. A man is lying on a pallet. For a moment Julian does not recognize him, for that flesh has grown very thin and pale. Then he remembers the road to Awhai, and understands why he has been drawn to Frederic now.

He hovers over the body, and calls Frederic's name.

The eyes of the spirit body open, though the physical form seems still asleep. With double vision, Julian sees Frederic lie still and sit up to look at him.

"My lord, are you truly here?"

"Part of me, apparently," answers Julian. "I don't understand it either, but that doesn't matter now."

Frederic sees the Sea Star blazing at Julian's breast, and smiles. "Rana reached you! They told me she was dead, but I could not believe it!"

"She's alive, all right, and the darling of all the People of the Sea!" He shakes his head, having no words to describe what Rana has become. "But something happened to her on this island before she escaped from it—do you know what it was?"

Frederic sighs. "One of Zoltan's men attacked her. Though Rana's body wasn't hurt her spirit was damaged. I hoped that she would be healed by getting away from here—"

"And so you nearly got killed yourself helping her!"

201

exclaims Julian. He is beginning to understand what's wrong with Rana, but he has no more time to consider that now. "How badly were you wounded?"

"I don't really know—I live more in this state than in the waking world."

"But why, Frederic? You have to recover and be ready when we come for you!"

"Forget me—it's too dangerous! Oh, Julian, forgive me! I don't seem to have the courage either to live or to die! I should be dead—then you would not have to risk yourself for me!"

Even bodiless, Julian's response reverberates. "Frederic, if you die, I will follow you down to the Land of Death and haul your spirit back into the world!" Now, Julian remembers clearly his journey to the Otherworld, and Frederic believes him.

"My lord, you called me back before, when neither of us knew what we know now. I will obey you, but you cannot know what pain—"

Julian draws closer, realizing there has to be some other reason for Frederic's weakness, and sensing that he is about to learn it now. But as Frederic starts to speak again another presence flows into the pavilion like a wave of darkness. Julian cannot see within it, and whatever it hides cannot see him, but even its presence is disrupting.

"Frederic! Remember!" Julian begins to withdraw. He feels a web of force reaching out to trap him, and with an effort of will snaps back to his body.

Julian woke with a cry and sat up in his blankets, shuddering and gulping in raw sea air.

For three days the air rang with the sound of hammer and saw. Bertram did not return, and gradually the men of Seahold accepted the fact of his treason. However, Julian's negotiations with the headman of Elkhorn had created a more cooperative atmosphere, and three of the young men volunteered to sail north on *Sea Brother*. On the fourth morning they slid the ship into the water, where she lay, trim and bouyant on the gentle swell. There was no cheering as they hoisted the big sail, but the people of Elkhorn had turned out to see them off, and as the wind began to move the ship outward, they waved farewell.

Julian leaned back against the rail with a sigh. Now he had nothing to do but watch the sunlight burn the mist away. Already patches of glimmering azure showed overhead, and a wave flared with lucent blue. Impossible, on such a day, to think that violence could ever stain the sea. But Julian remembered the dead otters they had seen on their way in, and the signal fire. He wondered if Rana were thinking of them too. A quick glance showed him her bright hair by the dolphin figurehead at the bow, and seeing Rana, he remembered his dream.

Or was it a dream? The visions that had come to him before Rana brought him the Sea Star had all been vivid, but their events had been a succession of images which required of him only that he *see*. . . .

His experience of the Isle of Birds had held the strangeness of a different reality. He supposed that the Master of the Junipers could have explained it, but the Master was far away. Even Frederic might know, but since he did not understand how he had reached Frederic in the first place, Julian had no idea how to contact him again.

For the moment he must content himself with dealing with what he had learned. Frederic was alive! Even that knowledge lifted a weight that Julian had not known he bore. Julian remembered his threat to seek his friend in the Otherworld and shivered with mixed dread and longing. There was peace, and release from all the stresses that bound him now. Did he have the right to force another soul to remain captive in a body of pain?

But there was nothing more he could do for Frederic now. It remained to consider the other thing that Frederic had told him, the knowledge that had nagged at his awareness for three days, and which he could no longer shut away.

Frowning, he looked at Rana once more. She lay on the figurehead as she had been carried by the dolphin. Was she dreaming that she was with the Sea People once more? Certainly she had good reason to fear the world of men. She had been sexually assaulted on the island. No wonder any reference to the act of love appalled her.

Julian's fist closed hard on the railing as images flooded his imagination—faceless men pawing at her, pinning her, tearing at her tunic to reveal white skin. . . .

Abruptly he saw once more the perfection of Rana's body as she rose out of the sea. The Sea Star had nestled between those young breasts like a murre between two waves. And then he had carried her ashore—how could he not have been aware of the sweetness of her body when he held it then? Julian's flesh quickened at the memory of Rana's softness against him and the Sea Star throbbed in sympathy, intensifying the response of his body into a spasm of desire.

When Julian came to himself again, sweat beaded his forehead. Automatically he glanced forward, and the gleam of sunlight on her hair struck him with something very like pain. Only the stress of the moment had allowed her to accept his touch. He knew now why it would not happen again. Julian shuddered in sudden revulsion. As a man, he accepted the guilt for what other men had done to her at the same time as he wanted to destroy them. And yet his fury was partly directed at his own appalled recognition of the same desire. Yesterday he could have comforted her as a brother, if she could tolerate even a brother's touch now. But after today, what solace could he offer her that would not be an insult? He looked at Rana and ached with an intolerable need for what he knew he could not have and should not even desire.

Julian was still watching her when he saw her stiffen and point, and realized that they were no longer alone upon the sea. . . .

Westward two black shapes lay stark upon a sheet of blazing gold. It hurt the eyes to look at them; impossible at this distance to see what they were. Trading vessels, perhaps, or fishing craft from one of the other villages on the bay? No one dared to believe in such innocent explanations. Only one thing was certain—*Sea Brother*, higher in the water with the sun full upon her, would be easy to identify.

Arn wet his finger and held it to the wind. "Wind's freshening from the southeast," he said. "We'd have to beat against it to get back to the village—" Everyone turned to stare at the three Elkhorn men, who had gone red and then pale.

Julian took pity on them. "Even if we could reach the village before they caught us, we can't lay that choice on the people. But there's little chance you lads will be recognized here with us—"

"Unless we're captured and questioned," murmured one of the Seahold men.

"We won't be!" exclaimed Rana, and Julian knew that rather than be taken by the reivers again she would throw herself into the sea. Robert stepped to Julian's elbow, his hand on the hilt of his sword, and Julian sensed his friend's unspoken determination to be killed himself rather than let his Prince be taken. That might have been intended to reassure him, but it only increased Julian's fear for his friends. Yet at the same time, Julian's pulse leaped at the prospect of battle. Perhaps he could kill

205

some of these men who were like the one who had hurt Rana. Perhaps action would burn away some of this intolerable stress of desire.

"Well, we can try to outrun them—" Arn began uncertainly.

"At sea? Those hulls of theirs go through the water like a hot knife through butter. Even with her bottom scoured, *Sea Brother* was never built for such speed!"

"Be quiet, Will—you're as bad as Bertram!" Rana turned on him. "We need to think what we can *do!*"

"Silverhair, you and Will were talking about a watchtower on the northern end of the bay," said Julian suddenly. "Do you think you could find it again?"

The harper squinted across the waves. Ahead of them the land rose to a series of cliff heads with forested mountains behind them. "When we're closer, yes, I think so. It's on the southern tip of the point."

"Head for the point then," Julian said to Arn. "If we can reach the watchtower ahead of the reivers we can take refuge there."

"Yes—" Arn's gaze measured directions and differences. "We might be able to outrun them that far. . . . Gully—get the foresail up, and Fernando, you help him. Will, be ready to trim the mainsail at my call!"

Julian pulled Robert and Silverhair out of the way as the men began to haul on the halyards and the foresail rattled up the mast. The ship bucked uneasily, then more orders from Arn trimmed both sails, and *Sea Brother* plunged forward. But the dark shapes of their pursuers were growing larger. They were less maneuverable under sail than *Sea Brother*, but the speed of their sleek hulls made up for what they lost in flexibility. Still, Arn knew how to squeeze the last bit of speed out of his own vessel. He stood at the rudder, balanced, watchful, completely focused on his task.

"I wish I had a patrol of our own borders now!" said

Robert, looking around him. "These lads may be artists with a fishknife, but have any of them ever held a sword? Do they even *have* swords?"

"Enough short swords for my own crew," Arn called from the stern. "And bows—I added them to ship's stores after Beltane!"

"Bows!" exclaimed Silverhair. "Well, that's something!"

"If the strings are sound. . . ." said Robert gloomily.

"Well, we won't know until we look at them, will we?" Rana snapped back. "They're stored in the locker. Come see—"

The wind was whipping the wavetops into lace around them, and each plunge brought a faceful of spray. Even to Julian's inexperience *Sea Brother* seemed to be carrying almost too much canvas for this wind. . . . Almost— the reivers were still gaining, and he knew that Arn would push his ship to her limits to escape them. Now it was up to him to do the same with the men. They pulled the sacks of oiled leather that held the weapons out of the locker, and distributed the swords. There were only four bows. Silverhair had learned combat shooting with the caravans, and Robert had been carefully trained in archery as in all the other warrior skills. Clearly two of the bows should be for them, and another for Rana, who had used a bow in hunting. Julian had some practice, but had never become skillful. One of the Elkhorn lads said he often shot waterbirds on the slough, and so they gave the fourth bow to him.

While the archers chose arrows and tested the pull of their bows, Julian handed out swords to those men who were not busy working the ship and gave them a quick arms drill. It was a disheartening task—the coasts had always been peaceful, and although the lads were strong and willing, there was a considerable difference between the skills needed for fighting a fish and a man.

Still, the exercise kept the men from thinking about the steadily narrowing gap between pursuer and pursued, as it distracted Julian from fear for Rana. The pale cliffs were becoming clearer as well, but so slowly! As they neared shore the water became calmer, spotted with dark patches of floating kelp. The wind faltered, backed, and just as Arn began to trim the sails to meet it, returned to its former direction. But now it was fitful. The reivers' sails flapped, then the dark squares changed shape and began to disappear. Oars lifted like opening wings, dipped, and caught the sun in a flicker of light as they lifted once more.

"They know we can't trust the wind," said Rana. "They mean to run us down before we reach shore. . . ." Her hand caressed the arrows thrust through her belt.

"Go on while you can, Arn," said Silverhair. "I can see the walls of the watchtower and the surf on the beach."

"The sharks are fully manned, and fresh, and they are built for speed," Arn answered, looking behind him. "I don't think we're going to get there in time. Better to use this ship as our fortress. On the sea, their own numbers may hamper them."

"It doesn't look good, Julian," Robert said softly. "Our people will fight as well as they can, but an hour's training won't fit them to face men whose trade is war!"

"How many men in each of those ships?" asked someone.

"Twelve on a side. . . ." answered Fernando. The enemy was close enough so that they could see faces now, grinning whitely above the inexorable sweep of the oars.

"Two ships—that's nearly fifty men!" Gully's voice rose. "More than twice what we've got here. They'll swamp us!" His voice was lost in a frightened babble, in which the word "surrender" could be heard.

"Don't even think it!" cried Rana. "That's fish-offal

behind us—not honorable men! If you give in you'll die just as hard, but if you fight you might live."

"Fine words, but the men are right—" murmured Silverhair. "It's going to be a slaughter. Julian—the tree people came to your aid when you faced Caolin. Can you use the Sea Star to call the People of the Sea?"

Julian turned, and saw the shadow of memory stark in the other's eyes—a windswept river island beneath a gray sky, and the figure of the sorcerer crimson against sodden grass just before he had struck Julian down. Remembering, Julian saw his friends across the gulf between the dead and the living.

"*I* did not summon them—" he said painfully at last. "It was Lady Madrone! If you can bear to remember what happened on Spear Island, you know why!"

Silverhair went white and looked away, and a sudden flare of self-knowledge told Julian that he feared the deaths of those he loved more than his own, and more than death, he feared their pain. But worse than anything that could happen to them or to him was the misuse of power.

"I would not have dared to involve the powers of earth then, when Caolin's sorcery threatened to destroy our very souls," he added more gently. "And this is only a battle of men—how can I jeopardize the Sea People now?"

He looked up and met Rana's clear gaze. As if she had spoken he understood her thought— *You see, Sea Mother, he is worthy of your trust in him!* Was Rana's approval worth more than her life? He shuddered as he imagined a raider's harpoon piercing her as the sea otters had been slain.

"But if the reivers beat us they'll capture the Sea Star!" exclaimed Arn.

"No—if it comes to that, I will give the Jewel back to the sea. . . ."

"And we will all die. . . . Perhaps that does not matter, but if you are killed what will become of Westria?" asked Robert.

Julian started to reply that Westria had survived for several centuries without him, but that was unfair. Robert had not been at Spear Island, but they had served together against raiders in the Ramparts. His friend would never believe that it had been more luck than skill that had enabled Julian to get them out of tight spots before.

He looked behind him. The sharkships were drawing closer. The painted teeth on their prows gleamed viciously. The sight reminded him oddly of something else he had seen—after a moment he placed it—an evilly effective carving of a shark that Bertram had made. *If I was a real sorcerer*, he thought then, *I would enchant those figures to fight for us now*. In vision, he saw wooden dolphins, otters, whales and seals bobbing over the waves. . . . For the space of a breath Julian stood quite still.

"I will not use the power of the Sea Star to compel the creatures of the sea," he said suddenly, "but this foe is their enemy as well. I would not refuse alliance with any who seek their own vengeance! Bertram's gear is still aboard, isn't it?" he went on, "Get it and see if you can find any figures of otters there!"

"You're thinking of the kin of the dead otters we saw!" exclaimed Rana.

"Yes—" said Julian slowly as Gully pulled Bertram's pack from the locker and fumbled with the knots. "I think the reivers killed those otters, wantonly and against the Covenant. Perhaps Bertram's talent can make up for his treachery!"

The Master of the Junipers had told him that there was a level at which symbols were one with their realities. That state could be linked with ordinary reality by a trained will. *I'm not trained*, he thought, *but I'm desperate! That will have to do.*

Gully sat up with a wooden figure in his hand. "Is this what you wanted—"

It was an otter carved from a piece of pine about a foot long. Bertram had taken advantage of the shape and grain of the wood to convey the sinuous curve of the body and the richness of fur. Delicate paws clasped a shellfish to its chest; a knot in the wood made a bright eye. Julian took it, and as his fingers caressed the satiny surface he seemed to sense a vivid joy in movement and the echo of laughter.

"Little brother, will you help us?" he whispered. He moved to the rail, holding the statue against him. "Sleek swimmer, shell-cracker, joker of the sea—Otter I name you, go seek your kindred, and if they will fight for us, bring them to us now!"

Julian's awareness shifted, and a vision of the dead otters was superimposed on present reality. For a moment he was conscious on both levels, and at that moment he projected all his conflicting emotions into the figure and cast it into the sea.

Then he straightened. "Arn! Head the ship into the thickest part of the kelp bed! When they close perhaps the seaweed will foul their oars!"

The deck tilted as the ship turned. Dizzied, Julian lost sight of the floating figure. The certainty that had moved him departed abruptly, but whether or not his rough magic had any other effect, it had distracted the men during those last moments when panic might have destroyed what little ability they had to resist their enemies.

But now there was no more time for emotion. Julian moved toward the stern and drew his sword. A great quiet seemed to enfold him, as it always did before battle. He swayed easily to the ship's gentler motion, realizing with a faint surprise that some time in the past weeks he had got his sealegs. Arn lashed the tiller and pulled out his own blade, and Will and Raymond settled into position beside him.

"Archers, the sharks are almost in range!" said Robert. "Aim into the midst of the boats and you'll likely hit something. See—they're splitting up now—they probably mean to board us from both sides. Rana, stand here with me, and Silverhair, you take the other side of the ship with the Elkhorn boy. We can divide our favors evenly—good thing we had an even number of bows!" Robert's voice had a soothing quality that steadied the swordsmen as well as the archers.

"I make it almost two dozen in the boat to starboard, and a few more in the other," said Arn.

"Well that's only three or four for each of us to kill!" Silverhair gave a short laugh. A quick glance showed him that Piper was safe in the sail locker.

"Those are good boats they have . . . the kind we will need. I hope they don't get damaged," Julian said calmly.

The harper smiled, love for his nephew for once showing openly in his face. He turned back to the enemy again, and his strong voice soared out above the gutteral chanting of the foe—

"Both land and sea my songs have known.
I have known loneliness and fame.
And yet I shall not die alone—
With such companions, 'tis no shame
To cease at last from wandering. . . ."

Julian felt an odd tremor beneath his heart as he recognized a new ending to Silverhair's walking song. Then the harper's voice was drowned out by the war cries of the enemy. Sunlight on water and drawn steel glittered blindingly. Julian raised his sword.

"Death! Death! Sharks to your prey!" shouted the reivers.

"Dolphins have teeth too," said Robert. "Archers, pick your targets—Draw . . . and . . . loose . . ."

Four bowstrings sang as the archers drew and released, fumbled for more arrows, and shot again and again. The first shots went wild, then the archers began to find their range. Julian heard a cry, and one of the sharks faltered as a thrashing oar upset the others' rhythm. But in a moment they recovered and came on once more. Silver-hair shot swiftly, scarcely seeming to aim; Robert, with disciplined skill. The Elkhorn boy crouched as if he were in a duck blind, but Rana drew and loosed her arrows like the Huntress, all her grace focused in deadly accuracy.

Sea Brother shuddered as the first shark slid alongside and the grappling hooks thunked into the rail. The other enemy had been slowed by the seaweed, but they were still coming on. Arn's crew stood shoulder to shoulder with knives or shortswords ready, and the archers dropped their bows and drew their own blades.

"Now may the Lady of Sea and Sunset hold us in Her hand!" cried Julian.

The ship rocked as yelling reivers clambered over the rail. A sword thrust at Julian's middle; he swept it aside and brought his own blade around to slice the swordsman's arm. A kick knocked another man backwards. After the first moments, Julian saw only weapons, arms, bodies to be dealt with as they appeared.

No one got over the part of the rail Julian was guarding, but elsewhere the Westrian line had broken, and now struggling clumps of defenders were surrounded by reivers. Julian's sword swept down as a foe sprang toward him, but this man had some notion of swordplay; the blow was parried, and Julian had to

213

retreat to gain space to strike back. He began to understand why Arn had stocked shortswords. As he attacked again, he heard a shout behind him and a headless body hurtled past. He leaped aside, saw his opponent's momentary distraction and thrust; the sword checked on the tough leather of the fellow's jerkin, Julian put his weight into it and felt it go through. He saw the raider's eyes change as his weapon clattered from his hand.

When Julian straightened, Silverhair was behind him. Back to back, they moved toward the stern. He glimpsed Robert fighting with his own peculiar grace, and a knot of struggling men around Arn and Fernando.

"Where's Rana?" he gasped. Silverhair jerked his head toward the bow.

Julian saw the girl's bright head bend, and for one terrified moment thought she had been wounded. Then she stood up, blood splattering from her blade, and in almost the same motion plunged it into the back of the reiver nearest her, caught him as he fell back, and drew it across his throat. There were blotches of red on her tunic, but if any of it was her own, her battle madness had prevented her from feeling it; her hands and arms were smeared with blood while crimson spattered her face and hair. He saw her lips drawn back from white teeth in a silent snarl.

But there was no time for either horror or pity. Now the tide of battle was sweeping toward them again. There were too many even now, and when the other boat reached them they would be overwhelmed. Julian struck out and struck again.

A cry from the bow pierced the din, and for a moment the fighting faltered. Everywhere men were turning to look at the ocean.

"What is it?" asked Silverhair. Julian strained to see.

Through a gap in the fighting he glimpsed the second shark-ship floating motionless a few yards away. The kelp was thick around it—perhaps that was why it did not move. But the men on board were active enough. He saw the flicker of steel—were they going to throw knives at the enemy they could not reach?

But the sounds that came from that ship were not battle-cries.

"The Sea itself fights for them—" came a shout. "Sharks, save yourselves!"

The water around *Sea Brother* boiled. Now moans of terror came from nearby. Over the edge of the ship came a sleek-furred head with bristling whiskers and sharp teeth set in a snarl. A sinuous body followed, four and a half feet of muscle long. Another otter appeared beside the first and then they were coming from all sides.

"Julian, you did it! They came!" breathed Silverhair.

"Reivers, save yourselves if you can!" shrieked Rana. "The beasts you would have slain fight for us now!"

Snapping and snarling, the otters slithered among the men, attacking those who seemed to fear them. Soon their jaws were as red as Rana's hands. The Westrians drew together, letting their allies carry the battle. Some of the raiders were still shouting furiously, striking at the lithe bodies of the sea-beasts; others leaped over the side to be dragged down by those who waited in the sea.

A man in a mail vest broke from among his fellows and leaped toward Julian.

"Strike!" he shouted, "Will you have the Times of Chaos come again? Fight on, and let us at least be killed by men!"

Julian and Silverhair advanced to meet them. The harper's sword darted in and out like a flame, but Julian felt a great wave of power lift him, and his blade swept down with a deliberate force against which nothing could stand.

In moments, the raider crumpled to the deck, his life pouring out of a great wound in his belly. There was no

215

fight left in the enemy now. They threw down their weapons and crowded against the crew of the *Sea Brother*, pleading for protection while the otters worried at their heels.

Julian felt his own battle-madness drain away. A line from the *Book of the Cataclysm* echoed in his memory— *"Then against Man the Oppressor was turned every hoof and tooth and claw, and the First People slew the Children of Men without pity or fear."* Appalled, he stared at the bloody deck, the empty sharkships, the bodies in the sea. And it was he who had called up these demons! But he had not thought beyond the battle—how was he to dismiss them again?

Instinctively his hand went to the Jewel hidden at his breast, fumbling away the wrappings to touch the bare stone. He felt a surge of power, and for a moment he understood that the blood that was flowing so freely was the same salt as the sea, and that the fury that had exploded here was as much a part of the ocean's cycles as a storm. But even bearing the Sea Star, he was still a man, and though the Jewel had not called the otters, it was the only means by which he might reach them now.

"Sea People, hold!" His voice cracked and he swallowed painfully. The otters paused, and heads twisted as they reared up on their hindquarters to look at him. Their fur was torn and bloodied, and their mouths dripped red. "Allies, your valor has saved us. Let your vengeance be satisfied!" The otters would not understand his words, but the words focused his will. Julian drew breath and strove for calm. "In the name of Sea Mother, I command you, let it be ended now . . . Go back to the kelp forests, my brothers, and live in peace with men!"

Julian stood in a dazzle of azure light. As through deep water he saw the beasts staring back at him. *Go in peace, my brothers* . . . he begged silently. *Wash yourselves clean of this stain!*

Then the otters dropped to all fours, turned a last scornful glance on the cowering reivers, and flowed over the side. Julian lifted his sword in salute to them as they disappeared.

Slowly the blue glow dimmed to the ordinary light of day. With fingers that trembled, Julian wrapped the Sea Star securely and hid it once more, then wiped and sheathed his sword. The sick-sweet smell of blood weighted the air. Across the deck he saw Rana. She was looking down at something, and though others moved around her, she did not stir.

Limping a little from a gash on his thigh, Julian went to her. On the deck in front of her was the body of an otter. A sword slash had gutted it, but the blood was already clotting and its eyes were dull.

"Rana—" Julian said softly. "Rana, it's over now. . . ." He did not touch her.

She gave a shuddering sigh, knelt, and gently laid her hand on the soft fur.

"On the Isle of Birds the otters slid down the rocks and rode the waves," Rana said softly. "That's what they're like, really, not these—monsters. . . . Sea Mother, forgive me! I didn't know—I didn't know!"

"Rana, *I* was the one who called them! Rana, look at me!" he said desperately. Was it her guilt she was confessing, or his own? *What use was all my contorted reasoning about power? In the end, it was all the same!*

Rana shivered, took her hand away, saw the blood on it and tried to wipe it on her breeches. But her breeches were bloody too. Julian saw her gaze move from legs to body, to her arms and hands and the gory knife that she had just set down.

"I killed men, didn't I?" Rana looked up, but her eyes

were unseeing. "I'm a monster too!" Suddenly she was on her feet, lurching toward the rail. Julian reached for her with an appalled certainty that she was going to throw herself into the sea, but when she saw the water she reeled back against him.

"No! The sea is clean—I can't pollute it! I have sinned against the sea and it will never receive me again!"

Julian's arms closed around her and her hands came up to grip his. Was he supporting her, or clinging to her like a drowning man?

"*Rana . . .*" The Sea Star was pressed between them, and Julian's heart spoke her name. Linked by the Jewel, he sensed in her a horror so great that his own guilt and confusion were forgotten. And her need forced him to do what he would never have dared for himself, to open himself to the Sea Star so that its peace could flood through them both, and bear away the pain as the blood of those they had slain was even now dissipating in the vastness of the Sea.

Chapter Eleven

"Rana, you must help me—" Julian knelt in the sand, not quite touching her. The clear, merciless light that filtered through the sailcloth sunshade showed him the tight line of her mouth and the purple shadows beneath her shut eyes.

"Do you think that feigning sleep will fool me?" he added roughly. "Rana, I'm not going to go away!"

"Don't you have anything better to do?" Her eyes were still closed, but her face was no longer quite so shuttered. Julian sighed and sat back on his heels. After the battle, Rana had fallen asleep in his arms. She had continued to sleep as the three ships limped into the sheltered waters below the point and the dead and wounded were taken ashore. The people of Soquel had seen the battle, and though refugees from the College of Bards still filled all the spare rooms in the village, the weather remained

219

warm, and the Seahold folk could be accommodated in temporary shelters on the shore.

When Rana finally woke, her despair had faded sufficiently so that Julian no longer feared for her. Now the danger was apathy.

"Everyone else is busy tending the wounded and burying the dead—" he answered sharply. "And you are mourning as if you were the first person who ever had to kill an enemy!"

"You don't understand!" Her eyes opened, dark with pain. "In the sea, only sharks kill their own kind!"

"Don't I? Let me tell you about my own first fight someday!" Julian's voice shook. He took a deep breath and added more calmly, "We call the reivers sharks, but we are sharks too. Man can be as cruel as any other beast in nature—perhaps more so, or there would have been no need for the Cataclysm."

Julian stopped. He had been treating her like a recruit shocked by his first battle, but she was right—that was not really the problem. The link between them was strong enough for him to realize that Rana was horrified now not because she had been forced to kill, but because she had *wanted* to. If only he could tell her that he knew why she hated the reivers so desperately, that the rape didn't matter. But of course to her it *did* matter, and it seemed to him that her awareness of his knowledge would destroy the trust that had begun to grow between them. Or perhaps he was only afraid to see her look at him with that sick disgust in her eyes.

As the silence between them lengthened, he heard the gulls lamenting overhead and the intermittent whisper of surf on the shore. Wooden wheels creaked as a wagon went by. Men were talking in low voices nearby, and he heard a burst of quickly suppressed laughter.

"That guilt is something we all must share, and may the Guardian of Men forgive us—" he said finally. "But

220

where will I seek absolution for the deaths of the otters? I thought that I could stay innocent by not using the Jewel, and instead I nearly started a new Cataclysm."

Put into words, the pain that he had suppressed during the long night while Rana slept was suddenly unbearable. He had meant only to distract her from her own grief, but suddenly his own overwhelmed him. The others had driven him half-crazy with praise for the success of his stratagem. Only she could understand that it had not been a victory.

"It was bad enough when Lady Madrone raised the powers of earth to help me, but she is one of them, and it is not for me to judge her. I called the otters myself— who will judge me? Rana—I have broken the Covenant of Westria!"

After what seemed an eternity, he felt the touch of her hand on his bent head.

"The Sea must judge both of us . . ." she said at last.

"But how?" he looked up at her.

"Through the Sea Star—we must submit ourselves to the Jewel. . . ."

"Rana, you must help me—" It was the same question with which he had begun, but its meaning was different now. Julian had tried to rouse her to help with the work of recovering from the seafight for her own sake, but his involvement of the otters called into question his right to bear the Jewels of Westria.

Rana's eyes were still haunted, but they met his steadily. He realized that she did understand. Westria was more important than her pain or his own. Then her gaze shifted beyond him. Julian turned, and saw Robert standing behind him, anxiety marring the purity of his features and shadowing his blue eyes.

"Julian, I think you should come take a look at Silverhair."

221

Julian stood up too quickly and for a moment his pulse pounded dizzily. "But he only had scratches—"

"I know," said Robert. "He collapsed a few minutes ago. He's sitting up now, but he doesn't look well."

Rana followed them to the other sunshade, where a little crowd had gathered around the harper. A buxom, auburn-haired woman whom Julian remembered having met at the College of Bards was checking his pulse. As Julian came up Silverhair started to speak, but she shushed him, held his wrist a moment longer, and then set it down.

"Siaran, stop fussing! I told you, I'm all right now!"

"Are you?" She raised one arched eyebrow. "Your pulse is still hopping like a rabbit, and your face is the color of old cheese."

Silverhair saw Julian and grimaced. "I was helping to unload that wagon, and for a moment I just couldn't breathe. I'm too old to fight all day and work all night, that's all!"

"That's the first true thing you have said, Farin Silverhair!" Mistress Siaran answered tartly. "Let your nephew wear himself out fighting reivers, and come back to the College with me!"

Julian dropped to one knee beside his uncle and took the older man's other hand. Silverhair was breathing more easily now, but his skin was still clammy, his thin face pallid beneath the white hair.

"The College of Bards is a collection of charred timbers—" Silverhair said bitterly. "I got worn out, as you call it, fighting some of the bastards that burned it, and there are more where they came from!"

"The College is Music, and it lives in men's hearts. When we rebuild our halls we'll need you to bring that spirit back again . . ." said Siaran serenely.

Silverhair sighed, and then suddenly he smiled. "Very

well. When we've made sure no one is left to burn them again, I'll come!"·

Something in that smile made Julian's heart twist in pain. In the past year he and his uncle had passed from a mutual exasperation through grudging respect to a love for which neither of them could find words.

"I need a live uncle more than a dead hero!" he squeezed Silverhair's hand. "You're not going to lift anything heavier than your harp until we're home again!"

He looked up and saw Rana watching them. *You see*—he said silently—*more than your soul and mine is at risk in this war!*

They carried Silverhair to a house in the village to recover, and after that there were other tasks, and decisions to be made. Two days later, having arranged for the captive reivers to be taken under guard to Sanjos and having recruited a half dozen fishers from Soquel to help crew, *Sea Brother* set sail once more for home, with the captured sharkships following like imprinted ducklings behind her.

Caolin was waiting with Ardra at the cove when Zoltan returned from a foray southward with the news that the two ships they had assigned to watch Montera were lost. It was Bertram who had brought the story, having heard it in Soquel as he made his way upcoast to the rendezvous. Shrouded in his dun-colored cloak, the sorcerer moved unnoticed through the gabbling crowd. Bertram had already told his story to Ardra and Lorca, and now he was trying to repeat it to anyone else who would listen, while the commanders moved off to confer.

"Uncanny, it was! Those furred demons slithered up out of the sea and devoured good men! That bastard they call Prince is a terrible sorcerer surely—it hadn't ought to be allowed. They should burn him before he turns all the beasts against their betters, the unnatural. . . ." Bertram's ramblings faltered as he met Caolin's eye. For a moment the old man stared as if he thought he should recognize this person who was watching him, without quite remembering why.

"Bertram!" Caolin spoke the old man's name with a peculiar pitch and intonation, as he had spoken it on the day when he bound Bertram's will to his own. Expression drained from the seamed face and motion from the old sailor's body. The reivers hardly noticed, too caught up in embroidering on their speculations. Caolin recognized the shrill tones of excitement, and beneath it an undercurrent of fear. Something must be done about that, or the whole babbling lot of them would panic. But first he needed to find out what Bertram had actually heard.

"Come with me—" the sorcerer made his way along the path and Bertram, expressionless and silent at last, followed him. When a jog in the trail gave them a semblance of privacy, he turned. As the old man's eyes lifted to meet his, Caolin's mind thrust inward, bypassing the surface editing of memory until he reached the actual sensory impressions that Bertram had received. He heard the villagers repeating what the crew from *Sea Brother* and the reivers had told them about the battle, and found the story, if anything, more disturbing than Bertram's own tale. With his awareness pulsing with a mounting fury, Caolin turned to go back to the camp, then paused and with a negligent flare of force wiped Bertram's memory of their interview.

By the time Caolin reached the encampment, Bertram was forgotten. The reivers had mishandled it! The Elayan scum had bungled their best chance to take Julian! They should have attacked when Bertram signaled from Elkhorn, they should never have let that wretched boy loose upon the sea with the Sea Star in his hands—easy, in retrospect, to see a hundred things the reivers should have done. But they had not known. The information that revealed the presence of the Jewel to Caolin was obscured by a general accusation of sorcery.

He would need a new plan now, and there was no longer time to manipulate his puppets into playing their roles. He would have to control Ardra directly, and that would no doubt be easier if Frederic were his creature as well. Now that he thought about it, it might even be better this way. He had planned to seduce the boy into his service to spite the Master of the Junipers. But Frederic's resistance so far suggested real potential. At times his stubborn fidelity to his Prince reminded Caolin painfully of the feelings he had had for Jehan long ago. But the sorcerer had learned too well that love and loyalty were dangerous illusions. Indeed, showing Frederic the emptiness behind the world's appearances would be a favor. The only safety was to embrace the darkness.

Ardra was still talking to her captains when Caolin entered the red pavilion and stood looking down at her prisoner. Frederic lay half-raised on pillows with a blanket thrown over him. After a moment he seemed to sense the presence of the sorcerer, and opened his eyes.

"My lord, much better you look today!" Caolin smiled effusively, clinging to his role while he decided how to proceed. But what he had said was true—Frederic's color had improved visibly, and he appeared to be gaining back some of the weight he had lost. There must have been more virtue on the medicines Caolin had given him than he knew!

"Yes, I do feel stronger." Frederic answered readily enough, but his gaze was watchful. Even when he had been semi-conscious he had seemed uneasy with the "healer", but that was no surprise in one who had studied at the College of the Wise. Soon, he would know the truth, but by then it would not matter any more. . . .

"My herbs do you good, eh? You take your drink again now, lord, and be very strong soon!"

Caolin knelt by the satchel in which he had brought a selection of remedies suitable for treating wounds and the usual illnesses of a camp, along with a few more specialized mixtures whose preparation he had learned from the sorcerer Katiz. It was one of the latter that he chose now, a dark liquid derived from the moonflower of Awhai. Frederic was no villager to be conquered with a swinging crystal and a word. But there was no need to engage in a contest of wills when the boy's resistance could be unlocked thus easily. He poured a little wine into a goblet, added the tincture, and offered it to his patient with an ingratiating smile.

Frederic swallowed obediently, then frowned. "This isn't the stuff you gave me last time—" he sniffed at it. "It's bitter. What is it, anyway?"

"Yes—very good," Caolin nodded as if he had not quite understood him. "Purifies the blood! You drink it all now, and finish getting well!"

"I've smelled this somewhere before, though. Maybe it was at the College." Frederic drank again. Suddenly his mouth puckered and he set the goblet down. "A drink that makes your mouth dry! Julian told me—" he stared at Caolin. "This is *toloache*! They gave it to Julian in Awhai!"

Caolin blinked. He had not known about that—but it was not important now. He smiled. "Yes—you are very perceptive, my lord. It is a mild dose, however, and it will do you no harm. . . ."

"Or good either! What are you trying to do to me?"

"My dear Frederic," he said in his own voice. "I am

going to talk to you, and you are going to answer me. . . ."

As Caolin spoke, he straightened, and let the semblance of the little healer fade. Frederic's eyes widened, and the sorcerer knew that within the deep hood he now saw only shadow. Already the boy's pupils were dilating. He licked dry lips and tried to control his breathing. Caolin smiled, knowing very well the disciplines in which Frederic had been trained. He would be fighting his panic now, but breathing would not help him once the drug activated the deeper levels of the brain.

Frederic's focus shifted suddenly, and his eye movements became jerky as he tried to track something that only he could see. He closed his eyes, then quickly reopened them as if whatever he was looking at showed up more vividly against the darkness inside his skull. With visible effort, he focused on the candle flame.

"Who . . . *are* . . . you?"

Caolin smiled. "I am your master, and the master of Westria." There was a silence while Frederic struggled to form words.

"No—you are . . . my enemy . . . Caolin. . . ."

The sorcerer nodded. Frederic had not wasted energy on shock or speculation. The boy's will was strong, and he was brave. He would be a worthy servant.

"Don't try to talk—" he said then. "I will talk, and you will listen . . ." He thought Frederic looked relieved, and smiled again. The boy did not yet understand. "You refused Ardra's offer of shared rule. She did not understand you, but I do. The spirit is stronger than the sword, and true power lies within. Men such as we are desire to know the truth at the heart of things. . . ."

Caolin saw Frederic's face twist, and a gentle probe slipped past the boy's surface awareness to catch the thought within—

227

"Then why are you trying to destroy Westria?"

"The old Westria has already been destroyed," he answered softly, sending his thought along the tenuous link between them, strengthening it as he went on so that his next words were carried as much by the power of his mind as by sound. "The holders raid their neighbors, the cities bicker with the provinces, the College of the Wise is an empty husk ruled by an old woman who lost her powers years ago. . . ." he paused, letting the images sink in. *"You know this is true—"*

"It is true . . ."

"Westria needs a new spirit in order to live again—" To this, also, Caolin sensed Frederic's agreement. *"And to make that happen someone who understands the inner powers must take charge!"*

The response was immediate. *"Yes! Julian!"*

"Of course, you are loyal to your friend," came Caolin's answer, *"But are you certain that he has the wisdom? Haven't they told you how he forced the sea otters to fight for him? Many died—for the first time since the Jewel Wars, the Elder Kindred have died in a human battle! Was that a right use of power?"*

"No! He wouldn't do that! Julian doesn't even want to use the Jewels!" Frederic stared as if his dilated eyes could pierce the shadow by which Caolin was veiled.

"Well, perhaps I was wrong. You are his friend and know him—what are Julian's powers?" Caolin could feel Frederic searching for an answer. He moved deeper into his captive's mind, past the distracting confusion of drug-induced images to the visions Frederic was summoning from memory.

He read there the doubt with which Frederic had at first received this battle-toughened, mountain-bred boy who was such a reluctant claimant to the throne, and the delight with which the Regent's son had discovered in Julian a dogged, enduring integrity that complemented his own more ebullient spirit. And then had come the first challenges—Caolin's interest quickened as he saw how their battles had appeared from the other side—and in Julian an upwelling of power that had astonished all of them. The memories continued, and Caolin saw Julian's lifeless body on Spear Island, and the light Frederic had seen in his face as he emerged from the Sacred Wood on Midwinter Day.

Caolin nearly lost contact as he flinched from that reflected glory. It was an illusion, of course, for which he would presently find an explanation, but it partly accounted for Frederic's dazzled devotion. It would not do to underestimate Julian in the future, for the untrained talent which had already once or twice balked the sorcerer was clearly greater than he had believed. Still, where Frederic saw virtues, Caolin saw weaknesses which he would make use of one day.

But just now it was not Julian he must deal with, but Frederic, who at the moment was lost in contemplation of the shifting images that the *toloache* had spawned in his brain.

"*Do you find them pretty?*" the sorcerer questioned him. "*They are only delusions—but I can show you reality—*" Without waiting for a response, Caolin began to alter the images, superimposing his own visions so that they became at once more recognizable and stranger, familiar objects that distorted into horrors, the truth beneath the surfaces of things that Katiz had shown him long ago. This extended beyond anything Caolin had done with his lesser servants, for Frederic was made of purer metal. It was a deliberate corruption of the psyche, intended to break Frederic's mind and leave him a willing tool.

"*Do you want to escape this? I will show you the way—*" Caolin perceived his captive's frantic struggles without pity, remembering his own. And then in Freder-

229

ic's mind he opened the door into darkness, wider and wider, until it was all he could do to maintain his own identity against the emptiness within. But as he reached out to draw the terrified spirit of the other back again, all resistance suddenly ceased. To Caolin's inner senses, Frederic had disappeared.

Shaking with reaction, Caolin fought his way back to waking consciousness. He crawled forward to see what had happened to the boy. Frederic lay sprawled against the cushions, but to Caolin's surprise, he was breathing. He looked, in fact, as if he had fallen asleep, but on his face was an expression of peace beyond pain.

From the northern point of Montera Bay the coast stretched west and northwestward in a series of bluffs and broken beaches. The wind had shifted to the northeast, bringing dry air down the Great Valley and out to sea. On land men must be sweating to bring in the harvest under a searing sun, and the breeze was hot as it skimmed the waves.

Beyond the shore, the land sloped up to the wooded coastal hills. *Sea Brother* and her two captives kept formation under shortened sail, heading homeward beneath a sky that was brilliantly clear except when a drifting stain of smoke told them that the hills were burning, for the spring rains had been scanty, and the autumn rains had not yet come. The coastal springs had shrunk to trickles, and any spark could set the land afire. Watching the smoke shadow the sky, it seemed to Julian that the reivers were only a symptom of a greater imbalance, and that the problem of defeating them and correcting it were the same.

But he could not do it yet. Julian knew that there were at least a dozen sharkships out there somewhere, eager to avenge their companions, but at sea, the brilliant weather was like a reprieve. Wounds healed, and faces that had been drawn with strain began to ease. The tensions that had divided them on the way to Elkhorn had been washed away by shared danger and, for the first time, all on board *Sea Brother* felt themselves part of one crew. They cruised past a shore patched with autumn's tawny hues whose colors ripened daily, and slowly Julian began to gain a kind of perspective on what had happened in Montera.

"Arn says that if this wind holds we should sight the Great Bay tomorrow," said Rana, coming back from the stern.

"Oh indeed, we are getting close to home—" Gully exclaimed. "I've been down this far after bluefin. If this were the season for them we could bring back enough to feed everyone in Seahold—three boats full!"

Julian smiled. "I think the boats themselves are enough of a prize. When we have made the seas safe again we can worry about fishing them."

"It's so peaceful now," said Marta. "What happened with the otters seems like a dream!"

Silverhair looked at them gravely from the piled sacks they had arranged into a comfortable seat for him. "Is there then no violence in the Sea?"

Julian saw Rana's eyes cloud and knew that she was remembering the Floating Island, and his hand moved instinctively to touch the Sea Star.

"In the ocean," she said slowly, "everything is either hunter or prey. But the Sea People kill only for food, and they are food for others when they die."

"I know how Mother Earth treats the dead," Julian answered, too intent to care if that reference to his own temporary burial shocked them, "but the ocean is different. What is the Way of the Sea?" Something tugged at his memory, and he stared at Rana, willing her to answer him.

"Like the way of the waves on the shore . . . Water is

231

meant to flow. It is only violent when it meets resistance."

"That's what I was trying to remember!" exclaimed Julian. "There was an old swordmaster with Lord Philip at Rivered. He used to talk about flow—he told us not to think too much or try too hard in a fight. The trick is to find the rhythm and let each movement flow naturally. An opponent who resists it will destroy himself."

"That's true," said Silverhair, "but what does it have to do with the sea?"

"This—" Julian lifted the silk bundle that hid the Jewel. "If I had understood the Sea Star, I would have known how to work *with* the Sea. I wish you could have given me what you learned on the Floating Island, Rana, when you gave me the Stone!"

She stared at him, and he understood suddenly what must have happened before she was taken to the Island by the whale. Rana had offered up her life to the sea, as he had given his to the earth. Must he be killed by all four elements in order to master the Jewels? He shuddered, knowing it was not death but surrender that mattered— going with the flow. His fingers closed on the Jewel.

I will do whatever I must do, and give whatever I must give. . . .

At that moment Will whistled to tell them that dinner was ready, and whatever further awareness Julian's thought might have led to was lost. By the time they had finished eating, the waves had swallowed the crimson sun, and all that the sky retained was its memory. Stars began to twinkle into life above them, and presently a bulbous harvest moon floated above the eastern hills. As it rose, it hardened and paled until the waves that sunset had gilded glittered with silver scales.

The sea was a tapestry of light, and beyond their white lacing of surf the hills seemed luminous. In such weather there was no need to seek an anchorage, and Arn had set a course parallel to the coastline. For a long time it seemed that human words could only insult the night's beauty. They sat in silence, watching the silent shore go by.

But presently the musical gurgling of water under the bows was threaded by another sound, at first faint, and then growing in confidence until one realized it was a flute's sweet singing, and that Piper had settled himself atop a coil of line and begun to play. For a long time he played alone, a wordless, wandering song like the wind on the sea. Then a faint chiming of harpstrings gave depth to the music, like sea-bells calling from beneath the waves. Flute and harp met and parted, in unison and harmony, now one and now the other leading the melody.

Julian had not realized that Piper had learned to play so well. Did the ability to create such beauty make up for the suffering that had left music the boy's only outlet? Did this perfect communication of flute and harp compensate Silverhair for the frustration of Piper's silent adoration? Such questions had no answers, but for this moment at least, no one could desire more than they had.

There was an aura of moonlight around Silverhair's bent head, and the burnished strings shimmered as if the music had become visible. Even the swan that crowned the curve of the harp seemed cast from silver now. The flute fell silent, but the harp gathered strength and sang full-voiced into the luminous darkness, then diminished to let the harper's singing seal the perfection of the night.

"Softly, the wind from the West fills our billowing sail.
Slowly, the ship turns to follow the moon's silver trail.
See how her way plainly shows in its glittering light—

*So guided, our ship shall sail safely, though dark be the
night.
Hear the stars' melody drift from the heavens above . . .
Sleep now, for the Power that protects us is love!"*

Silverhair's voice distilled the words as if the music
flowed through him, and before *Sea Brother* the moonpath lengthened as if it had been created by the song.
Where is it leading us? wondered Julian. *Surely such a
road leads to no mortal shore!* For a time the harp
embroidered on its melody, and then the harper began to
sing again.

*"Gently the ocean is rocking us, promising rest.
Sweetly it sings—dear one, come and find peace on my
breast.
The wind in the sails is whispering its own lullaby;
Safe in my arms I will keep you 'til morning is nigh.
Hear the waves laughing—all sorrow is gone and all
fear!
Sleep now, for when you awake I'll be here. . . ."*

The song finished, and then the music. The ship was
very silent. Silverhair had eased back against his cushions with the harp cradled in his arms. The others were
dark lumps on the deck. Except for Arn at the helm,
everyone seemed to have been lulled to sleep as well.
Julian got up, a little stiffly, for during the music he had
not moved, and made his way to the stern. Seeing him,
Arn yawned and then smiled.

"Are you sleepy?" asked Julian. "If you'll trust me
with the tiller I'll take it for awhile. On a night like this I
don't think even I could get us into any trouble, but of
course I'll call you if there's any change."

"All right—" Arn yawned again. "I think that song of
Silverhair's would put a naiad to sleep, and I am tired."
He gave Julian's arm a squeeze, and stumbled forward to
find his sleeping roll.

Left alone, Julian checked the lashings that held the

rudder steady, and then settled back against the rail. His body moved easily to the sway of the ship, and he realized that in some ways, at least, he had become accustomed to the sea. He could feel *Sea Brother*'s timbers flexing to the motion of the waves. Her motion told him what the wind was doing, and every creak of wood and vibration of rigging sent him its own messages. He would never have believed that he could come to care for a construct of wood and rope as if she were a living thing. Arn's passion for his ship was suddenly comprehensible.

That sense of union made the gaps in Julian's knowledge all the more painful. He looked down the shining seapath and sighed. In the crowded world of the ship, this was as close as he could get to being alone. And there were things he desperately needed to think through before they reached shore.

Only somehow he could not keep his mind on them. Rana had turned in her sleep so that the moonlight shone full on her face, and as he looked at her, Silverhair's singing echoed in his memory. She looked so defenseless, lying there—if only he could hold her safe in his arms until the sun rose! Julian felt an odd aching in his chest and realized that it was not with his body that he wanted her now, but with his soul. He had thought he had only the lusts of the flesh to contend with, but this was something more.

Whether it would outlast the intimacy that had been forced by this journey he could not tell. Whether Rana could ever be healed enough to accept any man's love he did not know. And with a war to fight and all his own inadequacies to be conquered, Julian dared not pledge his faith to anyone. He could not touch her. He could only watch over her rest, while this new emotion brimmed within him until he shook with the pain.

And then he could contain it no longer. But though he

had been sure he must scream, the only sound that came was a sigh. Released, Julian let it flow through him unhindered in silent offering.

Sleep now, his heart sang silently, *for the Power that protects us is Love....* And *Sea Brother* sped through the waves unhindered, while Julian watched over his beloved, alone with the moon and the sea.

Chapter Twelve

Sea Brother followed the moonpath across the sea. Julian, at her helm, lost consciousness of self and ship in contemplation of the beauty of the night and the wonder of his love. In this waking dream he remained while the moon completed three-quarters of her course through the midnight sky. They might have gone on thus until morning, but as the moon began to dip toward the horizon the glittering ripples solidified suddenly into three silver shapes that rose from the sea and fell back again in an explosion of shimmering spray.

Julian came half to his feet as the three dolphin-shapes leaped again. A shrill whistling split the silence. Rana sat up with a gasp and the others began to stir, mumbling and rubbing sleep from their eyes. The ship was shaken by an invisible turbulence; water swirled as something rose from the depths before her. With a gentle bump it touched her bow, and *Sea Brother* slowed, shuddering as the pressure of wind on her sail thrust her against the obstacle that held her.

"Are we aground?" came Arn's cry, and then before anyone could answer, "Quick, get the sail down before she tears herself apart—"

Stumbling and clumsy with sleep, the men struggled with the sail. Then the canvas flapped loudly and billowed to the deck, and *Sea Brother* halted, rocking gently beside the great mass of a humpbacked whale.

Arn seized the tiller from Julian. The others were hanging over the rail. Rana had already slipped over the side, and swam now with the dolphins. They could hear the chittering of the sea-beasts and the girl's responses through the lapping of the waves.

Slowly Julian moved toward the bow, the Sea Star clasped between his hands. His body shook to the slow, heavy beat of his heart. A great quiet held him, and even before Rana called out to them he knew what she was going to say. He had meddled with the Sea People, and now they had come for him. He was in their power, to save or to slay.

"Julian! You can't go with them!" Robert seized his arm, his fair face distorted by anxiety.

"Do I have a choice?" asked Julian. "That whale has been gentle with us. Would you rather he capsized the ship and left you all to swim home? They are not asking me, they are commanding, and they have the right, Robert. Even if they had not required it, I would have to go."

"You could die—"

"Any of us can die, at any time," Julian answered gently. "We are at war. But without the favor of the Powers of the Sea I cannot use the Jewel, and without the Jewel I cannot rule Westria. I must submit to their judgment. And I *need* it, Robert, in order to go on!"

"Julian, come—" called Rana from the water. "Long-Fin will carry us to the Floating Island!"

"At least take cloaks," said Silverhair in a tight voice. "It will be cold, out at sea."

"Should we try to stay here until you return?" asked Arn.

"No, keep heading for home. They found us this time—I'm sure they can locate *Sea Brother* again."

If they bring you back at all—Arn and Silverhair and all of them were thinking it. Julian did not need to hear the words. But what he had said to Robert was true—if he did not win absolution from the Sea, it would not matter if he came back again.

He put on the cloak Silverhair handed him and went to the rail. The humpback lay alongside, his black back almost as wide as the ship, his tail extending past her stern. Rana was already sitting midway along the broad curve; it was only a short step down for Julian to join her. He settled himself on the whale's back, wrapped the cloak around them both, and felt mighty muscles quiver beneath him as the humpback bore them away through the silver sea.

With a dreamlike swiftness they travelled through the ever-changing landscape of the ocean. Julian could not guess how far, for there were no landmarks by which to gauge the speed of their passing, and he did not know how fast a whale thus burdened might swim. But the moon was low on the western horizon when their progress slowed, and he saw ahead of them a large smooth area on the surface of the sea.

"It's the Island—" whispered Rana. "You see, what I told you was true!"

"I never doubted you," Julian replied.

"Didn't you? There were times when even to me it has seemed like a dream!"

She gave the sigh of one who wakes after a nightmare, but to Julian, it seemed that this was the dream. For Rana had spent the night within the circle of his arms after all, and no fear had tainted their unity. Whatever else might happen now, at least this one night had been his.

The Island lay across the moonpath. Beyond it, the silver trail narrowed toward the horizon, where it disappeared into a mist that merged sea and sky. As they neared the Island, the moon dipped suddenly and the mist distorted it so that for a moment what Julian saw was not a circle but a woman-shape that seemed to lift one hand in salutation and then was gone.

Julian felt, rather than saw, the dim mass of the Island looming beside them. The humpback turned to lie alongside it, and Rana gathered herself and scrambled outward. Hampered by the folds of his cloak, Julian struggled to do the same, and in moments found himself sprawled atop a resilient, sandy surface, blinking in the grey light of the hour before dawn.

A dark shape bent over them. Julian felt his shoulder gripped by a powerful figure that lifted him and Rana to their feet. He found himself still looking up at it, and his skin prickled as he recognized its more than human size. Assuredly he was now in the hands of a power older than man.

"Come with me—" The voice was deep, liquid, and it resonated in Julian's bones. "It is commanded that you wait here. . . ." Those strong hands propelled them forward. Lengths of kelp had been woven together to form a seat. Julian draped his cloak across it, and he and Rana sat down. The air was damp, and now he felt the chill. He shivered as if judgment had already been passed and he was awaiting doom. Some imperceptible lightening in the sky showed him their guard more clearly —tall and black-skinned and hairless, with powerfully muscled arms emerging from a long, black and white sleeveless robe.

"That's Orca—" Rana's whisper tickled his ear.

Julian nodded. He had already realized that this must be one of the Guardians, and now he saw how the human form represented the creature whose essence this being contained.

The east was growing luminous; an iridescence purer than the light of either moon or sun now glimmered in the air. The sea was shimmering also, as if mist was rising off the surface of the water everywhere. A pulse of color suffused the sky, as delicate as the inside of a shell. The world was all shell colors now—subtle rose and peach tones, aquamarine and silver and pearl.

Color and form shifted subtly—was it the changing light only, or was it something in the mist that moved? Julian gripped Rana's arm, and she nodded.

"Yes, I see it too . . ."

He felt her grow very still at his side, and then his own breath caught, for now he saw that there was indeed something moving in the sea around them, forms that flowed from one shape to another as they neared the shore.

Suddenly something leaped from the water in a fountain of silver spray. For a moment they saw the perfect curve of a dolphin's body, and then it changed, and when it landed it was a smoothly muscled young man with laughing eyes and silver skin. Almost immediately another, darker shape slithered up out of the water to join him, and the sleek, water-darkened fur of the seal became a short tunic that covered the body of a graceful woman with pale skin and long dark hair.

"The Seal Sister and the Lord of the Dolphins!" breathed Rana. "Oh, they are coming, Julian—here are all the Powers of the Sea!"

Julian knew it. He had expected it. And he did not know if his trembling came from wonder or from fear.

Now several gleaming shapes flashed out of the water. Julian glimpsed the blue-green scales and striped sides of a bass before it lengthened into a woman in shining green and silver whose cheeks were marked with the lines of tribal scars. Close behind him appeared the vermilion robes of the Guardian of the Rockfish and a green-brown halibut who seemed to be perpetually looking back over his shoulder, even in the form of a man.

A great shape seemed to fly out of the water, a sunfish ten feet long even in marine form, that settled onto the island as a woman cloaked in dark blue over a paler under-robe. The Sturgeon joined her, straight and silver as a sword; a great eel slithered out of the water, becoming a lithe, fierce warrior whose features were set in a wolf-like snarl. A ray like a giant bat flipped out of the sea, black wings turning into a cape that flared around a slim olive body.

Julian felt the Sea Star throbbing at his breast. Even to see this was an initiation. His awareness expanded to sense the energy that radiated from each of the Guardians; as they found places on the Island they were communicating in patterned pulses of power.

The translucent mass of a jellyfish heaved itself over the edge, turning into a dumpy woman draped in glistening fringes of purple-brown. Stranger creatures followed her, starfish and crabs and shellfish who retained their armor even in human form. Anemones rose from the sea like ambulant flowers.

The whales came, shrinking their great bulk to take their places with the others: the long-armed humpback and the giant blue. More dolphins joined them, black and white and gray, quivering with silent laughter. The great Sea Lion pulled himself out of the sea, his shaggy mantle fluffing out and fading to a lighter brown as it dried. The grotesque features of the Elephant Seal followed, the body below them massive even in man-shape.

There was a gap in the arrivals, then a quiver passed through the crowd as a pale pointed snout slid up over the edge of the Island, to reveal rows of shining teeth in a grinning gash of a mouth. Powerful muscles contracted, and the whole fifteen-foot length of the great white shark twisted onto the sand, then changed into a big man with pallid skin. Black eyes glittered as the others drew away from him, and the Shark's big mouth opened in a toothy, mirthless grin.

Looking at him, Julian thought, *If the judgment goes against me they will give me to him. He is the executioner. . . .*

Once more there was a silence. Without his noticing, dawn had come to the ocean. The newborn sun rose in a blaze of light, scattering a pale glitter on the waves. There was a splash, and out of that splendor burst a last, shining shape, a five-foot salmon that leaped as if she were scaling a waterfall and came down again clad in shining mail.

"Grandmother Salmon!" whispered Rana, and both of them made the salutation to the Guardian whom Westria honored as the Spirit-Keeper of the West. "She is the herald. Now Sea Mother will come."

At first Julian thought a cloud had shadowed the sea. Then he realized that it was not the surface, but the depths of the ocean that had been darkened by something whose dimensions increased as it approached until the waves were lightless for a hundred feet around. Turbulence framed the darkness, but above it the water was smooth. The short hairs prickled on Julian's neck; he stiffened as if he were already being dragged down.

A glistening tentacle snaked out to grip the edge of the Island and pulled the rest of the darkness closer. More tentacles writhed out of the water; the Island shuddered as they pulled the rest of the body upward. Then the whole ropy mass lay pulsing before them. From beneath the smooth mantle glittered two bright eyes. Julian had known that Sea Mother ruled deep ocean in this form, but he had not been prepared for the reality.

But now she was changing again. Water cascaded from coiling limbs as she rose, and limbs and mantle became a fringed and hooded cloak swathing a massive dark-skinned form with a sharply hooked nose. Slowly she settled again with her cloak spread around her, its slick surface gleaming a dark reddish purple in the sun. With the smooth unfolding motion of a falling wave the Guardians of the sea-creatures bowed.

"Mother of Oceans, we have heard your call and obeyed it," said the Sturgeon when all had recovered again. "But this is not the season for Council—why have you summoned us?"

"We are not the only ones summoned—there are two humans!" exclaimed Seal Sister. "What are they doing here?"

"Have you no eyes, sister?" said the Ray. "Look at the Jewel the man bears! Has he come to claim lordship over the Sea?"

"He has come to be judged by it—" the deep voice of Sea Mother rolled over the babble of questioning. "I call the Lord of the Otters into this circle now!"

With a start, Julian realized that he had not seen the one Guardian he should have most expected to be there. But it was always the right of the accuser to enter last of all. He bit his lip as a shape that was only too familiar slipped onto the Island, reared up on its hindquarters, and became a shaggy, brindle-whiskered man in a fur kilt who stood staring about him with bright eyes.

"Well, I'm here," said the Guardian. "Will you now get on with it?" His gaze met Julian's and he stopped, glaring. "I've lost too many of my folk to these humans

244

to be patient any longer. The blood of my people is on this man's hands!"

"I never meant to harm—" Julian began, but Orca's grip immobilized him.

"Silence, both of you!" said Sea Mother. "We will do this properly. This human is accused of breaking the Covenant between our peoples. Ordinarily such a one would be sent to his own King for judgment, but he himself is the King-to-be. His crime is therefore all the greater, and it calls into question his right to the Jewel of Power that he now bears."

A murmur passed through the assembly, and Julian felt his belly knot as he heard all his own self-accusations articulated so coldly. If it had not been for his duty to Westria, he might well have judged himself already, just as harshly as she was doing now.

"Prince of Westria—" now her deep eyes were fixing him, "do you accept our jurisdiction? Know that it is your right to appeal to the Guardian of Men. . . ."

Julian stared at her. In the Name of the Guardian of Men he had sworn to defend Westria, but though he knew the Lady, the Guardian was a brightness glimpsed only in his deepest visions, a glory that he, who had seen so many wonders, was not yet certain he had the courage to look upon. But he did not hesitate because of fear. What mattered now was not his life, but his ability to rule the elements. Even if a higher authority forgave him, as Master of the Jewels he must be accepted by the People of the Sea. He stood and bowed to her.

"Lady, if I have sinned against the Sea through ignorance, the Sea must correct me, and if by intention, it is the Sea's right to punish me. I will have your judgment or none."

She nodded. "So be it. Now for accused and accuser both we must choose advocates. Who speaks for the Otter in this assembly?"

"I will speak for him—" the voice of the Sea Lion grated harshly. "My people have also suffered from this enemy!"

"We have all suffered . . ." came the echo from many throats.

"They suffer from each other, too," muttered Rana, beside him. "But they are not putting themselves on trial!"

"And who speaks for the Prince of Men?" There was a silence, and Julian began to wonder if he must defend himself, and whether he dared.

"I'll speak for him, if I may!" It took Julian a moment to realize it was Rana who had moved, and now stood before him with her red head tipped back defiantly. "I gave him the Sea Star!"

"The responsibility for his possession of the Jewel is something we share," said Sea Mother. Her gaze softened a little as she looked at the girl. "But I recognize your right to champion him." She turned toward the Otter. "State your case now—"

"'Tis simple enough, Lady," said the Sea Lion truculently. "The Covenant they swear to allows killing only in self-defense or to preserve life, and this man brought the Sea People into a fight among men. He had the power of the Jewel—they could not resist his compulsion. They—"

"That's not true!" objected Rana. "He refused to use the Sea Star! That's why we had to call on the otters. He only used the Jewel to make them stop, at the end!"

"Maybe he didn't mean to use it, but he had it on him, and my people felt the power," put in the Otter. "If he doesn't understand it, he oughtn't to wear the thing!"

"Yes, perhaps that is the true problem," said Sea Mother thoughtfully. "But before we address it, I think the Prince should be allowed to explain the reasoning that moved his deeds."

Julian got to his feet and considered his accusers. He could sense the power in them, and knew that their true bodies were such as he would hardly dare to look upon. But he must try to make them understand.

"The Lady has called me Prince of Men. That is true—that is my heritage. But I am not yet King or Master of the Jewels, because another human betrayed his trust. The Jewels were lost when that man tried to use them to destroy Westria. Now the Earthstone and the Sea Star have been found. But this same enemy has arisen once more and seeks power over the land. If the reivers who have killed my people on land and your people on the sea are not his allies in fact they surely are in spirit." There was a little quiver of interest from his listeners at that, and heartened, Julian continued.

"Everything that I have done has been to preserve the Jewels and defend Westria. But I know so little! Only enough to realize how much power is here—" he touched the Jewel at his breast, "and how much damage I could do if I used it wrongly.

"And yet if the reivers had captured the Sea Star, it might have come into the hands of my enemy, and he would surely use it to do evil such as you, I hope, can hardly imagine! It was not to defend myself, but to protect all who are linked by the Covenant of Westria that I called on the otters for aid, knowing that they had already suffered at the hands of these reivers, and thinking that they might welcome a chance for revenge. . . ."

"No action is without complications," said Sea Mother, "though perhaps your choice had fewer than most. And yet it has brought you here, into our power."

"Yes it has, Lady!" exclaimed Rana. "And don't you want to know why he submitted himself to you? Why he didn't go home by land after the sea-fight? Why he didn't simply throw the Sea Star back into the sea? Don't you see—he was trying to protect you as well, all of you, because you are already part of this war! You, Lord of Dolphins—" Her finger stabbed toward the figure in princely gray. "Don't you know that the same enemies who held me prisoner have wantonly slain your people too? Don't punish Julian, help him, before they kill more!"

Julian stared at her in astonishment. What she had told them was true, but he would never have dared to say it that way. Her passion had done what his caution could not—he had found another reason to value her, and his heart soared. Then Sea-Mother spoke again, and he turned back to listen to her.

"My brothers and sisters, you have heard the accusation and the humans' plea. What say you now?"

The air sparkled suddenly as the Guardians linked in soundless communion.

"The Prince of Men did wrong to involve my people without thinking what would happen," said the Otter slowly at last, "but it is true that their hearts were already hot against their enemies; perhaps no compulsion was needed. I will not condemn him for what he has done, but how will you make sure that he does not do it again?"

The dark eyes met Julian's, and the human sensed the well of laughter that lay beneath his sorrow, and wished that both of them could leave their responsibilities behind and simply play. He had not done that for much too long.

"I will speak more strongly," the Lord of the Dolphins came forward. "The girl has been adopted by my people, and they love her. Those of you whose peoples live principally in the deeps may stand aside if you will, but we who range the coasts share the danger. We would help the humans against their enemies."

As he spoke, the Guardians began to move, separating into coastal and deep-sea dwellers. Now, two groups faced Sea Mother. Julian took a deep breath, and stepped between them.

"If you will not punish me, then it is your duty to help me! Lady of the Sea-Creatures, show me how to use this Jewel I bear, lest in my freedom I do you more harm!" For a moment he stared into the deep eyes, then he knelt in the sand before her as if he had received a sentence instead of a reprieve.

"We are only the ocean's creatures, not Ocean herself, and even the sea holds only a portion of the world's waters," she said softly. "To be Master of Waters you must submit yourself to the Element of Water utterly. Are you willing to undergo that ordeal, knowing that it will mean death if you fail?"

"No! Julian!" came Rana's voice behind him. "You still have the Earthstone!"

But Julian shook his head. Without water, the earth would die. In his dream, Rana herself had shown him that. It would be better to have no power at all than to only go part way.

"I seek the Initiation of Water . . ." he said finally. "Let it be as you say."

"So be it—" Sea Mother's voice strengthened suddenly. "Lord of the Waters, I call on you to receive this human. He comes with our blessing—teach him what he must know!" In the silence that followed, thunder rumbled, though there had been no cloud in the sky.

"Otter, Dolphin—take the man and throw him into the sea!"

Down with a rush and a tumble and hush farther still he was falling, endlessly inward and downward and onward as consciousness dissolved. Awareness spread outward then, indistinct, dissipating its focus, 'til all that he knew was the flow and the strong, slow swirl of the depths of the sea. Deeper and deeper the dark currents bore him; he sank through chill, still-unfathomed immensities. Yielding to pressures that would crush all resistance, he was borne through realms beyond the depths of the minds of men.

And Julian was that dark weight of Water and knew the deeps of the Sea.

Lightless and lifeless, the submarine current moved in the heart of the waters. Bearing a burden of minerals onward it spread, 'til abruptly it met with a barrier, recoiled and rose, growing lighter and swifter as deep pressures lessened. Suddenly light lanced the waters, life by light ignited, on itself fed and feeding, dissolution resolved into form welling upward in ever increasing complexity. Mind moved in the Sea, knowing the currents that curled around the continents, and how heat and cold compelled life to arise and fall.

And Julian was that rich brew of life, welling toward the surface of the Sea.

In wavelet and eddy, in ripple and riptide he swirled. Apparently aimless, yet obedient to the Moon's silent compulsion, he was the tide. Forever at ebb or flow, he moved with the waters, now the hissing scour of wave across sand, and now its presumptuous crash on rock that battered and beat back in a clatter of polished stones. In that tumultuous battle he fountained into the air as glittering spray, scattering droplets that misted into vapor as sun and wind caught and carried them into the skies.

He was Mist, formless, weightless, at the mercy of the wind, a myriad of droplets that sought to join. An invisible attraction drew the droplets together; the multitude gained density, developed identity, in company became a cloud. Larger and thicker, tingling with anticipation, unbearable tension released at last and lightning stabbed the sky. Thunder rumbled and drops grown too heavy began to fall in a flood of rain.

And Julian was the rain.

Pounding the hilltops, misting over the meadows, moisture gathered and pooled, brimmed over and trickled in a thousand rivulets to become a stream. Laughing, the stream swept onward, rippling over rocks and spurting through gaps, roaring over waterfalls and bubbling in the shallows, scouring out deeper channels through which it poured with gathering power.

Julian was the River, and now the river rolled slowly. Water channeled widely, spread over earth's dry flesh, began to penetrate and pass within. Percolating between particles, absorbed by rootlets and sucked upward, he was carried up the tree trunk, out through the branches into the round red globules it bore. Swelling that sweetness, the water was contained while more and more was added until the ripened fruit fell.

And now, crushed, released, down a dark passage it flowed bearing bounty, and yet it was not that bounty. When substance around it absorbed what it carried, it remained, ever-moving, ever-changing, dissolving, permeating thin membranes, dispersing through narrowing channels, pulsing to the deep beat of a red drum. In endless permutations liquid circulated through the body, filling cell and organ and vein. All structures existed only to give shape to water, water passed in and out of the body in endless repetition of the ancient cycle that led back to the sea.

And that Body was Julian.

He lay, tasting the sweetness of his saliva, conscious of the water that plumped out the moist, soft flesh of his body that was pumped by his heart, flowing freely through every vein. He heard a soft roaring and did not know whether it was the rush of his blood or the sea. The body which he had thought so solid was only a receptacle that enabled water to take a form and name. He knew then that with a thought he could be free of that constriction and flow back to his source and the cycle would begin again.

I am water . . . the thought precipitated in his awareness, *and I can never be destroyed no matter how much my form may change.* . . .

Wet droplets were falling upon his face, too warm and salty for rain. Julian opened his eyes and saw Rana bending over him. Now he could feel the wet clothes that covered his body and the resilient surface of the Island beneath him, but his senses expanded to encompass the moving depths upon which it lay. He felt consciousness dissolving again and forced himself to focus on Rana's face. The sun blazed from her bright hair, but her eyes were welling with tears.

"Surely I'm wet enough, love, you don't need to weep all over me!"

"Julian! I thought they had drowned you!" She sniffed and wiped her eyes with her sleeve. "They took you, and you were gone, and then suddenly you were lying here. Where have you been?"

"I think I have been everywhere. . . ."

He ordered his muscles to lift him to a sitting position, wondering whether he would slither like Sea-Mother across the sand. But apparently he still had bones, because they supported his body. The blue sea was dancing around them. The Guardians had gone and they were alone.

Rana sat back on her heels, staring at him with the beginnings of understanding in her eyes. He could see the swell of her breast beneath the tunic, and thought of his seed filling the hidden hollow of her womb.

The waters of our lives will mingle, and from that sea our child will be born. . . .

The conviction formed in his awareness as if someone had spoken the words. At such moments all his uncertainties fell away and Julian knew that there was a bright future waiting beyond all the present sorrows.

A deep *whfft*! came from the ocean nearby. Water vapor fountained above the edge of the Island, and the bulk of the whale followed it in an endless dark curve until suddenly the perfect sweep of the whale's flukes stood stark against the azure sky. For a moment he and Rana and the whale were all part of the same beauty. Then Julian realized that the whale was Long-fin, who had come to take them back to the world of men.

He reached out to Rana, but she was turning, trilling a delighted call to the whale. Already the moment of certainty was passing, but as he got to his feet, Julian thought that he would never fear the sea again.

By the time Long-fin brought Julian and Rana back to their ship, the sun was westering, and its lengthening rays dyed the sails of *Sea Brother* and her two followers, and the white cliffs past which they moved, deep gold. Arn already had *Sea Brother* under the minimum of sail needed to maintain control. The humpback matched her speed easily, and Julian swung himself aboard with a fluid grace that made the others stare. Rana could have told them where it came from, but to her it did not seem remarkable, for her memory was still haunted by the movements of the Guardians of the Sea.

Julian was aware how their eyes followed him, felt the pressure of questions they were afraid to ask. He remembered how it had been after he mastered the Earthstone, for once more he found himself without words to explain what had happened to him. At least this time he bore no scars to stir their whispers. He did not know that they saw the change in him every time he moved.

Arn bent on more sail, and the three ships surged forward as if they had caught the scent of home. Guardian Point slid past behind them, and then they were paralleling the long beaches on the sea-side of the peninsula. Smoke from Yerba Buena rose above the brown hills. The sun was kissing the horizon when they rounded the snarling rocks of Wolf Point and stood in past the rusty cliffs of the Gate at last.

The tide was nearing the end of the ebb, but a brisk wind blew in from the sea. Plunging and bucking against the current, the ships fought their way through the narrows and coasted into the quiet waters below Seahold with the last of the light. Gulls screamed overhead, alternately dark and bright as they wheeled against the sky, and the first lamps had been lit already in the houses on the hill. A bell clanged and they knew someone had seen them. As they eased in towards shore lanterns bobbed on the jetty; the whole village seemed to be there.

Julian stood in the bow beside Rana. He touched her and felt her trembling.

"What is it?"

"I have longed so for home, and now I am afraid!" she whispered. "What will I say to them?"

What can either of us say? he wondered then, but there was only one thing that mattered now.

"Say that we return with the favor of the sea—" He squeezed her shoulder. "And that now we are going to make the seas of Westria free once more. . . ."

PART THREE:

A Mingling of Waters

The sea shudders as molten magma boils from beneath it. Fish float white-bellied on the churning surface; sea-birds flap wildly and fall as noxious vapors fill the air. Creatures not so close feel the disturbance and dart away. They carry the news, and the great whales sing warning through the waters—"The sea has gone mad! You must flee, you must flee!"

Julian hears it. From the depths he arises. Silently he moves through dark waters, seeking the source.

Now the dead bob silently on stilling waters, but a wave of pressure moves outward, a ring of ripples that gathers power as it expands, coheres, gains size and strength and rolls across the unresisting sea. No high tide had ever the power of this wall of water. It has become the tsunami, racing away from the explosion that formed it like a demon escaping from a sorcerer's circle to devour and destroy.

Julian perceives the great wave's acceleration, plots its course, and understands what will happen when it strikes the land. Moving swiftly now, he soars towards the mountains and calls the clouds. With all the force of his will he compells them, piling one upon another until their own weight breaks them and they release their burden of moisture in stinging showers of rain.

From slope to stream, from stream to river the water races. Each tributary bears its contribution, the weight of the waters increasing their speed as they rush together to seek the sea. Scouring out new channels, the flood forces forward. Julian watches it—will it be enough to oppose the tsunami? Will it reach the sea in time?

Desperately he watches as the two walls of water race forward. The Wave is still growing, but the Flood rises within its banks, then suddenly it leaps them and begins to overflow—

"No! No! This is the land you are destroying!" Julian throws himself against the river, striving to contain it. But the flood he has unleashed overwhelms him, and he is carried away . . .

Chapter Thirteen

Six ships moved in formation over the calm waters of the Bay. Butterfly sails flapped as signal flags appeared at *Sea Brother*'s masthead, and the line turned, wavering as the crews struggled to trim their sails on the new tack and finally disintegrating as different rates of speed and skill took their toll. A horn blew, and the stragglers got their craft back under control, but there was still a great gap in the line.

"I don't know, Arn—" said Julian, watching them. "I was hoping to use the fishing craft as a kind of light cavalry, but if they can't keep together, the sharks will snap them up like sardines."

Returning in triumph with the Sea Star, with the memory of his union with the sea still bright, it had seemed to Julian that their victory was almost won. The weather held clear and warm, perfect for sailing, though landsmen manned the fire towers and watched the hills.

257

But as Julian tried to forge the motley assortment of men and vessels that had answered his call into a fighting force, he was beginning to understand that there were limits to what even magic could do.

"These are fishing boats, not horses, and every one of them is different. It's as if you took a goat and a cow and a buffalo and expected them to run in formation just because they all have four legs and tails. Just because two boats both have sails doesn't mean they'll act alike on the water, and our lads have no practice in maneuvering in formation," Arn added defensively.

"Well, the sharks do, and excuses won't save us when they ram our line." Julian frowned and lifted his horn again. It was a handsome instrument, a gift from Lord Austin, with rim and mouthpiece bound in silver worked with sea-beasts in bas-relief. Its mellow tones resonated over the waves, and the fishing boats beat back toward their original positions for another try.

"Did I tell you that Alexander of Las Costas is sending his greatship *Battle Gull* to join us?" he went on, trying to cheer himself. "With the Regent's ship and your father's that will give us some strength in the center of the line. We'll cram them with men, archers especially, and try to tempt the sharks into range. They can maneuver, but they can't fight and row at the same time. . . ."

"And they have to close with us eventually. If we can train enough men to fight on shipboard, we'll overwhelm them." Arn grinned.

"*If*—" Julian echoed, feeling his morale slipping once more. "The men and ships are beginning to come in, but will there be enough of them, and in time? I'd rather take out as many of the foe as possible before we come within their grasp. Lord Eric has asked me to come to Laurelynn and talk with some people who have ideas about using siege-machinery on the sea."

"Will you be back by the Harvest Festival?" Arn asked anxiously.

"I hope to be here, but is there some particular reason why?"

Arn shrugged and his wind-burned face got pink. "No, it's just that Bella's baby is due . . ."

Julian stared at him. "But I don't know anything about babies! Surely the women—"

"Oh, the women! They've made it very clear that I did my part nine months ago! But I may need someone to hold my hand! I'll sail *Sea Brother* straight for the foe whenever you ask me to, Julian, but the thought of waiting while Bella is in labor frightens me." Arn's face was red now beneath the fair skin, and Julian controlled his laughter.

"I'll make you a bargain, Arn—I'll stand by you now if you promise to do the same if it ever happens to me!" He held out his hand, and Arn grasped it forearm to forearm as they braced themselves against *Sea Brother*'s roll.

Morning sunlight poured through the long windows of the hall at Seahold and glimmered on the age-polished oak of the floor. Rana put a pile of folded linens on the end of the table that they were setting for the Harvest Festival. For several days before the Equinox the weather had been unpredictable, with high winds and a spattering of cold rain. But this morning had dawned fair and still. Lord Eric and Lady Rosemary had come down for the harvest ceremony, and Julian should have no trouble crossing the Bay on his way back from Laurelynn.

"Rana, come help me move this chair—" called Isabella from the hearth. She moved into the sunlight as she spoke and her tawny hair glistened like living gold.

"Can't that wait until the boys come back?" asked Rana. Her sister was already tugging at the chair and

Rana ran to take it from her. "Bella, stop! I'm sure you shouldn't be trying to lift anything now!"

Isabella straightened and rubbed at the small of her back. "I'm all right. It's just that my back aches a bit, and no wonder, with all this weight to carry around!" She leaned back so that her pregnant belly jutted like a ship's bow. Rana thought it looked obscene.

She set the chair down at the head of the table and sat down on the arm. "Well, it won't be long now," she answered neutrally.

Isabella eased into one of the other chairs with a sigh. "I feel as if I have been pregnant for *years*! Perhaps I should just squat down there with the rest of the pumpkins—" She gestured toward the fireplace, whose hearth had been decorated with ears of corn, late fruits, and piled pumpkins and gourds, and indicated her own swelling contours with an expressive hand. "If this child gets any bigger I'll pop like corn on a griddle and save all the bother of giving birth in the usual way—!"

Rana gave her sister a sharp look. For the past week Isabella had moved about the hold like a goddess of the harvest-tide, serenely complacent in her ripening. But just now she looked both exasperated and uncomfortable.

"Bella—" she said slowly, "Are you at all afraid?"

Her sister's brows knit, and Rana realized with relief that Bella was taking her seriously.

"I don't know. . . . Our mother and Arn's mother and all the old wives in Seahold seem to feel compelled to tell me about every difficult labor they have ever known. I think I must have heard everything that could possibly happen by now, and a lot of things that probably couldn't as well. But I still can't imagine what it will be *like*. I've tried to tell Arn how I feel, but he gets all worried at the thought of it, and then I have to comfort *him*! You'll see—" she added, as if Rana had spoken.

"I doubt it." Rana twisted the end of her braid around her fingers, remembering foul breath in her face and a hard male body battering against her own. She had not told her family what had happened to her on the Island. She did not intend to. She only wished that she could forget it too.

"I'm not going to marry."

"Well, not for a while, certainly—Arn and I knew each other so well it was inevitable that . . ." She blushed and broke off. "Don't take any vows just yet. There are some things about marriage that are very enjoy—"

"Rana! Bella!" Their mother's voice interrupted her. "How can we be ready in time if you cannot even put a tablecloth on?"

Both girls jumped to their feet as Lady Leonie came into the room, followed by their brother Cub with a pile of trenchers in his arms. Linens flapped as they shook them over the tables. Cub followed them, setting out the trenchers, and then the hall seemed to fill suddenly with people.

As others finished setting up the tables, Isabella took Rana's arm.

"Will you stay with me, sister, when the baby comes?"

Rana looked into her sister's face and saw in its shape the mirror of her own. She had privately intended to be far away when Bella's time came, but she could not deny this appeal.

"If you want me—" she said brusquely, and then squeezed Bella's hand.

Frederic laced his hands behind his head, took a deep breath, and then forced trembling stomach muscles to pull him upright. His head spun for a moment as he completed the exercise, but at least he had done one more situp than he had been able to yesterday. He sipped water from the bottle beside him. Then he turned onto his belly and tried the pushups again. This time he managed five before his wounded arm gave way.

Purple scars marked the places where the arrows had pierced it. They were healing now, but the muscles beneath were still strengthless. *I should not have been so quick to tell the Powers Above that I was giving up the sword!* he thought as he lay panting. *Unless the Champion is very merciful, I don't think this arm will swing a weapon again. . . .*

That might be just as well. It would get rid of one distraction from the Way he had chosen, the Way of the Adept whose weapons were of the spirit alone. But in order to follow any path at all he must be free, and he was not going anywhere, helpless as he had been. Whether his conversation with Julian had been real or a projection of his own unconscious, the truth was that he had to get well.

And now, of course, there was another reason for getting his strength back. He would rather be a closely guarded prisoner than an invalid at the mercy of the man whom Ardra called Eldron the Healer. Frederic was still not quite sure exactly what Eldron had done to him. He dimly recalled having drunk something, and since then he had seen flashes of color that reminded him of Julian's descriptions of his visions from *toloache*. But if the juice of the moonflower was indeed what he had been given, then the amnesiac effect of the drug might well prevent him from remembering what had happened after he drank it.

For a moment Frederic struggled to pierce the void in his memory. There was a sense of wonder mixed into it, and urgency, as if he had learned something of fearful import, something that Julian—if somehow he could contact him—must know. But there was terror in that memory as well, and consciousness sheered away from it, leaving him white and sweating for reasons that had nothing to do with his physical exertions.

A gust of raw sea air fluttered the tapestries as the doorflap of the pavilion was opened and fell shut once more.

"Frederic! Are you ill again?" Ardra let her cloak slip to the floor and knelt beside him, wiped the sweat from his forehead and put her cool hand against his brow. "No, no fever," she murmured, "but I don't like this at all!"

"I'm all right, Ardra. Please don't fuss so—" Frederic started to tell her what he had been doing, then bit back the words. It hurt to lie to her, even by implication, but her misjudgment of his physical condition might make it easier for him to escape one of these days. He turned over and looked up at her. "See, I'm better now!"

"I suppose so," she said dubiously, sitting back on her heels to look at him. "Your cheeks have more color anyway. . . ."

"So do yours!" he smiled. She had been out in the wind, and the even brown of her cheeks was deepened by a rosy glow.

"My greatship is here!" In the dimness of the pavilion Ardra blazed like a newly polished sword. "The *Lioness*! All this summer they have been building her for me and now she is here! Oh, she is a beauty! You must get well, Frederic, and I will show you—we will sail together in comfort, for *Lioness* can go anywhere!"

Her eyes grew luminous as she looked at him, and Frederic knew she was thinking of the two of them together in the state cabin, perhaps with silken sheets and a full moon shining on the sea. He remembered Ardra's body by moonlight; he remembered it too well, and he reproached himself as much as her in his reply.

"Even to attack my people, Ardra? A ship is not a toy—what will you do with such a weapon?"

She sent him a quick glance, her jaw set mulishly, then looked away. "You know what I will do, Frederic, for I have so often told you. I will conquer! I will win the place I deserve! Why cannot you believe me? I must do this or I will die!"

"You may die doing it—" he answered bitterly. "Julian is a greater foe than you imagine. Why cannot you believe *me*?"

Ardra laughed. "A mountain-bred stonecutter who never set foot in a ship until this summer? Perhaps on land he is what you say, Frederic, but what can he do on the sea?"

Frederic opened his mouth to tell her about the Sea Star, then let the words die unsaid. That secret was not his to reveal.

"I am not greedy, my lord—give me the coasts and the islands and the mainland may be ruled by whomever it wills." She laughed again, more lightly, and turned to rummage in the chest that held her clothes.

Bitterness rose in his throat like bile, overwhelming all his self-restraint, and any pity he might have for himself, or her.

"All of the coasts, Ardra? Or only those of Westria? Why are you encamped on this piece of desolation and not on the sunny islands of Santibar? It would be no new thing for a member of your house to turn against his leader—didn't your cousin revolt against Prince Palomon more than once before the old man finally died and left him the Lion Throne?

"Are you attacking Westria because Prince Ali would be too strong an enemy," he plunged on before she could answer, "or because it was Ali who sent you here? You talk of honor, you belabor my ears with tales of the fame you mean to win! But what are all those fine words worth in the end? Your rabble snaps at Westria like a pack of curs around a village—you have not even the decency to challenge her to open war!"

He paused, because the breath had left him, and sank back against his pillows. Ardra's face had paled to the color of putty; now the blood rushed back into it, making her even darker than before. In a single lithe motion she was on her feet, pulling the tentflap aside.

"Healer!" she shouted. "Find the healer Eldron and bring him to me! Our prisoner is raving, and must be drugged until he calms down!"

Frederic realized with dismay how weak his retreat into illness had left him. It had been hard enough to deal with Ardra when he was in full possession of his faculties —he should have known better than to enrage her when he was still an invalid. And now he had laid himself open another visitation from that so-called healer whose very presence made his skin chill, though he could not have said why. He lay still, fighting to master his breathing, knowing that his only defense was to try and endure what was coming now with dignity.

In moments, it seemed, the pudgy man in the dun-colored robe was easing through the door. He must have been hovering outside, thought Frederic. He wondered how many others had overheard their shouting. One forgot, sometimes, that the walls of a tent only provided visual privacy.

"Well, now, what is it, what is it?" The man peered at Frederic warily as if waiting for some reaction, and then, when it did not come, seemed to relax. "Has he been overdoing, then? We'll find something to quiet him—" He began to poke through the contents of the bulging bag that never left his side.

"Ardra," Frederic said painfully, "I never meant to

hurt you—I know the purity of your honor—I only wanted you to think about what you are doing!" She turned from him and seemed to stare at the collection of weapons that hung against the wall. "Ardra, please! You know I am not fevered—I only need time and rest to recover. Send this man away!"

"Now he begs me! Now he makes pretty speeches—" she said spitefully to the wall. "Now he remembers that I hold the power."

"The quality of strength is that it can afford to be merciful," Frederic added quietly. Why did she do this to him and to herself? Everything that he had said was true—both the good and the ill; he saw so clearly the bright spirit that was in her, and the evil she might become! "Ardra, show me that you are strong. . . ."

"But the speeches *are* very pretty," she added, turning. "Oh, Frederic, why do I let you enrage me so?"

"Here's what I was looking for!" said the healer briskly. He held up a vial of darkish glass with some unidentifiable liquid inside. "Feed him a spoonful of this and he'll sleep soundly; feed him a half-spoon full and he'll do whatever you ask!"

"Will you do anything I ask if I drug you, Frederic?" Ardra asked, smiling. "I don't think so. Even half-conscious, your will is stronger than most men's, and if I could force it, then I wouldn't love you! Why do you think I shout at you?"

Dizzied with relief, Frederic returned her smile.

"Oh, but if there has been shouting, then he must be quieted—" said Eldron, as if he had not heard. "Bad for him to be upset! Might make him ill again—" He poured some of the liquid into a spoon and approached the pallet.

"No thank you—I don't need it. I think if you ask the lady again, you will find that she agrees with me!"

"Do you? *Ardra*—" the healer turned and light flickered on the crystal dangling from the chain in his hand. "Do you hear me, Ardra? Do you understand what I say?"

The timbre of the man's voice had changed; there was a peculiar resonance to it now that set Frederic's teeth on edge, but he had no attention to spare for that, because all the animation had drained from Ardra's features, and she was staring at Eldron with that fixed, in-seeing look that Frederic had seen on her face once or twice before.

"Yes, I hear you—" came the slow answer. Then she waited, as if until he ordered it she would not move again.

"You have ordered me to give this man a sleeping draught. I am going to give it to him now. . . ."

"Yes," her answer came like an echo.

The healer came toward Frederic, who shoved the chest that served for a bedside table between them, and tried to roll away. The other man stiffened and looked down at him with something deadly leaping in his eyes. For a moment his features seemed to blur and Frederic blinked, trying to focus again.

"Ardra," said the healer coldly, "this man has disobeyed your order. You must hold him for me so that I can give him the medicine. . . ."

"Yes—" this response was as emotionless as the other, but Ardra moved swiftly, and she was strong. Despite Frederic's struggles, in a few moments she had immobilized him, and Eldron was forcing his mouth open with an expert pressure. He gagged, gasped, and felt the stuff go down. As he swallowed, the other two let go of him.

Frederic clenched his fists, but already his voluntary control over his muscles was fading. In moments, his body lay inert, but sight and hearing lingered last.

"You see, Frederic," said the other man very softly as

consciousness fled. "Ardra does whatever I tell her to. And so will you—so will you. There are many ways to break the will, and I know them all."

It was a little past noon when the people of Seahold gathered with their guests in the hall for the ceremony. Julian looked around him, wondering what he was doing there. A year ago at this time they had been celebrating the Autumn Balancing with the people of Awhai. Now the companions who had gone with him on his quest for the Earthstone were all together again, except for one.

Conflicting images jostled in Rana's memory—Frederic whirling beneath a silver moon with a rattlesnake draped across his chest; Frederic giving Julian his father's sword. It should have been Frederic who was standing there beside Lady Rosemary and the Regent today.

Arn's mother gathered her flame-colored robes around her and moved to the fireplace. Lady Katrine was a small round woman with silver-streaked dark hair drawn smoothly back over her ears, but Rana had noticed that a woman always seemed goddess-tall when she stood as priestess at her own hearth.

"At this service there is no altar," she began. "Instead, we face the hearth, which is the oldest altar." She touched a taper to the perpetual candle they had brought up from the family shrine and used it to light the fire. "However this is not only a Festival of the hearth but of the harvest, and in giving thanks for the harvest, we honor the powers of Earth and Sky and Sea from which it, and we, sprang. . . ."

She gestured to her husband, and Lord Austin responded with the old story of what had befallen humankind when the earth grew weary of its depredations, shaking down the cities as an old mare twitches away a fly, and refusing to feed their people.

Lord Austin was very like his son, thought Julian, but with his fair coloring faded to gray. And in another twenty years might it be Arn who was grizzled like an otter, facing Isabella across the hearth? And would the child who now bulged her belly stand watching them with eager eyes?

If Julian could not find a way to defeat the reivers, by the time the child was grown, Seahold might be nothing but a pile of blackened stones.

Lord Austin repeated the Covenant which had at last been sworn to reconcile humankind with the Elder Kindred and set bounds to its dominion forever, then began the prayer:

"Maker of All Things, forgive us and help us, who cannot perceive You as You really are. . . . Help us to keep the Covenant which we have made, to live in harmony with the Earth and with each other, and hear us as we address You in our hearts, each in the form we know You best. . . ."

Julian tried to pray, but awareness of all that was still to be done taunted him. He had sworn to rescue Frederic and Rana, but the girl had freed herself, and so far Julian had been able to do nothing for Frederic, nothing at all! It was not so bad when he was working, but how could he give thanks to the Guardians, not knowing whether his friend still lived?

He took a deep breath as the Master had taught him and once more sought the center of his being, forcing those other thoughts away. *Help us to keep the Covenant!* He begged silently. Once more he saw the dying otters. Once more he heard the judgment of the People of the Sea. *Maker of All*, he prayed, *save us from sinning against the Sea!* Awareness followed memory into cool depths. He sensed Rana and the Master there, and others—for a moment he understood the pattern of all . . .

"So be it." Lady Katrine's voice brought him back to

present awareness. It was only when he opened his eyes and met the Master of the Junipers' frown, that he realized that he had been broadcasting, and that others had glimpsed his vision too.

"Oh Thou Maker of All—the Covenant has been kept!" the Lady of Seahold went on with a conscious briskness that grounded them in the present again. "We have shelter, and clothing, and the good food that weights our tables, and as best we may we love one another, and all manner of good things are added unto us. Let us then consider and remind each other what new things we have to be thankful for in this year—" Her eyes rested on her son and she smiled.

Arn grinned and tightened his arm around Isabella. "I know what *I* have to be thankful for!"

Bella blushed, gave him a quick kiss, and blushed again. "I am thankful for the baby—" she said, "and because the baby's father has come home to me!"

"We are grateful that our child whom we thought lost has been restored to us," Lord Randal said, and Lady Leonie reached out to take Rana's hand.

"And I am thankful that my son still lives, and hope that we soon shall see him again."

Julian braced himself to meet Lady Rosemary's confident gaze. He had told her about his contract with Frederic in vision, but could they trust that? He tried to take comfort in the fact that Rosemary seemed to think so.

One by one the others spoke of gratitude for good fishing, for love or children or lives spared by battle and the sea. Rana cleared her throat.

"I am grateful to the Powers that set the Sea Star where it could be found, now when we need it most. And I thank them that we have a Prince who can use it as it should be used!" Her clear gaze challenged Julian, and for the first time he felt a measure of hope.

270

"And so are we all!" echoed the Master of the Junipers. He was backed, as usual, by the familiar unobtrusive shadow of Malin Scar.

"Then in token of our thanksgiving let us lay the fruits of Earth and Sea before the hearthfire—salt and water, milk and honey, bread and wine, squash and corn, and fish and herbs of the sea—" said Lady Katrine. In most parts of Westria, the list of tokens would have ended with the squash and corn.

Rana's brother Cub got to his feet, dancing with eagerness to do his part in the ceremony. The youngest always asked the questions, and this time that responsibility ought to have gone to Piper, who stood between his grandmother and Silverhair, watching attentively. Julian felt a spurt of anger at the fate that kept him from taking his proper part in the ceremony, the violence that had shocked the boy to silence, that still threatened them all.

"Why do we offer salt and water?" Cub asked the Master of the Junipers, who as the oldest person present was bound to answer him.

"We offer salt and water because they fill the womb of the Earth—the Sea from which life came. Without the water of life nothing could live upon the land, no plant nor animal or human being, nor can we live if salt is denied us. Salt and water are the very blood in our veins, and the giving of salt is a seal of peace among men."

How many times I have heard those words? thought Julian as Arn left his place to take the salt and water in their silver bowls and lay them on the hearth. *But now I understand what they mean. . . .*

The ritual continued as the other tokens were questioned, explained, and laid before the fire.

"We have laid these gifts of the Earth before our fire, but we cannot consecrate what is already more holy than we . . ." Lady Katrine said at last. "Rather, let these things consecrate us, and as we partake of them in our

271

Festival meal, thus incorporating many substances into our single bodies; let us, who are many, also become one!"

The Autumn Feast was the climax of the harvest which had begun in August with the Feast of the First People and the maturing of the corn. From now until Samaine, everyone would be busy storing and preserving what had been taken in. But now was the moment of ripeness, and the laden tables in the hall bore eloquent witness to the bounty of both land and sea. Julian wondered if the folk of Seahold had made a special effort because they knew that there would be little time for celebration in the weeks to come.

Platters of roasted fowl, earthen pots of rabbit stewed with carrots and potatoes, bowls heaped with the last of the salad greens, and little dishes of pickled sea-weed, candied fruits and flowers, nuts, and other condiments, appeared in a seemingly endless stream.

Julian stiffened as two servers bore in a whole baked salmon that had been basted with butter and herbs.

"Doesn't that look wonderful?" exclaimed Lady Katrine. "Arn made a quick dash out to sea to get it, for the salmon never reached the Dorada this summer, and the delay in the autumn rains has discouraged the autumn run."

They set it, succulent and gleaming with the steam still rising, in front of the Lord and Lady of Seahold. Julian stared, silver shapes flickering across his vision.

"Master, I can't eat this—" he said hoarsely. "I *saw* Her—the Spirit Keeper—She leaped from the water and shimmered into woman-shape. How can I eat salmon, knowing what I do now?"

"If that is the way you feel then you are going to leave this feast very hungry—" The Master's weathered features creased in a faint smile—"for how can you eat any of it, knowing that each form of flesh once held a spirit of like value, if not the same complexity, to your own? Even the fruits of the earth, as *you know*, have their own Guardians!" His gaze sharpened, and Julian's hand moved involuntarily to hide the tracery of silver scars on his temple.

"Yes, I know it," said Julian heavily. "Life feeds life, on land and in the sea, and I have only borrowed this form of flesh for a little while. . . ." He slid a piece of salmon onto his plate as if he touched a holy thing, murmuring, "Lady, as your body feeds mine, may mine nourish others one day. . . ."

For a few moments he was aware only of the tender meat fragmenting in his mouth so easily that it seemed as if it were melding with his own flesh indeed. *We are one* . . . he thought in wonder. *We are all One. . . .*

Then Cub jerked, jarring the table, and the rest of the thought was lost. Julian glimpsed mischief in Piper's face, and guessed he must have kicked the older boy under the table. Cub's face had grown angelic, but there was a gleam in his gray eyes. The servers came round with more cider, and as Piper started to drink Cub made a swift movement, Piper yelped and upset his goblet and cider splashed across the table in a golden stream. Lord Randal frowned ominously at his son.

"You boys can either leave the table now . . ." he rumbled, "or behave. I'm assuming that you want some of the pie?"

Two young faces turned toward him with identical sobriety. They seemed to communicate without words only too well, and they fell upon the desserts that were being brought in just as if they had not worked their way through the full five courses before.

People began to push back their benches and leave the tables. Lord Randal and Eric resumed a discussion of the best sources of wood for bows. Isabella swung her legs awkwardly over the side of the bench and stood up, then let out a gasp of surprise. In a moment her mother was at her side. Bella's skirt was darkening with a spreading stain.

"What's wrong?" Rana's face had gone white.

"Get a towel, that's a good girl! Now, Bella, sit down," said Lady Leonie.

"But what's the matter with her?"

"Nothing to fear—only the bag of waters in which the baby has floated these past months has broken now," Arn's mother said calmly. "Now go on—you will find towels in the oak chest in the upper hall."

Julian edged toward the door, knowing he had no business here now. But he moved slowly, for the awareness that after so much death a new life was going to enter the world filled him with wonder.

Arn hovered over his wife, ignoring her exasperated attempts to wave him away. For a moment she stopped talking, tensed, and then let out her breath in a long sigh.

"No, I am *not* in pain! And I did not know the baby was coming—I was uncomfortable, but I thought I had eaten too much, that's all!"

"But shouldn't you be in bed? Is there something we should do?"

"Now if you had been home, young man, instead of sailing the length of Westria, you would know all the things we have been teaching Bella," said Lady Katrine. "Do not worry, son—the first child always takes awhile. We'll get Bella changed into a fresh gown and then she can walk or amuse herself as she likes. It will be hours before the real work begins."

The women were all laughing now, and Arn's ears grew red. He turned to the Master of the Junipers in appeal. "You helped Prince Julian into the world—"

"Yes, and you must not fear. I will be here if I am needed, Arn. But for now we had better do as the women say—they know their business. Calm down, lad—" his face warmed in the familiar cragged smile. "Everything is going to be well."

Bella took her husband's hand and set it on her belly, which was hardening with a new contraction. He looked up and met Julian's eyes, and his anxious expression changed to awe.

Rana stood a little to one side, her fists clenched in the skirts of her gown. As Julian looked at her he realized that it was Rana whose face showed fear. But he dared not try to comfort her.

Chapter Fourteen

The waning moon was just lifting above the hills on the other side of the Bay. Below the terrace, dark waters sighed like a great animal asleep. The sea was calm, thought Julian, calmer than the woman who lay in childbed in the room over the Hall. Here, the only sound was the ring of Arn's booted feet on the flagstones; he was walking as if their sound could cover the moans of his wife as she strained to deliver their child. Soon enough they would call him back inside to watch with her. Three hours had passed since sunset, when Bella's labor began. It did not seem possible that it was still going on.

"Ah—it is much cooler out here!" Silverhair came through the door from the Hall, breathing deeply of the damp salt air. There was a burst of song from behind him, and the two young men turned.

"A toast to that, my lords!" they heard Lord Eric cry. "May Arn's son be as good a seaman as his father and grandfather!"

"Bella's doing all the work, and I'm doing all the worrying," muttered Arn resentfully. "What do they have to celebrate? And they're so sure it will be a boy. What if the child is a maid?"

"They will adore her—" said Silverhair. "I remember how Lord Theodor acted when my sister gave him his first granddaughter, who is now leading the armies of the Corona. Sweet Lady, it seems a long time ago!"

"Have you ever seen a baby born?" asked Arn.

"No," answered Julian. "All my foster-brothers were older." He shared Arn's silence, wondering.

"I have," Silverhair said after a while. "It was like the incoming of the tide."

A spurt of flame flared in the shadows as he lit his pipe. The glow wavered as he drew in and exhaled again. Then the door beyond him opened and they saw the figures of the older men backlighted as they came through.

"So this is where you've got to, Farin," said Eric. "Good idea. We all need some fresh air."

Lord Austin stumbled on the lintel, and Bella's father took his arm.

"Easy there, man," said Eric genially. "The grandfathers are not supposed to get drunk until after the baby is born!"

"And what about the father?" exclaimed Arn suddenly. "You've all sired children—you've been through this—how? It seemed like a wonderful idea to have a baby last spring, but now that it's happening I'm terrified! How could you bear this waiting—and after the first time, how could you let your wives do it again?"

Lord Randal gave a bark of laughter. "If you want to know the truth, boy, we were all terrified too. . . ."

"I remember once when we were caught in a storm, trying to battle our way back through the Gateway," Arn went on more quietly. "We rowed until it was agony to take a breath, afraid each wave would finish us. It seems to me as if what Bella is doing is just as hard. And she's going through this because of *me*! If there were only something that I could do!"

"Arn—do not take it so hard!" his father said. "Remember that Bella contributed something to the making of this baby too. Be patient and brave and comfort her with your love, and you may find it all seems different by the end. It hurts me to think about it too, but then I remember that if your mother had not gone through this, I would not have you!" For a moment his arm rested across his son's shoulders.

"I hope I was worth it. I hope this child will be!" muttered Arn.

"We men go into battle to slay," said Lord Eric. "Even when we are fighting to defend our homes. Women are more fortunate. When they go to their hour of trial it is to bring new life into the world." He held out his drinking horn to Arn, who took it and gulped thirstily.

"And every human being that walks the earth got onto it this way—" said Julian in wonder. "It seems impossible that women have been willing to do it for so long. Do you think they know what it will be like, before they begin?"

"Did you know what battle would be like when you first faced a foe?" asked Silverhair. "Does any of us ever know?"

There was no answer to that, and the men smoked in silence until an upper doorway opened, and a silhouetted figure beckoned.

"No, nothing's happened yet." It was Rana's voice. "But Bella's calling for Arn, so he had better come in."

* * *

Isabella's contractions were coming close together now, and hard. Midnight had passed unnoticed while her labor went on. Rana wondered how she could endure so long. Bella grimaced and whimpered with another contraction, and her mother sponged her forehead. Then it passed and she relaxed.

"You're doing very well, child—very well—" said Lady Katrine, patting her hand.

"Thank you—but how long am I going to have to keep doing it?" The last words came out on a gasp as her next contraction began.

"I never said it would be easy, did I?" Lady Leonie answered tartly. "If you don't want it to hurt, pay attention to your breathing."

"She *is* in pain!" exclaimed Rana to Rosemary. "Isn't there anything you can do?"

"Well, it is not *comfortable*, I admit, but have you never seen men working hard? They grimace and grunt too. She is working, child, harder than she ever has before." Lady Rosemary smiled.

Arn came into the room, pale but calm, and sat down by his wife, who gripped his hand. She tensed and cried out, twisting on the bed. Rana glared at him. *He* could go out and walk on the terrace with the other men, away from the pain. Bella had to stay.

"Relax—calm down, love, and breathe lightly. Remember what they've been telling you." Arn's voice was steady, but he looked as he had just before the sharkships attacked them, and Rana found her resentment fading. "Come now, pant like a dog, and let your muscles work. . . ." He patted her hand and she grew quieter.

Arn's mother had prepared cloths and hot water, and was bathing the birth-opening so that it would stretch without tearing. "She is six fingers open now—doing very well," she told them, straightening.

"The muscles must pull open the passage like a gate.

When the opening is eight or nine fingers wide, then the child can be born. But this last part is always the hardest, especially the first time," Lady Rosemary explained.

"Would it help to have music?" asked Arn. "Silverhair was telling us how he once played for a woman in labor."

"Not now, I think," said Leonie. "She needs to concentrate now."

Isabella was tiring. She moved her head restlessly against the pillow and whimpered even after a contraction had passed. And now when her belly hardened she cried out and gripped Arn's hand until her knuckles whitened. Her mother reached out to stroke her brow, but Bella struck her hand away.

"You lied!" she gasped. "You said it wouldn't be long! Make it stop! Make it stop now!"

Lady Leonie stood up, biting her lip, and went quickly from the room.

"Hmph!" said the Seahold cook, who was feeding the fire. "It is not even dawn—these young women have no strength! I remember with my first, it took from sundown until the sun was setting again . . ." She broke off as her mistress glared at her, but continued to mutter under her breath. "Well, the child will come in its own time, whether she fights it or no!"

The Master of the Junipers limped through the doorway with Lady Leonie behind him.

"You talk some sense into her!" she said as Bella screamed again.

Arn looked up with a profound relief in his eyes. His forehead was beaded with sweat, and when Bella let go of him, red marks showed where she had gripped his hand.

The Master smiled and moved toward the bed, laying a gentle hand on Isabella's forehead and on the mounded belly that hardened and relaxed, hardened and relaxed again. At his touch the girl seemed to calm, but she did not respond to his voice, and her eyes were vague and unfocused. She lay at the mercy of the spasms that racked her, crying out as each one came on.

This is monstrous! thought Rana. *This is not something you do—this is a force that seizes your body and tortures it against your will! But that will never happen to me—perhaps I might have lain with a man for the sake of a child before I knew, but I will go childless, if this is what it means!* It seemed to her now that the assault that had scarred her had been in its way a blessing, freeing her from even the temptation to submit to the body's terrible bondage.

"What's wrong with her?" Arn asked.

"From what her mother has told me, the labor seems to be going well, but this is the hardest time," the Master replied. "She must not run away from the pain. We must help her to work *with* it, or she will suffer needlessly." He looked around at the women. "We will need help from all of you now. Sponge her and give her a little to drink, and Katrine, massage her belly to relax it."

They pulled off Bella's nightgown, and for the first time Rana could see her sister's belly change shape as the constricting muscles tightened and let go. And still it went on, but instead of quickening and finishing the job, the contractions seemed to be farther apart now. Bella lay panting with relief at the respite, but the older women frowned. When Katrine measured her, she found that the birth-passage had begun to narrow again.

"Come now, love—you must relax and let go!" said Leonie.

"No!" whispered her daughter. "I don't want to. Why can't you just let me be?"

Rana stood by the Master. "What is happening?"

He sighed. "It's what's not happening that matters now. The longer this goes on the harder it will be for both mother and child."

"But *why?*" exclaimed Rana. She had wanted the labor

to end almost as much as Bella did, but now she began to understand that there were worse things than simple pain—like a swimmer facing a falling wave, the only way to survive was to dive through.

He made a little helpless gesture with his gnarled hands. "It could be simple exhaustion—but she is young and strong, she should have been able to bear this well. It could be that the child is too large to pass between the gates of her pelvis, and the muscles are tired of trying to open what cannot be moved. Perhaps the signals by which the blood governs labor have failed. It could be one of many things. . . ."

"You're saying that she could die, aren't you?" Rana hissed at him.

"It almost always goes well," his voice was even lower now, "but there is a danger. Go to her, Rana. She asked for you to be with her. Perhaps you can comfort her now."

Rana stared at her sister's contorted face and felt bitter fluid rising in her throat. "No! No, I can't—" She put her hand to her mouth and dashed from the room.

The sickle moon swung westward, tangling itself in the trees that topped the hill behind the hold. Rana could hear a murmur of conversation from the men in the Hall, but the terrace was all in silent shadow. Still shaking after her sickness, Rana sat down on the bench and leaned back against the cold stones of the wall. After a time the quiet seeped through her barriers and she grew still. And it was then, when she had opened her awareness to the night, that she heard someone move.

"Who's there?" Her voice rasped, but even as she spoke, she knew that it was Julian.

"I don't belong in there, but I promised Arn that I would watch with him," he answered quietly.

Rana swallowed despair. "*I* promised I would stay

with Bella! But I can't! It's horrible, and she might die, and there's nothing that I can do!"

She felt him sit beside her. She would have screamed if he had touched her, but it was the cold edge of a goblet that brushed her hand.

"Drink this—it's only wine, but it will steady you. . . ."

Rana took the cup, filled her mouth and spat to take the taste of vomit away. Then she drank thirstily, though she knew that the thin wine would not even lift the edge from her fear.

"It's going badly?" Julian asked.

"Yes—the labor has stopped." She gasped convulsively and drank again. "I hated to see Bella pregnant, hated to see how the birthing tortured her body, but this is more terrible. How can any woman start a child, especially if she knows that this is what it might mean?"

There was a short silence before he spoke again, and then it was with difficulty. "Rana, I know why it seems so terrible to you. . . ."

"What?" Understanding came to her suddenly. "Oh—you found out from Frederic?" She felt the blood heat her skin, then drain away. But Julian could not see. He was only a presence in the darkness, almost not like a man at all. She realized then that he had known about the rape for some weeks now and it had not changed him, except, possibly, that he treated her with greater care.

"What you do yourself is your choice, but your sister has already chosen," he went on. "Help her, Rana—"

His patience defused her anger, and all that remained was despair. "How?" she whispered then. "What can I do?"

Cloth rustled, and she felt him slip something over her head. "Take the Sea Star. The ocean is Mother—surely Her power can help somehow."

Automatically Rana's fingers closed on hard smoothness, and she started as she recognized the pulse of power she had felt once before. "But it's yours—"

"And yours also," Julian interrupted. "You know that is true. Go now, and do what it tells you to!"

Clutching the Sea Star at her breast, Rana came back into the birthchamber. Isabella lay still, her face turned to the wall. Arn was still sitting beside her, holding her hand, while the Master of the Junipers sat at the foot of the bed, his eyes closed as if he were praying.

"Arn—" Rana said very quietly. "Let me sit with her for awhile—"

He sighed, then nodded. There were marks like bruises beneath his eyes—in his own fashion he had been suffering too. She felt the faintest touch of tension stir the air and saw that the Master of the Junipers had roused and was watching her, but she refused to accept the weight of his hope by meeting his eyes.

Sitting down in the seat Arn had vacated, Rana set one hand on her sister's mounded belly. Bella's skin was taut, the muscles beneath it unyielding, but as Rana pressed down, something poked back at her from within. She stifled a gasp as she realized that it had been the baby, that there really was another human being inside there, struggling to be free. She laid both palms where she had felt the touch, trying to imagine what it must be like within.

And suddenly Rana felt as if she *were* the child, at the mercy of forces she could not control. Or was it her own memory of floating in the ocean that was surfacing? She remembered vividly now that she had found release only when she surrendered herself to the natural movement of the sea. And as if that thought had opened a gate, the Sea Star began to pulse and Rana felt all the power of the waters come flooding through.

Isabella shuddered and looked up at her with wondering eyes.

"Bella! Think of the ocean! Think of yourself as the tide, bearing the baby to shore!"

Rana's perception broadened. She felt the Master of the Juniper's steady support, and as he sensed her awareness, he began to reach out to the others and draw them into the link, channeling their energy to her in a steady stream. One by one they turned, aware without being told that something had changed—Lady Rosemary's trained understanding focused the more diffuse energies of Leonie and Katrine and the other women. As Rana became used to the inflow the Master delicately withdrew, and together the women filtered through Isabella's barriers and drew her into their common awareness, which was all women, which was the Goddess, which was the Sea.

Rana felt the tone of the muscles change beneath her hands, rigidity becoming a flexible resilience that rippled with the first of a new series of contractions like the sudden purposefulness of the waves when the tide has changed. The tension in Bella's face gave way to concentration. She lay in an active stillness, letting her muscles work without resistance, and the motion which had been a struggle earlier became a rhythmic surge. Five minutes passed, then ten, then there was a time when the pushes came and went irregularly like the eddies in a tide.

But Rana could feel a gathering of forces as if a great wave was rolling in from far out to sea, and in that moment she realized that Julian had been drawn into the link as well. Power blazed blue around them as Bella opened her eyes.

"Oh!" she cried. "Now I understand!"

"Push now!" said her mother, "Push as hard as you can!" Leonie helped the women to heap pillows behind Bella until she was half-sitting, and Arn settled onto the bed behind her, arms around her, letting her grip his hands. Now the two mothers braced themselves against her feet. Rana felt the muscles ridge beneath her hands and thought of the purposeful rolling of the breakers toward the shore.

Grunting, Bella bore down, her face set in a savage grin. Again and again she pushed, and the changing shape of her belly showed her progress. Power throbbed around them, and Rana no longer needed to touch her sister's flesh to know what was happening now.

"She's crowning—" murmured Leonie.

The Master finished scrubbing his hands and turned back his sleeves. Rana moved silently to the foot of the bed behind him as Bella took a deep breath and shouted. The curve of the baby's skull distended the edges of the birth-opening, which slid back suddenly to let the entire head through, streaked with birth-blood, tiny features screwed up in protest against this violent transition between worlds. The Master knelt as Bella pushed again and the rest of the body slid freely into his waiting hands. It was a girl-child, perfect and wonderful.

For a moment that squirming form, as wet as any creature fresh from the sea, was the only thing in the world. And to Rana, it seemed as if the world had been created anew.

Swiftly Rosemary swabbed the tiny nose and mouth with a damp cloth, the arched chest heaved, and the baby's color changed from white to red as she let out a long, indignant wail. The Master laid the baby on Bella's belly and together, she and Arn reached to cradle it between their hands.

"Arn—" whispered Bella. "Do you see what we did?" She looked up at him then and it seemed to Rana that there was suddenly more light in the room.

The baby mewed faintly and curled her tiny fingers while the Master tied and cut the cord. With one finger he made the sign of the circled cross on the baby's forehead.

"Thus do I seal you to the Covenant of Westria—" he said softly, "child of Earth, Water, Air, and Fire, and sister to all that lives!"

Rosemary lifted the child in a warmed blanket and took her to be washed and swathed while the other women bustled around Isabella, dealing with the after-birth, washing her and changing the linen, and putting her into a clean gown. Then they laid the baby against her mother's breast.

Rana looked down at her sister and the child. The baby was mumbling at Bella's nipple, happy to have found something satisfying in this strange new world. Bella pulled her gaze away from her child and met her sister's eyes.

"You came back—" Bella said softly. "You came back from the Sea . . ."

"Yes," dazed with reaction, Rana replied. "Yes, I did." She stretched out a tentative finger and touched the baby's head. Her hair had dried to a halo of honey-colored fluff. "It's the color of amber. . . ."

"Amber!" Arn repeated with the beginnings of a smile. He looked at Bella, who nodded. "The gem that is born of earth and sea—a fine milk-name for a sailor's child!"

There was a clatter on the stairs to the Hall and the door burst open. The two grandfathers, Lord Eric, and Silverhair tiptoed in and the women moved away from the bed to let them see.

"It is a maid-child," said Arn radiantly. "Her name is Amber."

Lord Austin looked at Lord Randal and they solemnly shook hands, grinning as though as if they would crack their jaws. Then they bent over the baby again.

"Well, well—" said Leonie indulgently after a little while. "You have seen that life goes on. Now do *you* go on and leave Bella to sleep. She has worked hard and needs her rest." Isabella's eyelids were already drooping, but she smiled as her mother kissed her.

"And you," Katrine said to her son, stroking back the damp hair from his brow. "I think that you too could sleep now."

Carefully Arn released Bella's hand and put his arms around his mother. "Thank you—I did not know until now what you did for me. . . ."

"Katrine, Rosemary—there's no need for us all to stay. I will watch with my daughter for the first few hours," said Leonie. Randal whispered something in his wife's ear that made her smile, then followed the others out. Nobody seemed to have noticed that Rana was still in the room.

She hesitated in the doorway, looking at the mother, daughter, and granddaughter. The face of the infant nestled in the crook of her mother's arm was tight-closed as the bud of a rose. Isabella's features had a serene beauty that Rana had never seen in her sister before. But Lady Leonie sat still as though carved from oak, and strangely, in that moment, her mother's face, worn and pale beneath her gray-streaked hair, was the most beautiful of the three.

Then Rana closed the door behind her and went out into the darkness of the terrace to return the Sea Star to Julian.

"My baby would a-sailing go
Upon the sea of dreams,
Where thoughts like little fishes dart
Among the silver gleams. . . .
*   La, lu, lay, Papa's gone away,*
To catch a fish for you and me
To eat this very day—"
Amber made an odd little mewing sound and Isabella

patted her back until she stilled. The lamps had been lit, and the soft light made a nimbus around mother and child. The Master of the Junipers beckoned to Julian, and the two men edged softly backwards toward the door. When they reached it, Isabella smiled farewell, but as it closed behind them they could hear her singing begin once more—

"She thought she'd catch a grunion,
She thought she'd catch a whale,
She thought she'd catch a great sea-shark
By biting off its tail!
    La, lu, lay, Papa's gone away. . . ."

"A beautiful mother and a beautiful child," said the Master as they moved down the passageway. "And all the more precious because we almost lost them—"

"I was terrified!" said Julian. "I could feel the tension coming from that room even before Rana came out and told me Bella was in danger. Earlier that night Arn was wondering how anyone could let his woman go through childbirth, knowing what it means. But in one week he seems to have forgotten all his fears."

"Yes, and so has she," answered the Master.

"I haven't!" said Julian with feeling. "Perhaps one of Robert's children can be my heir. I could never let—" He bit back the name he had been going to say, "I could never let a woman I loved suffer that for me!"

"No?" asked the Master, who had not appeared to notice Julian's hesitation. "But childbirth is not usually so traumatic, or the race would never have survived. I imagine that it will be easier for Isabella next time, now that she understands what to do. With all the worry about war I suppose they did not have time to teach her properly. But your Queen will have the Sea Star and the other Jewels. . . ."

"What do you mean?" Julian asked sharply.

The Master smiled at him. "What did you suppose I

meant? You know that the Queen of Westria must also be Mistress of the Jewels." They were at the door of the Master's chamber now, and Julian followed the old man inside.

Of course he had heard how his mother was invested with the four Jewels of Westria at her marriage, but he had never considered the implications. Rana had already borne the Sea Star, and he wondered suddenly what would happen if he put the Earthstone into her hand. But what right did he have to lay that upon her? Rana might never give her love to any man, especially after seeing her sister's suffering. And even if her spirit was healed enough to love, could he ask her to bear the weight that had killed his mother?

"Would you like some tea?"

Julian realized he was still standing in the middle of the room. He knew that the Master had been watching him and flushed, wondering how much of what he had been thinking the adept had seen. It was true that there had been one moment of contact during the birth when he had touched wonder, but it was hard to believe that could make up for all the pain.

"I would like your help—" Julian forced his mind away from speculations which were at the moment irrelevant, no matter how much they troubled him, to the problems that concerned them now.

The Master sat down by the fire, the lines of his body shifting subtly as they did when the Priest in him replaced the Man. He had recovered well from the blow that had felled him at Registhorpe when he shielded them from the sorcerer, thought Julian, taking the other chair. Only the limp and a slight sagging in the right side of his face bore witness to what had happened to him, though there were still times when he seemed very fragile. Julian allowed his fingers to trace the scars on his own brow. They had both been marked by Caolin.

"The night before we left Montera I dreamed of Frederic. Only at the time it felt as if I were really with him on that Island. Since then, I've learned that one of the things he told me is true—something I could not have known otherwise. Is it possible that my spirit really contacted his?"

"Quite possible," answered the Master, "especially if you were wearing the Sea Star. The Jewel is attuned not only to the element of Water, but to the sphere of the Moon which governs it. In the world of manifestation, its kingdom is the ocean, but in the world of the spirit it is the realm of archetypes and images—what you might call the sea of dreams. Through that sea the adept may voyage in his spirit-body, and meet with other travelers."

"Yes . . ." said Julian slowly. "Now I understand— when Sea-Mother threw me into the ocean I learned how to do that too!"

"I have tried to reach Frederic myself," said the Master. "But there have only been glimmerings of contact. I wondered if perhaps the link was being interrupted by all the water flowing between us, though at times there seemed to be some more purposeful barrier. But with the Sea Star, it would be much easier for you." Was there, perhaps, a hint of hurt in the old man's dark eyes?

"He didn't want to be reached," said Julian quickly. "He was trying to die. . . ."

"And—" the Master raised one bushy eyebrow.

"I refused to release him. I ordered him to get well." Julian hunched his shoulders in the gesture of embarrassment he had almost outgrown.

"That relieves me—" The Master eased back in his chair.

"Yes, but that was several weeks ago. I'm worried about him now, and I don't know why. Will you help me try to reach him again?"

"Now?" The adept bent forward, considering. "Yes, now would be a good time. The hold is quiet and we can work without distraction, and they will most likely be asleep on the Island as well. Take the pallet and blanket from the bed and lay them down before the fire while I ward the room—the body can become chilled when the spirit is away. I will guide you outward, and watch over your body until you return."

Julian pulled the blanket over him and closed his eyes. The fire was warm, and he felt himself growing drowsy. But no—it was not sleep that was taking him, for he heard the Master's voice quite clearly. Now the deep sweetness of that voice was the only thing he was aware of as consciousness of his body fell away. He floated in a swirling silver mist as once he had floated in the sea.

"Julian—your will determines where you will go here, and what you will see. Don't allow anything to distract you." The Master's thought is distant, but clear.

Julian feels himself grow more solid as he nods. He wills his form to take the shape of a dolphin, and with dolphin senses seeks the Isle of Birds. He perceives the pattern of energies that his spirit has already explored unknowing, and lets its currents guide him toward his goal. He is faintly aware of the line of light that connects him with the physical body he has left behind him, and through that lifeline he senses the steady support of the Master of the Junipers.

And now the astral Island looms before him. In man-shape he steps upon its shore. The murky life-fires of the reivers glimmer around him, but he is seeking a spirit with the pure glow of a star.

And he cannot find it! With growing anxiety Julian searches, and realizes finally that there is one place on the Island into which he cannot see. There is only darkness where before stood a pavilion, not even a darkness, but an absence, as if this spot alone has no existence in this sphere. His alarm is transmitted back to the Master, and Julian strengthens the link, letting part of the adept's consciousness flow through it so that he too can see.

"There—a barrier—" says the Master.

"Do you think that we can break it?"

Carefully they drift toward the darkness, and very gently press against it, seeking not to destroy, but to filter through. It feels like wading through a sewer, but increasingly Julian senses that what he seeks lies beyond it.

It thins, Julian thrusts forward and feels a flare of joyful recognition. And in that moment, whatever has formed the barrier seems suddenly to become aware of him, and the darkness solidifies. Julian panics, for here there is no direction, only a suffocating sense of evil that negates even the memory of light. Then his link with the Master tightens, and with a desperate wriggle he breaks free.

"I am glad—" said Julian when a second cup of hot tea had stopped his teeth from chattering, "I am very glad I did not try that alone! But what in the name of the Guardians did we run into?"

"Nothing to do with the Guardians!" exclaimed the Master. "It was a warding of darkness. You are sure it was not there before?"

"I don't—" Julian began, then stopped himself. "Yes, there *was* something the other time, just at the end, that swept me away. But it was nothing like so strong! Has Ardra imported a sorcerer to guard Frederic now?"

"*A* sorcerer? There are few who could resist my skill and your power," the Master replied. He was not boasting, and Julian felt his skin grow cold once more.

"But Caolin is beseiged on the Red Mountain!" He put words to the thought that had flashed between them as if to dispel it.

"Is he?" the Master asked heavily. "I am beginning to wonder. . . ."

Chapter Fifteen

"My daughter—" said Eva softly. "Why are you so afraid?"

"Afraid? Yes . . . I suppose I am," Rana answered her.

The flickering of the fire set shadows flowing across the beamed ceiling of the Moonlodge and etched new lines into Eva's worn face. Outside an owl called thrice and then was still. Rana's courses had returned with the dark of the moon, and after a morning of misery, she had let Eva persuade her to come away to the cabin where the women of Registhorpe conducted their rituals.

"The flow of blood is the sign of womanhood. On the Island, a man raped me because I was female. Because she is female, Bella nearly died giving birth to a child. Why should I want to be imprisoned in a body that can do that to me?"

She took another swallow of tea, recognizing the

flavors of yarrow with red clover and a little willow bark against pain.

There was a silence, then Eva's distress whispered through her darkness. "Child, child—without begetting and bearing there would be no world!"

"That's true!" Rana spat back at her. "And what does that tell you about the world? Blood begets blood!" She heard the hate in her words and hated it. Who was she attacking now?

"And sheds it too, sometimes!" Eva's voice sharpened suddenly. "You yourself have taken life, as I recall!"

Despair rose like a great wave of blood to sweep her away. "Yes—oh yes! I have killed!" She saw once more *Sea Brother*'s blood-slick deck, and the fighting madness in a man's face changing to horror as her blade sank into him. That had been the first one. Rana did not remember the others, only the brain-deadening babble, and blood everywhere. She ground her face against the coarse blankets, and her words died among their muffling folds.

"I killed them. . . . I wish they had killed me!"

And now, men and ships were gathering on the Great Bay, waiting for the deathwind to fill their sails. *I have sworn to go with them—begged for it*! thought Rana. *And when they meet the reivers in battle I will kill again. . . .* She had believed that she *wanted* the destruction of all those gross, cruel men with their broken teeth and grasping hands. But now her body was betraying her. Was it the killing, or her own desire for death that had caused this rebellion?

Or was it because she had seen the birthblood that gave life, and now death was an abomination to her? Despair's dark tide rose around her; unanswered questions and nameless emotions swirled in an undertow that swept her away.

* * *

She is rising from her blankets. She goes through the door of the Moonlodge—not the entry, but the low, hidden door through which the girls go to initiation. She has been through this door before, and she recognizes also the cavern in which she finds herself afterwards, even though it is not the little cave beside the sacred spring.

Rana knows this place, but she cannot tell how, for it is dark here, and cold, with a pressure like the depths of the sea. Why has she come here? Why is she alone? She begins to panic and strikes out wildly, calling—

And in the darkness a hand grips her shoulder, and a voice whispers, "Be still, and see . . ."

See what? But Rana obeys and finds that the blackness before her has become translucent. In that visible darkness she sees a great cauldron. A robed figure rises beyond it, and Rana trembles, knowing that something more than mortal is here. Dark draperies outline the form of a woman, but Her face is hidden. Only a white hand can be seen worn and gnarled by age. It is beckoning. . . .

And a shape comes out of the shadows. Gaping wounds mark his body, and in horror Rana recognizes one of the reivers she killed. But the Goddess grabs him, her sickle releases his blood into the cauldron in a dark flood, and then the empty body is dropped in. She bends over the cauldron, stirring with a ladle made of bone.

"Let it flow, weal and woe, let it go,
As you grow, you shall know, be it so—"

The chant rises and falls, and Rana's blood chills in her veins. Only the strength of the invisible presence beside her keeps her on her feet. But slowly, her vision of the cavern clears. Looking behind her, she realizes that the features of the person who has been upholding her are her own, and at that moment her double disappears.

The face of the Goddess is still invisible, but the walls of the cavern glimmer glassily. This is a cave of ice, and strange creatures lie frozen in its crystalline walls. But as the Goddess stirs her cauldron, steam swirls above it. A breath of moisture blesses Rana's skin. Where the steam touches the walls of the cavern, they glisten and begin to melt, and soon the silence ripples with the sound of falling water.

"Behold, the Cauldron of Life from which you are reborn!"

The Goddess reaches into the cauldron and pulls out an infant, blood-streaked, dripping, and squalling like Amber when she emerged from Bella's womb. Now, at last, Her hood falls back, and Rana gasps, for Her face is radiant. Rana recognizes the features of the pregnant Goddess whom she had seen in vision months ago. For a moment the eyes of the Goddess meet those of the girl, and She smiles.

A great gust of moist warmth blasts from the mouth of the cauldron. The walls of the cavern melt; the floor beneath her softens; Rana's bones dissolve—the world is flowing away. Once again, she floats in the sea's salt womb, feeling her essence merge with the immortal ocean until she herself is the ebb and the flow.

And then she rises into consciousness once more. . . .

Rana woke. The fire had died down, and at first she did not realize where she was. Her body felt boneless, but at ease. Then a coal snapped, and in the momentary flicker of light she recognized the Moonlodge. But the dull ache in her womb had drained away. Instead, she felt warmth soaking the pad between her thighs, and knew that the tides of her body were once more obedient to the moon.

But what had changed? She was still bound to stand with Julian in the battle, and she would probably be forced to kill, but somehow the aching, constricting horror had dissolved. What was different now?

Rana tried to visualize herself in battle, and realized

that her red fury had drained away. She would strike if she had to, facing the possibility of her foe's death as she did her own, but she would no longer see the face of the man who had attacked her in every enemy.

It seemed to Julian that half the population of Seahold had gathered to welcome him home. The weather had reverted to a summer brightness that was unseasonable, but he could not help enjoying the sparkle of sunlight on the Bay and the warmth of the air. The banner of Westria had been run up on the mast above him. As the barge turned, the wind caught it. The circled cross blazed suddenly, gold on green, and the people began to cheer.

"A warm welcome—" said Robert, behind him. For a moment it seemed to Julian that there was something wistful in his cousin's tone. But Robert knew how important it was to gain these people's loyalty, as well—perhaps even better—than he.

Julian nodded. Were they cheering because that banner proclaimed the Regent's support for the makeshift navy Arn had gathered here, or because they were glad to have him back again? Perhaps the people who waved from the ships or waited on the shore did not know themselves why they were cheering, but the sound brought quick tears to Julian's eyes. What mattered was that the spirit he needed to forge this motley assortment of ships and men into a fighting force was here, and he would use it, must use it, whether they knew or not what they had given him.

Then the barge was bumping against the dock, and Arn was reaching down to help him up, grinning delightedly. In the need of the moment, any lingering sense of guilt was swept away.

"The fleet seems to have grown while I was away! How many ships have we now, and how many men?" He asked above the hollow echo of their footsteps on the worn planks.

"Four greatships now—*Wind Dancer* and the Regent's ship *Waverider* were here when you left, and *Sea Otter*, back from her trading trip to Normontaine. *Battle Gull* is the other—she arrived a few days ago from Las Costas. Andrea Hardhands is her captain, and she lives up to her name, but she knows how to make that great cow of hers sail!" He pointed toward the largest vessel of them all, which flew the banner of a white gull on an azure field.

As they started up the broad stairs to the hold Julian glanced back at the bright banners that flickered from the anchored fleet's bare masts, as if an orchard of flowering trees had somehow taken root in the Bay. It was an odd conceit, and he was smiling as they passed into the shadows of the hall.

"Then there are six warships—fast rowing craft which can also use sail." Arn went on. "That includes the two we captured at Montera. I've put crews into them, and they're shaping well. Most of the other new men have been assigned as marines to the greatships and larger fishing craft. There are almost a dozen of those, similar to *Sea Brother* in size and handling. Then there's the miscellany—" Arn shrugged, "about twenty others that you could call boats, though that's all they have in common. The largest will carry no more than a dozen men. But they can all sail outside the Bay."

Lord Austin and the other major captains were waiting for them in the Hall. Julian reached the seat they had left empty at the head of the table and stopped there, taking a deep breath before he began.

"My friends, you seem to have made good use of your time," he spoke standing, holding their attention. "I hope that I have done the same. Though I bring no ships,

I found a thing or two in Laurelynn that may be of use to us. One of them is a man. . . .

"Master Artificer," he called. "Come in here! He has a name," Julian added, grinning at the captains, "but no one seems to call him by it. He is simply the Artificer."

They all stared as a stout, ruddy man with silvery side-whiskers pushed through the crowd. Close to, one realized that his broadness was all muscle, but though his big hands were stained and scarred, his eyes were as blue as a child's. Julian clasped his arm and drew him the rest of the way to the table.

"My friend, these men command the ships that will carry your machines. My lords—" He turned to the captains again. "The Artificer thinks he can construct a catapult that will work as well from the deck of a ship as on land."

The moon grew full and began to wane again, and the golden days of October sped by to the rhythm of hammers and the whining of saws. Under the Artificer's direction, carpenters built catapults for every ship big enough to bear one, and rebuilt them as the daily practice revealed problems in execution or design. In such beautiful weather, it was hard to believe in the reality of war, but the coastal villages were suffering almost daily, and the smoke of their burning stained the western sky.

The month was nearly over when a single sharkship made the mistake of pursuing a trading vessel through the Gateway into the Bay. Julian waited until it was well inside, then sent his own warships to overpower it and capture its crew. The ship they kept, but they gave the surviving reivers the oldest rowboat that would still keep out the water in which to make their way back to the Island. If they made it, they would be a burden to the enemy, for sharkships had no room for extra men.

And they would be a provocation.

Julian's forces were as ready as they could be without another year of training. Before the weather broke or his own men became restless, he had to bring the enemy to battle. But his scouts had been out to the islands twice without finding them.

He spent a sleepless night and an even more anxious day wondering whether he had done the right thing. But at sundown the lookouts gave the alarm, and a sleek sharkship slid into the cove below Seahold with a truce flag fluttering from her mast. Rana flushed with anger when she saw it. Zoltan's ship, she said it was, with Zoltan himself commanding. He brought the craft to a halt with her own depth of water still beneath her, and stood in the bow to read his commander's message in a voice that savored every insulting word.

"To Julian of Stanesvale, Pretender of Westria—" it began, but Julian let the others stiffen with indignation. What he wanted was the message, the message he had been hoping for. Ardra was summoning him to give battle in the gulf between the Far Alone Islands and the Gateway on the morning of the following day.

The sky was a clear silver and the hills blue shadows above a cobalt sea as the Westrian fleet filed through the Gateway and headed out to sea. Rana steadied herself against the rail as *Battle Gull* rocked in the swell. They had not given her a hauberk of canvas covered with hardened leather scales—not as heavy as plate or mail, but awkward enough when one was unaccustomed to it. Her cap-helm with its throat-guard of hanging mail was stacked on top of her round shield at the foot of the mast. The sword at her side was scarcely more familiar, though it was the one from *Sea Brother*'s stores that she had used at Montera. She should have stayed home with Bella, she thought dismally, even as she realized that the anxiety of

301

not knowing what was happening to the fleet would have been far worse than the grim dread she was feeling now. She tried to distract herself by a review of the signal patterns they had practiced so carefully.

And yet, as the big sails filled and the motion of the greatship grew more lively, it was hard to maintain her depression. At last she had escaped the landlocked Bay, and before her stretched the limitless plains of the sea. If only they could forget this madness of warfare and use this freedom. In a ship this size one could sail to the world's end and back again!

Julian stood at the prow, gazing toward the veiled horizon, with Silverhair and Robert just behind him. Did he feel the call of the sea as she was feeling it now? Or was he too concerned with his ships and his men? Rana stepped out of the way as the Artificer passed from one catapult to the next, checking the cords, as she had checked her signal flags, counting the piled river rocks they had collected for ammunition, repeating his instructions to the men. A funny old man, he was, so single-mindedly entranced with his machines. Had he visualized what would happen if his missiles flew true? Had he foreseen not only the smashed timbers, but the smashed men?

The helmsman held their course steady toward the Far Alone Isles, and the other ships emerged from the Gateway in an orderly line behind them. They seemed to move so slowly across the expanse of the sea. A seaman wet his finger and lifted it to test the wind. It was coming from the north now, as fair a wind as Julian could ask for, and they bounded along on a broad reach across the wind. If the sharkships came out from Bird Island under sail they would have to tack close-hauled to meet them, perhaps that was what had delayed them.

Someone shouted from above, and Rana strained to see, then reached for the signal line. A neat bright line of ships barred their way, so close they seemed to have materialized there. Rana's stomach clenched as an involuntary murmur stirred the men. Julian alone seemed unmoved.

His order set her to reaching into the bag for the flags, choosing and snapping them to the line automatically, now that the need had come. In a moment, the red and yellow pennons went rattling up the masthead, breaking free in bright splashes against the sky. *Battle Gull* leaned into the wind, curving to starboard as if she had taken fright at this sight of the enemy. The other ships followed her example in apparent confusion. Julian had hoped that the enemy would be tempted to give chase, and be within catapult range before they realized that the Westrians were not fleeing, but maneuvering into a crescent with the greatships waiting at its center to cripple the sharks before they could implement their usual strategy of grappling and boarding their foe.

Someone was counting the enemy ships as they passed them, his hoarse voice clearly audible in the hush of waiting—ten, twenty, twenty-five, a few more—fewer ships than the Westrians had mustered, but as many men. And behind the line of sharks Rana saw a greatship almost the size of the Regent's *Waverider*, a ship with crimson sails and a banner of the same color that displayed a golden lion rampant as the ship turned.

Julian shaded his eyes to peer at it, then beckoned to Rana. "You didn't tell me about this—"

"I didn't know about it!" she exclaimed. "They had nothing this size when I was on the Island. It must be Ardra's—the banner is certainly hers. . . ."

The enemy flagship completed her turn and suddenly the red sails shivered and began to come down. As she slowed they saw a boat being lowered. The line of warships parted to let it through, and a white flag blossomed from a lifted oar.

Julian's mouth hardened. Then he sighed, and in a low voice ordered Rana to signal again. The fleet was to hold position, but *Battle Gull* would have to stop to parley. Andrea Hardhand was already seeing to *Gull's* sails, and in moments they began to slow. The truce boat was nearing now. Rana touched Julian's arm, pointing to a figure in glittering golden mail that stood at the prow, balancing easily as the small craft swooped over the waves.

"That's Ardra—" she whispered.

"Yes . . . I remember seeing that armor by torchlight at Beltane," he answered her. Then he stiffened, and Rana's gaze followed his to the figure behind Ardra. His hair was a glint of paler gold, and there was another man behind him, though whether he was holding him, or simply holding him up, they could not tell.

"And that is Frederic," Julian said in a still voice. "They've bound him."

Waverider had taken position nearby. Frederic's brothers were there, and Lord Eric, who was staring at his son. Rana swallowed as she recognized the naked longing on his face, and wondered what it must be like to see your child in the hands of an enemy.

The longboat reached hailing distance and came about with a disciplined swirl of oars. Ardra had taken off her helm and they could see her dark eyes narrow as she recognized the Starbairn arms on the surcoat Julian wore. For a moment the two commanders measured each other, alike in their youth, but so disparate in every other way. Rana felt her own heart thumping painfully as memories she thought she had suppressed came flooding back to her. Then Ardra smiled.

"Welcome to *my* realm, 'Prince' of Westria . . . we are met as I have planned. Now you shall hear my terms. . . ."

There was an indignant murmur from the Westrians at

both the inflection and the words, but Julian's face seemed cast from stone.

"I ask three things only—" Again Ardra smiled. "First, your renunciation of any claim to sovereignty over the waters from Mist Harbor in the Corona, south to Santibar. Second, I require you to deliver to me or to those whom I shall appoint, authority over the villages of Los Osos, Montera, Elkhorn, and all other coastal anchorages. Third, you must pay to me each year a tribute of a thousand laurels upon Midsummer Day."

By the time Ardra had finished, the clamor from the two Westrian greatships almost drowned out her words. But Julian waited, his dark gaze holding hers, and Rana felt a flicker of pride in him. She supposed that legally this negotiation ought to have been addressed to Lord Eric. But the fleet had been raised by Julian, and perhaps Eric did not trust himself to treat with this woman who had made a prisoner of his eldest, most-loved son. Julian raised his hand finally, and the noise behind him died away.

"And if I will not agree?"

Ardra laughed. "What does that matter to me? What I have asked for I can take, with or without your will. You may try to stop me, but your men are untrained in our kind of warfare. I thought to give you a chance to save their lives, and the life of this man, whom I have heard called your friend." Her eyes seemed to burn as she glanced back at Frederic. He returned the look serenely, though his face was pale. She turned to Julian again. "If you do not agree—if you oppose me—his death will be the first of all!"

Julian hunched his shoulders, his first sign of anxiety.

"She won't kill him—" whispered Rana. "She loves him, I think. She can't—"

"Julian—don't listen to her! Forget—" Frederic's voice rang out suddenly, and was as abruptly stifled as

305

the man behind him hooked an arm against his windpipe and pressed down.

A word from Ardra moved her boat towards *Waverider*, where the Regent stood watching with his fist clenched on the hilt of his sword.

"You are still these people's lawful ruler," she said scornfully. "Will you make no move to save your son?"

Eric's face had gone first red, and then pale. He looked desperately at Julian. "My lord, may I speak to her?" His voice grated as if rusted by unshed tears, and Julian nodded.

"Lady—Julian Starbairn leads this force, and I will abide by his decision, but as you say, I am still Regent of Westria. As Regent I must protest if he accedes to any one of your demands! We share the duty to guard this land, and nothing can release us. The Prince will not shirk it for the sake of friendship, and I will not flee it even for love of my son!" Eric took a deep breath.

"If Frederic must die . . ." The Regent's voice cracked, then regained power. "If he dies, I will mourn him as if he had fallen in battle . . . and I will honor his memory. But if I betrayed my trust so that he might live, never for the rest of our lives could we meet each other's eyes!"

Eric was not looking at Ardra, but at his son, and though the seaman's arm still kept Frederic from speaking, his eyes were shining. Rana remembered when Frederic had despaired of winning his father's understanding, and thought that they had never been so close in spirit as they were now.

Ardra looked from the Regent to Julian, then at the disordered line of the Westrian fleet behind them. Then she shrugged and smiled.

"Very well—I see you are determined to die—" Her clear tones seemed to vibrate in the air even after her

306

men had upped oars and the longboat was speeding away.

But Julian was watching Eric, and though the older man's eyes were still fixed on the boat that was bearing his son away from him, the Prince bowed.

"Rana—signal the greatships to make all sail—" he said softly.

Bare feet thudded on the deck as the seamen rushed to obey. Men swarmed up the masts, lines creaked and pulleys squealed as the yards of heavy canvas were hauled into place again. And then there was another silence, for the hoisted sails hung limp, and *Battle Gull*'s only movement was a gentle rocking in the swell. There was not a breath of wind.

Andrea Hardhand was swearing in a continuous muffled stream, but Julian cast a swift look at the enemy. There was a blur of movement as the oars of the sharkships rose and fell with trained precision—or was it their movement that was making it so hard to see them? The crimson of the flagship seemed to be fading, and the longboat had disappeared.

"Artificer, can you sight your machines on them at this range? There's some devil's mist brewing out there—let them feel our teeth while we can still see!"

The old man barked agreement. He was already bending over the first catapult and targeting it on the nearest enemy. He released the lever, and the arm of the catapult thrummed forward. Twenty-five pounds of rock arced over the water to splash down between two sharkships. There was a flurry of activity on *Wind Dancer* as her marksmen tried to follow the Artificer's example. *Gull* shot again and again, and then Julian stopped it, for they could no longer see where the missiles fell.

Horncalls echoed through the thickening air. The enemy ships were signaling now, and Rana's signal flags would soon be no use at all. Suddenly snarling shark prows materialized out of the fog. The Artificer made a quick adjustment and cranked the catapult taut once more. The arm flicked and another stone sailed towards the dim shape of the enemy. This time they heard wood splintering, and then angry cries.

"First blood to us!" said Silverhair grimly. He glanced back, saw Rana still clinging to the useless signal line and swore. "Put on your helm, girl! We'll be in arrow range soon!"

Julian threw his weight against the lever of the second catapult. The great muscles of his arms and shoulders strained as he pressed down, then the resistance eased, his own grunt of relief was lost in the clacketa-clack as metal-shod teeth met, and the wheel began to turn. *One—two—silently he counted—five.* The wheel stuck, he eased back and saw the rope strained tight around the drum.

"Stand back!" Men scattered from behind the catapult. A quick glance showed Julian the boulder centered. He nodded and lifted his hands.

The team leader released the ratchet. Rope raced as the great arm whipped up in a swift arc that snapped the stone across the water. The arm smacked down and Julian felt the deck vibrate beneath him as it hummed to rest.

The air sang; a breath on Julian's cheek refocused awareness; short, crimson-feathered arrows were raining past him, thunking into deck and masts. He staggered at a sharp tap on his helm and an arrow rattled across the deck. Behind him someone screamed.

How could the reivers have archers? They had to row—but perhaps at such close range they could manage with fewer oarsmen, leaving the rest to use the bows. His own archers were scrambling into position by the rail, but mist hid most of the enemy, while the Westrian ships were still in sunlight.

Julian snatched up his shield and felt more arrows punch into it as he shoved his forearm through the strapping. The sea frothed as distant Westrian warships got into motion, but the sharks were too close for the catapults to play now. A bow-wave of mist curled before their prows and rolled between the Westrian greatships and their allies.

Suddenly *Battle Gull* was alone, and being forced into exactly the kind of battle Julian had hoped to avoid.

The Westrian archers used their ship's height to shoot down at the approaching enemy, but in moments she shuddered and heeled as a dozen grappling irons clattered against the rail. Julian plucked one cold claw free and hurled it back; around him others were doing the same, but men were falling around him too, as the reivers' arrow-fire grew heavier. The grapples clattered and scraped against the rail again and again, until with a grinding of wood the two ships were joined.

Julian leaped back and wrenched his sword free as reivers scrambled over the side. The Artificer roared as they knocked over his catapult; then grabbed the broken lever and began to lay about him. Julian started toward Silverhair; the deck tilted and he was flung sideways, a blade hissed above his head and struck splinters from the mast. Julian saw the blur as the reiver's arm swung back for another blow. Flexing thigh muscles absorbed the momentum of his fall and used it to power a stroke that brought his blade ripping upward through flesh and bone. Blood splattered like sea spray, then the lift of the ship spun the dying man away.

Two more leaped forward. Julian settled into a wider stance to balance on a deck that shuddered to the shifts of weight upon it and the underlying lift and dip of the sea. A blade blurred through mist. Julian's shield rose to meet it; the blow smacked the hard hide and shocked down his arm. He rolled with the blow, let it help bring his sword arm around in a long smooth swing that caught his foe in the side and sliced through.

The same movement brought the blade up to knock the second man's blow aside. But this one shoved his shield into Julian's face, breaking his rhythm. He drew his arm back and jabbed, awkward at such close quarters, but effective. Iron rings scraped, then parted as the blade went in. The fellow grunted. Julian met white rimmed astonished eyes as he tried to jerk his sword free. The man's weight bore his arm down.

A shadow reared up behind him; Julian thrust up his shield, still struggling to free his weapon. Not fast enough! The enemy sword clanged on his helm and sliced across his cheekbone. Pain sparked from nerve to nerve; Julian ripped his blade free just as another knot of struggling swordsmen crashed into his foe and carried him away. For a moment Julian stood gasping. He tasted liquid—blood or sweat—salt as the sea.

"Westria and Julian!" Silverhair's shout pierced the uproar and resonated in his bones. Julian felt his uncle's ecstatic fury, Robert's detachment, Rana's determination, the desperate defense of the others as if they were his own.

"For Westria!" he shrieked, unleashing all the energy bound up by the fears and frustrations of the last weeks and days and hours into the deadly sweep of his sword as he leaped into the battle again.

In the mist there was no way to tell time. Rana became aware of its passage only when she found herself standing still, panting, leaning on a bloody sword. She had somehow gotten separated from Silverhair, but the only reivers she could see were the dead. The deck was slimed with red that trailed in pink rivulets into the scuppers. A severed hand lay like an abandoned glove. She heard a splash, and then another. *Battle Gull*'s crew were throwing the bodies of their slain enemies over the side.

Her shield slipped from a suddenly strengthless arm and thumped on the deck. It was scarred and slashed. *I will have to repaint it before I give it back again . . .* she thought vaguely. Automatically she wiped her sword, sheathed it, and looked around for Julian. He was in the bow, binding a strip of cloth around Robert's arm. A breath of air kissed her cheek and rustled the sail. Now, when it was too late, were they finally getting some wind? The sound of shouting was borne to them by that breeze, and she knew that at least some of the other ships fought on. But everything was quiet here. Her bright braids uncoiled down her back as she began to pull off her helm.

A crash shook the ship; Rana staggered as the deck tilted beneath her. Wood ground wood, and the ship leaned in the other direction as the ropes of the grapples the first attackers had left behind were drawn tight once more. Steel scraped as silent men with suddenly blanched faces drew their swords.

Rana fumbled with the straps of her shield, then almost dropped it as golden mail flashed. Grimly she settled into a defensive stance. Reivers poured over the rail without attacking, and the defenders were glad for the respite, however momentary. Then they moved aside to let Ardra through. For a moment her eyes met Rana's, and the younger woman thought she read scorn there, and apology, and a desperate pride. But perhaps she had been wrong, for the helm made Ardra's face a stranger's. The girl retreated to Silverhair's side as Ardra and her reivers rushed past them toward Julian.

"For the Star Prince!" cried Robert, stepping forward.
"For the Lioness!" came Lorca's deep-throated reply.

Swords met with a clang, and suddenly men were fighting like sharks in a feeding frenzy. Rana took a good grip on her sword and set herself to guard Silverhair's back. The reivers charged them, were repelled, and came on again. A falling body separated Rana from Silverhair. Turning, she saw that he had lost his shield. He was using his sword two-handed now, chanting as he circled his foe.

"Shark's teeth are sharpest under the sea—
But above the brine, my blade bites better!"

Eyes glittered beneath the rim of the bard's battered helm. Whatever weakness had taken him in Montera was forgotten. Silverhair seemed now as brilliant, as free and as deadly as his own sword.

"Warrior, your comrades wait under the waves!"

The bard's next line was lost as the deck shuddered again and more reivers swarmed over the ship's other side. Rana got her back against the mast and took a deep breath. The fighting swirled around her, then eddied away, and she found herself facing Zoltan.

The Elayan leader was elegantly armed in mail which had been tempered to a steely blue. A crimson scarf bound his steel cap, and a crimson shark circled with mouth agape upon his shield. He stopped—perhaps he thought she was admiring him, then he recognized her and laughed.

"Do you think to mimic the *Comendadora* with that soldier's gear? Women belong in bed, not on the battlefield. But you owe me a life already, bitch! I will make sure you dishonor no more good men!" Gradually he had been settling into a crouch, and now he sprang.

Rana flung up her shield, felt the blow that knocked it away, and the scarcely lessened shock as it struck her helm. She tried to lift her sword, but now she was on her knees, blinking as flashes of light and dark burst behind her eyes. Inner vision showed her the Goddess of the cauldron.

It is just—Rana remembered the men she had killed —*Lady, my blood belongs to You!*

Numb, she waited for the second blow, and it took a moment for her to realize that someone had interposed himself between her and her enemy, and that the blow had fallen on another's shield.

"Hold, Zoltan! *She* does not want the girl harmed!" The voice was Don Esteban's.

"No lady's lapdog tells me whom I may kill! Stand aside before I cut you down as well!"

Lorca shifted his stance and grunted, lifting his shield. Then there was a rush of feet. Lorca straightened, and Rana realized that the press of battle had swept Zoltan away.

"*Niña*, are you all right? That was a hard blow!" Lorca turned, sword still raised, and bent to see her face. Rana tried to smile at him, then caught a glimmer of blue and silver beyond him, and the flash of a lifting sword.

"Watch out!" she gasped as the sword came down. Lorca's startled parry was knocked wide. He tried to recover, and Julian struck again. Rana watched in horror as the big man swayed and dropped his sword. Julian strode forward, weapon swinging high for the final blow.

"No!" she screamed. "He saved me from Zoltan!"

Julian stopped short, then whirled as a shrill whistle split the air. "To the boats!" came a clear cry. Two men dodged around him to catch Lorca as he crumpled and carried him away.

Rana dropped to her hands and knees. Her sight was going again, her eyes blurred with more than tears. Someone caught her and propped her against the mast.

She shook her head to try to clear it and gasped in pain. She had escaped Zoltan, but the cauldron of darkness was still waiting. She felt black waters rising around her.

It seemed very quiet suddenly. Then she felt the breeze.

"Wind! A wind is coming! Set the sails!" came the shout. Men began to move about; Julian was trying to persuade *Battle Gull*'s captain to go to the aid of the other ships.

"No, Prince—I've had enough of this," the woman replied. "My own Lord will not thank me if I lose his ship. 'Tis only by the Guardians' grace we have survived so far. I must use this wind to get *Gull* out of danger before they come again."

"Sound the retreat, Julian," Silverhair said softly. "We are in no case to give help to anyone, and the sailors will obey their captain no matter what you say."

Through the ringing in her ears Rana heard the bellowing of Julian's battle horn. The ship began to move. Then the spots before her eyes all flowed together and she sank into darkness.

Chapter Sixteen

Campfires dotted the edge of the lagoon of Longbay like fiery flowers. In the lean-to that *Sea Brother*'s crew had made for their captain, torchlight flickered deceptively, touching Arn's cheeks with fitful color. Or perhaps it was her own vision that was faltering, thought Rana, for her head still ached from Zoltan's blow.

"He looks a little better, doesn't he?" Gully's dark eyes were beseeching. "I guess that stuff the Master of the Junipers gave him helped him after all. . . ."

Rana nodded without conviction. The Master had bound up the great wound in Arn's side and given him a drink to dull the pain, but he could promise nothing. If death could be beaten by youth and hope then Arn would survive, for surely wife and child and ship were something to live for! But so much blood had been lost. . . .

Fernando and old Will sat beside the fire, boiling the

rice and dried meat the people of Longbay had sent down. Marta lay near them, herself wounded when she stood over Arn's body after he had been struck down. The other encampments were no better off. Barely half of the ships that had sailed so proudly through the Gateway that morning had made the shelter of Longbay's lagoon, and Ardra's sharkships lay in wait for them just outside.

At least the Master of the Junipers was here, with Lady Rosemary, so something was being done for the wounded. Unless infection took them later, most of those who had not been killed outright would probably survive. They had tried to make Rana lie down, but a knock on the head was nothing compared to what others were suffering.

"Rana—he's trying to say something—" said Gully.

Arn's pale lips were moving. Blinking, she bent close, straining to interpret the whisper of sound.

"Stop . . . the leak . . . dark water rising . . . no!" His voice strengthened. "Get *Sea Brother* free!"

"Arn—she *is* free! The ship is safe; Arn, and so are you—now please be still!"

"No—" he answered more softly. "Head out to sea. . . ." He smiled.

Rana stared at him. "Arn . . . *Arn*!" she shouted suddenly, and the men at the fire looked up. But Arn did not stir. Shaking, she picked up the arm that lay so limply outside his blankets, feeling for the thread of pulse that should have been there. Old Will stood beside her, and she turned to him.

"I'm too tense," she said desperately, "you try." She stood up and let the old man take her place. After a few moments, he laid his captain's hand back across the still chest. He had said nothing, but his weathered cheeks were glistening with tears.

Wordless, Rana began to back away. She had thought that Isabella looked obscene, swollen with child. But now she understood that the true obscenity was this empty shell that had been a boy her own age—her brother, and her friend.

As she stepped into darkness, she heard the wailing of *Sea Brother*'s crew begin.

"A fisherman sat on the sand
And sang of love though he had none.
The daughters of the dancing waves
Danced to his tune 'till he was done."

Now Bella has lost her love, thought Rana as she stumbled up the path toward the shelter they had set up for Julian. *But she doesn't know!* The tune came clearer as she approached it, and she recognized the singer as Silverhair.

" 'Oh fisherman, why do you stare?
What watch you there so wistfully?'
'I thought I saw two flashing eyes,
to my surprise they beckoned me!' "

The song was an old tale of the time after the Cataclysm, when the First People, newly restored to sovereignty, had been more curious about the world of men. Then she remembered how the Lady of the Madrones had tried to protect Julian at Spear Island, and thought that maybe those times were not entirely passed. But no one had intervened to save Arn.

"Marana danced upon the sea—
Her form was fashioned of salt-spray,
Her eyes from sunshine on the waves.
Her hair from moonbeams gone astray.
'Alas, I love a mortal who
What'er I do will never know,'
She sang, and watchers sitting by
Heard the wind sighing soft and slow."

Julian's lean-to was set apart from the others, though it was no better than they. Rana glimpsed Silverhair's firelit face beneath it, lined with marks of grief and battle that even the release of his music could not take away. Julian was lying on his belly with his face turned away from the fire. The Master of the Junipers leaned over him, sponging the patterned bruising on his back where some blow had driven the links of his mail through the leather padding. His skin shone bronze; the beautifully defined muscles of shoulders and back thrown into relief by the light of the fire.

"Where ocean's deepest currents flow
the earth moved once and moved again.
A little wave began to roll
and grew and grew unknown to men.
She cried, 'When this wave strikes the land,
Those on that strand will perish—all!
How can I tell my love to flee
this doom—he cannot hear my call!' "

Rana stopped beside a stunted live oak, fighting a wave of dizziness. She had seen Julian's body often enough on the voyage north—was it because she had just seen the lifeless body of another young man? Or was it simply her own weakness? She had sought Julian's comfort for her own suffering, but the pain she sensed from him, though it was mostly of the mind, was worse than her own. Could he carry the grief her news would bring him in addition to everything else he bore?

Julian winced as the Master put down the sponge and began to bathe the broken skin with a greenish solution on a soft cloth.

"They tell me we have scarcely enough men left whole to work the ships, much less fight them—" Rana, listening from the shadows, could feel the emotions beneath his surface calm. "—Even if they could, after this they would not follow me! You heard *Battle Gull*'s captain! What she said to my face the rest of them are saying to each other, but more colorfully. I cannot blame them. . . ." He sighed as the Master finished with the salve and with an effort sat up again.

"But I should not burden you with this—" he added as the Master bound a dressing in place. "Without your help here things would have been far worse."

Without meeting Julian's eyes, the Master began to put his medicines away.

"You have not asked me why I did not warn you of the mist, or tell you what the enemy will do now—" he said quietly. A little betraying color showed in Julian's face.

"I have thought that," he admitted, "but I remember the darkness that repelled us when we tried to reach Frederic on the Island. We could not have *known* what would happen, but both of us should have forseen *some* sorcery! My failure was in having no alternate strategy."

"Marana sought that might hall
where Sea-Mother dwells beneath the wave
and begged her for a human form
so that she might her lover save.
'Ah, sea-child, what know you of men,
who perish when an hour has passed?
Once you a mortal body wear
know you will share their fate at last!'"

Rana could feel, so clearly, all the things he did not say. But she did not *want* to know anything of men! Marana had been wrong to choose mortality. Far better to retain the immortal substance of a sea-sprite and live forever in the freedom of the sea! She choked back a sob and saw Julian stiffen. His hand went to the Sea Star.

"Rana—is it you?" he called softly, "Come here! Are you all right?" he added as, swallowing her grief, she came the rest of the way into the light of the fire. She nodded. She had pulled her hair forward to cover the bruise on her brow, and they all had reason for tears.

"Marana came out of the sea
with hair like moonbeams shimmering
and as she lifted them, her arms
as white as foam were glimmering.
'Oh take your boat and ride the wave—
your life to save, though this land drown!'
The fisher heard, but did not dare
greet one so fair; he warned the town."

Rana cast a quick glance at the harper, wondering if he was trying to cheer her, then Julian gripped her hand.

"Something *is* wrong! Rana, what is it?"

His words, or his touch, released her tears.

"Arn—died . . . a little while ago . . ." She shut her eyes as the words made it real once more. Silverhair had stopped playing. They could hear the distant lamentation now.

"I should have been there!" Julian's voice was tight. "*You* should have been there," he said to the Master, "not soothing my scratches here!"

"I left him sleeping—" the Master said heavily. "There was nothing more I could do. I hoped—"

"But if you had stayed—"

"What do you think I am!" For a moment the Master's control slipped, and they saw the human being beneath the adept's serenity. "I have walked in both worlds, but if I could save everyone, Julian, do you think I would have let either your father or your mother die? I am sent to teach, to serve, to show the way—but I cannot save them all!" Each soul's fate is her own!"

Julian flinched and hid his face as if to ward off the Master's anger. He was trembling. Rana started to move toward him, but stopped herself as the Master spoke again.

"It is hard enough for me to keep from blaming myself, Julian—" he said gently. "And you must not try to carry the burden all alone—"

"No? When Arn is dead, and Lord Eric fought like a man seeking death because I refused to save his son, and Frederic—" for a moment Julian shook in silent agony —"when my friend is a prisoner in torment because of me? If I cannot save them, why do men call me Prince? Why have I been given the Jewels?"

"Why should either of you take the blame?" snapped Silverhair. "The Elayan witch started this war and captured Frederic! Lord Eric would have had to fight her even if you had never been born!"

"But is it Ardra's doing?" asked the Master. "I think of that darkness that kept us from contacting Frederic on the Island and I am not sure—"

Julian looked up at him, some of the pain in his face changing to concern as the meaning of the Master's question became clear. "Do you think it is Caolin?"

"It must be!" exclaimed the harper. "That mist—the dying wind—they were not natural. This whole business has the stink of sorcery! That is why you have been given the Sea Star, Julian! I told you that you would have to use it in the end!"

Julian touched the Jewel as if to reassure himself that it was still there. "I must be sure. If I use it wrongly, I may break the cycles of the sea, and what the Jewel has caused not even the Jewel will be able to control. . . ." He looked at the Master of the Junipers in appeal.

"I cannot tell you what to do. The barrier is too strong, and emotion clouds my judgment here. Julian—" his voice sank to a whisper, "remember, I love Frederic too!"

Julian closed his eyes. As clearly as if he had spoken, Rana heard his heart cry, "*What can I do?*" He had just lost one companion. The death of another might be too much for him to bear.

"Ask the Sea Star—" Without thinking, she reached out and laid her palm over the shrouded Jewel. She could feel the rapid beating of Julian's heart beneath her hand. "You cannot use it as a weapon . . . but perhaps it can show you how to work with the forces that are already in the Sea."

His hand closed over hers. Rana realized that she was touching his bare skin. Julian's eyes opened, deep and dark as forest pools. Silence echoed around them. Then his gaze released her, and she jerked her hand away.

"You are right—" For a moment they had been so close, and now, though he had not yet moved, he was already far away. "There is no more to say. Let me be alone for a little while. I will make up my mind before morning, I promise you."

He got up, and Silverhair helped him put on his tunic and handed him his cloak without a word. Rana had risen as well. Julian took her hand and kissed it, bowed to the Master and Silverhair, and then he was gone.

"I will pray—" said the Master simply, settling himself again.

"And I will pray—" echoed Silverhair with a wry smile. Rana stared from one man to the other, and then at the shadows into which Julian had disappeared. She wanted him, but he did not need her now. He must bear his pain in solitude; could she do less than he?"

"I must go," she stammered. "Arn's people—" Shaking her hand, she ran from the shelter. Silverhair's song followed her into the darkness—

"The Wave rose like a moving wall,
upon the shore fell thundering,
and in their boats, the sons of men
tossed, terrified and wondering.
The waters swirled, when they were done
the town was gone; the people wailed.
The fisher could not find the maid;
his life was saved, yet his heart failed."

The moon had not yet risen, but light from the beacon at the other end of the lagoon kindled the crests of the wavelets that foamed about Rana's bare feet as she stood on the shore. How had she come here? She had meant to go back and watch by Arn's body. But he was there no longer. If his spirit still hovered near, surely he would have sought the freedom of the sea!

Freedom for Arn, perhaps, but not for her—not with Ardra and her sharks on guard just offshore. Frederic was there as well, and perhaps his despair was as great as Julian's, for he would fear that his continued captivity might well inspire some foolish and desperate action from his friend. It might yet do so, no matter how the Master tried to steady him. Foolish and desperate actions were all that were left to them now.

"And in that case—" Rana said softly to the darkness, "why wait for Julian to risk himself? He belongs to Westria, but I am free—" She smiled suddenly, realizing how little the danger meant to her if she got back out to sea. Julian was powerless to save Frederic. But perhaps *she* could find a way. . . .

Rana knew that her grief for Arn was driving her to this, but just because she had been powerless to help Arn, she was determined that Frederic should not die while there was anything she could do. She waded out further and took a deep breath. They said there were porpoises in the lagoon here. Soon she would see.

What came from her lips was a long, trilling call. For a moment she waited, then called again, adding the whistle that would identify her as one of the mer-folk to any of the People of the Sea. For a few moments there was silence. Then came a splash as a heavy body struck the water, and a burst of chittering almost too swift for her to understand.

"*Sharksbane*?" Astonishment stole the breath from her whistle. "Flasher, Pearlgray? Why here?"

"Wait, watch—Sea-Mother say. Flasher reports. Sharksbane look for you!"

Rana waded out until she could hug him, feeling her legs begin to ache at the chill. It would be much colder out to sea.

"Sharksbane help? Pull boat? Sister go to Shark-ships—"

"Bad men, dolphin-killers, dangerous!" came the whistled reply.

"Yes. Go quietly, hurt them—go now!"

It took her some time to argue him into agreement, but before the moon rose, Rana had found an unattended boat, and the dolphins were pulling her out across the lagoon. There was no challenge from the watchtower. If the guard saw them at all, he had other things to worry about than one old rowboat adrift on the tide.

Frederic flexed cold fingers and twisted, seeking not for a weakness in the bonds that imprisoned him in the chair—he had exhausted that possibility some hours ago—but for some fractional improvement in comfort. It had been a great mistake to let them see how much his strength had returned, but he had hoped to force the reivers to kill him before they could use him as they *had* used him this morning, as bait for his father and Julian.

The hanging lamp swung as *Lioness* rocked at anchor, light chasing shadow across the rich rugs on the floor. For a moment the expression of the man in the lower bunk seemed to change and Frederic tensed with hope, then the light shifted, and the familiar blunt features resumed their permanent immobility. The din of voices from on deck grew loud enough for him to make out the words, then faded again. The reiver captains were debating whether to launch a dawn raid on the tattered remnants of the Westrian fleet in the lagoon, or to draw off and snap them up when they fled for home.

But it hardly mattered which they chose. Either way, Westria's attempt to protect her coasts was doomed.

Then he heard a light step on the stair, and schooled his face to hide the pain.

"Don Esteban is dead, Ardra—" he said quietly as she came into the room, and winced as he saw the eagerness fade from her gaze. Moving more slowly now, she went to the bunk and smoothed the graying hair back from Lorca's brow, then slipped her hand inside his tunic to feel for a heartbeat.

"He died regretting only that he could serve you no longer," Frederic added implacably. "Do you still wish to be a Queen?"

Ardra whirled. "How dare you? You and your whore —he was trying to save her and your precious Prince murdered him!" She leaned back against the bunk and looked down at Lorca's body, the tears running unchecked down her cheeks. She had wound a turban of scarlet silk around her head, but she still wore the stained tunic that had gone under her mail. Without the armor she seemed so thin, as if only the power of her will sustained her.

Frederic's love for her betrayed him. "I am sorry. . . ."

The tears seemed to freeze. She sprang toward him, and his chair rocked as her palm met his cheek.

"Sorry! Don't you *dare* speak of pity to me!"

Frederic blinked, caught his breath, and then began to laugh.

"Dare, Ardra? I can dare anything now. . . . I am a dead man too!" He saw the high color leave her face. "My dear, have you not faced that yet?" he asked.

She sat down on the other side of the table, still looking at him, then hid her face in her hands.

"You know that Zoltan will have my head now that my value as a hostage is gone. What you gave to me is what he desires, and he thinks my death will prove him the better man." Ardra murmured something about ransom, but Frederic shook his head. "The men will not believe it now. Already they suspect your motives with regard to me—" he added gently. "I told you before. We both do what we must."

Ardra shook her head without looking at him. "No—I will not let them kill you. If you die too, who will there be in the world . . ."

"Who loves you, while knowing you as you are?" he completed her thought. She looked up at him finally, and he saw all the splendor of her spirit blazing in her eyes. "If I have loved you while hating what you do, do you think my love can be altered even by death?"

"How can you love me?"

Frederic smiled. "Shall I tell you again? Because you are as brave as the lioness on your banner, because—"

She shook her head and came to him, setting one brown finger against his lips. He kissed it and closed his eyes, wanting her even now. That was another burden that returning health had laid upon him, but he could not wish it gone.

"Believe that you will love me until death and after if it comforts you. I will not take that chance." She drew her knife, and Frederic's eyes followed its flicker in the lamplight.

"Will you kill me yourself, then?" he asked wryly.

Her face changed and she bent over him, sliding her fingers through his hair.

"Yes!" she said fiercely. "As you would kill me!" She kissed him, and then there was only fire and darkness until she released him again.

"I will let you go. . . ." Her voice was shaking, but her hand was steady as she she slid the knife through the first of his bonds.

"Ardra, you must make it seem an escape—" he breathed.

"Why? After today's victory will anyone dare oppose anything I do?" She laughed.

"Yes . . ."

Both heads jerked around as a man neither of them had ever seen came through the door.

"Who in the Kraken's name are you, and what do you* here?" snapped Ardra.

"You do not recognize this face?" asked the intruder pleasantly. "Then try this one—" He stepped forward, and they saw his features change into those of the little healer, Eldron, and then to someone else, until finally he wore the face of Don Esteban Lorca, and smiled Lorca's familiar, lazy smile. Frederic felt suddenly ill.

The shape-changer looked from Ardra's chalky face to the even paler face of the body in the bunk and smiled. "How convenient—this will make it easier to keep an eye on you." Then, seeing Frederic's severed bond he added, "Apparently I have come just in time!"

Frederic stared at him. He had learned to fear Eldron for his own sake as well as for Ardra's, but if this man was not the healer, then who—

But the man who wore Lorca's face was laughing, a laughter with all the world's scorn in it, that froze him like a breath of icy wind. And in that moment he remembered a cold wind on Spear Island, and how that laughter had taunted them as they stood at bay. And not only on Spear Island—that laughter was hidden in the dark places his soul could not remember—even at the thought of it distortions flickered across his vision again.

"You are so adept at changing faces," he whispered. "Have you forgotten your own—*Caolin*?"

Rage and confusion warred in Ardra's face as Caolin's changed once more, and they saw a young man with pale hair, straight and proud. He and Ardra faced each other across the table, and for a moment Frederic saw the girl's face as a darker mirror of the man's, with the same arched nose and high brow. He felt the deck shift beneath him, but he did not think that it was the ship that had moved.

"Caolin, the sorcerer of Westria?" asked Ardra with deadly courtesy. "I have heard of you. You seem to know him, Frederic—suppose you tell me what this means?"

But it was Caolin who answered her.

"He does not know me nearly so well as you do. . . ." He stared at her, and Frederic saw her face still as it had when Eldron entranced her, but this time it did not go all the way. She looked as if she were listening.

"The Voice I heard . . . my guide . . . it was *you*?" Her face contorted and she sprang at him. The knife flashed and Caolin reached for it. For a moment they struggled, then the weapon clattered to the deck. Still he held her, forcing her to look at him with her will—if not her body—still her own.

"Well," he said mildly. "Is this any way for a daughter to greet her father for the first time?" He let her go then, and she reeled backward to crouch, retching, by Frederic's chair. The smile was still on Caolin's lips. "Surely you guessed?"

Frederic's head spun as he tried to piece together things he had heard from the Master of the Junipers and from Silverhair. Caolin had a child in Elaya, and Ardra would be about the right age. *He* ought to have guessed, even if Ardra didn't know.

Ardra looked up at the sorcerer, her golden skin glistening with tears. The words seemed torn from her, one by one.

"Then is there *nothing* that is my own? Not my dreams . . . not my deeds . . . not my *name*?" Slowly she regained her feet. "Do you expect me to love you?"

Caolin grunted. "What use would that be? But as for the rest—you never resisted those dreams. Do you cease to share them because they came from me?"

Frederic remembered the radiance on Ardra's face when she spoke of the Kingdom she hoped to build, and held his breath. She was not responsible for what had been done to her without her knowledge, but if she consented to serve the sorcerer willingly, she would be lost indeed.

"I will make you a Queen—" said Caolin.

Ardra seemed to pull herself together. She twitched her tunic straight, pulled off her dangling turban and let it fall to the floor.

"Am I indeed your daughter?" she murmured, smiling strangely.

Caolin nodded, watching her.

"Then I have inherited one thing from you which I will not deny—" she went on—" and that is my pride! I would not be content with the fair lands that my . . . that he who thought he sired me . . . left. Do you think I will take the glory that I have bled for from your hand like a bitch who licks up the table scraps after her master is done?" She shook her head. "No. Go your way, *father*. I may fail, but I will reach my goal without your aid."

Caolin considered her. "I think you do not yet understand. Did you believe that this was *your* war? You have served very well to keep the princeling and that fool Eric out of my way. But now the situation has changed. What follows I must handle directly."

The last time you and Julian met, the powers he summoned bested you. Are you sure you are not keeping out of his *way?* thought Frederic.

"There need be no difficulty. We will dispose of this—" Caolin bent over Lorca's body and lifted it. "And I will take his place. You have followed my orders unknowing—you will find it easier now." They stared as with a single swift movement he shoved the corpse through the open window in the stern.

Rope cut painfully into Frederic's skin as he jerked in an instinctive movement to stop him. Ardra gasped and slumped to the floor.

"I see you are still trying to step into dead men's shoes—" Frederic said furiously.

Caolin gave him his full attention for the first time. "Dead men's shoes? Patience, colt—your father's are almost ready for you." His lip curled at the shock Frederic could not quite conceal. "But no, you are the tame priest's acolyte. You made a poor choice of master. Now then, when I was Eldron, what did I promise you?"

He stared into Frederic's eyes, and Frederic felt the darkness rising around him. He was dimly aware that Ardra was moving, but he could not pull his gaze away.

"Anything I might have been willing to learn from you, you forgot long ago!" he whispered.

Caolin's mouth twitched. "You wish to leave here, don't you? I will help you. . . .I will send you to the Red Mountain. You may find my arguments more persuasive there. And if I cannot win the Master's pupil away from him, there are other things I can do that will pain him even more—" He considered briefly, then laughed again. "Yes, perhaps that would be even better. I could

330

break your mind, and send what remained of you back to him, or perhaps I should send him your body, piece by piece, while your mind remains with me, or perhaps—" His gaze flickered.

Ardra had reached the fallen knife, and in one swift motion poised it to throw.

"Perhaps you will do nothing at all!" she cried. "Perhaps you will have neither him nor me!"

Caolin stepped towards her, his face terrible, and as she drew back her hand he raised his own. He spoke a word that reverberated in the tiny room. The dagger shivered into fragments that tinkled as they fell. Ardra screamed once, then crumpled with a completeness that proved her faint had been a sham before.

"She had done better to obey," said Caolin. "The end will be the same." His gaze came back to Frederic. "Did you love her? Well, perhaps I will pity you . . ." He raised his hand once more, and Frederic lifted his head almost eagerly to meet what was coming now.

There was a shout from above, and feet clattered on the stairs.

"There is a body in the water!" "Lorca?" "I see a boat out there!"

"Lady Ardra! Alteza!" Someone pounded on the door.

Caolin was taking Lorca's shape again. "Quiet," he called. "I am better, but my lady sleeps!" The knocking continued, and he turned to Frederic. "I will leave you a little longer to enjoy her company. . . . Patience," he added to the man outside the door, and then, his transformation completed, he opened it and stepped through.

Something moved at the stern window, scattering water across the floor. For one horrified moment Frederic thought Lorca had come back from the dead to protest Caolin's theft of his identity, then he realized that this figure was smaller, and that the lamplight was glinting on sopping red hair. Dazed, he stared as Rana sawed at his bonds.

Suddenly he was free, and he dropped to his knees beside Ardra's still form, pulling her into his arms, kissing her lips and eyelids as he called her name. He was vaguely aware the Rana was calling his, but though Ardra did not respond, her flesh was still warm, and he felt her heart beat beneath his hand.

"Frederic! He may be back at any minute—" Rana tugged at his arm. "That boat is waiting for *us*! We can get away!"

"Ardra—" whispered Frederic.

"She's not dead—they'll take care of her—come away!"

"No! I can't leave her to *him*!"

"Very well," Rana answered impatiently, "there's room for all of us if you can carry her—but please, Frederic, come now!"

Together they carried Ardra to the window, then halted as Rana bent and whistled softly. The shouting on deck had died down, and they could hear "Lorcas"'s voice giving commands.

"May Sea-Mother keep them from looking this way," breathed Rana. "I will go first, and you lower Ardra down to me. I will whistle when it is safe."

Frederic watched her slide soundlessly into the water and saw something move behind her, a sleek form that almost immediately slid under the water again. But there was no time for wonder. He used his last strength to maneuver Ardra's long body through the window, and fell through himself as limply as Lorca's body had gone. Something hard came up under him and he gasped for breath, then Rana was hissing in his ear, and he managed to grip the dolphin's dorsal fin as the creature began to move. Rana had her arm across Ardra's limp body, the other woman's head on her shoulder, and seemed to be moving through the chill water almost as easily as the mammal Frederic rode.

Carefully they eased through the water. There was a shout from the ship behind them.

"There by the stern—something's moving!" a man cried.

"Where? I don' see nothin'. What it look like?"

"A head, bobbing in the water . . ."

"At midnight? In middle sea? Maybe *la foca*—what you call, the seal! Is a boat we look for now!"

"Yes, I know that, but he told us to look sharp . . ."

Still arguing, the voices faded as the dolphin bore Frederic on. The lights from *Lioness* were sparks behind them when he saw the dark shape of the rowboat against the sky. A second dolphin floated in the water with the rope in her jaws. He steadied Ardra in the water while Rana clambered over the side and hauled her in, then felt an unexpected boost from the dolphin as she did the same for him.

Lying on his back in the boat, Frederic heard a burst of chittering from alongside.

"What do they say?" he asked, almost too dazed for wonder.

"Pearlgray thinks we were long in coming—" Rana answered him.

Frederic remembered the six months of suffering that seemed now, beyond all reason, to have come to an end. He gathered Ardra into his arms and fell back again, laughing weakly.

Chapter Seventeen

Mist swirled above the waves as if air were dissolving into ocean, blurring the distinction between sea and land, and diffusing the dawn into a directionless light in which all elements seemed mingled. Julian hurried toward the entrance to the lagoon, feeling the fitful touch of damp wind against his right cheek, and knowing that there was more moisture in the masses of cloud that were forming over the sea. He felt the water content of the air grow less as he came into the lee of the point, in the same way he knew that the waning moon still moved invisibly across the morning sky, and sensed the progress of the incoming tide. Night-long he had been one with the waters, and he knew, now, all that moved upon or in the sea. A storm was coming, but before it broke, Rana would be here.

In the camp, men were waking with hearts as dismal as the skies. During the night, more of the wounded had died, and the wounds of those who lived had stiffened, leaving them with no heart for battle by land or by sea. But as Julian passed their dead watchfires they turned and saw the Jewel that blazed unshielded on his breast.

"The Sea Star—" went the murmur behind him. "It is the Master of the Jewels!"

The awe in their voices did not concern him. That night Julian had traveled far from the world of humankind, and was not entirely returned to it, though the dual consciousness in which he functioned now allowed him to speak and move. He neither knew nor cared that to the men and women who watched him, his movements had the ease of flowing water. The Master had warned him of the dangers of forgetting his humanity, but in the past hours it had become clear to him that to have even a chance of saving his people, he had to become one with the Sea.

Robert emerged from the lean-to and stopped short, staring, as Julian strode up the hill.

"I want a stretcher and the men to carry it—" said Julian. "Where is the Master of the Junipers? He should be there too. . . ."

"With Lord Eric, I think—" Robert began. "The Master should be *where*? Where have *you* been, for that matter?"

"You can come too," Julian answered as he turned away, "but not too many others. He'll be very tired— "

"*Who*, Julian? What is going on?" spluttered Robert, limping after him. Silverhair put down his harp and followed them.

"Frederic is coming . . . Rana is bringing him home. . . ."

Julian waited at the entrance to the lagoon, letting his spirit reach out until he felt them nearing. A word brought the stretcher-bearers forward, muttering dubiously. Only the Master of the Junipers watched serenely as Julian waded out into the water, and only the Master was not surprised when the freshening wind parted the mists, revealing suddenly two dolphins who drew a battered boat through a silver sea.

For a moment a shaft of pale sunlight broke through and the dolphins lifted from the water in a single shining arc, fell back in a spray of crystal, and leaped again, curving away to either side in almost painful symmetry. The mists closed in again before they reentered the water, so that they seemed to have taken flight. But Julian was already pulling the boat the rest of the way to shore.

The keel ground on sand. Julian felt his detachment falter as he saw Rana sitting in the stern, white and shivering, with strands of wet hair hanging limply down her back and clinging to her brow. Now he saw the bruise on her forehead, and knew why she had left in secret. He would never have given her permission to go.

But she was smiling.

"Marana—once more you bring me a gift from the sea!"

Her eyes widened at the name, then her grin broadened, and he felt delight bubble through him from some previously unsuspected well of joy.

"You needed something to cheer you up again—" she said simply. But his heart shook within him as he realized what she had dared to bring this gift to him.

What I feel for her is something greater than infatuation—in that moment Julian understood it. *This is external whether or not she ever knows. . . .*

"I think she has brought you more than you expected," said the Master of the Junipers, joining him.

Julian looked down. Frederic was asleep at Rana's feet, but Julian had not expected the slim, tan-skinned woman who lay in his friend's arms. Then he recognized the golden armlets on her wrists and realized who she must be.

Rana shook Frederic's shoulder, and in a moment he stirred, the blue eyes opened and met Julian's. Frederic smiled, and Julian, still grieving for Arn, understood abruptly what his grief would have been if he had lost this friend too.

Then Frederic's face clouded, he felt Ardra's brow and sat up quickly, still holding her. The Master reached down to touch her.

"She's chilled, in danger of shock if we don't get her warm soon. But she is very strong, Frederic, don't despair!" He motioned to the stretcher-bearers, and Julian and Frederic together lifted the limp body. Frederic staggered as he stood, and Julian reached out to him, shocked by how thin the other man had become.

But Frederic was watching Ardra.

"What happened to her?" Julian asked softly.

"Caolin . . . blasted her somehow! He is out there, on the *Lioness*!"

Julian winced, knowing better than anyone what that meant. He scarcely heard Frederic's hurried account of what had happened just before Rana arrived to rescue them.

"Caolin's daughter—" murmured the Master. "I knew he had begotten a child while he was in Elaya, but not for what ends. Poor girl . . . poor girl!"

Silverhair whistled in wonder, then an odd smile lit his

337

face, and softly he began to repeat the ending of the song he had been singing the night before.

"He wandered on a barren shore
where still harsh waves were battering
the wreckage of a hundred lives
across the salt sands scattering,
and wept, and stopped—saw something where
the moon-pale hair like sea-wrack lay.
Chill lips he kissed; he held her there,
so cold and fair, until the day."

The stretcher-bearers lifted the stretcher and started toward the camp. Lady Rosemary hurried across the sand to meet them, with her second son running before her—a boy who was already as big as his older brother, with Eric's sturdy frame and his mother's bright hair.

"Mother! Alaric—" breathed Frederic. "Is Father—"

Alaric grinned, and grabbed him in a hug that nearly bowled him over. "Father's better! The Prince told him you were coming, and the Master says he will live now!"

And then Rosemary herself was there, holding her son as if not quite sure he was real. Frederic met Julian's gaze over her shoulder, and the Prince felt his throat tighten again.

This is too much emotion— he told himself. *And there is so much yet to do!*

But there was still a little time before the labor must begin, and Rana was getting out of the boat now, staggering as if she had not realized just how stiff she had become. In a single swift motion, Julian had his cloak around her and lifted her in his arms.

"Julian—my lord—There is no need!"

"If I am your lord, then obey me—" he said with mock sternness. But the Sea Star pulsed almost painfully as it was pressed between them. She must have felt it too, for her eyes widened.

"So, you were able to save Frederic after all—" Julian

fought for something to say to her. "I hope he thanked you."

"He was more grateful to me for saving *her*!" retorted Rana. "I didn't understand when I saw it starting on the Island. They're fire and water, but in her own way she loves him. Maybe they can be happy now!"

Rana's head rested on his shoulder as she gave way to her weariness. Julian felt the warm, live weight of her in his arms and for a moment found it hard to breathe. Faintly, through the pounding in his ears, he heard Silverhair's song—

"But when the sun soared in the sky
he felt her stir, and though the sea
still filled her eyes, within her breast
her heart beat warm and steadily.
He wed her, and upon their hill
their children still live, waterwise.
They fish the sea whose favor bright
shines in the light of their blue eyes."

Yes, thought Julian. *My sea-sprite has returned and I will never let her go again.*

"Rana—" he began, but suddenly people were all around them, cheering.

Was I really going to tell her that I love her? he wondered as they were swept back to the camp. *And what could she possibly have answered, exhausted as she is now*? There was no answer. The people were shouting, and Julian shivered in the first breath of the approaching storm.

"The storm *is* coming—I have felt its weight in the air, and its force in the swells of the sea. We must leave here, not to fight—but to flee." Julian took a swift step forward and stood, challenging them.

Rana pulled his cloak more tightly around her, for the canvas they had rigged to shelter this meeting was little

339

protection against the chill. All around her the captains were muttering. Their own experienced weather-sense agreed that the air-pressure was falling, and the wind had been backing southerly since dawn. But they did not understand what he proposed to do.

"Let it come then," said Andrea Hardhands. "We're safe at anchor in this lagoon. Why sail into the jaws of our enemies when the sea will avenge us soon?"

"Mistress—this will be no simple autumn gale! What I have sensed is a Great Wind. When it strikes there will be no pity for anything in its way."

Julian had covered the Sea Star again, but surely they could feel its force, thought Rana. Or was she the only one who felt it so strongly? Perhaps it was her own exhaustion that made her so apprehensive. When Julian carried her ashore she had felt safe for the first time since the battle, but now her head hurt, and the food they had given her lay like a lump in her belly.

"The sandbar that guards the lagoon will be no protection. This storm comes from the south! It will sweep across the bar and smash our ships against the farther shore. I chose this haven to draw the reivers away from the settled lands around the Bay, but we must get the bulk of the Lady Mountain between our ships and the sea if we are to save them, and we must get our wounded away. Even if the village survives the storm, they cannot shelter them all."

The villagers had not laughed at the warning. They knew these storms, and some of them were already loading their animals and preparing to flee.

"But surely there are paths over the mountains—with a storm coming, the last thing we want is to take to the water!" This was the leader of the armsmen who had fought on board *Battle Gull*. But the ship captains were frowning, and Rana thought that if it were not for the reivers, they would gladly run for the safety of the open sea.

"Any who can cross the hills under their own power are welcome to do so—" said Julian. "But the wounded do not have that option. Even if we had the beasts to transport them, they could not survive being carried that way."

"My lord and I will dare the waters," said Lady Rosemary. *Waverider*'s captain looked uncertain, but he nodded obediently.

"But what about the reivers, Julian?" asked Robert. "By the time the storm scatters them it will be too late for us to get away!"

"It's true," Rana added reluctantly. "Even without the Lady Ardra, Zoltan and . . . the other commanders will be waiting to gobble us up the minute we set our sails." She did not want to say Caolin's name.

"They will be waiting, but the trick that served them yesterday may serve me today! I will take one ship out under flag of truce, and delay them while the rest of the fleet gets away."

That seemed to satisfy them, and it was true that with any lead at all, this wind would give the advantage to the ships with a greater weight of sail. If Julian could buy them even a little time, they might hope to outrun the sharkships back to the Bay. To save their own skins they would let him sacrifice himself, Rana thought furiously. But he did not act like someone who was about to throw his life away. Only that had prevented her from saying so before them all.

"And just what makes you think that Zoltan is a more honorable foe than Ardra?" she hissed when the others had gone. "Not to mention Caolin! It was his magic that defeated us yesterday—do you think that he will have suddenly lost his powers?"

"Caolin wants the Sea Star—" Julian answered quietly. "Now I have something to bargain with, while he can no longer use Frederic to threaten me. The Jewel will be no good to him at the bottom of the sea. If he can hold me in talk while he tries to trick me out of the stone, he will not care if the rest of you get away. And the reivers should be told what is coming. They may not want to suffer for their leaders' greed."

"Hah!" Rana frowned at him, but privately she was thinking that what he said might well be true. "And what ship has consented to bear you on this fool's errand?"

"Lord Austin has offered me *Sea Brother*, with any of her crew who wish to go."

Rana winced. For a little while she had forgotten Arn. She supposed the Lord of Seahold might well wish to see the last of the ship on which his son had been wounded, and the man who had led him to his doom. Was *Sea Brother* a deathship? Rana knew only that she would rather die with Julian than watch him sail away.

"Well, I'm part of that crew—" she said finally. "And so is your cousin Robert, and Silverhair. Haven't they told you yet that they're coming? They will!"

"No, Rana!" Julian reached out as if he was going to shake her, then his hands fell away. "But if I forbid it, I suppose you'll just call up your dolphins and come after me—" His expression was twisted between amusement and pain.

"It won't be the first time!" Rana grinned, remembering how she had followed him when he went in search of the Earthstone. "My lord, I'm afraid that you are stuck with me!"

"Am I?" For a long moment Julian simply looked at her. Then he smiled with a sweetness that was almost pain.

* * *

"We have come not to beg your mercy, but to offer you terms. . . ." said Julian. *Sea Brother* and *Lioness* had retained only enough sail to maintain position during the parley, tacking back and forth against the wind. Rana suppressed an impulse to look behind her, where the Westrian fleet was drifting steadily to leeward, ready to make its run for the Gate. Everyone else was watching the Prince, whose silvered mail glittered in the light that shafted between the gathering clouds, and at the slim figure in gold who looked down at him from the deck of the *Lioness*.

It gave her an eerie feeling to see Ardra's semblance there, knowing that the real woman was with Frederic on *Waverider*, several miles away. Caolin's illusion was good enough to deceive the reivers as well as the Westrians. Julian had hoped that the loss of their leader might demoralize the enemy, but there was no point in trying to tell them the truth now.

"Are you counting on your miserable fleet to support you, princeling?" Zoltan spoke for his commander. "I suspect that at even now they are preparing to scuttle for home!"

Rana felt Gully and Fernando stir angrily beside her. Was this idle insult, or was the Elayan taunting them with full knowledge that that was precisely what Julian had ordered those ships to do? And if the enemy was second-guessing them already, how were they going to keep this parley going long enough for the others to get away?

"It is not I who will destroy you, nor my warriors, but the sea itself, Zoltan!" Julian lifted his battle horn. He had bound the Sea Star to its rim, and the reivers began to mutter as the stone blazed like sunlight on the sea. "Have you heard of the Four Jewels of Westria? They are no legend. This is the Sea Star, and it tells me that death awaits you all if you do not lay down your arms."

343

"Ardra" laughed. "Do not believe him! He may have a pretty bauble, but he is no sorcerer!" But even as Caolin spoke, he was leaning over the rail as if drawn by that bauble he scorned so.

From overhead came a mournful cry. Rana looked up and saw a line of brown pelicans flapping heavily shoreward. Behind them came wave upon wave of massed clouds, heavy with rain. But the reivers were facing north. Had they seen? Had any of them understood what the steady approach of those clouds must mean?

"Listen to me!" cried the false Ardra. "For I have real power!"

But the men on the warships were looking at each other, and some of them pointed to the sky. Zoltan bent to whisper to his commander. "She" shook her head and spoke again.

"Watch, and I will summon my own allies from the Sea!"

The sorcerer pointed to the space between the two ships, and something in the movement focused all attention. The clouds were gaining on them now, dimming the day, but no one noted them. It was the shadow in the water that drew all eyes; darkening, expanding, until suddenly a huge tentacle broke water, questing blindly. The rest of the monster came after it, a gigantic, undulating mass of coils.

"May the Lord of the Waters protect us!" exclaimed Marta. Her words died in a mutter of prayer. "It is the Kraken . . ." whispered old Will, his eyes still red from weeping for his young captain. Both crews watched, too transfixed by horror to even try to escape, as another dark tentacle hovered over *Sea Brother* dripping water like foul rain. The water bubbled, and the evil head of the Kraken rose slowly from the sea.

Rana remembered having said that she would never fear the sea again, and knew that she had been wrong.

Oars splashed wildly as one of the reivers' captains lost his nerve and ordered his ship away. The lifted tentacle swung towards it; the reivers rowed more wildly and rammed one of their fellows. In moments both ships were settling in the water. The tentacle swept down, and they heard the terrified cries of the men as they were dragged under and disappeared.

"Surrender, my lord," pleaded Gully. "If we don't she'll make it eat us all!"

Julian stood still, his hands clenched on the horn. "It is not true, I *know*—" he whispered, and then, though nothing else had changed, a brightness began to grow between his hands.

"I am no master of illusion—" he cried suddenly, "but I can show you reality!" And he lifted the battle horn to his lips and blew. Light and sound flared together in a single deep pulsation that rippled through the blood of the human creatures on their fragile ships and through the boundless depths of the sea.

Rana blinked, thinking, *Now it will disappear.* . . . But the Kraken appeared, if anything, more solid when she looked again. It was moving—it was *changing*! The head grew rounder, the eyes became somehow less evil, the color shifted from black to a deep reddish purple that she had seen before. Her heart began to pound—

"Sea Mother! Sea Mother!" she leaned out over the rail.

Now everyone was shouting. And the creature before them continued to alter. Tentacles were drawn back under the sea where they became the fringed edges of a cowled mantle. The hooded head lifted, human in form now but still far greater than human in size. From beneath its shadow gleamed two dark eyes. For a long moment Sea Mother floated eye-to-eye with Julian. The thin lips beneath the beaked nose smiled. And then, with a swirl that rocked the ship, she turned.

"Caolin!" The voice vibrated like the call of Julian's horn. "Caolin—next time, be more careful what powers you call! And do not mock the Sea!"

Suddenly Sea Mother sparkled all over, then her substance vanished, leaving an outline of pulsing lights that blinded human vision.

When they could see again, there were only the heaving waves.

On *Lioness* someone shouted. Where "Ardra" had stood, Rana glimpsed a red-robed figure with pale hair. Then the deck pitched beneath her, and she grabbed for the rail to keep from going over the side. Julian seized her and shoved her toward the foremast.

"Get the sail up—double reefed—" he cried, leaping for the tiller.

A gust of wind pushed them the other way like a giant hand. Rana pulled herself up, holding to the mast. The clouds were rolling down upon them in a white wave, driving the waters before them. Rana gasped as she got a facefull of stinging spray. *Lioness* pitched as she slid sideways through the waves. Two more sharkships crashed with a crackle of snapping oars, and they heard the seamen shouting for help as they were tossed into the sea.

Gripping *Sea Brother*'s tiller, Julian turned. "It is too late—too late—" he shouted into the wind. "Your choice is made! Pray to the Lord of the Waters to save you—I can do no more!" The ship leaped northward, racing the white-capped waves as her bow came around and wind and helm were suddenly in harmony.

"Is it too late for us, too?" asked Robert, his eyes on the clouds.

"She's weathered worse than this when the young lord was at the helm. . . ." Old Will's face twisted as he remembered his grief again.

Julian still had the tiller, as if its quivering told him what was going on beneath *Sea Brother*'s keel. His orders came clearly, and the ship leaned into the wind as they brought her around close hauled. Now they were plunging along on an eastward course, paralleling the brown cliffs of the coastline. Fernando and Marta controlled the lines to the big gaff sail like a horseman with a spirited team, easing them to spill wind at each gust, then pulling the sail taut again.

But every time they eased the sail, the pressure of the wind against *Sea Brother*'s side pushed her a little closer to the shore. Presently they could see the rocks that edged it tearing the waves to ribbons of foam.

"M'lord—we need sea-room or we'll be on those rocks before long!" said Will.

"Why not head back to Longbay?" asked Robert. "With this wind, we'd be there in no time!" Silverhair nodded agreement.

"That's a landsman speaking!" said Marta. "This wind would smash a landlocked ship against the cliffs! Better to get out to sea while we still have a sail, and ride the waves!"

Rana found herself nodding as she remembered what the dolphins had taught her. When the great winds blew, no sea-creature wanted to be anywhere near the hungry teeth that edged the shore. Julian gave the rusty cliffs an uneasy glance, and she realized that he felt the same way. Seen from this angle there was nothing comforting about the Lady Mountain.

The sail crackled as Marta let it luff, and when she trimmed it, the cloth began to part along the leech where the wind had frayed it.

"Ease off again!" ordered Julian. "We may not have a choice—" he began.

"Bend on the stormsails, lord—" cried Fernando.

347

"The captain tried to think of everything, and there's a trysail and a jib stored in the for'rard locker." Julian nodded, and Rana and Gully dragged out the folded canvas. After a few moments of confusion, *Sea Brother* steadied again, and Julian sighed.

"Arn, if your spirit is watching, I thank you. Stay with us, my friend, we'll save your ship if we can!"

Rana felt her eyes sting with something more than wind. Suddenly she was sure that her sister's husband was near the ship that he had loved as much as the girl to whom he would never now return.

But a ghost, however benevolent, could not help haul on the lines as they worked the ship around to the southwest on a port tack. A ghost was not flung bruisingly against the rail when a new gust hit, nor had he palms to be burned by the rope when a line jerked free. The stormsails flapped as they headed directly into the wind, blinking at the spray that lashed their faces. Then the boom swung over, and *Sea Brother* began to claw seaward on a broad reach across the wind.

The wind that drove *Sea Brother* harried the sharkships across the sea. Several foundered immediately, others after a valiant battle with the storm. A few, more seaworthy or better-manned than the rest, reached the coastline, only to be savaged by the hungry rocks that edged the shore. Bodies were tossed free and those that the curling currents did not take were swept landward to lie tangled among the seawrack on the shore, cold as the ocean mostly, although there were a few in which life lingered still.

Ardra's greatship shuddered beneath the blows of the waves. The sails had whipped themselves to ribbons early, and the first big seas carried all the fine scrollwork that had been Ardra's pride away. But as if unsatisfied by that sacrifice, the storm snapped both the masts. Water worked between straining timbers; each time *Lioness* wallowed down one trough between the waves it was harder for her to clamber up again.

Caolin felt the ship failing beneath him, and set himself to survive this test, as he had mastered so many others. He had enough authority left to order the sailors to bind him to one of the benches and let the next wave that crashed across the deck carry him away. As the water closed over him he sent his awareness inward, closing down all but the most basic body functions in an attempt to escape the fury of the sea. Inert and unfeeling, board and body were swept shoreward by the capricious powers of wave and wind.

And still that wind rose, buffeting *Sea Brother* until the mind grew as numb as the fingers with the never-ending struggle to hold on. Only Julian's voice seemed audible above the screech of the storm. Now they were heading into it, and it lashed them with whips of rain and flying spray. The dark rampart of the coast was lost behind them, and they held their course only by the relentless pressure of the wind. Rana did not know how long it had been when the trysail split. The jib was tearing, and they hauled it down too, and ran under bare poles at the mercy of the sea.

Rana had thought that she knew every mood of the sea. But she had not met this raging animal, the storm. She had called *Sea Brother* a deathship, while harboring the conviction that neither she nor Julian could be killed by the sea. She recognized that assumption only now, when she realized that neither whale nor dolphin could save them if they went overboard.

The ship shuddered as water cascaded across her, and Rana blessed the labor at Montera that had made her seaworthy again. She was fighting valiantly for survival, but without the help of the sail, the rudder could not keep them headed into the waves.

"—Make a sea anchor!"

Rana crawled closer to the mast to hear what Will was saying to Julian.

"Rolled sail—give us leverage!" Will gestured broadly. Julian nodded, and soon they were struggling to knot ropes around the tightly rolled sail. Rana could hear Gully, who was next to her, muttering.

". . . He knew about the storm. He knew, and he has the Jewel! He knew because he *called* the storm!" Gully shook his head piteously, then another wave drenched them, and he began to scream. "Stop the storm—you started this, now stop it—stop it now!" Dropping his rope, he flung himself across the sail at Julian.

Robert grabbed him and held on while the boy continued to rave.

"Tie him to the mast—" said Julian. At that moment the command did not seem heartless. There was no time to pity Gully's pain; roped to the mast his chance of survival was good as any of theirs.

Breath came in harsh gasps as they wrestled the makeshift sea anchor over the side. For a moment nothing happened; then the rope finished paying out with a jerk that sent them sprawling, and the sea anchor began to exert a counter-pressure to the wind.

But the crests of the wind-driven waves curved over them in white cascades, and the sea was lathered like an over-ridden horse with foam. Even old Will could think of nothing else to do, and when he himself was almost swept overboard, Julian ordered them all to tie themselves down. A new gust carried the top of the mainmast away, but there was enough of a stump left to be useful. Rana strained to help the others, and then found herself grabbed by Julian and tied to the pillar of the stern platform. Julian roped himself next to her, by the useless rudder.

The ship lurched as the sea-anchor tore away, and shuddered uneasily into the trough between the wave she had been crossing and the one that was looming above her now.

The wave rose like a moving wall, upon the shore fell, thundering . . . Rana remembered the line from the old song. But it was falling on *them*—an unbearable weight of water that drove the breath from her body. *Sea Brother* rolled sickeningly.

"*I can fight no longer . . . I owe my life to the sea—*" She did not know if that fragment of thought was hers or Julian's.

"*I can't let you die like this!*" That was Julian, but Rana's own thought crossed his—"*You have to live for Westria!*"

"*Julian!*" her spirit cried. "*Blow the horn!*"

"*Blow the Horn! Use the Sea Star!*" The imperative rolled through Julian's body, empowered by the union of their wills. With numb fingers he fumbled for the strap that held it and wrestled the end to his lips. Between one wave and another he filled his lungs and blew.

The music resonated in every cavity of his body, was borne by the pulse of blood through every vein. He felt as if he were falling down a well. Waves of sound tuned the vibrations of his spirit to their own rhythms. He felt Rana's body echoing that music, and then her identity flowed into his own. In the spirits of the others he heard its echo; his knowledge expanded to take in the sea around them, and all the creatures who rejoiced in the excitement of the storm. Human senses were transcended as consciousness deepened. In that totality of vision, for a moment he glimpsed the protean essence of the Lord of the Waters, and did homage.

The merged awareness that was both Julian and Rana

351

saw through the surface to the moving patterns within the waves. Instead of blowing spume they saw the undines, racing white horses whose manes and tales streamed backward in the wind. Rana's memory recalled the spirits who had almost tempted her into the sea when she found the Jewel. Julian's more recent experience on the Floating Island gave them names. Fear was dissolved by understanding.

This was not chaos, but an interaction of forces on a scale too great for human comprehension, an ecstatic eruption of energy as harmonious in its violence as the climax of human love. But for that very reason, it was no place for the fragile bodies and artifacts of men.

Julian raised the horn to his lips and blew again. Once more his awareness shifted. This time the tone was deeper, and it was the depths that echoed back its power. Something was down there, more alien than the Guardians who ruled the People of the Sea, less powerful than the Lord of the Waters, but potent enough in this, its native sphere.

Waves rolled aside in a great ring and the sea bubbled as something burst through to the surface, its size impossible to judge in this expanse of water, its form shifting as mind tried to find a metaphor for what eyes perceived. In this realm the only speech was symbol— symbol interpreted by the power of will. As a deeper vision had enabled him to see the form of Sea Mother through the horror of the Kraken, Julian now willed the transformation of the Elemental Power that had surfaced here into a shape he could understand.

Scaled flanks streamed water; sea-beasts bowed their heads like great sea-horses harnessed to a shell. The being that it bore in form was human, green-skinned, fish-tailed, bearded, crowned with pearls. One mighty arm a silver trident brandished, the other held a goblet, silver-wrought, from which pure water poured in endless stream. Julian recognized in this image the counterpart of the Gnome-king who had served him in the heart of the Mountain. Now, in the midst of the ocean, the Sea Star revealed to him its name.

Julian channeled the power of all their spirits into one call.

"*Nicsa, I command you—guide us home!*"

The trident lifted then in salutation. Julian grabbed the tiller as the elemental turned. Where there had been a wilderness of water now he saw a way.

*"Let it flow, weal and woe, let it go—
as you grow, you shall know—be it so . . ."*

The song surfaced into memory. There no need to fight the storm any longer, for they were part of it. The heave of the wave was the power to propel them. Guiding, not gripping the tiller Julian turned, easing off, holding fast with the flow of the waters, knowing the current, going with the current, they followed Nicsa through the undulant paths of the sea.

Time funneled into an endless present, but the day was darkening when they realized that the ecstatic energy of their ride had become a channeled swiftness that bore them forward at ever increasing speed. Lightning split the clouds to reveal glistening, blood-dark cliffs looming to either side, and the world exploded in thunder. Julian's expanded senses recognized the driving power of the ingoing tide and balanced the forces of wind and current that would keep them on course as *Sea Brother* shot through the Gateway and into the sheltered waters of the Bay.

For a moment Nicsa's chariot glimmered beside them. They saw the silver shine of his trident lifting above them. Then it too dissolved into gray darkness and the Elemental Ruler was gone. Once more, Julian blew his battle-horn, softly this time, for this was not a summons, but a farewell.

Even here, flails of rain whipped the water, and whitecaps scudded like frightened sheep toward the eastern shore. But one could think of untying the ropes and trying to stand. It was possible for the human voice to compete with the wind. Julian laid his hand over the Sea Star, still attached to the horn. The violence that had been natural to the sea would be devastating, unleashed upon the land. As he had compelled the Elemental, he summoned his tired mind to one last focusing of the will.

"Creatures of water, our thanks for your favor—return to your homes now, sleep well in the sea. . . ." he whispered, and felt Rana's hand close over his, balancing and steadying him.

"Let the clouds bear their burden in peace through the heavens—" he said more strongly. "The soft rain, the slow rain—let it fall now. Rain on the hillsides and rain on the mountains, rain on the forests as gently as love. . . ." His chant rose and fell. And as Rana echoed him, the power of the Sea Star muted to a gentle glow.

"Soft rain and slow rain, soaking and healing, female rain falling, send us your blessing. Transforming dryness and dearth, sweet waters, give life to the earth!"

"Look—" said Marta.

Above them, the lights of Seahold were glimmering through the shining veils of rain.

Chapter Eighteen

The wind slammed its load of rain against Seahold's western wall, rattling braced shutters and forcing a trickle of water between frame and sill, then fell away with an angry sigh.

Frederic cupped his hand around the lamp to stop its flickering. The storm that had chased the remnants of the Westrian fleet through the Gateway was raging still, but all the ships that had survived the battle had made it into the Bay. All except *Sea Brother*.

But there was nothing he could do for Julian now. Frederic had come, as he thought, to comfort Ardra, but admitting his fears for Julian he realized that he needed comfort too.

"Ardra?" He held up the lamp, saw a quiver stir the blankets, and came the rest of the way into the room. Shadow eddied in the corners and pooled in the twisted folds of the bedclothes. The day had not yet ended, but with the hold tight-shuttered against the storm night already reigned within. Frederic took another careful step forward and set the lamp on the oak table. After a moment he made out the curve of a back and shoulder, and saw that she lay curled with her face to the wall.

He put his hand on her shoulder. A jerk wound the blankets more tightly around her.

"Ardra—it's only me, Frederic. I couldn't get free before. How do you feel?"

"Have you come to taunt me?" Her voice came muffled through the blankets.

For a moment he looked down at her helplessly. Then, a sudden anger shook him, and he grabbed her shoulder and pulled her flat, forcing her to look up at him. He felt a cold breath on his cheek as the storm struck the hold again.

"I would be justified, wouldn't I? When I was your prisoner, you taunted me—and I endured it, Ardra, and more. Was all your strength in your ships and your sword? I don't believe it! Now is the time to prove your courage—now! Show me the steel I know is there!"

She lay where he had thrust her—skin dull, hair tarnished, with nothing alive in her but her eyes.

"Am I your prisoner, then? I thought so!"

He grasped her wrists, then suddenly twisted so that her hands were outside his. Reflexively she gripped back and they held each other equally.

"Yes!" he dropped to one knee beside the bed, holding her gaze. "Yes, as I am yours, and always will be, Ardra, even if the Cataclysm should come again! In strength and in weakness—"

"Only now it is your strength and my weakness—" she interrupted him. "I deserved that. Well, now you have me, do what you will. . . ." She let go of his hands.

"You're cold!" he said accusingly. The bed creaked as

356

he sat down. Ardra did not resist when he took her hand again and began to chafe it between his own, carefully, as if he held a wounded bird. But if so, it was a bird of prey. Frederic smiled a little, at the contrast he could feel between the fine narrow bones beneath the silky skin on the top of her hand and the hard muscles under the callouses on her palm.

"I don't want to own you! What binds you and me together has nothing to do with the world—I was a seeker of the Inner Ways even when I was your prisoner. I still am, and you are still a warrior. So fight!" A little warmth came into her right hand and he started on the other.

"With what?" she asked bitterly. "As you say—I am without ship or sword. You lost everything but honor, Frederic, but from me, even honor has been taken away!"

"You did not betray your*self*, Ardra—that is all that matters to me!" He kissed her hand, and looking up, saw the tears begin to sparkle in her eyes. "Listen—Julian was a leader before he ever knew who his parents were. That's just the way he is! And you are the same!"

"Am I? I will try to believe it if you say so, but that leaves me no more hope than I had before. If I had captured your prince instead of you I should have imprisoned him even more closely, and used his danger to threaten your land. I am enough Elayan still to know what the retribution for such a deed should be."

Frederic shook his head, smiling. "Be thankful then that Julian was not bred up in Elaya! He is not vengeful." He eased down beside her, curving his body around hers protectively as a burst of rain lashed the window once more.

"Perhaps not," she whispered in the silence that followed, "but there are others who are. Can you not hear?"

The momentary lull let him hear the patter of raindrops, the slam of a door somewhere below. And then, as if the storm had found a voice for its agony, he heard the keening of the women of Seahold.

"Tonight the son of this house lies dead in his own hall," Ardra said harshly. "Because of me . . . There was little kindness in the hands or voices of those who brought me here."

Arn . . . thought Frederic, remembering. *Arn is dead and Julian and Rana are still out there somewhere. Perhaps Ardra is right to be afraid. . . .* Instinctively he held her closer. She was shaking, he did not know whether from cold or from fear.

"I am alone. . . ."

"Never alone, Ardra—" He tightened his grip, searching for words. He felt her shake her head.

"Easy to say, Frederic my beloved, but not true! In some things you are still an innocent. Your loyalties are given already—how many times have you told me so! If your Prince lives, you must serve him, and after him, your masters at the College of the Wise. Would you give up your hope of reaching Awahna for me?"

Outside, the storm ravened across the sky, but still Frederic heard her whisper, "It would have been better if you had left me to die in the sea. . . ."

Mind and spirit quailed before the despair in those quiet words. But the body that knows life only gave its own answer as his lips touched hers. For a moment Ardra stiffened, then her arms closed around him and her flesh sought his with an urgency that equalled his own.

Lightning tore the clouds asunder; for a moment the window was outlined in fire, then sight was extinguished as thunder boomed and rattled above the hold. The roof roared with the sound of falling water, deafening. But other, deeper, senses responded with all the triumphant splendor of the storm.

And then came a great stillness.

Bodies rested in healing unity. The world around them hummed with the steady murmur of gently falling rain.

"Our loving will never be like anyone else's, Ardra," Frederic whispered when he could speak again. "Promise me that you will keep fighting, love, and I swear that I will keep faith with you."

She gave a shaky laugh and pressed her face into the hollow of his shoulder. It was answer enough, for now.

They were still together when a wild, incredulous cheering rose above the patter of the rain. Frederic raised himself on one elbow to listen and heard them shouting Julian's name.

Rain flattened the bleached grass of the coastal hills, soaking through the hard earth to the hidden seeds, runneling down each fold and crease to rocky draws choked with laurel and willow trees. Rain drummed on the prairies of the Great Valley, and filled the marshes where the tules rustled in the wet wind. Rain dashed against the foothills, darkening the red earth to blood-color and releasing the aromatic incense of the scattered pines. Rain splashed the stony moraines above the snowline and collected in icy pools where last year's snows had never melted away.

The rain penetrated deep into the parched earth, filling cracks and smoothing wrinkles, renewing and rejoicing the land. And when earth could receive no more, the water began to flow downward in a million chuckling rivulets, joining to become rushing mountain streams that hurried to lose themselves in the rivers that would bear their purified waters back to the sea.

It was still raining the next morning—a gentle drizzle that pattered soothingly against rooftiles and dripped steadily from rafters. Up and down the coasts of Westria men went out to see what gifts the storm had left them, and found among the driftwood and sea-wrack the shivered timbers of ships and the bodies of men. Mostly they were dead men, grey and waterlogged from their time in the sea. Elayans dead in the storm and some of the Westrians lost in the battle had found a single resting place.

But the ocean had given up some of its prey still living, and that afternoon men on mud-spattered horses carried Julian's word to the holdings nearest the Gateway. The bodies were to be sent to Seahold for identification, and any living Elayans were to go with them as prisoners.

The rain continued throughout the day, falling on Seahold with a relentless steady patter as if even the skies were weeping for the slain.

Two rows of paired ships faced each other across the silver surface of the Bay. Between their eastern ends two other ships were held by lines, but from their crews no sound came, nor ever would again. After another day of rain the weather had broken, although the massed clouds that filtered the afternoon sunlight promised more to come. But now it was Samaine, and with the pause between storms the gates were opening between the worlds.

Julian stood in the bow of *Waverider*, watching as men settled the last of the logs around the bodies, and saturated them with oil. Lord Austin's *Wind Dancer* lay anchored directly across from them in the other line. He knew that Rana was there with her sister, and wondered if she was watching as he was. He wished she could be here with him—she would understand what he was feeling now. But once away from the sea, he had realized how unfair it would be to lay the burden of his love upon her. She had to deal with her own grief and her growing.

And he had no right to speak to any woman until he had earned the right to speak for Westria.

One of the tethered ships was *Sea Brother*, ready for her final voyage with Arn at her helm. But this time his crew consisted of the other dead from Seahold. After all she had survived, *Sea Brother* had become a deathship in the end. Julian wondered if the powers of the sea would recognize her and make her welcome—he knew that the tightness in his chest came only partly from his grief for Arn and the others. For one day he too had been *Sea Brother*'s captain, on a journey even stranger than the one on which she was about to go. He knew her as a lover knows his first woman, and for no other ship would his feeling ever be quite the same.

The other craft was one of the warships they had captured from the reivers, and now it was a sharkship again, for there they had laid, with equal reverence if less elaboration, all the dead reivers who had been washed up after the storm. One of them was Don Esteban Lorca, whom he himself had killed—the one man of all that crew whom he would have spared if only he had known. Remembering that, he turned to glance at Ardra, who sat bundled in a cloak by the mast with Frederic behind her.

Her eyes looked like holes in a blanket, but she had insisted on being present when the funeral ships were set free. At her feet huddled three of the reivers. Julian considered them with a kind of wonder—only three men left alive out of the armada that had boasted it would make all the coasts of Westria a reivers' realm! They had clung to the bottom of their capsized vessel until it grounded below Wolf Point and they were found by Westrian searchers.

No one had reported finding Caolin.

Seeing Julian looking his way, Frederic squeezed Ardra's shoulder and came around the mast to join him.

"Are you all right? You looked so grim—" Frederic's eyes were bright with unasked questions. Julian supposed that he had changed a great deal since Beltane, but the changes in Frederic himself came from more than illness. They would have a lot to say to each other, when there was time.

"Should I be happy?" he asked. "One of those boats holds men I learned to love, and the other bears some worthy enemies."

"And at least one who was both and neither, from what I have heard," said Frederic. "They tell me that old Bertram was washed up alive, and before his heart failed him he had quite a lot to say."

"Bertram!" Julian remembered a summer night by the sea, and the old man capering around his fire.

"Apparently he camped below the Red Mountain last year, and after that he started having headaches, and there would be hours and days of which he had no memory at all."

"Why didn't he say so?" asked Julian.

"He was afraid—he thought men would call him crazy. The Master says it was probably Caolin's tampering with his mind that killed him, as much as the sea. . . ."

"May his spirit find peace—" Julian bowed toward *Sea Brother*. "I cannot hate him, knowing what the touch of Caolin's mind can do—" He stopped short, with an involuntary glance at Ardra. When he looked at Frederic again there was an unaccustomed flush on his friend's cheeks, but his eyes were clear.

"It is true—Caolin used her even more than he did the old man. But I believe that there is a core of integrity in her that he never came near. I believe that will save her—only she has been used to position and authority. The training of the College helped me to endure captivity, but what use is it for me to set her free when there is nothing for her to do?"

Julian nodded. In some ways he could understand this warrior woman of Frederic's very well. And even Caolin's support could not have enabled her to lead those sea-wolves if she had not had her own authority. Too many good people had already died—it would be wrong to waste such quality. He reached out to grasp Frederic's arm, wanting to promise—what?

"I love her—" Frederic said in a sudden, shaken, voice. "Caolin's daughter! I cannot think what my mother will say!"

"And what about Awahna?" asked Julian.

"The One Who is both Lord and Lady made Ardra and me!" Frederic answered strongly. "I will serve the Guardians better because I have learned to love her. Can you understand?"

Julian nodded, his glance flickering unwilled across the water to Rana. *I can understand better than you imagine*! he thought wryly. Looking back at his friend, he said aloud, "I will save her for you if I can . . ."

He felt another presence, turned and saw that the Master of the Junipers had silently joined them in the bow.

"Is it time?" Julian asked quietly.

"Almost—I believe they have finished readying the funeral ships now." The Master gestured at the rowboats that were pulling away. As he spoke, the gentle murmur of talk that had come from the anchored ships faded away.

"Yes—now—"

Julian lifted the horn to his lips and blew, knowing what emotions would stir in the hearts of at least a few of his listeners at that sound. But this was a gentle calling. And when the Master spoke, his trained voice seemed distilled from its echoes, carrying clearly up and down the line.

"The harvest season is over, it is the time for rest and recollection. Now the world draws in upon itself, preparing to endure the cold. At this time we remember the loved ones who have left us, for life and death comprise one perfect whole. Now it is time to loose the grief that binds us, lest love should fetter those we would set free. Call them now, my sisters and my brothers. . . . Call their names and make your peace with them before they go."

As the Master continued, it seemed to Julian that the silence had deepened, and suddenly he was sure that those silent ones who waited in the funeral ships were listening too.

"I call my son, Arn—boy, you should have been here, saying farewell to me!" Lord Austin's voice cracked, then he mastered himself. "But no man ever had a better son, a joy to remember . . . Go in peace, boy—"

"Oh, Arn, *no* . . . " It was a girl's voice, Isabella's, he thought from the bustle of women around her. After a moment they managed to calm her, and she spoke again. "Arn, I'll always love you, but I'll try to be good—Arn, I'll take good care of our child!"

Then Lady Katrine was speaking, and the others from the household, and finally Rana, saying farewell to a brother and a captain.

"I salute you also—" Julian found the words coming to him suddenly. "Arn, I survived because of what you taught me. Leave a little of your spirit to guide us still!"

From the other ships came farewells to sons and sisters, husbands and brothers. Almost every family in Seahold had lost someone. Julian's belly twisted again as he realized how heavy the toll for that mismanaged battle had been. Only the grace of the Sea had gotten him out of it with any kind of victory. What had possessed him to think he knew how to win a sea battle? It did no good to remember that Caolin's sorcery had made him the victim of Ardra's skill. He should have expected sorcery.

And now? he asked himself. *Dare I assume that Caolin lies at the bottom of the sea?* Reason said it must be so, but Julian had fought two rounds with the sorcerer, and he did not think that either of them could now feel confident of the other's extinction until he saw his body on the pyre.

There was a mutter of surprise around him, and Julian's awareness jerked back to the present. Ardra had risen and was moving unsteadily toward the rail.

"I call upon the men who lie in *Corvejon* to forgive me!"

None of the Westrians had thought to ask the sharkship's name, thought Julian, but Ardra was continuing.

"My pride led you into an evil battle, and I deserted my command. I should have been with you—"

"It's not too late for that," came a mutter from one of *Waverider*'s crew. Julian was turning to see who, when he heard a scream—

"She killed him! She killed Arn! Put her on the pyre!"

"Isabella, be still!" cried Rana, but all up and down people were whispering—.

"The Elayan sorceress! She did this—let her burn with the rest of that scum!"

Ardra had straightened, and for the first time since the battle Julian saw her spirit shining through. Frederic was holding her, but not to keep her from falling. She had a fey brightness about her, as if she did not care whether she or her attackers died.

"*Hold!*" Julian's voice rolled across the waters as if he had blown his battle horn. "This war was started by the sorcerer of the Red Mountain, not by the Lady Ardra! Would you respect her more if she refused to honor her men? It was Caolin's magics that trapped us. But we all knew we faced death when we sailed out there—if you are going to blame someone for our losses, blame me!" Julian was aware that Ardra had stopped fighting Frederic's hold and was watching him, but he dared not look at her.

"I killed at least one of the men on that warship, and I salute his spirit—" he went on more temperately. "Don Esteban, hear and forgive me—may all who serve me be as loyal as you were to your lady, and as merciful to their captives as you were to those I love!"

"But it was Ardra and her men who killed our people—" someone cried from a ship down the line. "She should pay!"

"She *has* paid—" answered Julian. "She has lost men and fleet and everything she fought for—"

"It is not enough!"

Julian turned in astonishment, for that cry had come from Ardra herself. She took a swift step forward and knelt before him.

"Lord Julian, I will serve you! Your men died because you did not know sea-fighting. In compensation I offer you my life and my skill!"

Those who were not too stunned for speech were still murmuring, but to Julian, what Ardra said had a rightness that made all come clear. His awareness blazed with fragments of vision; he saw her at the helm of a greatship larger than *Lioness*, and again on a barge approaching Laurelynn, with a small blond boy by her side.

"So be it!" he said loudly, and felt her calloused hands trembling between his.

Then Frederic was helping her to her feet again. She lifted her face to his, speaking softly, and Julian saw his friend's face brighten as if it were not sunset, but dawn. *For them, this is a beginning*, he thought. *How will the rest of us renew the world?*

The ship jerked as *Waverider* tugged at her anchor, and Julian realized that the tide had turned.

"Peace, my children—" the Master's voice silenced the babble. "Leave the conflicts of the living for another day! It is the dead who deserve our attention now. Landsmen place lamps on the graves of their loved ones, but those who gain their living from the ocean give their dead back to the sea. Now the tide is ebbing, and it is time to let them go. Compose yourselves now, and let them pass with love. . . ."

Once more Julian blew his horn, and before the echoes had faded the boats which had held the funeral ships tethered cast off their lines. Released, the two ships rocked gently for a few moments, and then the current took them and began to carry them slowly toward the sea. Seven pairs of ships made a guard of honor on both sides of the channel through which they would pass. Beyond them, the way was clear through the Gateway to the open sea.

As the deathships gained speed, archers standing in the bows of the first pair of boats drew and released arrows tipped with fire. They arched across the water, trailing dark smoke against the pale sky, to bite into the oil-soaked masts with a spurt of flame. The ships moved onward, *Sea Brother* a little in the lead, and the second pair of archers shot, then the third. Then it was *Waverider* and *Wind Dancer*'s turn, and Julian saw that Rana was shooting from the other side.

Flame ran along piled branches until *Sea Brother* was wreathed in fire. *May you go in glory!* prayed Julian. The air trembled to the roar and crackle of flames. Silverhair stood up behind him and began to sing. Julian found his voice to join him and heard the others beginning, even Piper, who clung to Silverhair's side. Ship by ship, voices roughened by sorrow were eased as they joined in the singing, until the music echoed back and forth across the waves—

"Into Thy hands, Great Mother, we surrender—
Sovereign of sunset, Ruler of the Sea—
all we retain of these whom we are mourning,
and send them homeward to their rest with Thee."

Already the two ships had passed the last of their guardians. As they moved toward the Gateway the last two ships in line weighed anchor and moved after them, ready to push them off if they began to drift ashore. Out to sea, the clouds were lifting, and the light of the westering sun blazed suddenly through a curtain of gold. Julian opened himself to that radiance, let it suffuse his spirit and bear him above all weariness and sorrow.

"All that we owe to this fair world around us
must be returned to its elements again:
like rain we fall, to mingle with life's waters,
so that once more the clouds we may attain."

Now the burning ships were speeding through the Gateway, their heading as true as if the spirits that rode them had indeed set a course for home. Their escorts tacked in a smooth circle to bring them back into the Bay.

"Boats, bear them hence, and peace attend their faring;
bodies we send into the sea's embrace.
Now may the Boatman give their souls fair passage
to harbor where they may look upon Thy face."

As the music ended the fire reached the ropes that bound *Sea Brother*'s sails, which unfurled in a bright sheet of flame. In a moment *Corvejon*'s sail followed, a square of pale fire against the brilliant sky. Moment by moment the bright shapes grew smaller, disappearing so quickly that when they vanished at last no one could say if they had gone out of sight or sunk suddenly into the sea. But Julian knew that they had sailed into the Light that is the final shore.

Gradually Julian became aware of his own body again. But some of the peace he had tasted remained. The dead were gone; Ocean's deep womb had received them. Now those they had left behind must wait for Her to give life back again.

Rana picked her way along the water's edge. The tide was coming in, lifting the boats that had been drawn ashore until they tugged at their moorings. A fresh breeze pushed a few puffy clouds across a sky washed clear of every stain, and tickled an occasional whitecap from the surface of the Bay.

It was so *clean*, she thought as she took a deep breath. So necessary a cleansing after the smells of food and baby's napkins, and the heavier miasma of grief up in the Hall. Even her clothes seemed soiled and heavy, as if they had absorbed some of the grief from yesterday's ceremony. But the dead were at peace now and it was time to take up the business of living once more. She looked at the swirling water, wondering just how cold it would be.

The regular squeak of oar against oarlock close by brought her head up, squinting into the light of the rising sun. For a moment she could see only the stark silhouette of man and boat against the bright water.

It is the Boatman . . .

Rana knew that too much mourning was making her morbid even as she remembered that the Boatman was supposed to pole a barge. And she knew only one man whose shoulders were that broad. Strong arms flexed, and the skiff shot shoreward and turned with a deft swirl of oars so that it still moved toward her even though it was broadside to the shore.

Her lips twitched with unasked questions. What was Julian doing out so early? Had he known he would find her here? The waiting boat was an irresistible invitation, its presence an answer to all questions.

Rana clambered into the bow and sat on the bench facing Julian while he maneuvered the boat out into the Bay. There seemed to be no need for conversation. Beneath the rolled sleeves of his blue tunic the muscles rippled along his arms as he bent and pulled, and the skiff slid effortlessly over the water. She had never before sensed such peace in him, and gradually her own tensions melted away.

She could hear the creak of rigging and a murmur of voices from the harbor—the fishing boats of Seahold were preparing to go out again, cleansed of the stains of war. Julian eased back on the oars as the first boat moved by them, gathering way as the wind filled her white sail. One of the sailors waved and Rana recognized Gully, crewing for Will's sister Vesta. She waved back, glad that the boy had gotten someone else to take him on.

Two more vessels followed. Rana named them for Julian as they went by.

"What are they after? I thought the fishing season was done—" It was the first thing he had said to her.

"Salmon . . ." Rana answered him. "When the rains swell the coastal rivers, the salmon begin their run. Sometimes they start coming as early as August, but this year there have been none. Dried and smoked salmon is what we store and trade. The sprouting of the winter grass and the return of the king of fishes mean that the drytime is done, and we know there will be food for the coming year. When the salmon come the world begins again. Listen—"

Across the waters came the sound of singing; the same

tune that the fishers had sung at the Beltane Festival. But the words were different this time.

"Now the summer sun is gone, winter's on;
Now the clouds are dark with rain, once again.
May the silver salmon come safely home—
Oh favor us who love the Sea, Lady, pray!"

"We need the salmon—they have to come soon!"

"Call them then," said Julian.

"With the Sea Star?" she asked him. Why did his dark eyes hold hers? Was he testing her?

"No need. You are the priestess. Speak to the Sea . . ."

Rana stared at him. He was not even wearing the Sea Star, but suddenly she felt its presence linking them, as if she were inside Julian's skin, breathing his breath, flowing with the rush of blood through his veins. She tensed, but there was a well of stillness in him that dissolved her fear. Shaken, she leaned over the edge of the skiff and thrust her hands into the sea.

For a moment the chill was numbing, then she felt the tingle of contact flare through her, as if she had a dolphin's senses in her skin.

"Grandmother Salmon," Rana chanted the words of the ancient summoning,

"Great Spirit of Emotion,
swim from your western waters, your grandchildren call
you!
Grant us your supple strength,
wash us with the waves of your wisdom,
guide us to the pool of rebirth.
Welcome, Grandmother!"

The cold water cleansed the soil from her fingers. She felt some of the darkness that weighted her spirit begin to wash away. *Sea Mother, send your children*! she prayed. *Give new life to the earth—give new life to me*!

She kept her hands in the ocean, realizing now that she had only to touch the water to share the freedom of the sea. And so it was that after a time she felt the change, and sensed the pressure of many lives approaching even before there was anything to see.

And then the first fish leaped from the water in an explosion of energy that yearned to test itself against the hazards that lay between the mountain stream where it had been born and the open waters of the Bay. Almost instantly they saw another—the great King Salmon in all his glory—nearly five feet and a hundred pounds of spring-muscled shining body that soared over the skiff as if he disdained both earth and sea.

Julian's hair swung back as he leaned on the oars. Rana saw the silver scars on his brow and remembered who he was.

"Did you know this would happen?" she whispered.

"I knew that something was needed, and you must be part of it—you, who gave me the sea. . . . I think that you will be part of everything, now."

She had no time for wonder. The fish were all around them, and Rana knew that at the mouth of every river in Westria the same thing was happening as the salmon scented the outflux of fresh water into the ocean. Along all those rivers the people would be rejoicing. In the north they would do the White Deerskin Dance to renew the world, but the new year was already beginning. Though humans with their nets and spears took some of the salmon, and the grizzlies and other fishers among the elder kindred claimed their share, that culling would leave the strongest of Grandmother Salmon's children to complete their journey.

Silenced by that splendor, Rana and Julian watched as the river of living silver flowed past them, and the salmon came home from the sea to mate and die and begin the cycle of life anew.

A f t e r w o r d

I would like to acknowledge my debt to several sources of information and assistance, without which *The Sea Star* would have been considerably less salty.

First, to the Whale Center of Oakland, California, my gratitude for their cruises to the Farallon islands, which revealed a whole new world just off shore from my own. The cruise itself and the preparation at the Center were immensely helpful. My appreciation also goes to the Monterey Aquarium for their wonderful living displays of zones in the Monterey Bay. Watching fish swim in their native habitat gives one insights impossible from a book.

Anyone who found the choice of an octopus for Sea Mother surprising should look at the work done by Jacques Cousteau and others to establish their intelligence and ingenuity. As far as I know, no one has been able to capture one of the great ones of the deep for study, so I stand by my speculations.

I would also like to thank Marvin Martin and Lynn McVey for checking out my sailing, and the Armchair Sailor Bookstore in Sausalito for providing just the resources a landlubber needed.

The summoning chant for Grandmother Salmon is included courtesy of April Stockley.

DIANA PAXSON

THE EARTHSTONE

Once more the Royal traitor has risen up to threaten Westria. Now he is infinitely more powerful for he has become the Wolfmaster, the wielder of fear.

The weapons that could stop him – the Jewels of Power – are lost to the world as Westria, leaderless, drifts towards doom. There is yet one hope, Julian, lost son of King Jehan and Queen Faris, lives. But he is untested, unblooded, his birthright yet to be proved.

He must journey, with Silverhair the Wanderer and the Regent's children, to seek the support of the unearthly Guardians of Westria.

Then, braving sorcery and assassination, he must search out and use the first Jewel of Power: the Earthstone.

Post·A·Book

A Royal Mail service in association with the Book Marketing Council & The Booksellers Association.
Post-A-Book is a Post Office trademark.

DIANA PAXSON

THE WHITE RAVEN

A story of the still-living past.

Set in an ancient fantasy world, in a time when King Arthur is still remembered, *The White Raven* magically recreates the epic love story of Tristan and Iseult – and of Branwen, healer and destroyer, servant and Queen of the Otherworld . . .

'A lovely blend of legend and realism'
Marion Zimmer Bradley

HODDER AND STOUGHTON PAPERBACKS

DIANA PAXSON

THE WIND CRYSTAL

'Truly it holds one spellbound in the old meaning of the word' *André Norton*

BOOK FIVE OF THE CHRONICLES OF WESTRIA

Prince Julian, lost son of King Jehan, had returned.

But before he could reclaim the throne, he had to prove his right by finding and mastering the four jewels of power, lost in the magical war that had killed his father.

Two he had found: the Earthstone and the Sea Star. Now the quest must begin for the Wind Crystal. For in the saga of treachery and wonder working that is the Chronicle of Westria, there can be no half way stage between success and failure. And in failure lies the end of all good and all hope.

Watch out for the final volume in the *Chronicles Of Westria: The Jewel of Fire*.

HODDER AND STOUGHTON PAPERBACKS

MORE FANTASY TITLES AVAILABLE FROM
HODDER AND STOUGHTON PAPERBACKS

DIANA PAXSON

☐ 50938 9	Westria 1: Lady of Light, Lady of Darkness	£4.99
☐ 52091 9	Westria 2: Silverhair The Wanderer	£3.99
☐ 52472 8	Westria 3: The Earthstone	£3.99
☐ 56250 6	Westria 5: The Wind Crystal	£4.99
☐ 56227 1	Westria 6: The Jewel of Fire	£3.99
☐ 50251 1	White Raven	£4.50

FREDA WARRINGTON

☐ 41903 7	A Blackbird in Amber	£2.95
☐ 40161 8	A Blackbird in Darkness	£3.95
☐ 05849 2	A Blackbird in Silver	£3.99
☐ 53626 2	The Rainbow Gate	£3.99
☐ 53816 7	Darker Than The Storm	£3.99

All these books are available at your local bookshop or newsagent, or can be ordered direct from the publisher. Just tick the titles you want and fill in the form below.

Prices and availability subject to change without notice.

Hodder & Stoughton Paperbacks, P.O. Box 11, Falmouth, Cornwall.

Please send cheque or postal order for the value of the book, and add the following for postage and packing:

U.K. including B.F.P.O. £1.00 for one book, plus 50p for the second book, and 30p for each additional book ordered up to a £3.00 maximum.

OVERSEAS INCLUDING EIRE – £2.00 for the first book, plus £1.00 for the second book, and 50p for each additional book ordered.

OR Please debit this amount from my Access/Visa Card (delete as appropriate).

Card Number

Amount £ ....

Expiry Date ....

Signed ....

Name ....

Address ....